W9-BPL-180

# Rails Under My Back

ALSO BY JEFFERY RENARD ALLEN

*Harbors and Spirits* (poems)

# RAILS UNDER MY BACK

A Novel

JEFFERY RENARD ALLEN

Farrar, Straus and Giroux

New York

Farrar, Straus and Giroux
19 Union Square West, New York 10003
Copyright © 2000 by Jeffery Renard Allen
All rights reserved
Distributed in Canada by Douglas & McIntyre Ltd.
Printed in the United States of America
Designed by Debbie Glasserman
First edition, 2000

Library of Congress Cataloging-in-Publication Data
Allen, Jeffery Renard, 1962–
    Rails under my back : a novel / Jeffery Renard Allen. — 1st ed.
        p.    cm.
    ISBN 0-374-24626-2 (alk. paper)
    1. Afro-Americans — Fiction.    I. Title.
PS3551.L39383 R35 2000
813'.54 21 — dc21                                99-038696

*To the women who made me*

# Contents

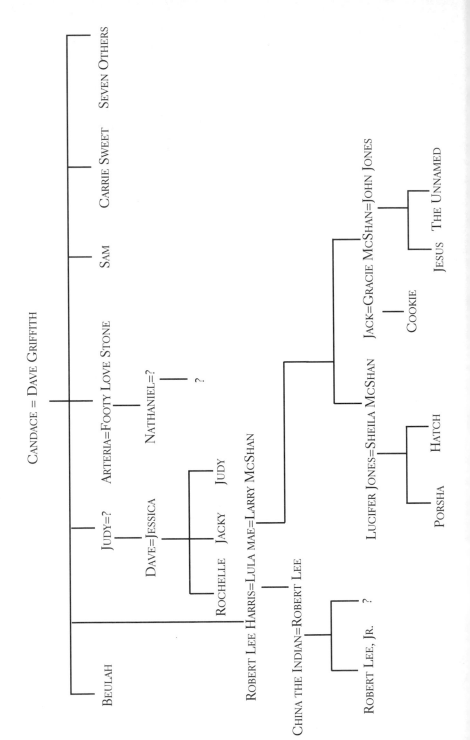

# THE GRIFFITH FAMILY

CANDACE = DAVE GRIFFITH

# THE SIMMONS FAMILY

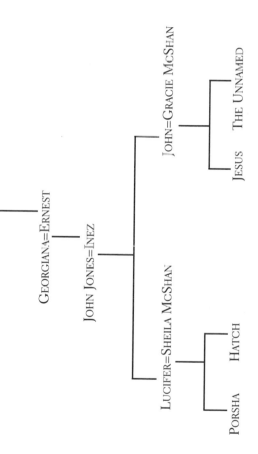

MAMMA THE INDIAN=WHOLE DADDY SIMMONS

GEORGIANA=ERNEST

JOHN JONES=INEZ

LUCIFER=SHEILA MCSHAN

JOHN=GRACIE MCSHAN

PORSHA    HATCH

JESUS    THE UNNAMED

*Hit me in the eye*
*Maybe then maybe then*
*I'll be better*

—TRADITIONAL BLUES VERSE

*Part One*

# SEASONAL TRAVEL

LONG BEFORE JESUS ENTERED THE WORLD, blades of southern grass sliced up the soles of his grandmother's feet. Her blood leaped from the danger, drew back into the farthest reaches of her heart, and the roots of her soul pulled away from the sharp earth which had nurtured her. But nothing escapes the laws of gravity. We martyr to motion. In step with the flowing sweep of her garments, an undercurrent of rhythm, she cut the final strings of attachment, her children, and on a rich spring day cut a red path to New Mexico—what business had a nigger there; New Mexicans had yet to invent the word—for a man eternally bound to a rakish fedora, his sweet face like a mask beneath it, pinstripe suit, diamond horseshoe tiepin, and two-toned patent-leather shoes. Drawn by the power of nostalgia—*Hold infinity in the palm of your hand and eternity in an hour*—she swept back two years later without a word about her lover, the father of R.L., her oldest child. A decade later he would be thrown through the windshield of his sparkling green (red?) Edsel (Eldorado?)—the squeal before the thud, the skid after—his decapitated body slipping the surly bonds of earth, sailing kitelike over a California highway, arcing over and beyond a thicket of treetops, to touch the face of God. Jesus was convinced that her exodus had strangled any impulse her surviving children—his mother and aunt—had to get close to her, and had ripped open his life, for an eye, like a shattered mirror, multiplies the images of its sorrow. The years only deepened the sorrow his family had in common. Even a hatred like hot ice could not halt destiny.

Jesus thought he could never recover from his grandmother's betrayal. While his mother and aunt had long purged their thoughts and feelings of the act—it escaping through the back of their heads, into space—it continued to haunt him, a wallet photograph that he carried everywhere. He moved with a sort of amazement in the world, anger fueling the furnace of his heart. With ceremonial rigidity, each day he wore red, symbol of his unflagging fury.

He leaned over and spit. The saliva held and gleamed, suspended, rust-flecked, then curved down to the pavement. Crashed, sizzled, and cooled. A red coin. He leaned over to pick it up, but the coin refused his touch. Sirens sailed into the sky, a spiral of red sound. He drew himself erect. A strip of white asphalt stretched hot before him. He walked. Only his brain moved. Tall earth-rooted wrought-iron fences hovered before a cluster of houses. And beyond the fences, black and green rhythm of trees. Trees full of birds, plentiful as leaves. The vapor-kissed spires and steeples of North Park. The sky in fanning torches and soaring flames. And heavy white clouds hovering, flying saucers. The street opened into a broader one, the space between two massive rows of skyscrapers black with a continuous throng, two busy streams of ants. He walked with long scissors stride for Lawrence Street, where he would catch the train to South Lincoln. The cradle of the week, the sunny street filled with competitive radios, anxious engines, car horns, hawking of wares, footsteps, and conversation—disembodied voices—a kiss blown from the lips of the square, floating, rising, and hanging above it. The sidewalk steamed with city sprinklers pulsing wet rhythm. Jesus sang:

> *Shine went below deck, eating his peas*
> *Til the water come up to his knees.*

He felt air currents from the movement of cars, shoes, skirts. Rumble and rustle tingling the blood in his rubber-soled feet. Suits and ties and skirts and heels were beginning to change color in the spring heat. A constant weight in their faces, the suits and ties lugged briefcases, newspapers tucked under the left arm. The skirts and heels sported ankle socks and gym shoes—*tennis shoes*, his grandmother called them—as if they gon shoot some b-ball in the office, arc crumpled bills (fives, tens, twenties) into steel wastebaskets. Cut a V for the express train into Central, slowed somewhat by purses bulging with thick paperback novels. A flyer curved around a lamppost: MOTHERFUCK THE WAR! A hang-tailed hound jogged out of an alley—Jesus hoped he would stray within range—and past a knot of beggars hunched over in a corner doorway, rained-on ghosts.

Kind sir, could you—

Hell nawl. Jesus did not pause in his walking. Get a job.

Go to hell and take yo mamma wit you, just for company.

Jesus kept walking.

Cheap nigga.

Jesus kept walking.

Goofy-looking motherfucka.

Bitch, Jesus said, stopping, turning at the beggar, facing the spit-thickened beard. Wash the fart out yo draws. He continued on.

He hadn't gone far when stench stopped him. Eighth and Lawrence, the subway entrance—*A blind man could find it. Follow your nose*—a funky mouth, with worn, broken, and dirty stairs like neglected teeth, descending to a dark throat. The subway breathed him in. He tugged at his ear, his fingers rough against the diamond there. He knew all about the purse and chain snatchers who rode the trains. Rough niggas versed in all tricks of the trade, killin, stealin, and gankin to get paid. Once, he saw a thief hack off a woman's earlobes with a straight razor to loot her diamond earrings. The thief wiped the blood from his razor onto her blouse, slowly and smoothly, as if buttering a bread slice, and Jesus wondered if the woman screamed from the sight of blood, from the pain, or from the sensation of reaching for her lobes to discover they were no longer there.

He had heart, a lot of it—fires could not burn it, water could not drown it, winds could not bend it—and would sport his jewelry. He thought: *Cutthroats. Praise them. Got to have heart to cut mine out. But ain't nobody gon fuck wit me. Jesus Jones. They are clay. I am stone.*

Two rails of level steel, the only clean things in the subway, ran from the darkness at one end of the tunnel into the darkness at the other end, ran over the piles of filth that filtered down from the street two levels above. Two rails that glittered like silver needles in the darkness, awaiting the shiny thimble of train.

A dark pulse at a distance. Jesus could feel it under his feet. He saw pale light, then deep shadow, then glistening train, train that came boring out of the tunnel, bellowing in the distance. Carrying distance to him. The doors opened quick and noisy like a switchblade. Jesus slipped inside the silver sleeve. Muscled a window seat, the window black, nothing to see, metal brightness around him. Suits and ties rested their briefcases across their laps. Skirts and heels parked with their legs crossed. Then, fresh motion. The train moved over greased tracks, a steady rumbling beneath the floor, the car shaking from side to side. The black subway tunnel was a hollow subterranean string stretching under Tar Lake and joining North Park and Central. And the car, an aquarium with passengers for fish. Better yet, a reverse aquarium, with the fish kept in and the water out.

Jesus curled up in his seat, jacket draped across his shoulders, neck, and chest, baby-snug. The car was cold, cutting to the bone. Lucky he had worn his thick socks. Still, the cold bit through; he shivered, a pinned butterfly. The train swept along the curve of a blind river (one of the city's twelve). Long after the curve had passed from vision, it boomeranged back, remained imprinted on his inner eyes, two spinning black half-moons. He liked double-decker trains and wished this were one. *Kind sticks to kind.* But you almost never saw them in the city anymore. Only in the suburbs. Every summer, the family—you, your cousin Hatch, and your aunt Sheila—used to board a silver double-decker for West Memphis, where Lula Mae live, riding high above the rails, your thermos heavy with cold soda pop, and fried chicken stuffed in a greasy shoebox, the aroma strong enough to haunt future passengers for years to come, odors of food and rhythm of rails. Eat that chicken, then lie back fat in your seat, gazing out the window. High hills rolled all the way to the horizon. Scraggly trees like squirrel tails. Cows still as stones. Each rail tie demands attention. The conductor would shout out a litany of stops. And you and Hatch would get happy.

Stop all that jumpin like monkeys in the jungle, Sheila said. You know better. Show some home training. Do that again and I'll beat the living daylights outa you right here on this train.

Lula Mae would be waiting at the station, accompanied by a redcap. A woman thick in the waist, taking up space. Tall, commanding vision from a toadstool of height. A creature of no color, so pale many believed her an albino. You were afraid of her white skin, the smell, the touch. Feared her black snakelike veins. And the figured scars on her calves. *Ole cotton patch. Crazy Junebug giggled giggled at her calves. Ole cotton patch. Tar baby. Tar baby.*

She saw you and kindled instantly. Over here! Waving. Go get their bags.

Yes'm. The redcap rushed forward. Loaded the suitcases onto his cart.

Give yo granny a hug. The thorny hairs on her bosom snatched you before you could comply or decline.

Lula Mae?

Yes.

Why you don't shave them hairs?

Meanness rooted up in the black veins of her neck. Cause they only gon grow back longer.

Come switching time, she would make you go out to the yard and strip your own branch of leaves. Whip the hard branch soft against your hardheaded behind. Whip your butt and legs with the ease of a conducter waving his baton. After a thorough switching, sweat greased the creases of her face. But if she had no energy to switch, if exhaustion had sunk into her bones, she settled for a quick open hand slap across your chops. Water would dam at the back of your tongue, a multitude of days threatening to spill out. You ran out the house and escaped to the red gravel road. Found there, frogs hard and flat as soda pop cans in the desiccating sun. So you would kick them—metal sound, scraping across the sunbaked road—or, if your fingers had heart, pick them up and fling them, Frisbee fashion, bouncing and skipping like a pebble on water.

BUT JOHN GAVE IT TO ME. For my birthday.
　Yeah. His daddy gave it to him. My Uncle John gave it.
　I turn seven.
　I don't care if Jehovah himself give it to you, Lula Mae said. Take that scorpion outa here.
　He ain't no scorpion, Hatch said. He a chameleon, a lizard.
　Houston got scorpions look jus like lizards.
　This ain't Houston.
　Lula Mae drew back her hand. I don't stand for no back talk. Sheila might, but I don't. Now take that scorpion outa here.
　You and Hatch carried Dogma the chameleon out to the red gravel road.
　He get crushed, you said.
　No he won't. He a chameleon.
　So?
　He can change color. Red. The color of the road.
　You laughed. What good that gon do him?
　He be invisible. Cars can't see him.

STOP THAT CHUNKIN! Lula Mae screamed.
　Damn! Can't have no fun!
　Yeah. No fun.
　Lula Mae was tight on you, shoes. Watchin you hard and hateful from her brick porch. You could see her eyes, looming, though the road was several hundred feet away. Preacher eyes trying to burn the devil out of you. *The sun looks through your western window. Carries the record of human deeds to the Lord each night.* Legs might escape her body—run to the yellow field across the road, high grass tall and safe, or so you thought—but nothing could escape her eyes. Even when you climbed high in a tree—a yolk sun cooking the sky, burning and blinding you, with cool air singing in the branches—her high-flying eyes would find you. Hurtful eyes that followed you everywhere, rocks in your shoe.
　Stop all that runnin! Yall catch heatstroke. Her skin was transparent under the sun, revealing a red tracery of veins. She snapped open her umbrella. Held back the day with her body, scraps of sky peering in past her

arms and trickles of light at her feet. She started into the road, red gravel crunching underfoot. You and Hatch followed behind her.

Why yall walkin behind me! Gon up there where I can keep an eye on you.

Small houses, kin to Lula Mae's, lined both sides of the road and Lula Mae greeted the occupants one and the same.

How you duce?

Fine.

Alright. How you duce?

Fine.

Alright.

Entered the barbershop, a bare floor, dust and splinters, a single white cloth apron draped across a single red leather chair, and a black plastic comb submerged—pickled—in a container of green alcohol, causing you to recall Lula Mae's false teeth at the bottom of a water-filled mason jar.

These here my grandsons. Cut them nice. Start wit the red one first.

The barber positioned you in the chair, pinned the apron behind your neck, and set to work. You sat there under the buzzing weight of the clippers, eyes peeling motion, a circle of red hair at the circular base of the barber's chair, skin from an apple. Then the barber resuscitated the drowned comb. Grabbed a fistful of grease. Set to work. There, he said.

Look nice, Lula Mae said. Real nice.

You fidgeted in the chair to chance a glance in the mirror. Your red hair: high and crenellated, a rooster's comb.


THE DOORS CRACKED OPEN LIKE BONES. Federal Station. First stop in Central. The car emptied. Jesus sneezed, coughed, Lula Mae's suffocating odor on his skin. Her rhythm inside him, is what he is. Ill will persisted in his blood. Someday—the promise stagnating, unstirred—he would pay her a little visit, yes, surprise her. Surely, she would stop in the middle of whatever she was doing, caught in his thick, molten rage. What would she say? Do? Invite him to her bosom, that valley of thorns? What would he say? Say anything at all, other than to pronounce sentence? What would he do? What could satisfy him, right the ancient wrongs? A white smothering pillow? A knife clean between the ribs? A shower of stones? A quick spray of gunfire and hot bullets bubbling the flesh? Or something slow? The body straining against a thick pony-tail length of rope, the pulley creaking, and the feet and legs lowering into a leech-filled well? Today might be the day. Board a train for West Memphis. Better yet, fly down there swift as thought and serve a death sentence.

Doors shut, closing the world out. He exhaled, expelling the rage, eased back in his seat, and tried to relax. He still had a long ride ahead. A long ride. All the way to South Lincoln. Red Hook. Two hundred blocks. Four hundred. Who could say? But nothing better to do today. Might as well chill with No Face the Thief. Puff live. He even toyed with the idea of taking No Face under his wing and schooling him. Thinking this with last night in mind.

YOU CAME ALL THE WAY from Red Hook to find *me*? Jesus tightened his one-handed grip on the steering wheel, strangling a snake to bring it under control, let it know who's boss.

You the man, No Face said from the back seat.

The words, like the vibration of a silver wire, sent a glow of light into Jesus's heart. Oh yeah?

Yeah. No Face pressed his face close to the back of Jesus's shoulder, close enough to kiss him. Jesus could smell his sewer breath and hear his heavy elastic breathing, which came and snapped back, came and snapped back. That's what they say.

No Face pinched the Buddha's unlit end and offered it to Jesus. Jesus took the hot end between thumb and forefinger and watched No Face in the rearview mirror. The dark magnified every detail. Jesus didn't look anything like No Face the Thief and was proud of it. No Face resembled a baited fish someone had snatched from the line and thrown back into the water. Short dreads like dynamite fuses. Face a ravaged landscape of dark hollows, craters and caves where the flesh had collapsed in on the bone. A checker-thick black eye patch. *Word, nigga poured acid into his eye to win a bet.* A nappy mustache, round nose boogers. Uneven brown teeth deep in his gums, ancient ruins. He tried to move near you when he spoke. You'd move and he'd move closer. You'd move again and so would he. Jesus trained his eyes back on the road. Hungry feelers, headlights searched the night. He took a long and slow suck on the Buddha; red warmth spread through his body; the streetlights brightened, then gleamed in full glory.

That's what they say.

Why they say that? Jesus looked at No Face, so clear a moment ago, now a small black oval on the rearview mirror. He turned his eyes back to the road. Aimed the unlit end of the Buddha at No Face's voice. No Face took it. Jesus smelled the seashells of No Face's armpits. Considered lowering the window to let the night in. But a frail yellow moon stuck to the windows and sealed them.

You know. No Face took a long toke, a deep sea diver sucking at the mouth of his Aqua-Lung.

Motion hummed a wave through Jesus. He and No Face floated in white space. Floated. He lowered his head, ducking danger—the car's angled hood.

That's what they say.

From what they say, Jesus said, *you* the man. Everybody knew No Face the Thief. Knew his rep. Bandit. Robbin folks wit his finger stuck inside a dirty paper bag.

Me? I'm jus a young brother strugglin in stride. No Face watched Jesus with his one bright headlight of an eye.

Where's the Buddha? The wheel was easy in Jesus's hands. He barely had to touch it. The bobbing headlight beams curved, pulled the car around a corner, and hit another car in the distance.

Ain't no mo.

Jesus heard the ashtray click open, then close.

You want me to fire up another one?

Nawl. I'm straight.

Got plenty.

You the man.

I work hard.

The curb curved the car in. Eighth and Lawrence. Like to see a brother tryin to do sumpin fo himself, Jesus said. Not like these knuckleheads hangin on the corner. He pointed to one or two of them, hardly motioning, his hand still on the steering wheel.

I work hard.

I bet you do. Yo, I'll holler at you.

Want some more of this good blow. Check me anytime. We'll have a session.

Bet.

Anytime.

Stonewall? He didn't have to ask.

No Face laughed a spiral up Jesus's spine. You don't know me from Adam. I'm from Red Hook. I represent. Red Hook. First building. Seven-oh-seven.

Bet.

No Face extended his hand over the seat cushion. Jesus shook it without turning around. Where I say?

I remember.

Can you find it?

Jesus laughed. I can find anything. The engine ignited. Sparks fired from twig to branch and made the car glow.

Jesus spoke to himself. *Hope he don't start geekin. I probably shouldn front this nigga, but you always need some sucka willin to work cheap.*


THE FLASH CAUSED A NEW FLOW, waves of people crashing through the doors. Union Station. Subway, not the distance-seeking trains stories above. Downtown. The Loop. Now, the Loop-jammed train would follow Central River, the spine up Central's back. He heard voices. Laughter. Halfway there. Halfway. 707. The first building. The first from where? He didn't let it worry him. Can't be too hard to find. He stretched his legs, exhaling to drag out what dragged inside, and smelled the sweet burn of pain. The residue of urban moonshine hit his stomach and pumped acid through his body. With the pain came a warmth, a shimmer, a pulse, a new brightness, haze. His sight blew a hole in itself. Shut down his eyes. Darkness.

He loved darkness. Shapes moved across the interior screens of his lids. Funny how the shut eye could fill with dark water, a well, where shadows and shapes swam, and empty circles floated like life rafts. He couldn't quite get the effect now. So he opened his eyes to the stares of the other commuters. Gave them his hardest look. As a child (seven, he figured), he saw a motion picture about a group of blond children who channeled destructive power through their stares. (Their eyes were probably blue, but that was before Gracie and John owned a color TV, or perhaps the movie was in black and white.) For weeks, he'd stood before the mirror trying to get that glow. And now, ten years later, he still had not mastered it, but he mustered enough power to send the eyes of the other passengers running for cover. He extended his long legs and put his kicks on the seat in front of him. Darkness made deep mirrors of the windows. His reflection stared back at him. Shaved head sparkled with sun, even the veins at his temples radiant as cables. He liked it that way, bullet-smooth, streamlined, straight and accurate. Shaved it every day with a straight razor. (Looking down on the very crown of his head, one would see faint black lines, like a claw print. He wore his scars proudly.) A slit of mouth. A thin pipe of neck. Clay-colored skin. Red freckles like dried blood. The naked razors of his long thin lips. The sharp angles of his jawline. The tentative touches of a red beard. Ears that stuck out antennae-like. And the big eyes, visionary and alert.

The train broke out of the darkness, rose at the sky. Jesus saw it with his body. Through the window, sunlight struck a glancing blow against his cheek. He followed the sun into himself. The car shook from side to side as if trying to rouse him awake. He opened the suction caves of his eyes. A constant stream of images rushed past the window: the cuts and valleys of the river (another one of the city's twelve), angles of sail jutting from water into sky, row upon row of three-story buildings—yes, he let his sight multiply— cluster upon cluster of projects, and an occasional house. A small bathtub toy of a boat puffed gray bubbles of smoke as it angled through Tar Lake— still today, motionless—pushing water before it and tugging a huge ship behind. He laid his head back on the dusty seat and felt the sun getting hot on his shoulders and neck.

A red roar. The train spit him onto the elevated platform a mile from Red Hook, the closest it could take him. With a dull gleam of clanking metal, it pulled away from the station, the wooden planks under his feet humming and vibrating. He stood on his perch and watched and waited. Double distance. Sight took solid shape reaching to his brain. The city hung enduring. Central and South Lincoln and a river stringing them together. He sought an exit. No silk thread of elevator to lower him through the web of scaffolding down to the street below. Instead, a twine of stairs, unraveling strands of metal that spiraled up from the street. He piloted these stairs, three flights.

In patient black lines and arrows, a bus sign mapped his journey. Yes, the bus could deliver him to Red Hook. But he wanted—needed—to complete the final leg of the journey on foot. *It's about heart.* He walked.

Streets gaping and torn with road work. Birds still as shadows. Swift-moving clouds. A haze of sunlight. He rubbed his eyes, which burned from being closed, and cleaned dry ash from his throat. One-eyed beer bottles poked from grass, watching him. Heat radiated in a circular fashion throughout his body. He moved carefully under the shocked eye of the sun, a calf trying out new legs. Engines erupted, rousing dogs in an alley, barking in the shadows, then the sun snuck into the alley and a dog bursted bright, chasing a light-winged pigeon. Scoped Jesus with ears erect, a TV antenna. Jesus hoped the dog would stray into distance. It did not. Jesus kicked a pop can and sent it clattering. At the end of the block, a wino lay curled up in a doorway, vomit rolling like lava down his lips.

Long time since Jesus had seen vomit like that. Long time. (How many years ago? Count them.) Decatur. Great-aunt Beulah, Lula Mae's sister, was bedridden after a heart attack. Her wasted frame barely made a ripple in the sharp-white hospital sheets (not remembered mounds of yellow flesh propped against her home pillows), plastic tubes following the lines of her throat, moving toward the curve of her slow-breathing chest, then trailing off. And John—this man he knew as his father, wild in the face, sensing the stuff in Jesus and Hatch, their young blood purring, gurgling, lifted high, struggling to be heard—John snuck Jesus and Hatch from under the hopeful eyes of the family into the morning, the sun's bare ribs poking through the clouds, Jesus and Hatch perched in the back seat of John's gold Park Avenue, a huge ship of a car. They went burning up the straight lines and smooth planes of the highway, John driving with perfect ease, one hand on the steering wheel, or no hands at all, using his knees (didn't need no guardrail to keep the car on track with John squeezing the steering wheel between his knees, narrowing the highway, making it skinny) or chest (man and machine leaning as one toward Kankakee); *he and Dave (his main man, running buddy, kin by marriage, adopted blood) would hold contests, one steering while blindfolded, then the other steering with his nose, teeth, or chin, or toes*; and one eye on the rearview mirror, yes the rearview mirror where Jesus's baby boots once dangled white—somebody had stolen them, along with John's radio and the whitewall tires—and kicked to the motion and speed, dancing; and the highway unraveling like a bandage, a narrow road darkened by trees and underbrush, the car rushing and bouncing, and him swaying to the motion—the two of you stuck your hands out of the open window, feeling the air rush past—his stomach sucking in against itself. John would wheel the car off the road and into every bare field, free of cornstalks, bearing down fast on hip-hopping hares, trying to run them out onto the road, but no luck, since rabbits were spasm-quick, breaking from one clump of brush to another, running for the high grass, thickets, the trees, just escaping by the skin of their buck teeth, and John tiring of the hunt; and thirsty, charting a course—the Kankakee River following and flowing beside the road, the river in his memory flowing brown, heavy, and slow (slow cause John never speeded inside city limits), always there, always working, never tiring, like Lucifer, my uncle, so-claimed—to a liquor store, over in Kankakee cause Decatur was a dry county then, and John bought bottles and bottles of gin, bottles and bottles of tonic water, John mixing drinks for the three of them, potent drinks in plastic cups, and they drank in the dense shadows of the pear trees—fourteen trees, count em, where they felled fruit with broom handles to satisfy hunger and adventure—in Beulah's backyard, leaves like thin fingers of cloud, a wandering smell of wetness, drinking through the afternoon and into the night, he and Hatch playing musical chairs but without music, without chairs, until Hatch babbled something about blacks in Africa being short on corn bread, and he, short on ham hocks; then it came, someone pulled the chairs from under their stomachs, it came, pink, flowing, stinking, he and Hatch taking turns, their stomachs rebelling, John laughing all the while, carrying them to the car, black John invisible in the night, diamond ring sparkling on the steering wheel. They couldn't have been more than thirteen.

He and Hatch were close then, the very name Hatch as familiar and comforting as his own. They were related by blood, and though they differed in shade—he as yellow as sunlight on an open field, and Hatch, evening

shadow—he could see in his cousin some trace of his grandmother's appearance. Kin in will and act. Cutting the fool with John. John, bet you
can't catch us! John chased them round and round the courtyard, them running on three-, four-, five-, six-year-old legs, their screams lifting from the
mouth of the copper-filled fountain. You boys scream like girls! John said,
chasing them, but actually restraining himself, moving slow, cause his short
bulldog legs contained a terrible momentum, the blurred speed of hot pistons. Close then. Double-teaming John on the basketball court. (John always won.) Cutting the fool in church, propelling their farts with paper fans.
Or pitching and batting in the living room with a broom handle and a
rolled-up pair of socks. And basketball with a bath sponge and lampshades
for hoops. Standing tall in the swings, the chains tight in the tunnels of their
hands, pumping their legs and knees, carrying the swings in arcs above the
ground, slanting into the sky, the chains shaking and creaking. Pedaling
their bikes with slim strong ankles, pedaling, fast eggbeaters, guiding the
bikes zigzag through the streets, wind whistling past the ears, drawing back
on the handlebars, like cowboys pulling back on reins, balancing their bikes,
and the front wheel rising for the wheelie, a cobra raised and ready to strike,
and the two of you rode the snake for a half block or more. And in quieter
moments, doctoring the broken wings of dragonflies with Band-Aids or cutting the lights from fireflies with a Popsicle stick and saving the sparkling
treasure in a mason jar. Driving down to Decatur, the speed of flight, fields
of cornstalks bent like singers over microphones, the sun sinking into the
fields like spilled wine, and the headlights stabbing through the darkness,
and scattered trailers like discarded metal cartridges, where John bought
Buddha—*weed*, he called it—from white trash.

Your seventh birthday John stormed out the front door, you and Hatch
two in kind, seated in a high-backed chair, clutching the armrests, Dogma
the chameleon—confused about color—caged in plastic across your shared
laps, and Gracie—the woman you know as mother, the woman who grunted
you into this world—holding her massive Bible at her side, weight that anchored her, kept her from being swept away.

Every hair on your head is counted, she said. Each strand has a name.

Well, John said. You ain't got to worry. I ain't coming back. He let the
door close.

Without hesitation Gracie turned from the shut door and slipped into the
spell of habit. Bathe, put on her perfumed gown, rub Vaseline under her
nose, grease the skin above her upper lip, lotion her body for the motions of
love, cook John's favorite meal, salmon or trout, place the food beneath two
glowing steel dishes for warmth, then retire—her small hesitant walk, steps

of a little bird—to her bedroom rocking chair before an open window over-looking Tar Lake, her Bible open on her lap, and patient as a fisherman, waiting for her John to arrive with his Cadillac ways. *Weeping may endure for a night, but joy cometh in the morning.* Rocking robin, rocking robin, beak-hungry for the spermal worm. Come moonlight, John bounds through the door, and a burning awakens her, wine color brightens her black berry face. John leaves quiet as dew the next morning, and she returns to her rock-ing chair.

JESUS HEARD A SOUND, corn popping over an open fire. Hooded niggas cir-cled a corner, drinking from a swollen paper bag.

What up, homes?

What up. He measured his words. He didn't look into the cave of the hood.

Want some? A hand extended the paper bag out to him.

No, thanks.

Yo, g. You kinda tall, ain't you?

You shoot hoop?

Yo, black. Kinda red, ain't you?

Funny-lookin muddafudda.

Blood-colored.

Three quick full steps took him beyond the voices' range. A can rolled down the gutter, its source of locomotion invisible. Red Hook shoved his head back—as if tilted for a barber's razor, straining the neck. Red Hook. Twelve buildings, each twenty-six stories high, a red path of brick thrusting skyward, poking the clouds, bleeding them. Each building a planet in con-figuration with the next, a galaxy of colors. Sharp structural edges chal-lenged anyone who entered. Word, heard stories about project niggas throwing bikes on unsuspecting passersby. And sure-eyed snipers who could catch you in the open chances of their sight. Can't miss me. A tall nigga like me stand out. And red too.

Jesus spit, saw the thought rise and fall. Above him, birds cried. He lifted his face to the sky—black specks of birds high above the buildings, their cries changing in pitch as they shifted in direction—and let it crush him. The sun was almost blinding. Thick clouds of black smoke, a ship's smoke-stack puffing up from the buildings. *Word, used to be able to drop yo garbage in the incinerator. Every floor had one. Til people started stuffing their babies down wit the garbage.* The shiny brick more like tile. A scorched dog black-snarled from the wall. In a rainbow of colors, weighted words screamed. Too much of it, lines and colors running together, a mess of messages. Inside a sickle, a half-moon, letters darkened and deformed, scrawled in a giant's hand: BIRDLEG WE REMEMBER.

Birdleg? Jesus inhaled the word into his lungs. Fact? Fable? Ghost? Memory was so deep as to silence his footsteps. Somewhere here was an honoring presence. Jesus felt it at his back. Shit, Red Hook! The jets! You can get caught in the middle of something. Rival crews. But he refused to allow this possibility to slow him. *If it's gon happen, it's gon happen.* His shadow swooped high and huge above him.

He entered a vestibule the size of a bathroom. *Felt it, more than saw it.* A cramped doghouse of shadows. Every vestibule inch quilted with more rainbow-strands of words. Bare shattered floors. Long rows of metallic mailboxes, most broken and open like teeth in serious need of dental work. And bottled-up summer heat. A metal stairwell rigged up and out of sight. Metal stairs? A broken escalator? *Word, stairwells often carried fire throughout an entire building.* Jesus knew. Stairwells are chimneys. Up ahead, the elevator caved. *Word, in the jets, elevator motors were mounted on each building's outside, victim to vandals and weather.* What if the elevator stopped between floors, caught in midair, like a defective yo-yo? What if flame climbed the yo-yo string? Are elevators chimneys too? Jesus entered. A hard aroma of piss. He pushed the button for seven.


DOORS SHUT. Pulleys groan into motion. Cables whine. Tug at the muscles of his legs and belly. Rust metal walls compress on him. He extends his arms scarecrow fashion, the walls in-moving as the car rises, and water rising inside him, cold, making him swell. He shuts his eyes.

Black weight drops like an anchor and knocks him flat.

Just relax.

Put your head down.

Iron fingers mine for the diamond in his ear. Hey, he warns. Be careful. That diamond cost me . . . Iron fingers squeeze his throat and crush the words. He chokes. Voices spin above him. He feels caressing fingers on his back—*whose?*—strokes of bird feather. Easy, boy. Calm down. His hands move rakelike in Gracie's plush living-room carpet. I said calm down. The anchor lowers. Two steel loops snap click and lock around his wrists. (He hears them, he feels them, but does not see.) Spikelike leaves rise high above him from the coffee table (ancient, he has always known it)—supported by four squat curved legs, wooden ice-cream swirls—above but close enough for him to make out small red-and-green buds. Wait, he says. I'm money. The two cops work on the pulleys of his arms—he is heavy with Porsha's cooking and the coin of life—drawing them, lifting him high above the carpet, table legs, table, plant pot (glossy green paper), the spiked leaves—bright red on the front side, but colorless on the reverse; veined and tissue-thin, lizard skin (Dogma the chameleon)—and small red-and-green buds, small planets from his height, small planets dissolving in distance. In his fury, he melts into his deep essential life, hard and heavy, a red stone, a fossilized apple. Gravity. The cops raise their nightsticks like black trees. *Don't give us any trouble.* He fights the anger shooting through his stomach. The door flies (or hands shove it) open. The two cops, Jack and Jill, thunder down three nightmare hills of stairs. A blast of winter wind, a cold wind whipped up by Tar Lake. His tongue covers, blankets his teeth against the chill.

Jack looks him in the face.

He smiles. *Can't break me.* Smiles. *Gravity.* Or frowns. His face is so cold he isn't sure. His red eyes shove two fossilized apples into Jack's teeth. Jack yanks down on the cuffs. *Get in.* He ducks his head under the siren roof and squeezes into the low ride. The engine squeals into life like a slaughtered pig. A thin rapid shimmer of exhaust and the cool wind of motion. Sweat cools out of him. His wrists itch raw with the rub of the handcuffs. He gazes through the wedges of mesh partition that separates him from Jack and Jill. Studies the back of their two capped heads. Then he sees a face in the rearview mirror. *Bitten by sin, Gracie said. Bitten by sin.* Two wild eyes burning in the darkness. *Yet, man is born into trouble, as the sparks fly upward.* The car takes a heavy curve. He shuts his eyes. Circular momentum.

He flutters up through the roof into the domed siren, red light spiraling through his veins. Springs out into wet darkness. Flares, flame to sky. Shines. Settles.

A particle of light enters his cell. Spreads like spilled ink on paper. He feels a flutter in his spine, his back, his shoulder blades. Peels away from the floor and starts to rise. White. Cold. Weightless.

Distance steadily shortens between himself and the light's point of origin. He discovers that he is actually part of the light, caught, a red worm on a bright line.

THE SKY MOVED IN WINDOWS. Windows without screens. Lean forward and look out and feel you are peeking over a mountain's edge. Jesus was thankful they were shut on this hot day. He stood very still. Here, one might stand forever and watch the world go by. Cars zooming across the highway. Birds circling above boats bobbing on the river (one of twelve). And the river itself reaching away into the horizon's gaze.

I said Buildin One.

No, you didn't. You said first building.

Same thing.

No. Big difference. Jesus turned and surveyed the cramped, narrow room. Ancient walls that had seen no paint for decades. Mushroom-shaped water stains. Exposed heating pipes dripping like a runny nose. He suddenly felt he was submerged, in a submarine.

Make yourself comfortable. No Face was kicked back against the couch, his feet on the coffee table, his shoe heels run-over, completely flat. His one eye followed Jesus's every move like a surveillance camera. He was as tall as Jesus—Jesus hadn't noticed this the night before—but all muscle, the legs and arms of his red jumpsuit swelling like pressurized pipes. He had groomed the previous night's mustache into a fine streak of soot.

Jesus flopped down on the love seat.

Where you park?

I didn't.

What?

I took the train.

You ain't drive?

Jesus looked at him, hard.

Yeah, No Face said. What am I thinking about? Fine car like that. Round here.

A single stream of sunlight, bothered by flecks of dust, flooded the room. Spread a bright patch like a tablecloth in the middle of the floor. Jesus squinted at the stark whiteness. Shadows spotted the walls.

Nice earring.

Jesus fingered his diamond stud.

Where you cop?

Downtown. At the Underground.

My nigga. No cheap stuff.

Word. You'll get one too. Look in the Cracker Jack box. Save your prizes.

What?

A woman entered the room from a box-sized kitchen. Like his cousin Porsha in age—late twenties—but not in appearance. Black and skinny. Legs thin as wineglass stems. *I can't dick nothing skinny.* Ah, No Face's mamma. A legend. Word had it, she once coldcocked a Disciple with her Bible and saved No Face from getting smoked.

This is Jesus.

The woman looked at him.

*Boy, where yo manners? Lula Mae said. Can't you speak? Cat got yo tongue?*

*No, ma'm.*

*Lower yo eyes. Don't look at me like that. I'll slap that frown off yo face. Gracie may stand fo some sass but I won't.*

We bout to handle our business, No Face said. Take them over to Mamma Henry or Mamma Carrie. No Face talked with a nervous, jerky flow of words. Take yoself too.

She looked at him for a moment. Soon as I get them ready.

Well, don't take all damn day. Stay in the kitchen til yall ready. Me and Jesus need some privacy.

She sailed out of the room and, once in the kitchen, shuffled across the linoleum in red cloth slippers, moving cautiously as if she didn't know her way around.

Who those mammas you mentioned?

Just these two old bitches that babysit them crumb snatchers sometimes.

Jesus could see No Face's mother through the kitchen door, washing the face of a little boy. Several breadboxes lined up like shoes along the counter.

Yeah, these BDs ran a train on her daughter and threw her off the roof.

Jesus looked at No Face.

Mamma Henry. Threw her daughter off Buildin Three. I sexed with her.

Who, Mamma Henry?

No Face looked at Jesus. Funny. Real funny. It's all good though. No Face grinned.

Jesus watched the woman. Where yo daddy?

Something flitted across No Face's mouth, jaws. He handlin his business.

In the kitchen, the mother extended a white plastic teacup to the boy. Go see if Mr. Lipton can put me a lil dish soap in this cup.

The boy headed out the door without a word.

Damn, that's how yall do it in the jets? Give and borrow soap?

It's cool. See—

Yall that po?

No Face's one eye widened, shocked, trying to see if Jesus had truly insulted him. You don't know me from Adam.

Yall some real country niggas—Jesus shook his head. Country. Thinking: Country like Lula Mae, who always buy that thick nasty syrup. Mole asses. He and Hatch wouldn't touch it. Too thick. Mud. So Lula Mae would give Jesus a coffee cup. Go ask Miss Bee for some syrup. Say please. And he'd go get a cup of thin buttery Log Cabin syrup and share it with Hatch.

A knock on the door. The mother hurried from the kitchen to answer it. A little girl, about six or seven. My mamma, she say can you give her some sugar.

I'll bring some. I'm fin to come see her.

Who that? Jesus said.

My sister.

Yo sister?

My *play* sister.

The mother stepped back into the room, one hand on the shoulder of each child. She looked at Jesus. Looked at No Face, expectant.

Go now, No Face said. Later, I make you straight.

She opened the door with no change of expression.

Nice mamma you got, Jesus said.

No Face looked at him, face working, as if trying to decipher Jesus's statement.

The doings of No Face's life circulated all over the city like the sewers. Everybody knew how No Face the Thief ran with a Stonewall unit, Keylo and Freeze, way way on the wild west side of South Lincoln. A coupla ole niggas—well, not *real* ole, late twenties—two jacks who always kept an inch beyond reach of the law's long arms. When they got high or bored, they would flip on him, take turns beating his ass, further damage to his already ruinous anatomy.

Where yo *play* daddy?

No Face looked at Jesus. He at work.

What bout yo smoked-out sister who suck dicks?

Ain't my sister. A slender thread of something in his voice.

I heard—

I don't care what you heard.

Jesus saw something in No Face's one good eye.

I ain't got no sister like that. You don't know me from Adam.

Whatever. Anyway, a blow job don't mean blow.

No Face tried to adjust his eye patch, fingers thick with anger. Tell you who my daddy is. My *real* daddy.

Who?

No Face was blank.

Where yo *real* daddy?

I already told you.

Tell me again.

Where yours?

Nigga, I ain't the one who frontin.

Who say I'm frontin?

Then what you doin hangin out in Stonewall?

Another stretch of silence. Aw, man. You don't know me from Adam. Those my peeps. Where you come from?

From out my mamma's ass.

What?

A round smelly hole.

No Face chuckled. You got to be somebody. Ain't nobody born naked.

People.

People? We all People round here.

Jesus watched No Face hard. Nigga, you ain't no—

Why you always be wearin red? Who you represent?

Myself.

Yourself?

Jesus nodded.

It's like this. If you stand for something, you should show it.

Jesus said nothing.

You got to represent something.

The words sounded across the entire length of Jesus's mind. Jesus red-rolled up one sleeve and revealed two lines of scars running up his forearm.

No Face cleared his throat with a scratch of sound. How'd you—

A Roman shanked me.

Man! No Face's eyes traveled the length of the scar. Look like a railroad.

Check it. Jesus nodded. See, you up here doin all this frontin at Stonewall, but I learned from the source.

What source?

You know.

Tell me about it.

Jesus thought hard and fast, brain working. Bright wings fluttered in his dark mind. Birdleg, he said. I used to roll with Birdleg.

Birdleg?

That's right.

Who—

Birdleg.

No Face thought a moment. Jesus's bald head gleamed in the room like a bright egg. What he learn you?

Listen and learn. Jesus repeated the words from memory. Learn to listen. More will be revealed in the end.

What?

Birdleg. The source.

Then, you got to represent something.

I told you—Jesus rolled down his sleeve and covered the scars—myself.

You selfish.

It ain't like that.

How it like then?

See—

Even T-Bone represent.

That crippled motherfucka, Jesus said. He pictured T-Bone. Wide body-builder torso and slim ballerina legs, riding a wheelchair like a Cadillac in Union Station, patrolling the platform, digging in the scene, racing the subway trains. Word, everybody knew T-Bone. Kickin up dust in his wheelchair, crippled but still kickin it.

Yeah, but he got more heart than some niggas wit three good legs. He ain't sorry bout what happened to him. I was there when it happened, No Face said, proudly, chest puffed out. See, it's like this. We had jus jacked that Jew, Fineberg.

You was in on that?

Yeah.

Jesus looked at him. *I see. He tryin to bullshit the bullshitter.* And once I caught one this big—Jesus held a fabled fish in his parted hands.

No, straight up. You don't know me from Adam. We had just changed that Jew, Goldberg—

Thought you said Fineberg?

Naw. You said that.

Nigga—

Like I said, we change that Goldfine Jew, then we get on the train and this crazy white man, this other Jew-lookin muddafudda, pull out his gat and start shootin at us. Jus like that. So I pull out my shit. I'm like—No Face rises to demonstrate—Boom boom boom. No mercy. And—

Nigga, you weren't even there.

No Face retakes his seat. How you know?

I *know.*

See, that how I lost my eye. I had the long demonstration like this. No Face took a sniper's pose. Then I went Boom boom boom and hot oil popped in my eye. No Face raised the patch and used two fingers to open the eye socket like a clam.

Jesus peered into the gray-pink insides. Nigga, that's disgustin. Why don't you get a glass eye or somephun.

No Face laughed. Stick yo finger in.

Make a nigga wanna throw up.

Go head. Stick yo finger in.

Jesus shook his head.

See, I'm down fo the hood.

Nigga, the only hood you down fo is the one I'm gon put over yo ugly face.

See, you don't know me from Adam. No Face closed his cavernous socket. I put in work. When I see a number three, my enemy. That's it. Dev-astation take over.

Nigga, stop dreamin.

But I don't use no street sweeper, mowin fools down on the run. No in-nocent bystanders and all that. See, me, I'm like this. If I want somebody, I park in fronta they house, camp out all night, drink me a little Everclear, smoke me some Buddha and jus wait fo em. Soon as they leave they house, I be like bam! Peel they cap. Staple a navel if I jus wanna fuck em up fo life. You know, make em carry one of those plastic pee bags. Make em wear dia-pers.

Like that, huh? A mission.

Hard-core. No Face patted his heart.

Then how come you ain't got no rep?

He looked at Jesus for a long moment. You don't know me from Adam. I got a rep. You jus ain't heard about it.

Yeah. I heard you a busterpunklyinmotherfucka.

Now why you come at me like that?

Jus stop frontin. I got proof. Real proof.

Man, you don't know me from Adam. I got proof too. I—

Jus fire up the Buddha.

No Face grinned at the words. Aw ight. Stroked his bare chin. You al-ready sampled my fine products.

I can tell you something. Jesus thought about it. He approached the words slowly. I got plenty enemies. Last Christmas. No, last Thanksgiving. No, Christmas. Yeah, Christmas. My family— But he didn't say any more.

No Face sucked his teeth. Can't trust nobody these days.

Jesus said nothing.

Can't get no respect.

Jesus nodded.

Tell me about it.


PORSHA MOVES like a mule. Slow and strong. A young, shapely woman in a tight black dress, bright red belt boasting her slim waist. She drapes a white cloth shroudlike over Gracie's long supper table. Sets the table. Lace doilies, cloth napkins (folded and ironed), silver utensils, gold-edged plates, and glass goblets. She positions two crystal decanters of dark dinner wine—Mo-gen David by the looks of it, tasty Jew wine that Sheila, her mother, *my aunt*, had stolen from the Shipco liquor cabinet or that Gracie, her aunt, *my mother*, had lifted from the Sterns—at each strategic end of the table. And two pitchers of minty eggnog. Balances steaming serving dishes on her raised palms. Carefully sets them down. Everything where it should be. The table creaks, sags from the weight.

Yall come eat.

The family blasts into the dining room like an express train. Porsha directs them: Mamma, you sit here next to Dad. Aunt Gracie, you sit over there next to John.

Jesus grins it over, grins cause Sheila and Gracie are sisters, but you must keep them apart. Can't stand each other. Always been that way, always will be.

And you boys sit down there.

Boy? Hatch says. Who you callin a boy?

Yeah, Jesus says. We men.

Seventeen ain't grown, Porsha says.

Don't start, Sheila says.

Dressed to the nines, as always, John removes his glasses, sets them next to his plate. He whispers something to Lucifer—*my uncle*—who nods in silent agreement. Two brothers, their hair spotted gray, strewn with ashes.

Aunt Gracie, why don't you say grace?

Okay. You must realize that in the last days the times will be full of danger. Men will become utterly self-centered. They will be utterly lacking in gratitude. For everyone who asks receives, and everyone who searches finds, and for everyone who knocks, the door will be opened.

Prayers circulate around the table. Sheila says, Let the peace of Christ control in your heart and show thanks. Porsha says her say. In connection with everything give thanks. Lucifer, John, Hatch, and Jesus mumble in unison, Christ wept.

Let's eat!

Jesus tears into his food, though the sleeves of his thick winter coat slow him somewhat. He watches the others as he eats, prickly aware of himself.

I was jus remembering something, Sheila says over the clatter of dishes. When Porsha was little, she couldn get enough of Jesus and Hatch. Feed them. Bathe them. Take them anywhere they wanna go. I tell you. Sheila smiles and shakes her head in memory and delight. She used to drape their wet diapers across the radiator. And bring them fresh cookies from school.

Oh, Mamma, Porsha says. Why you have to bring that up?

Cause I—

Sheila, ain't you got this boy tied to yo apron strings?

John, I don't see nothing on my apron.

Look again, cause the way I remember it, when Hatch there was a baby, he was always ridin yo hip.

As tired as I was. How he gon ride my hip?

You go to the grocery store and he ridin yo hip.

John.

You go to the Laundromat and he ridin yo hip.

Please.

Well, he rode it. Yeah, while you cleaned up yo house.

Dr. Shipco, Lucifer says, told me himself that Hatch rode her hip while she cleaned his house.

Dinner over, the family retires to the living room with two fifths of Crown Royal. The women take glasses and a bottle and retire to one corner. The men take the other bottle and another corner.

Give them boys a drink, John says.

Just one, Sheila says. One glass apiece.

What about Porsha? Hatch says. How come she can drink?

Porsha grown and livin in her own house, Sheila says.

But I'm livin in my own house, you say.

You ain't grown, though.

Don't worry, John whispers to Hatch. Got something for you. He slips Hatch a shapely paper bag. Don't let the women see that.

Time passes.

Lucifer and John grow louder with each successive tip of the Crown Royal bottle.

Liquor-possessed words slip from John's slack mouth. So me and some of the fellas at the dispatch tryin to start our own company.

Yeah.

We got the cabs. Most of the guys own theirs.

Still ain't gon buy yours?

John laughs, a laugh that begins little on his lips but expands to swell his stomach and chest.

Still ain't . . . Lucifer kills the words, staring at the laughing John with his heavy, stone-cold eyes, then uplifting the bottle and the weight dropping from the eyes, the mouth slacking into a smile, adding his laugh to the other. Jesus sees recognition in Lucifer's face, his own features and nothing else.

Brother. John shakes one bottle then the other. We empty.

Can't have that, Lucifer says.

Be back in a flash. John's slow fingers fit his spectacles onto his face, the sidepieces creating viselike pressure at his temples, pressure that scrunches up his face, features distorted, pained. He quits the house for two fresh bottles of Crown Royal.

Boy, you sho is tall. Smile gone, Lucifer speaks with his torso craned forward, the widow's peak at his forehead like a scorpion's tail. Jesus knows what is coming. The liquor helps bring Lucifer's true feelings to the surface. Where you get all that height? Lucifer says. And that red hair? Can't be from John. No. Can't be from my brother.

Come on, Hatch says. He tugs at Jesus's elbow. Hot, Jesus refuses to move, soldered in place. Come on. Hatch tugs.

Jesus and Hatch move to the bamboo patio with the big movie screen of a window overlooking shrubs, kept green and square by any wino willin to do the job for the buck or two John paid. Green but hidden today behind curtains of slanting rain.

Where you get that jacket? Hatch says. It's the hype.

Arms out, Jesus twirls like a ballerina so that Hatch may admire it. Red down (goose feathers that flutter when he walks) with a black leather circle centered in the back. From Jew Town.

The hype. I gotta get me one.

Cool. We should go down there. I'll take you to the store.

They slide their food-heavy bodies onto the oak rocking chair, feeling the baked ham and turkey, the candied yams, buttered corn, the collard greens and string beans, apple and peach cobbler settle into their bellies. Hatch pulls a brown paper bag from his blazer pocket, unwraps it, a brick of Night Train, the lil somephun that John had promised, that John had sneaked in under his jacket. Hatch crumples the paper, returns it to his pocket. Breaks the cap and offers Jesus the first taste. Jesus tilts the bottle twice, taking two huge swallows, a musical gurgle of liquor in his throat. The wine's heat spreads fanwise out from his stomach, filling his entire body. He passes Hatch the bottle. Hatch hits it, eyes closed. Passes it back to Jesus. So it goes. They share the wine while their legs pump the rocking chair in motion. The liquid spills forward in the upturned bottle. Jesus gulps. Hatch gulps. Gracie's plants lean into the absent daylight. They drink in silence, only the rhythm of the rocking chair and their breathing indicating that they are not asleep. Drink, until the empty bottle glints beyond their reach.

Guess they think we sposed to sit there and watch them drink.

One drink.

Yeah.

One.

One.

Won't even let us drink like a man.

Check it.

I mean she let Porsha . . . Jesus's mouth seems swollen, the words too fat to escape through his lips. He reaches up to examine them. Fingers tell him what no mirror can reveal.

Hatch brings the empty bottle to his lips. Damn!

Jesus recognizes in the gentle, absentminded movements of his hand something like a familiar melody. You remember?

Remember? Remember what?

Jesus shakes his head. Hard falling rain turns him to the window. Later. I'm out.

Where you going?

Business.

Business?

Peace. His legs carry him quietly out the back door, away from the loud adult voices in the front room. He stares down the deserted street back of the house. Somewhere in the distance, the thick-throated whistle of a freight train. Wherever he turns, he breathes water, drinks air. He throws his head back into steaming rain. Wind-whipped water pokes needles into his face. Yellow streetlights pop on.

He jets to his red Jaguar. Melts into it. Sits a moment, his clothes slippery, puddling on the red leather seat. Beyond the glassed-and-metaled outsides, the rain falls light now, spaced, fine and fresh. He teases the engine into life, and it purrs like a zoo cat house. The liquid world dissolves under the wipers' squeaky swath. Forms again, dissolves. He eases the car into the street. Works up speed. Streetlamps run in two straight lines. The g ride runs silk patterns in the rain. A rooster tail of water arcs behind.

The rain shuts off. He kills the wipers. The world looms close. A star-blanched night. The heavens wheel and march overhead. The road flies past in the cold glitter of the moon.

He poplocks out of the g ride into a wet, cold, shining world. The street shimmers and swims beneath the streetlamps. The rain has washed the air clean. He inhales deeply, savoring the taste. Pure breath.

Inside the store, he shakes off rain like a bird. His hands blunder upon the counter, shedding coins. He tries to pick them up, but they run and jump from his fingers. He feels the counter edge against his stomach. His hands return the last coins to his pocket.

The slant-eyed slope—gooks, John called them, gooks—opens his mouth in disbelief. Toothless. His gums loom red. A flame opens in Jesus's stomach. Swells through his blood and makes all his muscles loose and warm. Something kicks him in the back of the head. The slope's face spills into red dots.

YOU LOOK LIGHT, Jesus said. He surveyed the apartment. I'm gon help you change the weight of your pockets.

What you mean?

Change yo cents to centuries.

Huh?

Damn you stupid.

No Face looked blank, an empty gun.

We can hang.

No Face raised his head. Thought you said you don't represent?

I don't.

Then—

We can hang.

No Face fed on silence. Really? The eye watched Jesus in disbelief.

Yeah.

You jus sayin that.

Really.

Really?

Yeah.

And we can hang?

Yeah.

Really?

Straight up.

On the for real?

For real.

In one movement, No Face bounded out of his seat and dropped down like a shoe salesman before Jesus's feet. Thank you.

Hey!

Thank you. His tongue dripped hot saliva on Jesus's canvas kicks.

Just relax, Jesus said, feeling saliva seep through shoes, socks, between his toes.

Thank you.

Hey!

Thank you. No Face sat there panting at Jesus's feet.

Hey! Stop actin like a lil bitch.

Still on his knees, No Face raised his head, eye and patch studying Jesus's face. When we roll?

I should kick yo teeth out, Jesus said.

Sorry.

Damn.

When we roll?

We don't, Jesus said.

What?

I'm at another level.

Tell me about it.

What's to tell. It's a twenty-four-seven thing.

What?

Nigga, get off yo knees.

He did.

Find a seat.

He did.

Kick back.

He did.

It's like this. Everything you do parlays into the next day. All yo life. And that's the jacket you got to wear. Forever.

No Face looked at him, face slack.

Forget it.

No Face watched with his single eye.

Forget it. Just relax. Kick back.

No Face put a big glass pipe on the table. Jesus couldn't tell what it was shaped in imitation of, a trumpet, a rocket, or a dick.

Beam me up, Scotty.

Where your father? Jesus really wanted to know.

Ain't you already asked me that?

Ask you again.

No Face looked at him. He gone to work.

Jesus took off his shoes and removed the hot, wet socks. He put the socks inside the shoes and placed them neatly in front of him.

Turn off the lights.

No Face did.

Now close the shades.

Why?

Jesus looked at him.

No Face rushed over to the shades, snapped them down one after the other. Know any stories? Word, I heard you can tell some good lies. Tell me one.

Tell you bout the time yo mamma sucked my dick.

Hey, can't you stop talkin bout my mamma? Show me some respect.

Jesus didn't say anything for a moment. Then he told a lie about the nigga who could catch his own farts, the only story he could remember at the moment. No Face laughed all the while, uncontrollably, twisting and shaking, slapping his knees.

Know any more?

Jesus thought about it. Should he tell one of John's war stories? *See, West-side was tired of humping. So he shot himself in the foot. One problem. The bullet ricocheted off his anklebone and hit him square in the forehead.* Wait, that was one of Lucifer's stories. The one or two he told. John told this: *Water. We wanted water. Our feet was burnin after all that humpin. So we was beaucoup happy when we saw the resupply choppers flyin in. Beaucoup happy when we saw those choppers drop us down some buckets, some buckets of what we knew was some good cool water after a long thirsty hump. So we hurried up and opened one bucket and another and another. Fuck. Ice cream. Those lifers had brought us buckets of ice cream. Can you believe that? So we took off our boots and started stompin marchin in that ice cream. Humpin all over again.* No.

Come on.

I said I don't know any mo. Damn.

No Face went silent.

Jesus blew the trumpet. It hissed. Light began to glow in his chest, particles of smoke creeping outward through his bloodstream, penetrating muscles and bones, washing his stomach hollow, his whole body slipping inside it, a pit where heat and light coiled around him, a nest of snakes.

He closed his eyes.


THE AIR CONDITIONER HUMMED like a speeding train, you snug in the bed under a winter blanket, staring at the ceiling, which seemed strangely close. You heard the creaking of Lula Mae's sleeping bones from across the hall. Smelled her odor (Ben-Gay). Took stock of the day's wrongs. Wrongs inside of wrongs, this onion that you peeled from one layer of stink to another, from one eye-watering sight to another. Each wrong deed joined like stones on a path.

Hatch?

What?

You sleep?

Sound like I'm sleep?

Lula Mae mean.

Yeah.

Real mean.

Yeah.

Let's fix her.

How?

We gon walk home.

Kinda far, ain't it?

A million miles.

Oh.

We can make it.

You sure?

Positive.

Okay.

You packed your bags, you and Hatch. Moved ghost-silent through the house, sensing the presence of the attic far above—the roof slanting inward with the pitch of the rafters. You unlocked the front door—it always stuck when you tried to open it; the rusty hinges were informants—and moved out into the black reaches of night. You stood on the front porch, where a yellow light burned—a swarm of insects—and saw a world in full bloom. The sky like a dark open flower. A full-eyed moon. The sound of covert crickets. And the short, discontinuous fire of lightning bugs. *When they hold they breath, Hatch said, they fire come on. When they blow it out, they fire go off.* Heat. *Yes, even the nights were hot in West Memphis. Dark forgot its connection to cool.* You waded out into the night, waded, then dolphin-leaped the fence, a red arc of light. Damn! Hatch said. He lifted the silver cuff that latched gate to post. You waded. Hands jammed in your pockets, head thrust forward, you scowled down the empty road. Stepped onto the red noisy gravel. Luggage dragged you to the corner. Dragged too by the pulley of a fresh act.

Hatch's eyes began to water.

Why you cryin?

He did not answer. You turned to see Lula Mae giving chase with a switch.

SUNLIGHT AROUSED JESUS from sleep. He pushed himself upright on the couch, and sat there, groggy, trying to clear his head against the growing hum of morning traffic.

Damn! His flesh luminous with heat. His feet cold. He looked down at them. No shoes. He could see No Face, fuzzy, cloudy, dim. No Face! he screamed.

No Face's black eye patch glowed like the barrel hole of a fired gun. I be dog. We fell asleep.

Nigga, what the fuck!

Some powerful shit. No Face's head hung suspended between his knees, a heavy balloon.

Every inch of Jesus's skin was alive, seeing, watching himself move in a dream. Bitch, what did you put in that weed? Jesus grabbed No Face by his collar and jerked him to his feet.

Nuthin. Somebody had stuck a red moon and a black moon in his face where the eyes should be. I told you I—

You can get hurt like that, seriously hurt. Hardly getting the words out, throat clogged with hate, each word anger-clotted.

But—

Jesus shoved him back on the couch. The sunlight scorched Jesus's socked-but-shoeless feet. Where my goddamn shoes? Once again he snatched No Face up from the couch.

No Face pointed. Red color began to bleed from his eye. He adjusted his black patch. Over there. By the couch. Jesus pushed No Face down like crumbs off of a table. Mamma musta put them over there while—

Jesus quickly shoved his warm shoes on his feet. I ain't never heard of no Buddha making nobody sleep like that. Pass out. He checked his pockets. Found everything in order. I mean, it's tomorrow already. I mean. He sat down on the couch.

The pipe on the coffee table had been cleaned of ashes.

I be dog.

Where'd you get that shit?

From Keylo. He musta gave me some of that crazy shit. Whacked. Nigga always be jokin around.

You lucky I don't . . . Jesus rested the words.

It's cool, No Face said. We're cool. Hey, you wanna watch some TV?

No.

We can watch some.

Bitch, do it look like I watch TV?

No Face studied the words, magnified them under the lens of his one eye. Well, what you wanna do?

Jesus felt a hole in his stomach, growing and spreading. His hands ran an orbit around his belly. Got anything to eat?

Sure.

He followed No Face to the refrigerator. Watched him open it. Almost threw up when he saw old cooking grease inside a mason jar, brown and gray like a rotting limb.

See anything you want? If you don't, we go down to Mamma Henry's house. She keep our meat in her freezer. And Mamma—

I know, Jesus said. I can't wait.

They took out some leftover meat loaf and ate it cold and fast, then drank milk, right from the gallon jug, sharing swigs until the plastic container was whistle-empty.

You can take a shower. No Face's anxious eye watched Jesus. I got some clothes you can wear. We go shoot some hoop.

Jesus looked at him. You lucky to be alive.

No Face directed his good eye somewhere else.

Real lucky.

Look. The eye returned. I got some of my own shit.

I don't wanna try no mo of yo shit. I mean—

You don't know me from Adam. I told you, that wasn't mine. Keylo gave me that. Look, I'll take you to my kitty so we can smoke us some real—

Nawl. I don't wanna smoke no mo.

Cool.

You lucky to be alive.

We can pick up some oysters.

What?

Oysters. Wit hot sauce.

That's what you like?

That's what I like.

Funny. Spokesman used to eat that.

Who?

Never mind. Jus somebody from back in the day. You don't know him.

So why—

It's cool. You can eat. I'll watch.

I ain't hungry. Let's shoot some hoop.

Some hoop?

Yeah, you know. No Face curved his wrist in a mock shot.

Well—

What's wrong? You don't want to?

I don't care. I'll whup yo ass in a game or two.

Follow me.

They squeezed through a narrow neck of doorway, then hurried to the elevator, which began to lower like a rusty bucket. The walls came rushing in and Jesus had to fight the urge to extend his arms in defense. The elevator opened into a dark vestibule. No Face miscalculated the height of the vestibule step and tripped out into the day. Jesus blinked forth upon the sky.

Hey, boys. Give you five dollars if you can tell me what kind of bird this is. The words emerged from pitch blackness, a dark niche cut deep in the building's brick. A face, then a body—blue overalls with dirty suspenders, parachute straps—pushed into the light, fist holding the groin. A janitor, Jesus thought. He's a janitor, cleaning up after this nigga trash. He saw Jesus looking at him. Flicked his tongue fast and dirty.

Damn, No Face said. You see that? He a stone-cold freak.

You can get hurt that way, old man, Jesus said.

The janitor cupped his hand over his ear. What? What you say?

Hurt.

And I can get hurt getting out of the bathtub too.

Jesus turned up the heat in his eyes, red coals. The janitor winked at him. Dushan, the janitor said to No Face.

No Face did not answer.

Tell yo mamma I be up there to see her later.

Damn, Jesus said. You gon take that shit?

Aw, man, he can't sweat me. No Face waits a beat, watching Jesus.

Nigga, he talkin bout yo mamma.

You don't know me from Adam. He ain't nobody. That's Redtail.

Who?

Redtail.

What kind of name is that?

Well, his real name is Roscoe. Roscoe Lipton.

He yall janitor?

The superintendent.

A janitor.

Yeah.

Don't see how he can be nobody's janitor. Too fuckin ole. Nigga can hardly move.

Crazy too. Nigga be feedin rats and shit. Feedin em.

What?

Word.

Jesus shook his head.

I know. But guess what?

What?

He used to be a pilot.

What?

A pilot.

You mean an airplane?

Yeah.

Jesus tried to picture the old drunk in a cockpit. What he do, fly a bottle round his lips?

Nawl, in a war. Warplane. Flying Tiger. Hell from Heaven. He changed some enemies too.

That old drunk motherfucker?

Yeah.

He can't change his dirty draws.

He did.

Musta been a long time ago.

Yeah. Old nigga can't even hear.

I can tell that. *So that was why he did it, covered his deaf ear and cupped his good one.*

But he hear good nough to hear what he shouldn hear.

What?

He a transformer.

Jesus considered the possibility of this.

You do something, and he can't wait to snitch. Hey, he might even snitch on *you.*

Jesus looked at No Face.

Round here, he gotta watch his back. I almost changed that nigga a few times myself.

I bet. He walk like you. He talk like you. He yo daddy?

No Face watched—one red eye—Jesus hard for a stocktaking moment.

They began their journey. Above the river, a gull white-winged along a wave. A hang-tailed hound sat tough beside a garbage can until No Face roused it with a speeding stone. A ragtop speeded past, but slow enough for Jesus to be momentarily blinded by a flash of hand signals.

Trey Deuces, No Face said.

Right, Jesus said.

No Face took cautious steps crossing the street, as if fording a river. He walked, Jesus beside him, for several more blocks through a fog of belching cars, dragging his feet, tripping over his shadow, slow and purposeful, the blind motion of sleep. The morning increased, the wind rose, gusts of it shaking the branches, bringing a faint snow of spring petals, flake on sifting flake. Through rectangles of glass, Jesus saw men dipping their heads in coffee cups, sitting stiff with their beers or hiding their faces behind newspapers. He and No Face rounded the corner. The sun brightened in the distance, and Stonewall glittered white. Tall rockets of buildings, ready to blast off.

Damn, we walked that far? You ain't tell me we walkin to Stonewall?

Chill.

Nigga, you crazy.

You be aw ight.

A fenced-in basketball court loomed in the distance, thick shapes roving inside. Jetting along, Jesus and No Face found a stone bench and sat down to watch the game. Tongues circulated the circumference of the court. Homeys lined the fence, fingers poking through the chain-link holes, slurping Night Train and firing up missile-shaped joints. Floating heat. Sweat air. Grit that Jesus tasted in his cough.

Whirling colors, four men played the full-length of the court. Jesus took a good look. Two men in khaki pants and bare chests, and two in chests and blue jeans. Khaki One a tall (Jesus's height) man with a sharp-angled hair-cut like a double-headed ax (V from widow's peak to neckline). Bull-wide nose and thick worm lips. Wedges of muscle angling up from the waist and fanning out to a winged back. Big Popeye forearms. Dull white skin, as if faded from bleach. Whispered under his breath when he shot a free throw. Khaki Two a short nigga with carefully greased and patterned hair—a sculpture—and proud, bowed wishbone legs. He passed Khaki One the ball for a rim-ringing dunk. Serious hang time in the radiant haze. The opposing team took out the ball. Light-moving, the white man fell like an avalanche and smothered a shot. Drove the ball up the alley and around the other defender for the easy layup. Hoop, poles, and backboard cold-shuddered. The ball swirled around the rim before it flushed.

Good game.

Who got winners? Khaki Two curled up first one leg, then the other, checking his shoe soles. He pulled an old fighter pilot's helmet (World War I stick-winged biplane, Snoopy and the Red Baron) over his sculpted hair.

A scuffle flared up. No Face started for the court, Jesus followed him. Like a magnet, faces drew them in.

Keylo. No Face spoke to Khaki Two. Why you give me that whacked weed?

Give you? Bitch, I ain't give you shit. You paid me.

Jesus blinked. Focused. *Keylo?* So Khaki Two was Keylo, legend in the flesh. Word, drove an old red ambulance with a bed (stretcher?) in the back. His *ho buggy* he called it. Say he never changed the sheets.

Keylo approached, and Jesus imagined him choking No Face in the noose of his bowed legs. He smiled toothless, like a snake. Crunched his face, a single line of eyebrow above lidless rat eyes. Balled in a boxer's crouch. Rose on his toes with a dance in his body and pimp-slapped No Face upside the head.

Damn, Keylo. Why you always fuckin around?

Cause I want to. Keylo slapped No Face again. A storm of laughter convulsed the spectators.

Damn, Keylo. No Face's dreads rose like cobras. Quit.

Make me, bitch. Fists moving, Keylo circled No Face, dukes up, slow-moving like an old man. Circling, he fired slaps, loud as thunder in easy rain, stinging blows which rocked No Face, hard, fast-pitched blows to the soft mitt of his raised chin. No Face hung tough, refusing to go down.

Chill.

Laughter died down.

That's right. Chill.

Jesus searched for the voice's source. Khaki One. Sunlight streaked his greased flesh, accentuating every vein. Chill, he said, voice feverish, cloggy and hot, phlegm-filled as if from a cold.

Damn, Freeze.

*Freeze. Freeze.*

No Face alright, Freeze said. He hooked No Face's head under his elbow and stroked the idiot's bowed head. No Face grinned, tongue fish-flopping in his mouth. He alright. Freeze yanked down on No Face's head, then released it. No Face ballooned up to his normal height. Don't try to play him like a bitch.

I was—

Freeze cut Keylo off with a sharp glance. Shoved him into No Face. Kiss and make up.

What?

Kiss and make up. Freeze's biceps were round and solid, train wheels. Go on. Kiss and make up.

Keylo searched the crowd, pleading eyes and mouth.

Freeze cut a grin. The crowd flew into stitches.

You see the look on his face?

Yeah.

Had that nigga goin.

Yeah.

Thought he was serious.

Bout to piss his pants.

Shit.

No Face bobbed in place, grinning, cannibal teeth, appreciative, glad that Freeze had made a fool of him. Freeze slapped him on the back. You did good, he said. He looked at Jesus, and his eyes spoke recognition. Jesus was sure of it. You did real good.

Thanks, No Face said.

Something inside told Jesus that Freeze's compliment went beyond the battle with Keylo, addressed some secret subject.

Yo, Freeze.

The voice spun Freeze's head.

You had yo fun. A short dude spoke, coal-black face under a red baseball cap, brim backward, manufacturer's tag dangling from the side like a tassel on a graduate's mortarboard. You ready to do this?

Aw ight, Country Plus, Freeze said. If you hard.

I'm always hard.

So pick yo team.

Well you know I got my nigga here. Freeze nodded at Keylo. They slapped palms and locked fingers in some private ritual.

Huh, Country Plus said. So what else is new? Ain't yall married?

Freeze ignored the comment.

Give me MD 2020.

My nigga.

Cool, Freeze said. You can have him. Give me my man No Face. No Face swelled up with gratitude, chest out, lips inflated into a grin, one eye expanding expanding expanding, and he rose, tiptoes.

Thunderbird.

Damn, Freeze, Keylo said. You gon let this bitch play on our team?

Jesus breathed his first whiff of Keylo's gravedigger breath.

Give a nigga a chance, Freeze said. Even a bitch. He gave Keylo a quick hug.

Come on, Country Plus said. Choose another man.

Damn, who else? Freeze studied the crowd.

Pick him. No Face pointed to Jesus.

Freeze gave Jesus a fishy-eyed look. I want him.

That doofy-lookin muddafudda, Keylo said. He and Jesus faced one another, eyes colliding.

And I'll take Mad Dog. Okay. We set.

Jesus pondered the faulty mathematics. *That's only four. Four players, not . . .* No Face pulled Jesus into the huddle.

Yo, g, Freeze said. What's yo name?

Jesus.

Jesus?

Yeah.

Welcome, Jesus. I'm Freeze. Freeze extended his hand, and Jesus took it with his firmest grip.

Country Plus pulled a dime from his pocket and tossed it shimmering into the air. Call em.

Heads, Freeze said.

The coin fell to the surface of Country's skin. He slapped his palm over it.

See, Freeze said. You already lost.

What you call?

You know.

Country removed his palm. Heads.

See.

Country Plus stared into Freeze's face, the price tag dangling from his cap and jerking back and forth in the breeze like a hooked fish on a line. From this time forward, I will make you hear new things.

Whatever, Freeze said. You talk a good game. Let's see if you can play.

No Face unzipped his jacket and pulled it off, removed his T-shirt, and revealed his Mr. Universe torso.

Hey, Jesus, Freeze said. That's yo man. He pointed to Country Plus. Stick him.

Word, Jesus said. *Damn, how Freeze tryin to play me?* Jesus always played center, the tallest and strongest player on the court. And here Freeze was, playin him like a guard.

We skins, No Face said. Ain't you gon take off yo shirt?

Nawl.

Why not?

Nawl.

Yo shirt gon get all funky.

I'm aw ight.

Better take out yo earring.

Nawl.

Nigga yank it off.

Nawl.

No Face, Freeze said. Take out the ball.

No Face took out the ball. MD 2020 snatched his lazy entry pass and tossed an easy layup. Good steal. Country Plus congratulated his teammate, and his team—Thunderbird and Mad Dog—celebrated their first basket. No Face looked at Freeze with a drowning man's eyes (eye!), begging for mercy.

Country Plus threw Freeze the ball.

Wait a minute, Jesus said. It's their ball.

Wake up! Keylo said. You in South Lincoln. Red Hook rules. Stonewall rules. Stonewall rules.

Freeze took out the ball. Fired it to Keylo, who crouched low and ran it hard on his short, baby-thick legs. Country Plus's unit swooped down on him, a flock of small fast birds moving in streaks, sparrows in a room. Keylo froze in place. Fired the ball at Jesus, but Country Plus clawed it in midair, and in the spark of a moment swept Jesus aside like a swatted fly. Jesus gave chase with everything in his legs. Country Plus launched for the nest-high basket, his elbow catching Jesus in the throat.

Damn!

Don't sweat it, Freeze said. He took the ball out. Fired it in to Jesus. Jesus dribbled. Green-thumbed grass poked through the concrete and snatched at the ball. Tall weeds twisted around his legs. And puddles swamped him, quicksand. With each putting down of his heels, his whole body sank further into the court. Then Country Plus liberated the ball from his paralyzed fingers. Rode an invisible rainbow to the hoop. Reaming sight. The rim vibrated colors.

Freeze looked at Jesus. Took the ball out, fired it to Jesus. Jesus barely caught it. A large fish. It slipped from his hands back into the dark court waters. Country Plus clawed it up, bearlike. Lifted for the jump shot. Jesus jumped as hard and high as he could, springs in his toes. Fake. Country Plus had never left his feet. Now he took it casually to the hoop. Jesus landed back hard on the court, waves of hard concrete pulsing from his feet and through his body, mixing with waves of laughter circulating the court.

You see that muddafudda? Way up in the air.

Yeah. A real sucker.

Freeze took out the ball.

Wait, Jesus said. You take it in. The center is supposed to—

Freeze fired the ball hard into Jesus's defiant chest. Jesus watched him a moment, eyes working. He dribbled the ball up the court. Country Plus yanked it from his hands, a string on rolled twine. He dribbled, in front of him, behind his back, between his legs, while Jesus grabbed at the ball, again and again.

Damn, look at that mark nigga!

Gettin played like a bitch.

Country Plus blew past Jesus. Took it behind the backboard for the reverse lay-in.

In yo eye, punk.

Mark.

Trick.

Ranked and intense observers watched Jesus. No shifting, no craning among the still faces, the still eyes. Country Plus laughed in close, Jesus hearing himself, the laugh erupt from his own belly.

Be true to the game, Freeze said.

Jesus lowered his eyes. The ball went weightless in his hands, so he hugged it to prevent it from floating away. The leather skin peeled away to allow him to look directly into the ball's hollow inside, where shapes formed then started to move. Thick sweatbands pinch head and wrists. Sleeveless T-shirts loop skinny shoulders. Jogging shorts sag like oversized diapers. Layers of brightly colored socks curve like barber-pole stripes around thin calves. Converse All Stars, Pro-Keds, and leather Pumas scuff the court with rubber music. John, Lucifer, Spokesman, Dallas, and Ernie—the Funky Five Corners—geared up for battle. Chuckers doing chumps. John with his quick little hands, hands so fast they don't move when he passes the ball. And Lucifer, mouth open, his tongue hangin in the air, some magical carpet lifting him above the ground, the court, the basket.

And you shoulda seen that nigga shout out when he jammed the ball. Served up a facial. He'd be like, Take that, you punk ass motherfucker!

Quiet Lucifer?

Yeah. Quiet Lucifer. I dawked that in yo face!

One-word Lucifer?

One-word Lucifer. How you like that motherfucker! Feel good? Taste good? That tongue just flappin. And those big hands shakin in yo face like he jus rolled seven. Yeah, he had some big hands, but they was slow. Lucifer wasn't no good at handling the ball. Dribblin. Catching a pass. Spokesman told John, Throw it at his face. He'll catch it then. It worked. Same way with everything: Spokesman had an answer. Standing there, watching from the sidelines, rubbing his belly like a crystal ball. Tryin to science the game. Geometrize plays for the Funky Five Corners. *This is a human behavioral laboratory. You know, white smocks and white rats. Test tubes and Bunsen burners. Ideas lead to buildings and bridges. I like to think about yall, us, the team, the Funky Five Corners, and visualize yall, us, the team, being better players through my schemes.* He measure the court with a slide rule and a triangle, then write some figures down on his notepad, sketch some pictures.

*Damn, nigga. What you doin?*

*Always tryin to science something.*

*You may be Einstein but you ain't no Jew. Still black. Science or no science.*

One time he took these big-ass pliers and measured every nigga's head on the court. They let him, too, wanting to be part of the experiment, get written up. Spokesman. This other time he took this big magnet and poked it all around in the air and kept poking it. We jus shook our heads.

When he made his report he expected you to abide by it. He shook his head when you fumbled a pass. *A person your age and height normally covers three and a half feet with each step, so we must conclude that you shouldn't have taken more than ten paces. An unnecessary waste of energy.* Drew his lips tight with anger when you missed a layup. *Lucifer, be slow about obeying the laws of gravity.* And he was always placin bets. Oh, we can't lose. I got this all scienced out. John, if my right eye jump, we win money for sure. We won some money too. Serious money a coupla times. Lost some. Did we profit? Who can say? I guess it evened out.

YALL GON PLAY OR WHAT?

A cool breeze wafted onto the stifling court, stirring up the stench of wine and weed. Jesus breathed through his hard-winded nostrils, unsure whether it was time to breathe in or breathe out. Everything was off, out of whack. *Just need some more time. Gotta learn how to fly again.* He was drowning in dark waters, in spinning lights. Blood on his tongue. He surveyed the players, searching for that one face which would sanction his plight. Freeze cracked his anxious knuckles. Keylo checked his shoe soles. No Face hard-breathed. Then the sun awakened, clean and clear.

I said yall gon play or what?

Jesus saw in precise detail thick, ropelike veins stretched lengthwise in skinny arms and hands. Saw a red sleeveless T-shirt and a red baseball cap, brim backward, the price tag dangling from it. Jesus saw him. Jesus knew him. Engaged sight the pulse of his color. Red, he would get back in the game. He would—yes he, he alone, not his team—make a run.

He fired the ball to No Face, who fired it to Freeze, who fired it to Keylo, who fired it back to Jesus. Jesus held the ball above him, squeezed in one hand. He brought it upcourt, dribbled three times, blip, blip, blip, then took it up the alley, body curved, elbows high. He faked the layup, drew back for the jumper, kicking his feet ballerina-like in midair. The ball arched from his fingertips. Sunk.

Country Plus grinned. I gave you that one, he said. Felt sorry for you. He took the ball in. Lifted off his toes for the jumper. Jesus caught the ball in the palm of his hand, midflight, fly to fly strip. Swatted the ball to Freeze, who lifted for the easy basket.

You got lucky on that one, Country Plus said. He looked Jesus flush in the face.

Guess so, Jesus said.

Mad Dog fired the ball to Country Plus. Country Plus crouched low in the dribble, challenging Jesus.

Pass the ball, Country.

Nigga, stop showin out.

Jesus punched the ball from between his legs, scooped it up, and arched it into the net.

Country looked at Jesus, anger and frustration concealed like fishhooks in his eyes.

Thunderbird inbounded the ball to Mad Dog, who bounced it in MD 2020's direction. Jesus hopped on the ball mid-air, squeexed it tight between his thighs, and rode it for a second or two like a bucking bull. Country Plus faced him, crouched, arms out, yellow sweat covering his forehead. Jesus bobbed and weaved, then broke for the basket, elbows working, tearing off a layer of Country's flesh. Jesus soared in solar heat—he could stay up in the air long as he wanted—gave niggas plenty time to count each tread mark on his rubber soles. He looked down on the basket miles below him, and released the ball like a bomb.

Okay, okay. Don't get happy. Game ain't over.

Country Plus planted his feet, tent in a field. Wind, Jesus blew him flat. Jumped for the shot. The ball hit the rim. Bounced. Once. Twice. Freeze snatched the rebound. The enemy unit trapped him within a wall of raised arms. Freeze fired the ball to No Face. Perfect pass. Except No Face was three seconds behind the ball.

Bitch, Freeze said.

Damn you slow, Jesus said.

Bitch, Keylo said, you better stop fuckin up. Or I'll wrap my dick around yo head like a turban.

No playin bitch, Jesus said. Sweat dribbled down his nose, his mouth, his chin, every inch of his skin, every cell flooded with the energy of the game, the rhythm of his breathing. He studied his heart's double beat. Defense. That was the key. Offense through defense. Offense through defense. Fundamental. Time and distance. Count the pauses between bounces. Feel the game, deep down, somewhere behind the belly, near the lungs. Play as you breathe.

Country Plus rose like a wave for the basket, and Jesus chopped him down with one stroke.

Damn!

Jesus dunked and almost threw himself through the hoop. He landed on the court with easy footing, tiptoes, a ballerina.

That's game.

We won.

Country Plus lay flat and still on the concrete, like something you could stick a fork into. Mad Dog extended an aiding hand. MD 2020 and Thunderbird followed his lead, but Country Plus slapped their hands away, then raised himself warily, like someone trying to stand up on a rocking boat.

Next time, Country.

Next time.

Good game.

Yeah, Country said. Good game. He studied Jesus with nonforgetting, nonforgiving eyes. Good game. Catch yall later. He turned and led his unit from the court, parading his anger and his wound.

Jesus gave Freeze a high five, palms slapping. Slapped some skin with Keylo and No Face. Memory warm like sweat on his skin, of the Funky Five Corners—John, Lucifer, Spokesman, Ernie, Dallas—celebrating a victory.

You play a strong game, Freeze said. He greeted Jesus with a quick hug.

Yeah, Keylo said. He removed his pilot's cap, exposing a thick wave of

greased hair, raised and stiff, a parrot's comb. He turned the cap upside
down and dumped out a gallon of sweat. Liked the way you conned them
mark niggas, actin like you couldn play at first. He fit the pilot's cap back
snugly on his head.

You got it going on like a big fat hard-on.

Jesus said nothing. He wanted more game.

Straight up. Hard.

Ain't no man, woman, or beast can beat me, Jesus said, words warm with
his heart's heat.

You got that right.

Word.

You the man.

Aw, Freeze, No Face said. You don't know him from Adam. This nigga
can tell some stories.

Stories? What kinda stories?

Like—

Like the time he fucked yo mamma.

No Face looked at Freeze.

Keylo twisted off the metal cap on a cloudy, missile-shaped forty-ounce
bottle of malt liquor. Threw his head back and gulped down the liquid,
Adam's apple working. A big booty switched by. Some bitch got a big booty
around here.

Keylo, Freeze said, you got no class.

Freeze, you know I'm a dog.

Yeah. Sniffin a bitch's ass.

No Face burped some laughs.

Tell one of them stories.

Later for that, Jesus said.

Nawl, tell one.

You really want to hear one?

Straight up.

Word.

All ears.

Aw ight. Why not? Once upon a time, this nigga went to this bitch's
house. Her daddy come to the do. The nigga be like, I come to see your
daughter Sally. The father let him in. Sally roll into the room.

Roll? Keylo hunkered down to listen.

Yeah, in a wheelchair. See, she ain't have no legs. Got nubs up to here.
Jesus put the edges of his hands at the knees.

Damn. Head bent in listening.

Check it.

And she ain't have no arms. Nubs. Right here. Jesus put the edge of his hand at his elbow.

Shit.

What kind of bitch . . .

And she had this special wheelchair and all she had to do was throw her hips like this. Jesus demonstrated.

Oh, I see. One of them. Big-booty bitch.

Mad back.

Word.

Lumpin.

So the father say, Yall gon out in the backyard and talk. So the nigga and the crippled bitch go out. So he start kickin it to her. And she get hot, but she ain't never been fucked before. How you gon fuck a bitch with nubs? So the nigga see this clothesline stretched across the backyard. He gets an idea. He grabs two clothespins, then he takes the bitch out of the chair and pins one nub arm to the line, then pins the other nub arm to the line. He props an old wood barrel under her butt. Then he bump her from the back.

Damn!

Word!

Bumped that crippled bitch!

After he nut, he zip up his pants. Then he be like, See ya. Her father come out and find her three hours later. Pinned to the clothesline.

Laughter bounces around the court. Jesus is deep into it too, rejoicing from the gut.

And he left her like that?

Word.

Cold-blooded.

Hanging on the clothesline.

Word.

Heart.

But, nigga—Keylo shoved No Face's head back—that wasn't no joke.

You don't know me from Adam. I ain't said nothing bout no joke. I said a *lie*.

Bitch, stop lyin. Keylo stuck a big eyedropper into the forty and suctioned up liquid into the tube. When the dropper was full, he craned back his head, poked the dropper in his mouth, and squeezed liquid from the flooded ball at the dropper's end.

Funny story, Freeze said. He took Jesus's shoulders into the circle of his arm. Jesus saw that his own feet were no longer touching the ground. He bobbed in the air, bobbed in the circle of Freeze's sweat-warm arm. He could stay here, forever, and hang. Hang. Freeze released his shoulders. Anchorless now, Jesus concentrated, concentrated so as not to float away. Freeze walked a few steps, then turned to Jesus's trailing eyes. Keylo, he said, go to the sto fo me.

Damn, Freeze. I wanna check out another one of them jokes. Lies. Stories.

Me too, No Face said.

Gon on, Jesus. Bust another one.

Yeah. Bust another one.

Stop repeatin after me, bitch.

Keylo, go to the sto fo me. Buy me a . . . he nodded at Keylo's forty.

What about them stories?

Later for that.

Come on, Freeze.

Keylo.

Damn. Keylo tail-wagged off to the store—no, walking like an antelope, lifting hoof from knee.

And buy Jesus one too.

No, thanks, Jesus said. I'm straight. He fluttered his feathers.

No Face, go with him. Make sure he don't get lost.

Aw, Freeze. But I wanna hear—

No Face.

Damn. Hey, Keylo, wait up. No Face trotted off. Jesus watched him grow smaller and disappear.

A pigeon skimmed the earth in flight, then headed toward the sky, and the sky breathed it in.

Freeze worked his arms through his T-shirt, and covered his bare chest and back. Pulled a pack of cigarettes from his back pants pocket. Shook the pack until one cigarette eased its length, extended, like a radio antenna. Want a square?

No, Jesus said. I quit smokin.

Wish I could quit. Freeze pulled the antenna from the pack, tapped it against the back of his hand, then stuck it in his mouth. Using his thumbnail, he flamed a match. Where yo daddy?

What? Jesus said.

I said, where yo daddy?

My daddy? Jesus stood in a mass of tobacco smoke.

Yeah.

Jesus breathed in the silence. You don't know me.

Freeze watched the lit cigarette end. Where yo daddy?

Hey, you don't know me. Why you askin bout my daddy?

We got something to settle.

You must mean somebody else. He don't even know you.

He stole a bird from me.

Sound strikes what skin is meant to shield. Jesus wobbles. What?

He stole a bird from me.

A trapdoor shuts inside Jesus's chest. A bird?

Yes.

My daddy? Jesus fingers his chest, points to his heart.

Yeah. His name John, ain't it?

Nawl.

His name ain't John?

Yeah.

John ain't yo father?

Nawl.

Who yo father?

Jesus looked into the sky. Thinking: *I get it. No Face told you. Yall running a game.* He laughed.

You think that's funny?

Jesus drank Freeze's milk-white eyes. No.

Ain't John yo father? John Jones?

Yeah, he my father. So, what up?

Like I said. Freeze took a drag on the cigarette. Exhaled through his nose, dragonlike. He stole a bird from me. Light lay in four colors on his face.

You serious?

Freeze said nothing.

Jesus shook his head. Fingered the words in his mind, measured them, searched for color and sense. When did he steal it?

Freeze smoked the square down to the butt. Does it matter? He crushed the butt under his heel.

John know you?

Know me good enough to steal from me. Know me good enough to steal from me then run off and hide like a lil bitch.

Jesus let truth move inside him, let himself move around inside it.

So now you know.

Yes.

And you believe?

Yes.

Good. So then you know. Know what I need you to do. So then you know that I need you to—

I know, Jesus said. I know.

You know?

I know. And I will.

You will?

Yes. Yes I will. Yes, I'll do it.

You can always choose—

Wait, Jesus said. He halted Freeze's words with his palms. Pushed them back. Wait. Feet carried him away. He didn't want to hear any more. No reason to. No reason, will, or desire. He walked, putting time and distance between himself and Freeze's request, command, mission. Maybe Freeze did know John. Maybe. And maybe John had stolen from him. No surprise there. John was a thief. Water-slick. Easy in, easy out. And John was forever desperate, light, seeking to add some weight to his pockets. But would he accept any color or shape of pay? *God marked every sparrow, Gracie said. Every sparrow.* Gravity, Jesus carried the thought inside. Raised it. High. Descended down the spit-mottled steps of the subway.

# Part Two

# CHOSEN

# 2

THE TRAIN LEAVES AT TEN. John held two pieces of luggage—a suitcase and a flight bag—muscled out in each hand. Runs express. A ten-hour ride. Call you as soon as I get there tonight.

John's promise was like money in the bank. Gracie could count on it. In thirty years he had never missed a call.

You heard from Jesus?

Gracie heard nails in his voice. No. She recalled the day John tied Jesus's shellacked baby booties to his rearview mirror, the hanging boots running when the red Eldorado kicked into motion.

That boy slippin. If he keep it up, he be six feet deep.

I guess so. She carried two images of Jesus. The last thing she saw of him, Christmas Day on his way out her door, the black circle stitched dead center to the back of his red winter jacket, still and watchful a sinful black eye, clean and clear, smooth as the back of his bald head. And the first (minutes after his red birth), the empty cave of his bawling mouth challenging her to enter.

Don't worry. John put his hand in the small of her back, drew her in close. She watched his brown eyes, dark, wide, bottomless, two thick high piles of leaves. Maybe we could—

But she already knew the answer before he had fully shaped the question. Maybe we could have another one. To make up for the one we lost, Jesus. She slipped her tongue in his mouth. His met hers, and they held one another, hands and tongues exploring.

He drew back. Come on, now. You know I could stay here all day. But I can't. I gotta meet Lucifer. His brown eyes twinkled a warning, as they had done that morning more than thirty years ago—time is the seed—when she had answered his first knock on her door, when she had opened it—in those days you could open to a stranger without first looking through the cautious peephole, open without a second thought, as if the stranger had muttered magic words under his breath—and saw him standing there, the brim of his hat in the circle of his fingers, and his smooth thin girl-lips parting, blowing a bubble of words, Miss Gracie, I jus thought you might need some help.

*Gracie, Lula Mae says, why take the package when you can have the man too?*

*Maybe all I want is his package, you say. Maybe I don't want the man.*

*He's a nice boy.*

*I don't care. I don't wanna—*

*Why you always gotta be so stubborn? Sheila says.*

*Who asked you? You my sister. You ain't my mamma.*

*Well, Lula Mae says. I is yo mamma and I think you should—*

*Jus had to get in yo two cents. Your voice directed at Sheila. Gracie directs her. Next time, save it fo church.*

Come on, now. I gotta meet Lucifer.

I heard you the first time.

John cut a smile, avoiding an argument. He's at—

That figured. Before all the years and blood, he used to say, I gotta meet Dallas. His old running buddy, run off into a dust and dirt cloud of memory, his funky unwashed pea coat billowing out from his shoulder blades like a racing car's parachute. *John and Dallas: used to be hard to know where one began and the other left off.* Why don't you say what you mean?

What *do* I mean?

I have to meet Lucifer at Union Station cause I have to catch a train to Washington and march and check on the war.

Then to New York. John kept his grin.

New York?

Meet some old army buddies. You know. Spin. Spokesman.

New York.

The Big Apple.

Why they call it that?

The Big Apple? The early bird gets the worm. One hand on the banister's polished oak globe, John broadened his grin. Didn't even have to use his eyes. Kept them on a leash. Years ago, they had chased down her heart. He blew her a kiss, airborne, floating, light wings, landing, settling on her face. Be back Friday, he said. I'll call you tonight. Lock up good while I'm gone.

Be careful, she said. She shut the door.


GRACIE LAY ALERT AS A DOG, every muscle live and attentive. She rubbed them, tingling. Narrow bars of sunlight fell across the bed—*gray and yellow mix green*—where, moments before, John had lain rolled into the sheets, motionless, face against the wall. His body fit easily into the worn groove of their mattress. Earlier, the stiff wetness of his penis inside her—*Baby, yo pussy so tight; you got quicksand in there?*—then it resting like a beached whale across his belly. A warm breeze troubled the curtain. Heat started in her face and worked down to her stomach and legs. She drifted.

*The boat stopped and dawdled in the hot sun. She stood in the bow, knees bent and arms thrown back. Two pairs of red footprints walked off into the horizon.*

*Yes, I can swim. Water breathing in waves. Washing over skin. Wet fingers kneading the body's clay. Moving out into depths, stabbing down into icy blackness. Then cutting up, breaking the surface, rivulets of sand brown-running from nostrils. Setting back to water, to wash clean. Yes, I can swim. The cutting machetes of my strokes. Slicing depths into icy blackness. Breaking away. Again.*

Birds sang in full chorus. The mashed-in place on the pillow like the space inside a catcher's mitt, and the hollow of his body pressed in the sheets. Though he was gone, was not in touching distance, she could still hear his breathing, feel it, nearer to her than her own. With the first rays of sunlight, he always left her. The first white light before breakfast. This had been their arrangement for the last ten years or more, since the day he tried to throw her out the bedroom window. Memory wouldn't carry her that far back—Houston hanging like cobwebs in her mind, sun that seeds deep in famine soil, the shoving arms of the 'Sippi—only the carrying storm of John's words before the open window, *Bitch, you wanna leave?*

Hollow too in her chest where she expected pleasure, but she was determined not to let herself go back through the tunnel of years already passed, slip through mental cracks. Once, John had wanted to sleep inside her lungs and breathe her blood and be smothered. Now. Still, it was the aloneness that filled her with love.

HER FINGERS SLID INTO THE HOLLOW created by his absent body. The year he went away to war, she immersed herself in the darkness behind her closed eyes. Her fingers rooted between the thin leaves of her Bible. She fingered him and he returned the favor, visited her in dreams, his hair loose and black and streaming to the floor like a black gown about his body. She folded herself small and got right down in the foxhole with him. But she couldn't speak—had she left her mouth back home?—couldn't jingle the key of her tongue.

*Some of them niggas was crazy.*
*Yeah. Too crazy. Musta been born and raised in the jets.*
*They wax somebody, then flip that Ace of Spades on they fohead.*
*Like a black leaf.*

*See, those boys over there were babies.*
*Yeah, they called me old man. Imagine that.*
*But yo brother woulda done real good.*
*Yeah. R.L. woulda done real good.*
*His green eyes woulda hid him in the jungle real good.*

Waiting, listening, a world in the moment, and then he was back with her, key turning in the door.

# 3

JOHN THREW HIS HEAD BACK, holding his liquor in his mouth. Shut his eyes. Worked the liquor around behind his shut teeth. Swallowed. Placed his glass quietly on the table. Removed his spectacles. Lifted them to his mouth and blew ancient dust. He cleaned the spectacles on the tablecloth, rubbing hard—the same way he rubbed his marbles as a boy, polishing them for hours, raising them glinting to his eyes, then polishing them some more with one of Pappa Simmons's old rags—glancing up now and then at Lucifer. He fit the glasses firmly on his face.

Twin reflections of Lucifer's face floated on the lenses. Lucifer leaned in slightly for a closer look. Had he shaved before leaving the house? He couldn't remember. Each morning, he shaved off his red widow's peak, and it grew back during the night. The sky flared through the tree leaves outside the window. Spilled bright light across the table's polished surface. The wood glowed banked fire upon the lenses. Lucifer's twin reflections dissolved into rainbows.

John's drink threw a reflection on the tablecloth, a red-orange oval. He aimed the spectacles on a group of suits and ties who passed by the window—two magnifying glasses channeling sun heat to burn through the briefcases. Stormy Monday, he said, the lump of his Adam's apple curling the words from his throat.

Yeah, Lucifer said. Another day, another dollar. The sun hovered high and hot above Circle Boulevard, an avenue really, one long street ending at Union Station. But it was one of the city's busiest. A neat expanse of cement, two shoals of parked cars on either side of an open channel of moving traffic, with skirts and suits wading through—floating flesh, their shadows hopping behind them—to reach stores, restaurants, hair salons, expensive shops, the bus terminal, and here, the Club Car Lounge at Union Station. Dark circles of sweat under suitcase-weighted arms. A hot day out there, the middle of spring with temperatures in the nineties. Spring imitating summer. And a hard summer wind winter-whining, pushing the window, buckling the glass in waves. Lucifer saw his reflection in the glass. Water-clear light-brown skin condensing on the flesh beneath. Often, gazing into a mirror, he could not tell if he was inside the mirror or inside himself.

Nice work if you can get it. John spoke into his hands. Manicured nails. White, round and smooth like ten tiny eggs. Squeeze them eagles til they say uncle. He looked directly at Lucifer, or so it seemed. Sunlight played against the lenses, obscuring the eyes beneath. On what exactly were the lenses focused? Lucifer's eyes? His forehead? Perhaps John knew the old trick of watching someone's forehead instead of their eyes.

Sometimes Lucifer thought he could see right through John's brown eyes, jack-o'-lantern eyes lighted from deep within by private suns. Once in their childhood house on T Street—a long narrow rectangular structure like a cereal box knocked flat, one of those shoebox houses that soldiers squeezed into after the war—Lucifer entered the bedroom that John and he shared and found John sitting on the floor, head bent, face twisted over his raised bent knees, working his jaws vigorously.

John looked up, put his eyes on Lucifer. The flames blew out. Lu, why. John flicked his lashes in the spring summerlike light. What's up?

Nothing. Lucifer didn't know what else to say. He would never forget the unconcealed look on John's face, the eyes. John's eyes opened themselves. Lucifer entered, walking corridors and rooms, and more rooms and more corridors.

For as long as Lucifer could remember, women had been drawn to John's tobacco-brown eyes, the taste, the smell. John had sung women in three cities and two countries. Fought off the women who wanted the eyes, and fought off the bullying men who saw weakness in his short body. Ripe eyes. Ripe, till a fertilizer of herb or taste shrunk them to the size of watermelon seeds and he came home at three in the morning, if he came home at all, and filled the bedroom with his alcohol-coated snoring. Yes, back in the old days, in the basement apartment days on Church Street.

Those were his eyes in the old days. For the last ten years, John had worn round spectacles, twin clear moons. The spectacles had changed the eyes. You could no longer tell the color. Now, the two of them sat at a bright table amid a mass of sleeping shadows—figures at the other tables cut about with shade—and Lucifer noticed something new in John's eyes. A good deal more in the eyes than had been there last Christmas, and even more than last Thanksgiving.

How's the cab business? Lucifer said.

John's eyes flew to Lucifer's face. Lucifer had last seen John about a month ago when John had paid him an unexpected night visit.

Lucifer, remember how I was tellin you bout the cab business?

Yeah. Lucifer couldn't forget. All John had talked about since Thanksgiving.

Well, it's rollin. I jus need some capital.

Don't we all.

The bank turned down my loan request.

Lucifer said nothing. Night made mirrors of the windows. He looked in these mirrors, gaining time for thought. Sorry to hear that.

But, guess what.

Lucifer was afraid to ask.

This guy at the dispatch bought a car for sixty bucks at one of those government auctions. He sold it for six hundred dollars. Six hundred dollars. Can you believe that? Now, if I could buy six cars a month and sell those six, I could pull in six thousand dollars. Six thousand dollars a month.

It can't be that easy.

And in a few months, I could buy a whole fleet of cabs.

It jus can't be that easy.

It is.

Lucifer thought a moment. So you came here to tell me that?

What you mean? Man, we brothers.

It's just that—

You think Porsha might want to get in on this? She has money.

She's got a little saved. But her condo costs a fortune. Her car note. Clothes. Plane tickets. And she gives a lot of her money to that church.

That's why I didn't call her. John stretched forward the length of his neck to bring his mouth closer to Lucifer and give his words more force. You should get in on this!

Me?

See—John worked his smile—if you invest four or five thousand—

I ain't got no money. Sorry.

John's expression did not change.

Why don't you ask Spin? Or Spokesman?

John said nothing.

Or the Sterns? The Shipcos?

Them tightfisted Jews?

Don't hurt to ask.

Depends on how you look at it.

Well, I wish I could help.

Don't worry about it.

LUCIFER HAD NOT SEEN or spoken to John since that night. John had stopped attending the Saturday basketball games where he and Lucifer had officiated together at Red Hook. Lucifer called John's home, but John never answered the phone. Lucifer left messages with the dispatcher and Gracie and (even) with Inez. John never responded.

*Junior, why ain't you called?*

*Inez, this Lucifer.*

*Why you ain't been to see me?*

*I'm comin soon. How you doin? You heard from John?*

*Junior, when you comin to see me?*

Lucifer took the long train ride to Eddyland—*dusty trees and dense foliage hiding faded bungalows and crumbling courtyard buildings; backyards crammed with chickens moving in small crooked shapes of white and yellow; auto yards and factories gift-wrapped in concertina wire*—where John lived. His keys—one of John's extra sets—couldn't turn the locks. Lucifer tried the next day and the next. John never answered the door.


SLOW, JOHN SAID. Business is real slow. He laughed. He didn't stop. The drinks were starting to work, Lucifer's gin and tonic, and John's Jack Daniel's with water. John's third? fourth? It was to his taste today, though the old fire in John's blood had cooled. His heart no longer burned for firewater, the strong cheap stuff.

The drinking made Lucifer remember Sam's funeral, with John and Dave leading Beulah up to Sam's casket, each holding on to one frail arm, holding her up, Beulah weightless under her heavy, gravity-commanding black hat. Sam, I wish I had been there with you. If I could trade places with you. Mamma told me to keep watch. Be yo brother's keeper and yo sister's keeper. And keep watch. Pallbearers Lucifer, John, Dave, and Dallas lowered the silver-railed coffin into the ready grave. They purchased a few pints of 40 Acres Gin (John's favorite that night because it was Dave's favorite) and looked right into the night, moving. They stooped in the mouth of a rotten building, tasting smoky piss.

Let's drive down to Decatur, Dave said.

Why? Ain't nobody down there. Beulah here. You blind? Didn't we jus leave her at—

Let's drive down for ourselves.

Good idea, John said, agreeing to what he had disagreed with the moment before. Let Lucifer drive.

Lucifer took the wheel, though it was John's car (the red Eldorado?), using both hands, driving slowly and carefully, eyes tuned to the road's music. The music was smooth and slow and allowed his eyes relaxed sights. Manteno State Mental Hospital, a white castle in the distance, where many bloods rested their rusted armor after rotating back to the world. The old dog-food factory where many bloods found jobs. Cornfields, yellow-green arms stretching for the yawning sky. A rooster red-spinning on a farmhouse roof. His inner eyes kept returning him to Sam's coffin—his inner eyes penetrated metal, flesh and time—Pappa Simmons's bronze coffin blanketed with pink carnations and fully guaranteed not to let in any moisture for at least fifty years. *Inez had spent a good penny.* He felt the double weight on his foot, pressing down hard on the accelerator, strength he never knew he had, squashing it, a bug under his heel. He sunk out of himself. Drove the Dave-John way. Fast and dangerous. The car rocked in a loud rush of air. Allowed him quick spotted looks. His hands grew slippery on the wheel and every curve in the road slowed him down. He stopped the car, tires crying. Turned the wheel over to Dave or John. *He didn't remember which.* Dave and John took naturally to fast driving. *That's why Dave can turn the bottle cap on a wine bottle so easy, Beulah said.* John pulled off the highway, taking the back roads safe from observation, the car red-flying—swaying with only the loosest connection to the road—past instants of trees, quick spaces of yellow fields, black-spinning shapes, pieces of white moon scattered on the Kankakee River, and a motionless sky. The four tossed gin, talk, and song, back and forth like a volleyball.

I float like gravity.

Got thirty-six babies that call me daddy.

I'm the man to be.

The man to see.

That nigga was a lion, John growled. A lion. Them Muslims popped him. You dig? He was startin to steal they fire.

That's crazy. They need to put you in Manteno. John, turn the car around.

I know it's crazy cause I popped him.

Nigga, you couldn pop a piece of toast.

What you know bout poppin?

Know more than you and yo mamma too.

Still don't mean you know who popped the pretzel. So what you talkin bout?

Look, the three workers who fingered the Wizard were black.

So? Ain't no Muslims in—

Hell if they ain't. They be in all sorts of places, jus like yo mamma's stanky draws.

Yeah. On yo mamma's teeth.

Damn. That's cold.

It was a setup. They fingered Oz.

Like a bulldog finger a cat.

Nawl, like a bird dog rub his whiskers.

Dallas, you must be one of those dumb creatures God peopled the earth with.

Yeah. Daddy dumb. Yo daddy.

Well, nobody know who popped the pretzel cause that ginny popped ole Oz.

I'll taste to that.

Bet the Reverend be gettin his taste. And I don't mean this. Dallas raised the bottle.

He sho preached a good funeral.

Yeah. I always be smellin hellfire on the Reverend Sparrow's breath.

That ain't the kind of taste he talkin bout, Lucifer said.

Bout time that nigga said something. Nigga always be standin round quiet. Cat got yo tongue?

Nawl. He left it in yo mamma's pussy.

How you gon talk bout my mammy? We got the same mammy.

Shit. Lucifer went silent, amused at how he had entangled himself.

Any dog would snarl over the fine brown bones in his church, Dallas said. Hear Rivers and Sparrow double-team the bitches.

John looked at him, eyes blinking hate. Nigga, who asked you?

Moonlight lay thick on the thick cornfields.

Pull over, Dave said.

What?

Nigga, you deaf. I said pull over.

John curved the car onto the road's shoulder—gravel fled from the fast tires (you could hear it, feel it tap like drizzle against the windows)—and stopped. Dave took off his shoes.

Nigga, what you doin?

You that drunk?

Corn arms pulled Dave from the car. The three men followed him barefoot into the yellow fields.


HOW'S GRACIE? Lucifer asked.

*You gon do what?*

*Get married.*

*Why?*

*Man, I'm pussied out.*

*I understand that but why her? Kinda ugly ain't she?*

John took a huge ice cube into his mouth. Same ole same ole. His breath winged its way past Lucifer's nostrils.

You still keep yo keys under her doormat?

Where else I'm gon leave them?

Lucifer wanted to say, *Yall been separated what ten years now and still ain't divorced. Why yall still married? Shit. Don't see why you married her in the first place.* But he left it there. Years ago, Pappa Simmons had advised him and John, Marry a widow or a lady wit kids. She be thankful the rest of her life. But neither had followed his advice. Lucifer married pretty, John married ugly.

*What you lookin at? he asked Dallas.*

*Looking for that nametag on yo collar. Taken.*

*Man, I'm still free, dick blowing in the wind.*

*Ain't what I heard.*

*What you hear?*

*You boppin Gracie.*

*Gracie?*

*Yeah.*

*No way, Dallas said.*

*Where you hear that?*

*Through the grapevine.*

*Well, I ain't gettin it, but I plans to.*

*Gracie? Dallas said. Aw man you can't get them draws. She saved.*

*Yeah, savin it for me.*

*What you want wit that old stuff?*

*Ain't you heard, pussy sweetens wit time.*

The overhead fan hummed waves of cool air. John fingered something in his blazer pocket. His lighter? He pulled a box of matches from his pocket, pulled a cigarette, without producing the pack—New Life, still his favorite after all the years—scratched a match on the roughened side of the box, conjured a flame, studied the flame, and finally touched it to his cigarette. He closed his eyes and breathed the smoke in, then smoked the cigarette down without once touching it with his hand. Fired up another. For years, he had been trying to stop smoking. Or so he promised and claimed. *Gracie would leave the room whenever he fired up a square.* Apparently, his failing eyesight had not curbed his habit. Lucifer recalled hearing that blind people don't smoke. Seeing the smoke was part of the thrill.

Smoke drifted in the morning light and hung bright and heavy as silk. Lucifer fought a sneeze. He let his gaze drift through the huge room. A good deal of people moving across the thick carpet, wood buckling underfoot, soaked with alcohol. People drinking, laughing, and talking, around a bench-long damask-covered table, light-ringed, sampling plates of canapés, calamari, cheeses and crackers, spinach dip, shrimp and seaweed. *Never eat none that shit. They let it sit around for weeks. Get old. Get contaminated. Make you sick.* The place was elegant, more in line with top-of-the-line airport bars. A sparkling chandelier, wall sconces, tulip-shaped lamps, gilt-framed mirrors and paintings, pastoral scenes quiet and bright with flowers, lakes, and trees, abstracts with lines, dots, and colors. He hated the art, the lack of definition. Like grease stains.

Heard from Jesus? Lucifer heard the boy's birth, noises like an angry cat.

Jesus is Jesus.

Lucifer didn't say what he thought. Jesus. All bone. Long and skinny, a red river. Red curse of a son.

How's Hatch? John asked.

Lucifer pictured Hatch and Jesus in the back of John's gold Park Avenue, both boys hunched forward as if to hurry the car along. Lucifer, John, Hatch, Jesus—when had they last been together? Lucifer said, You ain't talked to him?

Sorry I ain't called. Been busy with the cab project.

How's that going?

Fine. John let the silence work for him.

How long is the ride to Washington?

Ten hours. Quick. Express.

Lucifer saw his reflection in the window and, looking through the glass, saw a pigeon rise in flight from the pavement, pulsing its wings in the sunlight. You shoulda told me. I woulda made plans to go. Lucifer followed the slow circles of two silent birds revolving high in the air.

Spokesman jus called me. No warning. John's spectacles followed the bird's movement. Last night. John leaned his cheek against the greasy windowpane. A fresh shave. Yes, a graying in the lower part of his face.

Why didn't he call *me*?

John bright-watched him. Thought he had. Thought you'd be all packed and ready to go.

Why didn't *you* call me to be sure?

John slipped past Lucifer's voice. After Washington, I'm gon spend a few days with Spokesman in New York.

Good.

And Spin.

Lucifer's heart generated a haze in his chest. Spin?

John grinned.

The shadows in the lounge swam fish shapes. Lucifer peered closely at a painting, black lines crossing into broken planes of violent color. Spin too?

John nodded.

Lucifer gave the painting another look. *Somebody actually paid money for that? White folks.* What about Webb? And Lipton? You meetin them too? Lucifer was shocked at the violence of his words. He could taste it.

Lipton? That crazy motherfucker? John shook his head. No. A bit of cigarette paper stuck to his lip. He lifted it off with a fingernail, rolled it into a ball between his fingertips and flipped it away. Jus me, Spokesman, and Spin.

FIVE YEARS BEFORE, after they had both been back in the world for twenty years, Lucifer and John shared parallel seats on a train headed for Washington. Seats close enough for them to exchange breaths. Cramped distance. Crumpled sleeping. *The slanted seat slanted dreams.* Bums lined the tracks like milestones as the train neared its destination, tossing their bottles at the speeding windows. Spin met them at the station in full uniform. He moved easy under a weight of medals. *Rallied a detachment, skillfully conducted a running fight of three or four hours, and by his coolness, bravery, and unflinching devotion to duty in standing by his commanding officer, in an exposed position under heavy fire, saved the lives of at least two of them.* Squeezed John in a choking hug. Then he hugged Lucifer with equal feeling. John's stories had failed to capture the lineaments of Spin's torso; the stories had never risen to his full height or lowered to his full weight. He was too large. No room for him in John's memory and imagination. The blackness of his beard made his lips look red. This was the man who had once bent over a mine with the ease of a shoe clerk over a foot. At last we meet, he said. Lucifer's feelings exactly. Spin was forever coming or going. He and John would pass without touching, two stars, an eclipse effect. With a toast that topped the music charts, Spin had pushed himself to another level of life and roamed the world from end to end.

I heard a lot about you.

All of it is true.

There it is.

They had loaded their baggage into Spin's BMW—the license plate read FNG, short for Fucking New Guy, Spin's band—and rushed to the demonstration, changing out of their civilian clothes into their neatly kept uniforms.

*So this is Chocolate City, John said.*

*Yeah, Spin said. Niggas melting in the sun.*

Spokesman met them there. He was as Lucifer remembered him from the old days, face-wise at least. Doofus-lookin motherfucker. Dark and fat like a church deacon. *His well-paying job at Symmes Electronics had put some flesh on him.* His eyes—large and black—lent the illusion of size. And his teeth sharpened the illusion. Two front teeth, a black gap of space between them, like walrus tusks, crooked, jagged. And he was still wearing those heavy brown shoes of brokerage, the kind where the heels never wear out.

Lucifer's feelings filled with light. He was part. John, Spokesman, and Spin were famous bloods once. (Perhaps they are famous still.) The Hairtrigger Boys. Drawn to trouble as much as to the trigger. Sharpshooters who ran night missions. Twenty-five years ago when Lucifer was in the shit, word wafted that the Hairtrigger Boys had returned to their base, mission-worn, and requested water, buckets and buckets of it. *Jim, we was ready to swim.* The lifers flew in three choppers that dropped three pails, trailing from three parachutes white in the night. With his buckknife, Spin opened the first pail. John and Spokesman—using his buckteeth—opened the others. White eyes, cold and paint-thick, watched them from the pails. Steaming vanilla ice cream! *Son of a bitch.* Spin removed his jungle-logged boots. *Fuck those lifers!* Spokesman and John removed theirs. *Motherfuck them lifers!* Spin hailed a starting distance. Spokesman and John followed suit. The three set off like javelins. Sailed through the night, straight, precise, arching high, then falling, falling, dead center. *Swish!* The Hairtrigger Boys stabbed and jabbed their boots in the ice-cream pails, stomping around, marching in place, cold-swishing. Singing. *I don't know but I been told. Artic pussy mighty cold.* There it is.

And here he, Lucifer, was, with the three of them, the Hairtrigger Boys. He was part.

Uncle Sam led the demonstration, a poster replica—Day-Glo makeup, red lipstick, Pinocchio nose—who rose above the crowd on oak stilts, tooting a party bugle that sounded with the thick power of a foghorn. The vets followed Uncle Sam, all armed with serious frowns and heavy flags hard to keep steady in the wind. Spin walked point—*he always did*, if you believed John's stories—his solid body swaying side to side, his voice carrying—*If shit did not exist, man would invent it*—and holding in the air like an extended tree limb.

Pulled by the full gravity of Spin's presence and decorations, Lucifer displayed his most spirited parade step. Stiff flags snapped a rainbow of shadows. A spell of keen witness. Lucifer squinted against the day. The sun dropped yellow grenades, small sharp cones that exploded in pricking yellow heat and light. Spin's head swam high in the air. Lucifer fell into space and floated. They marched, touching shoulders until the last. Medals and all, they made a tinkling circle around Washington.

When physicists locate a new particle, they start by giving it a new name, which helps them—

Lucifer was hardly listening. He could say the words just as easily as Spokesman, for Spokesman had left his dirty fingers on Lucifer's memory.

—identify its properties more reliably and leads more easily to the identification of still newer particles.

Spokesman spoke in a light voice with fast words running together. No waits in his voice. Tryin to science you to death. He drove the mind into dislocation, a broken angle where it couldn't hang on. *The T Street Church Street Sixty-third Street days. Lil Bit's Give and Take Pool Hall and Barbershop. Spokesman sat slouched down in the hard wooden chair, one leg folded over the other, scribbling something in his spiral notebook. Same way you saw him in the barber chair, pumped inches above the floor, head arched back and face working—cause Lil Bit allowed nobody to read or write while under his razor and clippers—brain calculating the volume of the room, how many shaved hair clumps it would take to fill this volume. Look, Spokesman liked to say, there a science to everything. He put science on the pool halls. Leaned over the table, working the cue stick between the crook of two fingers. Shutting one eye, then the other. Calculating angles and trajectories. Pulling his slide rule from his back pocket and measuring the green felt. Eight ball in the corner pocket. Crack! Rack em up, chump.*

*You'd see him talking to some fine lady on the corner, then scribbling something in his spiral notebook.*

*Nigga, what you doin? you'd ask.*

*I'm tryin to discover the simplest path between dick and pussy.*

Naming is how science enlarges itself. Let's get up early tomorrow and shoot some hoop.

You don't wanna shoot no hoop wit me. You get hurt.

Nawl, you get hurt.

I'm gon play Nazi, you gon play Jew.

You feel that way, let's play fo some sparklin stakes.

I don't wanna bankrupt you.

The day's last dregs mixed with the D.C. streetlights. Lucifer had never seen so many bums. *Here, in the city, you see them in the bus stations, the train stations—in the old days, they used to sleep near the rusting tracks, get drunk and rest they heads on the rails—a hand stretched out on a downtown corner, unlike the beggars in New York, beggars who are choosers, who will watch you cold and blank, or wear a sign saying something like Sick and Not Saved: Give.* They had entire camps, tents made from green plastic garbage bags. Cities within cities. *Recall the one, maybe the city's first, on the edge of Eddyland, only blocks from where John lived. Will our city shed the old image for a new one? Perhaps these green cities are rotten teeth waiting for us to fall asleep one night, then slip clean and quiet under our starched pillows.* He saw a man wrapped up in greasy rags, crouched in the doorway of a building leaning like a worn heel. Another man in the next building, only curled, and one in the building after that, pacing back and forth against the cold. He gave them all the last of his change.

A cluster of lights hazed in the distance ahead of them.

Let's go there, gentlemen.

John you can sniff out a bar from fifty kilometers.

A billow of distant music. Sure enough, a beer sign blinked, signaling their faces.

And I can hear the ringing of a register too.

Flash and cash.

And stash.

Well, good gentlemen, let's get hammered.

They entered the bar, tramped in single file. A round table in the bar's darkest corner looped them in. Spokesman bent down and moved his chair out twelve inches—he measured them with his eyes—in a spirit of gentle, uninterrupted abstraction.

Four of your best, sir. The good stuff.

So I been thinkin about startin my own business.

Spoke, what you know bout business?

More than you.

Spoke, John a businessman.

That I doubt.

Why?

You a businessman?

I understand the ignoble proclivities of the marketplace.

Hot damn.

He speakin cash.

Well, join me. Both of yall. Gon be plenty of money to spread around, money for everybody.

What kind of business?

Extermination.

What?

Killing—

Yeah, I'm gon call it the Black Widow Exterminating Company.

Lucifer felt he was inside an igloo. The frosted windows white-showed the world outside the bar. Alcohol-light voices lifted above the hum of outside traffic.

See, you'd always bomb the railroads first cause the trains carried arsenal and supplies from the factory to the field.

Member how they were still using those ole steam engines when the war started?

Man, they was slow.

I member gettin my assignment, then boardin the train and the coal from the engine blowin black smoke in my face. You could see it on yo tongue.

Naw. That was rationed tobacco.

Shoot, that wasn't nothing. What bout those wartime farts? Everybody eatin all that rationed food.

And burping up rationed food.

Lucifer searched for the faces behind the voices. Five or six old-timers crowded a dark corner. Yeah, old-timers. Grunts whose legs could no longer memory march (let alone hump). *Thousands turn out to greet them. They march with careless, natural precision. Throw their hats into the cheering crowd. Theirs is a regiment of men who has done the work of men.* Legs good for Ben-Gay and whining wheelchairs. One old-timer—Christmas tree-bright—stayed constantly in vision, a floating balloon, an advertising blimp flinging parade streamers from his talkative fingers. Medals covered his body, many attached with safety pins. Big safety pins too, with colored clasps. *Like the pins we used on Porsha's diapers.*

Damn, John said.

What?

I know him.

Who?

That old-timer.

From where?

Yeah. John stroked his chin. His eyes closed in recall. Yeah. Damn, I got it! John jumped up from the table as if a hot poker had sodomized him. That's one of Sam and Dave's old running buddies. Before Lucifer could get a word out, John bounded over to the other table and stretched his elbows across it in conversation. His lips moved silently. *Why he whisperin?* Two of the old-timers rose, the animated one and a second man, stocky and bandy-legged like a gorilla. The decorated man followed John. His shirttail stood out behind him, low-hung wings. His shoe heels had no roundness, worn down like clocks easing on to a final wind. The gorilla man bent his weight onto a cane. Took a few short steps, reaching out with the black hesitant eye of his rubber-tipped cane. Walked in a seesaw motion as if one leg was shorter than the other. He looked back. The decorated man shooed him forward, heading off a chicken in a yard. The gorilla man collapsed into a chair beside Lucifer. His cane poked Lucifer's shin. Excuse me. The gorilla man apologetically touched Lucifer's knee with the tips of his fingers.

No problem.

Let me introduce yall to some old friends, John said. This here is Roscoe Lipton.

Lucifer shook the animated man's hand, the bones close to cracking.

Howdy. The medals winked in the dark. I understand yall some kin to Sam and Dave, those Griffith boys.

That's right. They—

Crazy niggas.

Lucifer studied the man's black circling brows and his wide, unblinking owl eyes. He half remembered the man at Sam's funeral.

Then yall must be alright.

And this here is Pool Webb.

Glad to meet you. Pool Webb extended his hand—big, gorilla big—to Lucifer. The years had not loosened the vise in his grip.

Same here.

Yeah, me and Webb here go way back, Lipton said. He used to be the super at Stonewall. I worked under him. Now he retired. And I'm the super at Red Hook.

So yall from the projects? Spin said.

Well I—

I been wanting to start something at the projects, Spin said. Lucifer knew, after the war, Spin had worked as a youth counselor. Not just in Philly, Spin said, where I'm from, but where yall live too. Maybe a basketball program.

Let me know if I can help.

Me too, Webb said. He winked.

What bout yall? Spin directed the words to Spokesman, Lucifer, and John. Yall be interested? Maybe do some officiating?

Sure. Months later, the three men would keep the promise, as Spin would keep his when he formed the Royal African Company and held seasonal lotteries at Red Hook and Stonewall which gave away thousands of acres of free land in Kankakee County to the winning families. He would also start the Basketball Demons programs, Spokesman, Lucifer, and John officiating at the games, to keep teenagers out of trouble. But that was later. The old-timers held center stage tonight.

What you drinkin?

Can I buy yall something?

Lord no, Webb said. I stopped drinkin. Sugar.

*Meaning, sugar diabetes?*

Well, ain't no sugar gon slow me down, Lipton said. Nor no pig. Lipton dug his fingers into the bowl of pickled pig's brains.

They got any oysters?

Up there at the bar.

No. Those is eggs. Pickled eggs.

Pass those nuts.

Knew a nigga that loved oysters.

Musta loved him some pussy too. Webb winked.

So, where were you stationed?

In the Pacific. Germany for a while too.

*Auf der Stelle*, Lipton said, watching Webb.

Crazy fucker, John whispered.

Lucifer elbowed him. Be cool. Before he hear you. He bit back his laugh.

What?

A dirty deal.

Yes, Lawd. Driving cargo. See, they had us—

A dirty deal. Lipton was looking right at Lucifer, pushing his red eyes into Lucifer's face. *These words are meant for me.* A shit-low, piss-level dirty deal. Lipton's voice came with a loud, rushed intensity, as if he shouted from a distant cliff. Raise a kid, and you think it's over, that you done raised all a man sposed to raise, that yo work done, duty done, you think it's time to relax, time for a lil deserved rest—

*Why else come to the city?*

—but then she decides to wear clothes for concrete and he don't want to be bothered, and run off, Here, old-timer, take em, and dump the crumb snatcher on you like a lump of shit, Take this deposit, my payment—

*Pavement? Like the concrete clothes?*

—for all you done for me these thirty-three years. A low-down cocksucking cumchucking buttfucking shitducking dirty deal. And my girl . . .

The first unreasoning hush. Lucifer watched Lipton with stiff delight. Lipton spoke in birdlike bursts of rapid twitter. Voices crowded the bar, but only Roscoe Lipton spoke that night.

Need to put a sign right up here, HERE BEGINS THE TRAGEDY OF . . . Seen him once. My daddy. Pa if you want. A man under a Mountain Peak. Just back from overseas and got message in his stride. Stride right on to the railroad line. See ya later. I'm a railroad man.

Lucifer's tongue ran out to meet the tasty words.

And me? A scab at seven. A strikebreaker at fourteen, the age when you got enough muscle to wield a baseball bat. Lipton's dogtags spilled out from his shirt, swinging on their chain, back and forth, catching the light. Seven comes eleven and a man ready to marry. A lil piss of a room. Dark and dank. And stank.

Lucifer saw something. Added sight to sound. *A thin bar of sunlight falls across the hall. A single bulb burns from the end of a cord, shaded by old newspaper brown from the heat.*

Baby, my Baby. But the work wuz good. Payday, I'd come home and throw it—

*Greens. Stinky greens. Stinky steam lifting from a pot.*

—up in the air. All my money. Baby and the kids, they be jumpin for all that green snow.

Green sparkled below the surface of Lipton's eyes. *Seaweed.* Lucifer saw the eyes across from him, keenly bright, unblinking, unwavering, as far apart from his life as stars in the sky.

After the war, Baby and I come up here permanent. Well, not here, you know, back home, the city, Stonewall. Lipton tapped one row of medals. Muffled metal, a shovel patting down dirt on a grave. *Each bar of medal is a coffin. Some dead gook or kraut buried beneath Lipton's glory.* Didn't know a soul. But the Veteran Burial Club directed us. Set me up with a good-payin job. So I'm here.

*Yes you are.*

Couldn stay there. The town was a railroad division point, full of transients, bums, hoboes, hatless men in overalls. A thousand streets that ran as one street. The whiskey went down your throat cold, without taste. He had been a moonshiner before the Mountain Peak and the over there and the stepping-off stride, my daddy, my pa, a light-skinned man, lighter than *you.* Yellow, as high yellow as high could get. A yellow man who passed, hanging wit the other broad-brimmed big-city men miles away, another country, in Memphis. Then one time Mamma took me there. Pointin. There, she said. There yo daddy. There.

Lipton paused. Sighed.

So I tell them, my children, I heard it all. I'm tired. Don't give me no shit.

My girl, she come to me. What you doin here? I asks her.

Daddy, he beat me.

We all gets beat. That ain't no reason to leave home.

But—she start.

No ifs, ands, or buts. We all gets beat.

He likes to beat me. Smilin. Likes it. In front of his friends.

A family must stick together. He a good provider.

And he threw the baby food out the window.

Git back home.

No.

Don't make me use my belt.

He used his already.

Listen, he provide. And he gave me two grandkids. Two. To continue the line. If he spit, git down on yo knees and lick it up.

But my feelings changed. Daddy, Bobo said. Bobo, he my son. Cops had him all in handcuffs. Daddy, he say. Git her away from that nigga. Then they carted Bobo off and locked him up.

Way Bobo got round, all these kids out here might be kin. Even yours. Lipton's eyes rippled wet light. Yours too. The wet eyes whirled John into their two wet pools. And yours. Spin sampled his drink. And yours. Spokesman calculated. Sowing oats. Whole fields of em. Nuff eatin fo a life-time. But if he say jus this one, I believes him. This one, this girl named Sharmeta—Lady T they calls her, Lady T—now she faster than a biting flea, but I still raise her for my own. I believes him. Never know him to have no problems claimin what's his. That polio that twisted his legs and forked his feet couldn't slow him down none. Them crutches built him some shoul-ders and arms. Know how women like muscle. Flies to shit.

That's why I say, a dirty deal. You can put that on my grave. Raise a kid, and you think it's over, that you done raised all a man sposed to raise, that duty done, that service done, that it's time to relax, but then she decides to wear clothes for concrete and he run off.

John whispered, He really is crazy.

Uh huh.


IF JOHN WASN'T TELLING all to be told, the three and perhaps the five, with crazy Lipton and crippled Webb added—would have a Washington re-union, followed by a New York sortie. *I will not be there.* Lucifer took an-other gulp of gin, let it linger in his mouth, feeling both its smooth icy coolness and its heavy hotness. *I will not be part.* With his tongue he worked the ice cubes in his mouth. Light-headed with hunger—he'd hardly eaten any breakfast, so anxious to meet John—he had made the ride to Union Sta-tion, taking the long route, the El along and above the river, the river like a candle wick, innumerable strands washing and flicking. *The subway*—lights on the tunnel wall announcing the train's arrival, white snakes crawling along black tunnel walls—let you out on the second level of the Under-ground—yes, you could avoid the revolving doors, doors you always got stuck in, your legs slower than the spin, and avoid altogether the thick crowds of Circle Boulevard and Himes Square—then you took a fart-shaking elevator up through black-marbeled bowels into the station lobby. Lucifer's palm followed the curved edge of the wood table, back and forth. He and John had had a hearty breakfast, bowls of boiled eggs—*how Pappa*

Simmons *liked them, not runny or scrambled (food meant to be eaten, not fork-chased, he said) or sunny-side up, yellow eye watching you (food meant to be eaten not admired, he said)* — stacks of pancakes, each with a mountain of jam — *ah, your mouth watered for Georgiana's perfectly circular hotcakes, her homemade jam, sticky and tasty in the memory* — and plenty of meat, so much that they'd held a meat-eating contest: monkey-wrench-shaped steaks that banged against their trained intestines, fingers and fingers of sausage that poked their belly walls, and sonorous bacon. Indigestion fogged up their chest and stomachs. They agreed on a draw. Now, breakfast over and contest done, they listened with one side of their ears and talked with both sides of their mouths.

*Dallas wiped the bottle on his shirtsleeve, Nigga, I don't want the sweat of yo lips fo bread.*

*Jus hurry up wit that taste.*

*Dallas took a swig. Blood of the lamb, he said. He wiped his long, narrow dog face across his sleeve. Blood of the lamb. He handed the bottle to John.*

*That's right. Let a man show you how to do it. I hold suzerainty over you. So let me wrap my dick like a leash round yo neck.*

*Nigga, why you always gotta preach when you get drunk? Ain't signifyin enough?*

*John worked the bottle on his shirtfront, as if polishing silver. Is tiddies enough, without the pussy?*

*Dallas said nothing.*

*John drank, throat working. Brothers and Sistahs, he said, spreading his arms wide, we are gathered here today . . . He drank. Passed the bottle to Dallas.*

*John and Dallas shared the last inch of fire wrapped in the brown paper bag. Lucifer waited for chanted phrases of song and sermon. Dallas wiped his lips on his coat sleeve, wiped the mouth of the bottle, then took a taste. He extended the bottle to Lucifer. Lucifer looked at it.*

*Nigga, you act like you too good to drink wit us, Dallas said. Or maybe you jus too good to drink.*

*Nawl, I jus* —

*John slapped Dallas on the back. Forget it. He jus a little square. You know that. He took the bottle and drank. Aw. Blood of the lamb, he said.*

*There it is, Lucifer thought. I knew he would say it.*

*John passed the bottle to Dallas. Dallas killed the fire, the stars blinking black for a moment. He flung the empty bottle from his lips without lowering it, the glass spinning and glinting in faint starlight.*

We jus gon shoot the breeze. John spoke through a bright uproar of voices and a clattering of salad forks.

Spokesman gon science you to death, Lucifer said.

Man, Spokesman's cool. John held his cigarette in the scissors of two fingers, smoke rising lazily. He took a deep drag, exhaled smoke in rapid streams from his nose and mouth. Don't let his science fool you. If you coulda seen him in the shit you'd know. A very fine individual.

Lucifer watched John's face go red, animated with memories from a quarter-century ago. The drinks were doing their work. Lucifer shook his head to free his ears of water. He sho is a good salesman. He became deaf to the noise of the bar. He thought about the awards and the New York promotion Symmes Electronics had bestowed on Spokesman. Shit, Spokesman could sell dog shoes to a cat.

John's eyes watched Lucifer through the spectacles. I'll drink to that.

They lifted their glasses in toast. Their eyes met in the mirror. Immediately, John downed his drink and ordered another. Even with the spectacles, it was impossible to mistake John for someone else. As always, he was clean—a black blazer heavy for such a hot day, and white slacks with sharp creases. *He was his sharpest the first time he went to Gracie's house, his bad-ass suit cutting air as he walked. (Wind, step outa the way, Jim.) Even had a tie knotted round his neck, noose-squeezing the flesh.* The boy John happily darted around tree trunks but even happier to dive into the freshly ironed, stiff warmth of his Sunday service clothes—Yall come get dressed for church, Georgiana called, clothes ready. That was the sole reason he liked to go to church. Later as a teen, John would go to Jew Town and get good deals on the latest fashions and tailored fits. *Going to Jewrusalem to pick up some threads.* The Jews would chase you down the street and force you to buy something. *Come on, buy. You want that I should suck dicks?*

John's lips tightened on the pretzel, a woman's tongue. You know why they call it the Big Apple?

Why?

Cause *they* bitin a big plug out of it.

Who?

You know who. They never stray far from their nature.

You got something against—

No. I love bitches.

Lucifer fired down his drink. He saw Sheila's body reflected in another body. Tell you now—leaning over the table—got to have a lot of bucks in New York. Some expensive women there.

You act like I never been there befo.

I guess it's because we never went there together.

New York New York.

So bad they had to say it twice.

Only thing I don't like bout New York, no alleys.

Got that right.

No alleys, no place to piss.

New York New York.

Those slopes run it now.

That's what I hear.

You better believe it.

Man, someday those slopes gonna convert the White House into condominiums.

Shit, the mayor talkin bout sellin Red Hook to some slopes. Throw Stonewall in for free.

Man, those slopes are something else.

The Man got them in his hip pocket.

Mr. Slope, he *is* the Man.

They bent over in bellyaching laughter. Lucifer clapped, hard and fast, until he noticed some of the other patrons flinging stares in his direction. He and John had spent that morning, like so many others in the old days, conversing about the Man. They had developed a whole mythology. He was a white man (what else?) with white hair and a white beard, wore a white suit with matching shoes, drove a white Caddy, drank milk, owned a white cat, liked mayonnaise in his food, and ate only white bread (of course). The myth had spilled from them as they tried to keep their voices level, above the rising and falling alcohol sway, away from the monitoring eyes in the lounge. The myth took Lucifer away from his own situation. He and Sheila had gotten into an argument that morning.

*Have a good one, Sheila says.*

*I ain't going to work today.*

*What? She is dressing for work—the long train ride to the Shipcos in Deer-field—white snatches of cloth in both fists.*

*I already called in.*

*Well, where you hurrying off to?*

*John.*

*John? There is no mistaking the look in her eyes.*

*Yeah. He called while you was in the shower. He's going out of town.*

*We ain't heard hide nor hair of him in a month and he calls and you gon run off jus like that?*

*Well, I—*

*What yall up to?*

Look at that bitch over there. Not over there. Over here. The twin motionless glare of John's spectacles, motioning with his eyes. The one with the French braids. I'd like to teach her some mo French.

Lil brother, Lucifer said, ain't you got enough women?

True. But a man is an army. Gotta have your reserves.

There it is.

John kicked his legs to straighten his trousers. He finished his drink and ordered another. One for the show and two for the road.

The TV mushroomed into life above the bar. Flicked quick color-catching images. A rim and backboard shudder like birds. A black figure sprints down a runway. Takes to the sky. Rail-thin, Flight Lesson sails thirty feet above the court—bouncing on the pole vaults of his legs—in slow motion. *He can truly fly.* He feather-floats back to earth. Leaps into outer space. Reaches out his tentacle-long arm. Grabs a Cool Breeze. *Hermès Athletic Shoes and Cool Breeze, the winning combination.* Behind him, the moon shimmers like a half-dollar. Freeze-frame, he hangs in the air, perfectly still. Legs tucked under him like landing gear. Their last wedding anniversary, Lucifer and John had taken Sheila and Gracie to Air Waves, Flight Lesson's new restaurant. *Reservations. Black tie. C-note entrees. Five-dollar cups of coffee. Live jazz. Vinyl doggy bags.* Lucifer gave the waiter a heavy tip for choice seats. Flight Lesson dined with his family in a glassed-in booth at the restaurant's center.

Man, John said. He nodded at the TV screen in direct line of his sight. Dap coulda cut that motherfucker.

Yeah. Dap was made for basketball. A hoop machine.

A legend.

Pros chumps these days.

Spoiled.

Too much money.

And pussy.

Lucifer laughed a good laugh.

*You* coulda cut that motherfucka. John's spectacles were trained on the screen.

Yeah. In the old days.

There it is.

And you coulda beat him too.

Me? John curved the spectacles onto Lucifer's face. Nawl.

Yeah you.

Lucifer looked toward the end of the bar, where the bartender—he stood against the day; an aquarium-long piece of frosted glass filled up the space behind him—a rag knotted in his fist, tried to hide his interest in them. He wiped down the bar. Lucifer finished his beer in slow, deliberate swallows, then tabled the empty glass. Think *it* will do any good?

Nope. We had our day in the sun.

So why you goin? For Spokesman and Spin?

John thought about it for a moment. Nawl. For myself.

Lucifer said nothing. He thought he knew what John meant. He caught a flash. Smelled a thin gray streak, a match's trail. John met his eyes in the mirror. Immediately, he moved his eyes and tried to read time on his gold watch. 1300 hours, he said, grinning. Time for my train. He drained his drink. Lucifer saw the nerve gathering in him. The lenses snapped shut like a cigarette lighter. He blinked and burned off the alcohol. Stood.

Lucifer stood up also.

John pulled a thick pad of folded bills from his pocket.

Lucifer wanted to say, You're wasting time and money, but he had learned long ago that trying to stop John was like trying to dam a river with a Band-Aid. John paid the bartender with a single bill from the fat pad.

Keep the change.

Thanks. The bartender wiped down the bar. His eyes maintained their curiosity.

Lucifer lifted John's single small suitcase. Surprised at its heaviness. He had expected light, phantom weight.

Damn, nigga. What you got in here, bricks?

John grinned. Something like that. He hoisted the flight bag up to his shoulder, heavy-like, thick rope. Jus some extra things. You gotta be prepared.

Didn't the Man teach you how to pack light?

They walked through cavernous hallways, nearly empty but with spurts of hustle—Lucifer's steps so light he couldn't tell where he put his feet down— their shadows sliding along green- and violet-tinged marble walls. Girders and glass lifted above them and somewhere far above that the conical station roof, clean metal that spilled out into light. Their heels sounded against the last length of the tunnel. In the distance, smoking trains signaled a wavy beam of noise.

Wait, John said. I need some squares.

They stopped at a vendor pushed deep in the tunnel wall. In the old days, no vendors here. Only a blind man or two trying to drum up some pennies. John would drop a dirty washer or greasy ball bearing into the blind man's tin cup, then pocket a handful of yellow pencils.

Give me two packs of New Life.

Lucifer and John continued, the tunnel growing crowded now, passengers filing through, their dragged luggage echoing through the marble station chambers. Lucifer and John broke the tunnel's mouth. Steam hissed up from the tracks below.

John moved his flight bag from one shoulder to the other with perfect lightness. He was anxious for the trip. His face was burning with it. And his eyes—Lucifer caught glimpses of them—red at the edges.

He handed John the suitcase.

Remember the las time we rode the train together?

Yeah. The spectacles masked John's eyebrows, but Lucifer could see the eyes clearly, brown and lined with red threads.

We were goin to see Beulah, John said.

Lucifer couldn't recall ever taking the train to see Beulah. No. We were going to Washington.

Washington?

For the demonstration.

Right. Right.

Why you takin the train? Lucifer said. Ain't you a plane man?

What's wrong, can't this old cocksman learn some new tricks, some new shakes of the dick?

They both laughed. The vibrations bounced off John's spectacles, red balls. Lucifer felt a shocking surge and fall of blood. The red tail of some animal—like something that was always around, a live vine spiraling around a dead tree—curved hidden around the next corner.

*Shit, man we should open us a church.*

*Yeah. You know them reverends gettin them some.*

*Cash money.*

*Nappy pussy.*

Sure you don't wanna go?

Lucifer thought about five years ago. *Let's find us some cooze, John said. Lucifer could hear the gin sloshing in his brother's beer-barrel chest.* He looked at John's suitcase. Tulip-shaped locks. Wish I could. If I had—

John answered before Lucifer could finish. Sorry you can't.

Well.

Happy trails.

Lucifer and John embraced in a tight knot. John didn't seem to want to let go.

# 4

A GREEN BREEZE slipped beneath the curtain. On a green day like this word had arrived (Lula Mae speaking through a clipped Western Union letter because the T Street apartment had no phone) that R.L.—*he was my only brother, as Sheila is my only sister*—had died in a car crash in California. Beulah stood brushing her hair before the open window—*Pappa Simmons loved to comb his black, Indian hair before a full-length mirror, feeling slices of wind push through the comb's teeth, saying, By God, you're a handsome son of a bitch*—while Sheila guarded bubbling pots on the stove—she never could cook for shit—and Gracie enjoyed a passage from her Bible (the specific verse memory also hid), when the message arrived. Beulah read the letter to herself, her lips working silently, then stuffed it in her bosom.

Gracie opened her album to two photographs—she could never connect them, the R.L. in the photos separate from the R.L. in her memory and the hearsay that had become part of her memory of R.L. The first showed him sitting at a round table in a smoky room, playing cards with a group of other jacketed men. He gazes directly into the camera, expressionless, with the confidence of one who doesn't need to strut his good looks. The black-and-white photo couldn't capture his green eyes. And the second photo, so cracked and faded that the colors had started to bleed, R.L. standing in broad winging daylight, riding boots with spurs like sparkling stars. *Well, they used to sparkle when the photo was new, free of the grease of hands and age.* Chaps. Denim shirt and leather vest. A lasso looped around one shoulder. A Stetson, white and creased like a dumpling. And white gloves.

What kind of cowboy is that? Hatch asked. The toddler pushed his fingertips over the white gloves as if to rub away the color.

A real cowboy, Gracie said. I can testify to that.

Yeah, Sheila said. You remember back home in Houston how he was always sneakin Daddy Larry's broken-down horse out of the barn and ridin it to town, causin all that devilment.

*Gnawed steps leading up to the barn where Daddy Larry kept his one bright horse, skinny as he was, a long room with hooks and hanging collars and traces and hames and plowlines and ranked shelves where Daddy Larry stored kerosene and where his wife Ivory Beach—don't call her my mother, never that, step or otherwise—kept her mason jars filled with applesauce and preserves and molasses. And if she had her way, these same jars would keep the murdered flesh of her husband's three children—Sheila, me, and R.L.—pickled and brined, until she served his cherished seed with his Sunday supper.*

What kind of horse he ride? Hatch asked. I don't see no horse. Where his horse at?

He wasn't no devil, Gracie said.

Sheila looked at her. I didn't say he was. Did anybody hear me call him a devil? She searched the other faces in the room for support.

I heard you, Gracie said.

You know Sam and Dave and Nap was always puttin him up to something.

Gracie considered the truth of her sister's statement. Sam was the oldest of the bunch, uncle to his three nephews, who were first cousins. Dave the oldest nephew and close to his uncle in age, Nap next in line, and R.L. the youngest, wet behind the ears and eager to prove himself to his older kin.

They didn't have a bit of sense, Sheila said. She shook her cloudy drink.

Gracie considered it. Never thought he'd die. Die like that. On some highway in California.

R.L.'s death refused to yield to her powers. He never visited her in dreams, only spied on her through the keyhole from the other dimension. So she never knew what killed him. But her first kiss with John—the shock of his lips—carried her back, her first kiss in the shadows of John's new car, a red Edsel or Eldorado—what did she know about cars?—a replica of the instrument of R.L.'s death.

*I don't see why he wanna go out there in the first place, Beulah says. What business a nigga got being there.*

*R.L. made it his business, Gracie says.*

*Why don't yall hush, Sheila says. Hush.*

*You know they don't want us down there.*

*Who cares what they want.*

*Those crackers out there lynched him. Probably was waitin for him at the bus station.*

*Hush, Beulah. Hush.*

No one could afford the train ticket West to attend R.L.'s funeral. R.L.'s wife sent a single letter (translated through Robert Lee Junior, their seven-

year-old son) which said he'd been buried in . . . Beulah had stuffed that letter in her bosom too.

It was too much fo them white folks, Beulah said. A black cowboy with
some white-lookin Indian woman from Brazil.

Hush, Sheila said. You know that R.L. was killed in a car accident. You
know he liked to drive wild.

That's what those white folks said. Can't no cracka stand to see a black
man wit no white woman. And that black man speakin Latin too.

Portuguese, Porsha said. The girl blinked. People in Brazil speak Portuguese.

Beulah, you don't know what you talkin bout. Gracie shoved the words in
Beulah's face. R.L. died in California. He weren't in no South.

Anything south of Canada is the—

That's not right, Porsha said. Geography is my best subject.

Anyway, Gracie put down her plate of pig's feet, how R.L. even know
bout Brazil?

I don't know, Lula Mae said. He sent me jus that one letter. Them cowboy friends in California told him bout it.

California? Porsha said. California on the other coast. West. The Pacific,
not the—

Where the letter?

Beulah said nothing.

See, they gots lots of cowboys down there in the pampers.

Pampas? You mean—

That's what I said.

Aunt Beulah, Porsha said. Beg yo pardon. Ain't no pampas in Brazil.

Daughter, close yo mouth, Sheila said. What I tell you bout talkin
grown?

Yeah. Go geography somebody else.

Hush, Sheila said. You know ain't nobody killed nobody.

And I bet they didn't kill Nap either?

Hush.

Down there in that Houston jail.

Hush. I don't want to argue with you.

*Shit, Dave said. You know how white folks is. Jealous.*

*You said that right.*

*R.L. famous all over California.*

*Yeah. Rodeo man.*

*Say he could rassle a steer by his balls.*

*And ride a horse—*

*What you know bout it? Who tellin it?*

. . .

*You know how white folks is. Jealous. They kick him and that Indian girl off the train. And they spend the night out in the desert, that Indian girl snapping her umbrella open and shut open and shut to scare off them coyotes.*

Gracie stayed out of it. Far as she was concerned, California was Brazil was Paris was Timbuktu cause it was so far away she'd never go there. Beulah knew (Lula Mae had mailed her R.L.'s letter, the letter that Beulah showed no one, like the letter from R.L.'s wife that she hid in her bosom, repeating the message out loud for everyone's ears), it was on a spring green day that R.L. galloped off to Brazil, and it was on a summer green day that Beulah told war-bound Lucifer and John, See if you can find his grave. Robert Lee Harris. And don't forget to look up Robert Lee Junior. Harris the name.

Damn, Beulah, Dave said. San Francisco is a long ways from Los Angeles. So I've heard. One south, the other north.

Yeah, Sam said. And how you spect them to find *em* when we couldn't find R.L., when we tried and tried after the war, after they discharged us.

All I'm sayin is they can try, that's all.

We'll try, Lucifer said.

Yeah, John said, mouth tight, we'll try.

I can't believe yall, Sheila said. These boys are going off overseas, they are going off to . . . Don't you think they got enough on they minds?

We'll try, John said.

A few days later, George—the man whom John refused to call father, who made John frown and spit at the thought—issued his request. Don't forget to look up Port Chicago. They have it all cleaned up now. But still . . .

We'll try.

And don't forget my buddy on Leidesdorff Street, if yall need a place to stay.

We'll keep him in mind.

Steam and hiss rose from the tracks. Redcaps fetched luggage for tips. Lucifer kissed Sheila long and heavy, tongue working. He planted a kiss on Gracie's cheek, then boarded the train without looking back. John kissed Gracie, his tongue diving through her body. He handed her his car keys.

Houston, Fulton, Memphis, the city, Decatur, Houston again, St. Paul—Beulah changed towns and cities as easily as she changed the colorful hats she wore each day. (She had a coatstand in every room of her Decatur

house, octopus arms reaching for every visitor's jacket.) It seem like when I
came North something cold crawled over my skin, she said. *Standing on the
icy platform after she stepped down from the frozen train.* The cold crawl up
inside you and try to weigh you down. But I ain't no ways tired. And this
cramped-up chicken coop don't bother me none. *Cause she was on T Street
then.* I done lived worse.

Newlyweds, she and Andrew came up from Houston to the city, where
they found jobs in the war plant—*You and Sheila stayed back home in Houston, for how could Beulah take you with her when she had a new husband?
And there was a war to fight. Them krauts hate niggers, Daddy Larry said.
They got airplanes too, so ain't no hiding place. But you hid under the bed
from those flying Klansmen, arms over your head to protect you from their
steel lynch ropes that could drop down from the heavens and yank you back
up into them*—bringing everything with them, both the seen and the unseen. But Andrew could not escape the draft. They took him, flat feet and
all. When the war ended, Beulah moved to Decatur, and Andrew took to
the Pullman car.

And was the best man I ever had, Beulah said. After he got that Pullman
job, his pockets were always filled to the brim with gravy. And he spread it
thick, even if he was skinny, and forget sometimes, and was no-hearing.

Gracie remembered. And had a lean and easy frame. He was forever losing his hearing aid, dropping it in the sink or flushing it down the toilet like
some wedding ring; sides, what good was it? Wearing it, he still could barely
hear. The war did that to him? she asked.

The war? Beulah shook her head. From the day I met him And couldn
hear. That war mighta made it worse. I can't tell. All told, I had three kin
overseas, three fighting.

Sam and Dave enlisted. *R.L. caught the Panama Limited west for New
Mexico and ended up in California and became a cowboy and made enough
money to buy a brand-new Eldorado and a big farm and a lounge, and traveled to Brazil and brought him back a white-looking woman called China
the Indian.* Nap was too young to follow. (And you know he had those
seizures.) Koot say—and she would know cause she was his mamma—she
had to strap him in a seat and sit on him to keep him from going off with
Sam and Dave.

Sam and Dave were some dang fools, Beulah said. Couldn tell them
nothing. Hardheaded. Most peaceful days of my life when they went off to
the service. Them niggas needed giant feet to kick up enough dust to reach
me from overseas.

These two cutthroats troubled my days when I first came here, Beulah said. Miss Glencoe paid me every Friday and these two cutthroats use to lay fo me Friday nights on my way from the Currency Exchange. She shook her head. Never will forget them two. Tweed golf caps. Long wool coats that stopped jus above they puffed-out knickers and long skinny silk socks. They see me. Hey, downhome, they say. They tackle me, and roll me round in the snow like a rolling pin or something. I didn't tell And cause I didn't want him to jump in and get hurt. Sides, lotta times he worked nights. Now, these two devils bout tired me out after four or five weeks of they mess. I puts me a bread knife in my pocket and the next time I sees those two devils, I cut them every which way but loose.

Beulah, wit a bread knife?

Um huh—nodding her head.

How you gon cut somebody wit a bread knife?

Any knife'll cut if you mad enough.

*I told Beulah to get an ice pick and put it right there. Dave patted his chest.*

*Her bosom?*

*Yeah. Right up the middle.*

*Dave, how you tell her anything? You was still back home, Houston.*

*I had talked to her on the phone.*

*Phone? But yall didn't—*

*See, cause if me and Sam had been there and got a holt of them niggas . . .*

*Gracie, John said, don't listen to none of that nigga's lies. Dave been lyin since he was born.*

Weren't you scared?

Why? Ain't no reason to be scared. When St. Peter call you, better put on your runnin shoes.

Why hadn't Beulah run away or crumbled away? And was dead. Sam was dead.

*White-gloved angels shuttled you to your seat; red-feathered prayers shimmered in the stained-glass mercy of Christ. Reverend Rivers raised the full sleeves of his billowing robe and Reverend Sparrow did the same, but Beulah stopped their words in their mouths. Sam, if I coulda been there to hold up yo head, I woulda pulled the ax out. Sheila fanned Beulah. The organ soared a wave of music.*

*I tried to warn him, Dave said.*

*Hush, Sheila said. Hush.*

*That woman had burnt up her first husband to get the chump change he had. But you know Sam. Hardheaded.*

*Yeah,* Lula Mae said. *Out of his cotton-pickin mind since he was a baby. Sneakin liquor in his bottle. Sassin Mamma. Holdin his privates.*

*Hush.*

*I tried to warn him,* Dave said. *That nigga say to me, Dave, I'm honored. If a woman'll kill you, that mean she really love you.*

Maybe she was staying alive to keep Sam's murderer in jail, staying alive to make the yearly journey, from St. Paul to the city, to the parole hearing and scream, No!

Keep that bitch in yo jail! Or give me a minute with her.

Sam dead. And Dave died, too. All the meat stolen from his bones, like somebody had boiled him in a vat of the brandy (E & J) he so loved. Dead. Like so many others. Andrew. R.L. Nap. Koot. Big Judy. And Lula Mae was near dead. Death growing inside her. *Cancer will take us all,* Lula Mae said. *Your fingers press into her skin like clay. You lift her up into your arms, carry her from the chair to the bed, a dog carrying a weightless bone.* And all her other siblings, all her brothers and sisters stretching back to Carrie Sweet, the baby sister, younger than Sam, whom she had killed nearly a century ago. I dropped her on the floor and cracked her head.

GRACIE SHUT HER EYES. Two white squares fixed behind her blind lids, fixed, for a moment before gradually dissolving into blackness. Her breathing gentle and peaceful. She heard rustling babies leave the room one by one, their feet the sound of rain, and their leaving the sound of sky beginning to blow clear. Then an in-waft of hot light. She opened her eyes to green. She half rose on her elbow. Her keys lay in the square of yellow where they had spilled out from her black leather purse. She picked them up, placed them on the nightstand, slid out of the bed, slapped her bare feet across the wood floor over to her rocking chair. She moved her fingers over the chair cushion. The black velvet had faded to green. She sat down before the open window. The shadows were soothing after the glare of the sun. Outside the window, clouds swallowed the sky, and the sky itself like a blue sheet stretched across the sun. Thirty years ago, John had hit her between the eyes with his words and ways. Their first apartment they shared with Sheila and Lucifer, a two-flat on Sixty-first and May (Englewood). She descended two flights of stairs each day, heels clicking against waterlogged boards, sinking into the wood flesh. Babies rushed from cracks, hissing and spitting, and she kicked at them, heels high (a cheerleader), and forced them to retreat back into the baseboards. Nothing in the city was attractive then, especially not that street with its big leafless trees, tall green iron-ridged streetlamps whose cold white light reflected in puddles and wet car roofs, or the courthouse buildings with chipped pee-stained fountains and leaning gargoyles ready to tumble into the street. The place she remembers from, this house, John had given her for his sins (the down payment he borrowed from his mother Inez, a loan he never repaid). The first night he left her, the room went silent, and the quiet got inside her. Her placing her Bible on the nightstand echoed the slammed door of his departure. (At least that's how she remembers it now.) She woke to the sound of rain, bed rocking to the downpour's rhythm. She tried to get out of bed and the floor began to rock. She reached for her Bible. She was lifted off the bed bodily and carried through every room in the house, then she was returned to the bed. She listened to the rain's silence. This house for his sins, John having vacated it more than ten years ago, leaving only the shell of an old suit, his clean overalls hanging in the garage—and the large nuptial bed where he still steered her desires every night, only—like a sailor—to return to sea at the spreading rays of dawn, trailing a scent of that first fresh shore thirty years ago where she spread the fans of her legs to his waiting hands, where his tongue discovered the circles of her thighs. This house, yes, but the babies had followed her here, hidden in the corners of her suitcase, warm beneath her cotton night-gowns.

Ten years ago, John had tried to throw her out the window.

Bitch, you wanna leave? His words shattered her sleep.

John. What you doin?

You wanna leave? He lifted her from the bed babylike and carried her over to the open window. Go out right now. The city echoed through the window.

She felt cool night air against her back, the wind's soft fingers trying to push her back into the room.

John. No. These words with the moon behind them, yellow and forceful, long as shafts of corn. John. No.

And the city slamming shut.

After he left, it took her nearly two full weeks to grow used to sleeping in a house flooded with babies—especially the blue one who slapped her with his wet dolphin tail—and she would find herself awake in the night's stillest hour, in full moonlight, all motion having left the bed, listening to the dull pulse of the infants circulating through the rooms, bumping against the fur-niture, rustling the onionskin pages of her Bible, and listening beyond that to the slow suck of her firstborn's lips, because it was city Jack who captured her country eyes, sugared her up sweet, and put a moving inside her, her firstborn, a daughter, Cookie, wine-lipped Jack, in that other life before

John, in her very first apartment in the city—*a four-room railroad flat on T Street over in Woodlawn that boasted sixteen windows, concealing a single bathroom in the hall with a hole in the ceiling, where you squatted on the toilet under an open umbrella, guarding against the greedy eyes above*—which she shared with Beulah and Sheila.

Grunting, the driver hoisted the steamer trunk out of his cab and put it on the sidewalk. I'd take it up fo you, but, see, I got a bad back.

Beulah tipped him a nickel.

Thanks, downhome. He grunted off.

Four bad younguns stood on the stoop of their building.

> *My name is Ran*
> *I work in the sand*
> *I'd rather be a nigger*
> *Than a no-dancing white man*

Get on way from here, Beulah said.

We ain't doin nothin to you, granny.

Boy, watch yo mouth. I'll knock yo teeth back to Tupelo.

I ain't from no Tupelo.

I know where you from. I know yo kind.

Aw.

If yall was nice boys, you'd help us wit these bags. Can't you see my niece got all these here bags?

It took all four puffing boys to get the steamer trunk to the third floor.

Sho is heavy.

She got some gold.

Or some cold.

Or somebody dead in there.


THE SEEK-AND-FIND-HER MANEUVERS of the babies started after the train sliced off Sam's leg, smooth as bread or a tube of lunchmeat. Sam and Dave liked to jump the speeding trains. One miscalculated jump landed him in Mercy Veterans Hospital (years later renamed Dr. Martin Luther King, Jr., General Hospital, MLK, where Dave wasted away).

*No loss, Beulah said. That damn fool brother of mine left his sense back home when he came up here, Beulah said. He mightest well have left his leg.*

Sam shook for three nights with fever. His tongue spat out red words.

What's that he's mumblin? Gracie asked.

Something bout that Filipino woman, Beulah said.

What Filipino woman?

The one who had his baby.

What? This truly surprised Gracie, for Sam had never said word the first about it.

Back when he was stationed overseas. It ain't nothing, Beulah said. Over there, them women so po they'll do it all night long for a can of beans.

*I was so glad to get shut of them niggas, Beulah said. And when they get out the service, first thing they do come visit me. Well, first they go to California looking for R.L. Ain't there but a moment. Come visit me. I like to think they come to stay fo good. One night, I prayed to God, Please send them niggas back to Houston . . . I guess they heard God's call, or maybe they jus missed all that devilment. They took the first locomotive back to Houston. But those two weeks they stayed wit me . . .*

*Well, Beulah, I guess they didn't want to get shut of you, cause two years after that—*

*—they come for good.*

The doctors put a spoon in Sam's mouth to keep him from swallowing his tongue—*like you had to do when Nap had one of his seizures*—shaking, like he hadn't got spilled onto the tracks but had actually caught the train and was riding it. That fever so hot that Gracie saw red plumes spreading over her hands and climbing red up the sanitized white walls. Only Beulah could stand the heat of Sam's bed.

Sam, Beulah said. Sam.

Quiet down now, Beulah. They gon put us outa this room.

Sam, you want me to hold up yo leg? Sam.

Beulah, he can't hear you.

Sam. You the baby. Mamma told me to guard after you kids. Mamma told me—

The hours trembled on, and days. Sam shook off the fever. The doctors gave him a wooden leg, the same leg—no, they forced him to buy a new one, the termites crunching down to the roots of that first one—that, years later, Jesus and Hatch mistook for a toy when the family went visiting him, laid up drunk wit that lady who would steal his life, steal the wood of his head with her ax, *already knowing and planning her crime, cause she always fled the apartment whenever we visited, didn't want us to see the guilt in her eyes, read her war plan*—the boys knocking one another upside the head with the leg, or using it as a bowling pin, the same leg that Sam often set on fire when he got drunk and bounced down the stairs naked to smother it out.

Sam out of danger, Gracie returned home. She needed a Scripture to celebrate his recovery. She kept her Bible high on the closet shelf, away from cheese-seeking mice. She opened the closet and found a baby—the first of many she would battle or evade in all the years that have followed—nibbling the pages.


THE BIBLE was the only gift Daddy Larry ever gave her, four-leaf clovers inside, small dried bookmarks picked by his own Houston hand. She brought it with her when she came North. *Why come North? To escape finger-cutting cotton fields. To avoid bundles of cotton inside some cracka's house, shirts, skirts, socks, draws, and sheets. So, go North where yams grow in the sidewalks, lemonade flows from fire hydrants, and the sky rains silver and gold.* Bumping her Bible and her suitcases against seat sides on the whistling northbound steel-smoking hound that dragged her past black 'Sippi fields and yellow oceans of corn to this red gray green city. A rich, hideous city built of stone and steel and mist. Tall buildings—cliffs of solar glass—side by side, no elbowroom between them. Their shadows slanting across the train's steamy window. Beggars seated in their depths. Tar Lake at the end of every street. A flow of people moving up and down the avenues, circling a drain of boulevards. Winking traffic lights. Congested cars moving terrapin-slow. *Light or dark square cars, not the bright-colored round cars people drive today.* Great green buses driving a wedge through streets. Ties hauling suitcases. High-butt women in tight weaved dresses shaking keys. *I got a rainbow wrapped and tied around my shoulder.* Tough boys shoving their faces into each other. *One of the mysteries of city breeding.* Life in proportion to beauty. This place up North was not in God's world.

The conductor took her suitcase without her asking, and beckoned her to step down the train's narrow metal stairs where a small metal footstool awaited her on the platform. With one hand firmly holding the passenger railing and the conductor guiding her by the elbow, she turned her back to the platform, curved her Bible discus-like up to her chin, eased one heel then the other onto footstool, and took a short hop to city concrete. She retrieved her suitcase, thanked the conductor, then headed for the station lobby, past passengers training or detraining and cars steaming in wait.

Gracie! Beulah opened her arms like a strong machine, curved black hat like a snail shell on her head. Hair below her shoulders in one electrified whitening ray. She sucked Gracie in with vacuum power and speed.

Hey, Beulah. Glad to see you.

Beulah loosened her grip just enough to allow Gracie to angle, bend, and hug Sheila.

Gracie. Sheila's hand rubbed concrete circles on her back. Gracie. So glad to see you.

Gracie searched the words for warmth and truth.

You, redcap! Beulah screamed. Come take my niece's bags.

Once home, Sheila and Beulah allowed her an hour to bathe and rest, then guided her out of the apartment to discover the city. She can still remember smartly dressed city people betaking themselves to their chosen destinations, remember the casual walk to the Elevated platform, her first sight of a green commuter train, car doors rattling sliding banging open, and city people charging out like racehorses. Faces at every window formed a chain of countless eyes all staring at her. She clutched her Bible to her freshly bathed and powdered bosom. Train rocked and rumbled by.

This not our train? she asked.

No, Beulah said.

That's when Sheila explained the city's complicated network of trains and lines: subway and Elevated, A train and B train, express and local, rush hour, the Englewood line, Howard line, Jackson Park line, Evanston line, Ravenswood line. On and on.

Memphis had only buses. Surely city trains would shake her to pieces.

The three women boarded their train. Sat side by side. Gracie placed her Bible on her lap and folded her hands over it. The train began to move. Quicken. She stared out the green-flying window as a lens, clicking mental photographs at rows of shops and stores exposed to merciless morning sunlight, at streets boiling with life and trouble, pools of people linking into other pools, rivers of cars linking other rivers—things as common to northern city life as dog and dung on a 'Sippi road. She dug her fingernails into the green leather seat.

Beulah and Sheila shuttled her all over the city, the ins and outs, from the (seemingly) penthouse-high elevated trains to the sewer-low subways. She saw a subway minister for the first time.

It is written in the Scriptures, Be not deceived God is not mocked, for whatsoever a man sows he shall also reap the same. Good for good and evil for evil. The Lord has sown his good seed into the world today and should it fall on good and pure hearts it shall bring forth much good. So you have the faith, but you must plant it in good soil in order for you to do great things. But mortal soil cannot produce eternal things. One must place his faith in God. This is the best soil.

She would learn, here in the North, many preachers carried pulpits in their voices. Even frail-bodied subway evangelists like Mother Sister could paddle you with wood words. *They got wings for us to fly around. And water beds filled with blue rivers. But rent in heaven ain't cheap. Nor are flying lessons.*

Beulah found Gracie a job (day work) with the Sterns in Deerfield, a sharp, clean suburb a good hour north of the city. Train, carry me. Train, bring me back.


HER FIRST CITY WINTER. Snow. Pretty when it first fell. White and clean enough to eat, then later, gray and muddy with footprints or tire tracks. Snow coating the windows of cars, but the apartment windows heated from the warmth pulsing inside, free of frost, an occasional collar of snow on a ledge. Snow on the bare tree branches—bare branches curled, fingers reaching to grab the falling snow—half the branch white and the other half brown-gray, like flesh slipping out from a split pants leg or coat sleeve. The sky white—the fog white of after-snow—above the buildings. And cars making that washing sound you hear in rain or snow, beneath the motor's hum the sound of water spilled from a pail. Then the first killing frost. The frozen steel of subway and apartment pipes. The asthmatic breathing of the radiators. (Better than a rusted yard pump and the carrying stones of the fireplace, flames licking—coals really—crackling with heat.) Jack Frost nipping at yo nose and peeking up under yo clothes. Hawk trying to snatch off your draws. Winter laid a sheet of ice between you and yo kinfolk in the apartment. You looking out the white window and thinking, thinking, perhaps of spring—because in this city, winter often carried over into mid-spring, or came back in spurts both spring and summer, like an unexpected relative. Spring: the trees a green maelstrom of mad leaves and brown movement because the city's wind stayed with you year-round, folding into the seasons. And thinking further of autumn, your favorite season, when the city grew alive with color, the summer's last fires flicking new flames of heat and pigment, red and green and blue and white and pink and red-pink and brown-red and yellow-brown and not just the pinks and greens and whites of budding May. But fall so far away, not like the babies who stand in the trees all day and night, a few feet from the building.


HER FOURTH CITY WINTER—so it seems to her now—she boarded the train and saw the Burned Man for the first time. A short man and fat, every space of his blue-jean jumpsuit covered with buttons—sermons, slogans, prayers. A few clumps of hair, like an unfinished bird's nest. And his head a lump of clay kneaded onto his body. No neck, all head. Clean swathes of smooth brown skin—funny how burns leave brown scars, not black—and the face smooth too, no eyebrows or eyelashes or eyelids. He rattled his hot tin cup, the metal sound giving more momentum to the steel wheel grinding steel rails.

Brothers and sisters, I come from the Church on the Rock and I bring you these books—*pamphlets, flyers*—these revelations designed to bless each and every individual which shall read them seven straight days, seven days in a row. As of today, there are 916 confirmations of blessings, 916 people who had received glowing gifts from the hand of Christ. Just last night a woman phoned me, Brother Foot, I thank you. Christ reached out his hands and turned my rags to gold raiments. I won the lottery after reading your book seven straight days and seven days in a row. Sister, I said to her, All who believe in Christ shall hit the jackpot. There are no number runners fleeter of foot than the winged angels in our Father's heaven.

God sent his only son to save man. Praise be to his only son, our Lord Saviour Christ. The burned man rattled his cup. Please give what you can. Read these Scriptures seven straight days, seven days in a row.

Gracie removed a dollar from her purse. Dropped it into the hot tin cup. Keep your book, she said. She never rode the train again.

HER SIXTH CITY WINTER, Sam and Dave arrived from Houston—on a fleeing locomotive—in summer's clothing, and made all Englewood sweat from their sinful Houston heat. Daily they galloped from bar to bar, lounge to lounge, liquor store to liquor store; sundown, they posed against afterglow on corners, watching cars cruise down Church Street—

I gotta get me a car, Dave said.

The way you drive, Sam said. Huh.

What's wrong wit the way I drive?

You don't know? Sam shook his head.

I gotta get me a car.

—and rested at night, collapsed in the bug-ridden pastures of nasty women's beds.

TWO YEARS LATER, Sam and Dave got sent up the river for stealing hogs from the factory, dressing the hog up like a man in a long coat and Dobb, leaning its legs over their shoulders and holding it up between them, Come on, Wheatstraw, you drunk fool, know you ain't sposed to drink on the job. But of course, two years after that, after the arms of justice had released them, they needed a place to stay and crowded into the one-room apartment with Beulah, Sheila, and Gracie, Sam and Dave sleeping beneath the kitchen table on the red-and-white-checkered oilcloth—Damn, you niggas, Beulah said, get out from under my tablecloth. People gotta eat on it. Enough to spoil yo appetite—*the same checkered oilcloth where, later, in the house here on Liberty Island, John would beat Lucifer and Dallas (his pig's snout level with the board, as if this could improve his concentration) at chess, and still later, whip the pants off the boys, Hatch and Jesus, til Hatch mastered the game, beating John and Lucifer for their spare dollars.* Wasn't a week before every devil-may-care man on Church Street cussed their names.

You niggas need some work, Beulah said.

Them two Jones boys—Sheila began.

Lucifer, Gracie said. And John. The one wit those brown eyes.

Why you worried bout em? Sam wanted to know. You mus like them brown eyes.

—got jobs washing windows. In Central. Good money too.

Now, what we need with work? Sam said.

Tell her, uncle. We had plenty work in the joint.

Well, Beulah said, why don't yall go back there and press some license plates.

License plates? Woman, I worked in the infirmary. And he assisted me. Sam hooked his thumb at Dave, who sat stretched back in the wooden chair, leg hooked over the arm.

Look, I don't care if you—

Don't say it, Sam said. Beulah, you know I know you. Don't say it.

Beulah gave him a hard look.

Look, woman. Get it straight. We ain't workin fo no chump change.

And we ain't luggin round that kid no more. Dave flicked a nod at Cookie. Like to break my back. Shit, silks ain't serve me no hard labor. Jus a straight sentence.

Yeah, Sam said. We ain't her daddy.

And we ain't gon pretend.

Sides—Sam smoothed his conk with the palm of his hand, followed its movement of waves, wet leaves—we fin to light out fo California and see R.L. Surprise visit.

Yeah. Surprise visit.

The only way you lazy niggas get to California is if it come to you.

That's mighty fine wit me, Beulah. Mighty fine. But I ain't luggin round that two-hundred-pound baby no mo. Sam hooked his thumb at Cookie, who sat crooked and twisted in the wooden wheelchair—the one that Gracie, years later, stuffed in the pantry, beyond Hatch's and Jesus's curious reach, the toddlers mistaking it for a rocking chair—body both tense and limp, legs smooth, round and slack as ropes, tiny feet motion-ignorant on the running board. Nothing straight about her, even with the leather belt holding up her waist, face lax, mouth open, completely relaxed, or tired perhaps, just tired. Only her eyes moved, watching you come in and out of the room, blank and unblinking, dead fish stare.

Got that right, Dave said.

*I was so glad to get shut of them niggas when they went off to the service, Beulah said. War didn't change them none. Always askin, beggin, Sister, how bout lettin me hold some change. Then Dave go, Aw, Sam, don't ask her. She cheaper than Jack Benny. Sam and Dave worry me so that sometimes I wish they'd never come back from Bataan. Buried there wit all them Japs.*

Beulah worked nights—spring and summer—so she could attend baseball games during the day—That Paige, oh that Paige; his curveball hum like a Roadster—and Sheila worked nights so she could watch Cookie during the day. When you returned from work, you and Sheila would lift Cookie down the three flights of stairs—a trip someone would make for seventeen years until your gains ebbed away and Cookie drowned in a sea of pneumonia—so you could take Cookie strolling in the park. You took her there every day, through lazy snow or sun slanting with wind. Circle Park was beautiful then, fields of red and yellow and pink roses, fields wide as the moon. The sky large, white, clear: a huge drop of milk. The grass neat. The hedges trimmed. Wind in the air. The iron streetlamps free of rust and the stems so brown and tall, and the lantern so wide and green, you mistook them for trees. And you circled the lanes, palms firm-gripping the handlebars of the wheelchair—hanging on the course of your life. The stroll was just that easy; a single movement, a slight turn of the handlebars, returned you to the apartment door stoop. You removed the keys from your purse.

Why, Miss Gracie. John watched her with those brown eyes. You need some help gettin Cookie back upstairs?

Yeah, Miss Gracie, Dallas echoed. You need some help gettin Cookie back upstairs?

John stood there, hat in hand, head bowed, thin waves of hair shining, the cut of his eyes directed where the hat brim would be, stood there, before a spillage of leaves on the vestibule doorsteps.

Thank you, boys.

John and Dallas slipped out of their blazers—*no, Dallas wearin that old funky nasty pea coat*—folded them neatly over their shoulders, and stooped like stretcher carriers, hands positioned on the wheelchair. Okay, John said. On the count of three. One. Two. Three. John and Dallas lifted Cookie in the air and carried her up the stairs, never missing a breath, their heels tapping cutting rhythm. Set her down—Cookie slobbered a smile—and stood waiting before the front doors, watching Gracie.

Yall want something to drink?

Yes'm.

Yes'm.

Have a seat. They did as Gracie ordered. She got them cool lemonade in Beulah's mason jars. John tilted his head back and drained his jar, throat working. Dallas did the same. John watched her—she thought of herself, how her skin gleamed like black milk—feet several inches above the floor. He was so small and Dallas so large that Gracie expected John to hop in Dallas's lap like a ventriloquist dummy. But he watched her. She assumed the men wanted a tip. Took two quarters from her purse and pushed it into their hands.

Wish I could give yall mo money.

John watched her, eyes wide as stage lights. Why, we don't want no money. Here. He reached out and took her hand, his own moist with heat, and put the quarter inside it. Dallas did the same, parroting, watching her with wino eyes, flood-delta red eyes. She returned her hands to the safety of her lap.

The windows let in chunks—square after square, box after box—of summer. It was a hot day, and the sun made the screen shimmer. Yellow light—line after line—streamed inside her window and tangled itself with the glow of the hanging sheets.

Dallas, where you from? She said it to break the ice. She smelled raw oysters on his breath, the raw oysters with hot sauce that everyone in Woodlawn knew he bought from Brother Jack's Lounge, this only child of smooth-skinned Vanilla Adams, who worked the white folks' houses but never showed the wear, this boy who could fix anything that went bad, radios, toasters, space heaters, electric blankets, humidifiers, refrigerators, and (later, when people began to afford them) televisions.

I was born by a golden river in the shadow of two great hills, Dallas said.

Nigga, John said, stop that clownin.

You stop.

You still drinkin that wine? Gracie asked.

Dallas shaped the brim of his Dobb. John flipped his on, fit it in place, pushing down softly. Dallas did the same.

I takes a nip every now and then. How you know?

Nigga, she smell yo breath.

You a lie. Dallas put his nose into the cup of his palms and blew air, testing.

Don't mind him, Miss Gracie. He still kinda young.


IT WAS MONDAY ALREADY and the service had been a good one. *Moses parted the Red Sea, allowed the people of Israel to escape the waters through the hollow of his reed staff.* Gracie had carried the service home with her, like a take-out order. She could still hear the chorus of laughter and amens, ringing shouts and pleas, stomping feet and clapping hands. Cotton Rivers helped Reverend Tower back into his seat, the older man shaken by the force of his own sermon. Rivers was always helping. Draw his handkerchief at the first bead of sweat on Tower's brow. Some folks in the congregation called him Bird Dog, cause it was his job to hunt out the places on Church Street most needing redemption. His job to follow Tower, that Cleveland Sparrow tagging along, each holding up one sleeve of Tower's flowing robe, absorbing its power.

Someone knocked on the door, hard and fast, like a fire warning. Gracie opened it. John, hat in hand, head bowed, the wings of his eyes lowered.

Hi, Miss Gracie.

Why, John.

The careless lifting of his brown eyes. I thought you might need some help.


GRACIE HAD WATCHED LUCIFER AND JOHN grow from two pint-sized boys in railroad caps—John the pint, Lucifer (two years older) the quart—whose laughter disrupted Reverend Tower's solo flights—*I know there are some greasy souls here today, tryin to slip their way up into heaven*—boys who shot down his heavenly sermons like clay birds with their filthy tongues—*Though I speak with the tongues of angels, and have not charity, I am becoming as sounding brass, or tinkling cymbal*—slipped their snores into his verbal pauses, and Reverend Tower would wake them with biblical anger. *If you boys wanna snore, go to Catholic mass!* It was her duty to shepherd the children from the chapel to the bathroom, and there they would be, Lucifer and John, aiming two streams of urine at the ceiling.

*Nigga, you can't piss fo shit.*

*Piss better than you.*

*Well, can you piss this high?*

*Higher.*

And Gracie would feel some new feeling circling around her heart, circling and rising, while Lucifer and John held their faces tight, roping in their grins, until she snatched their ears, their hands panicking, trying to slip their worm-small penises into the sanctuary behind their pants zippers. The entire congregation knew they were being raised by the grandfather, Pappa Simmons, the squat nigga with a touch of Indian, or a dash, depending on who you asked—the roll of something wild in his yellow-red features; the gray of his eyes had crushed out the brown; *Was he blind?*; his words were so ancient they crumbled to the carpet before they reached your ear—and Georgiana, his white-looking wife, both worn down from sharecropping back home and hauling city sugar and mail sacks, their old flesh and down-home ways left in the dust by the quick city steps and ways of the boys. Yes, she had watched them grow from mannish boys in railroad caps, the skinny rails of their legs beneath baggy slacks, to teenagers, two young men in tweed or plaid golf caps and peg pants. How could she have known then that these two boys held men's seeds, that these seeds would someday crack open and the newborn beings would accept the agreeable weight of manhood, would carry the silver rails of Sam's coffin, help to bury the old seed. Yes, they grew, stretched out of their tweeds, their swelling heads shrinking their boy caps—they replaced them with man-holding Dobbs—Lucifer upwards and John sideways, til no britches could hold them, they going one way and restraint the other, Lucifer running errands, and John running the streets with Dallas and Ernie and Spider and the other bad niggas who kept up a heavy traffic between the clubs and lounges on Church Street. Couldn't pass a corner without seeing John and Dallas pitching pennies, tossing the coins easy and graceful like life rafts.

How you, Miss Gracie?

Yeah, how you, Miss Gracie?

She could feel their eyes warm on her behind as she passed. *Maybe not Dallas's eyes, eyes that did not absorb a flicker of light. Frozen wells.*

Then, who could have known that, years later, John would beat Dallas within an inch of his life, and still later, that he would strap her, Gracie, to the bed after she told him, You sleepin in sin, both asking and answering. She saw his belt raise but closed her eyes to its sting. She searched high and hellwater for her keys. Could find them nowhere. Believed John had robbed her of them, as he had first surprised her with the burning damage of his words. *Why you think I be out there? Why you think? I like you but I don't lust you.* So surprised she still didn't know what instrument he'd used to whip her, his belt or his tongue. He opened roads in her back and walked them. She sought her keys, found them in the space under the bed, locked the door on her way out of the apartment, and caught the first taxi. Trucks flew through the yellow-lighted streets. A yellow moon. *The moon's taking a piss, John said.*

She explained to Inez and George—the man John would never call father, spit at the suggestion—what had happened, the story both heavy and formless from the water in the words. *You thought George woulda whispered a word of it to Lucifer, Check on John. Go check on yo brother. George probably wanted to and maybe he did, though how could you tell cause Lucifer always watched you in flicking glances, as if you were more than vision could bear.*

George took car keys out of the cookie jar. I'm gon kill that bastard.

George, Inez said, now wait. Junior didn't—

Damn, Inez. Open your eyes.

But Gracie was the one paralyzed by a blinding fright.

George shook the car keys in Inez's face. Damn, Inez. Open your eyes. Shook them again.

# 5

WALL-TO-WALL PEOPLE—crowded dots in an impressionist painting—load the car. Don't be such a bitch, lady. What's wrong? Didn't you get what you needed last night? The hog is just ahead, shoving its way through the car. Damn, homey? Think you a football player? He slaps a grip on hog's shoulder. Feels a burning sensation in his stomach. The hog has cork-screwed him with its tail.

The hog runs for the mouth of the tunnel, three-toed feet slipping on the tracks like a woman in high heels.

He surges and plunges, a windmill, all legs and arms, snatching his feet up almost before they touch the ground. The hog spins on one leg—the chubby shank, the monkey-wrench calf—brings the other high in a wide arc, and catches him on the side of the head—the temple, right? the church at both sides of your head—then, hollow pain, like someone knocking a pipe bowl against a table's edge. The old roundhouse kick. Hog knows its licks and flicks.

He has to guard against the hands—paws?—the narrow fingers in-grown perfect for the old eye gouge.

He sees an opening. Drop-kicks the hog in the balls. (Know my flicks, too.) Son of a bitch, the hog says, hands over his balls, Adam holding the fig leaf.

They are tangled between the rails—which one is the third, the hot jolt of raw electricity?—rolling, two contestants in a mud-wrestling match. The hog stinks bad—pickle juice?—and is covered with scratchy, stubbly skin, three-day-old beard over the whole week of its body. It tickles. He locks his teeth onto the hog's tonguelike ear. (Wait, raw pork is bad for you.) Hog considers returning the favor, but it is dignified, the low blow beneath him. These humans . . .

He brings the butcher knife—the knife, how could he have forgotten it?—into view. Hog-squeals. He drives the knife between the second and third chins, a clean blow. He can feel a weapon on the hog, just as he knows it *has a navel. What makes it moo—grunt?—oink? So that's why they called it—*

A grind of gears—*a lawn mower? a car?*—started beneath the small high window above the bed filled with books stacked like sandbags. Hatch's early-morning skin felt the old mattress—he slept in the same old iron bed he'd had all his life; each night, the coiled springs kept squeaking even after he lay still—but the contours and niches did not fit his bones. *Somebody's been sleeping in my bed.* His feet dangled over the edge, awaiting the hangman's ax. He swung his legs from beneath the covers, rooted his feet on the floor, pushed his torso up, and sat on the bed's edge, leaning forward, chin resting on the pyramid of his fingers. His sleep muscles tightened trying to hold on to the heat and color of the dream. *The shit that can crowd your sleep.* Sleep slowly pulled its two black wings from over his face. Silver teased his vision. A dogtag bright-dangled from his neck. He squeezed its motion in his fist. It was perforated down the middle, like a salt cracker, so—Lucifer had explained when he gave it to him many years ago—that strong hands could snap it in two, half of the tag marking the body and the other half, the grave. He checked the bed for dampness. Early-morning voices and traffic sounds rolled over him. He had never been one to take all the nightmare images from the evening news into his sleep. Why now?

The previous night he'd had trouble sleeping. A jackal had thrashed its tail repeatedly against his chest. He had defended himself with a motion he remembered but his body couldn't perform. Turned on the bulb beneath the hooded lamp. Sat on the bed edge, then moved over to the chair before the window, shade drawn. Small light teased the room, pale, from a street-lamp. And the darkness beyond, full of the city's sounds. Then a tin-trickle of rain. He sat that way until a washed-out sky and a swollen sun drenched the windows with golden light. Fingers of dawn pulled him back into sleep, into dream.

*A recurring feeling. Above: sun—choking up his skin's natural oils. He thinks. Pulls up clumps of grass from a mental pasture, a black concentration of thought-force, chewing a blade or two to cut free thoughts. The sap of resilient spring. The sun eats its last shadow for the day. Night falls boulder-heavy, heavy drape to drop over the day, cloak to shelter you. A lizard scuttles green. Curled, the lizard curves around the circle's inside. Grunts and silence. Silence and grunts.*

The shade blew steadily in the window with a rasping sound. The mattress and springs coughed dry. The sun stood small in the empty morning sky. Rays of light spread wide, like the early-morning legs of a man above his toilet, pissing yellow.

He screwed his guitar in tune. Played a few invisible notes. His fingers re-fused the strings. Why? He showered and dressed, quickly. Pulled a book, *Myths of a Mestizo Continent*, from the half-bubble chamber of his drop-leaf desk. A gooseneck lamp junkie-nodded over the wooden desktop. Once, the brass desk lock had hidden all his important belongings—magazines, books, his songs, poems, rhymes, and letters—*Yes, letters. Damn. I've wrote Elsa poems, songs, rhymes; still she ain't mine; should I try letters? Elsa. Elsa*—from the eyes of others. Especially Sheila's nosy eyes. He would not tell his mother Sheila about his hard night. She'd already applied remedies to lighten up his sleep: put a doormat before his portal so the spirits could rest their shoes; sat a glass of water on the mat to quench the thirst of their long journey from *there* to here; and tacked a Scripture above the inner door—*Just in case these evil spirits*—BLOOD SAVE ME. She had a theory: his posters—Bruce, Jimi, Bird, Trane, Jack J., Joe L., the honored dead whose names popped and blinked from these paper gravestones rooted to the walls—had attracted restless spirits. The dead call us to re-member.

The carpeted stairs creaked softly as he came down. Sheila stood framed in the open bathroom door, eyes dead set in the mirror. One hand hidden inside a Parisian washcloth—a pot mitten, a hand puppet—a souvenir from the Shipcos. A long monologue of soap and silence. Hot light flamed her taffy-colored skin. Reddened her skirt—diaphanous, flowing (flaming creases, rippling) in heat-blinding white—and matching pumps. Her hair sprawled a black uncombed shawl about her shoulders—like her aunt Beu-lah's hair—not the usual ponytail. The air steamed from her recent bath, the smell of scented soap and powder—musk? opium? honey?—and her la-bored breathing. She picked up—with hands callused by the rhythm of work, skeletal hands, the skin sail-tight, hands the Shipcos (and others be-fore them) had molded for her through thirty-five years of bronzed labor, hands that carried fine-papered books from the Shipco residence (*They ain't gon miss them. They got plenty more*) to here—a brush from the porcelain sink edge.

Good morning, she said.

Good morning. Lucifer already gon to work?

Your father went with John.

Uncle John?

Sheila nodded.

Hatch had not seen or heard from John in over a month. Nor had Inez seen or heard from him. Gracie relayed Hatch's messages to him, but he had yet to respond. Which had prompted Hatch to take the train ride out to

Eddyland and try John's extra set of house keys; John (or someone) had changed the locks. Why ain't he called?

He didn't say. The light is different where she stands from the light that surrounds him.

What you mean Lucifer went with him?

Your father sposed to meet John at Union Station. John's going out of town for a few days.

Why?

I didn't get all that. Lucifer rushed off in such a hurry.

Is something wrong?

I know bout much as you do.

Where Uncle John goin?

Do I look like John?

Hatch thought it over. He was not part. Neither Uncle John nor Lucifer wanted him to be part. Hidden rendezvous. Well, he said. Catch you later. I'm going to go see Inez.

One hand swam—a dolphin—along the white sink. Dived into a low glass of clear water. Brought teeth to the surface. Drowned dentures. Clean. Applemeat-white. Slapped them into her mouth. When a stranger or visitor caught her off guard, she would hide her toothless mouth (gums and more gums) with her hand and speak through her fingers. This embarrassing ritual would cause Hatch to shrivel, fade, then flare up in silent, unexpressed anger.

*Sam never could drive for shit, Dave said. I know. We runnin buddies for years. Never could drive. But he insist on drivin with that wood leg. We drivin down to see Beulah. John loaned me the car and I loaned it to Sam. Cause he beg me the whole night. Nephew, Sam said, after all I done done for you. You can't let me drive? And he kept on beggin. Sheila say, If you let him drive this car, you better let me out on the side of the road. And you know how Gracie is. She read me from the Bible. Sam keep at me. Nephew this and nephew that. I let him drive. Sheila don't get out. And Gracie don't open her Bible. Drove along fine for a mile or two. Then it happened. One, two, three. Faster than you can snap yo fingers. They couldn't separate the teeth from the glass.*

She faced him. When you talk to her?

Last night.

How she doin?

Same ole.

Sheila shook her head.

She—

Hush.

*Hello, Inez?*
*Jesus. How are you, baby?*
*This Hatch.*
*Oh.*
*How you doin?*
*Terrible.*
*How's George?*
*A long pause. Fine.*
*Well, I want to come and see you.*
*Don't come. You know I'm sick.*
*But—*
*There ain't nothin good out here.*
*I'm gonna come see you.*
*You'll understand someday when you old.*
*Be there tomorrow morning. Bout nine.*
*Don't come so early.*
*Okay.*
*If you gon come, come on then.*
*I will.*
*Bring Jesus. Bye.*
Well tell her I said hi.
I will.
Get you some breakfast before you leave.

I will. Hatch was already in the kitchen. Aunt Jemima's face floated up from the oatmeal box. Steam lifted from Lucifer's untouched nest of hawk-eyed grits. *Hawk grits soar to the nest of your ribs.* Toast floated on steaming coffee.

And some meat. You need meat. One day you'll see. Your body need meat in the mornin.

*Little chance of that.* Okay. Hatch drew open the refrigerator. Cold rushed out. Throat working, he guzzled some apple cider, straight from the jar. *Hope she didn't see that.* Held the edges of a toast slice and moved the butter knife in rhythmic strokes. Took a few slices of toast and some scrambled eggs and made two sandwiches. He eyed the ham on the bright white plate. *Leave that man's pork right here on the table. Take a pitchfork and feed the devils pork. Didn't Christ put demons in a herd of swine? Ain't the pig a graft between a rat, a cat, and a dog?* Stuffed the sandwiches into a paper bag and stepped out into the screaming morning.

Second Street. *Deep Second, Uncle John called it.* Edgewater. *Woodlawn long gone. South Shore too. An axis of distance.* Hatch suffered a furnace of sky. The sun's still yellow wheel. Birds winged high in a windless sky, their voices—yes, voices, high above in the blue-red arch—circling, circling—like explorers—new terrain. The air poked sharp, threading the lungs. A trumpet to the blood. Strange. Cause no wind. Unusual, here in this city of one big lake (Tar Lake) that lifted a hawk from the icy nest of its waters and flapped you in the wind of its cold feathers (stalactites of feathers, dripping winter year-round)—this lake imitating ocean. Like a traveler who had not seen land for months, he saw the world with new eyes. All the colors vivid. Saw two black lines of birds—red-tipped beaks, beaks dipped in inkwells—stiff on two black lines of telephone wire. Trees in green leaf. Brown blazers of barks covering their trunks—*And tracks. Networking through the bark; the seed must absorb water to rehydrate;* Sheila's green thumb had impressed this lesson, in the middle of his forehead—and brown sleeves of bark enveloping their skinny limbs.

A radio coughed on the horizon. Hatch tugged his horseshoe earlobe.

*Hello my friend*
*Sky, so happy to see you again*

*Do you know, Brother*
*What the wind's blowing down*
*Have you seen, baby*
*A million million peoples coming right on down*

The song retracted from Hatch's ear. Jimi. They bustin Jimi. The radio gurgled, cleared music from its throat. In the chambers of his mind, Hatch busted a rhyme.

*This is Genuine Draft*
*Master of all sorts of darts and arts and crafts*

*Back again my friend*
*So wipe the suds from your mouth and wipe on a sin grin*

*Dropping science and my mix ain't thin*
*Friend, I can chemistry you again and again*

*I view the colored heart from close range*
*And get mo strange than a Col trane and another thang*

*Stakes snakes states skates shakes*
*Wobbling and snaking making crooked trails and trailin flakes*
*Brakes and grapes and drapes and crates*
*It's my aim to take*

*Yes, My my my my my*
*Just me myself and I*

*Sharp as Shaft as tack*
*Here to kick the facts about how*
*the decks are stacked and whacked*

*Slice you up and put you down*
*Like toast in the toaster twelve miles underground*

*I'm a hardcore worker to the bone the bone*
*Got more rocks than Fred Flintstone*

*But even a rock man got wages to pay to the biblical pages*
*Victim to them skeezers like Eve*
*time way back befo the ages*
*I'm tellin you, bro, my girl got me goin through laboring stages*
*Cleaned me out, pay me coolie wages*

*Called me on a Monday another day another dolla*
*She say yo homeboy what's up I bought you nother flea collar*

*Come over quick let me see if it fit yo little ass*
*Shriveled up bastard, yo money last long as passed gas*

*You see what I mean, flip?*
*Thought I was captain of my ship*
*But she slapped me down a tip*
*Unctuous bitch got me losing my grip*

He trimmed his tongue. Unctuous? Check that. The ear trieth words as the mouth tasteth meat. Cause the whole language resembles the body of a trained athlete where every muscle, every sinew, is developed into full play. One day my ear will take me far. Hatch's tongue rolled in his mouth, the pea in the whistle.

*Slipping and sliding right down her manhole*
*I'm all covered with shit, black sheep lost from the fold*

Loud spit flooded his song. No, smells ambushed his nose. *Smell like dried doo-doo on a doggy day.* Realization barked in. Packs of unleashed jackals—all dyed in the same flaming color of spring (summerlike) heat—trotted in ducklike lines, sniffing out somewhere they might nuzzle their greedy snouts. Sunlight glared on their white shirts. Their clothing said blood. At the next corner, more jackals lay in wait. Wet dripping tongues tasting the day. Chiseled white fangs hungering to bite off the feeding hand. *Sic em, boy!* Paws shaking in tune to color and noise. *Every time Jack looks in yo face, he sees a mirror of his crime. And though he stacks the plates of grace, he ain't never done no time.* The best way to take jackals to your heart is to get as far away from them as possible. But Hatch had nowhere to run. He timed his movements against the rhythm of the street. Their ears caught the beat of his feet. These sound-sensitive jackals, red ears like sharp twitching flames. Red-tailed jackals blazing off to buy some coal or get their ashes hauled. Pure products from the deep red doghouse. *It must not be hot, that one can burn in it forever and never burn up.* Their mouths moved, but silence came out—a wordless gap—for their words rusted together in one red voice. Hatch pushed forcefully through them, a river in the middle of a red sea. Where had they come from? Who'd dreamed them? *A handful of light in his palm. Then a wild pitch spinning black out—* The thought cooled off in a hot breeze. *What Spin say on his record? A burned goose laid the golden egg of civilization.*

A red light halted him. He rubbed his throat. His voice hurt from the song. He pulled the sandwiches, greasy, slippery, from the paper bag. Took healthy bites. *Damn. Is there any taste in egg white?* Green put him back in motion. He rarely slept at night free of jackals, tail-whipping him, biting his chest, tugging his dick, clamping a tight bottle-cap anus over his mouth, or laying a heavy cloud of farts above his bed. Jackals at night and jackals in the day. He ate in large bites. The food was warm and slow and solid inside him. He felt it hang in his guts, bats in a cave. His stomach shook loose and steady around it.

A man flapped on the corner (VV and Second streets). Breathed vapors of yellow ribbon. Miniature flags (cloth)—small enough to deck midget coffins—waved in the free air. Miniature flags (plastic)—American, African (the red, black, and green), Puerto Rican (or Mexican?)—buzzed in his hair. At the next corner, a flyer red-beckoned from a lamppost: DO YOU WANT TO DIE OVERSEAS? A hand had scrawled in black marker beneath it, Niger

Go Back to Afreeca. *Punk, learn to spell first.* I ain't gon fight in no war. Not like Uncle John and Lucifer. Sam and Dave.

*Did yall have fun?*

*Fun? Nephew, did we have fun?*

*Fun? Man, them silks is something else.*

The lockstep life. The snap of servile salutes. Butts upended for the company chaplain. *Let God's winged horse root in you. Let the thunder of his hooves become your beating heart.* Jackal shit. Pure jackal shit. Not for me. Hey, no sand bunny ever called me nigger. Still, many fools out here eager to throw themselves under the hooves of the beast.

*If they was so bad, how'd they make it through the army?*

*Same way they made it through Houston, Beulah said. If Dave could tell one lie, Sam could tell two.*

*But didn't the army—*

*No. Them niggas steals off the truth. Steal a meat bone from a dog.*

The memory chased its own tail.

*Be patient, Beulah said, cause what is hot today will be cold in the end.*

He took more bites. The sound of his sticky chewing seemed to come from somewhere outside himself. He felt under the constant gaze of the sun's watchful face. Like a ray, it fell everywhere. *Red.* His eyes roamed the street, tiny bicycle wheels. He ate and walked. Some jackals paraded up and down the street—yes, paraded, proud-flying their colorful flea collars—while others rushed to catch the El. Pulses thumping, Hatch finished the sandwiches a moment before he arrived at the El's steps. He took them slowly, one by one. Seated in a cramped booth—an outhouse was bigger—the ticket agent took Hatch's money and slipped him a transfer with the evident sense of exercising a well-earned right. Dumb bastard. What did the agent know? Hatch knew. The El ran its orbit around the city, making stops here in Central, in Eddyland to the west, Kings in the east, South Lincoln, North Park—all the city's five boxes. Careful of his book, he removed a neatly folded Kleenex square from his back pocket and wiped his greasy hands on it. He dropped the soiled tissue into the foul depths of a garbage can. He watched the still logs of the rails. How heavy were they? How much did each weigh? How many men did it take to— A jackal leaned in near to him. And another. His legs found clean space. He kept his toes well behind the yellow line before him.

*What'd you feel?*

*Nothing, Sam said. But I could taste the rails. Iron. Blood.*

Life happens in a flash. As a boy, he'd read that humans have lead in the bloodstream, had believed the tracks might snatch him—*call* him, a steel mother commanding the child inside after a day of play—like a magnet. *Now* he knew, the speed, the momentum could suck you up.

He was not part. Lucifer had gone off to meet Uncle John. And he was not part. Lucifer knew how close he was to Uncle John. Uncle John surely knew. Why hadn't Lucifer awakened him? Why hadn't Uncle John invited him? Come along and be part. Why?

A STRONG SMELL OF FRESHNESS AND EARTH pushed through the open window. Gracie saw green among the gray. Lula Mae had left for New Mexico on a day like this. Rose above the strong-limbed earth and roared off into the great yellow world. It must have been spring, for the onions were the first vegetables to fill the air with aroma, their hollow stems poking black blades through the soil. Last spring, Lula Mae had returned. That is, she had come here to the city. (By bus? train? No, the plane.) Came to attend a ceremony honoring her grandson. White and timeless. Gracie watched her, wondering, How long? How long has it been? When had she last seen Lula Mae? Years ago at Beulah's house in Decatur? Or Big Judy's funeral in Fulton? Ceremony done, she flew back. Came and went. Came and went.

Then in the fall—*before or after Thanksgiving? you no longer remember*— Sheila had phoned her in the wee hours of the morning. Gracie, Sheila said, Lula Mae have cancer. The words echoed in the receiver. I jus called Beulah.

You called Beulah?

We better get down there right away. Porsha said she'll buy us plane tickets. Sheila hung up.

Gracie and Sheila caught the first plane smoking and flew to West Memphis. Sheila filled in the details. The hospital had released Lula Mae. She had already begun chemotherapy and shark cartilege treatments. She never spent an unguarded moment; women from her church's Senior Citizens Club provided, made sure she wanted for nothing.

The clouds outside the window were frozen swirls of thick white like cake frosting. Gracie couldn't remember the last time she'd visited West Memphis. Perhaps she'd gone with her sister and their sons on one of their childhood summer trips. Yes, that was it, to the best of her recollection. She shut her eyes and sought to retrieve some specific image or moment from her last trip, and seeking found none. Lula Mae was no welcome guest in her thoughts. And for this reason she had refused to travel to West Memphis. If only she could put some healthy mileage between herself and Sheila's know-it-all face.

Lula Mae's house and yard remained unchanged in reality and memory. The silver (spray-painted) garden chairs curiously in their element on the mowed grass. Blue sky visible at breaks in the rows of tall peach, pear, and apple trees. Trees that curved a horseshoe around the sides and back of the house. The little house (Lula Mae called it), a trailer propped up on cinder blocks that you reached down two splintery planks stretching from three cement back porch steps, always white and clean in the sun. And the house itself, green and white with the same stone porch. Gracie's old key still fit the front door.

Sheila, is that you? From her pillow-propped position on the bed, Lula Mae reached up and gave Sheila a forceful embrace. Sheila. They hugged long. Gracie stood at the bed smiling. She held her smile until she felt her face pulling out of shape.

Lula Mae released Sheila, then gazed with twinkling eyes at Gracie's face. Gracie bent for her hug. Pulled Lula Mae close, carefully, not knowing how touch might trigger pain. Lula Mae was equally lax. Must have used up all of her energy on Sheila's hug, for Gracie barely felt the two child hands that briefly pinched her back.

Yall came right away.

We came right away.

I can't believe it. Lula Mae wiped away her tears with bare colorless hands, wiping hastily without regard to her appearance. Tear stains criss-crossed with the shadows under her eyes and nose cast by the bedroom lamp and streaks of face powder. Her shrunken wig seemed too small for her head, hardly capable of hiding the patched gray. Gracie stepped back and almost stumbled.

LULA MAE SUFFERED A SPELL OF COUGHING before going to sleep. Gracie and Sheila settled themselves in chairs, unspeaking, and kept vigil through the night. And that night carried into more nights over days then months. The first week of every month, Gracie traveled by plane to West Memphis for a bedside visit. Sheila went every second week, Gracie returning as Sheila was leaving, Sheila returning as Gracie was leaving. Sometimes they waved at the airport.

FOLKS SAY, if you stand on the corner of Church and Sixty-third Street, you will eventually see all the people you have ever known or met, so when

Gracie first came to the city, she stood there, hoping Ivory Beach would pass by. She would beat the devil out of Ivory Beach. She saw, smelled, and felt the feverish rush of the city. But the wicked offers of men drove her from the corner after an hour of watching and waiting. The next day, she returned. And the next. It was this corner that taught her the life of evil. One day she saw a low, cloudy flutter of pigeons. She felt teeth on her behind. She made it to the solitude of her bathroom, removed her panties and checked herself in the full-length mirror, where she saw tiny marks, like a fork's indentation. She sat down on the toilet.

The rush of water relieved her of the day's filthy offers. She felt something clamp on to her behind. A baby held her buttocks in its gripped teeth.

A HOUSTON WONDER, Daddy Larry's three-legged cat ran faster than a dog wit six legs.

Gracie, Sheila said, catch that cat.

I'm tryin.

Can't you run no faster?

You, Sheila. You, Gracie. The stone of Ivory Beach's voice plopped at their feet. You girls stop aggravatin that cat.

Yes'm.

Don't yall have nothing better to do? Where that boy? Ivory Beach watched them, short and round, from her long-legged stool, a baby in a high chair. Her fat black face yielded a set of thin white teeth. Cat got yo tongue?

No, ma'm.

Where that boy wit them green eyes?

He walk to town.

Wit who?

Our kinfolks.

Nap, Dave, and Sam would sneak to the farm and steal apples, then take R.L., *that boy with them green eyes, that boy that ain't a McShan like his two sisters*, ditch-swimming.

Yo kinfolks?

Yes'm.

How come you let him go to town? Ain't yall older?

No, ma'm. He oldest.

Still, ain't yall sposed to be watching him? Ivory Beach knocked Gracie upside her head so hard that her thoughts rattled . . .

Don't, Sheila said. You hit her again, take the devil and his crew to get me offa you.

Ivory Beach watched her, unspeaking.

*Why, Miss Sheila. What you doin here?*

*Came to pay you a visit.*

*After all these years?*

*I waited.*

*Don't you look at me like that. You was an evil cuss. Should be grateful that I raised you.*

The next day, they found buckets of tick-red water in the barn.

Sho look funny, Gracie said.

Stink too.

Red river.

Nawl.

Paint.

*Larry, when you gon git that paint?*

*Next time I go to town.*

*Now, you been sayin that right near fo ten days.*

*And I might say it fo ten mo.*

*Larry McShan!*

*Looka here, woman—*

*Don't I deserve some spectful kindness? I, yo wife.*

*White folks the only one wit red barns.*

*Might be po, but this place don't have to look like the ground of no pigsty. The firewood should fit the cookin.*

Nawl, stupid. Blood.

You a lie.

That's Daddy Larry's blood.

Gracie said nothing. Both she and Sheila knew about the unseen world preached to Ivory Beach since the cradle—this woman from the backwoods swamps. Each night, the woman drank steaming horse tea. God knows what else she did. Who could tell the extent of her powers? Daddy Larry if anybody. He owned a tobacco patch—a *real* patch too, a few quilt squares—and Ivory Beach tended it. She rolled him fresh cigarettes, but he unrolled them and chewed the tobacco for snuff, a rusty coffee can serving as his spit cup.

What we gon do? Tell R.L.?

Nawl. You seen him kissin that heifer.

*Here, Miss Ivory Beach. Here some sugar fo you.*

Daddy Larry die?

He ain't dead yet.

Cause if he did die, then Lula Mae—

Or *she* make us hers.

The next Sunday after church, Daddy Larry gave Sam and his three nephews, R.L., Dave, and Nap, a nickel each to red-paint the barn.

You boys been stealin my apples? Ivory Beach said. Everyone still called her by her maiden name. She made the best applesauce in Chickasaw County.

*You needs to start you an applesauce business, R.L. said.*

*Cookin run in my family. My mamma the one invented Coca-Cola. She sold the recipe to a white man in Virginny. Fool run in my family too.*

Miss Ivory Beach, Gracie said.

Ivory Beach looked at her, saying nothing. You boys been stealin my preserves?

No, ma'm.

What yall doin?

Workin.

Paintin yo barn.

Miss Ivory Beach, Gracie said, Daddy Larry gave them a nickel apiece.

Anybody speakin to you?

No, ma'm.

You, boy wit the green eyes.

His name R.L., Daddy Larry said. Robert Lee Harris.

Don'tcha try to eat that nickel. Eats up everything else round here.

R.L. raised his toothpick arms high above his head, sucked air in and poked his chest out, then jackknifed. He walked on his hands.

Boy, stop that.

Git down here wit me, Miss Ivory Beach, R.L. said.

What? Why I ain't never heard such foolishness.

R.L. snapped his rubber-band legs and landed back on his heels. He smacked dust from his hands. He put two twig arms on Ivory Beach's shoulders, making prisoners of her head and neck.

Boy, what you doin? Let me go. Small butterfly hands fluttered up to the locked arms, but too late. R.L. planted a kiss on her cheek, lips purple on the black flesh, a living coin.

There! There you some sugar.

*He ain't die in no Eldorado. I know that for a fact.*

*Nawl, them crackas killed him jus like they killed Nap.*

*Jus like they woulda killed Sam and Dave. If they had caught them.*

*Yall, hush, Sheila said. Hush. Ain't nobody killed R.L. Ain't nobody killed Nap. Accidents.*

You younguns better learn some respect. Why, Lula Mae light outa town like she killed somebody. And I seen the devil hound on her trail. Aint no leash in Texas gonna hold it.

She ain't go to no Texas. New Mexico.

Texas, New Mexico—ain't no difference. Still the South. And a sin is a sin. She looked at Gracie. See, it's all in the bloodline. Good breedin shows.

The blue sky burst into yellow, thin, like Ivory Beach's chicken neck. She always had plenty of chores to give work to R.L.'s idle mind. Cleaning up the horse shit. Sorting the good peas from the bad peas. Plucking hair from the hanging hog on hog-killing day. Shucking corn.

R.L., Sam said, that lady got you doin lady's work.

Damn her dirty draws.

Double damn them.

Yeah. I feel like I been rode hard then put in wet, R.L. said.

*To get to Brazil, he woulda had to come back this way, cause California—*

*Porsha, hush.*

*What business a nigga got playin cowboy?*

*Don't know but I ain't a bit surprised he became a cowboy.*

*Damn them three rascals, Beulah said. White folks be damned if they didn't lynch em. Some colored folks love cracka mo than corn bread but not them three rascals. All I know is I get a call from Dave sayin that they gotta spirit outa town. R.L. had run off to California.*

*I thought he went out there to find his father? Mr. Harris?*

*Beulah continued, deaf to the question. Nap was dead.*

*Ain't nobody killed nobody, Sheila said. Beulah, you know Nap had those seizures and he get to drinkin and wouldn take his medicine.*

*And Sam get on the phone, Beulah said, and tell one version bout stealin out of some white woman's house and Dave git back on the phone talkin bout stealin her love. Whatever they did, they did it together. They both gets on the phone, cryin somephun bout crackas lynchin a boy in Fulton. Strung em under a railroad bridge and burned him up wit a blowtorch. Burned him so bad that his family didn't get no remains. First wind come along and blow his ashes from that rope. So I wired em some money.*


QUEEN OF THE MOUNTAIN, she bounced off the dresser in the old barn. Bounced, above and beyond. Went sailing over the side. Spread her wings only to discover they didn't work. Her stomach hit the edge of an open drawer, her flesh curving around it.

Sheila's lips moved silently.

At first Gracie felt no pain. Hers was the sudden feeling of falling down a well into the deepest solitude. Then she saw the pain, red spiders crawling down her thighs.

Gracie, Sheila said, You awright?

The words rolled heavy in Gracie's head.

Gracie? . . .

She'll be dry as an empty riverbed, the doctor said.

She was thirteen.


NOW, YOU AND GRACIE take this applesauce to Brother James.

I don't wanna be round no dead folks, R.L. said.

I don't either, Gracie said. She was thinking about the doctor's words. *She'll be dry as an empty riverbed.*

Ain't nobody dead. Do like I told you.

Sister James's house lay in the bend of the road, set far back from the trees to catch the best chances of light. *Why anybody want light in this 'Sippi heat?* The fever had gotten so bad that Sister James's naked black body glowed with heat. Not one sister of the congregation could get within ten feet of her without blistering.

Take the water from the well, Gracie said.

Why, girl, that water poison. Kill her for sure.

Listen. Take the water from the well. Gracie knew exactly what to do. Knowledge breaking like rushing waves inside her.

Lord!

Holy!

Heaven!

Fetch Miss Ivory Beach! Tell her come see bout this child.

That girl—the sister pointed at Gracie—one of them McShans.

You know Larry over there wit that three-legged cat. Triflin wife ran off—

And that one—the sister pointed at Sheila—touched. Born with a caul. So they both might be touched too.

Listen, Gracie said. Take the water from the well.

Sister, an older sister instructed, do as she asks. The lesser evil won't kill her no quicker than the more.

Sister took a bucket of water from the well. Gracie stuck her face in the rusty cool, bobbing for apples. She filled up the balloons of her jaws. She walked over to the bed and stood directly above Sister James. Arched back her head and sprayed a loop of water from her mouth, a thick stream that thinned and sputtered, then sizzled against the sick woman's naked skin.

Christ!

Moses!

Praise the Lord!

She makin the Good Book live!

It's the devil's work!

The sick woman's sweat knotted, a silver train that moved inward from the four corners of her body and congealed into a single large bead between her breasts. Gracie lifted the bead with two fingers. She snapped it in her mouth gumdrop fast.

That night, Sheila and Gracie discussed the day's events. Gracie realized that Sheila also possessed the slow fire of power, had always had it. *The Lord lends us his body to do good work.* Sheila explained the properties of roots, the democracy of ghosts, the committees of dead souls. *But who had told her? How did she learn?*

Look, Sheila said. Other folks live inside us. Yo body like a used road.

Gracie saw this, footprints up and down her body's inner roads. Well, I thought dead folks sposed to be *light*.

What you mean?

Like ghosts. Ain't they like sheets? Can't you put yo hands through them? Ain't they fulla air?

I think so.

They sho don't feel light.

Sheila said nothing.

If they gon walk inside somebody, least they could take off they shoes.

From then on, Gracie lived a life of iron prohibition, laying the gleaming metal bricks of her soul—smoke, drink, dance, frivolity, gossip, fornication, and profanity being the sins to be avoided, sins that would take an edge off her powers. She scaled up her belongings from this world and rode off to the next. Practices and prohibitions she brought North in her black steamer trunk. *Keep an eye on yourself, for fear you also may be tempted.* She would never forget that train ride. The long cold tube of the coach. She was fleeing Lula Mae's house for the station, and in the same image she was on a train looking down on flooded tracks, seeing a dead horse floating—its mane spread like a lily pad about its head—bobbing with the slow current. Two men at Union Station offered to carry her trunk; Beulah and Sheila arrived and chased them off with threatening eyes and purses—*Be careful of these city niggas*—this trunk heavy with the memories of every person back home she had helped, all the lights and shapes she had broken her soul into and shared with the less fortunate, all crammed into those brief years of power.

It was the most natural thing when Reverend Tower asked her to put in work for the church. Unlike the greedy-hearted brothers and sisters who only showed their face on Sundays, she went to Mount Zion every night of the week—*stay the course*—Reverend Tower's voice lifting the waters of her spirit—

*I won't tell my sins, for what is one man that he should make much of his winters, even when they bend him like heavy snow.*

*Preach.*

*I can see it all from a lonely mountaintop, the story of a mighty vision given to a man too weak to use it, the story of a people's dream that died in bloody snow.*

—in those days when Cotton Rivers was a poor deacon, those days before Reverend Tower died *and John, Lucifer, Dallas, and Rivers lowered him into the red soil of Woodlawn Cemetery (where Sam would later be buried), where he could watch over the souls of those he'd guarded in life* and the congregation light-lifted Cotton into the podium of leadership and power on the tips of their praying hands, Rivers weighing the souls of the congregation to find the heaviest ones, Rivers forming a partnership with the Reverend Cleveland Sparrow, pastor of the Holy Victory Outreach Church, the two men trading pulpits Sunday to Sunday, church to church, then sharing the same pulpit, and eventually setting up a pulpit at either end of the stage (at both Rivers's Mount Zion and Sparrow's Holy Victory); on the right side of the podium, with his right hand raised high in the air, Cleveland Sparrow always released the high ship of sermon—

*Abundance is belief in the Lord Christ.*

*What you say, Cleveland?*

*Cotton, I say abundance is belief in the Lord Christ.*

*Cause, our Gawd is the wealthiest being in the universe.*

*He is the owner of the trees.*

*He is the owner of the dirt rooting the trees.*

*He is the owner of every golden fruit born from the trees.*

*The stained glass flashed with the rhythm of moving shadows, the shadows of moving tongues.*

*He is the owner of the worm that spies in the fruit.*

*Yes, Gawd is the owner of the hollow beak that drinks the worm.*

*Gawd is the owner of the animals that eat the bird and the fruit.*

*He is the owner of four-walking animals that eat the fruit.*

*And Cotton, he is the owner of two-walking beings that eat the animals. You and me.*

*A blast of organ.*

*Yes, Sparrow. Man who holds dominion over the earth.*

*But Gawd is the owner of heaven and earth.*

*Who collects our rent.*

*He is the owner of the seas.*

*He is the owner of the fish in the seas.*

—buoyant, floating on the hands and prayers and amens of the congregation, the congregation that Rivers and Sparrow shared, as they shared snatches of sermon and prayer from the cup of fellowship, as they shared tithes and choirs, as they shared watching eyes; the preachers formed the Deacon Twelve, twelve deacons who spent every moment peeping through the bush of righteousness to observe the activities of every brother and sister of the church and to carry reports of sin back to Rivers and Sparrow so they could wash those sins in the waters of sermon; Gracie put in work for the church, visiting the sick, preparing meals for the hungry, adding the thin reed of her voice to the choir, and teaching the Sunday school class.

Christ taught and his teaching was so powerful that it mastered all nature. Birds flew about him and settled into the nest of his hair. Fish left the water and sprang into the cool waters of his lap. Tiger and lion lay down next to sheep. Wind and river flowed upward to his upraised hands. Pebbles followed his steps. Cause Christ made new roads from his winding shawl, white clean roads. If we stay clean, we keep wax out of our ears, and then we can keep our ears to his path. Do you all understand?

No one spoke.

Let me put it like this. Do not be misled. Bad associations spoil useful habits. Do you understand?

Yes, Miss McShan.

Lucifer, explain the passage to the class.

Well, you shouldn't hang around wit no bad niggers.

The class laughed.

Crude, but good. The Good Book says, A wise person will listen and take in more instruction, and a man of understanding is the one who acquires skillful direction. If any one of you is lacking in wisdom, let him keep on asking God, for he gives generously to all and without reproaching; and it will be given him.

Miss McShan?

Yes, John.

Do God come before my granddaddy?

*The devil come befo Pappa Simmons, that no-church heathen.* The Good Book speaks, Gracie said. And the word is living and its flesh never ages like the flesh of anyone's daddy, or, uh, granddaddy. Do you all understand?

Yes, Miss McShan.

Good. Let us sing.

*He's got the whole world, in his hands . . .*

—in his pants.

John, what did you say?

Just singin, Miss McShan.

He lyin, Lucifer said.

Nigga, shut up.
Both of you quit. Let us sing.

> *Raise me up*
> *Take me higher*
> *Lift me out of the fire*
> *Raise me to higher ground*
> *So I can see*
> *Turn the key*

—And my dick don't get too tight to pee.
John, what did you say?

# 7

NEAR THE CLOSE OF A HOT DAY—a lean, white spring—he sat, book in hand (*Man and Mestizo*), before an open window of Uncle John's Eddyland apartment, killing time. A vapor trail hung in the air, chalk-white. The window commanded a view of a long vista of riverbanks that cut into the horizon. The river like a plate of metal, reflecting the yellows of the day. Hills—he remembered these same hills from a dream when he was a kid (under Gracie's roof, lying in bed next to Jesus), but he couldn't remember the dream—that gradually flattened toward the river. *Hills? Well, not exactly. A few ridges rising out of the flat plains. Lumps in the carpet.* And the state line beyond the river. One world outside and one world inside.

From the window, he could see over the wall at the end of Canal Street to the busy avenue that ran two miles to the riverfront. Canal Street ran eastward to the lake. A broad and restful street between two rows of large buildings. Ran past little shops and delicatessens, boutiques and department stores. Tourists moved with tired confusion in the blazing heat. Shoppers walked stiffly and lazily between the thick traffic, like marionettes, clutching their packages and bags against their bodies to guard against swift-fingered and swift-footed thieves. He observed their rich and faultless clothes. Noticed the shape of their hats and the box of their shoes. How they carried their hands. Niggas drove by in streamlined bombs of cars, sound systems flinging music out into the street. The edge of the building cut Fifth Avenue off from his view. Well into the evening, yet the sun still well above the horizon. Earlier, the day felt like rain, but now the air was uncommonly clear. The world glowed. Windows sparkled. Rooftops shimmied and danced. A passing fire engine clogged his ears with alarm, cutting light from the siren's revolving red eye like laser beams on the ceiling and walls.

A wind sucked the shops out and he breathed the smell of fried chicken, chitlins, candied yams, and greens. The horizon clicked, turned. Noise and light lowered. He thought he could hear the bright sound of the river.

The sun couldn't reach Uncle John's side of the street. The apartment was completely dark and Hatch could barely make out furniture in the shadows. One wall, squares of mirrors that multiplied the reflection of any who stepped through the front door. A plain black doormat, hard as a board beneath your feet. A blind television.

Hatch was pissed. Patience expired. The plan: Uncle John would quit work early—he drove a cab seven days, twelve hours a day minimum, from seven in the morning until seven at night; some weekends, Hatch helped him wax and polish the cab until it glowed like a UFO—and meet Hatch here by five-thirty. Here it is, damn near six and the concert start at seven. He probably chasin some woman. Puttin on dog. Or fuckin round wit Gracie. Fuckin Gracie.

*Why'd you get married?*

*A dog don't like a bone, Uncle John says, but he likes what's in it.*

Can't understand why Uncle John continue to deal with her, put up with her ugly face and ways. A *married woman, Uncle John says, she the sweetest thing in the world.*

Hatch was pissed. Yet one glance at Uncle John's face made him forgive much. Canal Street had become the room so he hadn't heard a door rusty on the hinges, the click of key in lock, song rolling in thick waves off tongue

*Mean little girl*
*You should kneel down on yo knees and pray*
*I want you to pray to love me*
*Pray to drive yo sins away*

Hatch.

Uncle John.

Sorry I'm late. Uncle John smiled. His eyes moved behind the spectacles, which magnified them and camouflaged his fatigue. Tiredness showed in his shoulders.

Hatch felt Uncle John's smile in the muscles of his own. That's okay.

Slow day. Uncle John approached, a certain stiffness in his walk, moving in rhythm to his thoughts. You know me and some of the guys at the dispatch tryin to start our own service. He snatched Hatch in close for a hug. They embraced in a room of melting walls. They were the same height.

Hatch drew back. Let's go.

Give me a minute to wash up.

The concert start at seven.

I jus need a minute. See, we jus need some capital and—

What?

The cab service.

Oh. That's all you talk about.

You got to put in the work if you want the rewards.

Them Jews gon give you some money?

Which Jews?

Gracie's. Them people she work for. The Sterns.

No.

You ask em?

I ain't waste my time. I got better fish to fry. In a single gesture, Uncle John shed his clothes. Hatch turned to the window.

Give me a minute.

Uncle John, where yo binoculars?

My binoculars?

Yeah.

What you need wit binoculars?

I want to watch Randy's hands.

Who?

The nigga we going to see.

I thought you said he white. Hatch heard the bathroom door close. Heard the shower spill open. He imagined water rolling down Uncle John's tired muscles and the muscles giving the water more speed and force. He could feel the water, feel it roll, feel it rise in his chest.


UNCLE JOHN'S SHINY YELLOW CAB was imprinted with a moving image of Hatch as he approached it. The sun made two white spots on Uncle John's spectacles and blotted out his eyes. Uncle John seemed the focus of the day's heat. It shone in his face, in his voice, his walk. He opened the back passenger door from the inside. *Company regulations: no passenger can sit in the front seat next to the driver.* Hatch ducked inside the car. As a child, he and Jesus would take turns peering over the steering wheel of Uncle John's gold Park Avenue. Then Uncle John would take the wheel and spin them into the world.

*Take us to Fun Town.*

*Yeah, Uncle John. I wanna ride the Ferris wheel.*

*You know why they invented the Ferris wheel?*

*Who? Why who—*

*Nawl, why?*

*The army did it. They used it to elevate artillery spotters above the treetops.*

*For real?*

*For real.*

*Wow.*

Uncle John pulled the cab away from the curb, down the thin black strip of street, a plane down a runway. Uncle John was the pilot, Hatch his co-pilot. The cab rode so smoothly that Hatch had no sense of a road under the tires, sled over snow. The sun followed at a distance. Above, clouds of many shapes drifted in the evening sky, hard and congealed the closer they were to the horizon, vaguer in outline higher up. Hatch held the binoculars carefully, for they were one of the few mementos Uncle John had brought back from his tour overseas.

The windshield stretched a veil hiding Hatch and John from the eyes of outsiders. Thick windows and the air conditioner's hum blocked out the city's natural night sounds. Uncle John sent the cab spinning around a corner—Hatch gripped the binoculars to keep them from sliding out of his lap—down a greased ramp; then one bounce, two bounces—the diving board stiffens—and the cab sprung out onto the expressway. Uncle John and Hatch rode through the bright hot spring evening. The buildings gave way to houses and the houses to cornfields. Countryside speckled with barns, silos, sheds, and shacks.

Are we headed to Decatur? We look like we headed to Decatur. Damn, Uncle John. We going the right way?

A shortcut.

John singing.

> *I'm a tail dragger. I wipe out my tracks.*
> *I get what I wants, and I don't come sneakin back.*

A shortcut?

Uncle John took I-54, increasing speed. Hatch, you a backseat driver now? I drive every day. Don't you think I know how to go?

I just thought— Hatch saw his face framed in the rearview mirror, then fingered the dogtags Lucifer had given him years ago. Fingered them for assurance, to know they were there at his chest. Habit. Custom. New steel organs.

> *I got a mean red spider*
> *And she been webbing all over town*
> *Gon get me a mean black spider*
> *So I can tie her down*

His face slid over to the window. Now he remembered. I-54. The expressway they always took to Camp Eon back in the Boy Scouts days. Steel mills. (Most of the city's steel had come from here.) Yellow hard hats mushroom-like. The iron pulse of steady hammers. Showering sparks, an arc of red-hot tracers brightening night sky. Trolley tracks that ran to the mouth of Tar Lake. Bridges like hats above the lake, like upper and lower dentures that parted to permit a tongue-ship to enter the mouth-harbor. A mountainous ship held still on the waters. And in the distance, the low houses of Crownpin and Liberty Island. *And Gracie.* If you watched it long enough, the island would travel the length of your vision, float from one end of the horizon to the other.

Hatch heard bells. Baby-boot bells. Tinkle-tinkle. Round silver balls. The white ghost of Jesus's baby boots kicked with the cab's motion. Two white shoelaces flowed like milk streams from boots to rearview mirror. Whale-like, the back seat swallowed both him and Jesus, their eyes barely window level, excited, holding their breath. Then in Gracie's kitchen, Jesus's clumsy hand knocked a glass of milk off the table into Uncle John's lap.

Uncle John rose from his seat and stood up, his chair falling backward.

Jesus blinked.

Boy, look at what you done. Uncle John's hands, palms forward at his sides, as if displaying stigmata. He picked up Hatch's glass of milk and poured it empty into Jesus's lap. There, he said. See how that feel? That should teach you to think befo you make a mess.

Jesus did not move, his lap like a basin full of soapy water.

Elsa sure is fine, Uncle John said.

Thanks.

Mexican?

Nawl. I already told you. Puerto Rican. Mixed actually. Puerto Rican and—

Did you knock?

Hatch stirred in his seat. You know me, Uncle John.

Maybe I don't. Did you knock?

Hatch said nothing.

Come on, you can tell me. Did you knock?

Nawl.

What? You didn't knock?

Nawl. Not yet.

You crazy or something? Fine woman like that.

She—

It ain't about her. If you fly right, you'll never get anywhere.

Hatch scratched his chin.

Look, bitches are like cattle. Wherever you lead them, they will go.

Hatch thought about it.

You practice today?

Practice every day.

Good. God helps those who help themselves.

God?

Uncle John grinned. Hatch caught the joke. They looked at each other and laughed.

Women like musicians.

Hatch said nothing.

You can play music, you can play a body.

Rougher road now. The tires hummed, vibrated into the roots of Hatch's teeth.

Music is sweet and everything good to eat.

How much rent they charge you on this cab?

A hundred a week.

Damn. You might as well buy a house.

Could buy the cab. But it'd be worn down in five years.

Damn. Bet Jews own the company.

Probably. Got some regular white trash frontin for them. You know them Jews.

Yeah, I know them. Hey, you used to hunt. Ain't Hanukkah a duck call?

Uncle John chuckled. You real serious on them Jews. But I'll tell you one thing, on the Jewish holidays I don't make no money. When Jews don't do no business, nobody does.

Yeah? I can believe that. Hatch thought about it. Uncle John gon make his money. Always has. Always will. Now Lucifer is serious. Strictly business. The wee bird satisfied with the crumb. But Uncle John. Hatch tested the binoculars. The world came pressing in upon him.

They reached the high road outside the city limits. Uncle John pulled the cab to the side of the road. Hatch exited, walked around the rear of the cab—two POW stickers on the fender, soldiers in silhouette—got back in the car, sat in the passenger seat next to Uncle John. There beside his uncle, he truly felt like a copilot.

They let you fly those stickers?

Ain't said nothing yet. Maybe they ain't notice.

That's good. Yall bring back any contraband?

Just them rugs I gave Gracie. And them robes. *Gracie draped the robe over her shoulders. Blooming branches of embroidered silk and bright, soft dragons.* Spokesman got all kinds of shit though. He woulda brought back the whole damn country if it weren't strapped down.

How'd they choose you for the job? I mean, how'd they choose you for the Hairtrigger Boys?

I shot this sapper from a tree. Bull's-eye. The center of the forehead from a distance of four hundred yards.

Wow.

And at Fort Campbell, I'd done pretty good on the range.

Hatch watched the high sun, the last of a brassy day. He sat and watched and thought. Copilot.

You heard him before? Uncle John said.

Who?

Who? The silk you gonna see, that's who.

Yeah. Well, I gotta coupla his albums. And he's done a lot of music for war films. Bombs. Machine guns. Helicopters. You know, sound effects.

Oh yeah. Well, how come I ain't never heard of him?

He ain't rich and famous like Spin.

You know Spin. He gon make his market

Jus like you, Uncle John.

Jus like me.

Hatch and Uncle John tossed the laugh between them.

Don't you be banging your head against no walls.

What?

Ain't that what they do at these concerts?

Uncle John, you got it all wrong.

I wasn't born yesterday. Uncle John put his foot on the gas. The engine roared into life.

Nawl, you'll be born tomorrow.

There it is. His voice slid beneath the engine's growl and resurfaced. He was not wasting words tonight. A raw deal. He had gotten a raw deal. Inez. Gracie. John's Recovery Room. The Funky Four Corners Garage. He had had his share of downfall. A raw deal. Such is your luck. Such you are called to see. And let it come rough or smooth, you must surely bear it. Uncle John had taken it all and was ready for more. Cabdrivers need razor-thin instincts, given the con artists, thieves, and gangstas who'd shoot you in the back of the head for fun. Alert observers whose survival depends upon knowing people, knowing exactly how much to give and how little to take.

*Never pick up a pregnant woman. They think they don't have to pay. Like it's some honor to bring another crumb snatcher into the world.*

They drove down the highway drowning in steamy evening sunlight, the shut windows vibrating from the air conditioner's hum. Beneath the cool noise, Hatch thought he heard rings of laughter from surrounding cars. Uncle John kept one eye on the road and one on the speedometer, trying to keep the cab within the legal limit. The cab went on, smooth and swift, powerful. Uncle John's palm light on the steering wheel, almost hovering above it, bird on a limb. The cab seemed to bring out the tenderness, fast but smooth, unlike the big old bullying Uncle John cars that elbowed other vehicles out of the lanes. Uncle John would whip the car in and out of traffic, bearing down upon other cars until they slewed aside with brakes squealing. He would shoot across intersections, speed up at the sight of a slow pedestrian, speed out of the city onto the highway, the engine screaming, the lights of the other cars falling fast behind, spinning in the distance, flying saucers.

How come you don't drive the way you used to?

You get old, you slow down. I ain't as quick. The reflexes. Uncle John flexed a wrist motion.

The sky turned, white light washing to the red of daybreak and sunset. The sun raced down the sky and the moon raced up. That suddenly. Fallen light lingered, the road lit as if by distant fires. Bright enough for Hatch to decipher silver letters:

OBJECTS IN MIRROR ARE CLOSER
THAN THEY APPEAR

Darkness dissolved the glare on Uncle John's face. His eyes enlarged behind the spectacles. He clicked on the searching beams of the headlights. The streetlamps popped on one after another, a string of firecrackers. They rode in silence, wrist-deep in shadow, white lines caught in the headlights' gleams.

Do niggas really be jumpin from the plane wit two cans of Schlitz beer? Tall boys?

Uncle John grinned. Lucifer tell you that?

Do they be screamin Geronimo?

I don't know.

Why not?

I never jumped.

What?

I never jumped.

What you mean?

See, we weren't airborne.

But—

We were air mobile. No paratroopin. Uncle John laughed at some memory.

Ah, Uncle John, why you holdin out on me?

Average army stuff.

Hatch said nothing.

Sorry.

Hatch let the silence seep in. Uncle John was in the reach of his life. He saw him in the same eyes that he saw Jimi. Nothing could hold him like his uncle's words. Uncle John had returned from the war and settled like fine dust on his surroundings. The army ain't no place for a black man, right, Uncle John?

Uncle John looked at Hatch across the wheel. Well, lot of guys I was over there with have sons that enlisted. I mean, these sons in the service *now*.

Man. The headlights lifted and bored ahead into the tunnel. They brainwashed or what?

Uncle John laughed. Not exactly.

What you mean?

Figure it out. You the thinker.

Jus like you lunatics, always speakin in code.

There it is.

There it is.

Uncle John said nothing for a while. Ain't you never thought about it?

What?

Why the military took the both of us, why they took both of Inez's sons?

I don't understand.

You know that the military is only sposed to take one?

Hatch didn't know.

That they sposed to leave one for the mother? You know that's why they don't draft the only son?

Yes.

Well, why did they take both of us, why did they take both me and Lucifer?

They drafted yall.

But how could they? Didn't I jus say—

Look, Uncle John. Jus what are you tryin to say?

Think about it.

Hatch rocked in his seat. Rocked. Stopped. You jokin, Uncle John. You jokin, right?

It's not important.

You jokin, right?

Uncle John said nothing.

You gotta be jokin. I know you jokin. Huh. Why would you do something crazy like that?

Dark had set in solidly. Black. Smooth. Headlights like smoke. Ghost shadows of factories and steel mills.

Why you always jokin? I know you are.

CHIC RICKS: The night magnified the marquee's yellow undertones. A structure congealed into shape. Uncle John swung the cab from the tarred pavement to a gravel road, cab and men lurching from side to side. Pickup trucks crowded the parking lot, fat rats.

Wait a minute, Uncle John said. Is that the club?

The marquee lights danced and winked in the black night. Uncle John kept the engine running.

I guess so.

You guess so? I thought you said a concert. Does that look like a concert hall to you? Uncle John's silver-rimmed spectacles flashed. An auditorium? A theater?

Well—

That's a club, not a concert hall.

The marquee was a converted beer sign. Two long and low brick walls showed in the distance, and a badly placed doorway.

It'll be okay.

What?

It'll be okay. Man, they here to hear Jimi. Jimi!

After a few beers, Jimi, Johnny, Tommy—what the fuck do they care.

But it's Jimi.

Jimi? Disbelief in Uncle John's eyes, his words.

How could Hatch explain? Jimi was dead but Randy was the next-best thing. A disciple, following in Jimi's footsteps, true to his sound and vision.

A long metal caterpillar crawled out of the tunneled space of Uncle John's fist. Uncle John broke the caterpillar open, pulled what was inside out. Then he made the inside part float butterfly-like in the yellow marquee light. Let them see this, he said. He moved his butterfly in a sharp line across an invisible throat. Okay, that's good. They saw it. Now, let's go on in.

The air inside the cab went heavy against Hatch's legs and arms.

Come on. Let's go in.

John's butterfly glinted bright in the night. Hatch jammed all his fears to one side of his brain, and hoarded solutions on the other side. He started out the cab.

Wait. Uncle John touched Hatch's arm with his nonbutterfly hand. Let them see this some more. He floated the butterfly in orbit around the steering wheel.

Sharp silver light penetrated Hatch's arms and legs and pinned him to the leather seat.

Let's go.

Hatch did not move.

Damn, can't you hear? Let's go on in.

Leave that here. Hatch blinked.

What? John trained his red-filled spectacles. What?

Leave that here. You ain't got to do all that.

You want me to jus walk in? Jus walk in? For this Tambo and Bones stuff?

Tambo and Bones? Hatch had never heard of the band.

You expect us to get strung up so you can hear some silk shit?

The words freed Hatch. The blood of emotion swiftly flushed through him. He fought to get his own words out. Jimi ain't—

Call it what you want.

Anger rushed to his face under Uncle John's stare.

I tell you what, Uncle John said. Jus fuck the whole thing. Fuck the whole thing. He folded the bright butterfly back into its caterpillar. That's fair.

What?

We going home. He dropped the caterpillar into his blazer pocket. Whirled the car back onto the road.

Wait a minute.

You wait.

Hatch took a deep breath to calm himself.

The cab rocked side to side with speed. Uncle John fired up a cigarette, his first for the night. Inhaled and breathed and disappeared inside the smoke.

Hatch rolled down the window as quickly as he could, traffic sounds and city sounds entering the cab, night air sharp on his face.

John singing.

> I made a mistake gamblin
> I spent my money wrong
> I bet on my baby
> And she wan't even at home

Hatch began to sway lightly to the music.

# 8

WHENEVER GRACIE SWELLED into her first three months of pregnancy, like a poisoned roach ready to explode, she spent each morning in the rocking chair before the open window on May Street and watched the great circle of the sun pass from one corner of the room to the other. In the last three months, she would swell into sleep, become an extension of her white pillow. *Drifting with searching hands or hands searching pockets. Blood swelling to rigid breasts. Breasts swollen with the approach of your period or with milk for shower praise of birth. Milk that would create praise in the baby's skin and sad remembrance of boiling rivers crossed.* John would tell her something, then she would realize that days and even weeks had passed, his words carrying her back. Twice it happened—

*John saw the baby. Doctor, why he so red?*

*Give his color some time.*

*Redder than them leaves.*

—and each time she tried to warn him. More told in the telling.

John breathed very close to her in the bed.

John?

Yes. He put his lips against the back of her neck.

Something's wrong with the baby.

What? He raised up on his elbows.

Something's wrong with the baby.

You in pain?

Not exactly.

What is it then?

Jus these strange feelings. *It* don't feel right.

With her mind she had practiced manipulating the infant and her umbilical cord, string and puppet, trying to strangle the life.

John looked at her, engraving in her mind forever his look of fear. Tomorrow, we'll go to the doctor. See if he can help.

John—

He watched her with rain in his eyes, but he wasn't making any noise. We'll go now. He cradled her in his arms, took her out in the rain, rocking in his arms. A boat, rocking, rocking, in the rain. He opened the door of the fire-red Eldorado without using his hands—to this day, she didn't know how he'd done it—and set her gently on the seat. The car smelled new, the tight leather seemingly ripped with the least movement. So she kept very still. The engine roared, driving back the sound of the rainfall, wet constant footsteps. Rain rushed down the window, the twin wipers switching and flicking.

NEITHER HAD SUSPECTED her warm inner circle of life. Every detail of the night held vivid in her mind. Mockingbirds in the moonlight. Curtains blowing in the night air. John began as always, putting his lips on the back of her neck, then turning her around, a kiss on her forehead, placing a coin of light there, then putting his tongue in her mouth, heavy, diving through her body. Gracie could still feel his last hard thrusts—her womb full of raw menace—and his seed burning inside her, filling the vessel of her body with sticky heat. Afterward, she lay cradled in his arm, then drifted off to sleep. Something light and chill breathed upon her. A door slammed in her stomach. She awakened to a torn silver sky.

John, my stomach hurts.

John looked at her stomach. *Normal enough. Flat and hard with the same navel, round and bright as an eye.* He put his palm over it. *Waves of heat washed across his fingers.* Does that hurt?

Well . . .

It's that time of the month.

No. More than cramps. But I can take it.

John took her into the circle of his arm. They lay like this for a while. Then John gathered her in his arms like firewood and carried her down the stairs. Same way he carried her up the stairs later after it was done. Walking with ease, from the white globe and up the white railing and the white staircase that climbed toward the blue-and-white flowered wallpaper of the second floor.

But I'm not dressed.

He didn't answer. He placed this most delicate bundle inside his red Eldorado.

The car hummed through wind-torn streets. A gleaming empty sky rushed past the window. Yes, the car—the red Eldorado, the smooth-cruising red Eldorado, not the black Cadillac with power windows and locks (custom items in those days), and Jesus's erratic baby boots kicking on loose puppet legs—shot down Church Street. Rough black faces pushed into the traffic, not heeding the red lights. And the red Eldorado fled faster than cycle or streetcar, boat and steamcar, train and jet plane. Gracie's mind reeled full flash, rumbled down an unknown street. Her head stuck to the cutting thorns of her body. She thought she heard a shadow of song on the radio. The song spit and spattered.

The doctor's white smock took her by surprise. I think you have a tumor, but we need more X-rays to be sure.

Just hurry, John said. Can't you see she hurtin?

I can take it, Gracie said. It ain't too bad. I can take it. Red and black ants crawled inside her, working, moving things around. Pain was the one thing that never escaped her, life moving through days raw and wide. Shark-gray clouds in throbbing blue sky, and bird wings curving and cutting. Where did pain begin? Long ago. Certainly that was why the first two hurt so—those aliens lodged in her body, aliens that told her what and when to eat, when to piss (and how hard and how fast), shit; that made her scratch her vagina in public; that made her milk leak from her breasts (two white eyes peering out through her black blouse)—that was why they clawed away with thirsty fingers at her dry womb walls for nearly three days—

*Doctor, cut that thing out of her.*

*Ain't nobody cuttin me. I'll die first.*

—then shriveled like prunes.

But an hour after John brought her to the hospital, the invisible baby dropped easily from her womb, unraveled as if from a light ball of twine. A living baby in the raw, red-smeared with blood, black-smeared with grease, buoyant in the doctor's rubber hands, astronaut, the umbilical cord trailing behind, trailing in dark, quiet, sanitized space.

A small room in a small apartment made smaller by the city's crowded sounds and Beulah's listening ears. Made louder by the train that thundered by, yes, thundered, the train one long stream of torrential weather, shaking you in your bed at night—ah, the El trains were in touching distance, just reach your hands out the back window—shaking the ancient bones and aching muscles, flaking plaster from wall and ceiling. There was the single white sheet before the sink and clawfoot tub, and it was here that Sheila first revealed the burns spotting her arms and legs, light-colored scars, sand on dark skin. Gracie never learned why Sheila came out the bathroom nude, neither arrogant nor innocent, perhaps unaware that Gracie was in the room, perhaps knowing but not caring since they were sisters, perhaps carrying both feeling-seeds. Gracie had heard different versions of the story—it happened before she was born—but all agreed that Lula Mae had left her baby girl unattended before her fireplace. Mr. Albert Post—so he had named himself, this orphan, stuffed in a white man's mailbox in Tupelo, umbilical cord wrapped like a turban around his stone-small head—passed Daddy Larry's farm and heard the baby's screams. He rushed through the door and saw a bundle of fire on the stones of the fireplace. Lifted the burning baby into his arms, juggled flame and heat, and ran quickly, motivated by both heroism and pain, for the pump. The fire had already been smothered in his arms by the time he reached the pump seconds later. He dunked the blistered baby like an Easter egg into a rusty pail of water beside the well.

Beulah said that Albert Post visited Sheila every day for the ten years he remained in Houston, though neither Sheila nor Gracie had any recollection. Albert Post was nothing like these city men, Beulah said.

A man is a man, Gracie said.

I see you know everything. One day you'll learn that fat meat is greasy. *Beulah looked at the two sisters. Yall sap's runnin.*

*We jus women, Sheila said. Jus women.*

*Who asked you? Gracie directed the question to Sheila. She gave Sheila her hardest look.*

*And runnin early too, Beulah said.*

*Mind yo own business—still talkin to Sheila.*

*Who mindin yours?*

*Don't worry bout it.*

*Keep yo hand on it and nothing can get in it, Beulah said.*

Never *could* tell Beulah nothing. She love to weigh, to gravitate, to settle. She jus gab gab gab. Never seen nobody had so much to say about other people's business. Sniffing the dirt out of they clean clothes. Then gab gab gab.

*She shoulda opened her legs mo and her mouth less, Sam said.*

*Ain't that the truth, Dave said.*

Gracie had tried to tell Beulah about what had happened in church.

She was studying the vibrating words of Reverend Tower's tongue in the celestial roof. Thinking about the church in Houston that had no ceiling, just rafters for you to look through and see God. Thinking about the Memphis church that was hardly better. Thinking how Reverend Tower, the pearl of all city preachers, insisted his church mirror the pearly gates and roads of heaven. She could only wonder about his old church, but the new Mount Zion had a tower that poked the belly of heaven. Yes. Now she understood the eternal validity of the soul. Then she experienced the oldest feeling in the world. Something clawed her ass. The same something slapped its paw over the harp strings of Reverend Tower's voice and cut his song in its tracks.

She had scars to prove it, four long red lines that ran from her ass to her nape.

Beulah looked at her, her words not meriting a blink. You been drinkin wit that drunk fool Jack?

She tried to tell Beulah about the child, the alien lodged in her womb, chopping and kicking. The hiss words that snaked up from the pit of her belly. She tried to tell but couldn't. (By habit, she tells everything twice, once to get the words out, the second time for memory.) She knew what the results would be if she opened her mouth. Less told in the telling. So she drew herself tight, curved her umbilical cord into a noose.

WAS IT ANDREW who rushed her to the hospital the night Cookie was born? Or Sam or Dave driving And's car? *Did Sam have two legs then?* She seems to remember freight cars that ran by the stinking stockyards, long hooting locomotives drawn by a single engine.

Her sixteen years, Cookie never spoke a word. Her mouth slack, never giving her grunts the muscle they needed to push clear words. And where Jesus, the lone survivor of her womb, had etched his name on the walls of Gracie's belly, JESUS WAS HERE—to this day she urinated razor blades—his two dead siblings—who could tell what they were, these still births, the first with rubbery skin, gills, flippers, and snorkel, and the last, a two-headed cat with a pigtail—left no trace of their presence, their names erased chalklike from a blackboard. Though they disappeared, for weeks milk remained, mocking white trails of what she had endured and lost and what she might still endure and lose again.

ONE BABY STOLE A CANDY CANE from Jesus's Christmas stocking. The toddler clutched it by the throat, beating out its life with his bottle. The toddler grabbed another baby, the loop-bodied one—heads at both ends of the loop—and strangled life out of the throats. For those two quick minutes in her life, Gracie believed that Jesus had come to protect her.

EVENING SUNBEAMS set the dust to dancing. John sat with his arm thrown over the couch, his two brown eyes like setting suns, his body short and squat like Daddy Larry's smokehouse, perfect masonry, and his careful head sinking into his broad shoulders. A real downtown man. Gracie watched him from the other shore of the room, smelled the bright polish on his shoes. The soul travels quickly from a body touched by sin, she said, repeating Reverend Tower's words.

Ain't we all touched? John said.

Get out from among them and quit touchin the unclean thing and I will take you in.

John looked at her. He cut a grin. Took her hand hot into his own. Well, Miss Gracie . . . He played with her hand, searching each finger of memory.

Maybe he knew, all these children who ran her life, line by line. She still didn't know why they hadn't slain her, why each infant seemed to be allowed one feeble attempt at violence before it was snatched back to hell — or wherever it came from — sucked back, spaghettilike into the mouth of its creator. Rising for a single gesture of violence, then the bucket pulled back into the well. Until tomorrow.

Seek ye the kingdom of heaven and all things shall be added to you.

Does that include you, Miss Gracie?

*What them two boy-men doin wit them old women?*

*Don't look old to me. Least not the pretty one.*

*But they is old. Pretty can't hide age. Ugly neither. Them McShan sisters is robbin the cradle.*

Perhaps, she said. She extended the banner of religion, the white hand leading through the dark. *Will he clutch it and follow?* Hope you're takin care of your soul? she said.

Don't get down to Thirty-fifth Street that often, John said. His breathing had stilled.

Gracie didn't crack a smile. Power is no jokin matter.

Little green apples and all that.

You sound like that damn fool Dallas.

Years later, John would beat Dallas until he was blue in the face — first time she would see anybody black go blue, coal change to ocean — for reasons she forgets. Years later, Dallas filled John with the alcohol-flavored notion for the Dynamic Funky Four Corners Garage — John opened it with money he borrowed from Inez, money he never paid back; after a month or two, he dropped the Dynamic; Spider tended the register and books, (Engine) Ernie did all the actual car repairs, while Dallas and John drank and looked on — though John did come up with the clever idea to perch an old black Cadillac on the garage's roof. But that was later. This was now.

I'm the man walked seven seas. Done drank an ocean of sand. I can change a gray sky blue, but I can't get next to you.

What do you want from me?

Jus some kindness. Some lovin kindness.

Gracie thought about the passage that had directed her life. *Let each of us keep seeking, not his own advantage, but all that of the other person.*

For all his crude ways, John carried his giving heart hot in his hand. After his first visit, Gracie saw him as a young man no longer. He began to shine. There was a blinding light inside him, a blinding light that lit from his stomach to his head. Outside the inside light, she could not watch him directly, but she knew the motion of his heart. Whether a skullcapped November night or a bareheaded July evening, John could not get enough of her. He gave her wings to escape the gravity of the church and nest in its rafters. He flung her into the wilderness of sudden discovery and made her a citizen of another world. He filled her life, filled the whole world of feeling for her. She could hear his seed's approaching call. Bells of jubilation. She heard them peal in her sleep, a distant rhythm. She desperately awaited the night he would rip the veil of her virginity.

She did not wait long. Memory, hope, and reality meshed and clicked.

He massaged her with soft words. *Tell me more and then some. Whisper on to Doomsday.* And she embraced him, dived into his veins—*you go to my head*—splashed in the brown ponds of his eyes, her own shut eyes opening the black lens of her imagination. His teeth—he carried a toothbrush and baking soda balled up in tinfoil and white-brushed his teeth six times a day—gripped on to the black whirlpools of her areolae—and hers consumed his flesh—though she resisted its call, closed her hearing skin—because they had gone no further than innocent hugs and wet kisses, though she wanted *it* and got it, their flesh making loud slapping noises. Yes, he stuck it right inside her, a red-hot poker, and hot blood poured lava-like down her thighs, filling up the room, ready to set the bed aflame and afloat. The next morning, she examined her thighs. Two black streaks on the inside, like burned rubber. The smell of singed flesh. Through nights of muscular love, he forged her a new self. Afterward, she lay on the bed, moon and stars curled between her toes, him hard-breathing beside her.

*See yo belly.*

*I seen it befo.*

*Don't be a fool. He the father of yo child. And he ask fo yo hand in marriage.*

*I don't care if he ask fo my feet.*

But that first time. Eyes flicking with sleep, she woke that morning, nightgown a twisted rope around her waist, to a blood-red sun in white sky, the marriage sheet on display. *Them hilly-billies in Decatur hang theirs, Beulah said.* Birds sharp as naked blades, flicking light. Yes, dog days summer in mid-June. The sun burning red then yellow then red, alternating waves. At that very moment, she knew, a baby baked in her stomach—she could feel it

twist and tumble against the oven walls—while, now, these others were trying to crowd back in. Babies. Pushing their greedy faces in windows, belly-
fat faces, these blood-hungry urchins. Babies. Line by line, waiting to snatch
her out of the briefcased and Sunday-dressed crowd. Babies. Trying to crowd
into her belly where they don't belong.

Her first day in the city, she saw a beggar in the tunnel between Dearborn
and State. He was unlike the other beggars she would come to meet, blind
men who yellow-shoved their pencils in your face, musicians who snared
you with the cheap strings of a blues guitar, and fresh-tongued men. *Sistah,
could you spare some lovin?* No, he was different. He sat on a mouth-down
(water outspilled) metal pail, the stump of his leg pointing like a cigar in her
direction, tambourine-rattling his tin can—like those snuff cans down
home—and said nothing. She kept her distance in case the brown coins
should splatter. Going to work and returning from work each day, she saw
him, the metal voice of his can a continual presence for months then years.

One day, he was gone. She boarded the train.

*How much they payin you? Sheila asked.*

*Ten.*

*Ask for more. I get fifteen, twenty sometimes . . . Gracie?*

*Jus stay outa my business.*

It black-shoved through the tunnel, shaking, rattling. Then rain clicked
against the window. Tap dancing. She turned her face to the window. A baby
watched her with a fist-tight face, the train trying to shake him loose, and
him holding on with one iron-gripped claw, the other pounding against the
glass. The train's metal voice screamed, Halt!, the steel wheels (so many
mouths) slitting the rail's throat. Dry blood pasted on the glass.

Once, John and Gracie drove down to Decatur to see Beulah. A baby
stuck his face bright in the windshield (a cop's flashlight) and nearly scared
the wheel out of John's hand. The car swerved off the road and into the
bushes, branches whipping against the windows and doors, thudding rain.
John squeezed all life out of the brakes, squealing. The car—red Eldorado?
Cadillac? Park Avenue? Yellow cab? memory refused to speak—rocked to a
halt. The world fell silent.

My Lord, John said. Gracie took his head into her arms. My Lord. What
was that? Gracie could hold back no longer. She began. Told him all to tell.


THE RED ELDORADO was their private place. Away from the world, squeezed
into the back seat. *How you like my bed? John said.* Theirs except when Dallas, Sam, Dave, and Lucifer (and Spokesman perhaps) invaded, took it over
with a steamy blanket of talk.

*Man those slopes over there was something else.*
*Prospectin for gold.*
*Buildin railroads.*
*Least they din't finger none of yall gravy.*
*Yeah. They didn't finger none of yall gravy.*
*The Hairtrigger Boys.*
*Cause we could shoot the golden hairs from the devil's head.*
*Coulda been a sharpshooter myself.*
*Yeah. We coulda been snipers.*
*Sniper? Ha! That nigga wasn't no sniper. Them lifers had him searchin fo gold.*

But she knew how to *look* at John, a certain lowering of the head, and lifting of the eye. And John would shout, Yall niggas beat it! They stole feels and kisses from each other's body and breath. Her breath rose and fell. At least three times a day, she spread the sails of her thighs for him. She kicked his tongue down from the roof of his mouth and made it learn every crevice of her body, from her nostrils, to her eardrums, from the indention at the back of her neck, to—and only his tongue could speak her secrets.

John screwed with his eyes open, perhaps afraid he'd miss something. She didn't moan or wiggle around cause that made him come faster. *And it might be another moon before he got hard again. Cause I don't lust you, John said. That's why it take me so long to get hard again. I want you. But I don't lust you.* Those first years, he always spilled his seed on her belly—that barren desert where nothing unwanted could grow—cause he could afford no chances, taking many already, giving up the well-paying window washer job in downtown Central (the Loop) and setting out on his first business venture, he and Dallas opening John's Recovery Room. That's some chump change they payin, he said.

Yeah, Dallas said, some chump change.

I'm gon get me a real piece of money.

ONE SUNDAY AFTER church, John and Lucifer—surely by then they had stopped attending service, had *become* the service, running missions with Reverend Tower to the dens of sin on Church Street, his bodyguards, *Lucifer pulls down the pimps' gold draws for the hard paddle of the reverend's Bible, and John heaves them back up*—decided to take Gracie and Sheila to visit their parents, Inez and George. The sisters understood the importance of the invitation, for such an invitation precedes proposition. Imagine Gracie's surprise, Sheila waiting beside her on the trimmed lawn in front of the church and them chatting, small talk about the sermons and the new generation of young devils in Bible class, and John and Lucifer pulling up in the red Eldorado, then the gravity lifting from Sheila's face, her mouth brightening, and Gracie thinking it was because Sheila felt she had Gracie in a trap, the woman had backslid right into Sheila's righteous arms, then Sheila opening the back door of the car (Lucifer never was much on manners, chivalry) and getting in, Gracie thinking that Sheila would chaperon her, put her Beulah-like nose where it didn't belong into Gracie's dirty business jus because *she* had made that one mistake when she first came to the city, the Jack mistake, the Cookie mistake, made it cause she was young and naive and country—there's always someone to point the finger of blame, old folks say; Never let yo right hand know what yo left hand is doing—Gracie thinking this, but seeing different, and finally knowing different, awakened at the sound of *their* noisy kiss.

Look at them two lovebirds, John said. He motioned to Lucifer and Sheila, brown eyes delighted. Gracie, come on here.

Gracie's feet wouldn't move.

Kiss done, Sheila kept her face turned, forward, staring directly out the windshield as if she could steer the car with her gaze alone. Gracie slid onto the front seat beside John. He clicked the engine and aimed the long nose of the car into the street. The car whirred along. Gracie spied on Sheila in the rearview mirror, hoping to catch some indication of emotion. Sheila's face was expressionless, smooth stone. The entire trip, no one said anything, a curtain of silence falling before each of their faces, a block of silence—*cause you felt it*—heavy inside the car.

They parked in the shadows of the trees in Morgan Park, and walked over the dusty cobblestones that horse-hooved the sound of their clicking heels. John used his key to enter the house through the patio. George sat bent over the table before the *Daily Chronicle*—he never read the *Defender*, the black newspaper; its numerous spelling errors were an embarrassment to intelligent black readers and a boon to white—magnifying glass to eye. He looked up at her, eyes two marvelous globes, red-flecked and weakened by all the places he (and Inez) had traveled. (Travel is seeing, sharpness of notice.) They'd had a good life together. He was a retired blueprint worker for the Evanston Railroad, who had started out as a railroad dick right after the war. Nothing serious, he said, jus chasing turnstile jumpers, kicking off drunk white men from the suburbs, nothing serious like these cutthroat hoodlums today who slice you open just to see if your blood will run.

Inez sat at the table across from him. Junior, she said.

Gracie didn't know if the pet name was meant for Lucifer or John.

Mamma, this Sheila.

Mamma, this Gracie.

How yall doin?

Fine.

*Just* fine, Gracie said.

Glad to meet yall. So these the girls yall been talkin bout?

I heard a lot bout you too, Gracie said. John get his good looks from you.

Inez laughed. Oh, boy. Junior was the blackest baby I ever seen.

How could this be true? Inez and John had the same light tight skin, the same compact physique, though he was wider.

Lucifer came out light then got dark, Inez said, like a yam toasted in the oven, then went light again.

Later, in the privacy of the car:

I like yo Mamma.

Yeah, John said. Mamma. She been a woman all her life.

Gracie pondered this for a moment. Let it pass. I like George too. Yo stepfather.

Step? He ain't step nothing to me.

But, he seems like a nice man.

Gracie, you jus don't know. I seen it. John spoke, anger in his face. He got land. Oil wells. All sorts of stuff. And . . .

John, you ain't—

He got a long way to go befo he be my step anything.

Inez had met George right before the war—or right after; this she always forgets—when Lucifer (born when the war began) was learning his first sentences and John was still wrapped in swaddling clothes (no, he was born when the war ended; two years apart, they are two years apart)—John, a fine package dropped in the lap of Pappa Simmons and Georgiana. Georgiana was dead now, and George and Inez cared for Pappa Simmons in the basement of their house, dodging their neighbor's complaints about the whooping hound-dog baying of the Indian (as he thought of himself). Pappa Simmons had collected a set of bitter memories, stored them like preserves in his pantry, and put ice in his voice when he told you about them.

Lots of folks had already come up, he said.

*You took a path that led over the hill so that you could reach the station without having to pass through the streets of the town. You forced your way through the brambles that crowded the narrow path, your head bent sharp-angled to the road. The hill was steep. You breathed deeply.*

They lived in places lot worse than the one yall live in, he said. Inez, member that first apartment over on Peoria?

Pappa, don't drudge up the past, Inez said.

We had to walk to the market and buy coal fo heat.

And it were six of us in one room. Me, Pappa, and Mamma and this other family. You had to be very private cause it was always somebody else in the room.

Hell, but that ain't nothing. There were this one town where everybody jus packed up and leave. Even took the church. Put the Bibles and benches and rafters and doors and floors in they suitcase and got the first train fo North. And when they got here, all them down-home country spooks crowded into one flat. Pappa Simmons caught his breath. When the depression kicked in good, you shoulda seen us niggas shuttlin from street to street, from house to house, tryin to find some place to rest a heavy head.

That's the truth, George said.

Gracie would learn (because the four of them visited the two of them— or three, if she counted Pappa Simmons—every Sunday) that George spent most of his time on the patio (summer heat or winter cold), where he enjoyed his ball games on the radio (never on TV, not the little black-and-white portable one he and Inez owned then, or the large, heavy color one they purchased later). The radio also carried him country music. The only colored person she knew loved country music. *I think it relaxes him.*

See, George said, it's all about the military-industrial complex.

George?

He lifted his face from the paper, faced her, one eye bulging, swollen planet-big behind the magnifying glass. He lowered the glass. He wore a pair of glasses—*five* eyes—turtleshell, the kind you had to keep pushing with your index finger to keep them on your face. He removed them quietly to the glass table.

I never saw no action. We just loaded ammo from the cargo ships to the carrier. Port Chicago.

Well, Gracie said. Maybe white folks will give you a second chance.

George looked at her. No, he said. If anybody get the chance, it'll be these two boys here. He nodded at Lucifer and John.

*Boy? Who you callin boy? We men.*

George, they don't want to talk bout no war, Inez said. White folks is goofy.

But George foretold. Almost a year to the day the four said their wedding vows, John and Lucifer would be shipped off.


JOHN POUNDED THE SCREEN so hard it bounced against the doorframe. For an entire week, he visited her, bringing roses and rosy talk. The bottom fell out of the sky, coating throats and lungs with a foot of dust. Then the summer rain washed away all heat and dust. Flowers freshened the air with their scent.

The congregation lifted and crashed a swell of voices.

*I go forward for my God*
*I go forward for my King*
*I go forward for my Lord*
*I go forward*

Sheila, I think I love this boy.

Gracie thought Sheila would reply in kind, I think I love Lucifer. What we gon do? She didn't. Speak to Father Tower, she said. She called all preachers *Father*, a carryover from her Catholic schooling in Memphis.

Gracie did. Reverend Tower was a tall, built man. His arms were too short to box with God but had the right thickness of power to last a good round or two.

Gracie first reviewed her life in the Truth. Spoke about her three years of power and her sudden, unexplained loss of it. How she'd read the Bible trying to get it back.

I see, Reverend Tower said. He frowned down upon his desk, as if Gracie's story was a puzzling fossil.

Reverend Tower, she said, how come God don't show himself to us?

Sistah McShan, Reverend Tower said, niggas today got too much pride. They can't bow low enough.

Gracie continued to relate her life story. Talked and talked.

Sistah McShan, come right to the point, Reverend Tower said. I beg you. Storytelling doesn't like idle talk.

Should I stoop so low as to marry this boy? Gracie asked.

Sistah McShan, pride is the root of all evil, the termite that eats away at the tree of life. Only the Lord walks water with dry feet.

Reverend Tower didn't live to hear the wedding vows. The day of the double ceremony, Gracie walked in a narrow lane of faces she knew or had seen in passing or had heard in hearsay—just as she could hear her slow feet and the white silence of her gown beneath the organ's roar—for it seemed that all of Woodlawn was there, and nobody walked the thick red-carpeted aisle—so thick, you stepped carefully, lest you sink your footing—of the Mount Zion Baptist Church with dry feet, for Lula Mae (up from West Memphis), Beulah (up from Decatur), Big Judy and Koot (up from Fulton), Sam and Dave, Inez, George and Pappa Simmons, Dallas, Ernie, Spider, and Spokesman all bowed their heads like dripping trees and kept up a steady flow of tears. Surrounded by the glow of roses, even the organist cried.

Gracie and Sheila clenched their muscles against the hidden voices of the church. *Marriage don't stop gossip.* And they ran and ran and ran, so the church eyes and voices couldn't keep up—John was fast; he could snatch flies out of the air, could turn off the light switch and be in bed before the room went dark—especially the twenty-four eyes of the Deacon Twelve. The four newlyweds moved into a two-bedroom apartment, Sixty-first Street and Kenwood. Woodlawn. Sight limited to red, yellow, and green street-lights and, further off, the El scaffolding, trains passing like banners over the tracks, chewing and spitting rails. The apartment that would see John and Lucifer off to war.

GRACIE, JOHN SAID. He stroked her bangs and slick feather waves of hair. My Gracie.

John, you a natural-born fool.

They danced, John spinning her body, pulling her thighs and hips into tighter circles. The boards of the floor began to flex and squeak. He was above her—though she stood a head taller than him—and she could bury her face in the pillow of his scalp if she so choosed. She was lost somewhere, deep beneath the surface of her body, swimming away from her previous life. She allowed herself to be carried away by the sweep of blood.

The danger increased with her increasing belly. Hundreds of threads streamed out from her navel. She was so weak it took her half an hour to reach the bottom of the circular staircase.

John, my stomach hurt.

John opened his eyes. Sit down. Right here.

The black willing blood of the baby bubbled inside her. Her umbilical cord popped electric life, a telephone that transmitted the infant's threats: *I'm gon fuck you up.* Gracie laid her hands on her belly, and felt the baby kicking the hard table of her stomach, its hot hatred sending spark-filled smoke streaming up through the coils of her intestines. She felt it, a lump of clay that had squeezed into her. And so it looked, a totally smooth face, cause someone had forgotten to punch in the eyes and had punched every-thing else too small, a pinhole nose and mouth.

Where the rest of it? John said.

At the funeral for the second unborn (John believing that burying this one would make him feel easier inside), John's unseen words sizzled in the air while he watched the first clumps of dirt that thudded on the lunchbox-size coffin. *You rotten inside. Polluted.* And she remembered how she had felt earlier, at Cookie's funeral, John standing beside her, his arms tight around her shoulders to keep her from sinking into the mud.

Cookie's free now, Beulah said. She ain't gon suffer no mo. Up there in God's heaven.

Sho hope it ain't St. Peter's heaven, Sam said. He balanced on his three legs. Cause if it is, hope she brought an extra wing.


ONCE THE BABIES PINNED GRACIE IN THE STREET, between two rows of identical buildings, two lines of identical trees, one baby at each corner, stop sign–red. Their hands caressed switchblades. She screamed for help. The buildings watched her flight. Heads stuck out windows then drew back. Windows fell like guillotines.


ONCE JOHN SLAMMED TO A SKIDDING HALT to keep from running a deerlike baby down. What was that? he said.

A baby.

What?

She explained.

He drew back, as if she had shoved the stinking child in his chest. From then on, she remained silent about the attacks, fearing that any utterance would embalm her in her own words. Instead, she spoke about the ghosts of former times, a thirteen-, fourteen-, fifteen-year-old girl working miracles.

Can you still do it?

She gave him a tight look.

I mean, did you grow out of it or something?

Do you ever grow out of being yourself? One forever hears the calling.

John chuckled. That was some racket. We sure could use the bread.

She gave him a leather look, lest she knock him upside the head with her Bible. And he would come to learn, power was untouched by the test of water and time. She could tell John where he was and who he was with to the exact minute, to the number of thrusts it took to make some nasty woman come.

Once, in the middle of downtown Central, a baby began spreading its wings, flapping, and she, taloned, began lifting into the air, three feet high and rising. Luckily two kind pedestrians had the courage to grab one leg each and pull her back to the earth. (Since that day, she never left the house without her steel shank boots or fortified heels.) Enough was enough. She phoned Sheila.

Well, Sheila said. Put a glass of water beside all the doors and windows, then—

Sheila.

—nail a Scripture above each door, then—

Sheila.

—change the direction of your bed.

These are babies, Sheila, not haints. Still, she took her sister's advice. The babies drank the water—and on a few occasions peed in it—and crayon-scribbled on the Scriptures. One night, she woke to the spinning of her bed, a whirlpool's suck. Another night, a spitball of Scripture woke her to dawn's first light. She phoned Sheila.

Well, talk to Father Tower.

Sistah Jones, Reverend Tower said, have you spoken to John bout this?

No, sir. Well, not exactly, you know how he is wit religion.

Reverend Tower raised the arches of his thin eyebrows. He ripped four pages from his Bible—loud leather-ripping—choosing them seemingly at random (or maybe the finger saw what his mind directed). Funny because she had never seen him read the Good Book from the pulpit.

Sister Jones, he said, set these Scriptures before every door of your house.

Gracie took the pages. Yes, sir.

Now, I should warn you, the power of the Word can only be compelled with the necessary spiritual energy. That's why I asked you about John.

Yes, sir.

Once home, she made floor mats of the pages, to wipe clean the souls of all who entered. The babies defecated on them.

Gracie went to see Reverend Tower.

Sister Jones, we'll mission. I'll bring the congregation by to pray.

No, Father. Her heart ran away from the words. Terrified, she saw what she could not speak. *Face flapping in delight, the baby lunges, striking from near the ground with the sharpened bone of his hand. The reverend falls.* I got my own prayers.


DAY IN AND DAY OUT, all around her come and go, turn and turn, trot along beside her, a snowflake variety of babies, old and young, small and large, fat and skinny, homely or cute. One rainy day, a baby came crashing through the front door, whirling its yellow-and-black spiral legs, bringing in wild rain like a whale spouting sea. That was as far as it got, dissolving into the wet wood fragments.

Shit! John was pissed about having to buy a new window. Lucifer, Dave, Dallas, and Spokesman spent spare moments helping him improve the house. Added more tile, and wood floors, cabinets, storm windows, stair-ways, a garage, a new fireplace, doors, rooms, stoops, and had even raised the roof for a third floor. All this while John struggled to meet the monthly mortgage. Fuck! You know how much this gon cost me?

It wasn't my fault. A baby. She got the dustpan, he got a broom. He helped her sweep up the mess, the broom straws, a yellow blur.


EXCEPT FOR THE ODOR OF HER BEDCLOTHES, the house was absent of human presence. Sunlight swept across the room, wiping out the last of the morning shadows. Clean bare silence. John. Her voice carried in the small music of the morning. John. She liked this window, for it afforded her a full view of the city. Thousands of pigeons wavered in the fish belly-colored sky above a wide plain of rooftops. Stooped gargoyles guarded the streets. Pointed houses like tents in the distance. Yes, this place up North is not in God's world. *Checkerboard city, John calls it. You make yo move, then hop along to the next trick.* Tar Lake. The waveless lake chose a direction and flowed like a great river from one end of the horizon to the other. She could watch wool-capped sailors grab her unborn, spear them, then anchor-toss them into the water, toss them to a time remote and dim. She could study each event moving across the surface of her life. God's eye sees through all souls, Reverend Tower used to say. Can God see the ghosts of her unborn infants inside her, circling and circling, arms reaching out? See the infants outside, hidden there in the trees? John's departure ten years ago—like his departure this very morning, moments earlier—held like a shipwreck in her memory where no thoughts could flow past. And this memory that was almost memory that was almost thought that was almost reality that was almost memory spilled over her days.

If she could pull language into her mind then the memories would follow. If she said everything twice, once to get it out, then the second time for remembering, she could draw it all back to her bosom. Reel in a half-century of words. But time refused to move, this stranded horizon ship, so far off that no details reached the eye. She tried to picture its features, but her imagination did not extend to the unseen.

She knew what she must do. Pin down its shape. Rediscover time with the pulsing of its own blood. Like the raw fact of the rocking chair that fit the curve of her body. It might be the horizon itself—each rock a shift, a change, chair, horizon, chair, horizon—or possibly the water. *Wood, water, wood, water, rock, water.* She liked the chair, its sound, its unpillowed hardness.

How could she tell him that the past she had put away, that the other thing remained, though no longer with the staying fragrance of flowers? That now she knew, Jesus, her womb's second survivor, had ripped open the layers of petrified sorrow, that he—invisible to their knowledge of him, blind to sight and mind—had kept his fists tight on the reins of her umbilical cord, steering her destiny, that this son had fashioned them this new house, this bludgeon which had shattered their common life. But the old line could reach the new life. Their nights together formed memories underneath their pillows, Tooth Fairy's gifts. Their breathing remained unbroken, dawn to dawn, sunset giving away to stars, and stars to morning clouds, wheeling across day and night. All the past pounding had forged, beneath the sheets, a place remote and calm as stars laid across night sky.

She locked her eyes on him and looked inside. She pulled the inside of him out, wiped it clean, and set it before the sun, where it would receive warmth and light. His sins were now the forgotten shadows of his past, as the moment of salvation is a blinding light.

Still sun grew on green water. In the vast spread of this house, she sometimes felt she cast breaths inside a live belly. A region without light. Walls of sensitive skin. The hum of ocean. The acrid fragrance of fish. And she spent her life waiting for the whale to cut the surface of green water—a cracking of trees in the front yard—and spit her writhing from its mouth onto the shore—a thud on the front lawn.

The swinging trees rustled in a shot of unexpected wind. The sun wet her face. Her breath went short. The ache in her throat ran deep into her chest. The air's pure scent spoke of fresh rain to come. All the old will slip away like clothes shed after her deliveries. Life having been breathed into the lungs of the dead must be taken away again before death can be returned to. As the lightning cometh out of the east. Long-winged angels lift from the brow of God. She could see them from her perpetual rocking chair. Feel the wind to come.

She rose from the rocking chair and pushed her keys deep in her purse.

# 9

THE RECTANGULAR WINDOW afforded Hatch little to look at, the walls of the tunnel like two long black brushstrokes. The train took a curve with industrious roar. The ceiling bulbs buzzed and flickered, and the cab went from light to dark, dark to light.

The concert was a month old yet so ancient that it made him cough. The almost ancient feelings reinstated themselves. Sensation lingered on his fingers. He had never told anyone what had happened that night. *And I never will.* Concealed like his dogtags. He and Uncle John would share this secret to the grave.

The train fast-flowed, rushing water from a hose. The city blurred past. Hatch drifted. Think of Uncle John's spectacles, two glass river rafts. Floating down some highway. Floating over your face. And the eyes themselves, round color. Brown balls of tobacco. Or two clean circles of fire when liquor had burned away the color. Think. Think.

The train squeezed to a stop at Union Station, vast, blazing. The car emptied and filled. Continued. The car's tubular insides mirrored the saxophone curve of Elsa's neck. The car's bounce, the float of her breasts.

*How's your Mexican girlfriend? Porsha said.*

*Puerto Rican. I told you, she Puerto Rican mixed wit—*

*Whatever. How come you didn't invite her to Christmas dinner?*

*Well—*

*He hidin her, Uncle John said. In the doghouse.*

He planned to meet Elsa today after his visit to Inez's.

*Why don't you come over, Elsa said, her voice small and inviting inside the phone.*

*I'm sposed to spend the day wit my grandmother.*

*She needs the whole day?*

*It's just that I don't get to see her but once a month.*

*You know, Dad will be at the parlor.*

*I know. He's there every day. People never stop dyin.*

*A soft laugh bounced from Elsa's lips. He pictured them. It gets better, she said. Mamma will be there too.*

*Is that right?*

*She has to vacuum out the coffins, comb hair, apply makeup, paint fingernails, dress the clients, flower arrangements, that kind of stuff. Help Dad out.*

*I see.*

*So I'll be all alone, nobody here but me and Raoul.*

*Raoul?*

*My cat.*

But that would be later, much later. He had a long ride to Inez's house in Morgan Park, the southernmost part of Central. A long ride. Elsa was hours and miles away. He flipped his book, *Man and Mestizo*, open. As he read, he began to feel a comfortable place inside himself where he could peek out and judge safe from penetration. Two half-pint hoodlums snatched the book from his hand, Kleenex out of a box, and frog-jumped onto the platform. They boldly flashed him their sign, thumb and index fingers curled ino a C, then blazed an escape, feet drumming across the platform fast and heavy as rainfall, nylon jackets billowing behind them as if the policing wind were clutching and tugging at their backs.

Slow-moving silence. Hatch stirred in his seat. He could feel the eyes of the other passengers on him. His tongue dry and stiff in his mouth, a dead rat. A bad way to start the day.

He closed his eyes and invented his own darkness. And he roamed in this private space while the train pushed like a diver through tubular black. It rose—he saw it and felt it—and tilted him out of his thoughts. The morning pushed hot through the moving window. Opened him. The train sped. Distance changed kind. He tried to ignore the melting of familiar landscapes: crowded streets, a river lake-still and lake-steady to cast reflection, and the sun-catching skyscrapers and flag-decked buildings at the city's heart.

The train spat him onto a wooden El platform. He spiraled down three flights of stairs to earth. The light was slower here in Morgan Park. The sun sprayed lazy light in banks of red discs. Through the hot grit of day, he took deep-reaching steps for the bus stand.

AHHHHHHHHHH

Shut up.

Ahhhhhhhhhh

Shut up. I'm tellin you.

Ahhhhhhhhhh

Wait til we get home. I'm gon whip yo butt. You won't be hollerin tomorrow, no sir.

Ahhhhhhhhhhh

What you cryin for? Talk. I don't understand what you sayin.

Ahhhhhhhhhhhhh

Ahhhhhhhhhhhhh. I can holler too. Ahhhhhhhhhhhh

Ahhhhhhhhhhhh

No sir, won't be hollerin tomorrow. I'm gon tear yo butt up . . . Don't stop now. Might as well finish cryin. We got only three more blocks.

The toddler resumed crying.

Shut that baby up, Hatch said. In floating bus space, he rocked slightly in his seat.

What? You come up here and make me, punk.

Ahhhhhhhhhhhhhhhhhhhhhhhhhhhhhhhhhhhhhhhhhhhhhhhhhhhhhhhhhhhhhhh

Jus get the fuck off.

You make me, punk. Bitchass nigga.

She exited the bus. Stood on the sidewalk, hand on hip, and screamed at him, head jerking to the words. Still not satisfied, she hoisted the toddler above her head, champion weight lifter, then ran toward the bus, as if she would throw the toddler through the window. The bus pulled away.

Dumb bitch. He said it to himself. Fuckin hood rat. His seat offered no comfort. Inez live too damn far away. Too damn far. A long train ride, then a long bus ride. Shit. A flow of streets unfurled behind him. Sunlight angled across the river. The sprawl of the city and the sun like its glowing heart. With sniper-sensitive sight, he followed birds through the bus window, black images through blue sky, flying well and very low, with a calm, favorable wind. To his left (in the distance), the Central River pulled its drying legs together. To his right (near), Tar Lake stirred under a slow flood of sun. Formless substances afloat, each separate from the other, but each also kin to water, the element which will, in time perhaps, dissolve them into a new solid identity. A ship sailed for some unknown destination. *I know everything about that ship.* By simply stretching out his hand he could touch it. Ship lights bubble up and bob on night water. Anchors and chains ring, cowbells. Awaken you as Uncle John slips in silence through Gracie's front door. Moves like a bat in the dark, as he navigates the steps to Gracie's bedroom. Dallas's drunken ghost knocks and bumps against the stairs behind him. He peeps into the room where you and Jesus sleep, the hall light glowing behind him, and Dallas's ghost too, his eyes fired and twisted.

Gracie's house was completely surrounded by Tar Lake. Though the lake was but a short walk from the house, Uncle John would pack his fishing gear in the trunk of his yellow cab—well, back in the day he drove a red Eldorado, then the green Cadillac, then the gold Park Avenue—park Hatch and Jesus in the back seat, and drive the few blocks to the lake. *We don't wanna walk. We like to ride.* Hatch, Jesus, and Uncle John would play their favorite game, hide-and-seek. The boys would race down the hill toward the water, arms windmilling, and dive down into the tall grass. Uncle John would sneak up on them without a sound. Then Jesus would snag a black worm onto a rusty hook. Cast his bait. Motionless rod and motionless line in the current. Hatch would relax with a book and cast his thoughts into the black water. His fingers could handle the toughest guitar strings, but not twisting, slippery worms. Uncle John would ready his rod, clean the horsehair line— *stronger than wire,* he said—polish the gold-colored hook with his silk handkerchief, then tug on the bait, a red-snapping fiddler crab. Patient—*Patience catches a fish,* he said—he might spin a tale or two. *I remember this one time. This time, once, when this guy got shot. The bullet made his clothes catch fire. The weirdest shit. The bullet hit him in the thigh. A flesh wound. But his clothes caught fire. And the fire burned him crisp.* He would catch small, green, finger-thick catfish. *Be careful of them whiskers. Cut you like a razor.* He would clean his catches right there at the lake, nail a hammer through a head and pull off the skin in a clean stroke, easy as removing a sock. *Now, if yall really wanna catch something, we gotta drive down to the Kankakee River.* One night, Uncle John bought Gracie a bowl of goldfish, which she placed on the fireplace mantel next to Cookie's photograph, commanding a watery view of the living room. *Uncle John, why they call them gold? Ain't they orange?* She gave Hatch a few sparkling fish to take home with him. One jumped like a pole vaulter out of the bowl he had carried all the way from Lula Mae's lil house in West Memphis. He stood and watched it. Felt sea spray in his belly with each flop of the fish's tail. Felt his heart jump inside his ribs. For hours he watched it, beating out its rhythm.

He didn't chase the memory. Braided sun whipped the bus from side to side. Whipped him across the face.

*Junior, you comin to see me?*

*Inez, this ain't Junior, I'm Hatch.*

*You promised to come see me. Junior, you promised.*

Why was he going to visit Inez? Making this long journey? Why? Well, Inez was his grandmother. More important, Inez was Uncle John's mother. Yes, Uncle John's mother. The why. The reason. So he must journey, must pay respect.

*Junior, what time you comin?*

Sun spindled light. Junior? Why she call Uncle John Junior? Lucifer was the firstborn. Doesn't firstborn make him Junior? *I was young. I was new to the city. We all make mistakes cause when you young, you think you know everything. I wouldn't listen to Mamma or Pappa. I met him in the Renaissance ballroom. Used to be down there on Sixty-first and Ellis, right across from the Evans Hotel. See, in those days you would dance before the men came out to play their basketball. We danced. The Turkey Trot.*

*Well, what was it like when yall came here?*

*Hard. It was hard.*

*Hard how?*

*You shoulda met Pappa. He could have told you all about it.*

*Pappa Simmons ain't here. He dead.*

*You shoulda met Pappa.*

Sun shattered in flakes against the window. Hatch blew them away. Inez. The rubbish heap of old age. He would spend all afternoon and most of the evening with her, but, by morning, she would carry no memory of his visit.


A CAR DROVE BY on muted tires. The sidewalk steered him past a weed-and-bramble-filled lot that he once had believed was an alligator-and-cottonmouth-spawned swamp. A sidewalk made all the more dangerous for its narrowness. The sidewalk opened into a quiet unpaved street. Under construction to remove the old cobblestones hollow-sounding against your heels (like horse hooves), cobblestones that hollow-held the sun's heat and black-blistered your feet, wore down car tires (so George often complained).

Trees sparkled in the morning sun. Hedges square and trim, grass patiently mowed. A line of range houses all brick, all built for returning soldiers after the great war, the war that George knew firsthand. *He saw action. But how can anybody see action? Action something you do.* George (old and nearly blind) kept the house up and refused all offers of assistance, climbing a shaky ladder to fix the garage roof, shoveling snow from the walk and driveway, hosing watery blackish substance from the sidewalk. Hatch had never quite pieced together the chronology. The only wedding photo showed George in his army uniform and Inez in a knee-length party dress. So they had married during or after the war. Lucifer was born the year the war began. Uncle John two years later. Pappa Simmons and Georgiana took them in.

Hatch followed a short narrow cement path around the side of the house to a low white picket fence that opened into the backyard. A small patch of garden with furrows like dirt roads. Beans and peas and tomatoes and cucumbers and lettuce and turnips and mustard greens. A bird pond—*you and Jesus tried to build a birdhouse with some old sticks from the alley*—of white stone that had stood here as long as Hatch could remember. Plenty of birds today, splashing and chirping. He thought twice about it and retraced his steps to the front door.

Hi, Junior. Inez speaks as if someone had punched the air out of her.

Hi, Inez. Short, slight, childlike, her round yellow prominently boned face—level with his—and wormlike wrinkles shining between the dark wings of her hair. Her body frail as tissue paper, limbs thin sticks for a toy airplane, and you are afraid to touch her, to feel her skin, afraid that she might roll up and crumble under your hug. But you must hug her. She shrivels in your arms.

Let me look at you. She pulls like skin away from your body. So big. Ain't you all growed up.

Yes.

How's Lucifer?

He's fine.

How's your mamma?

She's fine.

And your sister?

She's fine.

And your wife?

You mean Gracie. She's Uncle John's—

How's Beulah?

She's fine too.

You speak to her lately?

Sheila called her the other day.

You remember that time we all drove down to her house?

Yes, I remember.

It was me, George, Junior, Sheila, now who else?

You know.

We had a fine time. I really like Beulah. She and I are one of a kind.

*Why did I come here?*

One of a kind.

Hatch considered the comparison.

Junior, you know anything pleasant in the world?

He ignored the fact that she called him Junior, Uncle John. Guess not, he said.

What's wrong with people today? Her face shows pain in every wrinkle.

They stood in the small living room crowded with furniture and memories. Nothing had changed. The room had remained untouched all of Hatch's life. On the wall above the long squat television, two glassed-and-framed prints of birds of paradise on either side of a glassed-and-framed charcoal portrait of Inez—*we got that in Mexico; he drew it for one American quarter, one American quarter*—fat-cheeked and plump, nothing like the way she looks now. On the wall behind and above the leather couch, a mosque-shaped mirror, dotted with colored glass. *We got that one in Turkey.* Two glassed-and-framed photographs above and behind the sitting chair, GOD SAVE THE KINGS—Dr. Martin Luther King and his family seated on a couch, reading the Bible; *Lula Mae got that one, I'm sure*—and CHAMPIONS OF THE PEOPLE, stills of King and the murdered Kennedy brothers.

And all these strange kinds of sex.

That's right, Inez.

The world gets worse and worse.

That's right, Inez. *Why did I come here?*

I'm glad I don't have long to stay.

Don't say that, Inez.

I wade into the deep water, tryin to get home.

Inez—

And when I get there, I'll sit on the river.

You ain't going nowhere, Inez. You gon be with us for a long long time.

I'll sit on the river. Let's go out to the patio.

They did. The enclosed back porch lay in sunlight, wood-paneled walls with black knots like spying eyes. Inez and George spent most of their time here with a huge wall map, the many places they had traveled pierced by red thumbtacks.

Hatch eased into the worn cane chair where Porsha said that Pappa Simmons, who died the year he was born, had sat and told stories. She had never told him the nature of the stories, only that he'd told them and to her.

George brought his coffee and biscuits to the glass table—*you* were always afraid to eat there, the plate banging against the glass, afraid table and meal would crumble beneath you—with a small portable radio blaring out the news, his reading glasses balanced across his nose, and holding up a magnifying glass before the newspaper. He liked his coffee black; he took his first gulp, throat working, without blowing off the steam.

Pale colors ran in his eyes, fish in a cloudy aquarium. After the war, he had found work as a blueprint reader for the commuter railroad and booked passage to blindness. You could stand two feet in front of him and your face would be no more than a black balloon. Inez was losing more than her sight.

George?

Yes, Hatch. He returned the cup to the saucer with the least bit of sound.

What kind of work did you do? He could never get it straight.

Well, when I first came up from Arkansas, I got a job in the stockyards.

Worked that for about two years, then I got this job workin for these two Jewish brothers.

Reading blueprints?

No. It was a machine company. We made the templates used to stamp
out car parts.

I see.

Yeah. George pulled off the top of one biscuit. Steam curled from its soft
white insides. It was just a mom-and-pop operation when I started. Big business now . . . Those two Jewish brothers smelled like dead fish, that heavy
fish odor.

Man.

Back in Russia, they managed a fishery. Good people. Fair. But I also
made a dollar a day. Service pay. That was good money in those days.

How'd you like the army?

George thought about it. See, it's all about the military-industrial complex. That's why they going to war now. George rose up from the table and
walked into the kitchen.

Yo father was here, Inez whispered.

Lucifer?

Junior.

Uncle John?

Yes. He left something. Let's go out to the garage. I'll show you.

Hatch took Inez's arm—light and brittle as a twig—and guided her to the
garage. Partitioned in two, a space for the car (ordinary, nondescript, pale
blue and gray), tools, and fishing gear, and a screened porch overlooking the
patio and yard. He had spent many hours on that porch, book in hand, rocking, on a large swing meant for two people.

In there, Inez said.

He helped her into the garage proper. She took an object down from a
wooden utility shelf. An ordinary basket, full of baby's breath.

He and that woman left it.

What woman?

It's some kind of spell. I been meaning to ask yo mamma.

Hatch recalled the time George got sick, weak in the legs, and Sheila instructed Inez to put a picture of a horse beside his picture. Horses have
strong legs. And burn a candle. Red might be too strong, make his legs too
powerful. So burn a red and a white candle.

Inez quickly put the basket back on the shelf and led (pulled, reined,
rider and horse) Hatch from the garage.

Why would Uncle John want to put a spell on you?

She pushed him into the screened porch.

Inez? Why would Uncle John—

That man, George.

Hatch glimpsed the old swing—smaller than he remembered it—and a few old clover-shaped church fans for cooling down the Holy Ghost.

He is low. The dirt washed off turnips.

George?

Yes. That man there, George. He got powers.

Hatch said nothing.

He knows everything I'm sayin. See, he can touch something and then he sprays me with something while I sleep. George. That man there. Married all these years. Married. To dirt.

George opened the patio door. Inez's wrinkled mouth went tight, a drawstring purse.


HATCH DRUMMED HIS FINGERS on the glass table, which yielded his reflection. He saw himself churn Inez's ice cream. Saw himself drop fresh cream and fresh cubes into the bucket then turn the handle with all the power of his skinny kid's arms. He saw himself skin apples for Inez's applesauce. Shell peas for her soup.

You hungry?

No. I ate. He lied. Memory brought hunger.

If you are hungry all you have to do is speak up.

No—

But you know, I don't do any cooking. These hands. She raised them. One day when you're old—

Inez?

—you'll understand. George, Junior is hungry. He want some chicken.

Inez?

Some chicken. Think I can drive like this? I'm not dressed. She smoothed her palms over her white cotton housecoat. Shuffled her matching house-shoed feet.

You can stay in the car, Inez. George spoke from down the hall.

Wait, Hatch said. I don't want any— He let it go. You want me to drive?

No, Inez said. You relax. You are a guest.

The three left the patio, walked out to the garage, and took their places in the car. Hatch in the back seat and George shotgun with Inez. She curved the car onto the gravel-covered alley. Took the alley slowly, then curved the car onto the street.

Okay, George said. Now make a left at the corner.

She did.

Stay on this street.

She did. She drove, steadily, both hands on the steering wheel, face intent on the road and George's directions.

There it is, right up there.

How was poor-sighted George so precise? Was he speaking from memory or instinct?

I see it. She eased the car into the lot.

Park over there.

She did.

Keep the engine running.

She did. She carefully took neat, clean bills from her purse and handed them to Hatch. There you go, Junior. Buy a box.

Yall want any?

No.

Buy some for yourself, George said.

Hatch ordered the cheapest box and pocketed the change. Boxed chicken under his arm like a football, he ducked back into the car.

Now back out the way you came, George said.

But the sign says—

I'm telling you the right way to go.

But those arrows there—

Inez, just do what I say.

She didn't.

What are you doing?

She said nothing.

Inez, what are you doing?

Shut your damn mouth unless you going to drive. She swung the car into the streaming avenue, just missing another car. She drove on steadily. Drove past their turn. George said nothing. She turned left and moments later, they were back at the chicken shack. This time she turned right, at the wrong corner. It went on like this. They circled the chicken shack again and again and again.

Make a right at the corner, Hatch said.

Okay, Junior. She made a right.

Now, there's the alley. Turn left.

Thank you, Junior. She turned, car bouncing, tires crunching on gravel. See, they fixin the street. Junior, you see?

Yes, Inez.

Those cobblestones ruin the tires. She pulled the car before the garage. George got out. Hatch got out.

I'll park it, George said.

Okay. Inez made her way for the house. Junior, come on.

You see what jus happened? George whispered. You see? George took Hatch's silence as acknowledgment. She spend all her time in that garage. All her time. He blinked back his anger. Tell yo mamma to call me. I got to tell her something very important.

I will.

Be sure and tell her.

I will.

Better yet, tell your sister to come out here.

I will.

Tell her.

I will.

# 10

SHEILA LEANED OVER THE EDGE of the platform—a wood-and-iron structure rising stories above the street—to see if her morning train was coming. A yellow oval shimmered near her face. A young Oriental woman watched her, small, prim, and delicate in a red dress suit. Her hand held firm to the black leather purse strapped over her shoulder. Her eyes were sharp and curved, glinting swords. *Hear they don't like to be called Oriental but Asian. Oriental like saying Negro. Or nigger. Bet she own a cleaners. Or a restaurant. Or a grocery store.* Turned her face away when she and Sheila locked stares.

The rails looked white and fragile under the sun. Sheila often wondered what Sam felt when he fell under the speeding train and lost his leg. *Nawl, I didn't pass out. I tried to get up and walk away. Crawl away. I remember looking up at the third rail high above me. I felt like one of those limbo dancers.* Cause after it happened, all he did was look her in the face from his hospital bed and say, Niece, I gotta learn to use my wings again. Then he looked at Lucifer. Sam and Dave were big on teasin Lucifer and John.

*He say war or whore?*

*Yall been fightin a war or a whore?*

*What kinda fightin yall do over there?*

*Sam, these niggas ain't do no fightin.*

*Yeah. Ain't been gone but a year.*

*What kinda fightin can you do in a year?*

*Shit, take a year to learn how to kill a man good.*

Boy, Sam said, that train reared back like a horse to keep from hitting me. Lucifer didn't crack a smile. Like worn-out brooms, his eyebrows cast shadows over the soft light of his black eyes.

Sheila could not remember where Lucifer the boy ended and Lucifer the man began. The stern face of the seven-year-old child she had seen for the first time at one Sunday service was the same stern face of the forty-seven-year-old adult she had seen this morning, the boy-man-husband who would never set foot in a church today. *Unless somebody died.* With her white fingers, Georgiana would dress her two grandsons for church—fine clothes too that her white hands scrubbed and washed and pressed for; fine clothes, not the cheap tight-fitting wash-once-and-wear-once Jew Town clothes—greased their thorny naps, shiny as grapes, and hurried them off to Mount Zion. Georgiana would hammer home the importance of religion, cause, as everybody knew, Pappa Simmons spit when he heard the word ligion. He wasn't much on ligion, or anything else white after those crackas back home had cheated and tricked him out of everything he had. *If I'da kept my hand on the plow, he said, I'd still be back there in bad man boss's cheating fields. So much fo the weak will inherit.* Lucifer and John—Sheila seems to remember that damn fool Dallas as one with the Jones brothers; yes, she recalls three boys, a trio, so she sketches Dallas in one or two remembered scenes, a faint image like chalk on paper, a tentative figure that scatters and disappears at blown breath—would cut the fool in church. And Beulah would spend Sundays at the baseball park—*Damn, fool, can't you hit no ball? Don't be scared of it. He pitch mean but knock his teeth out!* So after service, Lucifer would fix her a plate of food, carefully placing her buttered roll so that it wouldn't topple off of the plate, and bring it to her at the T Street apartment Sunday evening. Miss Beulah he called her. *Thank you, Beulah said. You a fine boy. An angel. Wish I could make it to church. But I can't.* Lucifer also mowed the courtyard—mowing with Pappa Simmons's rusty scythe, mowing with that same expressionless face and the same hollow eyes. He would always take time to speak, *How you, Miss Sheila?*—and carried Sheila's groceries.

One morning, he spoke:

Miss Sheila, may I speak to you?

Lucifer.

I never seen nobody get the Holy Ghost like you.

Sheila didn't know if she should blush. Had he embarrassed her?

I mean. I never seen nobody do it that pretty.

Her eyes lit up inside. Yes, it had happened to her last Sunday, as it seemed to eventually happen to all of the church's sisters. Bloat with the Holy Spirit. *Music beats round the rim of your ears. Air flows solid and cold with fire. Your lungs crumble, sprout legs, then run free of your body, leaving a black hole in your bosom. A stranger enters. Yes, a stranger inside you, shaking the bars of your chest, gnawing through the iron with her teeth, flailing her arms, kicking her feet, running from one corridor to another and screaming FIRE!, breaking free of the cage and into the light, running dead into the glowing face of the spirit. So you must keep moving cause your body is FIRE!, red ants ravaging skin. And the striding shadow of the spirit riding you, holding on, with one hand thrown up in testimony, against your strong steady bucking. White-gloved ushers hold on too.*

You know John and Gracie spending time together.

She looked at the set of Lucifer's shoulders. He was over six feet tall and weighed better than two hundred pounds, though he wasn't a handsome man. Yes. I know. *Seen the spirit in her eyes.*

Well, I decided. You the one I want. He said it real matter-of-fact, like asking for a job.

Is that right?

Yes, ma'm.

She thought a moment. Decided to feel him out. A levelheaded young man. Both feet on the ground. An earthling. So unlike his brother John. What makes you think you can have me?

Jus informin you.

Sheila didn't know what to say.

Jus informin you. His eyes were clear black stones, hollow and unchanging, eyes without taste or heat. *Keep em open while we do it. Keep em open.*

Thanks.

You welcome.

Anything else?

Well. He paused, hesitant perhaps. I don't want nobody but you.

Really?

I don't *ever* want nobody but you. He was still, quiet, waiting, a ticket conductor.

From then on, Lucifer met her in the courtyard each morning. Miss Sheila, thought you might need me to carry yo bags. She let him carry the bags to the El. Then she rode the train and took two buses to the Shipcos' house in Deerfield, far beyond the sprawling arms of Northern Central. After work, she returned and found Lucifer's waiting eyes on the platform, unmoved, heavy as stone. So it would be. Morning and night, Lucifer stood heavy on the platform, the wood boards swaying beneath him. I don't want nobody but you.

He rarely revealed emotion, whether happy or sad. *He kisses the flesh around her slip straps.* He had put time into constructing this face. Spent his life building the hard outer hull, only for her to be drawn into the soft inner life. *His tongue works two places at once.* He invited her inside. *His tongue wiggles between the halves of her breasts.* Walk around. Explore on any terms you want. I don't ever want nobody but you.

Sheila heard, Here, these for you. Two black pearls heated her open hand. Light flashed against the black pearls and the whole world rearranged, a black flood.

With his reliable wings, Lucifer launched full flight into the dark future. She followed.

The first time he came inside her, he jerked twice, and she felt him plop out two seeds of sperm, two black seeds that bided their time. That was Lucifer, still, quiet, waiting.


BIRDS SHATTERED THE GLASSY TRANSPARENCY of the morning. Soared, suspended in air, light pulsing in their wings. Waves of air heated Sheila's face. The Oriental woman's eyes rushed toward her, two black circles coal-burning, flicking and fading. With something sharp at heart, she looked around the bend, silver rails curving and disappearing behind a building corner. The train appeared, gliding slowly and silently several hundred yards down the track. These slow Els, slower than the subway, even during rush hour. *Sheila, Hatch said, these trains so slow. How come they jus don't fly?* She always took the subway home through the rapid shortening evening. El in the morning, subway in the evening. Each day: half and half. She didn't like the subway, trains smashing through the darkness, darkness black as the space inside a hoodlum's hood, so she took the Dan Ryan or the Englewood El to work. But they an eyesore. What you see outside the window. Dull glass in vacant lots, trails of bold grafitti, cementless chimneys, the bowed legs of collapsing porches, burned-out buildings like moth-eaten suits, rusting cars like rotting apple cores, and garbage stacked high.

Somewhere down in the street hammers and saws were busy. The sun was up, all the way clear of the distant lake behind Red Hook and Stonewall. *Metal. Everything is metal.* The lake enclosed the projects in a bubble, like a toy paperweight. Sheila expected shaken plastic snow to fall. In the far distance a freight train curved into view like a black snake. She counted fourteen cars. The long train like a chain linking the two projects.

Perhaps these trains would stop at Union Station, where Lucifer had gone to meet John this morning. Ain't heard a word from John in a month, then he up and call and Lucifer rush off to the station, a dog returning his master's stick. And miss a day of work, too. But she could forgive Lucifer. Brothers are brothers. Forgive him. I'll jus let him *think* I'm mad. Might earn me something.

Sides, John ain't my problem. I don't sleep wit him. Gracie do.

Gracie was like the ancient women back in the old days at Mount Zion, bitter and alone, crying about men long gone when their own wrinkled flesh had caused their suffering. When their own blindness had shoved their heart into the dark outdoors. They take their pain out on you. Snap bitter words with the least justification.

Gracie hadn't been in the city a quick minute before she bring Jack home (T Street) to meet Sheila and Beulah. Sheila took one look at Jack. Compassion wilted. She wanted to beat him to death with his hammer-heavy wine bottle. His beard blackened his yellow skin. Sheila tried to touch his outstretched hand but couldn't. Beulah gave it the lightest squeeze. His red eyes wouldn't look Beulah in the face. Later, Beulah told Sheila in private that back home she had dated Jack while Koot dated him. My own sister. I lived in one town and Koot another. By accident we found out.

Sheila told Gracie.

Mind yo own business, Gracie said. He mine.

Didn't really surprise Sheila. Gracie liked to graze in other people's meadows. That's why she had to leave Memphis.

*Don't you know that's the easiest way to get killed? Lula Mae said.*

*Lula Mae, Beulah said, let me talk to her.*

*Why don't you talk to yoself, Gracie said.*

Beulah loaded up thirteen black steamer trunks, and John, Lucifer, and Dallas heavy-hauled them down the two flights of stairs, loading two trunks at a time into John's red Eldorado, one in the red open trunk mouth (trunk for trunk), and the other canoe-fashion on the roof. Seven trips to Union Station, and another seven trips to carry Beulah's twenty-seven boxes (how could this small apartment have held so much? where had she hidden it all?), the Eldorado stuffed so full that only John could squeeze inside it, the stacked boxes causing the red roof to sag above his head, the car to creak along. (Christ, Beulah. You gon wreck my ride.) Left a free space in the apartment on Kenwood (Woodlawn)—*Cookie's expanding wheelchair had forced yall out of the T Street apartment, elastic wood stretching as age pulled Cookie long and slack*—which John and Lucifer filled, and the four of them, the two sisters and the two brothers, transforming that closet apartment into nuptial chambers, the apartment they shared for the single year before John and Lucifer went off to war, and that they shared for seven more years after John and Lucifer returned. Gracie and John would spend time in the red Eldorado, while Lucifer would touch Sheila behind a hanging white sheet. He always touched her with cool fingers (maybe he had soaked them in ice water) that went hot.

Dallas followed John everywhere like a compass. The two would sprawl over the living-room couch laughing about some private joke. Dallas followed Sheila with angry knowing eyes.

*Dallas lay like a pinned butterfly beneath John. John leaned forward, pushing the stakes of his knees further into Dallas's shoulders. Then John hit Dallas, hit him and kept hitting him, quick straight stiff punches that did not miss.*

*If you gon get beat up, Dave said, you might as well fight.*

*Lucifer, you said, ain't you gon do something? You gon let John kill him?*

*Lucifer did not move. Waited.*

You (and Gracie and Lucifer and John) had witnessed John's transformation from boy to man, the boy-man whose face expressed every feeling quickly and vividly. The man was something to see. Lucifer, John, and Dallas had shared a basement apartment on T Street. Three steps down, then a hall leading to gray cement walls that breathed Dallas's smell, the stink of old drink. *40 Acres. Cheap wine.* Your nose watered the minute you entered. Once a week, in those months before you and Lucifer married, you mopped and wiped down the walls with ammonia. But the stink remained, as if the walls had been painted with vomit.

Even the lame, the deaf, and the blind knew that Dallas and John would hit every port of call (white port, cheap wine) on Church Street, from Seventy-third to Sixty-third and back again, in a matter of hours. Sing those foul corner songs that demanded foul corner faces, twisted mouths, broken curbs. Drink made dangerous words slip out of Dallas's mouth. When he got drunk, his eyes would get wide and black, two open shoe-polish cans, and he would try to rumble. *John, Dave said, you better tell this nigga something before I shoot him.* And what could John do? Drunk-stumble into somebody's door, so hard that the door jumped in its frame.

And everybody knew that John liked to lay with woman, that itch he had to scratch. *Mind yo business, Gracie said.*

Marriage did not change John. He brought his business to Gracie's doorstep and invited it inside. What did Gracie do? Let it happen. Right under her nose (how could she not smell the stink?), right in her home. *Mind yo business. Stay outa mine.*

Sometimes Sheila would watch Gracie pouring out tea, swinging her leg beneath the kitchen table, lifting a spoon to her mouth, and hated her for these things, murderous actions. Then, all of their years together would rush at Sheila. *Five, ten, fifteen, twenty, all hid? all hid? You and Gracie and R.L. and Sam and Dave and Nap playing Catch Me and hide-and-seek in the thirteen pecan tree clusters that surrounded Daddy Larry's house and barn. Five, ten, fifteen, twenty, all hid? all hid?* The boiling hatred would simmer down to pity. Gracie, Sheila would begin, don't you know—

It's my business, Gracie would say. He mine.

After Porsha was born, John would strap the baby in his Eldorado and take her red-speeding through the streets. Sheila told with her eyes what her mouth wouldn't speak. John bought a red wagon and pulled Porsha everywhere in it. *Same way he used to wheel Cookie (Jack's product) around in the park when he courted Gracie. Her body was liquid in the wheelchair. Her muscles moved under your fingers like water-filled balloons.* Lucifer would return from work each day with some gift for his daughter, usually something cheap, depending on how far his little money would carry him. John offered candy, cookies, and pop. Gracie watched it all.

Babies grow fast. Before you knew it, Porsha was starting school, learning how to read and write and add and subtract, figuring out this and that. John would light a cigarette and begin to speak, leaning his elbow on his knees. What you learn in school today? He watched his niece with his brown eyes, dry, ready to catch sun and flame.

How to think, Porsha would say.

She was all in your business, surprise you, standing straight and staring, like a paper doll in a pop-up book. Why the door closed? What yall doing? Why you on top of her like that?

Gracie and John moved to the two-flat on Seventy-second and May Street (Englewood) with a false fireplace—no chimney, all cement. *Then, when Jesus was seven or so, John bought the house on Liberty Island with a real hearth where a fire could burn. Gracie put Cookie's photograph—remember the day that you, Beulah, and Gracie bathed, dressed, and groomed Cookie and took her to the photographer—on the mantel above it: the dead muscles of Cookie's face and the loose eyes that looked in two directions at once; a white-and-pink bow; a pink dress with white collar and black belt; black patent-leather shoes; Cookie against a background of white cloud, its imprint surrounding her body, like a gem in a box.* She kept a six-pack of Big Bear malt liquor in her new refrigerator, drinking half the six days of the working week—yes, that was in those days when both you and Gracie worked on Saturdays—and drinking the rest on Sunday, finishing the last can late in the evening while her favorite show popped and buzzed on the TV screen. Stopped drinking the beer after John talked bout her so, complained how it stank so on her breath, how her gut started to swell like the toothpick-skinny drunks on Church Street, like the ever-present slow-moving Dallas with flat tires round his belly.


THE THOUGHT OF GRACIE brought Sheila back to the Oriental woman's face. Sheila caught the woman's eyes. The woman did not turn away. The eyes in the reflected face continued to look at her. Sheila felt transparent under the gaze. I forgot to comb my hair? Didn't wash my face? Got a booger in my nose? My legs ashy?

The train arrived with a smell of hot metal. Not the one she needed. Framed in the windows, the frozen-forward faces of passengers. *But they different in New York, Lucifer says. Here, the seats face forward overlooking the tracks—as if you were the conductor, you think—but there, you face the other passengers, keep yo eyes to yoself. Yes, you think, looking but not seeing, eyes turned away, curving and swerving with the tracks.* The conductor shouted, STANDING PASSENGERS, PLEASE DO NOT LEAN ON THE DOORS. Cause you might fall out of the doors, like teeth spilling from a mouth. The train drew off.

Roughnecks rolled down the platform steps. She clutched her purse strap tight, kept her hand firm on the skillet inside her purse. Her previous weapon, an open knife, Hatch's old Boy Scout blade (cause switchblades illegal) rusty to the touch, though it still cut; carried it till that day she left it on the sink and lost it to the drain; sides, knives are slow to the cut. Used to carry a pistol, wrapped up in a white footy—really did look like a foot, cloth stretched tight—til it fell out of her purse, stomped against the kitchen linoleum and blasted a hole in the wall, inches from Hatch's stomach. Tried Mace; one day on the bus, it released in her purse and nearly suffocated the passengers. So she settled on an iron skillet no bigger than her palm. Purse snatchers. Cutthroats. Rapists. Junkies. The mayor was even talkin bout puttin video cameras on every street corner. Fine with her. Sometimes she wished those doors would open and spill—spit?—out some of these bad niggas from the foul-and-rotten mouths of projects in Central, Eddyland, Crownpin, and South Lincoln. Kids nowadays got a patent on devil. They walk loud and talk loud and drive loud cars that zoom by in the silence of night, blaring music, shoving you out of sleep and rearranging the house. Most nights, Sheila slept through the noise, but Lucifer—*His reflection in the glass of her eyes is the transparent mask of a man.* The runaway world. The sharpest eyes can't see the arrows of death, Father Tower used to say. Bad intentions cannot travel so far as good.

The younguns in this dashing city, what do they know? Where have they been? Their eyes see nothing but their own nightmares. Father Tower used to say, There are plenty fountains of knowledge beside the roadside. It's up to us to drink. Perhaps, if these young hoodlums could taste the cleansing sweat of labor. The way of work and knowledge are one and the same, idle body, idle mind. The devil works overtime.

Somebody got to witness for the Lord. I'm too old. *You prefer the privacy of your own Bible, though your fingers almost too tired to flip through its pages. Tired of left-handed fellowship, you left the church a few years—two?— after Father Tower's death, after Cotton Rivers climbed to the pinnacle of Mount Zion's rock, setting up a pulpit at either end of the stage, and he and that Cleveland Sparrow exchanging sermons, extending a long length of white Scripture between them, branched birds sharing a single worm.* Said, somebody got to witness for the Lord.

Here I am, Mother Sister. Years of seeing, Sheila knew her well. A fat yellow woman, a lump of butter, spilling into two pink house shoes. Hair pulled back into a long ponytail, stretching the lines of her face. You may not know it, but each of you is my spiritual baby. I bring words of Scripture for nourishment. The milk of salvation. I am here to lift you up so that your short arms can reach the teat of your redemption. For the Lord Christ said, As Moses lifted up the serpent in the wilderness to save the backslidden Israelites, so must the Son of God be lifted up, so that whosoever will believe in him should not perish but have everlasting Life.

My children, do you want everlasting life? It is written in the Scriptures that the Lord Christ said, Lift up your eyes for the fields are white and ready to harvest, so pray to the Lord of the Harvest to send forth laborers into the field. The laborers are paid good wages. Better than the white man's wages downtown.

Each day, Sheila gave her a dollar and felt better for it. *God needs soldiers. Tomorrow is not promised to us.*

Mother Sister wasn't like some of these really crazy ones who got all up in yo face, a bullhorn, screaming, Repent! The wages of sin is death! The Lord will stamp your passport to hell: Blaspheme! Fornicator! Homosexual! Whore! Dope fiend! Drunkard! The crazy ones who say, God don't tolerate this, he don't tolerate that. Christ is coming. Take care of yo soul. No, Mother Sister wasn't bad. Nor the Burned Man. Each day Sheila gave him money too—a quarter—while most passengers turned their faces to the window.

*Heard he really saving that money fo an operation.*
*What happened to him?*
*Got burned up in a car crash.*
*That'd give anybody religion.*

No money could sway Lucifer. His feelings about religion had petrified into one silent shape. Once, Sheila and Lucifer had boarded a crowded bus. He found a seat and she found one behind him, both directly on the aisle. She could watch the taut ropes of his neck. The squareness of the back of his head. Whisper over his shoulder. For the next few stops, passengers crowded into the river of space that separated the two rows of seats. Stood tidal wave-tall above them, swaying to the bus's motion. A man vacated the seat next to Lucifer and he slid over to the window, opening the vacated seat for her. Before she could rise out of her own seat, a bean-bald young man snapped down into it. Sheila started to tap his shoulder, say, Sir, this man is my husband. Would you mind? But people today full of devil. Every word was a challenge. The man fumbled in the pockets of his blazer, stealing glances at Lucifer. Hi, the man said.

This was her opportunity. He had spoken and without venom. She saw the mug-shot profile of his face, every feature straining under a permanent smile.

You know you hear bout so much evil these days but rarely do you hear of the wonders of God. The man waited for Lucifer's response. *Here is my chance. I could ask him, Kind sir, this man is my husband. Would you mind exchanging seats so we could sit together?*

*Why, ma'm. Not at all.*

Guess so, Lucifer said. He was looking directly ahead, not at the man.

Bet you never heard of DDT?

*DDT?*

Guess not.

Disciples Against the Devil's Tribulations.

Oh.

*Oh.*

Now, do you attend church?

No, Lucifer said, saying it more with his eyes than mouth, cause they were in constant motion, whipping back and forth between watching the man and looking straight ahead.

Why not?

Well, it's kind of hard to explain.

Try as best you can. Don't be embarrassed.

Well—

I'm not asking anything from you. See, we Disciples are just a few men who get together on Thursday nights and discuss the glories of the Bible. We don't even have a church. Sometimes we meet at the Medina Temple, or the New Riverside Multimedia Church, even the Cotton Club.

*That disco on Hayes and Twelfth?*

But most of the time, we just meet at somebody's house. Brothers discussing the Bible's wisdom. How does that sound to you?

Fine.

The young man watched Lucifer with his permanent smile.

It's just that, see, I'm leaving the city, so I—

*What?*

For good?

Yes.

Where are you moving to?

New York.

*What?* Sheila stiffened at Lucifer's lie. *You are not. Oh, I see. Clever.*

Lord. The capital of sin. They got what, six million people there?

Ten.

That's a lot of sin. But you know, I'm sure DDT has a church there. Look them up and tell them you met a Disciple here who told you how God desperately needs your services.

I will.

You know, I used to live right over here on Forty-third. I used to stay up in the house all the time, lonely, alienated, didn't have many relationships. You have many relationships?

Guess so.

You married?

Yes.

Good. Cause if you ain't you could find some nice sister Disciples in New York. See, we always say, the devil put the *d* in evil. I used to do evil and I thought I was all alone up there in my room. See, I used to have this problem. With masturbation.

Sheila pulled the lines of her face taut, towing in her grin.

Yes, I would be up there in my room, my hand working up sin rather than flipping the pages of the Bible. Then I met a Disciple. He talked to me just like I'm talking to you now. I went to his house that Thursday. And these brothers were so honest they blew me away. It was an awesome experience. Right away I told them about my problem with masturbation.

This one brother told me, Every night, pray to Desire. And I did and after seven nights I didn't have my problem anymore. The Lord stepped in and kicked out that problem I'd had for nearly eight years. And you see, I'm not embarrassed to talk about my problem with anybody. Cause the problem means the cure. Gotta let people know about a good doctor. Ain't that right?

Right.

The Disciples are just awesome. And if you gon be a Disciple, you gotta be ready to suffer for the Lord. See, people don't want to suffer. They want a comfortable life. But every day can't be a McDonald's McCherry Pie day. Sometimes you got to eat just meat and potatoes. Sin lasts for only a little while. Take the *s* out of sin and you will get *in* to the kingdom. Moses and Abraham got their tickets punched to glory. Do you want to get into heaven? Do you want to go where there ain't no pain and suffering and crime and lies and overall evil?

Yes.

You seem like a pretty intelligent guy. Think God can use your talents? What do you do?

I work for UPS.

*What? You work at the airport. Crownpin.* Why had Lucifer lied? He would never see this man again.

Would you like to deliver glory in the kingdom? Doesn't that sound awesome?

Guess so.

Then you must be ready to roll up your sleeves and go to work for God?

Lucifer said nothing.

It is no accident that I am sitting here talking to you. Let God blow you away. See, I used to have a problem with masturbation, but today I have many relationships. Cause the Bible says, the body is the temple of Christ. The body belongs to Christ. Am I right?

Yes, Lucifer said. I'll look up the Disciples in New York.

Good. What kind of music do you like?

Jazz, I guess.

Well, I like classical music, though I listen to a bit of everything. Soul. Rap. You like those Christian rap bands?

What?

You ain't never heard of them?

No, Lucifer said. How does it sound?

Well, I never got to hear it good. But I saw some bands on this cable station.

Hm.

You ever heard Peter and the Wolf?

No.

Awesome. I listen to it all the time where I work. You know—

Well, Lucifer said, this where I get off.


A SECOND TRAIN banged by the platform without slowing down. The Asian woman watched Sheila, bulging black eyes, ripe plums. Sheila caught a glimpse of something else. Roundness stretching out the thin frame, as if the woman's belly were metal being drawn out by a magnet. The woman saw where Sheila was looking. Hid her stomach behind her small black purse. Might as well hide a watermelon behind a napkin. Can't be done. *Two of mine died on the vine.*

Hatch born seventeen summers ago, the summer of the cicadas—last year, they came a season early, mistaking spring for summer; or (perhaps) after seventeen years, too impatient to wait for summer; or (perhaps) their folded wings felt the coming heat (it would be the hottest summer in the city's history, sky red and the soil baking your feet)—the summer after the spring that the country pulled out of the war that had called both Lucifer and John, the year the cutthroats killed the Reverend Cleveland Sparrow. *Yes, niggas were changing even back then. They beat the reverend (Father is too good a word for him), made a bloody crown of his brains, punctured his body with the thorns of their ice picks, then propped him up on the altar, arms spread as if floating, over the open waters of his spilled blood. Cotton Rivers found the body of his partner in God, and he pined away in a matter of years (three?), this young man leaving behind a young wife and a new son, leaving the church in the young arms of his only son, Cotton Rivers, Junior, who the congregation knew as the New Cotton Rivers, the (now) fourteen-year-old evangelical who, through the clean channels of the TV screen, converted the pimps and prostitutes of Church Street and Cottage Grove and Stony Island and Hollywood and Broadway and all the other cesspools that flowed through this river-rhythm town.* From the moment of conception, he'd given her no peace. Nausea. Diarrhea (brown rivers). Dry skin. Cramps. More diarrhea (brown lakes). She thought labor would bring blessing and release, but he didn't want to leave her womb, fought her for thirty-six hours until the doctors had to cut her open. Then the fatigue wouldn't quit her body. *I'd been out of the hospital four months. Still tired. I mean tired. Tireda than when I was pregnant. Beulah had said it'd be a boy. They the ones tire you out. Fill you with morning sickness. Make you labor. Beulah was right. Porsha had come easy. But Hatch . . .*

From the first, Hatch loved words. Had to talk to him constantly or he'd cry. Sucked his bottle dry and left milk words inside the empty glass. *I WANT MORE.* And at night, he kept his hand at your mouth, touching, exploring. His first teeth—two buckteeth—looked like books. Had to read him a story before he went to bed and one when he got up. And he learned to read almost before he could talk. *In his room, neatly stacked books cover his windowsills like row houses, many that you carried home from the Shipcos' one stone-heavy book at a time.* Following the text with his index finger, word for word. (Some books he will flip through quickly, as if his forked fingers are divining for rapidly evaporating water.) In grammar school, he always won the class spelling bee—*but you had to whip his time tables into him*—cept that one time the letters knotted up in his throat, and the veins in his neck strained as they tried to draw up the words, and the tears fell.

One kindergarten afternoon (or was it Head Start?), he phoned her at the Shipcos'. His class had gone on a field trip (to the Aquarium? Planetarium? Zoo? the Museum of Science and Industry? the Historical Society?). *Our city had a black founder, Hatch said. His name was Marcel Vin. He established a trading post at the mouth of the Central River and lived there for seventeen years in a crude log cabin with a Potawatomi woman and twenty-three works of European art.* Sheila, he said. I had an accident.

What?

I had an accident.

What?

An accident. I got some bowel movement in my pants.

Just like him to say it like that. Book say it. His hands had grown books. *You speak to him, and he closes the book upon one finger to keep the place.* Maybe it was the books that made him turn serious. Made him stop smiling. And maybe one of the serious books put the idea in his head that God didn't exist. *One had hooked him on the theory that anything he could imagine had happened somewhere sometime. Flying monkeys. Talking roaches. Hyenas that work as stand-up comedians.* One day, he approached her, face serious.

Mamma? I got something to tell you?

Yes?

You ever heard of the Lord Christ?

She said nothing. What kind of question was this? He knew religion was no joking matter. Had she not brought him up in the church? Had they not attended Father Rivers's sermons three nights a week, where music weaved in and out of the preacher's words, hid like termites in the wood of your Bible, soaked into the after-service corn bread, chicken, and cabbage, followed you home, echoed in your bathwater, muscled into the sack of your pillow, added an extra pump to your man's loving, and tapped you on the shoulder when you tried to sleep?

Well, Mary gave the Lord Christ these toy clay birds. Guess what the Lord Christ did wit them?

You been reading your Bible? She had bought him the abridged one, the children's edition, the version she had given Porsha years before, after Father Tower recommended it.

Sometimes. Guess what the Lord Christ did?

She was afraid to ask. What?

The Lord Christ, he took the first one, see, and rolled it in his sandbox. Then he painted the wings yellow. Then he dipped the beak in some red jelly. Then he brought it to life as a goldfinch. Hatch's face was completely serious. Guess what the Lord Christ did wit the other one?

Where'd you read this?

The infant Christ, he dipped that second bird in his milk and brought it to life as a dove. Hatch walked off, his back and shoulders stiff and stooped. *Them big buckteeth, Lula Mae said. He got too much mouth. Boy, stop that chunkin!*

Seven. He musta been seven—cause his face became like Lucifer's face; cause he had stopped smiling; you saw the buckteeth only when he spoke— when he asked her, If God is good and God is great, why he do that to Cookie? Hatch wore Cookie's photograph like a mask.

Her lips grew tight with anger. She wanted to say, God works in mysterious ways, but she needed something fresh. The young won't touch anything old and wormy. What do you know about it? she said. Cookie passed befo you was even born.

And it seemed that every day that followed, he had a new challenge.

*If God made man, who made him?*

*Why God test Job? Ain't cruelty a sin?*

*Why did God tell Abraham to kill his son? Would Lucifer kill me?*

*Noah was mean. Cain ain't do nothing wrong. He wasn't naked.*

*If the Lord Christ so kind, why he put them demons in them pigs? I like bacon.*

*Why the Lord Christ put his two bloody paw prints on Judas's face?*

So she told him, Stay on the track. Cause a train can't run but on two rails in one direction. *Hold on, lest your hands slip from the rail and you go splashing into water. Hold on.*

What if it gon crash? Hatch asked. Should I still stay on track? And can't trains back up? She slapped the smart words back into his smart mouth. Cause religion was more than ligion; it was the whole thing, not simply using part of the thing and hiding the rest, like Gracie, who made the Bible her poker face.

Last Christmas dinner, Hatch had even refused to say grace.

God is good. God is great. Thank him for our food. Amen. Porsha passed the pea of prayer to Hatch.

Hatch sat with his face bent over the plate.

Hatch, your turn.

Hatch watched his plate.

Hatch?

I can't think of nothing.

Christ wept, Gracie said. Christ wept. Say it.

Hatch watched his plate.

Say it, Porsha said. Why you always tryin to be a nonconformist?

Shut up.

Who you tellin to shut up?

You.

Boy, you ain't talkin to one of yo little friends. I'll knock—

*Say it, Lula Mae said. Before I knock them big horse teeth out yo mouth.*

Nephew, John said, brown eyes blinking behind his silver frames, jus say it. So we can eat.

I don't remember nothing.

Couldn't say nothing when he was sposed to, only when he wasn't. Hatch's brain heated up too fast, putting words where they don't belong.

But John said Hatch was too slow. *Nothing fast enough for John.* Sheila—

John adjusted his silver-rimmed spectacles, watched her, his eyes like two brown animals caged behind glass—when you gon release this boy from yo apron strings?

Now, John, you know I ain't got him in no apron strings.

Damn if you don't. Do you know that he almost fell in Dave's grave?

*Yall be sure to lay a wreath on Daddy Larry's grave.*

*Where he buried?*

*That man Lula Mae work fo show you. Thinking, Cause he lies close by the river near the dark fence where the troubled waters flow and toss his body to and fro in the casket and the pigs used to run to him like puppies.*

*And don't forget the rest of yo kin, Big Judy and Koot and Nap.*

I didn't, Hatch said. He watched John, face saying, Why you do this to me? He forever tried his best to keep step with his Uncle John.

We lowering Dave in the grave and the next thing I know, Hatch here—

I didn't, Uncle John. You lyin.

Boy, Sheila said, watch yo mouth.

He lyin.

Sheila slapped his mouth closed.

Last summer—the summer after the cicada spring; *yes, buried in the blind ground, surely they prophesied the coming heat*—she felt the slighest lifting of her heart when Hatch told her he had found a job playing Reverend Ransom's Sunday service at the New Promised Land Baptist Church. She felt light inside, even if he only doing it for the money. She dropped to her knees like an exhausted cross-country runner, arms raised in victory, and lifted praise to the Most High.

SHEILA HEARD A CLICKING SOUND, like a train bumping over tracks. Black water towers rose above distant buildings like bad hats. *They got water towers all over New York, Lucifer said. Hear they work, too.* She felt a strange sharpness, a cutting sensation. She saw two eyes dry and black. Heard a clicking sound, sharp eyes working, cutting her open, perhaps searching for some secret reservoir. The young Oriental woman's thin lips were drawn as if framing a difficult question. The blood went thick behind Sheila's eyes. The Oriental woman looked both ways over the tracks, and kept looking, like someone crossing the street, her black gaze flying and buzzing past Sheila with each turn of her head. Birds cut through the silence. Then she saw the shaggy tremendous form of her train, an invisible smoke-colored shape—for she heard it before she saw it—hovering above the arched curve of track where it came around the building corner, smooth as water from a hose, this silver train with shadow on its roof, a seepage of moisture somewhere between earth and water, then the water level with her vision, the sound too, rushing and flowing, fish-flopping out of dark deeps, washing a metal sound, a thumping pail. The train hovered in the approaching distance, shaking steady on tracks, wavering, as if caught in a slow drizzle of rain, and the Oriental Asian woman looking both ways, hand clamped tight to her purse, and for a second that was more or less than a second, holding Sheila in her gaze, and Sheila seeing a thin black wing of charcoal-sketched eyebrows, and two black eyes punctured into a porcelain-smooth doll face (for she really was a doll, small and smooth and perfect), and the doll lips creaking open, parting to smile (would you call it that?), shout (call it that), silent beneath the train's roar, or as if the wind-loud train itself had lunged out the tunnel of her mouth, then the Oriental Asian woman moving with ease, flowing, and disappearing, not as Sheila might have imagined it, a slippery log rolling out from under her, no, not like this, but sinking, the anchor of her purse drawing her down, or the platform itself collapsing beneath her, a ringing chorus of rails.

LUCIFER FELT THE SHUDDERING RUMBLE of an approaching train. A rush of air at the side of his face. The train arrived so fast it seemed to fall toward him. The doors collapsed open. Passengers spilled out the silver insides, while new passengers poured in and refilled the depths. Root-stubborn, his feet refused to move. Sheila, one foot said. Sheila, the other answered.

STREETS OPENED TO HIS EYES. Rows and rows of glittering parked cars. Shopwindows rippling with reflections moving to and fro, fading and fleeing like ghosts. Billboards flashing the fast colors of advertisement. He walked, glancing over his shoulder, trying first one shop, then another. He had to find the right gift for Sheila, the right gift to set things right. When he had left the house earlier that morning to meet John, he'd tried to kiss her. She would have none of him.

*A kiss? Why don't you kiss John?*

He walked heavy through the spring crowd. He was all water, from the crown basin of his head to the ditch of his feet. The wells of his skin sweated rivers under the red dot of the sun. *Yes, his feet were heavier than John's luggage.* He tasted sweet summer dryness.

He circulated about another section of stores and shops—looking over his shoulder, glancing down the street with a steady eye on traffic—the buildings so close to the curb that one could drive up and purchase an item without getting out of the car. Some of the stores even had a drive-through. The spokes of the shops extended out from the hub of Union Station. *Like after a firefight, after you dropped the airpower and the next morning you went into the bush to check the damage. Dead gooks laid out like random pieces of iron.*

Kind sir. The bum spoke above a squall of traffic. Could you spare a quarter? Veins formed a black net in the outstretched palm. I hate to beg.

SHEILA FISHED IN HER PURSE for a quarter, and in that moment before she placed it in his hand, everything in the world grew quiet but his heart. Something catchy about a woman almost tall as you. A slight downward tilt of your face into hers and your lips touch. He had loved her for as long as he could remember, smooth-skinned woman—*and after the years, her caramel skin sweet as ever, her figure taut and fine, in both his memory eyes and his real eyes*—who chastised him in church, her perfume close and heavy. *His mental hands were forever hunting, trying to lift up her skirt and touch.* Later, a man, he told her, I used to come to church every Sunday just to see you. He spoke truly. He had bowed his head and mouthed prayer, while his inner mouth hummed another wish. *God, give me this woman.* He had placed his pumping red heart across his humble kneeling knees. *White red green orange or purple swirl in the dress that balloons around her stockinged legs.* Sheila mostly dated men from the church—Mount Zion Church, rows of varnished benches hard to the butt, steeple-shaped windows, stained-glass Christ with a flowing river of golden hair and two blue doves for eyes—and her sister, Gracie, was dating John. *Rumor had it that back home, down South, Gracie had, well, you know. Cause there was Cookie, the daughter. Rumors warn, John would eventually learn that Gracie's love never did anybody any good.* One day when the apple trees were heavy and white, Lucifer felt her move like the smallest of earthquakes—*his skin slippery against hers*—felt her heart beating under his lips.

You don't want that woman, Dallas said.

Why not? Lucifer said. He sensed a slight possibility that Dallas knew something he didn't.

Women are excess baggage, Dallas said.

Dallas would think that.

Sides, you don't want *that* woman. Been so long since she had any, I bet you her bed buried in cobwebs.

Lucifer looked at him, mouth hot and tight.

Dallas blinked, catching the sun directly. Man, those McShan bitches stuck up, got their asses way up on top of the church steeple.

Nigga, John said, you jus mad you ain't got nobody.

Dallas flinched at the words. He musta known it was true, cause Gracie said (and Sheila told) that he'd talked to the double preachers, Cotton Rivers and Cleveland Sparrow, about his trouble with women. Gracie would know.

*Have patience, son, the patience of an angel, Cotton Rivers said. For centuries, Cleveland Sparrow added, they've been waiting to try out their wings.*

Dallas had surrendered to his problem, settled for the whores on Church Street—the ones he could afford and the ones who would accept his money. He still talked a good game.

*Man, I went to the Coal Bin last night.*

*Whoopedoo. What else new?*

*Picked up this fine woman.*

*Nigga, you couldn't pick up a spoon.*

*Nawl, I picked her up. Little Red Riding Hood.*

*What?*

*You the firs nigga I ever heard of jerkin off to a fairy tale.*

*Nawl, that's what she called herself. Little Red Riding Hood. Had on this red cape. It stop right here.* Dallas placed the edge of his hand beneath his groin. *Man, I tore that pussy up.*

*Nigga, stop selling wolf tickets.*

*I ain't—*

*Did you touch it?*

*What?*

*Did you touch it?*

*Course I touched it. How else I'm gon get it in.*

Dallas held bright in Lucifer's memory, a young fat face shadowed under a hat's brim. So you gon lead Gracie? Dallas said.

John didn't look at him.

Nawl. She the woman I'm gon marry. And later, he told Inez, Mamma, these the women we gon marry.

Junior, Inez said.

But we don't have no money fo the wedding.

*Rivers and Sparrow don't come for cheap. And they charge more for a wedding than a funeral or a baptism.*

Junior.

And that's what she said at the wedding, the handkerchief wet in her hand, Junior. Pappa Simmons holding her up and George holding him up. A joint wedding, a joint ceremony, a joint sermon—Cotton Rivers and Cleveland Sparrow, silver-voiced; every time they opened their mouth, a coin fell out; *Christ is the stone the builders rejected, the spiritual rock from which the water of life springs. This stone is extracted from you, for you are its mineral*—and a joint line of twenty-five or twenty-six fancied-up cars—JUST MARRIED—Lucifer's car in the lead—well, Ernie's car that he'd borrowed, a rambling, slow, beat-up green thing, destined for the junkyard—since he was the oldest, and John's Eldorado (the mighty red machine) and the other cars honking behind him, slowly moving down Hayes Street, a bright and noisy procession of vehicles with tin cans rattling in tow and backstreams of fluttering crepe paper. He would not enter a church for fifteen years (Cleveland Sparrow's funeral, same year Hatch and Jesus were born). Cotton Rivers put pennies over his dead partner's eyes—the double preachers were double no more, the once blazing rails now a single track—tears streaming from his own. The congregation shut their eyes in prayer. When they opened them, the pennies were gone.

KIND SIR, HOW BOUT A NICKEL THEN? Even a penny would help?

Lucifer fished in his pocket for change. Tossed a quarter into the black-veined net.

God bless you.

THE UNDERGROUND housed exclusive shops. Lucifer entered the low red building separated from Union Station by a covered walkway. The Underground grew from the stone innards of the station, a Siamese twin. Eight levels of interchangeable structures—skywalks and skyboxes, catwalks and treadmills, marble waterfalls, silent escalators, glass elevators like transparent cocoons, layers of shops like the tiered galleries in a coal mine—that did not quite connect. Air itself was an invisible web holding it all together. Robotic surveillance cameras trawled the crystal floors, portaging live images. Lucifer plied their tracks. Hovered in one beat and out the next. His reflection was fresh and new in the shopwindows.

TWO COPS LED A BOY OUT OF A STORE, sunlight glinting on the handcuffs that bunched his wrists. Sunlight crawled yellow spiders up the boy's bald head. The boy offered no resistance. Lucifer studied him—some sign of familiarity? a boy Hatch's age, Jesus's age; other signs of familiarity?—and he watched Lucifer back, throwing the hard stones of his black eyes. Red Hook eyes. Stonewall eyes. Project kids stared at you that way. Tough kids that the Blue Demons basketball program hoped to soften. You officiated a call, using the fingers of both hands, forming them into a triumphal arch. They'd say Shit! or Fuck! or Damn, money. Can't you see?

Look, I'm jus tryin to be fair.

Fair? What's up wit that? Fuck fair.

And their eyes said more. *I'll beat you down. Steal yo money. Cap you. Pop yo life and yo wife.* Many a time, Lucifer clenched a red angry fist, ready to break and bruise some punk's face. But his anger met a wall. His skin.

The morning's alcohol flooded down from his brain into his eyes. *No mo drinkin wit John. I'm too old.* The boy's face shifted before him, two cloud-thick puddles. Lucifer flexed and unflexed his fingers to rid them of stiffness. The boy stiffened and drew back, a muscleman tugging a train.

# 12

THE TRAIN SHOT THROUGH THE LONG GRAY TUNNEL into an even blacker dark. In the car's unstained light, Porsha shook, a reed in the wind. Times like this, she wished she had driven. The city shouldered a notorious reputation for its thick traffic, scant parking facilities, and maniacal drivers. She never drove to an assignment. Watched the dingy windows of the train each day. Her green Datsun 280ZX that Mamma called a *man's vehicle*—

*Mamma, everybody drives cars like this now. Why don't you retire and get you one.*

*Daughter, I ain't ready to retire.*

*Think them Shipcos care?*

*I ain't ready to retire.*

*Ain't you tired?*

*Mamma said nothing.*

*Why'd you do it? Why'd you do day work all yo life?*

*I always knew I had a job*

—was parked safely in the garage on D Street at Hundred Gates, where she lived. She'd caught hell the last time she'd driven it.

The day has claimed her with its demands. She parks at the corner store, Cut Rate Liquors, goes in, and comes out with bath beads. She is thinking about the night ahead, a hot bath and Deathrow's hotter touch. She puts the gear in reverse, is about to turn her head back over the seat and back out of the lot when some young short punk—even today, here on the epileptic train, his face was a blur; they all look the same, baseball cap, Starter jacket, ankle-high gym shoes—some unsuspecting life moving in the darkness, approaches her car. He stoops to line up his face with hers. Hey, baby. Can I get a cigarette?

I don't smoke.

He looks at the paper bag on the seat beside her. You lyin bitches ain't shit. He raises up. She eases the car back. Feels a burning sensation in her nose. Ribbons of blood spray from her face, red-wetting the green leather steering wheel, the green leather dashboard, the rearview mirror, and the windshield.

Damn, homeboy. Why'd you hit that bitch like that?

Don't fuck wit me.

She brakes the car, throws it into park. Picks up the chunk of red brick lying next to the paper bag. In one motion she clicks out of the car yelling Yo, homeboy; he turns; she fires the brick whistling at his teeth.

He got the worst of it. No stitches for her, only a nick over the bridge of her nose. Some swelling for a few days—the second and third days were the worst, the bridge so puffy and swollen she could barely see—but nothing to rob her of bread and butter. If the brick had hit some other part of her body, another story. Cause her body was the only story that mattered.

Her beauty ran south of her neck. She thanked God and Mamma. Mamma had made her wear a girdle as a growing girl, as Mamma herself wore one. *Had Lula Mae started this family custom? Aunt Beulah?* Keen insight. Prophetic. The sacrifice had paid off. She made her living as a body-part model.

The train's lurch shifted her head to Deathrow's remembered shoulder. Her mind full of last night's argument.

They had horsed around, then lay resting, the two of them, under the sail-white canopy of the bed, continent-wide, limbs tangled, the second wind in their channeled muscles—sailors recovering from a shipwreck.

Clarence?

You know my name.

I don't like that name.

It ain't bout what you like.

A lump of words congealed in her chest. Dammed her breath. She forded them. She and Deathrow made up in bed. Deathrow took her to new heights of feeling, his lips smacking the waters of her thighs, his tongue propelling her clit, then diving into the well of her asshole. She arched, sending rivers of shivers through her body.

Yes. Yes. Eat it, motherfucka.

Afterward, he lay on the bed. She moved her hands over his body. It was like iron. She could find no softness. She nibbled at his boomerang-curved dick. What's this?

If it looks like a duck, if it quacks like a duck, if it wobbles like a duck, it is a duck.

Quack. Quack. She nibbled some more. Blew hot air past the hollow eye of his dick, making it whistle.

Aw, baby. Don't tease. Smoke my pole.

She went hard at the words.

He sensed her stiffness. What? He raised up on his elbows.

She watched him, hard.

Yo pussy ain't no mo important than my dick.

Huh, well maybe I should be giving my pussy to someone who thinks it is important.

I didn't say that it ain't important.

What are you tryin to say?

Drop it. Jus drop it.

No, I want to know what you meant.

Drop it.

She did. She had learned to put up with his tongue. Red Hook had woven him. Judge the sample by the cloth.

He settled off into the first flutterings of sleep, a curved shape. She squeezed her eyes shut. Slowly, her body faded away, dissolved into the white sheets.

The next morning, he was quieter than usual. What to make of his silence? His sharp features often made his moods look worse than they were. She tried to conversate while they bathed and dressed. He would nod or mumble a word or two. She would bounce back with a question. There followed a long elastic silence. What should she do next? She knew how to handle his bad mouth: with a thick titty stuffed in it. But how could she break his silence? She decided to harbor her words and release them in the full light of day.

The sun was ripe. His sudden and harsh anger last night had set a warning in the sky. Something red and hungry hung in the air.

She hooked her arm in his and guided him toward the subway station.

Are you mad at me?

No.

You're mad at me?

No.

How come you so quiet then?

I jus don't feel like talking right now.

Why not?

I jus don't.

Why not?

I would have to talk to explain to you why I don't want to talk.

She thought about it.

The day formed a red tube of silence that shuttled them to the subway station.

Okay, he said. We're here. I'll see you tonight. He put both hands on her shoulders and pulled her forward. Kissed her light on the lips.

What kind of kiss is that?

His eyes, full of hardness, held her. Loose paper curled in its own turn-
ings. He pulled her close and gave her a wet searching kiss.

That's better, she said.

Have a good one.

You too. Off to work?

Nawl. I gotta go home first.

Home?

Yeah.

She knew *home*, Red Hook, boiling with life and trouble. She wanted to
say, Be careful. She prayed for him silently. *God keep and protect.* You want
me to drive you?

Nawl. You be late fo yo assignment.

You want to take the car? She reached into her purse for the keys.

Nawl, baby. That's alright.

Really, you can take it. She always let him drive when they went out on
the town. Now, she was offering something more.

I can't park no car like that around Red Hook. I'd have to drive it all the
way back here.

Well, can't you ride with me on the train?

I would but I gotta pick up my wares first.

I thought you said—she dropped it. Studied his sharp face. It did not hide
his knowledge to know. With unsure fingers, she touched his baby-smooth
cheek. Okay, she said. Be careful, she said.

He kissed her fingers. Smiled his confident smile. I will.

I love you, she said.

I love you too. He let her fingers fall to her side. He walked off with long,
wide, muscular strides, undulating, stepping over oceans, continents.

See you tonight.

He spoke without turning around. Okay.

She said a prayer for him, uttered loud the Lord's speechless name.


DEATHROW CAME FROM SOME FAR-OFF LINE OF THE HORIZON where sea
touches sky, carrying his only cargo. The wide expanse of his body. The
waves of his muscles. And it was this force—the crushing pressure that lay
beneath his skin—that he showed to the world. But he showed her another
face. That sticky child face when they ate bubble-gum ice cream, her favorite, tongues sharing their rainbow-covered fingertips. And he gave her his
every free moment, riding the train all the way from Red Hook in South
Lincoln, dragging his wares along, to her apartment in Hundred Gates
(North Shore), an hour trip, or more.

*Hmmm. You're so young but so independent.*

*You gotta be. I'm trying to save enough money to start my own business in the Loop. A cafeteria. A coffee shop. Something like that.*

*I could help you, Porsha says. How much you need?*

*Thanks. I really appreciate it, but I gotta do this thing.*

A typical evening, Deathrow kicks off his shoes the moment he steps through the door. Lies his untroubled flesh on her bed. Grabs her butt with his great rawboned wrists and hands and pulls her to him. Runs his fingers over her face, using them to draw her new features. Rubs wave after wave of exhausting caresses. The warmth eats its way deeper and deeper inside her. She slips a movie in the VCR, wondering how long it will be before he slips his hand down her panties—his sweaty palm cool against her hot butt—and tickles her asshole. *They rarely made it through a movie.* How long before his body raised away from himself to hers. At the moment he prepares to enter her, she slips into the bathroom, using the excuse, I got to pee. She rubs two dabs of aloe vera into her pussy, a trick she'd learned from Mamma. Aloe tightened an orifice. After fucking—his spent penis a beached whale—he takes great delight in the two small holes in each of her earlobes—four holes in all. (He has a single hole in his left ear that many took as the troubling sign of a thug.) Ever see *Rosemary's Baby?*

You know I have, she replies. Horror movies are her favorite.

Now, one hole meant you worshipped the devil. You got four holes. What that mean?

She gets a damp washcloth, puts it over her forehead, a migraine shield. They lie sweating, skin to skin, beneath a heavy odor of flesh. Bone to bone, their ribs fit like a boat. *She has learned his body by heart.* Deathrow encircles the pillow with a sigh. Sinks into sleep with the speed of a stone in water. A storm breaks in his breathing. He wrestles and bucks, with jerky, electrical motions.

Her heart tightens. She thinks, still agitated, for his stormy breathing tosses her, leaves her on a shore of unrest. How to anchor herself? Take a sledgehammer to his stone heart? Wake him?

Once, she tried to wake him. A scream scratched its way through his teeth and he sat up swinging. One blow caught her full on the forehead. She retaliated, beat him senseless with the heel of her shoe.

The rise and fall of his sleeping chest calms her.

*A rib cage bleached white in the desert, bones curving toward the sky, frantic ants moving in the hollow in between, taking him into the colony beneath, for he has a full cutaway, revealing the canals that snake for miles beneath the sand, torpedo-shaped larvae in the queen's nest, and a worker transporting a beetle ten times its size back to the sand's surface. The sun has hardly moved.*

*Off in the distance, the square figurations of a ranch. A ball of tumbleweed rolls him closer until the ranch is a fixed block in his consciousness. Several horses escape the corral and run toward him at full speed, all thunder and fury, black manes streaming out behind them, but the pounding of their hooves upsets the image, unsteadies it, blurring the black and white patches on their bodies. Four cowboys give chase, catching at the bridles, lassos of blood spurting from their headless necks. Then bones—*

Morning. The ridges of Deathrow's shoulder blades form two humps under the sheet. He snaps upright in bed. Mornings give him an *attitude*, as if the new light has failed to wash away the old dreams, fails and floods him with renewed poison.

He sits with his face bowed in his hands, waiting for his head to clear.

Baby, what's wrong? Her hand feels out the shape of his back.

Nothing. I get these headaches sometimes. Kickin like a motherfucka. Bars of sunlight edge through the blinds and section the bed. He kicks his feet from beneath the sheets, lifts himself from the bed, and staggers over to the window. He peeps through the blind slats, tinkling like chimes. She watches: The vault of his butt and legs. The wings of his back and sides. And his squarely trimmed hair, a designer trim—not her preference but better than many she'd seen: that soup-bowl shave like the Chinamen in old railroad photos, or the pool-table cut with nappy pool balls and braided sticks— the city's skyline etched into the back of his head—a round sun miles above skyscrapers and Tar Lake—that mirrors in miniature the view beyond the closed blinds.

What you looking for?

He faces her. His abdominal muscles cobblestones. Yo mamma. He was born in Red Hook. They don't pull punches. And lately, every word came torn raw and bleeding from his throat.

I don't play that Mamma stuff.

Alright then. Yo daddy.

Maybe we should stop seeing each other. Never get a boy to do a man's job.

Who you callin boy?

Yo mamma.

Aw ight.


THEY'D MET, LAST SUMMER, on the bus en route to an assignment. She was looking good that day in her bright green dress that revealed her exact shape—hips flaring out the skirts—and matching pumps, the wide pirate's belt tightening her already slim waist and sunlight washing her smooth unstockinged legs. She caught many thirsty eyes drinking in every detail of her. The wind blew high, snatching at the dress. Cars pulled over to the curb and drivers signaled or honked their horns. She boarded the bus and found a seat. Across the aisle, her eye-slide caught a fine nigger, smooth, dark, light eyes, good build—every muscle straining to tear through his skin. He saw her watching him. Grinned. Blew her a kiss. Just like that.

Yo, baby. I'm Deathrow and you fly.

Not the best line but better than many she'd heard. *Baby, you makin me cry wit that onion between yo thighs . . . Yo, sugar. Make me a diabetic . . . I'm the plumber of love, wreckin homes with a foot of pipe . . . Let's get butt naked and fuck.* But a sin-sweet voice.

No, I'm not fly. My name is Porsha.

Well, Porsha, you got a phone numba?

Maybe. You old enough to count? He was young, but what was that thing about men reaching their sexual peak at nineteen? *I've been to the mountaintop!* (Later, she would discover that he was twenty, older than she had first thought. I always have been bad at math.)

Baby, I can count. Do lotta other things too.

She took him at his word. His eyes were hooded with secrets. Hmmm. I better give it to you then. She produced her business card.

He read it. Body-part model?

Um huh.

What's that?

I'll tell you about it.

He put the card in his shirt pocket. Stood and walked into the aisle. She observed his wishbone legs. (Later, whenever he made her angry, she would look at his legs and fuck with him. Hey, cowboy. Forget yo horse?) He stooped over his seat, hauled up a heavy cloth sack, his wares—incense, batteries, socks, scarves, jump ropes, umbrellas, telephone cords, body oils—sticking out the top. Santa Claus, she thought. He faced her. Extended his big hand. Pleasure to meet you.

She took the big hand in her own. A terrible excitement shook her. An old feeling. Ancient. Uncle John would pour popcorn into her girl-small hand—*I'm scared, Uncle John*—and the pigeons would swoop down and peck and feed. *It feel funny, Uncle John.* The same, she said.

Deathrow exited the bus, rolling his tight butt.


A PYRAMID OF LIGHT filtered from the projection room, specks of dust dancing in its blinding whiteness, to a wide screen that hemmed in the horizon. Your empty eyes filled up with white moving. Empty ears vesseled words and sounds of black surprise. Deathrow's face tinged blue and orange by the bright images shifting over it. A perfect first night out. A good-looking man and a low-budget horror movie. Grainy shots of two sisters, a castle, hooded rituals and Latin chants, and a frothing red-fanged witch who drags her victims, pleading, screaming, kicking, and bleeding, into the dark world behind the waxy plane of an oval mirror. Jump to 1940. A woman drives a knife again and again into a second woman prone beneath her on the bed. The mirror watches. Jump to the present. A third woman purchases the mirror at an antique shop. Once home, the mirror menstruates. Masturbates. Moans. Metamorphoses into a cavernous vagina that swallows the pet poodle. A psychic warns the woman not to fuck in front of the mirror. She does so anyway. The mirror swallows her lover. She seeks the psychic's help. The mirror swallows the psychic. She seeks the help of her best friend. *Don't white folks know when to leave? Jus leave the damn house.* The mirror possesses the woman's best friend, turns her into the red-fanged witch. You worked the popcorn out of your teeth with your tongue. A struggle ensues. The images come together. Form a magical whole. Everything moves. Everything immobile inside you moves. Frame after frame, you watch what your eyes cannot see. The screen gathers in your own image. You feel the electric rush of heat when Deathrow sticks his tongue in the socket of your ear.

THEY HELD HANDS in the late summer light and strolled through Circle Park, forested with a full and secret view of the harbor crowded with visions of amateur sailors and jewel-named ships. *Esperanza. María Concepción. Helena Nataría.* She walked very close to him, occasionally bumping her hip against his. The sun sank low, from glowing white to dull red, without rays and without heat. They sat close on the grass, Buddha-fashion, beneath low-hanging leaves, sharing bottle after bottle of wine—zinfandel, her favorite, neither sweet nor dry—which they chilled in the river where the last flames of sunlight glided like snakes. She felt the warm wine break a hot path through her stomach, growing hotter and sharper as it moved. Then the sky died down to the color of smoke. Points of light flicked rhythm from the lighthouse. Her breathing reached deep, where no air had ever come.

Damn, I gotta pee, he said. He pushed to his feet, legs heavy with water.

Need some help?

He did not hesitate. Yes.

She stood straight up, managing the wine better than him. Unzipped his pants and took his dick in her hands. What with one thing and another, before she knew it—

IN THE FIRST WEEKS, she discovered his secretive feet. He would keep his socks on during sex; and he would never allow her to see his bare feet. *One of life's greatest pleasures is charting the fine lines on the soles of the feet.* She pondered and planned. One day, she asked him to take a bath with her. (She loved baths, would sit in the tub an hour at a time.) They both disrobed. He raised a socked foot, ready to stick it in the water.

Uh oh. Take off your socks.

What?

Who heard of anybody taking a bath with they socks on?

With slow fingers, he removed his socks. And there *they* were, feet, like badly carved canoes, the sides scarred and rough, the skin mildew brown.

What happened?

Birthmark.

A birthmark?

Yeah. And he never said any more.

AFTER THE FIRST WEEKS, he stopped opening doors for her. Never pulled out a chair to seat her. Walked on the side of the sidewalk farthest away from the street. *The man should be near the street. Pappa Simmons had told her that this custom dated back to the days of horse and buggies and unpaved roads. If the wooden wheels of a buggy should spray an angle of mud onto the sidewalk, the gentleman's body would shield his lady.*

*Woman, you said. Say woman. Lady signify.*

*Pappa Simmons blinked.*

*Lady like callin an Asian Oriental. A black person Negro.*

Once, they met for dinner outside Davy's Garden, her favorite restaurant, where fig-leafed and sandaled waiters and G-stringed and pastied waitresses served the tasty low-calorie semi-vegetarian dishes that she needed. To start, he was late—he was often late, as if there were two worlds, he a member of the one lagging slightly behind ours—but he offered no apologies, and she didn't get angry, let it slide, put her tongue deep in his mouth. He played his palm over her ass.

Stop. You embarrassing me.

He gave her ass a firm slap.

Later, she said.

He opened the door and went inside. She waited outside. A minute later he came back.

What's wrong? he said.

Be a gentleman. Open the door for me.

What?

Open the door for me.

His eyes widened. You ain't handicapped.

Niggas ain't shit.

So what does that make a bitch?

Yo mamma the bitch.

Why you comin at me like that? What I do?

Being a young ignant stupid low-life no-class punk-ass muddafudda, that's all.

He grinned. Can't we just chill?

She looked at him.

Sound like a personal problem to me.

Yeah, you the person.


SHE LIKED HIM, though he was rough around the edges, and didn't hold the sharp weapons of money and power. With him, there was always something new under the sun. And not just the lovemaking, the wild gyrations of a twenty-year-old. *Nineteen? What difference does a year make?* They spent nights in Circle Park, near the Japanese garden, drinking and screwing. (She had scars on her knees to prove it—hi-riding the saddle of his crotch—manageable scars, nothing she couldn't hide with a dab of Nu Nile cream.)

*He puts his ear to her yawning vagina.*

*What you doing?*

*Trying to hear the sea.*

But he wasn't stuck on sex. He knew the value of a hug and would hold her all night sometimes, her head on the boulder of his shoulder.

Equally drawing were his wild dangerous moments. Once, they were standing in the lobby of Davy's Garden, waiting for a table.

How long will it be?

I already told you, sir. Fifteen minutes.

Me and my baby want to eat.

I'm sorry, sir. Fifteen minutes.

Deathrow knocked the host's head back with a short quick punch. Just like that. The host straightened his tie. Found them a table.

On another occasion, Deathrow shrouded his empty plate with his white napkin, then took Porsha by the hand and led her to the men's bathroom. (She had not finished eating. His quick teeth always finished before her.) He tipped the bathroom attendant about half what dinner would cost. Instructed the attendant to, Give us a minute. Shoved the attendant out the door, bribe money in hand. Locked the door. Checked the stalls. Washed his hands and her hands—his soap lathered them a single skin—one finger at a time. Undressed. Naked, eyes closed, they climbed into each other, a thin black seam. She held her breath. Their work was sweat and light, sweat and light. When they were done, they made a distance from one another and breathed, outstretched on the warm tile floor, smiling, faces pressed against stone.

And then there was the time he just up and grabbed a waitress at Davy's Garden. Some homely white girl who was working another table. Grabbed her by the arm and pulled her face next to his as if he had a secret to tell. He put his tongue in her mouth. He let her go. She cleaned her lipstick from his mouth with a cloth napkin. She tore up the check. He sat back in his chair, belly poked out with satisfaction.

Did you have to do that?

He looked Porsha full in the face. Clean draws can't hide a nasty booty.

They would talk for hours in the darkness, their lips almost touching. So she learned that he got to his station in life by magic.

It ain't where you come from, he said. It's where you're going.

She considered the truth of this.

Gotta take chances if you wanta get somewhere in this world.

What you know bout chances? Young boy like you.

Aw ight. Watch that boy stuff.

They breathed in the darkness, his slow hand on her body.

I know bout chances. *A bitch is a bitch, but you got a vicious body, the curves that make a nigga wanna gamble.* See, at Red Hook there this old bitch—cuse me, *lady*—

*Woman.*

Right. Woman. Anyway, there this ole ass woman live on the top flo of Buildin Three. Everybody say she a witch. Say she give you power if you go up in her. Some say she learn it when she lived way down South. Some say she got it from eatin cat food. Others say she throw parties fo the devil. All I know is, she got power. Power. And she got it to give. Why you think Freeze climbin so high up the ladder? He ain't no better than me. Only thing is, he knocked her boots.

Freeze? Who's that?

You ain't never heard of Freeze?

She shook her head. Should I have?

Well—drop it. It ain't important.

But—

Drop it. I'm fin to tell you about power. See, that's the way it goes, either knock they boots or knock em upside the head.

Why you talkin like a lowlife?

I'm jus tellin you how the niggas see it.

I ain't talkin bout them. I'm talkin bout you.

Sorry, baby.

Finish tellin me.

Well, people be scared of Miss Emily. Miss Emily, that's the name of that ole witch. Nobody mess wit her. I mean *nobody*. And they always speak when they see her. They be like, How you today, Miss Emily? Fine. All she ever say. Fine. Ole bitch be throwin—

Do you have to use that word? It's disrespectful.

Disrespectful? Baby, I got a lot of respect. All sorts of respect.

He kissed her on the cheek. A bird peck.

Anyway, Miss Emily always be throwin her liquor bottles out the window and bustin somebody head. You see her bout once a week. Be ridin round on one of those lectric wheelchairs and shit, you know, those ones that go *real* slow. Everybody be calling her Lectric EEL. EE. But we jus thinks it. Keep it way back in our mind. Call her Miss Emily to her face, cause she got power. Most ole folks be all scared to even leave they apartment and come out in the hall. And somebody crippled and ole too. But EE, she ride all round on that thing, all over Red Hook, circle all the buildings five or six times, jus creepin long in that slow lectric wheelchair. And you know the jets, all them buildings and shit, every lap bout eight blocks.

Porsha didn't know. She had only driven to Red Hook once or twice to pick up Deathrow.

Niggas speak to her every time she pass. They be like, How you, Miss Emily? Fine. Do her last lap and she go right into the elevator on that thing. He pulled back, pausing to word it right. Like a worm in a dirty hole, or a roach in the wall or somephun, and ride up to her apartment.

She look jus like a witch too. Big-ass head with these two little tiny dots for eyes. And can't hardly see. All this thick green stuff on her eyeballs. And her body all skinny and wrinkled up. Hands all balled up like crabs. And her arms all wrinkled up like some tree branch.

Don't sound like nobody wit power to me, Porsha said.

That's because you don't know power when you see it.

How you know what I know?

I know.

You don't know as much as you think you know.

You gon let me finish?

I ain't stoppin you.

Well, this one day, I see EE ridin round and goin slow as hell, and I jus walks right up to her, jus walks right on up to her and say, How you today, Miss Emily? then I whips out my dick.

What?

Straight up. Pop goes the weasel.

I don't believe you, Porsha said, thinking, Maybe he did.

For real.

You tellin a story.

You know I don't lie.

Porsha thought about it. Well, what she do?

I'm fin to tell you. I whips it out and shakes it a little, right in her face. I say, Trick fo trick. EE open her mouth and smile at me. Got all this gray shit on her teeth. Like steel wool or somephun. She say, Chillen are such a comfort to the body.

No she didn't?

Straight up.

What you do?

What you think? I wore my jimmy.

Niggas ain't shit.

Better believe it.

Fairy tale.

Only fairies tell tales. And you know I ain't no fairy.

What am I going to do wit you?

All the good things.


DEATHROW WAS BETTER than most of the men she'd dealt with. Trifling niggas. (One boldly told her: Baby, I'm only out for one thang. The pussy and the money.) Especially Les Payne. Fine nigga. Tall and muscular. Honey-brown skin. *I got a weakness for these good-lookin browns.* The rod of his penis printed against his tight jeans. Eyes you could leap into, singing and splashing. Rolled his own cigarettes (liked her to roll them for him) with Top paper—to make everyone think he fired up joints as normal people fire up cigarettes—and sweet-smelling tobacco. That was during her only year of college—Freeport University, downstate, a stone's throw from Kankakee County, Decatur, Beulah—a decade ago.

She met him at a Greek Club dance. *Ah, remember it.* Couples revolved around each other like spheres. Orderly motion. Beneath the long, skinny, white arms of the searching hall lights, she buoyed her way, mapped it out, speaking and receiving many flying words of friendship, her long fingers fluttering in every direction, clawing up cookies, cake, pie, potato chips, punch. *Girl, you ate like a pig back then. But the engine was working and you could burn it off.* She shone in her best outfit, a gown of polka-dotted tulle with short sleeves and puffed shoulders, a wide red belt cinching her waist. She removed a silk handkerchief from her purse and cleaned her fingers, one at a time. She shot a challenging look around the room. The man she would come to know as Les invited her to dance. Immediately, they were locked in a tight embrace among a whirlwind of incessantly moving feet. She felt so light in his arms. He kept his mouth close to her ear, and his tongue . . .

I gotta go. They had danced for hours.

Why? The stroke of midnight? His eyes searched her body. Your dress gon turn into rags?

She let slip a laugh. Not quite. Tomorrow's Sunday. I got things to do. Cooking. Cleaning. Church. Things.

Can I help? He batted his eyes, quick church fans.

She felt the slightest rising of her heart. No.

How bout tomorrow? Dinner at yo house.

Maybe. Give me a call and we'll see.

Next day, he called. She heard his eyes through the phone receiver, fluttering and flapping. She accepted the previous night's invitation. Cooked him a down-home meal. Her neckbones were his for the sucking.

They quickly established a lovers' routine. A fast drive away from the campus, Les Payne's old Mustang lurching like a gurney. They drove with the windows down, laughing big laughs, cornfields breathing in their faces. A midnight walk through the fields, holding corn-scented hands. Wet moonlight changed the fields into a sea of rippling yellow and green waves. They paused in an open spot, a circle in the corn. Settled down into the blind dirt. Les Payne's kisses moved like ants over her body. He breathed hard before he entered her, laboring like a steam locomotive. Afterward, they drove down to a quiet spot on the Kankakee River. Let the cold river water wash the manure from their bodies.

He would drive her home every weekend, two hours away. He's a real showpiece, Mamma would whisper.

Is that all you can ever say? Porsha said.

Okay, I'll tell you what Beulah always told me. Don't throw away dirty water until you have clean.

Porsha prepared dinner. Les Payne snapped his napkin taut and folded it across his knees. Cut and ate his food, knife and fork machine-clean and precise. Uncle John trained his loaded eyes on Les Payne's face. (Porsha had made sure to invite him.) He never touched his fork.

Mamma talked.

I had the easiest time with Porsha. During the pregnancy, I mean. Lucifer got morning sickness. And he standin there in the delivery room, lookin like he bout to pass out. Doctor gave me a cesarian. But with Hatch? Mornin sickness. And he was always kicking. Seemed like with spiked heels. All the pain. I thought it was because I was old. But Beulah said, Sheila, it's a boy. Yes. It was, too. Ten pounds, twenty-three inches. I thought I was gon die. And the doctor didn want to give me a cesarian. To this day I don't know why. I thought I was gon die. Lucifer and John stayed in the waitin room. I told em, You better not pass out, tired as I am. And I told the doctor, yes I told him, Sew me up and leave a hole for my husband.

Uncle John raised his fork. Poked words into Les's face: Them pretty boys got sugar in they blood.


THE CAMPUS PHOTOGRAPHER, Les used his lens like his mouth, an instrument of sweet talk. Baby, let me jus take one more shot of you. God, this lens don't do no justice to your beauty. Can't capture all that body. Stroked her breasts, her legs, her butt. You got a bad-ass body. Smokin. Man, wish I had a body like that. He showed some of her photographs (probably in boast) to a professional friend who called her in for a shoot. The photographer put a paper bag over her head—*you could weather the insult for the two hundred in cash he'd paid you*—and shot her in evening wear—*ah, you flushed red with embarrassment, a glowing coal; you sat and the crinoline broke like cinders*—short dresses, miniskirts, bikinis, and lingerie. The photographer lined up jobs for her, fashion layouts for black magazines and ads for local newspapers and catalogues. Les Payne had given her a career.

The career made her accept all of Les Payne's excuses, the many hours he spent at the frat house—or so he claimed—with his frat brothers. Baby, it's about unity. Togetherness. Brothers trying to get something in this world—batting his eyes the whole time. After all, he had branded the fraternity sign—Delta Sigma Pi—greasy and black on his biceps. *Or had he carved it?* What troubled her: He had acquired a name for prowess among the women at the university. Couldn't go nowhere for him winkin at some woman or some coed grinning his name. She took all she could. She asked him, Who squeezin yo lemon?

What?

You heard me.

Baby, that was all in the past. I'm a new man now.

Where the old man you left behind?

He kissed her. Baby, I'm straight. The words rolled out of his mouth like smoke.

That night, she prepared for her weekend trip home. Gave him her apartment keys. He would stay and study, needed book time away from his frat brothers. She loaded up her bags and hit the road. Rode the bus as far as the city line, rolling columns of streetlamps. She exited the bus and caught the next one back to the university. Opened the door and caught Les Payne on a downstroke, doing it in *her* bed, the moonlight so bright that the two bodies shone yellow against the sheets.

She quit college after her freshman year. Moved back to the city. Found an apartment on South Shore Drive with a generous view of Tar Lake. Signed on with an agency. Things were looking up.

Hang-tailed, Les Payne came crawling back. *Say, baby. Could you see your way clean?* Wouldn't leave her alone. Plead for hours on the phone. *His mouth peeled off in pages.* Send her cards. She gave him another chance. Her trust regained, the hang-tailed hound sneaked off for a bone.

It was time for a change, time to dust the broom, but she couldn't drop him. He had put his flame in her. She sought Mamma's advice. Between pauses of her raised teacup and the clink of its return to the saucer Mamma told her how to get rid of a boyfriend.

Daughter, write his name on an egg and toss it into the sea.

The sea? Ain't no sea round here.

A river then. The waves will carry him away.

She drove—not the 280ZX but her first car, the spanking green Camaro bought with her new modeling dollars—to the Kankakee River. She tossed three eggs for insurance.


LOOKING BACK, she could see all the lovers from her life, singular yet source-same, like the pages of a book.

*She rises on the pyramid of Uncle John's back. The afternoon air dances under the trees. She can touch the leaves.*

*A lot of dogs get run over chasing after that stuff.*

*What stuff, Uncle John?*

*You know what stuff.*

Sugar Smallhouse, the exception. Central Vocational High School, eleven, twelve, thirteen years ago. Like the school's coolest dudes, Sugar liked to bop. Intricate steps, shuffling feet, twirls, twists and splits performed by two male partners, dressed in self-named zoot suits. Broad-brimmed Dobbs. Long-lapeled blazers. Bright silk ties against blinding white shirts. Diamond stickpin and matching cuff links. Baggy pants with high waists, held up by red suspenders. Two-toned patent-leather shoes. Hair slicked with Never Nap cream. Shiny conks with warp waves flowing back like ridges on a seashell. Sugar Smallhouse was the best dancer, could dance his head off—maybe it was the way he ended a step by removing his hat, then shaking it like a tambourine—and the cutest too. *Jus a sucka for them light-skinned mens. I always been.* Their first date, they danced so close that she could feel his heart heaving and crashing against her breasts. He said next to nothing. His rarity of words would last the length of their three-year relationship. She had messed with—kissing (*bustin slob* they called it), touching (*feeling on*), grinding—a few boys, but he was the first she would let completely inside her. Pinch her nipples tightly erect. Finger her deep inside. Tug at her panties. Slide them over the curvature of her hips. Part her legs with cool hands, then something wet and cold on her burning pussy. She raised her head slightly, looking down, seeing his closed eyes, his tongue lapping like a dog, then pushing into her and her head falling back. He refused to believe he was the first. *Where the blood?* But she felt the pain of his slow, dry entry. He was forever grateful for her bodily gifts. If he had a penny, half of it was hers. Wise in love, he could never catch on with his studies, no matter how much she drilled him, and he graduated—*remember the prom, Sugar in his black tux and you in your royal-blue taffeta dress, walking slowly and carefully, holding it up around your waist*—only after falling to his knees before the principal, begging and crying. Please, sir. Please.

Get up, son. You'll ruin your suit.

Off he went to the navy (radar training?)—and she to Freeport University—rather than work full-time in his father's clothing store. They exchanged a few letters the first months.

*You datin now?*

*Got to sometime, Uncle John.*

*Any of those niggas act a fool, you come see your Uncle John.*

*Yes, Uncle John.*

*You come see me. I'll set them straight right and quick.*

Deathrow was the closest she had come to Sugar Smallhouse—though he was darker, a quarter after midnight—to matching that *feeling.* Sugar was inside him, a secret astronaut directing his life, directing him back to the love she'd lost. If you dug deep enough beneath his hard exterior, you found many a kind bone. His life extended into hers, clusters of lines reaching out.

The night before she was to move into her new loft at Hundred Gates, he phoned her.

Meet me at the apartment.

The apartment? Why?

Let me bless it.

Bless it?

You know, *bless* it.

They blessed the apartment, naked floors and walls echoing flesh and sweat.

Hatch and his best friend Abu arrived early the next morning at the South Shore apartment to help her move. She looked forward to a new apartment and a new neighborhood. Her body needed its sleep; sanitation trucks blew garbage odor through the bedroom window; to the siren of the truck and the call of the odor she awoke every morning; besides, it was time for a move; she had lived in South Shore ever since her return to the city from Freeport.

How come your cousin ain't helping us move? Deathrow said.

My cousin?

Jesus.

She had never uttered Jesus's name in Deathrow's presence. Her embarrassing secret.

Where's Uncle John? Hatch said.

I ain't heard from him.

He ain't called? Porsha saw the concern in Hatch's eyes. Hatch was fashioned in John's image. A shadow of John's face in his, an echo of John's voice in his.

No.

Damn, Abu said. He was Hatch's twin, only shorter, darker, fatter. His chimpanzee ears twitched. He promised.

I know, Porsha said. He told Lucifer he was coming. After Les Payne, she had come to trust Uncle John's gut feelings about a man. She would introduce a man to Uncle John on the first date. I know what men want, Uncle John said. She was anxious to hear his evaluation of Deathrow.

Don't worry, Deathrow said. I can drive the truck.

Deathrow put his mouth and muscle to good use. He instructed the others as to what objects to remove from the apartment first. (Days before, he had shown Porsha how to pack and seal her boxes properly.) He loaded up the truck with each object exactly positioned. Shackled the furniture so that it couldn't move. Drove the truck. Once at Hundred Gates—yes, she would love it here; live leaves ran green lines up the building and curtain-shimmered in the wind—he directed the unloading. It took eleven or twelve hours to load and unload several tons of items: her Bible, her globe, her wrought-iron bed with the white ship sail-canopy (she had attached chimes to it, sonorous seashells strung from a straw net, like a second miniature canopy), dresser, chest of drawers, tables, chairs, couches, love seats, sleeper sofas, refrigerator, stove, dishwasher, washing machine and dryer, and stacks and stacks of boxes: her South Shore apartment had been stocked like a museum, full of objects—dolls, dresses, coin banks (scared-eyed niggas with hollow grins and watermelon lips), old cloth for quilts, browned newspapers, perfumes that had lost their scent, doll-sized wooden Indians, a clay nigga foot (*Nigga toe*, Lula Mae called it), crystal knickknacks—from Lula Mae's lil house, the trailer propped up on four corners of bricks in Lula Mae's backyard, which you reached by stepping down three cement back-door steps and walking across two long, splintery wood planks to its metal door. The loft had been a dance space, then a gallery, then a radio studio, then a television studio. Perfect for her. Huge, an entire floor. A church-high ceiling. Two walls were solid windows. She could look down onto the web of a great tree. Sunlight smeared one wall of windows in the kitchen and dining room, and the small series of picture-frame windows in the bedroom. Through the fractured blind slats, she could watch a bird wing past. Moonlight made the floorboards silver. In the bare room—she had yet to hang draperies—voices moved like shadows on the walls and shadows danced across the ceiling. The windows were long, bright, shadeless rectangles of light. Without warning—light and dark, equal halves of a slowly spinning ball—they shaped to lengthening shadows.

The room steamed with hot silences. The purple glow of the tropical aquarium, the whisper of currents, gurgling bubbles, and fish rippling in bright streaks. Deathrow bobbed over to the aquarium, his footfalls echoing against the hard wooden floors. Tried to scare the fish with ugly faces. Fish unscathed, he rapped on the glass with his knuckles, hard.

So you from South Lincoln? Hatch said.

Yeah. Red Hook.

Red Hook?

Yeah.

Really?

Straight up.

You know T-Bone? Abu asked, eye cocked to catch deceit.

Hell yeah. Crippled motherfucka. Ridin that wheelchair like a Beamer. But he straight.

Man, *he* from Red Hook, Abu said to Hatch.

What?

*He* from Red Hook.

Man.

A moment of silence. A feeling silence.

So, Hatch said. So, well, what's it like?

Deathrow grinned his grin. When a man in the house, he said, all the bullshit stops. He slapped Hatch on the back.

Damn.

Damn.

You ever heard of the Blue Demons?

You mean that basketball team?

Yeah.

I seen them play a few times.

My Uncle John ref for them.

The same Uncle John who was sposed to drive the truck tonight?

Hatch nodded.

Deathrow thought about it. You know, I think I know yo uncle. A short guy, right?

Hatch nodded.

Look something like you?

Yeah.

Damn. Small world.

Sis, *he* from Red Hook.

*He* from Red Hook.

I know.

Sis, you know you don't owe me nothing for helpin you move.

That's right, baby. Deathrow kissed her.

Buy us some brew, Abu said.

Nigga, you know you can't hold yo liquor.

Yo, money. What you drink?

Be pissin all night.

Watch yo mouth in my house.

I don't drink no beer, Deathrow said.

What?

Man, how can yall drink that shit? Taste like piss.

Stop talkin low-life.

That's because beer and piss got the same ingredient.

What?

Pee.

So it went. Hatch, Abu, and Deathrow: their forms and talk awakened memories. Shades of blue pasts. Hatch, Abu, and Jesus as rusty-butt boys, the three sitting before her monkeylike while she greased their naps.

She gave them money for liquor.

Deathrow kissed her before he stepped out the door with the other two.

Be back soon.

You better.

Awaiting their return, she kept her hands busy, arranging, rearranging, unpacking boxes, dusting, sweeping, mopping, cleaning.

She felt very small and tight inside. Her mind wandered. Imagined the worst. She sat and tried to settle. Time flowed.

Hours later, the three of them came back, drunk and stinking, speech thick. A night with devil in the wind, beating, pounding evil against the windows, and a handful of stars.

What took yall so long?

We were talkin.

What?

Jus talkin.

Yeah. They were tellin me all about Jesus.

Jesus?

Yeah.

And Uncle John.

A measure of silence—Porsha expected Deathrow to lean in for a kiss; he didn't—then torrential tears. Hatch first. Abu followed. So too Deathrow. Tears distorted their faces. Sobs came wet and deep. The three babbled words from some unknown dictionary. Then their heads fell back like heavy stones, their bodies sinking into the floor, in the hollow created by a ring of boxes.


DEATHROW HAD YET to turn the final corner of maturity. Porsha moved in the world with complete faith that he would in the fullness of time. She devised ways to speed up his growth. Last Christmas, she had bought him a black trunk full of new clothes, a Bible at the bottom, leatherbound and smelling like new shoes.

That's your passport to heaven, she said. She braced herself for some sarcastic reply.

He ran his hand over the worked leather. Thanks, he said.

Perhaps her very look had drawn out of him the answer she wanted. She went further. It is the traveler's map, the pilgrim's staff, the pilot's compass, and the soldier's sword.

I don't know bout all that. He grinned. But it sho is some nice leather. I never knew you were *this* religious.

I am, but I ain't no fanatic. What about you?

I believe.

Since then, she had chanced on him reading the Bible once or twice. And he had promised to attend the Great Awakening with her on Sunday to fellowship with the New Cotton Rivers, the fourteen-year-old evangelist who steered the souls of his congregation, the New Riverside Multimedia Church. The Great Awakening would be the evangelist's first live appearance in four years. The Full Gospel Assembly, seven hundred and seventy-seven golden-throated singers, would accompany him.

Okay. I'll let some fat fried chicken-eatin preacher take my money.

Every preacher ain't like that. This one's good. Builds houses for the homeless.

Need money to build houses. Most church folk ain't got nothin but chitlins in they purses.

Well, he got money.

What's his name?

The New Cotton Rivers.

That nigga on TV?

Yes.

Who be wearin them gym shoes and that joggin suit?

How else can you keep up with the Lord?

Right. He way younger than me.

Age got nothing to do with knowing Christ.

And he—

Will you go?

I don't know.

It would mean a lot to me. She put her cool hand to his hot chest.

Okay. If you insist. Maybe he'll do some—

She didn't waste a minute. She called and reserved two tickets for the Sunday appearance.

Nothing like a good show, he said. I wanna see that preacher turn silver to gold and cotton to silk.

His promise, his tentative steps toward Christ, were good signs. No man had ever gone that far for her. But she wanted him to go further, touching distance, and accept God in his life, accept the voice resounding in her skull. *These are candied kisses from God. God is the author of healing. I pray for sweet mending.* I'll put no man before my God.

One day he might even be elected to the Tubes of Testimony, Rivers's missionaries, and help spread the gospel, roll the biblical light off of his hands and set the day ablaze. *May the sun fly high. Spread wide the peacock-tailed fan of truth and light.* This possibility eased her heart.

The train eased into Union Station. She rose from her seat, renewed. The doors parted. Passengers waiting on the platform divided, a clear open path between two rows of rushing bodies. She calmly waded through. She told herself, This will be a good day.

# 13

HER STEPS SEEMED SLOWER THAN USUAL. She rationed her breath as she climbed the long avenue of stairs up from the basement to the kitchen, laundry basket draped across her outstretched arms, a fireman carrying a child from a blazing building. She rested the heavy laundry basket against the wood railing. Waited for her second wind. It never came.

She continued up the stairs. The floor beneath her fell away. She dropped the laundry basket to the linoleum with a noisy splash. Snatched her a chair from the table and put herself in it. Shut her eyes and took a deep-chested breath. Her breathing was noisy. Wind and wheeze. She tried to quiet it. Crisp pain coursed through her body. She opened her eyes. The room was twisted, its objects warped, moving into one another, planes and lines falling away into white space.

*Mamma, why don't you retire?*

*Don't start.*

*Why don't you?*

*Hush.*

The pieces floated into place. Her heavy eyes anchored them.

Mrs. Shipco?

No reply.

Most mornings Sheila and Mrs. Shipco would share a cup of coffee here at the kitchen table. Mrs. Shipco would trace endless circles in the brown liquid with a spoon before she took her first sip. Return the cup to the saucer, then lift her head and the cup with it. *She always wore her blond hair straight back behind her ears, draping her cheeks and nape. She had never changed the style or length in all these years.* She would finish the cup in one gulp, rhythm in her throat. She would begin talking, tense, wrinkles moving like currents over her brow. Close her eyes to help her words along. That done, she could talk with ease. Sheila would swim in the current of words in the morning kitchen. Let it carry her. Add words of her own. She wished to talk today. Needed to talk, tear truth from the tracks. Mrs. Shipco?

*Hi, Sheila.*
*Hi.*
*You didn't have any trouble with the train today?*
*No.*
*That's good.*
*Well, I sorta did.*
*What happened?*
*Oh, nothing worth telling.*
*I'm all ears.*

Mrs. Shipco rarely left the house. The past few years, arthritis twisted her like a vine around her bed. Uprooted her daily routine: swimming, yoga, crafts, and classes at the university—noncredit courses; she already had a Ph.D. in sociology—the same university where she had met Dr. Shipco some forty years ago when they were both students. He came from poverty. (Sheila remembers the day Dr. Shipco and his sister—older, also a doctor—sat in the living room, barefoot, shared a bottle of dark wine and celebrated their first million.) She paid her tuition from insurance money obtained after her parents' death. *A boating accident.* He was a Jew. She wasn't. He was ten or twelve years older—Sheila always forgot which—but a handsome man, when he removed his glasses, brown eyes heavy with learning, and a neat mustache.

Dr. Shipco?
No reply.

Dr. Shipco had been forced to close his practice after his heart attack. He had never heeded Mrs. Shipco's and Sheila's warnings to slow down. Rushed out the house every morning carrying a briefcase weighted with patient files and the latest professional journals.

*Aren't you going to have some breakfast, Dr. Shipco?*

*No, thank you, Sheila. I have to squeeze in a new patient.* And when he wasn't seeing patients at his office or at the hospital, he would see them here, upstairs, in his study. *You could never see yourself going to a psychiatrist. Only a fool discusses his business.*

The day it happened, Sheila was stuffing clothes into the laundry chute when she heard him call her from his study. Sheila?

The moment she stuffed the last shirt into the chute, he called her a second time. Sheila?

Sheila hurried down the carpeted hall. Yes, Dr. Shipco.

Please open the door.

Sheila pushed the door open. Dr. Shipco was leaning far back in his leather chair, as if his upper body was trying to flee from hot steam rising up from the desk in front of him. The phone receiver was stiff in his raised left hand. A ballpoint pen remained where he had dropped it on the pad beside his right hand.

Sheila, Dr. Shipco said. My heart feels like a baseball in a catcher's mitt.

Mrs. Shipco! Sheila tried not to scream. Heard Mrs. Shipco approach from the master bedroom down the hall, the balls in her arthritic knees squeaking like rusty faucets.

Don't upset her, Dr. Shipco said.

Philip! Mrs. Shipco placed her hand flat in Dr. Shipco's chest.

Sheila pried the phone out of his hand, one finger at a time. Dialed 911.

Martha, I'll be okay. If we all talk quietly.

Dr. Shipco remained conscious and quiet and gave Mrs. Shipco and Sheila specific instructions for his comfort and care until the paramedics arrived.

Now, three mornings a week, Mrs. Shipco drove him to the gym for mandatory exercise. And the hours they once spent at the university or the practice, they now spent reading together in bed.

Dr. Shipco? Mrs. Shipco?

Still no answer.

I'll check the Shipcos' bedroom. In a few minutes. After I rest. Can't deal with any more stairs just now.

*How horrible. You saw that and you still came to work today?*

*I didn't want to miss a day.*

*Sheila, you should go right home.*

*No need to miss a day.*

A cuff of water froze her ankle. *Lord, I peed on myself.* Sheila looked down. Nelly's wet nose was sniffing at her feet. Nelly, get on away from here. Sheila gave the black fox terrier a light kick to push it away. Nelly inched back to her feet. Nelly was one black ball of short wild hair, like somebody's napply ole head. Nelly sniffed, wet. Then she started to howl. Shit! Mrs. Shipco ain't home. Sheila hated when Mrs. Shipco left the house, because Nelly would howl and howl and howl until she returned. Wishful, Sheila checked Nelly's bowl. It needed no food. Habitually, Sheila would have to slide the bowl directly under the dog's nose. Nelly could no longer actually see the food. Sheila had been after Mrs. Shipco to have the dog put to sleep. But Nelly was one of the family. Just like Laddie, that old collie, had been. Shipcos musta owned Laddie fifteen years.

*Fifteen of our years for one of his years, Sheila said.*

*No, Sheila, Mrs. Shipco said. He's twelve.*

*That makes him—Sheila calculated—one hundred and five.*

*Not fifteen. Seven years.*

*So he's—Sheila calculated—eighty-four.*

*He's making it.*

Mrs. Shipco had waited until Laddie could no longer walk before she loaded him onto the front seat of the family station wagon and caressed his fur and snout all the way to the veterinarian's office. Brought Nelly home the same day.

Nelly howled. Sheila's nerves had tolerated enough. Sheila picked up the dog and tucked it under her arm like a football. Carried it outside and lowered it into the fenced-in pen—oak rails and post—that ran parallel to the two-car garage. Nelly howled once or twice, blinked her unseeing eyes, then curled up on the gravel.

*Now I can get some peace.* Sheila went back inside.

She retrieved the laundry basket. Dumped the clothes onto the kitchen table. Readied her iron and board. Her hands burrowed into the pile of clothes. Starchy heat massaged her fingers and palms, a warm after-dinner cloth. Her warm hands worked. Backwash flooded her throat, a flake of something dry and nasty. She had a city inside her. An entire kingdom. She had been an hour late today. Eyes had held her back. Eyes that see everything they care to see. Her vision helpless as the image formed itself, upside down, backward, salmon-driving up into the streams of her tears. *But your witnessing morning is now a part of somebody else's memory. You don't want it. Give it away. You were conscious of shoes, so many different clicking colors, walking by you while you stood and waited, wading in ocean, so much surrounding you. Voices drawing from you, moment to moment. You were conscious of boarding the train, the train moving, jerking to a stop, then moving again. Besides, everything that happens makes sense. So Father Tower used to say.* And what happened this witnessing morning— Well, it ain't anything to miss work over. She has worked for the Shipcos for over thirty years and can count the numbers of days she has missed on all twenty of her fingers and toes.

The first time, she took the day off to mourn President Kennedy's death. The second time, five years later when the other Kennedy boy was assassinated. That same year, she left work early when Dr. King was assassinated. *Maybe King died before the Kennedy boy. So long ago. Memory fools. Kennedy and King. Unformed shapes and sounds in grainy black and white surround the words. Sounds and images faint and indistinct. Did I imagine them? More touch than sight or sound. What holds one funeral from the other? Makes one name, one man, one brother distinct from the other?*

I can't tell you how many times I seen that hotel.

Flitting and fitful points of light flickered on the television screen.

That's right. Mrs. Shipco gulped down the rising in her throat. You used to live in Memphis.

Used to pass by there almost every day.

After everything else that's happened, now this.

Sheila understood. Mrs. Shipco would get a certain look when she knew Dr. King was to appear on TV. A faint smile of anticipation would soften her face.

Sheila went home and soaked her feet in Epsom salts. Watched black and gray images burn down the city. She might have joined them but her feet hurt too bad.

She took off for Sam's funeral, Big Judy's funeral, and Koot's funeral. She would take a few days off for Lula Mae's funeral.

These past few months, she had missed more days than in all the previous years, flying down to West Memphis—*outside the window, the shadow of the moving plane toy-small against the white clouds*—twice a month to tend to Lula Mae on her white deathbed. Lula Mae's toenails curved out from under the white sheets, long yellow bird claws. Sheila would remove the sheets. Look right through Lula Mae's white skin, water. The bones delicate underneath, sprung with tension, the splinters of a collapsed bridge. And further down, the lumps of cancer like river stones. Sheets missing, Lula Mae would awaken. Take one look at Sheila and color would climb high in her bosom, neck, and face.

Sheila would pull back the curtains and raise Lula Mae's face to the light. Lula Mae would chew the pain and talk until she could talk no longer. Sheila would replace the white sheets. Search for the long scar across Lula Mae's stomach, the scar she and Gracie—when they were girls—would finger as Lula Mae deep-breathed sleep. The scar had disappeared. Dissolved in memory. The clear white belly mirrored Sheila's face.


WHEN SHEILA WAS PREGNANT, she hauled the freight of her belly to work. Unimpeded by the weight, she worked while her stomach domed under her blouse. Washing, kneeling, scrubbing. Got rounder each day, so round she thought she would bounce away. Her energy did not subside during labor. Rapid breathing reflected her rushing mind. So much to do with and for a new baby. Sweat spread a blanket of wet weight over her. Her mind and chest slowed. She breathed heavy in the darkness, breath twisting up like smoke. She climbed the smoke up into a white room with a silver sun. Saw the forceps move in position. Pull. Pull. Something long emerged, a brown banana. The baby's head. Don't worry, ma'm. We can shape the head. It's soft like clay. *Kids can give you such a scare.* She took a day to rest, then gathered the baby up in the pink blanket and hurried out of the hospital. She had never had so much energy in all her life. She could leave Porsha, her firstborn, in the cradle for hardly a minute. The baby lay on its back, the legs and arms pumping outward like a turtle. She took it high and awkward in her arms. It opened its eyes, whimpering. She rocked it. She carried it everywhere in a back sling. Carried it to work, not because she could not find or afford a babysitter, but because the magic had not burned away.

Sheila would awaken—having dozed off in the middle of mopping, dusting, polishing the piano, vacuuming the floors, cleaning the windows, folding the laundry—and find the baby lying in one of the Shipcos' old cradles, Mrs. Shipco leaning on the cradle's high rail, and trying to tease out laughs with a rattle.

IVORY BEACH, SHEILA, and Gracie drew water from Daddy Larry's well—drawing water was women's work—washed laundry and carried the baskets to town, not on the crowns of their heads as the old folks liked to do, but sack-heavy in front of them. Gracie always fell behind the other two. You, Gracie, Ivory Beach said. I'm older than you and if I can carry mine, then— She meant to say, My basket is heavier cause it's stuffed full of herbs—*beneath the sun-clean sheets*—for the white folks in town. Come on here, she said. Ivory Beach didn't like Gracie. Especially when the sun made Gracie's birth-black skin three shades blacker, *like it did the red summer day Lula Mae went away, watermelon red cause it is the scent of watermelon that always reminds you of that day.* Blackbirds should be shot and eaten, she liked to say. Sheila could carry with ease. Labor was buried deep in her nerves and muscles. The three of them white-scrubbed the laundry and carried it to town over the hot sand road, the road that was like a river of heat so you walked in the grass.

Beulah got Sheila and Gracie a job, their first, in Fulton. Mr. Harrison would drive twenty miles to Houston to pick them up. Drive twenty miles to take them home. Many a Sunday, Beulah, Sheila, Gracie, and R.L. would sup with the Harrisons. Yall welcome here, Mr. Harrison said, from now to Moses. Beulah, Sheila, and Gracie divided up their work. When Sheila and Gracie rested, Beulah would nap in the same bed with the Harrison children. Why, Beulah, you the prettiest nigga I ever seen. The kids would stroke Beulah's long hair. White men in the town tipped their hats when they saw Beulah. How you today, Miss Beulah? Mr. Harrison owned Fulton.

Yall need anything, he said, yall ask. He was always good for an extra five dollars here or there. Mrs. Harrison gave Beulah, Sheila, and Gracie blouses, skirts, and dresses. Shirts, suits, and pants for R.L. Why, R.L., you got the prettiest eyes I ever seen on a nigga. The Harrison boys would take R.L. to the picture show and they would all sit in the white section, rowdy and loud. And when he got older, they took him drinking. Sometimes bring Sam and Dave along. Mr. Harrison found them good jobs at the sawmill.

Beulah moved to Memphis. Once she'd saved enough money, she sent for Sheila, Gracie, and R.L. Beulah met them at the same smoking train station where a few years before they had waved Lula Mae off to New Mexico. Beulah got Sheila and Gracie day work. Each morning, Beulah would send Lula Mae a letter by special mail: *Come back to your children.* Lula Mae came back. Beulah left for the city.

Two years later, Beulah sent for Sheila. Sheila would always remember the world outside the train window. A kaleidoscope of sounds and color, loose fragments of houses, trees held together with dirty clotheslines and patches of sun-drying laundry. Day rounding into night, then the city, a tapestry of steel and light. Here was where she would live and work, live and work.

The following Monday morning, Beulah took her to meet the Shipcos.

*Now remember about the daughter, Beulah said.*

*Lynn.*

*Yes, Lynn. Young but nasty. No home training. Take off her panties and let them drop anywhere. The kitchen table. The piano stool. In front of the fireplace. It don't matter. Nasty.* They gave her a chair and with all the usual hospitality offered her a refreshment.

As you know, Miss Dear works for us on Saturday. We wanted her to work the full week, but she is unable to. She is a wonderful woman. She said you were the next-best thing.

Sheila smiled. Beulah taught me everything I know.

Miss Dear probably explained that—

Oh, yes. Beulah told me.

And I will need help preparing Thanksgiving dinner.

Fine.

Are you available Christmas Eve?

Yes.

Philip's family flies into town.

*Napkins folded into crane shapes. Bread loaves like airplane hangars. Sneak a bottle or two of Mogen David into your purse. Your family will drink them—and Crown Royal—on Christmas.*

I see.

The Shipcos' faces told Sheila that they had satisfied their hunger, thirst, and curiosity. Sheila changed clothes and went to work.

SHE PLACED THE HOT IRON on top of the stove to cool. She set about folding the clothes into neat squares. She put the laundry basket into the utility closet. The clothes were clean and neat and permanent.

This was what life had offered and she had accepted. She would hold other jobs briefly, even attend a free, city-sponsored nursing program. But day work was permanent, beyond the whims of bosses and supervisors. Safe from politicians and fluctuations of the economy.

Yes, she had come to work today. What had happened this witnessing morning was nothing to miss work over. *City life. I seen worse.* A poor excuse to miss work. There's no water wasted at this well.

*You should retire, Porsha said. Ask her for a pension.*

*I don't have to ask her. She'll give me one without my asking.*

*Well, retire then.*

*And do what?*

*Porsha thought for a moment. Spend time with your husband.*

Often, she found comfort in the knowledge that Lucifer worked equally hard. They sweated the same sweat. That's one reason why it was hard knowing that Lucifer had gone to meet John this morning and missed work. Lucifer had put John before his job.

His actions could not change the simple fact, she would forgive Lucifer, as she had forgiven all else, safe in the knowledge that John would be gone with the train's whistle, but Lucifer would remain, waiting for her in a form she could touch and love.

# 14

PORSHA HUGGED HERSELF. Wards Tower—the tallest building in the city— was cold after the outside heat. The metal exterior hid the green insides. Seeding grass edged with blues and lavenders. Red and yellow rose sprouted into petaled life. Peach and pomegranate limbs reached out to touch her. Bark of pomegranate enfolded bark of peach. Scentless green. Real or artificial? These plants and trees had no plastic shine. She inspected them closely, searching for brown edges, signs of decay. Detected a brown spot, here and there. Real to the touch but perfect, too perfect. If it hadn't been for the walls, you might believe you were strolling through Circle Park. Walls spoke geometrical patterns, petroglyphic figures inlaid with shards of glass, broken tile, and what looked like shining bits of bone and teeth.

She entered the elevator. Selected her floor. The doors hissed closed. She rode the elevator alone. Heard nothing and felt nothing. Came reeling out the elevator under the influence of speed, fifty flights in half the seconds. Brightness blinded her for a moment. One wall of the hall was windows. Outside the windows, sky spread a red song. Sunlight fell in whispers. Booming prisms of sun and shadow below. Birds veered, the moving shadows of their outstretched wings black against the blue water of Tar Lake. The lake rolled like a painted sea. Water echoed in silent, solitary swells. Her raised eye caught a sailboat on water, red sail like a waving handkerchief. She continued down the sun-shafted hall.

The door she needed was the shiniest black, lacquered like a Chinese screen. Eyebrow-pencil rivers. Thin trees with cat-o'-nine branches. Wing-eyed men battling dog-sized dragons. An engraved brass plate: THE RAYMOND OWL STUDIO PHOTOGRAPHY. A tension rode her back. She always felt nervous on an assignment. To relax, she would slide her face behind an imaginary white veil. But why was she nervous now? She and Owl had worked together for years, well over a decade, and they met every week. He always had work for her, even when business was slow. And while the average photographer eyed her through his open fly, Owl was professional, strictly business. Her one complaint: he always misspelled her name on the checks he wrote—

*Porsche*, like the car. She had done some of her best work with him. Like the beach shot. Her body stretched across the horizon with the ocean behind it (Tar Lake, actually). Her body duplicated in numerous poses to cover an entire beach. The best. He had even taken the shots in her first portfolio, fifty soft-focus stills of her breasts, hips, legs, and rear end. She and Owl had a history. But that history didn't count for much at times like this. She always needed a moment to calm herself before she entered his studio.

The door opened to her shaking touch. The open door magnified the small insides. Lights, reflectors, screens, tripods, backdrops, and props positioned with ritual precision. Each detail bore Owl's touch. He rarely worked with an assistant. He even did his own hair and makeup.

Porsha?

She recognized Owl's voice. Yes. It's me.

Make yourself at home. I'll be with you in a moment.

She entered. She saw herself repeated over and over. *Everything is one, the New Cotton Rivers said, born of the perfection of a unique light, and multiple things are multiple only by virtue of the multiplication of light itself.* The office ran four rows of mirrored walls. She checked her figure. Mirror, mirror on the wall, who's the finest of them all? She thanked God for her infinite perfection.

Porsha.

In the deep shade, at the farthest end of the studio, a figure ran backwards and forwards. Was it beast or human? She could not tell. The figure rolled through the reflected shadows. Broke into light. Owl's bald head bulb-gleamed. His orange jumpsuit forced bright color into her eyes. He always wore an orange jumpsuit. Perhaps a carryover from the days when he had worked as the coroner's photographer.

He stubbed out his cigarette in the jar lid that he used for an ashtray. (He knew she couldn't stand the smoke.) He was a short man, the shortest she had ever seen. He might have made a successful paparazzo, slip his tiny camera through a guarded peephole, this man small enough to slide under a door, camera and all. He came forward with his hand extended, his eyes full of light and fire.

She took his warm hand into her own. He pulled her forward a step or two. Bowed slightly from the hips. She lined up her cheek with his lips. He kissed her.

How are you? Owl was so close that he almost put his eyes in her mouth.

No complaints. She eased back a step or two, trying not to be noticeable. Jus fine.

Sorry to keep you waiting. I had problems adjusting a lens.

Don't be silly. You weren't long.

Owl gave her a moment of concentrated attention. That's what I like about you. His knowing expression shook her. Not only are you professional, but you're kind, too.

Every word pulled the knot in her belly tighter. Thanks. How's everything with you?

You know, chicken today. Feathers tomorrow.

She forced a laugh.

Have some breakfast? He motioned to a small card table behind him laden with toasted bagels and rolls, steaming coffee and tea, and colorful juices.

No, thank you. I already ate.

Some spirits?

No, thanks. Kinda early for me.

Each to his own. He fixed himself a drink.

Damn.

What's wrong?

I forgot my briefcase. Deathrow had snared all her attention. Made her forget her leather briefcase that harbored the tools of her trade: dazzy dukes, biker shorts, a thong bikini, a miniskirt, a teddy, and assorted garter belts and stockings.

Don't worry about it. I need you to model a new line. You'll find the out-fits in the dressing room. Start with whatever you like.

THE BLACK TRANSPARENCY AND GLOW OF HER SKIN caught the candlelight. The candlelight threw black shadows that repeated the profile of her face, her throat, her arms.

Okay, give me something soft.

She curled into the most delicate gesture, a root searching for moisture, circling out.

Okay. Now walk toward me.

She undulated rather than walked.

Butter. Pure butter.

She drifted in a well-tight place. Broke the surface. Trawled the wet floor. Spun. The concentric dartings of fish through clear spaces of water.

Ah huh. Ah huh. Yes. Owl spoke slowly and carefully as though every word was costing him money. I like that.

She shimmied. Small white shells rattled on her ankles.

LIGHT STUNNED AWAY COLOR. Two white tunnels trapped her vision. To overcome their length, she had to look straight ahead. Her eyes rolled in dry sockets. She crawled through the tunnels on all fours beneath bone-blackening heat.

That's it.

Her spine curved around air. She stretched the elastic wealth of her body. Her hands and feet curled into wheels.

The eye watched. Large, like black velvet, with a flashing diamond in its center. The outside world disappeared whenever it blinked.

Good.

The shutter recognized. Ignored.

Okay, now, pick up the jacks.

She did. She rattled them in the well of her fist. Tossed them. A song spilled out of her.

*A dollar to school.*
*A dollar to church.*

What? Owl said.

Nothing. A song. Sweat raced down her body, a rivulet of snakes. She heard the steel eye snap, butter beans popping into a steel pan.

HER BODY ILLUMINATED in the steady, biting light of lamps, she released the full army of her skin.

The eye ran for cover.

Wonderful. I don't know how you do it.

Easy. She had slipped behind the mirror inside her head. She was looking at herself through his eyes. Her whole body spoke of pleasure.

Yes. That's it.

Sweat sheen gleamed on her. It moved when she moved. She knew what he liked. He didn't spray his models with water. Preferred natural sweat. It caught the light truthfully. *I see a shot, I can tell right away if it's water or sweat.*

More.

He spoke in a pecking way, picking up corn, feed.

She fluttered in fowl flight.

Yes.

Her body clarified. Bled light.

Pig meat. Real pig meat.

She threw her head back.

I like that. Keep it. More. Uh huh.

Her body caught the velocity of the camera's desire. She pranced out of herself, blowing about. The clicking lens and clucking tongue invited her outside.

Good, Lord!

She galloped fully now. Pranced back to the center. Settled down to a trot. That's it.

She bowed her head. Her body drifted toward rest. She watered at the well. She steadied herself, like someone recovering from a fainting spell.


SOME SPIRITS?

Thanks. She checked her figure in the mirror. Smoothed her blouse. Pulled her skirt here or there.

What would you like?

Zinfandel, if you have it.

I do, but I don't think it's chilled.

That's fine.

He found the bottle. Popped the cork. Waved it under his nose. His face spoke fire. He put the cork under her nose to smell.

Umm.

He filled a stemmed glass and she accepted it, water cool. He didn't pour himself one. Sat the bottle on the card table in easy reach.

She sipped. Umm. It's good.

Yes, I bet. The smell was delightful. Owl lit a cigarette—his hand shielding his eyes from the unbearable brilliance of the flame—and in its flare she saw that he was laughing silently. That was great. With rapid wrist motion, he waved the flame out. I always like working with you. He leaned forward and tossed the black match. It sounded against the metal jar lid. He sucked heavy. Lifting his chin, he blew the smoke high. Professional.

She waved the white words away from her face.

Oh, I'm sorry. How stupid of me. The smoke. He reached for the improvised ashtray.

Wait. Don't put it out.

Are you sure?

Positive.

Smoke formed a white gown above their heads.

I thank you for allowing me one. He sucked. I've been tryin to quit. But I can't seem to do without them.

They say that it's not easy.

His eyes followed her words. No, it isn't. It comes with the work. You know me. He dried his face and hair with a towel. Slave to the image. He folded the towel into a sharp square. Dropped it into a wicker basket. Sweat had formed two crescent moons under his arms.

Her body started to respond to the cool and quiet machine-generated air. Sweat froze on her skin. Her nails raked away frost.

But I like working with you. He sucked on his cigarette. You're easy to work with. Our sessions always go so quick. Most of the models, you have to tell them everything. He stubbed out his half-smoked cigarette in the jar lid, a flattened top hat. They own no poses or gestures. Or they copy something they saw in a magazine. But you—

Porsha sipped her wine. She didn't know what to say. Didn't want to say anything. Wished he would stop talking. Just stop talking. Allow her to enjoy her wine and the habitual calm that followed a shoot.

Then you have to shoot the same shot six, seven, eight times. Stupid. They can never get it right.

I try to do my job.

Waste a whole day. Time is money.

She finished her glass. Well, guess I'll be going. She aimed the stemmed glass at his chest.

He took it. Sat it next to the unfinished bottle. How about another glass?

No. One is fine.

He studied her face. It's been a pleasure.

Same here.

You got any other—

A video later in the week.

Good, good. He tried to light another cigarette. The match wavered from side to side in his unsteady hand. Any plans for tonight?

Not really. I mean—

Oh, don't explain. I just thought I'd ask. We've been working together how many years now? Six? Seven?

Ten.

Ten?

Uh huh.

Ten?

Yes.

That long?

She nodded.

Are you sure?

Yes.

Time flies.

So they say.

And I hardly even know you.

I got a man. Her words pushed his face back. She hadn't said it. Some forceful other had taken control of her mouth.

Pardon?

She snorted. Let me put it this way. My granddaddy, well, my great-granddaddy—he used to say, Never chase two rabbits at the same time.

Rabbits? His small forehead was lined up with her lips. She considered putting a hot glob of spit there. You don't understand. I—

Wait. Jus wait. She shoved her palms at him. I already told you, I gotta man.

Hey, you got me wrong. His chin was so thrust forward that the muscles in his neck stood out. I was just tryin to—

Whatever.

He dropped his head. She studied him. His head, cow-bent in shame—I'm sorry—chewing the cud of his words. He eased his head up. Their eyes held for a moment.

Look, I'm sorry.

No, I understand.

I'm really sorry. One of those days. I have some things on my mind. *Deathrow.* I didn't mean to snap at you.

Hey—he stubbed out his cigarette in the jar lid—it's okay. He stepped into touching distance. We all have bad days.

For a moment she did not answer. She crossed to a window overlooking the curved lake and the city's charted skyline. I'm sorry. She watched the bronze world outside the window.

Hey, it's okay. Tell you what, let me give you a few. On the house. Your boyfriend would like them.

Thanks. You've done enough.

Please, allow me.

No, really.

Are you sure?

Yes.

Well, enjoy your day.

Thanks. I will. She faced him.

If you don't mind my asking, what's your boyfriend's name?

Clarence.

Clarence. Well, tell Clarence I said hello.


SHE ROLLED LIKE COAL from the oven of the building into fierce afternoon light. Unclean light. The sun immobile in the sky. Yellow-red-white fault-finding color. Nothing to fear. Unlike some models', her deep black skin suffered no aging in the light. The sidewalk gripped her feet with concrete hands. Her legs said stop, sit down, lie down, go to bed—right here in the crowded street. She heard a gurgling in the depths under the sidewalk. Long ago, she had studied a map of the city's lower parts, the sewage system with its drainage lines and tunnels. The hollow skeleton beneath the city's concrete-and-steel skin. She could smell heat rise from her body, buttered with sweat.

Yuck. I need a bath.

Two tall stacks pumped metal steam in thick clouds that thinned and streamed a white message high above the rooftops: BATH. Ah yes, of course. Why hadn't she thought of it? The New Cotton Rivers's bathhouse. She dragged her stinking body there.

Once inside, she presented her membership card and found a cubicle. She quickly undressed. Eased the fresh shroud over her head and pulled it over her work-slick body. Her shroud ran silk against her exploring fingers. It was soft and loose. Brushed against the tops of her bare black feet. She tiptoed across the marble floor to the chapel.

The New Cotton Rivers believed that the body must be heard. You must rub Christ right into your bones so the flesh can sing praise. The Prophet 1 Faith Stimulator—patent pending—was the machine he had invented for this purpose.

The white-gloved attendant taped a black cross over each eyelid. The crosses felt like fingers, touching her, caressing, probing. Each cross transmitted three thousand biblical pulses a second. The attendant attached a crystal crown and made sure that it fit snugly around her forehead. Holding the sleeve of her robe, he guided her across the white tile to the freshly drawn bath. The water appeared still, motionless, but her feet entered and spoke of bubbling warmth.

She lowered herself slowly into the perfumed waters—frankincense and myrrh—careful not to disturb the crystals at the bottom. *Crystal serves to stabilize and balance our energetic system. It has positive and negative poles. It orients us more than guides us, concentrates the attention and drives our spirit to God.*

Wine?

Yes, please.

Red or white?

Zinfandel. If you have it.

I'm sure we do. One moment please.

She drew up her legs, a bird with folded wings. The attendant returned shortly with her glass.

Thank you.

Enjoy.

Once the attendant left, she disrobed.

Toes arched on the white porcelain knobs, she studied her steepled knees. Her skin tingled in the touching water. She felt the sweet solid flesh of her own bones. Wet pressure enveloped her whole body, squeezing the breath from her lungs. A pain shot through her, and another and another, then a distant echo of the first, contracting and expanding in slowly accelerating rhythm. Mercury, her blood rose and sunk, rose and sunk. Warmth spread below her waist and relaxed the knot in her belly. A familiar feeling. When she got her period, she would sit in a tub of hot water all day to cool her joints.

Clean reflections played over her dark thighs.

> *Little Sally Walker*
> *Sitting in her saucer*
> *Weeping and crying for someone to love her*
> *Rise, Sally, rise*
> *Wipe ya weepin eyes*
> *Put ya hands on ya hips*
> *And let ya backbone slip*
> *Shake it to the east*
> *Ah, shake it to the west*
> *Shake it fo the one you love the best*

She saw blood beneath the water and thought the soap had cut her. She tried to use her washcloth as a sponge. Squeezed it in between her legs. Red roots extended beneath the water.

Lula Mae!

The roots lengthened.

Lula Mae!

Girl, hush all that screamin. Lula Mae shut the door behind her. What's wrong wit you. She approached the tub. The blood reflected on her white face. That's when Porsha knew, the blood belonged to her as wind belonged to sail.

We better get ready to go up to the Rexall, Lula Mae said. She untied her headscarf and thrust it at Porsha. Here, this a clean rag. I jus put it on. Dam your blood.

———

WHITE LIGHT FELL gray as new rust on the sidewalk. The crowd swept her along, a cork in the current. A wind blew now but she could not tell from which direction. Something long and wet pushed up her arm and licked her elbow. Scat! The dog trotted off, trailing the red leash of his tongue. The dome of Union Station rose up ahead, surrounded by its shops and stores, a tidy sweep of stone. Her shadow ran two straight lines along the marble walls of the station, veined green and black.

The earth is the Lord's and the fullness thereof, the world and all that dwell therein.

What you say? The cashier spoke from the glass wicket. Light flooded it. The cashier moved as if swimming.

*Told you*
*I got a right*
*I got a right*
*To the Tree of life*

What? The cashier took her money. Do you want a transfer?

Cherubs nested in the neural tangle inside her skull, the dense network of cordlike fiber—handpicked by God himself—that obtained, stored, and transmitted information from the front backwards. She watched their wings, veined and transparent, insectlike. Scriptured wings. Walk with Jehovah, shoulder to shoulder. The Prophet 1 Faith Stimulator patent pending had done its work.

What?

She charged through the turnstile, boarded the train, found a seat, and turned her face to the window. The train pulled into motion. The windows shook, drummed deep inside her. Don't bother me none. Her body was stone.

A legless man came rolling down the aisle on a wooden board. He rattled his change-filled can. Give if you can. Rattle and roll. Give if you can. Rattle and roll. She took a quarter from her purse, leaned forward into the aisle, and, like a game contestant, tossed the quarter at the moving can. She missed. He picked it up with stained fingers. Flipped it into his can. Looked at her with red eyes. Said through his masklike beard, That's the way yo do it. He rattled and rolled to the next car.

The nerve. She settled back into her seat.

She saw a brilliant sun through the window. A few sailing (fishing?) vessels speckled the lake. Flocks of phosphorescent birds. Wards Tower loomed over the Loop—a towering mass of soaring walls reflected in the terminal black glow of its windows—against a radiant sky, a mile-high, gray and black tombstone. The city was a flat prairie that spread outward from the lake. No mountains or other natural formations to relieve the endless vistas of water, land, and sky. But cliffs and peaks constructed out of steel, glass, and stone. She saw a plume of smoke rise from the harbor, fan out and lift, black fingers reaching for the sun.

SUNLIGHT TEARS THE RAFT APART *beam for beam tides and tongues stream metal and a breeze to witness the hour you mud-colored creature water wiping out the salt of your wounds rocking cliffs pearl-colored clouds. The circle closes, the net is being hauled in. You ride the monster's back, sheeted with flame, a live rocket. Avoid its sprout, red tentacles, flaming vines. Dawn ruins it. Wakes of yellow flame. Seaweed. A thousand years deep.*

She pinched her leg to force herself to stay awake. *Coffee? No way. Bad for your breadwinning body.* Glad she hadn't driven. Once, stalled in choked traffic, she had drifted asleep at the wheel to be awakened by a concert of furious honking.

A hot wish rose in her body. Deathrow. With his body she could exhaust all the day's games and pretense. Deathrow.

# 15

THE NIGHT HELD STILL outside the rolling train window. The glass framed a clean black box. Hatch reached for Elsa's hair. Smooth and black, pulled tight in a ponytail, or combed forward—this he hated—a curved wing on each cheek. He reached for her waiting scent. *Dream it to yourself.* Elsa entered the night spaces of his brain.

The cleanly dressed congregation greeted one another in the bustling calm following Sunday service. He knelt on the podium, prayer-fashion, and placed his guitar into its padded case, soft, shapely, a protective womb. Case/guitar he gripped close, then hoisted it up and slung it over his shoulder like a rifle.

That was glorious. Reverend Ransom rolled forward, polished shoes—twin reflections of Hatch on the toes—inches above the red-carpeted podium floor. He took Hatch aside—Abu was still packing up his drum set—and discreetly produced the weekly cash.

Thank you. Hatch took the cash and quickly divided it into two equal portions.

That was simply glorious.

I'm glad you enjoyed it.

Reverend Ransom continued to hover above the floor, quiet, smiling into Hatch's face. I have something else for you. He produced a business card. Floated it over to Hatch. CARIBE FUNERAL HOME. A CENTURY OF EXPERIENCED CARE FOR YOUR ETERNAL NEEDS. Explained: Close friend and colleague, the Reverend Drinkwater K. Bishop, was in desperate need of a musician for his funeral services. Go see him tomorrow. The Lord does provide. Hatch quickly slipped the card into his pocket.

The following afternoon, Hatch met the preacher-mortician in the floral chambers of his office. The undertaker explained, fingering his paintbrush mustache, that he had tired of the typical organ sound. Every funeral parlor had one. *Even the angels are bored.* He wanted an instrument that sounded equally celestial. My chariots need some new shoulders at the wheel, he said.

Hatch couldn't stand funerals. *Down-home spooks in their Sunday best. The chemical stench of preserved death. Dearly departed cramped in the casket. (Strange to see how death gets hold of the flesh.) White-skinned Dave eternally at rest in the black casket. Uncle John puts a brick of E&J—Old Rocking Chair, Sheila said, that was Sam and Dave's drink—in his stiff pocket. Bad enough he'd drink you out of house and home, Sheila said. Bad enough he wouldn't lift a finger to help raise those kids. He was the biggest liar. Oh, he could lie. Told Lula Mae that I smoke reefer. Big mouth—her tongue flopping up and down like a vessel on stormy sea—Beulah commenced to whooping and hollering. Sam, if I hada just been there to hold up your head. The preacher—Rise in the flesh up to heaven—resurrected the dead with the saliva of his voice. Once at the cemetery, the pallbearers (in ant formation) carry the morsel of casket to the rim of the grave. Dust dust and ashes, fly over my grave.* And he had never played one, but he took the assignment.

IT WAS A CAB like all the others, small and functional, bug-shaped. *Aerodynamic.* Uncle John, yo cab ride smooth as a Cadillac.

Don't it. Spokesman worked on it.

Hatch, Uncle John said. Bet you don't know this one.

> *When Adam and Eve was in the Garden of Eden*
> *They didn't know til the good Lord walked out*
> *Say, when Adam and Eve was in the Garden of Eden*
> *They didn't know til the good Lord walked out*
> *Eve turned around and soon she found out*

Uncle John, that's corny.

Where Abu?

That nigga sleep. He was sposed to come and help me with my gear.

You ain't get him in on the gig?

The—

That's yo running buddy.

The undertaker didn't ask fo no drummer.

Uncle John shook his head.

Well—

Uncle John kept shaking his head.

Maybe next time.

How he payin? The undertaker I mean.

Good.

Good?

Yeah. Real good.

Good for you. Get that money.

CARIBE FUNERAL HOME swam into focus. The letters formed large bright yellow boxes like at a supermarket.

Thanks, Uncle John.

Break a leg.


THE FUNERAL HOME was an apple, red outside—cherry-wood panels—and white—oak walls and pews—inside. The assembled marched like a long line of black ants up to the raised coffin. Small clouds of handkerchiefs at their faces. Wept before the body stuffed in eggshell velvet in a gleaming bronze casket. Looped back to their seats.

Preacher Bishop started them out slow. *Brothers and sisters, how often I have gathered thy children together, even as a hen gathereth her chicken under her wings. But such is the life of man.*

*Yes.*

Hatch whipped organlike waves from his guitar.

*Because Adam fell from grace, each of us must fall into the hands of sin, let Death lower us into the grave.*

*That's right.*

Reverend Bishop caught fire in the assembled's faces.

*But the grave is not our home. I say, the grave is not our home.*

*Lord said it ain't.*

*As newborn babes desire the sincere milk of the Word that they may grow thereby, you gather at the table of my sermon.*

*Take yo time.*

*Let us sit at the Lord's table. His breasts are full of milk and his bones are moistened with marrow.*

*Preach.*

*Brothers and sisters, one of ours has fallen but we must keep the bread of life fresh.*

*Fresh he said.*

The breath of prayers and sermons floated in the air. *He has made his bed in darkness, but as long as I am in the world, I am the world's light.* Hatch's breath grew fat. He concentrated on producing his thick music. *Yes, I'm pressing on the upward way. New heights I'm gaining every day. Our Father, lover of my soul, let me to thy bosom fly. Gabriel will wrap you up in his wings and fly you out of the storm.* He felt the wings of an angel hard-flapping overhead. *Shall we gather at the river where bright angel feet trod?* The assembled roared in front of him. Laughter touched him from behind. He turned his head to investigate. There he saw a woman among the odor of roses, standing in the doorway of the hall leading to the undertaker's office and holding a red-and-black sailor's cap on with both hands so that the winds of Hatch's music would not blow it off. Dark hair spilled in deep folds. And smiling. The coiled spring of Hatch's guts twisted and raised him from his seat. He was lifted up in a sea of music, pouring out of him, churning and eddying about him in warm spirals, burying him in a glittering shower.

Later that night, Hatch loaded his instrument and effects into Uncle John's trunk.

Uncle John, take these home for me.

What? Do I look like an errand boy?

I know I drive a cab but—

A fille. I met this fille. Elsa.

Uncle John smiled. Show her who's king. He kicked the cab into yellow motion. The sound of its backfiring faded at the end of the street.


HATCH AND ELSA cleared the last ashes of music from the chapel.

I like the way you play. Elsa brushed her hair back from her forehead. Her eyes were bright.

Thanks.

You play with a band? Her eyes burned two nails in his heart.

I got my own band. He had to unpin the words.

Your own band?

Yeah. Third Rail.

Nice name. I sing a little.

Oh, yeah. Well, we need a backup singer.

I don't sing that well.

Don't hang your harp upon the willows.

Elsa smiled. So you're a poet too.

Could be. Could be.


FREEPORT? MY SISTER WENT THERE. Well, just for one year.

I should talk to her.

Elsa had moved their conversation to the seclusion of her father's office. Are you lookin forward to going to college?

Yes, I am. I plan to study accounting, then I'll do my year of mortuary school.

Massive furniture, shadow presences in the room.

It runs in the family?

I guess so. My dad wants me to do a year or two at the seminary.

The seminary?

Yes.

Bet you already know how to preach. Yo father sure can.

I really want to be a model.

A model?

Yes.

Why you want to be model?

What do you mean?

You're a talented individual. Why waste your talent?

She thought it over, fingers at her ruminating chin. Are artists born or made?

Made.

So, how's that different from modeling? Natural talent.

He thought about it. My sister's a model.

Now I know I have to meet her. Are you going to introduce us?

Well, she's not that kind of model.

What kind of model is she?


NOBODY IN OUR FAMILY HAS A GRAVESTONE. Nobody.

Why not?

No money.

Money? They aren't that expensive.

No?

No.

We don't even have a car. My sister does. And my Uncle John. Hatch thought it over. People in my family barely get a decent funeral.

You have to watch what funeral home you choose. Have you ever heard of Sleepytime Incorporated?

I've seen them all over the city.

They are nationwide. They have a warehouse where they stack all the bodies. They've lost a body or two here and there.

What?

Yeah. A coupla times they tried to convince a family to have a closed-casket funeral because they had lost the bodies. Empty casket.

Damn.

And they also do mass incinerating.

What's that?

When they put more than one body in an oven at a time. Like they might cremate a baby with an adult. Or two kids together. The ashes get mixed up. The family thinks they have Bill's ashes, but Bill's are mixed with Sue's, Larry's, and Baby Tom's.

Damn.

It happens all the time.

I know one thing. They don't do no good funerals down South.

Next time somebody in your family dies, let us handle it.


WHAT'S YOUR SIGN?

Cancer, Hatch said.

Pisces.

*Two fish.* My sister a Pisces.

Oh. Then she must be a good woman. Elsa smiled.

Hatch returned it. An easy silence in the room. He looked at his watch. Wow! You know how long we've been talking?

I can imagine.

Let's do something.

You like Chinese food?

My favorite.

I know a restaurant.

At the restaurant, Elsa showed him how to eat shrimp fried rice with chopsticks. There was something magical about it, working the sticks like puppet handles and seeing the rice rise on invisible strings to your mouth.

Let's have coffee, Elsa said.

Coffee? That's for old folks.

So we can talk.

Okay.

I know a place where they have quality coffee.


MY GRANDFATHER, MY MOTHER'S FATHER, was a cigar maker in Puerto Rico. He died long before I was born. But my father's father died a few years ago. He had a funeral home down South and he had pictures of the old days and was always telling stories. He had two horses that pulled the funeral procession. The horses would cry if someone was going to hell. And they would stop twice if someone was going to heaven.

Hatch and Elsa blew laughter back and forth between them.

Who gave you those? Elsa's fingers reached out and seized his dogtags. Blind to him, they had slipped out of the V of his open collar.

Lucifer.

Steam rose like a white bird. Her fingers made two hot wafers of the metal.

Lucifer? She studied the dogtags closely. The hot metal sizzled and sang.

My dad.

Was he in the army?

Yeah. He and my Uncle John.

She studied the tags. Red shadows played over her light brown face, two small red coffins.

This is good coffee, he said. They were drinking thick brown coffee in thimble-sized cups.

Thanks, she said. She released the tags. They went instantly cold.

He sipped. She sipped. He tried to keep his reckless eyeballs in check, keep them from surveying the saxophone curve of her neck, the float of her breasts.

Who learned you this coffee? he said.

My mother.

She the Puerto Rican half of the family?

She laughed, molasses-thick laughter that sweetened the air.

Am I that funny?

No, honey. She took his hand into her own. The sheen of his skin seemed to add a shimmer to her own. She gave his hand a light squeeze, then returned her own hand to her lap. Give me your cup.

My cup?

Yes.

He handed her the thimble. She upended the cup, dumped the sediment into her saucer. She peered into the hollow. Let me read your future.

My future. You believe in that stuff?

She parted her lips, a light smile. She looked into the cup. He leaned forward to see what she saw. Patterns. There were actually patterns inside the cup.

Well, what you see?

Your future.

Well?

A bird.

LET'S GO TO THE PARK.

The park? he said. It's winter.

So.

Collar turned up, he agreed. The coffee had formed a warm sanctuary inside him. He felt free from the fears that had choked him in the funeral parlor. They left the coffee shop and took the train to Circle Park.

They strolled in the cold night. The sky sat awake above them. The air clean and stinging the nose. From a vast black vault, stained with city lights and stars—the floodlights of heaven—millions of snowflakes drifted down silently in a straight path. Brilliant moonlight transfigured her red-and-black sailor's cap, her black wool scarf and matching gloves, her body-hiding coat which reached down to her ankles, and her black leather boots that came above her knees. They strolled through darkness spangled with wet snowflakes. The night widened around them. Except on those lucky occasions when the moon shone just right, Elsa's face was lost in the shadows. Tracing a huge circle, Hatch and Elsa covered the entire park.

They found a quiet bench. He sat down facing her, so close their knees touched. They spoke in the perfumed darkness. He saw her in sharp detail in the moonlight. He hoped the darkness would protect his face, make him appear even the slightest bit handsome. He took both her hands in his. He kissed one hand, gently, a small trembling bird.

In the subway, they held hands while the panting monster of a train screamed down the tracks. He took her home through the flying underbelly of the city and on the El, the city's high skin above. She invited him inside. The Bishops had painted every room of their house yellow, pink, or purple.

You know us Puerto Ricans, Elsa said.

Damn.

It's even too much for Dad sometimes.

The colors mean something?

Nothing that I know of.

Wood furniture, banisters, walls, and floors. Hatch had never seen so much wood in a home. A forest in a house. Damn.

I had a wonderful time, she said.

Me too.

She kissed him with a foreshadowing of tongue.

He ran back to the El, with a thread of breath almost too thin to pull him up the stairs. Caught another train. He sang silently while it barreled down the tracks.

> *Lil piece of wheat bread*
> *Lil piece of pie*
> *Gon have that yaller gal*
> *Or else I'll die*

The words almost spilled into sound. Once home, he tried to settle back into his skin.

WINTER DEEPENED. HUGE wet flakes of snow streamed past windows. Gray slush in the streets. Then the hawk wind rose from the lake. Frozen birds rattled in the cold.

A crystal net of ice covered the city. Hatch rose early to meet Elsa in the privacy of her father's office. A patch of pink sky gave the illusion of warmth in the room. *Hatch.* A smile warmed her face. He was as welcome as violets in March.

ELSA MET HIM at the door in a black dress of ruffled organza and forearm-length black gloves. A cross gleamed gold on her bosom. She accepted his bouquet. *Aren't you sweet?* She buried her face in the flowers. *I got something for you.* She pinned a gardenia in his lapel. Pinned one to her dress.

Hatch led her by the arm toward Uncle John's borrowed cab. Elsa's trailing bows swept a clean path.

*Are we going in that cab?*

Yeah. My Uncle John loaned it to me.

*I could have used one of the limos. Never be afraid to ask.*

It wasn't that. I had the money. See, it's my Uncle John's cab. My Uncle John. See, well, it's sorta hard to explain.

*Please, Uncle John. Jus this one time. Special.*

*That's my livelihood. Why don't you ask Porsha?*

*Porsha? Man, she scared to drive her car. Know she ain't gon let me drive it.*

EVERYBODY BLEW GAGE and juiced back and jumped black. The dancers rocked the hall, a big sea-tossed ship. Elsa shook her butt like a rattle. She was as good a dancer as he was a clumsy one.

*Beulah. Why they call it the Lindy Hop?*

*Cause Lindbergh hopped the ocean in that plane of his.*

Hours later, white exhaust trails guided them from the dance to a cruise ship. The ship set out in full moonlight from a harbor of colors. Sang softly on the waters. Hatch pointed to the cathedral's cone towering above the docks. A flock of stars. He and Elsa leaned on the railing and studied the sedentary waters of Tar Lake. A big fish jumped on a string of moonlight, thrashing the very heart of the water. *You see that?* Lightning and thunder far out on the lake threatened rain. They tossed their gardenias onto the waters. Sailed into the early hours of the morning.

In the back seat of Uncle John's cab, Hatch and Elsa harbored the night. The rolled-down windows offered a cool breeze. Dark shone clear as day. May had drawn out every leaf on the trees. Hatch nibbled with soft kisses at Elsa's forehead, her eyes, her cheeks, her lips, and her neck. He felt the spires of her nipples poke through the soft dress. He tasted the moist loin of her mouth. Then he played the slow length of his tongue over her fast body. He put out his hand to fondle her charms. Elsa railed one word, Respect, then fit the pieces of her clothes together. His hands stopped but his mouth could continue. He could Spokesman her. *Baby, a circle is a circle, an angle an angle.* He could Uncle John her. *Bitch, why don't you jus relax. You know you want it.* He could run Jimi's voodoo down. *Well, I march right up to a mountain. Crumble it to dust in the palm of my hand.* It's our own little world here tonight, he said. So let's forget about yesterday or tomorrow. The time is now.

Your watch is fast, she said. She moved into her own seat. Sat on her own vine, under her own fig tree.

There was a hard silence in the cab.

*I wish*
*I was a catfish*
*Swimming in the deep blue sea*
*I'd have all you pretty women fishing after me*

Look, I'm not mad at you, she said. She put a light kiss on his lips. The hairs on his body rose treelike. Then the bird left the branch to return to the sky. Swift time flew on silent wings. Months later, Elsa was still sitting under her tree and his bird was still in the sky. She had yet to uncover the nest, reveal the unknown treasures of her inner life.


HE LEFT THE TRAIN, stepped out of a warm steel tub into naked air. He ran the five blocks to Elsa's house. (He was almost twenty-five minutes late. Inez was to blame for that.) House in sight, he slowed his feet. Pressed his hand into his chest to congeal his scattered breath. Searched for sweat under his arms (found none). He took the stairs one at a time. He rang the bell. Politely waited. He rang the bell. Politely. Waited. He pushed the doorbell again. Waited. Polite. Patient. His blood flushed and faded. He pushed the doorbell. Then he held it, held it, held it—couldn't let it go, finger and ringer electric one—so long that his finger began to hurt. The world fell silent, intent upon his response. He ran to the nearest phone. The phone handle mocked the rude round rhythm of Elsa's mouth. He dialed her number. Heard the answering machine click.

HE FUMBLED HIS KEYS before the door. The keys clanked loud as chains. He managed the keys in the lock. Pushed the door open. Night invaded the house. Wrapped it in longing sleep. *Elsa. Elsa. Elsa.* His fingers found the telephone in the dark. Dialed the number. The answering machine clicked.

Hi, Elsa. It's Hatch. I was jus there. We musta had a mix-up. Guess I'll try you again in the morning.

His eye leaked, dripping sight. The bed called, reverse gravity. Pulled him up the stairs. Pulled him beneath the covers. He sank down into the feathers of nested sleep.

# 16

LUCIFER DECIDED to return to Union Station for a final drink. He longed for the table near the window where he had sat earlier that day with John. The sun poured yellow surprise into his eyes. The bar was closed, the desired table sealed off from sight and sound behind a steel blind. Strange hours. He would have to find another bar. Bounded on the one side by Union Station and on the other by shops, the large square curved out of sight like a pebble skipped over water. Bus lines cut through the square from every direction. What he could not find here he could find in the narrow side streets that flowed into it.

It did not take him long to find a bar. He entered to a red carpet stained in places. The bar was filled with a fashionable crowd who blew opaque smoke and white laughter into mustard-colored walls. He found a table before two narrow windows overlooking the square. Hot-looking brilliant clouds swelled beyond the glass. He winked. A waitress watched him with eyes of shocking blue. She smiled with blood-smeared lips.

What can I get you?

He told her. She got it.

He could hear the clear ringing sound of wheels drawn close to the curb. He turned his glass around in his hand. Bubbles rose from its depths. He sunk back with collapsed shoulders. He had spent the entire afternoon searching for the right gift for Sheila. Far beneath feeling, it rested like a sunken treasure at the bottom of his pocket. Painly obtained, easily forgotten.

He emptied his glass at a gulp. Waitress, another.

He looked out into the fading sun and saw two reflections of the waitress going from table to table, drink to drink. Outside shade and inside light made mirrors of the windows. It was getting late. He reached for his glass. Brown, round, and empty: a bird's nest. Ah, he had forgotten. The liquor had flown out of the glass and into his belly. And hatched. He could feel young life moving through his body. He rose. His shadow remained seated. He gave his shadow a moment to get it together. His vision contracted the two waitresses in one. My check, please. The waitress scratched on a pad with a beak-sharp pencil. He paid his bill. Slipped a tip into the waitress's flapping soiled apron. He smiled his best smile. She had attended him with the soft and careful movements of a nurse.

Thank you, sir.

You are quite welcome.

Have a pleasant evening.

The same.

With that, he turned to the door. The knob reached out to shake his hand. Come again.

I will. Holding the knob in his hand, he turned once more to the waitress. Then he went out, the sun dropping behind him. A belt of shade gradually began to rein in the day. The ark of his head rocked unsteadily on the mountain of his neck. He took his breath backwards. He directed his steps back to Union Station, his shadow crawling along beside him. The streets looked unfamiliar, though he had walked them dozens of times. The sidewalk thick with people in evening colors hurrying in all directions. Rush hour. He looked at every couple as they passed. Watched every moving figure for some gesture, some form, some trace of Sheila. Seeing him, pedestrians turned to look at each other. Cars hissed on the wet street. (Had it rained?) Their movement made him aware of his own. Thoughts of Sheila walked in the open beside him. He found himself in front of the bar.

He tried again. He entered the station of Sheila's body on this street, at that corner, through this facade, and under that grate.


THE SQUARE QUIETENED, the stores emptied one by one. The light from the streetlamps managed to create a dim, fragmentary illusion. He turned a corner. The sidewalk glimmered like powdered light. Sparse traffic washed past. Taillights red-danced up ahead. The bar blinked in again.

He turned another quiet corner.

# 17

WHEN SHEILA MADE IT HOME, Lucifer was waiting for her, his eyes in the exact same spot where she last saw them that morning.

*I gotta meet John at the train station. He's going to Washington.*

*About the war?*

*Yes.*

*Short notice.*

*Well, they jus told John and he jus told me.*

*You gon skip work today?*

*I already called in. A sick day.*

*Jus like that?*

*Well—* He thought about it. *It's no big deal. It really isn't. I jus want to see John off.*

*I hope you're not going.*

*He looked at her.*

Twice he'd left her. First, to run off to the war. *He was one of the first niggers over there. But they didn't make him go. John went and he followed. Yes, he was carried to Asia on the foolish winds of John's draft. He might follow that fool John anywhere. Brothers are brothers.* And years later, he returned to the war—four trips to New York or Washington, four that seemed like one, beads strung together, a necklace of the big city's bright lights—searching for what he had lost. Might he leave again? She cut off this possibility, snapped the beads, ground them to powder. That's why, each day, she mixed Go and Stay Powders in his morning coffee.

Where's Hatch? she asked.

Upstairs in his room.

Hatch!

No, don't call him.

He's sposed to be out with Elsa.

Don't call him. Lucifer took a half-step forward, as if he had trouble recognizing her. He smeared a light kiss on her cheek. I bought you a lil something. He held a small box out to her. I bought it at the Underground.

The Underground?

Yes.

How can you even shop there? Sheila had lost herself the one time she shopped there. Ugly black walls that—rumor had it—were one-way glass and that concealed surveillance cameras and robotic eyes. Each shopper's voice roared a seashell's echo. Yes, it was the deepness that bothered her. Like being inside a big well. The elevators glass buckets drawing up lakes of people. Every floor ("level") a marble square of tiles awash with people, merging into eddies and disengaging into new thick paths, varied schools of colorful fish. Babies sucked on the Aqua-Lungs of their pacifiers. Sucked the air thin. The world rushed and swam. She elbowed her way into an elevator. Pushed the up button. The elevator went down in one long rumbling roar. She burst from the open doors, a bull into the ring. Took five flights of escalators, riding their light free-running whine. Rode up into sunlight and oxygen.

I went there for you.

She took the box. Unwrapped it with all the enthusiasm her fingers could muster. A yellow bird rested in a nest of white cotton.

You like it?

Is it my birthstone?

I don't know. But the man said that it's a precious stone.

A Jew will say anything.

You don't like it?

She said nothing.

They had these gems on sale. *Emerald. The deeper the green, the better the stone.* Brazilian. Don't you like it? Lucifer did not move. Stood there watching her, waiting for an answer, breathing. The moist air of his breathing carried her. *John, Lucifer, and Dallas heavy-hauled Beulah's black steamer trunks—seventeen trunks, yes, recall them, seventeen—down two flights of stairs, loading two trunks at a time into John's red Eldorado, one in the red open trunk mouth (trunk for trunk) and the other canoe-fashion on the roof. Seven trips to Union Station, and another seven trips to carry Beulah's twenty-seven boxes (how could the small T Street apartment have held so much? where had Beulah hidden it all?), the Eldorado stuffed so full that only John could squeeze inside it, the stacked boxes causing the red roof to sag above his head, the car to creak along. (Christ, Beulah. You gon wreck my ride.) Beulah's departure left a free space which John and Lucifer quickly filled, and the four of them, the two sisters and the two brothers, transformed the closet-small apartment into nuptial chambers. Gracie and John would spend time in the red Eldorado, while Lucifer would touch Sheila behind the hanging white sheet.*

Looking up, she caught his eyes in the light of her own. It had taken him what, seven, eight years to save up enough money to buy her a wedding ring, seven, eight years to replace the gold wedding band as he had vowed shortly after they married. Of course I do. Help me put it on.

He took the necklace. It hung between his admirable fingers, the bird gold-swinging. Navigational fingers which steered her heart. He always touched her with cool fingers—maybe he soaked them in ice water—that went hot. He touched her now, as he had in the one long-ago instant.

# 18

HUNDRED GATES ROSE behind a ragged screen of pine trees. When Porsha saw it, tired left her body with the sweat. Glad to be home. She made her way quickly inside and up to her loft. Once inside, she studied the spring evening. Behind clear rectangular panes of glass, she looked out over the treetops, a beautician above a client's hair. She must prepare for Deathrow.

She bathed for the third time that day. Powdered and scented her private parts.

Her eyes shined in the silver box of mirror that held her reflection. In paradise, her eyes might not have shone so brightly. She brushed her teeth. Lula Mae, Mamma, and Gracie had all lost their teeth by age thirty. *R.L. had milk gums, Mamma said. Maybe it was something in the water we used to drink. Maybe what we ate. We didn't know back then.* And thirty was looking her in the face, two years down the line. She brushed. She would halt destiny.

She checked the answering machine. One message, one voice. *Porsha, hey. How you doing? This is Hatch. I went to see Inez today. She wants to see you. She says that it's important. You can call me if you want to. Talk to you later. Bye.*


TIME WAS OUTSIDE, looking on. Looking in. Deathrow was late. Freighted with waiting, she seated herself in a comfortable chair and flipped through a magazine. Her trained eye recognized her body pasted beneath another model's face. Two or three years ago, she could easily identify her body in a photograph. However, as of late, other models had started to imitate her body. Her poses. Her gestures. Her texture. And photographers used lighting that glistened like juice on berry skin like hers.

She turned the leaves of her magazine.

*A three-year-old confessed to drowning her baby cousin in a bucket of bleach and water.*

Should she call Deathrow?

*. . . idea on the very cutting edge of the mortuary business. These plastic tombstones are cheaper, lighter, and more durable than stone. And etched letters are virtually eternal. In the near future, they will be all the rave.*

She was no longer reading. The print offered a resting place for her eyes. It occurred to her how little she knew about Deathrow's origins. She had not seen a single twig of his family tree. Roots sunk in darkness. Red Hook had given birth to him. I ain't got no family, he'd said. I'll tell you this, he said. I been to hell and back with gasoline draws. But like I said, it ain't where you come from, it's where you going.

THE MOON ROSE HUGE AND RED. She had been waiting more than an hour—one identical hour repeated over and over again—sitting, and thinking of Deathrow. Had he fallen into nested sleep? The phone rang.

Hello?

Bill?

Bill?

Is Bill there?

You got the wrong number.

Is this—

She slammed the receiver down.

She dialed Deathrow's number. The line rang and rang while she twisted and untwisted the telephone cord around her finger. The receiver grew pregnant, became too heavy for her to hold.

SHE LIKED TO LIE ON HER BED in the dark, run her hands over her naked body. The image she saw in the mirror, the body she could see with her eyes, her fingers saw differently in the dark. The mountains of her breasts and the valley of her hard stomach were only shadows and shapes, smoothed of all desire.

# 19

THE SMELL OF GASOLINE ruins the cold winter smell of the day. The blaze is beautiful as it catches, weed by weed, the hedges haloed with fire, a sound like ocean, the pond shining, white as the mountains behind it. The skating is good. The balance, the ease, the sense of sailing over hard surface, the blades cutting a whistling trail of white flakes. Figure eights are his favorites, time beating in the skate rhythms of the hourglass shape. Crunching, the ice gives in like a trapdoor. He sinks. He sees the sun through the ice, a weak hanging bulb. The deeper he goes, the dimmer the light. And he is falling quickly, as if weighted, clawing out at the finger-refusing rungs of a cold ladder, the ice coming away in his hands. Bubbles rush past his face, the cold cuts through his body as he reaches for the bubbles, chain links that will pull him to the surface. Not worried about drowning; in fact, he can breathe perfectly well. It is the falling, the lack of ground beneath his feet that's troubling. He wedges to a rest, directly in the center of the ice, unable to twitch a muscle. Can't even turn his head. He uses his teeth.

The phone's rhythmic ringing cuts through sleep; slices of night black-break away in a steady beat like the clanking of a train over rail ties or a hatchet falling to the chopping board, again and again. Black light freezes the hours.

Hello.

Lucifer?

Know that voice anywhere. Gracie?

John's gone.

What?

John's gone.

His heart fluttered—a soft rushing noise—wings unable to break the cage of his chest. What do you mean, gone?

I *feel* it.

He weighed the word. I see. The clock on the nightstand, glowing face and dial: 4 a.m.

Please come.

He looked over his shoulder. Sheila's left breast peeked at him from over the sheet. Okay, I'll come. See you soon. He hung up the phone without waiting for a response.

Who was that?

Gracie.

Gracie?

Yeah.

Gracie?

She had a feeling—

Behind him he heard Sheila roll over in her sleep.

Moonlight came silver through the window. It made objects look different, gave them glowing skin. He moved to the chair before the window and raised the shade a little. An edge of street. Splotches of light, the glow of the streetlights. The sky, a star-eaten blanket. Then slow rain and an occasional tire hissing over wet streets. Illuminated night allowed him to see a watery blur of trees that surrounded the house. Gracie's call put a hole in his rest. A *feeling*.

John the engineer. Places his school ruler flat across his clipboard, curves the ruler along the clipboard and angles the train out of the station, his mouth motion-wise under the ruler's control, accelerating, screeching— rails—easing off speed.

In the T Street apartment, Lucifer and John shared a tunnel-like room lined with Georgiana's canned food. Lucifer's bed faced the window—year-round, the windows stayed shut against the stink of the stockyards—the sun flashing between rushing clouds and, at night, the moon walking in light. A bed too short for him, his frosted toes hanging over the edge winter mornings. Woke early on those mornings in a humming house, while John slept in reaching distance of him, and Georgiana and Pappa Simmons in their closet-sized room. Walked through the coal-steaming apartment, wood buckling under his toes, buckling and crackling, popping like squeezed knuckles. Bathed, scrubbed his skin, shaved off his red widow's peak—*yes, shaving it, even as a child* to protect himself from sharp laughter—with Pappa Simmons's straight razor, then returning to bed and lying there, naked, warm, beneath Bingo's wet dog smell.

The first thing Pappa Simmons did every morning, regardless of weather, was step out onto the back porch naked and check the sky, the wind. He was not red or yellow or white, but some shade between autumn and winter; his old blood ran cold and thick, and his labor-bowed legs were too slow to keep up with two growing grandsons. He never said much, kept up a black cloak of distance, fixing this or that thing around the house, hammer in hand and nails in his mouth. Georgiana polished your shoes, smoothed the wrinkles out of your clothes, combed your naps—rather, you combed your own naps before you entered her kitchen (her bacon crackling on the stove and fresh glasses of lemonade or tea on the table), lest she do it and leave you tender-headed—and checked your ears for roaches. Dress you like twins on Sunday. Put your hands (smooth) in hers (weathered) and walk you to school or church.

I don't like that white woman touchin me, John said.

She okay, Lucifer said.

She was equally tight-lipped, speaking to stress the evils of sin, foretelling that either the dark wing of Satan or the bright cloak of God would trouble John's sky if he didn't change his ways.

Pappa Simmons had catapulted himself beyond the arms of religion. Counted the numbers of days since he last set foot in a church. *I'm a workin man, he said. Ain't never made no livin wit my mouth. That's a rotten way to make a livin.* You never heard him mumble a word of prayer. And he threatened to shoot Reverend Tower if the preacher ever stepped foot in his house. But he and Georgiana spent evenings in the living room reading from their Bible.

SOON AS HE THOUGHT HIMSELF OLD ENOUGH to board the train without supervision, John rode it with his running buddy Dallas. Miss Adams, Dallas's mother, didn't mind. Dallas was with John, and John was his brother's keeper. Lucifer could recall no moment when Dallas didn't exist on T Street. John and Dallas riding Bingo—a huge hound the height of your navel—saddle and all, like a horse up and down Church Street. Boy-men now, they rode the trains, working cons, three-card monte, the shell game— nickel-and-dime stuff. Small and swift, John zoomed from childhood directly into the world of power and feeling. Roll an occasional hooker on Church Street or milk fag-bar fairies for drinks.

*I been a man all my life, Sam said.*

*Nigga, hold yo horses. We jus hustlin them fo some drinks.*

*Yeah, Dallas said. We jus hustlin them fo drinks. No harm in that.*

*You can get mo than drinks, Dave said. If you talk to em the right way.*

John, Pappa Simmons warned, don't let me catch you actin a fool behind alcohol again.

John and Dallas shaped masks from Chinese chop-suey boxes and rolled a Jew Town tailor. *Officer, they looked like robots.* Them Jews sure do bleed a lot, Dallas said. John looked at him, face tight, eyes flicking.

John swaggered through his days and staggered through his nights. Runaway child running wild. A boy rushing into the future.

John, Pappa Simmons said, pack yo bags. Georgiana watched from over his shoulder, silent. You grown now. Be out my house by sundown. And take Lucifer with you. Ain't worth a damn if you can't guard over yo own brother.

Lucifer, John, and Dallas moved into a basement apartment on Church Street, a cellarlike door opening onto a flight of cement steps down to a small vaulted room—the floor one large slab of stone, and the walls, slabs too, mixed with splinters of brick. The apartment kept a permanent chill. Rats ran over the exposed pipes. The floor sloped invisibly away to dark corners and walls. Formerly the Red Rooster, a jazz club. (The drugstore above later became a church.) How had dancing bodies cramped into this tight space? Loud talk and laughter, clinking glasses and crashing cymbals, blaring horns and bottles set down hard on tables woke you in the night. Drunken shadows moved in the darkness.

*Flyin home*
*Fly like a motherfucker*
*Flyin home*
*Fly*

John and Dallas come home bone-drunk and pass out on the floor. John singing his sing. And Dallas, silent, in that vomit-smellin pea jacket year-round, and slumped like some old rug lying about. Part of Lucifer was glad that his roommates spent most of their time hanging on the corner of Sixty-third and Church—Brother Jack's Lounge behind them and Lil Bit's Give and Take Pool Hall and Barbershop down the street—holding the stones of their groins and signifyin.

*Flyin home*
*Fly like a motherfucker*
*Flyin home*
*Dallas, yo fly open.*


ALL OF CHURCH STREET cursed John's and Dallas's names. Lucifer had come to believe that it was the force of John's high-stepping activities that kicked Georgiana into her grave. Her shut windows could not keep out the odor of rumor. John's dirt, like sewage, flowed back to her.

That boy gon come to ruin, she said. After all we done. She flopped into a hard kitchen chair, heavy breathing, hand clutched to her bosom, pale—her color restored only after Lucifer fetched her a glass of water.

Try not to worry yourself, he said. He just tryin his wheels out.

JUNIOR, Inez said, can't you do right by me?

Sho, Mamma. He kissed her.

Why you act so bad?

I want to do better. I'm tryin. He gave her a sincere look. Mamma, I need your support.

My support?

Me, Ernie, and Dallas tryin to start us up a business. He left out Spider, the bookie, who liked to use his cuff links for brass knuckles.

A business?

Yeah. Tired of workin fo the Man's chump change.

What kind of business?

It's legal. A car shop.

What you know bout cars, other than driving like a crazy fool? And that Dallas—

I don't need to know nothing. Ernie know everything there is to know. Ain't that right, Lucifer?

Lucifer nodded.

Engine Ernie they call him. That nigga can—

Don't bring that street language in my house.

—play a motor like music. Ain't that right, Lucifer?

Lucifer nodded.

He was born under a hood.

How come Lucifer ain't said nothing. He part too?

John said nothing.

He ain't part. Lucifer, you ain't part? Why ain't Lucifer—

John calmed her with a kiss. Held her close. You know me and Lucifer.

Junior. She gave him the money.

The Funky Four Corners Garage gave new life to old clunkers. The revived cars flashed reflections in their paint and chrome. Sparkled like dew. All went well until an engine blew up in Ernie's face. Then Spider bowed out of the partnership, taking along his earnings and investment. *It's been a pleasure doing business with you.*

John didn't quit. Pleaded with, hugged, and sweet-talked Inez.

*A lounge? Junior, that's a place of sin.*

*Mamma, ain't nobody gon do no sinnin. Some dancin. Some talkin. Some preachin. Drinkin of spirits. Jus like church.*

Opened John's Recovery Room with her money. All went well until Dallas, on his own initiative, purchased some cheap 'Sippi moonshine and put it on tap, hog piss, devil's spit that burned like slow lava through your system and made you pee fire and fart dynamite.

Nigga, John said. He punched Dallas squarely in the nose. Nigga. Curled his fist again, but held back when he saw that Dallas was slow getting up.


SAM AND DAVE put John and Dallas up to all that foolishness. Had to be them. Lucifer had long known in his heart. Them niggas ain't worked an honest day since they got fired from Hammer Meat Packing House. Beulah telling it—her talk about Sam and Dave was like her far-reaching stories about the South, like the South itself—telling how they would dress up a hog in trench coat and fedora, walk out the factory yard with it between them. *Come on there, Wheatstraw, you know better than to drink on the job.* Got caught but the white foreman was willing to forgive and forget, and them niggas hog stealing again the next week, caught, not so lucky this time, three-year sentence to Joliet State. *Jet* ran the article: "Sam and Dave Griffith: Fools of the Week."

Had to be them. By the time John bought the red Eldorado, Sam was living off disability—oh, that leg-stealing train—and Dave was surviving on Jesse's welfare check. Beulah told that too. *She puttin all my business in the street. How she like me to show everybody her dirty draws?* How Dave got Jesse pregnant when she thirteen. *Hayseed-eatin country bitch, Dave said.* How three babies popped out of her womb in three consecutive years—but weren't there some twins? Lucifer remembered twins. *Three pearls, Beulah said. Three crumb snatchers, Dave said.* Dave cashed his paycheck at the liquor store. Might as well have used the money to feed them dead hogs at the factory. Fed them kids sugar water. Put newspapers on em for diapers. And Jesse. Jesse. Well— Lucifer could tell it from here, what Beulah both knew and imagined. How Dave could always get some from Jesse—*My sweetness*—how she remained a reliable piece until she had the stroke that sucked the life from the left side of her body and confined her to a wheelchair; *Dave ran her til she had a stroke, dang fool,* eyes buggin, her left arm hanging limp across her lap, trembling like a bird. So I took them poor kids, Beulah said. And brought em here to Decatur.

Sam ain't never have any kids? Lucifer asked.

Sam never claimed any, Beulah said. Cept one by this girl when they was stationed over in the Philippines. One. A Filipino. The only one he claimed. But who knows all the places his blood done run.

# 20

SHEILA DRIFTED AWAKE in sunlight. The rising sky lifted like a blanket. Faint sounds rose in spirals up the stairwell. *Hatch?* She reached for Lucifer. Discovered a warm hollow where his body had lain. *He sleeps very still, legs straight, hands crossed on his chest, an ancient mummy.* Strange. He never rose before her. While he slept, she would make breakfast and prepare his lunch. *Work-bound, he carries his lunchbox solemnly, like a miniature coffin.* Ah, so that was him downstairs in the kitchen. He was preparing to bring her breakfast in bed. Not if she surprised him first.

She found him in the kitchen, shaved and fully dressed, drinking his coffee in five scorching swallows. *Black. He likes it black. With four lumps of sugar.* Ah, he would go early to work. Make up for missed time. Set right to right. He caught her eyes as he lowered his cup, and his fingers suddenly became unable to compass both cup and sight; the cup banged against the table.

Sheila.

Clumsy. She smiled at him in the remembered fashion. Touched the yellow bird at her throat, floating in its element. Swept into an empty chair at the table. Ran her bare toes up the thick hard logs of his thighs.

Sorry.

How are you this morning?

Fine.

Why you up so early?

His head rocked unsteadily on his neck. I gotta go.

What?

I gotta meet Gracie.

Why?

His look rose and settled on her, then flew away.

Don't you remember? The phone call last night.

She watched him.

Remember, she called last night? You know, John. His eyes floated everywhere in his face. Away from her.

John again?

She had a feeling about John.

Two days in a row.

Well, she called. He rose from the table. What am I sposed to do? She called. Said John's gone. He crossed the room and stretched her insides.

# 21

Sunrise found Lucifer taking the long train ride to Liberty Island, his heart ringing and echoing against the warm bed he'd left. Coffee lay in a hot ball on his stomach. And Sheila lay somewhere even deeper.

He blinked behind sunglasses, looking through tinted glass, looking through the train's speeding window. Bright streaming skyscrapers rose above his twin lenses as the train left Central, shaking and shivering like a dope fiend, and passed over metal scaffolding to the island. The horizon licked the bright slapping waters of Tar Lake. Licked sun from his glasses. Sun-day. A day that reminded him of Sundays reminded him of Porsha reminded him of Pappa Simmons cause it was hot and bright and Sunday when he and Sheila carried the newborn to Inez's house, first showing her to the old man, spending the last of his years on the screened patio watching the grass and soaking in the quiet, and they made the trip every Sunday after that, Porsha making the journey by herself when she was old enough to learn the El, coming to hear the old man's aged words—*wrinkles slacken the face, loosen the tongue*—words that memory and possibly the fear of death had forced out of him, and it was on a Sunday when Death took him, snatching him from under Porsha's frog-witnessing eyes. *She never grew out of her ugly.*

Beneath his dark shades, an old feeling of stolen sleep. *Each day, he rose early, the sun scratching his back.* Gracie had robbed him of needed sleep. *Healing in long sleep.* Perhaps she had robbed him of even more. Sheila's mouth formed into a taut line and tightened about him. For the second day in a row, he had crossed her. In the kitchen this morning, his eyebrows had raked in her startling form. He had shaded his eyes so that he might see only a little of her face at a time, first the chin, then the lips, then the nose, then—skip the accusing eyes—then her forehead. Yes, she was angry that John had drawn him away for a second day. If she knew all that he had thought and felt as night softened to dawn, she would understand why he was on his way to meet Gracie this morning. *Once she knows—I must tell her, I will—she will understand.*

He reached Twin Lakes station, walked to the Davis Street exit, and ran down five flights of El platform stairs—cool wind blowing past his ears— hoping the speed would wake him. Liberty Island. Cobblestoned alleys gave hollow force to the sound of his footsteps. Tall yellow fire hydrants. *You only see those in museums.* Tree-lined streets. Gardens smearing the air with scent and color. Groomed lawns and neat squarish brick houses. Liberty Island.

The hot ground came up through his shoes. He pressed Gracie's door-bell. Removed his glasses. Fixed a smile on his face. Over the years, he had learned to hide his disgust for her.

She opened the door. Lucifer.

Shadows spilled out the house.

Gracie.

Sunlight filtered the shadows. The stairs curved upward just beyond her. Black. Black as a worn ass. She had lost some flesh. Always been a toothpick. A skinny chicken bone. *Caught in John's throat, his chest.* Two scroll legs meant for stomping prayers in church.

*You and John gripped your dicks like fire hoses. Pissed high as the hellfire ceiling. Pissed down Reverend Tower's hot sermons. Fat women with Bible-weighted pocketbooks chased yall out.*

*You, Lucifer. You know better. Being the oldest.*

*Zip up your pants.*

*Do something constructive. Fix Miss Beulah a plate and take it over to her place. And take them nieces something.*

*You fixed Miss Beulah a plate (fried chicken, buttered dinner rolls, candied yam, and greens)—them nieces can fix they own—and ran to keep it warm.*

*My, my, Lucifer. Ain't you sharp in your suit?*

*Thank you, Miss Beulah.*

*Miss Beulah smelled good, like rusty tubs of rain.*

*Where that mannish John?*

*Playin with Dallas.*

*Dallas. There's another one for the devil. Miss Beulah tasted her chicken. You ain't bring my nieces a plate?*

*I forgot.*

*Well, help them there with that ice cream.*

*You did. You turned the cooler's handle while Gracie and Sheila added ice, salt, or milk. Ice cream done, Sheila sat you down at the table and white-stirred some into your bowl.*

Gracie watched him, the curve of the staircase behind her. *There are curves in this house.*

They embraced as though through glass.

# 22

PORSHA WOKE with Deathrow imprinted all over her. Her nipples raised tepee-like. Deathrow had worked them, painting with his fingers. Morning entered, cool and clear, through the open window. Sunlight edged under the closed blinds and formed a yellow square of concern on her bedding. She shed her sheets—onion skins, layer upon layer; one skin for sleeping, another for loving, another for eye-burning tears—and opened the blinds to the full blast of day. What night had blurred began to take definition again. The humming warmth of the Prophet 1 Faith Stimulator patent pending still roared through her body. *Rise. Rise. Rise. Rise and shine.* She never slept this late. How dare he?

She showered. Perfumed her body. Massaged her private places with a healthy sprinkling of powder. Slipped on a red loose-fitting dress, black-belted at the waist. Slipped into fishnet stockings and high heeled satin shoes that accented the curve of her calves. She rouged her cheeks and drew another face for herself. Haloed her mouth with lipstick red and apple-shiny. Now the final touches. Four gold apple earrings Deathrow had bought for her. A necklace of real pearls she had bought for herself.

The full-length mirror returned her reflection. Coal-black eyes burned between inflamed cheeks. Coal-black body made the mirror steam. Yes, she liked what she saw.

She separated her garbage, tin and aluminum in one bag, plastic in another, glass and bones in still another. Tuesday. Today is Tuesday. Recycling day. I must stick to routine. North Park was the only square of the city with a recycling program. PRESERVE THE FUTURE. Funny how today's milk came packaged in yesterday's plastic. She put the garbage in its chute and the valuable waste in the recycling bin. Routine.

She hurried up her belongings. Hurried out her loft.

The sun held in sharp relief against the sky, though the stars still shone. (Today, the stars would be visible until noon.) Gnats swarmed in red light. She fanned them away from her face. Deathrow swarmed inside her. *All flesh is insect-harboring grass.* I must put myself out of his reach. Ah, a new day. A new rooster crowed. Forget Deathrow. By this road they would come to understand each other more clearly. She moved with arrogant rhythm through the chessboard streets, sidewalks red in the sun and black in the shade.

A dog barked pointed teeth. She rooted, held her ground. *What's with these dogs?* The dog trotted off, tail waving batonlike.

She took the rushing ride out to Inez's house.


WHY WOULD INEZ WANT TO SEE HER? What could be so important? She couldn't remember the last time she had visited Inez. In the old days, in the real old days when it was possible to tell Uncle John anything cause she was the black apple of his brown eye, every Sunday Uncle John would drive her—in his red Eldorado (or was it the black Cadillac?) with power locks and windows, custom items in those days; the two of them blasting along at dangerous speed, car mistaking itself for plane, shouted curses and angry stares from fellow drivers reminders of their passage; they passed a river; she held her breath, figuring that if the car crashed into the water she'd be pre-pared—to Inez's house to visit Pappa Simmons. Pappa Simmons could talk. The body was weak, decaying—he had barely enough strength to walk to the kitchen, the bathroom, or the bedroom without George's assistance—but he watched you with intense cold eyes, very black, sparkling like lumps of coal. He could see forwards and backwards, he could lift you up on the fork of his tongue, carry you to the heights of witness and testimony. He was the only adult on Lucifer's side of the family who would talk and tell, though he had little to say about Lucifer's and John's father—Inez testified, the boys resulted after an *indiscretion*, though the father was around long enough to pass down the peas of his name—though he rarely mentioned his wife—they met at the church picnic, her sitting beneath a chinaberry tree, mouth greasy with the last of her fried eel—the only two black spots in his memory.

Sunday was the nervous thread that pulled her through the week. The vi-brating pulse that awaited the hour when Uncle John would arrive.

Now, Pappa, John would say, don't talk my niece's fool ear off.

Two things I always been good at, Pappa Simmons said. Work and talk. I reckon I'll dig my own grave. Might even preach my own funeral. He faced Uncle John. Uncle John returned his unturning stare. Junior always been big on eye work, he said. He work when you lookin. Body blind when you ain't.

They remained then, looking at each other, looking, directly, for longer than they would ever again.

EACH SUNDAY, she rose early, with the first tentative fingers of sunlight, and fled the warmth or coolness of her bedcovers to catch the train—*Relax, Sheila. I'm gon ride wit her the firs few times myself. She be alright. Shoot, I been ridin the El since I was what? . . . nine. And she eleven. Or damn near. Sides, George said he'd drive her home. Instead of gettin on my case you need to ask George why he won't pick her up*—safeing it, as Mamma had instructed, meaning that she boarded the car with the most people and sat near the engineer in the shut metal cabin. She wasn't scared. Riding the train unattended couldn't be any more dangerous than riding attended in Uncle John's speeding Cadillac. So she took the hour ride from South Shore to Morgan Park, a land of un-city light, light that belonged someplace else where palm trees circled sand and sand ringed ocean black with unblinking sharks.

Inez would be departing as she was arriving. She took in the surroundings with a slow familiar glance. She wanted to be a stranger to it, wanted to see it with fresh first eyes. Adventure.

How's my granddaughter? Inez said. Porsha entered the circle of Inez's open arms. Inez hugged her tight, then pushed her at arm's distance for observation. Inez had a round face with a short triangular nose. Why, didn't yo mamma dress you pretty today. Look jus like a doll.

Thank you, Inez.

Inez carried a healthy portion of yellow flesh. Not fat or skinny but properly proportioned to age and build. Gravity was doing its work. You came to go with me to church? I can't get these two heathens to set foot in a church.

Well . . .

Pappa be here when you get back.

Inez, Pappa Simmons said, can't you see that girl don't wanna go to church?

Like I said, Porsha, Pappa be here—

Leave her alone!

Inez, you want me to drive you to church? George said. Pappa be okay until I get back. Porsha will look after him.

I can drive myself.

Okay. Inez. Jus tryin to help. George eased himself out (to the garage, to the basement, to somewhere) with his newspaper, reading glasses—thick lenses, fogged like pop bottles—and low-volumed radio whispering a baseball game or country music. *He listen to all that hillbilly music, Hatch said.*

Inez gave Porsha a kiss. I'll see you when I get back.

Okay, Inez.

Why, ain't you pretty today. She gave a final look. Now, where's my purse? And my keys? Singing as she searched.

> And the angel's wings will hum
> Thou kingdom come

Inez, Pappa Simmons said, what kingdom is that?

Read yo Bible, Inez said. Pappa, you too old to be so blasphemous. Hope you don't find out bout that kingdom no time soon.

Red clusters of canvas and boats slow-sailed on Tar Lake. The sun projected images on the bright-covered glass. Names, locations, places. The window became a moving map lit with places she'd never been, with names she'd heard roll off Pappa Simmons's tongue: Cairo, Gimmerton, Rains County, Thrushcross, Misketuch, Mobile, Sabine Hall. Names she could find on any map or globe and some she could not. Ah, she liked the way they sounded. Liked the way Pappa Simmons said them.

Pappa Simmons came to her now, bright and sparkling like a swimmer stepping out of a pool.

His skin was white as shell, and his eyes, completely white.

*Inez, you asked, is he an Indian?*

*Part.*

*Which part?*

*Inez laughed.*

*George, you said, is he an Indian?*

*About as much as I am.*

She liked the way white skin wrinkled at the corners of his eyes and mouth—little rivers running back to their source—probably from too much talking.

I may be white but I ain't no woogie.

I know, Pappa Simmons.

You know why I'm so white?

No, Pappa Simmons.

I got hurt a little.

She said nothing.

When I were born.

What happened?

Aunt T saw me and ran alligator-quick to the swamp. It took them four days to find her. He paused. Mamma saw my color, and she wiped me and wiped, with a clean rag, using her spit, searching fo my color.

PAPPA SIMMONS SAT STRAIGHT AND RIGID in a cane chair on the raised screened patio downlooking the backyard, grass-covered, with a patch of vegetable garden—sun-filled furrows—parallel to the concrete walkway parallel to the garage, trees hanging in green suspension, the steady whir of insects and the birds chipping at the green marble pond, he holding a newspaper like a sacred script, lowering it and putting his intense eyes on her. She looked far into them.

Girl, get you some ah them pinder.

The air rushed in and shaped the words. Yes, Pappa Simmons. She pulled up a seat to the theatrical workings of his mind. Grabbed a pinder fistful from the bowl.

They sat very close, she in the rocking chair and he in the cane seat, his forehead shot with red veins, his breath hot in her face.

Good you come here rather than church, he said. When a man's got the spirit of the Lord in him, it weakens him out. Can't hoe the corn. Milk the cow. Do the things need to be done. Rains County learned me that.

Yes, Pappa Simmons.

I never been too big on ligion. Church, I mean. Now, some say the closest a nigga get to heaven is the lynchman's rope. Some report and lie. I don't. I ligion. But not church. Home got more ligion than church. God can hear yo prayers jus as good in the bedroom as from the church bench.

Yes, Pappa Simmons.

*Christ been down to the mire*
*You must bow down*

He studied her—she never forgot the strange excitement she felt when he looked at her—rows of lines like pews in his forehead. Don't be ashamed, my chile, cause you was hatched from a buzzard's egg. Inez pretty as the day is long but she short on sense.

Her sense-driven mind revolved around the axle of his conversation.

How yo mamma?

Fine.

And a fine woman too.

Thank you, Pappa Simmons. I'll tell her.

I'll tell you like Whole Daddy told me, Die in defense of your mother.

Yes, Pappa Simmons.

Ain't much else worth dying for.

She ate the pinders, a handful at a time as his mind worked rakelike, combing among the dead leaves of memory.

Backthrust in the cane-backed chair—and if he wasn't sitting, he was standing (on two vines for legs, vines hidden under the dark cloth of his pants) before a mirror, silver mane flowing down his shoulders, or sometimes he sat small under a big Panama hat, with a bright yellow band like a collar of sunlight, saying, Ernest Simmons, my God you're a handsome son of a bitch—where cool breezes whistled through the wire mesh of screens, the old man watched her with grim and cold intensity. (Come smooth or rough, he had surely borne what he had seen.) His bow tie (sometimes a four-in-hand) motionless in the breeze. Yes, he sat very still, telling stories, only his lips moving (and hers, eating) and the cannon voice drowning the outside sounds.

He had a need to relate his life, to tell his story in full detail, from the moment he rocked the cradle up to the event at hand, but he knew how to tell stories, and you could feel him thinking, moving his mouth over the words, experimenting with them, tasting them, searching for colors strange even to him. She rode along on the endless stream of his voice. And they traveled here and there, here and there, carrying story. Lucifer and Uncle John were blessed, blessed to have lived in the house with Pappa Simmons for all those years. To shine in the treasure of his voice.

It is unwise for a man to tell more than half of what he knows.

Yes, Pappa Simmons.

From the earliest rocking of my cradle, I member Whole Daddy talkin bout Juneteenth and Jubilee and niggas pattin Juba and stompin Jublio and the flame of laughter and celebration that spread from one farm to another. Niggas drunken to a proverb. Dancin so hard the devil can't sleep beneath they movin feet.

Whole Daddy talkin. Mamma and Aunt T rather feed you than talk. Get more words outa a dog.

A day go by that Whole Daddy didn't talk bout it. You get him to quibble and reveal here and there a lil piece bout Rains County and Sabine Hall, then you memory and invent.

Whole Daddy was a small man, like me, wit same silver hair, wild and kinked.

*Jet trail. Yo hair is a jet trail. Rocket sparks.*

Sabine Hall was the only mansion in the county. Cuthbert Page had won it in the county lottery. The previous owner or perhaps the county itself had built the big ole mansion and a lil mansion the like, the cottage out back, twin in appearance, where the guests stayed.

She saw and heard. A diamond light from another time cut through the day.

Columns magnolia and white. And inside, posts walnut and newel. Oak floors that walk yo reflection. A calliope from some riverboat. Blinding silverware. And fancy paintings of woogies dressed stiff and proud and bright rivers and thundering horses.

But the size swelled and impressed. The mansion was big. One house wit a lotta lil houses inside. Nobody ever stop to count all the rooms, lacking will and time. Rumor this nigga Jupiter fled. Paddies never found him. Rumor Jupiter ain't go no further north than the attic of Cuthbert's mansion. Attic hide ten families and more easy. And Jupiter lived there, in one room or another, maybe comin back to the firs room and starting all over again. Lived there dead or lost. Never knowing that Cuthbert Page the father fall and Calhoun Page the son rise. Never hearing the bells of Jubilee.

Cabins stretched on both sides of the mansion like wings. Log cabins with thatched roofs. Looked like arks. Make no mistake, every cabin was a fine place to live. Sturdy built on a lot behind a rail fence and some thornbushes. A nice chimney and a nice fireplace. A stack of candles. Good candles too. Made from beeswax, not soap. Cotton mattresses and blankets. Page dressed his niggas in fine linen. No sackcloth but calico and cotton. Fed them well too. Plenty of food every two weeks. Good food too. (Not jus fat and meal. And none of that hardtack.) With coffee. Page wouldn give a chile a piece of bread if it weren't buttered and sugared on both sides. Chillun used to steal chickens off neighborin farms, raid watermelon and tater patches, jus for fun.

What Page didn't give, the land provide. See, in Rains County, the earth give off a deep redness. If you know how, you can dig down into the dirt and put a little sugar in it. Taste jus like cake.

Yuck. She had never heard of nobody eatin dirt.

Bout any food you imagine flow from the red of that land. Peaches, watermelon, strawberries—

Porsha closed her inky eyes and created night. Sketched places and faces in the black lands of her mind. Going there to know there.

—raspberries, celery, orange, grapefruit, cabbage, sweet corn, squash, turnips, cucumbers, collard greens and mustard, too, pumpkins—

Pumpkins? You mean like Halloween? *You carved and Uncle John carved. The smooth orange head felt like a warm belly in your hands.*

Yes. And string beans and butter, garden peas and black-eye, tomatoes, beets, tobacco, rice, lemon, cane, and sorghum. Pecans and walnuts sprouted up wild, papershell so soft you can crack them with finger and thumb. And green apples.

In August, you hang up yo tobacco to dry. Put the peanuts on a white cloth to dry in the sun.

Each word was a perfect jewel in the open light.

But hard work to eat. Even though Page buy every labor-saving machine and then some. Sometimes the soil baked hard enough to break hoe, pick, or shovel.

*All dem pretty girls will be there*
*Shuck that corn befo you eat*
*They will fix it for us rare*
*Shuck that corn befo you eat*
*I know that supper will be big*
*Shuck that corn befo you eat*
*I think I smell a fine roast pig*

And plenty of ponds, rivers, and lakes. Catfish, perch, trout, eel, cooter, gator, and what have you.

Gator?

You bet gator. Whole Daddy go git a ax handle and chase a gator when one come floppin up past de chinaberry trees at the front gate. And forests with coon and deer and possum and rabbit to hunt. You been hunting yet?

No. I'm a girl.

A girl? You mean Junior ain't learn you to hunt?

No.

A girl or no girl. Ain't nothin like it.

You learn Inez?

You watch the bird on the branch. The bird gets sharper by your watching and the bird not knowing.

You learn Georgiana?

Quiet and careful. What will it do? A hen you know. How it moves, how it eats, how it lays eggs, how it sleep. But a bird on a branch . . .

WHOLE DADDY WAS JUS TEN OR ELEVEN when he came to Sabine Hall— bout your age—and he spent forty-four or forty-five years there. Came when Cuthbert Page was leaving for the war. Last time Whole Daddy saw him live or dead. Night before Page left, Whole Daddy dreamed of him counting money. The next morning, Page gathered up his traveling shoes. And left them unworn, cause it seemed he wasn't gone but a quick minute when the letter arrived, He dead.

Ten or eleven when he came, but his memory already long. No day dawned befo he came to Sabine Hall. He often told about his firs job where he lay on the cold floor next to his master and mistress bed. Wake them at the proper hour. Help them bathe and dress. Check they commode. Smell their waste to see if it healthy. Clean and wash the commode. When he got a lil muscle, they sent him to work the fields. He slept in a lil hut-shack. No window in his hut-shack. The only light get in when you come in or leave out the open door. Wind and rain come in and the cooking smoke won't go out. A lil hut-shack to worry the head down on the bare floor, beaten earth, perhaps a toss or two of straw, but don't worry that. So tired usually you eat dinner raw and sleep befo you rest yo eyes and befo yo feet member if it's Monday or Friday. But he was honery. After they work him hard, he'd run off and hide out in the woods a few days. Then he'd come back and take his whooping. Traded him in when they got tired of whooping him. Like I said, he was honery. He never found a place to rest his hat. Farm to farm, bent over in the fields season to season, sun to sun, seasoned on one farm or another, farm to farm, a new master each year, workin side by side wit his master in the field, farms so po and shabby he be lucky if nother nigga there to pass time wit. Farm to farm, field to field, till he landed at Sabine Hall.

Cuthbert Page was the most famous man in Rains County. He once traded with this judge in Yawkatukchie a passel of crazy niggas fo a passel of uncrazy ones. The uncrazy niggas carried him home on their backs. Burpin drunk and laughin.

He work fast and hard like a reborn man. Ran rough and smooth over raw country people. From where? Rumored London, Scotland, Wales, Ireland.

She knew those places from maps.

Niggas taught him his daily bath. He repaid in kind. Any nigga could go to his back door, plate in hand. And he learned them to speak the English language without corruption. I don't want no dummies round my son, he said. What he hear, see, speak, he learn.

Then he ran off to Greek.

> Massa and Missus have gon far away
> Gone on they honeymoon a long time to stay
> And while they's gone on that lil spree
> I'se gon down to Memphis pretty girl to see

Greece, she said. I know where that is. Geography was her favorite and best subject. She pondered the globes of people's eyes. Studied longitude and latitude, the lined bottoms of feet and the palms of hands, measuring degrees.

Said one or two words to his son, the mamma being still and dead, and no more turn his head, and run off to war. Stabbed to death wit an ear of corn.

Three days after he died, a hailstorm hit the county. Fist-sized ice fell from the sky and knocked out the windows, punched holes in the roof. A storm came every day at noon fo three days and lasted exactly three minutes. (Whole Daddy timed it.) Calhoun Page the son took it as a sign. He wrapped himself in mystery, devoting his time to fasting and praying.

He decided to free any nigga wanna be free. By county law, he couldn't free no nigga. So he offer to buy them safe passage to Canady or Library.

Canada? Liberia? she said. I know where they are. I can show you on the map up there. Pointing to the red-tacked map nailed to the wood-eyed wall.

Some niggas went. Whole Daddy stayed on. Canady and Library, them jus words.

Page drew up a deed so if he died the niggas would own some land. Everything legal. Written in stone.

Page opened his front door to any nigga who wanted to sup at his table. And that ain't all. Built two or three lil red schoolhouses, learned over by the best teachers in the county. Teach the niggas figgas along wit words. He built fifteen chapels with the best wood, full of preachers of strong lungs and learning. He prayed with the niggas, led them in song, caught the motion of their bodies and did as they did. Preach in any pulpit that grant him privilege. *Masters, give unto your servants that which is just and equal, knowing that ye also have a master in heaven.* And he wrote letters to the newspapers.

*Always I felt the moral guilt of it, felt how impossible it must be for a master of men and an owner of souls to win his way to heaven. I must give an account of my stewardship. My sins form a part of those hidden things of darkness, which are linked by a chain into the deepest realms of hell.*

Page fired the overseer, some dandy from a Memphis garbage heap. Page wouldn't honor white trash wit his spit. He sold the driver, an evil cuss ripped from a cruel vine. He wasn't much good nohow. His whip create more sound than pain. Seeing that was the case, he took Whole Daddy outa the fields and put him in charge of em.

Whole Daddy ran a tight ship. He rung the bell before daybreak. He kept the books—he wrote in the neatest hand of the county—and if a slave sweat a good day, a good week, a good month, a good season, he allow them what Page allow them, time to work off the tation, be drovers, drivers, steamboatmen, draymen, carpenters, store clerks, and what have you—good works to make cash.

Whole Daddy. Overseer in name and title only. Spent most his time overseeing Page's garden and his own. Raising the hogs. And tending the horses.

Horses? They had horses on the tation?

*Did he wear a hat? Hatch asked. R.L.: when he went out West.*

*Hush, Sheila said. Hush.*

*Did he listen to all that cowboy music?*

*Hush.*

Do dogs have hair? Horses, you bet. Whole Daddy knew him a horse. He'd heat an iron bar red hot—

She saw it, like the tip of a dog's red dick.

—then he'd hammer it til it sent out a shower of sparks. He'd put that hot shoe on a horse. It smelled like burnt horn. And the horse would turn its wise eyes and say, Alright there, Mr. Whole Daddy. Go on. I won't make a fuss.

The warm air and sun breathed strong passion in Pappa Simmons as he spoke.

Rarely did Whole Daddy leave home without bridle, halter, blanket, girt, horsewhip, and saddle. Go ridin off holdin the reins stiff like he was frozen to death. He rode some of Page's horses into the grave.

Whole Daddy was a cowboy?

Not exactly. A drayman, drawing work from the harvest horses. And Page's coachman too. Drive him wherever he need to go.

Pappa Simmons shut his eyes. Two eyeballs under two closed lids, bulging the skin out, protruding bellies.

So those last thirty, thirty-one, thirty-two years befo Juneteenth, Whole Daddy lived the good life. Walked on time-slowed feet. He would overseer and dray and go to auction and purchase niggas.

Well, this one auction, Whole Daddy bought these two girls fo his own private matters.

Those ten or eleven years befo Whole Daddy came to Sabine Hall, those eight or nine years he was there before Cuthbert died, Whole Daddy had put so many long years in the fields his shoulders bent like cane stalks. These two Indians were field-bred too. The same slumped shoulders. The same black tongues. Indian girls.

Indians?

Yes. And twins.

Twins?

Indians and twins.

Indians can't have twins.

Couldn tell em apart. Nola and Idelia. The one who birth me. One my mammy Idelia and the other my aunt T Nola. They had raven-black hair and wings that fly bout they heads whenever they get excited, which was rare, since they both talked bout as much as a log. But beautiful. I member the sound of they walking hips. Like cooter shell. Whole Daddy married the one that become my mamma. Maybe he married them both. Cause you couldn tell them apart and I don't know all there is and ain't to tell.

Me and my brother, recent saint of memory, grow up wit the four fussy red hands of these two sisters. Barely women when Whole Daddy marry em but old in work and season.

Well, they duddied up, usin money Page prescribe. Page hired the best preacher. Whole Daddy's choice. They jumped the broom on Page's front porch all cluttered wit saddles, bridles, bale cotton, hoes, rakes, a washstand, washbasin, pitcher, towel, and wash bucket. Page squeal a note or two on the fiddle. Then he throw a sumptuous feast.

REBS COME RIDIN TO SABINE HALL and tell Page to git ready to fight. Said, All yo nigga foolishness fine peacetime, but this wartime. Said they'd give him three days and he'd better come, else they'd come and git him. He said, Guess you'll jus have to come and git me. I done already served.

The war came. Some woogies holed up in they houses all circled bout wit sharp stakes they niggas build. Other woogies run off to the war, blessed with traveling dust they niggas sprinkle on they feet.

By and by, word came. Whole Daddy ride horseback up and down and all about ringing the dinner bell and yelling above the clanging, Free.

Pappa Simmons rested his tongue, a humming ache of silence. Porsha studied his silence, a red stain in the light.

Nightfall, Whole Daddy gather up his hunting rifle and stepped bold as daylight into Page's bedroom.

Porsha saw it. Sun pushing through a window, bogarting.

Ernest, Page said. By and how, what's the meaning of this? You free.

Whole Daddy ain't say a word. He commence to workin. Raid Page's larder. Clean out Page's wardrobe, cluding his best pair of shoes. (They wore the same size.) He looked at Page. Follow me, he said. Page followed him out to the kitchen. Whole Daddy cleaned out the pantry provisions. Follow me, he said. Page put on his hat. He followed Whole Daddy out to the stables. Whole Daddy cleaned it out, then he put all his cleanings into Page's buckboard. He fixed the two best horses. Took Page's best shotgun. Follow me, he said. By God, Ernest, Page said. Can't you see? Page was still in his nightgown. Get in the wagon, Whole Daddy said. Page got in the wagon, where the two Indian twins sat waiting. Howdy, Page said.

They rode bout three miles. Then Whole Daddy stopped the horses and stepped down from the wagon. He spread his arms wide, marking off the best fifty acres on Sabine Hall. All this mine, he say. Far as yo eye travel yonder and yonder and yonder and yonder too. I repeat, all this mine. Enter on pain of your life.

Okay, Ernest, Page said.

Since the hailstorm, Page had tried to be a better man than his father. But you can't run wit the hare and hunt wit the hound.

What? she said.

Whole Daddy said, I'm gon come back fo some mules and hogs. Now get on back home.

Page tipped his hat to the ladies. Walked the three miles home.

They bedded down in the wagon. Whole Daddy sleep between the Indian twins. Those first weeks, Whole Daddy and the Indians keep one eye sleep and one eye shut. They didn't take no chances. Never know if a cup of courage replace Page's morning coffee. Never know if the old paddies come ridin. So they ain't take no chances. They greet visitors down the sight of a rifle.

Whole Daddy and the Indians set to the sweat of work. Whole Daddy was a glutton for work. That's why he stuffed his belly with three plates of food at each meal. Wore out his boots in a week. He say, In the morning sow yo seed and until evening do not let yo hand rest. Labor is the deck. All else is the sea.

He and the Indians sawed trees, split logs, cut and trim timbers fo a foundation and laid a line of Page's bricks fo the house. Built the house with scrap boards from Page's lumberyard. The house was nothing fancy. Front room, two bedrooms, a kitchen. They built a fence. Dug a well. Cut and hammer an outhouse. Nothing fancy. Jus a plank of oak stretched over a hole in the ground. When it rained, Lawd. Pappa Simmons pinched his white tomahawk nose, red.

They build a barn, a smokehouse. (The smokehouse my favorite place. Manfred and me, we be playin out behin the smokehouse, whipping each other wit chitlins.) And a hogpen. Fenced off with a shelter jutting from the barn. Hogs closed off in stalls.

Chickens. Yall ain't have no chickens?

We had a coop. They built that too. And planted the harvest. Know how? *Press a hole with yo heel. Drop a seed. Now cover it wit yo foot.* Hard work. Pick worms off the growing crops.

Yuck. Slimy worms.

And we tended the yard. Oranges, grapefruit, tangerines, and what have you. Any kind of tree you can name.

Porsha looked out the window at the tumble of vegetation in Inez's garden.

The Indians always take the dirty clothes down by the spring where stones sparkle like big white diamonds under the running water. Scrub your clothes clean clean. By and by, they build them a springhouse.

Them Indians could cook up a storm. Jack salmon wit some black-eyed peas and wild raspberries. My favorite. And squirrel.

Squirrel?

Yo mamma ain't never make you no squirrel?

No.

I'm gon have Inez cook you one.

No, thanks. Yuck.

The Indians sold ginger cakes and whiskey. And they made shoes and seams. Spinned and weaved. One would treadle while the other wind fast. (You got to wind fast and take the thread right off the spindle, else it get tangled up.) Then they switch.

When he could catch a day or two away from the farm, Whole Daddy labor on the county railroad. Ride down and work a day here, a day there fo something extra to fill his pockets. He was a trackwalker. Walked ten miles a day hammering down loose spikes.

DON'T KNOW WHEN I WAS BAWN. Whole Daddy write it in his Bible. (The one he took from Page.) Then somebody lose the Bible. So, don't know when exact, cept Whole Daddy say sometime around hog-killin day. So it musta been in December or January. You know how to kill a hog?

No, Pappa Simmons.

Get yo rifle and blast him right here. Pappa Simmons pointed to his forehead.

Porsha shut her eyes. At the back of her mouth, behind her clenched teeth. She tasted metallic gunfire. She opened her eyes.

Then slit the throat.

She closed her eyes. Red seeped through.

Dunk that hog in a vat of boiling water to get his hair off. Make him pink and white. Pink white. Now he ready fo the smokehouse. You bind and skewer his hind feet, then hoist him high on a pole in the smokehouse. Rip him ass to throat so the insides clean out.

————

IT RAIN ONE DAY and it cold next day and it rain again and cold again. Storm slow down work but it ain't stop it none. You got to eat. Take two spoonfuls of turpentine. And fish oil to make you thick inside.

Yuck! Double yuck!

Mamma get sick, bone-sick. Whole Daddy work while Aunt T watch, then Aunt T work while Whole Daddy watch.

You ain't going to die, is you?

I'll have to. You want me to live forever?

Whole Daddy take the pillow from her head to ease her dyin. Turn her bed east facin the crossroad. And he cover up the clock wit a hog sack to keep her spirit from stealin into the glass. But she didn't die. She didn't die the firs night or the second or the third.

Aunt T and Whole Daddy grew tired of workin and waitin. By and by, some of the church women come over and sit wit Mamma all night, singing them church songs. (Whole Daddy and the Indians tend church regular.) People tend her like she tend people. Come mornin, all of them sisters gone. Nowhere to be found.

What happened?

Water burst from Mamma's body. Them church sisters run off. Scared.


AUNT T FOUND THE SHARPEST KNIFE and cleaned it in her skirt. She cut a line on her forehead so that her blood could mix with her tears. Then she cut her a gown from a flour sack and a veil from some mosquito netting. She and Whole Daddy put Mamma in the box and rest that box on two chairs, then they call in a preacher who know how to whoop and holler.

We make ash of the body.

Ash?

Aunt T spread Mamma's filthy ashes over her face. Then we bury her out in the yard behind the house, plenty near the creepin gators and the diggin and shovelin coyotes. Whole Daddy hammer a cross three foot high to re-member where we put white roses every day. (We grew our own.) He put Mamma's favorite quilt over the grave.


WHOLE DADDY SAT DOWN on the front porch wit the double barrels of the shotgun across his lap. Aunt T sat beside him. Old. They couldn't do much else but watch me and Manfred work.

THE COUNTY SENT A WOOGIE to take the farm, the barn, the smokehouse, the hogpen, the outhouse, the springhouse, and everything else in and outa sight. The county hit like a flood and carry it all away. What the Lord give, he sho can take. He can even take what he don't give. The woogie say one word, Taxes. Death taxes.

Suh, I said, beg pardon but there must be some misunderstanding.

Manfred came right out wit it, You can't steal what ain't yours!

The woogie look at him. Nigga, go hire you a lawyer.

WE LEAVE RAINS COUNTY with one hundred twenty-six dollars Whole Daddy had kept tied in a knotted rag and buried in an old barrel out in the barn. Wasn't nothing to keep us in Rains County, make us wanna stay. Shake the tree and see what falls from the branches. Sides, niggas talk. (Don't we?) In the city, the fire hydrants full of wine and all the grass green onions and there taters neath the sidewalks. Mighta gone to Library if we knew how to get there.

Had to steal away durin day cause the white folks guard the railroad at night. Guess them white folks thought rightly no nigga stupid nough to leave in broad daylight. Broad or narrow, me and Manfred git.

Packed everything I owned into a grip. I wuz lookin good the day I left Rains County. Never will forget. A duster.

A duster?

High dicer.

High dicer?

A derby. Lil hot fo the summer. Frock coat. Vest. Paper collar. Watch chain all shined. And my brother was lookin good, too. (Folks took us fo twins, only he was taller.) Straw hat. Spats and high boots polished with Bixby's Best Blacking.

If I live nother hundred years, I ain't gon forget that railroad station. Station house no bigger than a toolshed and this lil ole red-faced woogie in striped overalls, like a convict or somebody on the gang, wheezin behin these three lil rusty iron bars wit his red face stuck in a piece of window. You can tell he think he high dukey there behind his window. One of those real nasty woogies, the salt that make the cracker.

How yall? he say.

Fine.

A good day fo travelin.

Yes indeed.

Two tickets fo two niggas, Manfred said.

I stomped on his foot.

That woogie's eyes snapped out of his face, like red whips. Niggas?

That's right, Manfred said.

We don't low no white niggas in this here county.

Yes, sah.

And we don't low none to leave.

We won't tell if you don't, Manfred said. He winked at the woogie.

Boy, you need to school you some manners. The red-faced woogie take the money and slid the tickets under the bars.

Manfred had to have the final word. Make sure his money rang loud on the counter. Thank you, white folks, he said.

We wait fo the train on a piece of knobby plank they called a bench under the station porch. Then it come.

Inside Porsha, the story grew and grew. She could see it, the locomotive puffing short blasts of black smoke that held, lingered in her memory, then grew, a long black plant.

I stand there and watched the moving walls of that train as it come rushin in and past, fast as a flood.

A few woogies get off and yawn and stretch.

We want the Jim Crow car, Manfred say. See, Whole Daddy had told us many stories about travelin woogies. Nasty. Spittin in the aisles.

Son, you know we don't low that.

If I'm payin, I'm nigga.

Suit yoself.

So we board at the noon whistle. Ride in the Jim Crow car. Niggas give us a curious eye, tryin to pretend like they ain't lookin. We right up front near the engine. Cinders jus fly right in through the window.

She faced him in light where red was missing. Shadows of dreams passed along his forehead, clouds over water. *So you fled across a black land similar and same to the black land that birthed you. The train rushed on. And your heart raced to keep pace. You leaning to the window, watching the fleeing countryside, the tracks hill-rising and valley-plunging, and your heart leaning into your chest, trying to flee your tight skin.*

But that car was dandy. Real dandy. Red carpet. Lamps glintin on the ceiling. Leather seats soft like a pretty lady's skin. This shiny-buttoned porter bawling out the stations. And the woogie conductor wit his shiny ticket puncher.

We stop to water the engine.

Water?

That's right. Just like a horse. They ran on steam. (Live and learn.) And we go on.

That train snort and burp and cough and fart and ginny and shake. And the walls shove you and the ceiling shovel you on top of the head and peo-ple camped and cramped bout and the flo rollin this way and that spillin people into yo lap this minute and out the next.

Damn, Manfred, I say. Move over.

What? I ain't on you.

See, I ain't never been on a train befo. Wasn't like no horse or no wagon or nothing else. That locomotion get in yo stomach and it spin round and round and round. I had no eyes, no ears, no nose, jus a mouth. Next thing I know, I spilled all over my brother's shoes.

Yuck. *Disgusting,* she thought, not saying it.

Christ! Manfred said. Christ! Jus like that. Jumping back like it was hot water.

He hand me his initialed handkerchief. (Aunt T had stitched us both one.) I wipe my mouth.

Christ! he say. What bout my shoes?

I get my handkerchief. Clean his shoes. Then I throw both hankies under his seat. The train wuz still movin but I felt better. And the train started to slow down.

*Then the train slowing down but your heart still rushing. Yes, the train slowing into town. And your body a gathering of tremendous effort. Cause this you must do and it can't wait. A sea of faces white-waiting on the platform. Like hot stones, they draw the water from your body. Something breaks and rushes away.*

I felt worse again. All I could do to dam my bowels and keep it from run-ning down my leg. I tell Manfred, I gon get off.

What? he say.

I can't stand it.

You seasick again?

Do fat ladies eat?

We proceed. See, the conductor said. That's what yall get fo niggerin.

I was so glad to feel land again. But standin there on that platform, I feel something else too. Red eyes on me. Feel like a fish in a bowl and I'm hopin these woogies don't kick the bowl over.

Manfred, you get back on the train. I'll catch the next one.

Couldn't you go on a boat? she asked.

Nigga, you crazy? Think I'm gon leave you here?

Why didn't you go on the boat? she said.

You know what'll happen if these woogies discover us? Better one than both. I'll find you.

Yall should have rode a boat.

Know how many colored folks in that city?

I'll find you.

So we talk like that, him fussin and me fussin. Manfred knew what I knew. Life don't sit still. It may wait a minute. So when time come to get back on that train, he get on. He ain't look back. And I ain't seen him since.

Where was you?

Mobile.

Mobile, Alabama? She could find it on any map.

No. The other Mobile.

Oh.

I get me a room in a boardinghouse. Live regular wit the woogies. Every now and then, a wonderin eye peep you, but the mouth say nothing. If somebody woulda asked, I woulda told. That's how I am. Always was, always will be.

Well, I got me a job workin on this bridge. Know how to build a bridge?

No, Pappa Simmons.

Well, you got to build both ends at once. It meets in the middle. Building backwards.

Why?

Ask me if I'm an engineer. Well, I ain't. I jus knows it meets in the middle. Building backwards. Well, I eat cheap and sleep cheap and save my money.

When we finished the bridge, I get me a job hauling sugar sacks at the process factory. I work and save. I bought me a brand-new Model T with cold hard cash. A man has to get around. My barking Model T scared all the dogs. And all the woogies laugh. Ernest, what you got there? they say. An automobile? You think worse than a nigga. Soon, they come beggin me fo a ride. I oblige. Charge them a nickel to ride in it.

So I ride and work, ride to work, work to ride. Well it went like that fo months and years.

Then the Broad River Baptist Association held their annual picnic. I ain't never been to the church. Like I say, I ain't big on church. The Scriptures got mo religion. I pray. God, kill all the woogies but leave all the niggas. But I figured I'd go to this here picnic.

Why?

I was gettin on in years.

I don't under . . .

How you today, white folks? All the niggas look at me. This here a Jim Crow picnic, they say.

I'm Jim Crow, I say. You see, I had let them believe what they believe.

Well, fix you a plate.

I joined in the hospitality. I saw this girl, sitting out under the chinaberry tree, legs stretched out white and stockinged. Eatin an apple. Takin lil polite bird bites. She was a small woman. Small. Bird bones. If you glance her with the tip of yo elbow she snap right in two.

Porsha thought about it. Mamma remembered his wife, Georgiana, as a sickly woman with olive-colored hair. (Pappa Simmons rarely mentioned her, the name trembling on his lips, rattling the cage of his flesh.)

Yes, distant stovewood am good stovewood. Her all dolled up in a choir robe with gold sash. Didn know that in a few weeks we become a divine institution. I'd been waitin fo the right gal to come along. Nothing should be plucked until it's ripe.

I joined her under the tree. We talked. I invited her for a walk in the trackless forest. Then I took her rowing on the lake.

> Her teeth and lilies are alike
> Sing, fellows, for my true love and
> The water will take the long oar strike

Come sundown, I drove her home in my Model T. We screamed above the barking engine. Simple as that.

If you want to catch you a gal, give her something nice occasionally to wear, and praise her up to the skies whenever she has anything tolerably decent.

When the woogies see me in town wit this girl, they knows I was a nigga. Mobile ain't but neigh big. Everybody got one foot in they do and one in yours.

Come morning, I'm fired. (Each day begins wit a lesson and ends wit a lesson.)

I had worked my way up to foreman. I worked my people hard and ain't tolerate no nonsense. Mr. Simmons, they say, he mean as the devil. I try to teach em to work and save, work and save, work and save. Don't spend every fool penny.

Boss man say, Ernest, you a good worker and bout the best foman I ever had. And I ain't got nothin gainst niggas. But—

I understand, suh, I said.

Here yo pay, and here yo half-day. I know you wouldn want me to give you mo.

No, suh.

And Ernest?

Yes, suh?

Good luck. A nigga need all the luck he can git.


GEORGIANA WAS A LAZYBONES. Her mother and father let her do nothing but sit around all day. Watch them work. Lazybones. And many a time I talk to her something fierce to get her to lift a light finger. A man should never strike a woman. Rather trespass on an angel.

Wasn't but two things a nigga could do in that town, wash or field. Unless you was a preacher, but the town already had one.

Did yall share—

By and by, befo you could blink good, Georgiana swell up and start to totin her belly round. We work, bear a child, work. Cept them woogies never pay you what you earn. Georgiana pray. I complain. Pray. Complain. Ain't much else you could do. Then the night riders—

Night riders?

—mail me a letter. *Nigra, you act like you don't know who running the show.* They wrong. I know.

That's when I decide to come North, train or no train. Locomotion or no locomotion. We took what money we had and some we didn—I earned, see, saved; I earned and saved—took and stole away in the night.

How old was Inez?

I don't member exactly but she was jus a girl. No older than you.

Inez often spoke about the three of them crowded into their first apartment, on South Park (later renamed King Drive after the beloved doctor-reverend). A kitchenette—*railroad flat,* she called it—heated by lumps of coal that warmed the iron potbelly stove. She taught Pappa Simmons to read by the stove's light.

*But I thought you said Page taught all his niggas to read? If he did, then Whole Daddy surely learned and shared.*

Why'd you come *here?*

Cause we followed the train and the train followed the bridge over the river and the river ran all the way to Cairo.

In Kankakee County?

Yes. We stopped in Cairo to change trains. You could go east or west or north. I asked the conductor, What's the nearest city? He told me, Take that train, the one going north. We did. We here.

But Inez said—

I don't care what Inez said. I tell you without lie.

EARLY AFTERNOON. The sky had already died from red fire to ash gray. Gray sidewalks, tar patches in the asphalt, vacant lots sparkling with old glass. Inez and George lived here in Morgan Park—far south, past Woodlawn, past South Shore—a two-hour train ride from North Park. Porsha strolled along the brick sidewalk with cold sun on her head.

She found Pappa Simmons palely asleep in his favorite talking chair. Pale but also on the edge of color. The red he had pined for, so many years—how many? it took her several minutes to count that number on her fingers—in reaching distance. She summoned George. He look funny, she told him.

George listened for his pulse, checked his heartbeat.


FRAGRANT COOKING brought Porsha to Inez's bosom, a white welcome table, again and again. Inez, you got any of that applesauce? I'll take four biscuits, please. Did you make more? Yes, cherry preserves. Inez, can you cook me one of those hamburgers? You ought to go in business. *Now Inez can cook, Pappa Simmons said. She learned from the best, but she can't hold a match to the best. But apples up here ain't nothin like the ones we had back home. And the meat don't taste live.* To indulge in these culinary delights, Porsha marked the fourteenth day—why the fourteenth? the day after unlucky thirteen? she liked even numbers? the halfway point of the month? (well, that would be fifteen, or even sixteen) or perhaps it took the first two weeks of each new month for her to channel enough strength to weather Inez's storm of pessimism?—of each month in her datebook. In this way she could remember to visit Inez. Then Inez started to forget. She forgot her recipes. She forgot the day of the week. She forgot all that happened the day before. She forgot your name. She mistook you for Mamma, insisting that Mamma's aging face was masked behind your fresh skin.

Even if Inez was standing right before your face, she wasn't *there*. Worst of all, Inez kept no portrait of Pappa Simmons readily visible to the visiting eye. You had to search through dusty photo albums to find his face and form. Photographs don't lie. *Inez was a looker in her day. Mad pretty. And George made a handsome soldier.*

In the failed daylight, Inez stood on the walk before the house—one of the small, low houses that George claimed the government had built for soldiers returning from the war—her thin frame etched against the sky, as if she had been awaiting Porsha's arrival. Colorless beside the marigolds, tulips, and roses (red, pink, and yellow). The rotten handwriting of time scribbled up and down her face.

Inez. Porsha kissed her on the cheek. Felt wrinkled skin beneath her lips.
How are —

Terrible.

*Can't you ever look at the bright side of things?* What are you doing out here?

Junior was here today.

John? Today? When?

Your father did something terrible.

My father?

He stole all my money?

He did what?

He stole my key.

Wait a minute. Lucifer. He —

Stole my key.

Key? What key?

To my safety-deposit box.

Porsha held up her hands as if to push Inez away.

He got all my money, my bonds, my stocks, my savings, my valuables, my certificates. Everything. Inez was crying now, hands over her face, the fingers larger than the shrunken head. Porsha guided her up the porch steps, hands on her thin shoulders, through the door, past the flower-filled sitting room — cream-colored plastic-covered antiques, and clam-shaped glass bowls offering candy — through the cramped living room, no larger than a chessboard square — the sketch of Inez done in Mexico, two photographs, Champions of the People (King and the Kennedy brothers), and God Save the Kings, that hovered above Inez's head on the chair where she always sat, the latest issue of *Jet* on the TV stand — past the guest bedroom where Porsha had always slept when she visited, patting Inez's back — burping a baby. Inez, get some sleep. Everything will be okay. She helped Inez to bed. Tucked her underneath ancient covers.

It don't matter, Inez said. I'm going home. Going home. Soon. Soon. Good Lord break of day. And with that, she fell asleep, eyes shut painfully tight.

Porsha moved down the hall to the patio — as a girl, you imagined it an island, separate from the rest of the house, separate from everything else; deserted island populated by you and Pappa Simmons — where George sat at the glass table, bent over his newspaper, eyes swimming beneath his reading spectacles and magnifying glass throwing his face in large relief. The portable radio blared the baseball game.

Porsha. He looked up as she entered. His eyes, despite the spectacles, were watery and weak.

Porsha flopped down onto the couch beneath the world map where red thumbtacks indicated all the countries Inez and George had visited: Morocco, England, Italy, France, Brazil, Mexico, Egypt, Turkey, Spain—*Spain would be an island without the Pyrenees*—and more.

George put the magnifier down on the glass table, clicked off the radio. His eyes were uneasy behind the heavy reading glasses. I didn't hear you come in. His white sleeveless T-shirt fit snugly against his firm flesh. He shifted his feet, gloved in backless house shoes.

Inez was out front.

Out front? George removed his glasses. I thought she was in the bed.

No, she was out front.

I didn't hear her go out. She gets worse and worse. I can't watch her every minute.

Why don't you get some help?

George watched her.

You know, have someone come in a few days a week?

I already looked into that. You know how much they want?

Porsha watched him. No. How much?

George eased back in his seat. I'll tell you it's a lot. More than I can afford. We're not rich.

Porsha fought back her words. *He got all kinds of money, Uncle John said.* She sat, not speaking, until she settled down inside herself. Was Lucifer here today?

Lucifer? Lucifer never comes here. You know that. John was here.

Today?

No, last week sometime. The week before. He wanted money.

Same ole same ole. John always wanted money. Family legend, Inez gave him ten thousand dollars cash to open a lounge, and another ten thousand to open a garage, five thousand down payment for Gracie's house, and a thousand here and a thousand there to pay his taxes, keep the hounds abay, and stay out of jail. John had squandered a good deal of their money, tens of thousands.

Inez says that Lucifer stole all her money.

He ain't stole nothing. I took her safety-deposit key and moved the money into a new account. In her state, you can't tell what she might do. And no matter what John does, she will always— He's got some scheme now about buying cars cheap at auctions and sellin them for high profit. Guess he'll never learn. He's been tryin to get her to sell the house.

I need to lay down, Porsha said. Flame spread a red plant through her body.

What's wrong?
Nothing.
Are you okay?
I'm gon lay down. Rest before I head back.
Okay. Tell your mamma I want to see her.
I will.
Don't forget.

SHE LAY ON HER BACK and watched the cloud-dark ceiling. Memory hovered like rain. The air heavy with perfume. Beneath the perfume, other scent. She could breathe in the air-carried aromas of other nights. She always had trouble breathing here. No fresh air. The one small window above the bed that George had nailed shut against burglars—he didn't like bars, the black wrought iron so familiar to every house on the block and in the neighborhood—until Inez had forced him to remove each nail—A guest has to breathe, she said—one by one. He had removed them with a grimace, as if extracting his own teeth. Then Inez had him stick an air conditioner into the window. Porsha had memorized in this room all the shadows and how they changed, memorized the exact spaces between things. Limited choices. She could sleep either here or in the basement bedroom, the humid, damp, and musty room like another world beneath the house, where Pappa Simmons had spent the last years of his life. The room you reached down the pantry stairs. (After all, the stairs were the pantry, Inez's mason jars neatly arranged on shelves, book-fashion. You could actually fold a thick wooden door over the stairs and seal off the basement, lid and cigar box.) Had they buried him down there?

The real man in the flesh, not the memory, would come to the guest bedroom and look in on her.

Girl, how can you sleep in there? He pinched his nose. You'll suffocate.

I'm okay, Pappa Simmons.

Well, come shut the roof for me.

She followed Pappa Simmons, the old man walking slow, slow, concentrating on each step. He moved so slow that you hardly saw any movement at all, and by the time he made it to the pantry, you felt you had walked and waited miles.

Need any help?

Jus shut the roof.

And the small old light white red man slow-moved down the pantry stairs, one by one.

Good night, Pappa Simmons.

Good night. Don't let the bedbugs bite.

She shut her eyes. Slipped beneath the covers. The comfortable buzz and hum and scratch and whirl of cotton and thick wool—the air conditioner blew chill—to warm the night. A steady wave of snoring rode through the house. Lying there now, the bed holding her above the floor, she turned again and again. Shaped in the darkness. Shaped.

*He trots along the vine-matted trail, erect in the saddle, head motionless, flicking his rod over the horse's flanks to keep off the flies. His spurs rake the mount's belly until it bleeds. Dry branches crack beneath hooves. He bends his head down and presses it against the horse's neck. Tries to put his mouth next to the horse's ear. Angry breathing. Hard hooves.*

# 23

WHERE EVERY SOLDIER tugged home a thick, brick-heavy album of snapshots proof positive that he and his buddies were true swinging dicks, John brought back only a few photos, all black-and-whites touched up for color, like the posters of jazz singers fronting the nightclubs on Church Street. Lucifer's favorite, the one he held now in his hand, previously angled in the corner of his bedroom mirror, where it so angered his wife: John arcing for a dive into an ocean, arms thrown back birdlike (winged flight) in peculiar light—light full of years—suspended for an infinity.

Lucifer returned the photograph to his wallet, a secret deposit that only John could clarify and claim. He gazed steadily at a patch of night in the train window—earth and sky folded in darkness—until the darkness revealed a long line of trees like dancers at John's Recovery Room, and a scatter of swift-flying swallows in the sky, their wings folded in the moonlight. He followed them as they swirled then flushed into Tar Lake. He watched the city blink and drift and wink and glitter and sink away. He longed for sleep but his mind was like the train, a rocking blue-steel cradle.

*John ain't called.*

*What?*

*As the Lord is my witness, John done a lot of evil things but he never once missed a call.*

Yesterday, he had been convinced that John's blood had cooled. Now it had flared up again. His disappointment mounted to anger against himself. *Watch him,* Pappa Simmons said. *Watch yo brother. Be his keeper. He startin to ramble. And he can get inside of anything, even if it has a fence around it.* He had arrived at a splendidly clear understanding of the problem that engaged him.

Lucifer had packed light, a single bag. (*Travel light,* Pappa Simmons liked to say. Travel-bound, Pappa Simmons and Georgiana never needed more than what their tackle box could hold.) Dodged Sheila's point-blank questions.

*How are you gonna help John? You know as well as I do, whether it be God or the devil, his spirit ain't never seen no rest.*

*He's my brother.*

*John. John's just an excuse.*

*An excuse for what?*

And stole away. With a firm and sure step, he took the path that led to Union Station—the great concourse of steel and stones, the soaring arches, train whistles arching and echoing—twice in as many days. Many years ago, he had followed John to war and now he was following John again, destination New York. Perhaps further.

HE SQUEEZED THE WHITE LETTER in his shocked hand and carried word to Pappa Simmons and Inez. John been drafted.

Pappa Simmons stood with his hat in his hands trying to catch the words. Inez ran from the room, her yellow face wet with failure.

John slapped Lucifer on the back. Let's go get drunk. Celebrate.

The high wind that carried you flylike into the shit began at Fort Dix, the downstate holding station only minutes away from Miss Beulah's Decatur. There, you yellow-waited and waded through cornfields, pondering the steel-blue actuality of war.

*Mister Buster Brown Mister Buster Brown*
*Don't let nobody turn you around.*

Then they sent you eight hundred miles away for basic and airborne training to Fort Campbell, set on a forest-covered and brick-shadowed hill—great sweeps of pine poked the skies; Christmas, you chopped down a tree and shipped it to Sheila by train—surrounded by thick underbrush and swamps, huge water oaks with gnarled roots reaching for the salt shore. (You felt and tasted salt, but you didn't recognize this water as ocean.) By day, you learned to ride wheezing wind, your body breathing easy. And fireflies blinked points of light in the night-darkened forest—a firefight, only quiet, noiseless. Then they boarded you on a train—black earth sprawled outside the window, place folded into place, the train a continuous loop of image and motion—headed for California. From your angle at the window, seeing inward, tree-covered and snowcapped, and later another state, clouds like frozen smoke above brown-skinned mountains. Each ridge a fist, running knuckles and joints. Blood began moving inside you. These mountains were made by the Lord. They showed his hand, every brown finger and thick knuckle of it. Foothills rolled with scattered balls of bushes. Bushes pale green, almost silver. Later, the flare-lit ridges of more mountains. Then the mountains themselves, still and white. A second ridge of gray-veiled mountains, the afterimage, the negative. Night also revealed the first palm tree you ever witnessed, dark-wrapped. So this must be California. Houses shoulder to shoulder. Out the left train window, skeletal frames of new houses under construction, desalination plants. And out the right train window, a million lights flickering through a rolling valley in the shadow of a brown stone monster. Fresh morning brought fresh light. Fresh red-colored sun. Green tufts on brown-bodied mountains. Green cemeteries. Palm trees with trunks thick as elephant legs, swaying slightly, their bladed leaves scraping the air. High streets like vertical statues. And a streetcar, a slow movement of color going up a hill. You spent one night in Port Chicago—you saw ocean (fish billowed in slow motion beneath the water) but never got to touch it—then they shipped you off by early dawn drizzle. You pushed off for shores of another world.

THE WAVE CURLS and throws you down with a dash on green beach like a trash heap before miter-shaped mountains. Ground that is terra firma one minute, dirt, mud, or water the next. Jungles slow and green as turtles. Man-high elephant grass—rolling patterns of water that shift and never settle—corralled off by half-submerged bamboo fences. Brown grass lined with the delicate shadows of barbed wire. Motionless heat, the sun falls, lead rain.

Here, everyone is vulnerable to blood. Flies smell through the flak down to the flesh. Sir Charles knows his shit. A ready-made nightmare in black pajamas. Sneaky too. Contaminate your C rations with black leeches. Or crawl up your unaware asshole—this Oriental suppository—a confirmed cholera kill. And beware of Mamma-san, her clit curled like a scorpion's tail.

Here, distances change, thanks to the trickery of mountains and plains. Faraway things seem close and what's close seems faraway. Time dense and real. Once you are short, you begin to see yourself as from a distance, like standing at the depot and waving at yourself on the train; you think in blocks of time no longer than a day, enter its passage on the improvised calendar scratched into the side of your helmet.

It hit you like that. You step from your bunker, all sense of time having left. Or you hear a mortar round whistling in. You jump up, snatch your rifle, dash into your flak jacket. You run for the bunker and jump. Sarge taps you on the shoulder. Go back to sleep, he says.

HUMPING. The legs doomed to muscular habit, carried by gravity and the sheer weight of sameness, for a body in motion tends to stay in motion, your lungs range wastes of air, and you move with erect urgency, on your way to meet a woman, your eye on the sparrow, the hairs of your body arched, wired to the landscape, running hot messages to the legs, advance a moment, only to wheel back in the shadows, your light quick bones, your eyes swollen to the world, both watcher and watched, body thrusting blindly through the jungle greens, and as the winds veer, you do also, running like a night-bound bird from beneath the sun's touch, heat adding fifty pounds to your back, so you drive on like sharp steel, holding to life and breath, wet earth sinking beneath your rhythmic boots, a musical shuttle, your hungry stomach, a bellying canvas, echoing emptiness, hollow pools of mud, but the jungle unfurls new shades of green, the rustling tissue of the leaves, fluttering with a distinct texture, sweat darkens your skins, salt fragrance, the wait-a-minute vines fasten your ankles, the waist-high bush ever-ready to deal a low blow, limbs scratch your face and neck, but your skin soaks in the blood and sweat, staying your powers, this wet heat, your sweat cold and singing on your skin, don't fall asleep now, put your back into it, haul a heap of memories, smothered chicken, sweet potato pie, a brew, your queen-sized bed, all the sweet pussy you had there, creepy sweat, making the helmet crawl on your head, white light changing, the horizon sharpens, the jungle again, shade out of sunshine, and you roll the great hull of your chest, oscillating your body like a gull, smooth sailing, steady motionless wings, the mountains now, flapping up there in the wind, ever-shifting movements of the whole body, twisting, wringing out blood that stinks like brass, barbed wire veins aching in a knot, but the legs are king, untouched in the eye of the storm, relaxed in silence, they smell the jump ahead, keep them in motion or freeze up mannequin-like, so your breathing speeds, your pulse quickens, pulled like a tide through the day, and in the white wake, a force stretches inside the marrow of your bones, a new sweat breaks over you like a crashing wave, emptying your mind, the drift of it everything, heat and image fade, drawing the fatigue out, peeling away dead flesh, old skin, bringing the second wind, you burn clean, blow skin, all of your muscles filling out, accomplishing the last few feet, your body feeling the dark set, fixed past motion, past color. Enough for today.

Truth to tell, as a technique for staying alive, humping seemed to make as much sense as anything. You're a killer. Let your nuts hang. Though humping brings back all the feelings of self-pity you experienced after a thorough childhood whooping, after Pappa Simmons's motion-hot belt scorched a black map into your behind. *Dream it to yourself. You sit in a wheelchair, paralyzed. Pappa and Georgiana cry behind you, their guilty tears wetting your shoulder. Forgive us, we didn't know. You say nothing, hate stitching your mouth shut. A year later, you are dead. Pappa and Georgiana are carried out from the funeral parlor, bowed over with grief. Forgive us, we didn't know.*

Your first months in the shit, you move wrapped in terror. Birds of fire rush for cover inside your head. You jump here and there with the histrionics of a bad actor rehearsing for the carnival of your death. Fucking New Guy. Slowly, by degrees (three months in the shit, you figure), a grunt learns to relax. By then fear has become so much a part of your flesh that it no longer bothers you. Your heart develops a reasonable rhythm. You master the fine points of killing and survival. For humping makes you tough and smart and capable, as the sun heats your helmet and scorches into your brain memories of your kills, from your first confirmed—*Charlie came through the tall elephant grass You let loose a whole clip—don't overheat your weapon; squeeze the trigger in three-second bursts; and remember that every fifth bullet round is a red-tipped tracer—sixteen rounds right in the face. From the chin up, the face disappeared as if from acid. The body stood there and shivered. Took two steps forward and fell—*to your most recent, your weapon resting easy in your arms, forging a new self, a matching of heart and muscle and will that force the old self into a premolded present. Tiny steps perfect in their knowing of the drum, follow the wound that is the river back to the sea. Relax. The worst that could happen, you could die. At least the humping would be over.

THE COMPANY CAMPED on a high saddle of the mountain. Been in the shit all day, humping bush and dragging through swamp. You dig a foxhole and fill up sandbags to fortify the trench. That done, you try to piss. Take a shit. Stubborn, pee and shit refuse to leave your body and be stranded in this foreign land.

You settle down on your haunches. View the night jungle through the starlight scope. (Nothing moved. Nothing ever moved. A dark flutter of leaves, perhaps.) Besides, halfway up the hill, your eyes have adjusted enough for you to discover that darkness contained its own light. And light here required shadow there.

You look up into the sky. The stars seem quite close through the branches. You count them, name those you know, identify the constellations. Rest is an illusion. Like the earth, those stars wheel in constant motion. All luminous stars are dead stars. You fix your eyes on a single star. Gather in its cold light. A gentle arm touches you.

You close your eyes doll-like once your back touches the ground.

---

LIGHT RACES to meet your eyes. The sun wakes you. Rise and shine. But the company has moved on without you. Shit. You study the situation. The world draws together to one center before you. You stare into the mountains, a green screen that hides the war. In many spots the trees thin to let in sunlight. Not a sound. Such quiet, such peace. What should you do? Will they come back to find you? Should you search for them? Surely, if you stay here, Charlie will find you. If you move, you might find Charlie. Flesh surprise flesh. You directed your gaze at the sky. Big whitish clouds massed together. God is up there somewhere.

# 24

SHEILA ALWAYS FEELS TRAPPED DOWN HERE, in this steel box sliding over iron rails. She gives her body over to the rocking and swaying of the train. Her feet are stinging, need a pan of hot water and vinegar to draw out the tired.

Are they really nasty like people say? Shaneequa scrunches up her face, a frown line or two in her young smooth skin. Her white head wrap forms a swirl like vanilla ice cream. Her face is turned toward Sheila with the window behind it, a black rectangular frame, and Sheila stares in stunned admiration. Shaneequa is the best age to be, for a woman, a year or two short of twenty-five, before age invades the skin, sets in, stays. I mean, nobody can be that nasty.

Their daughter is, Sheila says. She take off her panties and let them drop: the floor, the piano stool, in front of the fireplace, the kitchen table — it don't matter.

Nasty, Shaneequa said.

Enough to make you sick.

Nasty.

And she had plenty of home training.

You ever think about retiring?

And do what?

Lots of things.

You sound like Porsha.

*Did you ask them?*

*Hush. Don't bother me.*

*Mamma —*

*Now, I done told you not to bother me.*

*They'll give it to you if you ask them.*

*How you know?*

*Cause the Shipcos are good people.*

*Maybe, but that don't mean they have to give me anything.*

*If you ask, you could move —*

*Now, don't bother me. I'm tired and don't want to hear none of your fool-ishness.*

*Wish Sam was here, Hatch said. He'd ask them.*

*Who asked you anything? You tryin to aggravate me too?*

*How bout Dave? Porsha said.*

*Dave? Wit his drunk self? Hell, you might as well get Lucifer.*

*Dad? He never open his mouth fo anything. Barely mumble a word of praise or complaint.*

*John.*

*Yeah. Get John to ask em. He ain't scared.*

*Look, ain't nobody askin nobody nothing. I can ask myself. And I'll ask them when I feel like it.*

I'm gon work til I can't work no mo.

I got to buy a car, Shaneequa says.

You know it, girl. Save yo money. I might start riding with the car pool.

Why don't you buy a car?

Me?

Shaneequa nods.

You must be jokin. I don't know how to drive.

You can learn. Porsha can teach you.

It's too late for that.

Steel meets steel with a jolt as the brakes grab and spring, shaking rhythms. The string of cars halt. Several boys enter the car from the door at the end of the corridor, slapping daps, rolling their hips, holding the knots in their groins. Shaneequa leans forward over her shopping bags. Sheila could not move if she wanted; her body is a deep dry well of exhaustion, from the last round of labor, calling out for water. Shaneequa's gesture exposes the small butterfly pin stuck (floating) over the back of her right shoulder. She wears a new pin each day, always some variety of butterfly.

Sheila nodded at the boys. These younguns, she said. Can it get any worse? You wouldn't believe what I saw yesterday when I was standing on the El platform.

What?

This Asian— She thought about it. Should she tell? No. She would save it for Lucifer. Get down in his thoughts and have him share them with her. Oh nothing. Jus these durn younguns. She shook her head. People wonder why they so bad. Raised in the streets. Out of the frying pan and into the fire. She shook her head. People don't understand that a train can't run in but one direction.

Yes, ma'm.

One night, Porsha and Nia, Porsha's lifelong friend, had brought Shanee-qua over to dinner.

Mamma, Nia said, this is Shaneequa Chase, my Stylist of the Month. Actually, she my stylist of every month.

From what little she knew, Sheila had gathered that Shaneequa was a bright young woman quick to see the possibilities of any new venture. She would go places. She had much to learn and Nia and Porsha could teach her. Nia and Porsha, two peas in a pod, a fat one and a firm one, one form-less and spongy, the other shapely and hard; a lima bean and a pea—their relationship stretched back to childhood, like the rows of paper dolls they loved to cut from magazines. Nia and Porsha were serious in both work and play, strictly business in money and men, having sampled everything in the fish-giving sea, though Porsha was particular about what she tasted, while Nia was catch-as-catch-can. She seemingly had a new man every week, though she never let any man stand in the way of her money. The dominoes fell and she gathered up her chips.

> If anybody ask you who sing this song
> Say it was ole Kneel Down Nia done been here and gone

Through the success of her Ship of Beauty (OPEN 24 HOURS), Nia had more money than she could shake a stick at—heck, a whole forest. And money really did grow from trees in her neighborhood, Hombreck Park in North Shore, where they watered the grass—fine-combed lawns sloping in every direction—with the sweat of hard work. Old houses untroubled by the face of modern construction. Occupants raised goats, chickens, and, believe it or not, horses and cows. A little bit of country life for people with city dreams and city habits. Nia lived in a big Victorian house, which she'd pur-chased for a steal at a government auction, hidden behind a screen of green trees, trees of an age and grandeur rarely encountered in the city. You could relax on a rough-hewn lawn chair, reach for the pitcher of cool lemonade on the raw-lumber table, and watch a marble pond where ducks and water lilies floated, watch the brown green blue yellow life of nature. Nia lounged around in her bathing suit, the ruts of the rattan chair pressed into her fat thighs. She flopped around the house in hemp sandals, purchased in Mex-ico, hair flying all over her head.

Nia's success served as both accusation and witness. Sheila had choices. Her life might have gone different. All we have are choices. She realized that now.

By her own account, Nia worked Shaneequa hard. No wrong in that. Someday Shaneequa would feast on the golden fruits of her labor.

What time do you get off?

Two o'clock.

And you ride the train all the way back to Red Hook alone?

Shaneequa nodded. That's why I need a car. She sat there, pocketbook on her arm, gloves in hand, the butterfly motionless on her back. *Looked real. Not metal or ceramic, real.* The white shawl wrapped around her head, holding out to the world's inspection a round dark face with Indian cheekbones and shiny brown eyes. (Sometimes she hid them under a cloud of dark glasses.) The ankle-length dress inches above black calf-high boots, laced loop for loop, the strings taut over the leather.

*Are you a Muslim?*

*No, ma'm.*

*It's just the shawl and the dress.*

*I do it to keep the men away.*

*Girl, why you wanna do that?*

*What? Nia said. Girlfriend, don't you like mens? She flicked her tongue fast and dirty.*

How bout some modeling on the side?

Shaneequa turned her face away, the white shawl blush red at the edges. You sound like Porsha. She always tryin to get me to model.

*How much longer do you plan to model? You'll be thirty soon.*

*Not soon, Mamma. In three more years. You act like thirty is the end of the world.*

The boys passed them—Shaneequa's butterfly fluttered slightly, testing its wings—and found seats at the other end of the car.

Man, he act like a bitch. The boy's voice mirrored his face, hard and rough.

Word.

See, a ho can pussywhip a nigger.

Yeah.

Look at Jerome. Henpecked. His bitch and her best friend gang up on the nigga.

Birds of a feather flock together.

Yeah, tsetse fly.

The boys shoved around rough laughter.

The train hit a curve—the tunnel tightened around it like a fist—the riders pressed hard against the rim. The boys resumed their filthy talk. Sweat began to sheet Shaneequa's forehead.


COATED WITH FILTH, electric lightbulbs stretched toward the tunnel's black mouth. Paint peeled from the walls—scabs from a wound—exposing the white undersurface. Sheila took the stairs slowly. Closer to the street now, sunlight pushed through a window, splattered against the oily walls, a fluorescent river, streaming down the sides and pooling into cracks on the tiled floor.

Heels ticked by clocklike. Night rushed in. Traffic moved, an unguided circle. Buildings flecked with tiny squares of yellow light. Houses hazed in smoke. Each streetlamp provided a small oasis of light. She felt pain in every step. This was the part of the journey she hated, walking under the eye slide of the drunks, drunks who cast foul shadows, crowding in and staring, pushing their breath in your face. Hey now, fine girl. Evil spirits possess bums at night, enter the empty tenements of their souls. She kept her hand firm on the skillet in her purse. Times like this, she wished she owned a cattle prod. Or a stun gun. Maybe even a real gun. It was very dangerous to live even one day.

Man, look at that caboose.

Yo, baby.

Hi, she said. She always spoke. Kept walking.

My, you a pretty one.

Everyone always noticed her good looks. (She was the spitting image of her mother, only a shade or two darker.) The shadow-circled eyes (like women in silent movies), the round face, the glossy black ponytail that heightened her high cheekbones, the thin neck, and the smooth caramel skin. *When you smile, Lucifer said, it gives your age away. She thought about it; when she smiled, the lines of her face stretched tight, vibrating with age.* But the hands— *Yeah, Lucifer said, they give you away too. He kissed them, running their roughness against his smooth lips.* She had tried to protect them, snapped rubber gloves over them for forty-four years. Labor bit through. Her hands. Her body part the most like her mother's. But her sixty-year-old mind inhabited the same body she'd had at seventeen. Gravity had yet to take its toll, come drooping and sagging. And her respectful dresses and blouses hid her burns—not many really, four—one for each limb, each the size of a leather elbow patch, cause Lula Mae had left her baby by an open fire. How? Why? Beulah said that Lula Mae had gone to town to purchase Christmas gifts, while Dave claimed R.L.'s father had paid Lula Mae a visit—and Mr. Albert Post happened along to discover her. For all the years since, Sheila had tried to imagine Lula Mae's face when she discovered Albert Post ducking her baby in a bucket of water.

Yo, bitch. Why you walkin away?

The walk home seemed long tonight, and she had to will each foot to step one at a time. *Step on a crack, break yo mamma's back.*

Give you five dollars if you suck—

Sometimes, after she heard or read about a torched bum, her heart lifted on flicking fingers of flame. Thank heaven for hell. She and Lucifer had moved to this neighborhood to enjoy the deeper currents of life: solitude, safety, sanctuary. Five years ago, Edgewater was the haunt of style and fashion. And the move from South Shore to here shortened her daily commute to work. Then the projects started spilling out roughnecks like sand from a broken hourglass. There was talk of privatizing Red Hook—a group of Japanese businessmen had already put in their bid—converting it into a luxury high-rise. After all, Red Hook was but a short walk from the Gold Coast. Soon, they might be forced to move again.

Bitch.

Keep walking, bitch.

Bitch, you think you better than me or something?

Yo shit still stink.

The city flowed up to her. (There are tides in the body.) An old wish returned. Her thoughts fled thirty years back down the sidewalk. *Miss McShan, I don't want nobody but you.* Life struck straight through the streets. *I don't ever want anybody but you.* The pavement vanished, slanting away into darkness.

*You said, Yes, beneath the splintered scaffolding. Yes, drawn into a ball against the dawn's wet chill. Fierce summer stars swimming through blue sky. Cause they left you there, in the light's concentrated pool, perhaps expecting you to spill forth in a bright cascade of silver dollars. They left you there and you said, Yes, and he opened the door, shutting away the outside air. The lock clicked, skin setting off to light. Her eyes watching your eyes. Burning eyes, shoving hot pokers into your face. The heat can carry you to your inward-spinning self. Streaming through you. Lift skin to sky. Ice will flake and sink away.*

She felt lighter inside now, nothing left to hide. All she had to face now was the knowable weight of Lucifer's eyes.


The sheets were clean, fragrant, tight, white, stretched in the broad wide band that she had shaped that morning. She rushed to the bathroom. The tub was clean, white, and empty. Many a night, she would bathe Lucifer's work-worn body in a tub of red leaves. Then he would massage her, rub memory back into her muscles. She felt an echo of her morning's anger.

*Where you goin?*

*He's my brother.*

She snatched up the phone.

Gracie, where's Lucifer?

Sheila.

Where's Lucifer? If necessary, she would bleed the meaning out of Gracie.

He was here.

Is that all?

I don't know. I told him about John.

She said nothing.

Don't worry, Gracie said. Blood is thicker than love.

# 25

PORSHA SHUT THE DOOR FIRMLY against sticking layers of old paint and floated out into the open flower of the night. *Will Inez even remember that I visited? Know this: I won't visit her again.* Millions of fireflies—*fireflies? this time of year?*—supplemented the blackness with gold light and winking rhythm. Silent music. But sound also laced through the night. Shimmering crickets. A passing car, muffler firing and fender clattering chainlike.

You called a cab, ma'm? The driver's face bloomed in the night light.

Yes.

The driver held the door open for her.

Thank you. She ducked into the cab and sat back by the open window. The driver shut her door, floated on a lake of shadows to his own door, and placed himself behind the wheel.

Where to, ma'm?

The Ship of Beauty on—

I know the place. In Woodlawn right?

Yes.

Enjoy your ride, ma'm. The driver put the car in motion even before he had shut his door. Service is rare these days. She would be sure to give him a nice tip. A dangerous profession. To be driving at this time of night in this neighborhood. She had phoned the dispatch certain that no cab would answer her call. *I shoulda called Uncle John and had him pick me up. Ain't seen or heard from him in so long.*

The long afternoon had left the night luminous. Light and shade were so mingled that the houses looked transparent.

The driver eased the cab onto the expressway, then kicked it into life to duplicate the motion of passing vehicles.

The speed saturated her with a soft relaxed feeling. She was taking a chance on going to the Ship of Beauty. She had not phoned first. (Nia kept her ear tuned to gossip. And she could talk. Bend your ear until daybreak.) What if Nia was at home? Well, she'd take a cab to Hombreck Park. What if

Nia was home in bed, with a *friend*? That she had no answer to. Truth to tell, she much preferred the Ship of Beauty to Nia's home. (Nia knew a thing or two about keeping a comfortable home. She had found Porsha's loft at Hundred Gates—*Girl, you gon be large, so live large*—and helped her decorate and refurnish it.) Nia kept a clean house, at least to the unsuspecting eye. Nice and clean everywhere but the bathroom and kitchen, areas where guests never visited, with the exception of Porsha. (If you had to go, she would direct you to her next-door neighbor's toilet.) Nia didn't even allow Mrs. Charles, her own mother, to enter these rooms. Roaches had invaded them. Small wonder. For days at a time, dirty dishes lay like sunken ships at the bottom of the kitchen sink. (Nia would rather buy a new set than wash the old.) And dirty bars of Popesoapontherope censer-swung from the bathroom faucets.

Nia, girl, look at this mess. You ought to be ashamed.

I ain't got time to worry about no dishes. Life is too short.

Can't you get a maid?

What for?

Porsha grabs up the loose socks, towels, and garments lying about on the mattress and stuffs them down the laundry chute. She arranges the dishes in the dishwasher. Empties the smelling garbage. Scrubs away the old dirt that lassos the tub.

House clean, she and Nia relax on the bed, eat popcorn—with plenty of butter, salt, and hot sauce—and laugh at gruesome movies.

She needed to see Nia tonight. The need burned upriver to her heart. Their friendship held strong and unabated across twenty years' time. The thought circled about her mind. She urged the cab forward. Ah, it had already entered South Shore. She saw the buildings of her childhood, realized that the cab was taking her both backward and forward in space.

> *Chitty chitty bang bang*
> *Sitting on a fence*
> *Trying to make a dollar*
> *Outa fifteen cents*
> *She missed, she missed, she missed like this.*
> *She missed, she missed, she missed like this.*

Two motion-chasing loops, one loop traveling to where the other had already been. Two girls turned the rope, while a third girl, turkey-short and round, jumped.

> *A dollar to school*
> *A dollar to church*

The fat girl lifted and wiggled her meaty legs and butt. Hopped on one foot, hands on hips. Bent over, skirt raised and naked butt high in the air, a huge moon shining through the yellow-shimmering branches of the jump rope. And switching from side to side firm as a tree branch. Now, she was actually twirling between the two ropes, a hog on a spit.

The bottom half of the rope slapped the ground while the upper turned a lazy loop in the air.

Hey, new girl, the fat girl said. You know how to jump double Dutch? The fat girl's jaws were like two biscuits on her face.

Sure.

You do?

Porsha nodded. They had just moved from Kenwood to South Shore.

Well, if you don't, you turn, you know how to turn don't you, like this, you turn and I jump.

Porsha did as instructed.

What's yo name?

Porsha.

My name is Tanzania.

Tanzania?

Tanzania nodded.

What kinda name is that?

It come from Africa.

Yeah, you big as Africa too, a boy said. His grin glinted like his glasses, thick cloudy lenses held on his face by an elastic strap that pinched his slick-bean head.

Shut up, old four eyes.

Least I ain't got four stomachs.

Yo mamma.

Yo greasy grandmamma.

Curtains blew in tall windows, white to mute the sun. Sunlight formed a lattice from garden to roof. Roses shivered like birds in a bath. Roses—yellow, white, red—were Mrs. Charles's obsession, every object in the house as fragrant as her garden. She kept her garden body-clean. Clean enough to lie down and sleep in, which she often did. Her neat rake patterned paths—ah, soothing to the eyes—leading to pure air. The garden involved constant preparation for a secret something.

Mrs. Charles, the shape and size of her daughter, and Nia ate at an infinitely long table covered with huge pots and plates, the centerpiece of an equally long room in the large house they shared. They worked their knives and forks with the force of the most ancient, stable habits of etiquette, and they enjoyed a glass of red or white wine as the meal required.

The backyard was off-limits to everyone but Nia and Porsha. Their private green haven. *This is our skyscraper dollhouse.* Mrs. Charles had constructed a farseeing tree house with fireplace kinder. Converted old tires into swings. The neighborhood double Dutch champion, Nia taught Porsha all her moves. Porsha taught Nia everything she knew about maps and globes. They would lie on their bellies in the grass, the whole world spread out before them. They would tickle their tongues with bladed leaves and assemble countries, piece by cardboard piece.

Porsha came to prefer the Charles home to her own.

NIA NEVER ALLOWED FAT TO SLOW HER DOWN. She was fast. She would organize the neighborhood girls into a Soul Train Line, seeing who could dance the nastiest. Porsha tried to be fast—she told her first boyfriend, Let's kiss with our clothes off; wide-eyed with fear, he refused—but she couldn't keep up with Nia. Nia knew all the latest dances, the Bump, the Dog, the Bone, the Superfreak, the Heart Attack. When boys rubbed up against her, she would rub back. *I don't want you. Ole fat girl.*

One day, M&M—Malcolm Martin—bumped up against her booty. Nia turned around, ready to slap the taste out of his mouth. Sorry. He smiled, teeth big and even and white.

Yo mamma sorry.

I ain't say nothing bout yo mamma.

Yo greasy ass granmamma.

Why you want to be like that?

Yo fat greasy-ass sumo-wrestler combat-boot-wearin great-granmamma.

Later that day, M&M flashed Porsha a sign—smeared red crayon against lined notebook paper—from his desk on the other side of the room: I LIKE YOU PLEASE GIVE ME SOME PUSSY.

In the after-school playground, M&M greeted Porsha with his energetic pelvis. I'm all dick.

You nasty buzzard, she said.

Boy, Nia said, why you always actin so mannish?

Ain't nobody said nothing to you, fat and black.

Nia kicked him in the nuts. A short explosive grunt parted his lips. *Damn. She broke his balls.* How you like that, poot butt?

Yo mamma.

Nia slapped him upside the head.

Excuse me, but I don't fight girls.

Nia slapped him again.

You jus mad cause I don't want none of yo fat stuff, stank ho.

Nia slapped him yet again. M&M put up his guard.

They squared off. Nia floated on her toes, belly-buoyant, bee-stinging with her jab, trying to draw the blood of honey from his face. He crouched, his glasses—he was blind without them—level with her moving belly. Classmates cheered them on, put octane in their blood. M&M roundhoused a blow, his lunging body throwing him into empty space. Then Nia let go with her own punch. M&M felt—cause you could see it and hear it—her whole body against him, just above his glasses. I speak severely to my boy, Nia said, I beat him when he sneezes, so he won't thoroughly enjoy the pepper when he pleases. M&M recovered, landed two blows to her stomach. It went on like that, Nia impacting a heavy blow and M&M connecting to the stomach. They took a break here and there over the course of the battle and fought on until they shook hands from sheer exhaustion.


NIA AND PORSHA TOGETHER were guilty of what each did alone. Mamma whipped them both.

Once, Mamma caught them rolling a joint in the bathroom. Nia looked up, the joint pinched between her fingers and held before her mouth like corn on the cob. Hi, Mrs. Jones, she said. We jus tryin this experiment we learned in science class.

Mamma laughed a full ten minutes. Then she wore out the girls' behinds.

Why you whip me, Mrs. Jones? Nia said. You ain't my mamma.

Well, Mamma said, tell yo mamma that I whipped you, so she can whip you too.


ONE DAY MRS. CHARLES sat Porsha and Nia down at the kitchen table. You girls are almost grown, she said. Will be women soon. Bodywise. It's time to teach you girls about the birds and the bees.

Porsha's stomach tightened in anticipation. Nia grinned.

When you use a toilet away from home, be sure to raise yourself a few inches above the stool. Don't let your rear end touch the seat.

Nia looked at Porsha.

And if you sleep with a man, in the morning you shall wake and find a baby under your pillow.


MRS. CHARLES CLEANED NIA'S ROOM with the force of habit. You just keep doing well in school, she said. That's your job. Mrs. Charles allowed boys to sleep over since Nia said that it was the only way she could study.

Saturdays, Nia and Porsha would gather up Hatch, Jesus, and Abu and take them to the museum, circus, or rodeo.

Men like women wit kids, Nia said. Why you think they always be callin you *Mamma?*

THIS IS FINE.

Are you sure? The cab followed the downward slope of the street.

Yes.

The shop is—

I know.

Whatever you say, ma'm.

The street was well lit. People were about. Yes, she would get out here and walk a block. She needed the extra time to gather herself.

Thank you. She paid the driver—the fare in one hand, a heavy tip in the other—and exited the cab.

Thank you, ma'm. Have a pleasant evening.

You too.

The driver pulled away with a smile on his lips.

She walked down the lean yellow street. Trees bloomed in the dark and smelled like someplace far away. Church Street. Woodlawn. The old hood. (Well, not quite. The old hood was both Woodlawn and South Shore.) The Ship of Beauty, Nia's all-night hair/nail salon, travel agency, and tax referral service, was dry-docked in such an unattractive part of the city where all the streets were named after foreigners. Euclid. Galileo. Vincennes. Racine. Not to mention the people. That's why she had bought a car, to go directly from home or work and avoid streets besieged with beggars, bums, hoodlums, and swaggering seeking youth.

Give me a dime, baby, and I'll tell you a golden story.

No, thanks. She felt her hair tightening. This affliction always began the moment the Ship of Beauty floated into sight. Moon shadows speckled the two-story building. Hard to believe this building had once housed Uncle John's garage (lounge?). John used to bring her here often. Nia purchased it from the same bank that had foreclosed on John. *Those Jews foreclosed on him, Mamma said. That musta been the winter of '67, when we had that bad snowstorm. Nobody went outside for two or three days. John came out and couldn't find the lounge, then he realized that it was buried under all the snow. Then Dallas came back from 'Sippi with that pee-hot wine. When the snow melted, the Jews foreclosed.* If only John possessed Nia's money smarts. Nia had reaped and sown. Ambition (desire) was her biggest crop. She was not one to stand still and contemplate her accomplishments. She planned to open an upscale salon-agency downtown. She wanted Porsha to invest, become an equal partner.

Porsha could see lights and shadows moving about on the upper floor of the salon. Good. Nia was here. She tried to spot Nia's face in the window. Sometimes you could see her there in her office perch, where she leaned her elbows on the sill and sneered down into the street. *Come on. This is mine. Start something. Please start some shit.* It was the only window you could look in or out of. Nia had installed stained glass—shipped from the cathedral at Chutreaux (or Chartres or Notre Dame, one of them French places)—everywhere else. (Nothing about Nia was cheap.) You got to spend to earn, she liked to say. One day, she would retire and buy a beach house, a window opening on the ocean like an oyster, palm trees—full of fresh green coconut balls cuming white milk into her breakfast bowl—rising above egg-white sand, a yard with a dock, and a shed with two yachts.

The glass doors parted without Porsha having to touch them. *Welcome aboard. The captain will be with you shortly.* French tile formed a compass rose on the floor. A fountain threw a high musical rush of silvery water that fell in a constant spray into a marble basin fringed with violets and lilies. Copper and silver fish shimmered beneath the silver surface. The ceiling hummed music. Eastern? Caribbean? African?—Porsha couldn't say which. The walls carried the smell of Dallas's gasoline-laced 'Sippi moonshine. Nia had papered them with jungle scenes. Potted palms lined the halls. Nia had crowded the shop with objects from her travels around the world. Full-sized sculptures cast full-sized shadows: A puppy-sized jade bitch with mother-of-pearl teats and crystal eyes that she'd picked up in Mexico. An iron-rusted elephant from India. *The swami sold me some holy water from the Ganges River. He put a drop on my forehead and a drop on my tongue. You will have two sons, he said.* Slanted silver divi-divi trees (with the one hairstyle) pointing west from Aruba. *Follow the divi-divi and you'll never be lost. It will circle you back to your original departure. Departure is destination.* African masks followed you with hollow eyes. A framed encyclical (purchased from the Vatican) darted gilded light. Silk prayer rugs branched over the room. Japanese rice-paper paintings floated like flowers on water, shifting place and position even as you looked.

*This lil Jap guy called me a coon, Nia said.*

*What?*

*A coon.*

*You fo real?*

*Yeah. He said, So glad to neet you, Nia-coon. So I told him, You short-slanteyedjapmotherfucker, who you callin a coon? Don't you know that I'll kick yo puny ass? Then he said it again. Ah, Nia-coon. I'm sorry. Did I offend you?*

Spiral-legged tables held up bird-shaped Etruscan vases and Tunisian amphorae that erupted with roses so radiant and fresh they seemed artificial. Each reading table was centered with a handmade Navaho tablecloth from Santa Fe. Bubble-shaped hair dryers rumbled like space capsules, rockets. And a full bar where you could enjoy two drinks free on the house. (The third cost.)

Each beautician attended her client in a transparent receptacle, the cool shade of a hidden grove. The base of each chair was a genuine redwood stump. One client flipped through the latest issue of *Uplift*, hair done up like the Bride of Frankenstein. Porsha took the beauticians in at a single glance, without distinguishing one from the other. Tangiers, Archangel, Algiers, Baltimore, Tunis, Tripoli, London, Carthage, Mombasa, Fez, New York, Benghazi, Dublin, Suakin, Seville, Port-au-Prince, Seattle, Guinea, Messawa, Bahia, Zela, Kilwa, Hong Kong, Newport, Brava, Aden, Mina, San Francisco, Muscat, Cardiff, and Cape. Like one woman repeated many times. Each wore tiger-skin hot pants, halter, and sandals. Hair rose two feet above their heads and curved out into a huge anchor. For Nia's last birthday, they had all, Porsha included, chipped in and bought Nia a cake—the last thing she needed—a strawberry (her favorite) spaceship on a chocolate launching pad under a sprinkling of cherry stars.

Hey, Porsha.

She received a concert of glad welcomes and perfumed laughter from the beauticians. She answered them in chorus.

Porsha.

The sight of the beauticians and adornments made her eyes feel full.

How life treatin you?

Good.

I saw your mother today, Shaneequa, the captain, said.

The words flew behind her. She watched the pretty girl under a sailor's cap. Red cravat twisted in sailor fashion. Pen poised over the log. A butterfly fluttered over her back. Oh yeah? Nia in?

Shaneequa closed the log over the pen. You know where to find her.

Porsha nodded. She took the upward-rising stairs—the beak of a ship on a wave—two at a time.

The office door was parted. She would knock before she entered. Once she had thrown the door open to surprise Nia and caught her kneeling before some good-lookin brown. *The Bible say, Nia later said, Not that which goeth into the mouth defileth a man, but that which cometh out of the mouth.*

Men liked her. She often went the whole mile on the first date. And she had an educated pussy.

Knock knock, Porsha said. She pushed the door wide, not waiting for a response.

Nia sat before her desk, calm and monumental in the office light. Porsha, is that you? Nia raised her head—coils of yellow hair—sleep-heavy.

Nobody else. Porsha entered.

Nia's seat was arranged like the ideal house, everything in easy reach, including the globe—a replica of the world as Europe knew it at the time of Columbus's expedition to the New World, patterned with monsters, behemoths, sea dragons, and misplaced or missing continents and islands—that Porsha had given her for a birthday present many years ago (high school?). A bird could not ask for a better nest.

Girlfriend. Nia put a last piece of a sandwich into her mouth. *That girl been all over the world, Mamma said, but she never been further than the other side of a pork chop.* Mary Poppins. She rose up out of her seat. Pop up anytime. She forcefully approached, waves to the shore. Every part of her body danced. She sported snazzy palazzo pants. (Her designer was divine.) She always wore loose clothes—unlike some fat women who put on the tightest thing so the fabric stuck to every jellied curve—and her makeup was expertly handled.

The women hugged—Nia's body spanned the swaying fabric—and kissed.

Nia pushed Porsha to arm's length. Smoothed her clothes. She raised the lid on her cookie jar (from Nebraska) and peered into its depths. Like some tea?

No.

How bout a glass of sherry? Nia poured herself one.

Porsha laughed. I see you already had a few.

Nobody been drinkin no liquor. You ain't the police.

Porsha pulled a chair close to the desk. How life treatin you?

Workin like a bitch.

Heard that.

I left a message on your answering machine.

Girlfriend, we must be thinking on the same track.

Guess who came into the salon today?

Who?

Wanda.

That triflin bitch?

Girl, let me tell you, she started some shit with Seattle, and you know Seattle don't take no shit. A fool and her seat were soon parted.

What?

Yes she did. Seattle hauled off and slapped her.

No she didn't?

Yes she did.

I heard it all.

So how was yo day? Nia amused herself by cracking her joints in anticipation.

I went to see Inez.

How she doin?

Same ole same ole.

I see.

Porsha patted her hair. Can you do something bout these naps?

Let me see. Two fingers fluttered into Porsha's hair. Um huh. Jus like
I thought. Symptoms in yo hair. Go on over there and sit down in the
chair.

Porsha did as instructed. The high chair afforded a view of Church
Street. (She might have seen far without the obstructing trees.) Strange glass
rippled the world outside.

You just wash it?

No. I mean—

I can tell. What I tell you bout washing yo hair and going right outdoors?

Well, I—

Don't say a word.

Nia's black hands moved light and fast in her hair. *She can truly minister
to your scalp. Know how to make a head feel good.* I'll give you a few curls.

I like yours. But don't dye it.

Why not?

Girl, you know that ain't me. Porsha relaxed under Nia's exploring fingers. Her body sank deeper and deeper into the chair's warmth.

So how's Deathrow?

Porsha pushed the word out, no hesitation. Fine.

How come he ain't with you tonight?

The words washed from side to side in her mind. I don't know.

What you mean you don't know?

I don't know.

What, he actin a fool?

Did I say that?

The problem is you ain't said nothing.

You won't let me.

Thought yall was an item? Bout to make lil feet for shoes.

Porsha said nothing.

I see, you got a meat shortage. Girl, if you can't hold it in your hand, you can't hold it in your head.

It ain't that.

I tell you, men these days is jus too triflin. Pitiful niggas out here won't even give you a good fuck. I don't blame these prostitutes. You might as well get paid.

It ain't nothing sexual.

It ain't?

No.

Oh, I see. He can't keep his pants on? He found him some side meat.

Did I say that?

That's it, you can't keep yo man?

I don't know if I want to keep him.

Why not?

He ain't called. We was sposed to get together last night and I ain't heard from him.

Um huh, missing in action. I never did like Deathrow.

You never told me that. Porsha could recall only one complaint. She had told Nia about screwing Deathrow in Circle Park. Yall did it in the park? Nia said. You crazy. Even I wouldn't do it in the park, and at night too? A couple got shot there two nights ago.

He's not a man. He's a pair of pants.

You said you liked him.

Nia scrunched up her face. He's jus like Virgil.

Virgil?

You heard me.

Several months ago, Nia had phoned her, excited. Bring Deathrow over for dinner Sunday. We celebrating.

Celebrating what?

I found him.

Found who?

Virgil. He the best man ever wore shoes.

Aren't you lucky.

Sure. I need that dick.

Go slow.

I gotta have it. I'll retrieve it if he cut it off and toss it away. Like a dog fetching a stick.

Virgil was a yellow, snake-hipped man. Nia took his arm and put it about her waist. Porsha sighed inside. Recalled Uncle John's injunction against *pretty men*. They sat down to eat. Nia cooked a good meal—rabbit and snails, a recipe she'd picked up in Spain—though a bit spicy. (She cooked everything with hot peppers, even using the heat-containing seeds.)

What do you do, Virgil?

Nia answered for him. He's a preacher.

I also repair TVs, Virgil said. That's my van out there. Have a look.

Porsha parted the chintz curtains. A plain black van waited on the street.

I'm a journeyman repairman. Certified.

Nia crossed her knife and fork. Everybody ready for dessert?

Sure.

Nia served Trinidadian black cake.

Honey, can I make you a drink?

Thank you, baby.

Whiskey?

Why don't you know preachers don't drink whiskey? They drink gin.

Drinks in hand, the men retired to the living room to watch the basketball game. Virgil responded to Deathrow's every glowing comment about Flight Lesson with a routine, Yeah. *Virgil, Deathrow said, he kinda quiet.* The women spied on them from the kitchen, cleaning, looking, and talking. Porsha did most of the cleaning and Nia the talking. You shoulda seen it, scented rose petals floating around us. Red memory flickered in Nia's eyes. That was some bath.

Sounds like fun.

Fun ain't the word. I love Virgil. He makes me leave my body. And I think I make him leave his.

Porsha thought about it. Good in bed?

Heavens yes. He got sex organs everywhere. Like they say, You can't keep a good preacher down.

Porsha excused herself and went into the bathroom. She got down on her knees there on the bathroom floor—Portuguese cobblestone—and prayed that yellow Virgil wouldn't be the skinny straw to break the fat camel's back.


NIA RECRUITED PORSHA to help give some life to Virgil's apartment. Bare walls. Bare floors. Bare rooms. It would take longer to tell what was not in the house than what was in.


NIA AND VIRGIL vacationed in Mexico.

I had a wonderful time at Mardi Gras, Nia said. The men put the dog on this blanket and bounced it into the air.

That's cruel, Porsha said.

No it's not. Damn funny.

Cruel. Even though I can't stand pets.

Virgil didn't warm up to the country. *Never have liked Mexican food too much, Virgil said. Beans give me gas.* He didn't swim; he discovered that he was allergic to salt water. (It left him blind for hours at a time.) He refused to have his portrait painted. *Isn't it enough to be obliged to drag around the face God gave me?* And no photo contained the couple in the same frame.

Baby, Virgil said, I really like you. But could you move out the way. I really want to get a picture of that church.


NIA BUTTERFLIED HER WAY from wonder to wonder, but when she gave a man the boot, her decision was decisive, like running water, like rising light.

You crossed the line, Nia said. You better haul yo freight.

Why? Virgil said. You gon make me? I know you big. I know you look like a man, but you ain't a man.


NIA RECOUNTED THE WHOLE SAD STORY to Mamma.

Girl, Mamma said, what'd you expect? Preachers don't like yo type. Any gal can make a preacher lay his Bible down. But it takes a long, lean gal to keep him from picking it up again.


NIA AND PORSHA packed wine, cheese, and luau that Nia had prepared in a Spanish picnic basket, rented a little boat, and spent the entire day on Tar Lake alone—water slapping the sides of the boat, the boat moving not at all—watching the clouds and listening to the rippling of the waves, silent and listless.

Girl, Porsha said, I didn't know you knew how to sail.


SO WHAT YOU THINK?

Porsha faced the mirror. Her reflection bounced back. Girl, you know you can do some hair.

Good. You owe me.

What?

I'm going to the Silver Slipper soon as I freshen up. I want you to come with.

Porsha shook her head. I'm tired.

Why don't you jus come and have a good time.

Another time.

When either of them broke up with a man, Nia would take Porsha to the Silver Slipper, a dyke bar where they could dance freely without men hitting on them. Let the bull daggers flatter them and buy them drinks.

Let me see your hands.

Porsha extended her hands like a criminal awaiting the cop's cuffs.

Um huh, just as I suspected. You need to wear gloves. If you get the slightest nick—

My career will be over.

Sit down at my desk.

Porsha did as instructed.

Nia fetched her instruments from a Chinese Chippendale stand and carried them over to her desk. She pressed Porsha's fingers into two bowls—blue Chinese porcelain—of water to soak. An exquisite scent of detergent, olives, oil, and juice rose from the water. Nia removed one hand from the water, rested it on a cushion—light, a bird on a branch—and went to work.

I don't know why you won't take better care of your nails.

That's why I'm here.

Nia worked the file across Porsha's nails, bow to violin.

So, you gon start dating other people?

I don't know.

Why not?

I don't know.

Admit you wrong. You can't save yo face and yo ass too.

Porsha coughed a laugh or two.

What about that photographer?

Which one?

The cute one I met at that party.

Owl?

Uh huh.

Please.

He ain't your type?

Maybe he's yours.

Nia chuckled. I'd break that lil man. Look, next week I'm going to Angria. Why don't you—

You know I don't travel overseas.

That's why you turned down that job in France?

Yes, she had turned down the job, her first film offer, a chance to put her still body into hot motion. In fact, she had turned down all foreign assignments.

Girl, your taste buds broke. You lost the flavor of money.

No I haven't. I got expenses.

To win big, you got to take some chances. I learned that from the Jews. They are the last word in the game of smartness. Nia rose from the table and walked to her desk. She always had such advice. She kept a stack of Porsha's business cards on file at the shop and pitched Porsha to each and every client.

Forget Deathrow and take a trip with me.

I don't know.

Using all her might, Nia spun the ancient globe. So, girlfriend, where you want to go? The earth blurred in rapid motion. Nia let her finger ride lightly upon the whirling surface. Nia girdled the earth so fast she was everywhere at once. She always made double reservations on the slight chance that Porsha would travel with her. Nia would call her from some country and talk for hours on end about its wonders. (Nia was crazy like that.) She never sounded like herself, a stranger from another world. How about Toledo?

Ohio?

Not Ohio, Spain.

The globe slowed to a stop. Ah, Brazil.

That's not Brazil. There's no Brazil on that old globe. Porsha knew every country's size and shape.

Let's pretend. Wait till you seen those men in Brazil.

Only once in her life had Porsha pondered travel to Brazil. Porsha had looked up Brazil in her fourth-grade atlas of the Encyclopaedia Britannica. Six thousand miles from home and three time zones. She could walk there in fifty-four days if she didn't stop to eat or sleep. If she swam or walked across the ocean.

*Uncle John, teach me how to swim.*

*Sure, girl. Bout time you learned. Seen those babies swimming over there in Russia?*

*I ain't swimming there.*

*Where you gon swim?*

*To Brazil.*

You said half of them are fags.

No, I said bi. Gay or bi, they'll make you forget Deathrow.

You need to stop. Nia used every pretext to get Porsha out of the country.

Don't you need vaccinations?

Shots? Girl, you ain't going to the rain forest. Come on. Go with. Dare to know.

Not overseas.

Okay, where then?

She loved New York. Whenever she worked there, she took a room in the tallest hotel in midtown where she could watch the shadow-covered water towers. Night edges of the buildings. Lights. (Yes, the lights.) And off in the distance, the lit pyramid of the Chrysler Building. The Empire State like a steel ice-cream cone. Central Park, the city's green heart. Two rivers and an ocean, the water all one color until the light struck it.

Only a po rat got one hole to crawl in.

Are you going to do my nails or what?

Nia studied her for a moment. A sigh expanded her heavy breasts. She carried a deep wide bowl over to Porsha's chair and sat it before Porsha's feet. Then she seated herself on a low stool and put Porsha's feet in the water. Bursts of quivering ran up Porsha's legs.


NIA PAINTED PORSHA'S FINGERNAILS AND TOENAILS with garlic-laced polish. Okay, put them in the machine.

On bulrush sandals Porsha skied over to the machine (from South Korea). Placed her hands and feet in what looked like two bread boxes joined at precise distance, hands to feet, by a lamp pole. The machine dried her nails instantly. She checked the results. Her fingers and toes flashed like ten red moons. Thanks, she said.

Don't mention it. Nia freshened her drink and looked out the window. You gon go all the way back home?

I'll get a cab.

Ain't you had enough for one day? I'm telling, not asking. Nia's profile was full of authority.

Porsha admitted it to herself. Yes.

Here, lie down. Nia motioned to the office's chaise longue.

Minute-scarred, Porsha reclined on the cool leather.

Nia lowered the blinds. Closed them. Killed the lights. Filled the room with black.

I need some light.

Nia put the lights on, dim. She floated up and placed herself before Porsha, direct and uncompromising. Here. Behind black bars of fluted light, Nia held out a cup to her.

She took the warm cup.

It'll help you sleep.

Thanks. She sipped the tea. Concentrated on it, the heat flowing down her throat, the sweetness of the sugar.

Well, I'll see you in the morning. Smoke-black, Nia swayed above her, suspended, sustained.

Don't stay out too late.

You know me. Nia turned to leave the room.

You still going Sunday?

Nia stopped as if Porsha had hit her. Sunday?

You know, the Great Awakening.

Nia said nothing.

You won't even have to drive. The Arkmobile would pick them up—Porsha, Nia (and Deathrow?)—advance paid.

I'll let you know. Nia quit the room, tossing her body.

Porsha tried to rise but fatigue had nailed her to the chaise longue. Thick shadows warmed her blanket-like.

Moonlight struggled through the closed blinds. The blinds formed a net that caught all of the night's light. A luminous raft, the chaise longue floated. The moon dripped away in blood. If night held its course, stretched long and quiet, she would rest. Forget all her body's deeds.

*She kicked off her leather sandals and felt the warm sand on the soles of her feet. A sailboat rocked close to the coast. They walked along the sand with buckets, gathering treasures left by silvered waves on wet sand: coral, shells, starfish, bits of polished wood. The beach's curve wound from the open sea to the bay's half-moon, dotted with slow sails. And the sea itself, still and vast, a green plain.*

*The yacht moved slowly out of the bay. He watched her from the cabin's depths. The motor kicked loud and waves opened before them in divided crests of spray. She looked across the yacht's rail. The distant coast made a shimmering reflection of itself in the heat waves above it. He pointed. There, down there. She leaned over the rail. The coral waves of a sunken galleon swam into focus. Tonight, she would offer him her experienced hands and mouth.*

# 26

How Elsa doing?

I was sposed to see her yesterday.

You didn't?

Hatch shook his head.

So why didn't you?

Hatch sucked the missile, let fumes crowd his mouth.

So what's up?

Nothing. Let the smoke seep into his chest. Guided the hot missile into Abu's hands. Abu sucked deep. Left gray jet trails in his mother's night-darkened living room.

Ain't she gon go to the concert with us on Sunday?

I don't know.

So when will I get to meet her?

Hatch fanned his hands, propelling smoke through the open window. Soon

Soon?

Soon.

She that ugly? Bowwow?

Man, just bust that tape.

Abu clicked in Spin's new tape, *Hip Hoptaplomeres.* Shadows trembled, greyhounds awaiting release. Sound gradually filled the hollow speakers, water in a tub.

I really meant to pick up those tickets yesterday, Hatch said, but, like I said, I got tied up at my grandmother's house.

Why didn't you get them today?

I didn't feel like doing nothing. I was like, Let me jus chill.

Well— Abu toked. It's all good. We can get them tomorrow. He passed Hatch the hot joint. Who sposed to open fo Spin?

Goy Boys. Hatch sucked to the depths of his lungs. The joint was a proboscis drawing in the smoky night. Smoke lifted, forgot the joint from which it ascended.

Goy Boys?
Yeah, you know. That Jewish crew.
Ain't what I heard.
Well, that's what the ad said.
Heard it sposed to be Southern Cross.
Them born-again rednecks?
Abu nodded.
No way. You heard wrong.
Abu curled his legs in, Buddha-fashion. He formed a pyramid of rising fat. How you know?
I know.
I know this, whoever gon open, they gon be live.
Word.
Spin don't associate wit no busters.
Word.
And you know he can flow.
Way above the top.
You know Spin.
Hatch did. From the first flash of consciousness, he had consumed a daily staple of stories about the Hairtrigger Boys—Uncle John, Spokesman, and Spin—tales that sweetened his ears by day and nurtured his dreams at night. A year ago, Spin's *Noosepapers* had made it into the top ten. Accompanied by his military crew FNG (Fucking New Guy), Spin toured and twisted the world. Opportunity darted across Hatch's vision. Hatch decided to reacquaint himself with Spokesman. (How long had it been?) *Spokesman. The one on whom nothing is lost. You could ask him anything and he'd answer you, cause he spent all of his time in book and knowledge joints: the Woodson Library, the Museum of Science and Industry, the Field Museum, the Biblical Conservatory, the Cultural Center, the Shell Aquarium, the Armory Museum, the Planetarium.* Uncle John drove him to Symmes Electronics—in the Underground—where Spokesman worked. *Why you wanna see Spokesman after all these years? Uncle John said. His face was perfectly clear, sharp and defined.* Spokesman was bald as a thimble and just as bright. Through walrus teeth, he talked, half laughing, with money in his voice.

Spokesman discussed the almanac he had been working on the past four or five years, writing and rewriting the same ephemeris over and over again. (In bulging, badly packed envelopes, he mailed Uncle John, Lucifer, and Spin samples of his sweat-stained words.)

Scared or not, anxious or not, the electric air made Hatch light-headed. His head balloon-bobbed. Hey, he said, you heard from Spin?

Spokesman drew his head back, as if lip-deep in shit.

Music sawed the silence in half. Moved in the room with them, between and beyond.

> Let us cross over the river and rest under the shade of the trees
> Be born again in our BVDs

Turn it up, Hatch said. I can't hear it.

Abu turned it up.

> I am an Antichrist
> I am an Antichrist

That's blasphemous, Abu said. He clapped his palms over his ears.

> Don't know what I want
> But I know how to get it

Stop actin like a Christian, Hatch said.

I am a Christian.

I know. Hatch knew. Abu was a son of the church.

> Went to the river to be baptized
> Stepped on a root and got capsized
> The river was deep and the preacher was weak
> So (hear me, nigger!) I'm Walt Whitman with an AK-47
> I went to seventh heaven at eleven from
> the bottom of the goddamn creek geek

Always trying to be sarcastic, Abu said.

Hatch didn't answer. In the dark, sitting apart, Abu was no more to him than a voice.

Air spun into itself. Blinds sucked in and out by an open breeze. Dusky windows like sluggish eyes. The room blue-glowed, Mrs. Harris's China luminescent in the dark.

Hatch took a hit and passed Abu the joint. Abu accepted it with one hand, the second hand guarding his chaste ear.

Hatch lay back on the floor. Hard floor planks pushed wood hands through the Persian rug and against his back. Iron fibers raked his neck. Yes, once plush, this Persian rug was now tattered and rough. When Mrs. Harris gon buy a new one? Here, years earlier, Hatch and Abu had wrestled —

Hatch had the physical advantage, his height and strength making Abu's limbs and skin elastic, and always won in a matter of seconds—when they had free run of the house. The Persian rug magic-carpeted them through every room of Mrs. Harris's house, bumping into this item and crashing into that one. They would hear Mrs. Harris banging clusters of keys outside the front door—her WELCOME mat greeted all visitors at the back door, where she made everyone, including Mr. Harris, enter to prevent them from tracking mud or dirt on her Persian rug—and they would smooth the rug in seconds flat. Caught, they would flee the wings of Mrs. Harris's fluttering hands.

Abu, hear that? Hatch's fingers popped the song's beat. It'll fit right in with our new mix, Eve of Adam's Destruction.

I don't know if I'm down wit that mix. Abu toked—the tip glowed red—in his parents' absence. Bathroom attendants, they worked nights downtown, shining shoes and passing out towels and cologne for heavy tips. Abu passed Hatch the joint like the Olympic torch.

Jus listen. It's only a song. Stop being such a Christian.

I am a Christian. Abu wiggled his chimpanzee ears.

Well, least you ain't one of them Muslims. Knocking yo fohead against the ground a hundred times a day. Hatch stubbed out the joint in the Persian rug. There, now she would have to buy a new one. He looked at Abu with Uncle John's eyes, a measuring look. (This always reduced him.)

Abu turned away.

Hear that beat in between the beat? The words rose above Hatch's face and drifted into Abu's space. The words watched Abu, fat, earthbound.

I hear it.

Ah, if he would only *listen*. One might as well plow a field with butterfly wings as try to teach him music. His fat seemed unfit for molding. Hatch had turned him on to jazz. Funny cause back in the day, Hatch and Abu would trip on Mr. Harris's listening to his jazz. In his den, Abu's father kept the largest collection of jazz records Hatch had ever seen. Decks and decks of them. Perfect for the mixes. Cave after cave of albums to dig through and explore. Hatch and Abu would spy through the den peephole, see Mr. Harris sitting between the decks—his skinny insectlike head bowed, his eyes closed—rocking to the sounds.

Didn't they play that one in *The Flintstones*?

Nawl. *Mr. Magoo*.

Nawl. *Mannix*.

Nawl. That was *Plan Nine from Outer Space*.

They would laugh until their bellies hurt.

Did you hear what I said? Abu said.

Learn something about chords.

Why? I'm a drummer.

Forget it. Why explain? What was the use? Hatch was tired of carrying Abu on the cuff. When they had both played clarinet—Mr. Stingley, the red-faced band teacher, wouldn't allow a drum or guitar in his band; *This is a marching band; you should be able to handle that one clarinet. When I was a boy, we had four. A, B-flat, C, and E-flat*—in the school band, Mr. Stingley had to keep at Abu. Abu, what note is that? A quarter note? Then why are you playing a half? Mr. Stingley stood above Abu and struck his own leg with his plastic baton to the rhythm of the score. *Camptown Races?*

I should kick you to the curb and make that move to New York, Hatch said. Leave yo ass here.

Go on then. You jus talkin shit.

Try me.

The music gushed and bumped and hissed.

Ain't Uncle John jus go to New York?

Nawl, Washington. To stop the war. Then he sposed to swing through New York and holler at Spin.

Wish we was opening for Spin Sunday.

Word.

Maybe Uncle John could hook us up.

Look, Hatch said, my Uncle John ain't no messenger boy.

Abu watched Hatch, swaying a little. I ain't say he is. That don't mean he can't put in a good word or two. Won't cost him nothing.

And it don't cost nothing to take a shit either.

Abu's breath came out straight and sharp.

In the dark, on the floor, Hatch guarded his secret hope: Uncle John will put in a good word or two—hell, a whole library of praise—and Spin will be the Jawbone to break Hatch into the business. *Hallelujah!*

I seen some of his new video.

Ain't it the hype?

Way above the top.

*Spin's henna-painted face red-blinks in and out of focus. Congeals into a dotted map of gook hearts.*

Slammin.

> *This is Spin and I'm back again like the wind*
> *Cause I'm in my sin my friend and then*
> *If you want to go far, square, somewhere*
> *Get out of your punk ass chair (on the dare)*
> *Word, I'm gon put something cool in the air*

Hatch listened to the music that swelled the speaker, listening but not hearing. *Words is like spots on dice. No matter how you roll em, there's times when they won't come.* Carried Spin's words like a captured bird. Birthed his own rhyme.

> *This is Genuine Draft*
> *Master of graft and craft.*
> *I'm blowing on and on and on (won't stop)*
> *Step to me wrong, strong*
> *You get shot and end up in a Ziploc*

Damn, Abu said. What's up with that?
Something wrong?
Yeah, something is wrong.
You don't like my rhyme?
Nigga, you stole it. You stealin.
Stealin? Hatch said. No. Spin's words *traveled* to me. He nodded to the sea's sound.
Traveled?
Yes, traveled. Long ago, Hatch had faced the ugly truth that he couldn't sing. Though he savored each note twice, the words came out bitter-tasting. His recorded voice never sounded like himself—thin, a sewing string vainly attempting to vibrate sound—how he heard himself *inside*.

> *Redball, don't resist (pump yo fist and twist)*
> *It's on, I'm kicking up a storm like a communist*

So he studied Spin's music, made mental pictures of each song. Words came. Phrases came. Visions came. He learned to sketch the thing itself before it was a thing. Travel inside himself and discover secrets in the silence.
You stealin. Plain and simple. False prophets follow heavy on the heels of true prophets.
Now you gon church me?
Maybe you need some church.
The smooth, clear music moved on undisturbed, waterlike.
Put in our tape, Hatch said.
Abu squelched Spin's song. He clicked in the requested tape. Third Rail.
Now, new music rose, an unexpected match flaring up in the dark. Abu point-blank on the wheels of steel, backtracking the whacked, doctoring measured doses of beats. Both hands buck wild on two turntables, working the discs in opposite directions. Telescopic grooves. (Yes, Hatch had pro-

duced the mix—looped it to tape—and Abu cut it.) Ah, here was the next song. Abu's hands flickered once or twice, then died. His rhythms fell away from the fullness of the song. A scratched record, repeating the same beat, jumping on the same groove, no mix no mission. *Listen to your heart. No. Not like that. Listen to your heart.* Notes floated, aimless, chaotic. *It's like exercise. The heart changes. That beat in between the beat. Fast, then slow. Fast. Fast. Slow. Fast. Slow.* Hatch's ear strained to bring the pieces together.

You hear that?

Hear what? Abu said.

That.

Abu said nothing.

Can you play it?

Abu breathed in the darkness.

*Abu? What are you playing? Mr. Stingley said.*

*Nothing, sir.*

*Nothing? I can see that. I can hear it too. My ears are too old for this.*

*Sorry, sir.*

*Notes of the same key respond to each other.*

*Yes, sir.*

*And if you wet your reed you will blow better. You can't blow anything with a dry reed.*

*Can't I jus bend it?*

*Bend it? Wet it! What do you think I've been saying to you? I must be talking for my health. You can't play anything with a rigid reed. Can't I bend it? What is Mr. Nelson teaching you in that science class? Nothing in the universe is perfectly rigid.*

You jus think you better than me cause you had more theory.

Theory? Nigga, I read the same books you do. Indeed, they shared books, creasing a page with two sets of thumbprints. *We were here!* Folded both page corners (top and bottom), two dog ears for double listening.

So. You read more.

No, that's not the problem. See, you need an eye single to the music.

Don't try to sound smart. You had more instruction.

Not as much as you. Abu had trained under the most refined drum teachers.

You had *better* instruction.

Memory sounds in the slowness of the pause. Ripens to red visions.

Hatch's one guitar teacher had been Hank Hazlett. *Listen and bounce it back.* Hank taught Hatch the basics. *See that's your tonic, your dominant, and your subdominant. Music got to have that or it won't swing.*

*Okay.*

*And when you bend a note, you try to hit the notes that ain't there, the missing notes of the scale. That's the blues.*

*How'd it get up here? I mean, the blues, how'd it get all the way up here?*

*The music followed us here. Cause the 'Sippi River ain't nothing but one long guitar string.* Hank was an old man. A belt of white hair circled his head, squeezed out wrinkles in his face and neck. He had led a trio in his short career as a professional musician—

*We played our first gig downtown . . . a Chinese restaurant.*

*What?*

*Baby, them chinks love them some jazz.*

—and harbored a trunkful of stories.

*But I was talkin about the junkies. Baby, most of them cats were junkies. Hank leaned in close and put distance between the words and his wife's pious ears. And H makes you all constipated. Imagine Trane digging up his crack, trying to pull out a rock-hard lump of doo-doo.*

*Ah, man.*

*And thieves. H makes you steal. Bird would steal your mamma's draws, brown stains and all. Steal the flea collar off a dog's neck. Bird only looked after himself. He used to say, This is a solo flight and you may take no one with you. Talkin in that phony British accent.*

*I never heard nothing bout that.*

*Had to put on airs cause that H had taken everything else he had. Why you think he played a plastic horn?*

*Creative. He wanted to be—*

*Miles used to have to loan him a suit to play in. Skinny old Miles and fat old Bird. You know he was lookin silly. Sleeves too short and flood-high pants. But Miles took the H train too. And you know Bird and Miles were sissies.*

*Come on, Hank. I know Miles was on the H. But I never heard—*

*H, horn—he and Bird would toot anything, if you know what I mean.*

*Hank—*

*H brings out the fag in you. Make you do things you wouldn normally do.*

*Hank—*

*And Billie, you know she was a mess. She would kiss a roach for a quick fix. And she would eat anything for a buck. And I do mean anything. The joke was, she had sensitive teeth. Get it? Sensitive. S-i-n. Sen-sen.*

Hatch laughed, belly-hard. Then his laugh caught in the mitt of his throat. He spoke to himself: *I shouldn't be laughin about Billie, Lady Day. Show some respect,* he told himself. *Respect. R-e-s-p-e-c-t.*

*And she had this little dog named Melody.* Billie'd come in the club and sit down at the bar with a stiff drink—*you know how that alcohol ate up her voice. Used to sing so sweet. Billie's bounce. Well, she come into the club and sit down at the bar with a stiff drink and spread her legs. She never wore no draws. That dog start to lickin her and lickin her like greasy chicken.*

Hatch shook his head. *Now, why'd you want to tell me something like that? Hank, you talkin bout Lady Day, man, Lady Day!*

*By the way, she didn't like to be called Lady. (Prez called her Mamma. Bless his soul.) She said, Lady, that's the name for a dog.*

The pinnacle of his career, Hank shook hands with Charlie Christian. *Yeah, we were workin this gig and Charlie came in as we were leaving. Ole Charlie was tough. Lots of cats used to copy his style. Convert their style to co-incide with his.*

After Hank gave up the life, he put in thirty years at a paint factory. *I played a gig here and there. Man, I used to work with all those cats when they came to town. Prez, Monk, Bird, Miles, Trane—I used to buy all those guys hot dogs. I still can't understand it. Why do a guy want to be a junky to play a horn? a guitar? That's why I gave it up in 1945. I was afraid to go on the road.* The paint had wrecked his body. He stood reed-thin, knees squeezed together like a girl needing to pee. Took him ten minutes to quit a room.

Face to face with Hank, Hatch's mind often drifted, trying to image two persons in one, the young Hank, the hepcat—cuff-linked shirt, suspenders, painted tie, patent-leather kicks, and a sky red as autumn day—in the old Hank. The language was there—*I had this long cord. The longest in the world. Made it myself. I'd leave the stage and go table to table, running riffs and hustlin in tips. On Sunday nights we'd go down to Lamb's Cafe when the symphonic session was on. We going to church. But most nights the cats hung out at the Red Onion. The P.I.'s wore these big diamonds, big as dimes. Seen a few bigger than a quarter. And the hot women wit those big behinds. That was the place for cats to jam. But people wasn't paying much mind to what was happening onstage. Then the cats in the band would start to mess up. I used to ride the drummer for not playin the sock cymbal on the afterbeat. Mop-a! Like that. Mop-a*—but the flesh was long gone.

His wife, a yellow woman with a healthy wave of straight hair—*Used to be fine in her day. Wish I had known her when she was eighteen*—often inter-rupted a lesson. Hank, ain't you tired? You know you need your rest.

Mary, wait. Hatch pay his five dollars for thirty minutes. His time ain't up yet.

She was a follower of the New Cotton Rivers—*Hatch, why don't you come to church with us Sunday. Sky Church (the closed-circuit temple) is in a re-fined neighborhood*—and would often shout biblical curses.

Each week, Hank showed Hatch the same two tunes, Red Top and Take

Five. *Music ain't nothing but mathematics. Play chromatics, scales, that kind of stuff. The theory part. You know what I mean?* Week after week, Hatch improvised on the changes, missing riffs and hitting wrong notes. *That's okay. Coltrane said there ain't no wrong notes. Play sharp fives, flatted fifths, ninths, whatever.*

One day, Hatch played the tunes, blew the changes, paid Hank five dollars, took back the Trane albums he'd loaned Hank, waved Hank farewell, and shut the door firmly behind him.


PUT SPIN'S TAPE BACK IN, Hatch said. Take that shit out. His ears were exhausted from Abu's raw beat dragging the music —*that I wrote, that I produced*— down in its flow.

Abu killed the music instantly, fingers pinching out a live match. He slapped in Spin's tape. There. You happy!

Hatch made no reply. He shut his eyes. The speaker extended out of itself, slowly, gradually, sail-like. Sound approached, a distant train, faint, humming. Reached him in the darkness. Motion touched every cell of his body. He entered the blackness and found a space inside the accelerating music.

*The lane went straight beneath the moon — the sky thick with stars, blurring the constellations on the rare chance that you could identify them — boarded on each side by shadow-thick trees, the branches like thick black cords, weighted under the heavy moon. Yes, tunnels of trees rose in night's full leaf. You tried to feel with your feet as you walked. Paths first pale then invisible in the moonlight, felt rather than seen. Paths uneven as lumpy scars beneath your feet. (And after a rain, muddy potholes stewed booted feet.) Only Mr. Baron had the gift — this Peruvian Indian, adopted by German-American parents when but an infant, ever-present under his ridge-high Smokey the Bear hat (campaign hat, he called it), with his ever-present knife-straight tie, dark green to match the light green of his uniform. The only one who could negotiate the dark, the only one who knew the path without hesitation. The troop was guided by the compass of his eyes. It's his Indian blood, they thought — he had that Indian-black hair, pomaded to keep it from blowing wild in the wind like a smoke signal; and he was short like most Indians but packed in white skin; when you thought Indian you thought red, least Pappa Simmons's yellow-red skin in Porsha's photographic words; the handlebar mustache also refused the word Indian; and he preferred a sleeping bag to a swinging, swinging hammock, though once or twice you saw him nap on the hard forest floor — stumbling, stretching out their direction-seeking arms like blind men.*
Sang:

Genuine Draft and aft to adapt
and wield with musical skill
a rhythmical staff
to beat the shit out of these red beets
and make you stomp yo goddam feets, chief

Saturday night. Tents arranged around the center of the camp where a fire burned. Each tent sat on a wooden platform, raftlike, and inside the tent, two rusty coffee cans, one filled with water, the other sand. Abu loved building the fire more than the fire itself. He collected more twigs of dead wood, dry brush, and grass than any other Scout. Built a house of wood on a foundation of four thick logs. You loved the fire. Quiet and dark. Explosions of dry rhythmic crackling rose in the dark through the black sky. And leaping flames that preceded the invading heat. Warmth and light. The troop sat in a circle on the ground, arms around knees pulling them close to the chest and drawing the circle tighter. Eating hot dogs and marshmallows flavored with smoke and grit. You felt the cool knees of the Scout next to you. Caught the pulse. Around the breathing body—red veins of smoke bleeding the night—someone issued the call, struck double syllabled song for the rankin session to begin.

A ding dong dong dong dong
A ding dong dong dong dong
A ding dong
  Abu sho got some ugly teeth
A ding dong
  Brush em wit his ugly feet
A ding dong dong dong dong
A ding dong dong dong dong
A ding dong
  Hatch got some nappy hair
A ding dong
  Brush it with his dirty underwear

That was Stumpy's favorite song, Mr. Baron said.
Stumpy?
You saw Stumpy in the slim shadow of a tree trunk. You prodded the fire with a stick, roused clouds of soft brilliant sparks that sailed up into darkness. Stumpy melted in bark. Everybody in the camp knew the legend of Stumpy, but Mr. Baron spoke history, made him present, reminded the troop of the Scout who had lost his left arm under the accidental ax of a fellow Scout. For the last forty years, Stumpy had haunted Owassippee, choosing opportune

moments to dismember Scouts with his double-headed ax, or freeze the red fearful blood in their hearts with his red eyes. Mr. Baron told the story to tenderfoot ears, novices.

Stumpy soared in the dim blue night air above the smoke.

Where does Stumpy live? Where does he live? The forest is his house.

You kicked the fire into blaze. The great red light strove and burst the sky aflame. Fire chased away the cold.

Platoon Leader Jones, Mr. Baron said.

Yes, sir? you said.

Are you trying to burn down the forest?

No, sir.

You let the fire die down. Cheeks puffed out, you had only to blow on the ashes where the pile of red sparks waited. Above the forest, Stumpy watched Owassippee, where flickering campfires shone like vast unsteady stars along the horizon.

Platoon Leader Jones, Mr. Baron said.

Yes, sir?

Keep charge. I have a meeting in the mess hall.

Yes, sir.

Mr. Baron lifted off of his haunches. The forest swallowed him.

Harris, you said.

Yes, Abu said.

Tend the fire.

Okay. Abu knelt down beside the fire, stick in hand.

The logs burned slowly with hot, invisible flames. The fire burned for warmth—Abu added dead limbs when ordered—firelight on faces.

Ding dong dong dong dong, you sang.

A ding—

You hear that!

Yeah!

What was it?

Nothing.

It came from the woods.

Can you see anything?

No.

Make the fire brighter.

Yeah, make the fire brighter.

Abu made the fire brighter.

The troop draws out their knives. Whittle chips of wood, until the wood runs out. Whittle chips of song, until the song runs out. Chips of shadow, un-

*til the shadows run out. Chips of moon, until the moon runs out. And then,
sliver by sliver, Stumpy's dark body forms.*

*Look! Stumpy!*

*Help!*

*Night wafts in. And wind fans the fire. A red flame crawls out from under
the white coals. Stumpy breaks through the comouflage of smoke.*

Eyes closed, Hatch was better able to contemplate the entire course of his
life. Abu had been there for most of it. Their years were one. Shadow of
time. Shadow of blood. Morning and night, minute and month ran shape-
lessly together, the days rolling steadily beneath them, kith and kin.

MY NAME ABU. What's your name?

Hatch.

Glad to meet you.

Hatch says nothing. He is not glad.

Where you live? The roly-poly boy with a soda-stained red clown mouth
asks.

On Seventy-second Street between Constance and Bennett.

Hey, I live right round the corner from you.

*Why he speaking to me? Why did he choose me? I don't need nobody to
play wit.*

Yall live in a house?

No. A part ment. We got mice too.

Yall got mice?

Yeah. Do yall?

Yeah. You better watch out. Them mice grow into rats.

Damn you stupid. Don't you know nothing? Mice ain't no rats. They a
different species.

Oh.

Hatch looks Abu over, needing bigger eyes to sight fully his fat. What's
that you wearin?

My uniform.

Uniform?

Uh huh.

You in ROTC or something?

Nawl. Kids can't be in no ROTC. My dad was. I'm a Scout.

A what?

A Cub Scout?

That like a Boy Scout?

Yeah. And Weblos. Cept we little kids and they big.

Okay.

You want to become a Scout? Join my pack? Pack Five Hundred.

What's a pack?

A group of bears.

Bears?

Baby bears.

Hatch thinks about it. Abu does look something like a baby bear. What I get if I join?

We go on trips, make fires, learn how to use a compass, recite our oath, go—

Is that all?

Abu watches Hatch for a moment. Well, my mother a den mother.

A what?

A den mother. And we have lots of fun. We—

Do I get to wear a uniform like that?

Yeah, but yo parents gotta buy it.

Sheila buys it. Stitches yellow square numbers (500) into the blue khaki shirt, her needle musical in the cloth, a baton calling forth rhythm from the yellow square keys. She starches and irons the shirt. Starches and irons the crisp blue pants. Buys and blocks the half-globe blue baseball cap. Buys the yellow kerchief and shows you how to roll two corners into tight pigtail braids so that the remaining corners form a neat triangle—a bear cub centered inside it—beneath your nape. Slides on the kerchief holder. Polishes your best black shoes.

Uncle John! Uncle John! I'm a Scout.

What?

A Cub Scout of America. How you like my uniform?

ABU BOWS HIS HEAD at the sound of thunder, clasps his hands at clapping lightning, shuts his eyes at the sight of televised floods, and fears a tornado in every wind. He forms a steeple with his fingers, then whispers a prayer over his hamburger and french fries. He performs a slow order of dutiful chores. Mrs. Harris (mother and den mother) gives him permission to play. Abu and Hatch spill out Hatch's collection of Hot Wheels cars—I only play with the best; they like real cars, like my Uncle John's—roll them over rugs, under tables, up walls and banisters, down noisy pipes. They make tow trucks of their hands—*We can pull them anywhere*—and motors of their mouths. *Rrrrr rrrrrr.* They puzzle over scale-detailed trains. They spend hours of bent concentration constructing model tanks, battleships, and airplanes, military and civilian. Battle monsters (Godzilla, King Kong, Dracula, the Werewolf) against Superheroes (the Hulk, the Iron Man, Spiderman). Then they pit skills. Abu beats Hatch at checkers. Hatch can sense no strategy in the game and blindly moves the plastic discs from one black square to another. But he beats Abu at chess, game after game, hour upon hour—*Look, Hatch. We don't stop playing until I win a game*—and always under twenty moves.

*Who taught you how to play?*
*My Uncle John.*

They wear serious faces, masks, as they move the chess pieces. Hatch remains silent, focused on the magic of the unspeakable. He absorbs the plastic power of each piece. The pieces flow mobile with a self-determined plan and will. His hand moves knifelike, cutting patterns.

Abu, Uncle John says. His eyeglasses are like flying saucers, high and still, reflecting over the entire position of the board. Move your rook to—

Stop kibitzin, Uncle John! You jus mad that I beat you.
*Uncle John, who taught you how to play?*
*Spokesman. He says it's based on medieval warfare.*
*Spokesman knows everything.*
Well, who taught you how to play the game?
You did.
Don't forget it.


HATCH AND ABU walk far and fast—Hatch leads the way with a firm military step—until one or the other (usually Abu) says, I quit. They discover a place so far away that it has no name. Grass, trees—the place breathes green. The ground slopes down into a deeper green, an area entirely shaded from the sun where you can pick patches of sunlight from grass beneath an oak tree. Lie and read. White water flows down over clean black stones. Fill your empty canteen with the clean-tasting water. The river glows with the full benefit of the sun's rays, down to the stones shining like jewels. Birds and fish move in a single stream. Sunlight skims the waves; the water flashes like a buckle. You imagine it the sea, crimson as fire, and the patch of land at its center, an island retreat. You touch the water, and it replies, Yes. No matter how much or how far you walk you will never find where it begins or ends. At one point, it spills white steam against the surrounding rock—you toss a stone and listen to it plunge roaring into a black watery pit—rising yet somehow still, breath set in steel.

Wet, they sit in a dry space against a tree. The sun soon follows. Makes a square patch on the bark. Dissolves in your thoughts.

Say, you say, man is the measure of all things.

What?

Jus say, I hate God.

Don't say that, Abu says.

I repeat, say, I hate God. You speak in a place where you can wrestle with your shadow and never lay hold of it.

No, Abu says.

Afraid?

You don't believe in God?

No. Why should I? He does terrible things. *Why would he let Cookie deform and die? Kill Nap? Kill R.L.? Chop off Sam's leg?* If God exists—you poke out your chest—let him strike me dead.

You better not say that. Abu scoots away from you.

We are dwarfs on the shoulders of gods, you say. The words roll across the surface of your tongue. Words you had discovered in your wide reading. We can see farther into the distance than our parents and grandparents could see. Wise up.


DOWN DOWN IN WEST MEMPHIS, Lula Mae rewards you with a present, a sunburst Sears, Roebuck guitar.

*You doing good in school, Lula Mae said.*

*Well. I'm doing well.*

*But I hear yo math ain't too good. Strive to put the bottom rail on top.*

The train ride home, you sit the guitar in the seat beside you—*Red, move outa the way. Sit back there. And keep yo hands off it: it ain't no toy*—and touch it like a friend. Home, you perch on the edge of your bed. Slant the guitar across your body. Brush the elevator-cable-thick strings but barely raise a note. Hit it harder, Jesus says. You hit it harder, give all six strings— you counted them—a firm karate chop. The hollow body echoes a sound like a rake scraping concrete. Damn! Jesus laughs. Hit it another way, he says. You do. And this way and that way and the other. In the days that follow, your novice fingers grope for the dark strings at every opportunity. You hit them again and again, determined to produce the sounds inside your head. The strings become necessary, loud blood flowing through six red veins. *Even today, your hands will sweat when you don't or can't touch them.* You climb inside the deep dark well of the guitar and gaze silently about. Sound and sight enter from a bright world far away. Hours pass. Then you hear footsteps approaching from down the hall. You hide the guitar in the cave under your bed. Sheila throws the door open to the sound of your musical snoring.

*Dear Lula Mae,*
*I am well. I got one tooth out the chair fell on it. I want to see you. I got the*
*book you sint. Sheila read too stories in it. I still got the guitar. I like them*
*when I coming to see you again?*
*Love Hatch*

At the first opportunity, you lug your guitar to school for show-and-tell. (It was either the guitar or your chameleon, Dogma.)
*Where you get that guitar?*
*Down South.*
*Down South?*
*Yeah. Down South. My grandmother gave it to me.*
*What she doin down South?*
*She live there. You ain't never been down South?*
*Nawl. I'm from here.*
At the next show-and-tell, Abu presents a drum set to the class—*Copycat! Monkey see, monkey do*—the price tag still attached. *I can play music too.* A full set, not the kit with a single planet of drum, but the whole bright constellation of cymbals, tom-toms, cowbells, snare, and bass traps.

*Dear Hatch,*
*Be a good boy. Don't aggravate your mamma. Racket and confusion her.*
*Learn to play that thing. And jump at the sun.*
*Love your grandmother*
*Lula Mae*

You lug your guitar over to Abu's house. Mrs. Harris puts the two of you in the basement and shuts the door.
*What we gon call our group?*
*Third Rail.*
At home in your room, you continue to practice. You finger notes and miss them. Fingers snap off strings, soundless. Try again. Fingers jump back, riff-ready. Switch to the right track. Gradually—seconds, minutes, hours, days, weeks, months—you begin to *hear* it for the first time. Records are black seeds which sprout musical trees. You hack through foliage. Perched birds sing on six twanging limbs.

SO YOU PLAY GUITAR? Uncle John asks.
Yeah.
Bet you ain't never heard Jimi?

Jimi who?

Listen. Uncle John spins the record.

Sound surprises. You hear a guitarist who is also an orchestra. One man who is six. Oak, cherry, redwood, pine, rosewood, mahogany—six limbs bunched in a single trunk of sound.

Hear that? you say to Abu.

Hear what?

I gotta learn how to play like that.

What? Hear what?

MRS. HARRIS (Geraldine you call her—behind her back) leans over the church piano, her fingers spread web-wide on the keys.

> A *little gold in the church*
> A *prayer in the name*

Her round, flat, black skillet face shows no movement, a black dot of musical notation. Choir-robe sleeves rolled up, her hands run slow across the ivory tracks.

> *I got fiery fingers. I got fiery hands.*
> *And when I get up to heaven, I'm gon play in that fiery band.*

She mixes sin and syncopation, tongue hanging out the side of her mouth, music-thirsty. She keeps a glass of water on the piano but never drinks it. Holy water? She bangs heavy chords. She is a grinder, not a tickler.

Reverend Ransom constructs three-hour sermons to shore up the frailty of his voice. He can't make print crackle into life. Weak, lengthy sermons that fail to rise above the gold-edged page, to flutter about the congregation's head and bother them to rise. *Though ye have lain among the sheepfolks, yet shall ye be as the wings of a dove that is covered with silver wings, and her feathers like gold.* Sermon done, Reverend Ransom leads the congregation in fifteen minutes of song. The congregation is unable to move in their seats—except for an occasional fidget to relieve sore bench butt—never rock wood or transform their stationary pews into musical chairs.

Tough luck. No fun, no terror. You have never attended a service where someone does not get happy, shout, and dance the Holy Ghost. A first for everything.

*The choir's strong voices carry the song. Forked tongues lifting Sheila like*

*meat from the bench. She throws her arms and spine back in a dead man's
float. White-uniformed nurses attempt to pull her back to earth. The song
slows. She descends. White-uniformed nurses keep her fast to the bench. Fan
her to cool the hot fuel of her spirit. She leaps straight into the air and
screams, her eyes rolling one way and her body another.*

My dick bigger than yours, you say.

Be quiet, Abu says. We in the house of the Lord. He might hear you.

You got a lil dick, a Christian dick.

Do not let vile words defileth your mouth.

My dick taller than a mountain. Higher than Moses.

Be quiet.

Fatter than the ocean. And deeper than Jonah.

Shut up. Reverend Ransom lookin at us.

My jockstrap slung the boulder that slew—

Children should not talk in church. Brimstone words blister your face.
You face them. Reverend Ransom's finger points antenna-like at you, sounding the depths of your heart. Boy, I shall have words with you.

After service ends, you remove the holy water from the piano, drink it—
*Ah, still cold*—burp, then follow Abu into Reverend Ransom's chambers.
The reverend rises from his desk and moves toward you. His knees drum as
he walks. With one look (the all-seeing eye), he takes all that he wants from
you, empties you out. You are old enough to know better than to play in
church.

You listen to his words. Turn them over in your mind. Study their size,
color, and texture. You can use words, too. Yes, *Father*, you say.

Reverend Ransom blinks. The edges of his black robe billow back in retreat.

Yes! you shout inside. I've won! I've beat him! I've hacked him down. See
the blood spilling red rivers into his eyes.

Reverend Ransom steadies his running eyes. Channels them for an attack. So you think you know it all. His hand disappears inside his black
robe—

*Oh, Lord, he gon shoot me.*

—reappears with a dustpan. He holds out the dustpan between his fingers, a dangling apple. A Scout should know a thing or two about perform-
ing service.

You take the dustpan from him.

And you—he speaks to Abu. He shakes his head.

Sorry, sir. I tried to guide him.

The reverend shoves a law-heavy broom at Abu's chest.

Get to work.

Yes, sir.

Guide him with that.

Yes, sir.

You know where to find anything else you need.

Yes, sir.

Reverend Ransom turns his wide, tall black back to you and Abu, a mausoleum. One more thing.

Yes, sir.

The reverend cocks his head over his shoulder without turning around. He burns directly into your eyes, the cleansing fire of the Lord.

Yes, sir, Abu says.

*Why you say something? He talkin to me.*

Don't forget the basement.

Yes, sir.

You and Abu work. Work. Abu's broom switches like a dancer. Your dustpan catches the rhythm.

Why your preacher talk about snot?

He ain't say nothing bout no snot.

The Lord's nostrils.

The two of you sweep the aisles, dust the pews, and clean grime from the wings of stained-glass angels.

Abu, why is black people blackest at the bottom of their butt?

Stop.

You know the round cup part. Like a bunch of mud settle there.

Stop. Why you keep sayin that? We in church. You want the reverend to come back?

Is that old shit? Brown shit crusted black?

You blasphemous. I been baptized.

Baptized?

Ain't yo mamma baptize you? It's time.

I ain't no Christian. Christianity the Jew folks' religion.

No it ain't. Jews don't get baptized. They get circumcised.

I'm circumcised and I ain't no Jew.

Be quiet and clean up.

Aw right, you say, we finished here. Let's do the basement.

Two narrow flashlight beams lead you to the basement.

Let we sweep, you say. You shine the light.

No, you hold the light. You don't know how to sweep.

I can sweep better than you.

No you can't.

I'll shine the flashlight and I'll sweep too.

I ain't gon . . . what was that? Abu says.

Your mamma.

I'm serious.

Yo greasy grandmamma.

Stop rankin. We in church.

Yo, I jus heard it too. Sound like someone walkin.

Maybe it's the preacher.

Why would he be down here?

He always—

Probably rats.

Rats?

Or a monster.

Ain't no monsters in church.

You hear it again. Loud this time.

You point the beam. It came from over there. The beam glows a yellow eye on the closed door before you.

That's a closet. I think.

You lean your ears to the door. Hear the noise again. Bleating? Beating? Breathing?

Open it, you say.

You open it.

What's wrong? You chicken?

Yeah. So you open it.

You take the doorknob warm in your hand. You turn it. The door will not open.

It's locked, Abu says. Let's go.

No, you say. Give me that broom.

What you gon do? Abu hands you the broom.

You pluck two yellow straws. You kneel in the darkness, lean your ear to the lock. You put the two straws in the lock with one hand and work them like chopsticks as Uncle John had demonstrated. *Learned it in the army. You can open anything.* Listen for the heart. The heart sounds. You right yourself. The door opens with little force on greased hinges. But you and Abu don't enter the room. Stay well behind the threshold.

I thought you was gon go in.

Shut up, you whisper. Who's in there? you say, aim your voice into the darkness. Search it with your light. Crates. Boxes. And more crates and boxes. Your eyes loosen and tighten. Reverend Ransom? You feel Abu's warm hand on your shoulder. Two red eyes peer from a dark corner. Look you in the face. You lift and aim the beam. A face springs up under the flashlight. Wings flutter.

I BEAT YOU AGAIN.
    So. Least I ain't bad at math.
    Least I *know* my math.
    I know mine too.
    No you don't. You a Christian.
    What's that got to do with anything?
    Don't you go to church?
    I give fellowship every Sunday.
    You believe in the Father, the Son, and the Holy Ghost?
    I been baptized.
    The Trinity fits no law of mathematics.
    What?
    How can one person be three?

THE AIR MOVES at a roiling boil. Heat you can touch. Heat that will never cool in the memory. You and Abu join hands—skin to skin, sweat to sweat—in the double field trip line—the buddy system—and march onto the yellow school bus. The driver revives the idling engine. Kids cheer. The driver maneuvers the big steering wheel and forces the bus into traffic. The sun shines merciless in blue sky. A glowing showman glistening with sleight of hand, tricking your eyes into hot shifting vision. Burns and blurs them into two halos. Song floats in the bus's cool silver insides.

> *Five little ducks went out one day*
> *Over the hills and far away*
> *Mother duck said quack quack quack quack*
> *But only four little ducks came back*

You don't join in. Keep your quiet hands in your lap. Watch the moving world outside the window. All the streets run in numbers.
    A silver flower pushes metal petals through the bus window. A battleship grows in the grass-filled garden parallel to the Museum of Science and Industry.
    Look. You nudge Abu. That's a destroyer.
    No it ain't. That's a battleship.

Boy, you don't know nothing.
Yes I do. Can we walk the plank?
A destroyer ain't got no plank.
Oh. What's it doing in that garden? Why it ain't floating on no water?
You say nothing. Shake your head.


THE MUSEUM is the biggest house you've seen. Acres of walls. Lengths of steps like giant rows of teeth. Marble columns and pillars that hold the sky above the earth. Frieze-giants carved in stone.

Dutiful schoolchildren quit the bus and slip through revolving doors, one upon the heels of the next. An enormous globe lights the mezzanine. *The earth's magnetic lines of force flow from south to north. Continental Drift.* Look and learn. The museum harbors the siftings of centuries: two layers of fossil-rich earth caged off behind glass. *Those fossils can bite!* You view the heavens through a long tube. Cold metal sends shivers through your naked eyes. Stars blink and talk. *The light from a star takes ten years to reach us. Hence, when you wish upon a star, you wish upon the past.* You and Abu— *Follow me*—enter a cabin-sized hot and cool tank. *Heat travels. Insulators. Conductors.* Muscle a pulley and chain that rolls a bowling ball over a smooth rubber course only to return it to the place of origin and shoot it into free orbit again. *A loop is an antinode, the node being the point, line, or surface of a vibrating object free from vibration.* A round antenna blinks, vying for your attention. *A loop antenna is used in direction-finding equipment and radio receivers.* A rattlesnake snaps crescent fangs. *The copperhead is related to the rattlesnake family, but he does not rattle.* Film animates the origins of life. *Whales used to walk the earth.* Dinosaurs stand frozen over lacustrine ponds. *One egg of an elephant bird provided an omelette for fifty people.* Rows and rows of stuffed birds—*birds can fly for thousands of miles without getting tired and can sleep with open wings on a moving stream of air*—hover in perpetual air. A hummingbird flaps a haze of invisible wings. *The hummingbird flies backward.* A homing pigeon curves its course. *A tiny crystal in their brain is supersensitive to the earth's magnetic flow, which is received through their feathers and nerves.* You rub a model brain until it glows like a crystal ball. *The brain doesn't feel pain directly.* Man evolves from ape in caged glass fragments—*natural selection selects and rejects from an indiscriminate flow of innovations*—an upward plane of gradual height. *There is a metronome to evolution. Ninety-nine-point-ninety-nine percent of all species that once existed are now extinct.* Bananas reach for you with plastic yellow fingers. *Musa paradisiaca is a seedless cultivated species of berry. How then did it arrive in our hemisphere before the arrival of—*

I ain't know that a berry, you say.

That ain't no berry, Abu says.

Nigga, read the sign.

Abu reads the caption stenciled in negative light. So what? Yo mamma a berry too.

Yo greasy grandmamma.

Abu slaps you across your nape.

Punk. I'm gon kick yo ass.

Try it. You can't catch me.

Yo fat ass can't run.

Run fast enough to keep up wit yo mamma.

This ain't no time to be talkin bout nobody's mamma. We can do that later. Look and learn.

*The paruru species is an extraordinarily poor volunteer. It is difficult for this variety to spread quickly without a very active crusade on its behalf.*

How come everything got a foreign name?

How come *you* got a foreign name?

My name ain't foreign. It's black.

You move inside a giant stone head. Speak through its hollow mouth.

Abu, tell Geraldine she can't live in here.

Tell Sheila that.

You enter a hall of flowing mirrors that pull you along—powerless, let go, ride it out—swim your shape into shifting images of possibility. From the crest of a waterfall, you look down on a miniature of the city. Tar Lake loops around all five boxes of the city. Slims at the state line. Your eyes roam all points of the compass. They sharpen. The city stretches. So vast and yet so small that your eyes can take and piece together snatches of geography, yards, alleyways, rivers.

See, you say, that's Central.

That's where we live.

Yes.

Can you see my house?

No.

There go Eddyland to the west. Abu's eyes spin like compass arrows.

That's where my Uncle John live.

North Park to the north.

That's where my sister live.

Porsha?

Who else.

South Lincoln to the south.

Kankakee County just south of it.

That's where my aunt Beulah live.

Where?

Kankakee County. Decatur. She old. Real old.

Kings to the east. Liberty Island, a shapeless object stuck in Tar Lake, completely surrounded by plastic water.

That's where Gracie live. And Jesus. They jus moved there.

In all that water?

Yeah. But Uncle John know how to make the lake stay away from they do.

Buildings backward, you walk through century-old cobblestone streets. Board old streetcar trains iron-bolted to the floor. *During the morning several negroes amused themselves by riding up and down in the various cars. We are unable to discover any reason or justification on the part of a few young men in creating riot and discord.* A whistle burns blue air to black ribbons. *Whistles were used as signals.* One toot mean, *Train approaching town.* Two toots mean, *We passing through. Jus passing through. Ain't stopping. And the conductor stood in the caboose, swinging his red lantern.* A locomotive works its rapid elbows. You and Abu dodge the big mean-looking steam eye. Climb into the black engine room. *The sound of a train always reminds me of the clanging of steel doors, Sam said.*

*You got that right, Dave said.*

Grab at the slow smoke of the engine.

*One man stood on the track waving a warning light. When the train stopped, the armed robbers boarded the train and robbed the passengers of $20,000. Authorities couldn't track their mobility. They were everywhere and nowhere.*

Look over there.

You look. Shield your eyes at the brightness of a silver-fluted monster.

That's a rocket, Abu says.

No it's not. You need glasses. That's a streamliner.

*Zephyr. The first diesel-powered engine, 1934.*

You think you know everything.

*Matter cannot move itself.*

*Kinetics. The science of movement.*

*Physics. The study of movable bodies.*

*Theology. The study of the immovable mover.*

*Metaphysics. The study of—*

Blackness calls. Find yourselves armored in oxygen. Moonscape shadow. You two walk slow-motion. Jump. Float. Float on. Float over old Cadillacs, balloon-round.

Running boards glimmer under hot lights. Chrome bumpers shine one against the other. Engines churn black ink. It's all here. The world's first cars look like carriages. Cars of the twenties like trains. Forties, *cars*. Fifties, missiles. Sixties, jet planes. Seventies, speedboats.

That's Uncle John's car.

No it ain't.

He used to have one of those.

How you know?

I heard. I seen pictures. I rode.

Look. Abu indicates the World War II fighter planes spider-suspended at slanted angles from the ceiling, silk-seen, on invisible strings.

You and Abu run swiftly beneath them, guarding your heads. You pilot Abu through an iron tunnel to the battleship.

This gotta be the destroyer we saw on the bus.

Battleship.

Sight deceived: CLOSED FOR REMODELING.

Damn, it's closed.

Double damn.

You study photographs that line the corridor. (They study you.) Fighter jets on a vast deck like insignificant mosquitoes. Ant-small men swab tunnel-long guns. Damn. Look how big that ship is.

Yeah. And look at them big guns.

Yeah. Real big. Bigger than this battleship.

Bigger than this whole museum.

Bigger than the whole damn neighborhood.

Bigger than the whole country.

Bigger than the whole wide world.

The iron tunnel opens onto a maze.

A bunker. That's what this is, a bunker.

How you know?

A warren of corridors and rooms. Tiled roof. Whitewashed walls. But the walls are really doors. DAZE MAZE. Abu squeezes a buzzer. A door spits him out of the room into another, sopping wet and crying for his mother. You continue on, determined to win the prize, a red wax bull. One room hides another room clicking clocks of every shape and description. You take several more wrong turns, wind your way through more identical corridors. Your sense of direction deserts you. You try to double back. The corridors all look alike. The same tiles. The same light. Perhaps you have only orbited the main chamber. You crawl through a tunnel-like vent. Rise into space. In front of you, a sign reads THIS IS IT. A thick red arrow points down to a lever. You pull it. Moments later, the wall spits out the wax bull, red and warm to the touch.

You run to Abu with your prize. Told you I would get it.

Man! Abu says. He blow-dries his tears. Licks his snot. Let me see it.

You let him touch it.

Man. I wish I had one.

You coulda got one.

I know. What do we do now? Anxious, Abu hops on one leg then the other as if he must pee.

Follow me.

He follows.

Bull in hand, you know what to find and think you know where to find it. You claw the air. Duck under light. Squeeze through the dark. The air quick around your head with spastic machinery. Ah, yes. Here. Here.

Is this a real coal mine?

Yes, you answer. Come on. Let's go in.

He comes.

You board blackness. The coal car rattles down through the dark. You see Abu's face floating in the crowded blackness.

Wait a minute, Abu says.

What?

This an elevator?

Yeah.

It hold all these peoples?

Yes.

Why it going so fast?

The cables grip your guts. You bleed icy sweat. Surrender to the will of your body. Your bowels fill with an explosion of loose brown mud.

What happened?

Nothing.

What's wrong?

I had an accident.

Don't worry, Abu says. His head is covered with thickly woven coal-mine cobwebs. You can wear my draws.


THE SADDLE LIFTS YOU HIGH. The horse warm underneath you. You smell its sweat. The horse snorts like a dope fiend. Tail swipes at hot summer mosquitoes. Its motion helps you to think. But riding requires effort. You can't sit and let the horse take you where it wants. You must direct it with iron, muscular force.

Wait a minute, Abu says. How many stories is this? My horse is too tall.

That ain't no horse. It's a pony.

I'm gon fall off.

Just hold on to the reins. These horses are trained. He's walked this path a thousand times.

How do you stop it? It's walkin too fast.

It's not walking. It's trotting.

I can't hold on. Abu bounces in the saddle.

It's actually easier to hold on when the horse is galloping. That's why jockeys can ride so easy. I'll show you.

Your heels stab the horse's ribs. *Can't break them, no matter how hard you kick.* The rapid light beat of hard hooves on packed earth. A run of space. You sail. Your flying feet never touch the ground. The road flows under the horse's flicking hooves.


FAMILIAR MOVING BODIES, jangling colors, wandering fragments.

Sound off!

One two.

Sound off!

Three four.

Change count.

One two three four one-two, three-four.

Line it up. The troop can never hike in formation. They blow like lost sails behind you. The concrete road vibrates in your boots. Small red trees line it on both sides. Taller ones behind. And vines like twisted snakes.

> *I walk in moonlight*
> *To lay this body down*
> *I walk in starlight*
> *To lay this body down*

The troop cuts the fool and bends the forest with their voices.

> *Beans beans, good for your heart*
> *The more you eat, the more you fart*

> *Beans beans, the musical fruit*
> *The more you eat, the more you toot*

Simmer down, Mr. Baron says. Let me hear the sound of your feet.

Abu taps your shoulder. Hatch, give me a swallow of water. I'm sweatin.

His sweat runs red—he drank a canteen full of well water—then silver, then red again.

No, Mr. Baron says. Horses sweat, men perspire, and women glow.


AUTUMN FILLS THE GRAY-BROWN EMPTINESS between summer and winter. The world aglow with color as trees shed gusts of dead yellow leaves. A breeze holds up their fragrance. The woods stand tall and black—*Ah, the woods, where you could take a long swig of the dead-black wine and make your way out of this world*—sun in the treetops, sun on the branches, sun hazing the lake. You and Abu race through a yellow field bleached with rabbits. Race down the Hill—a steep crust of land, an upturned nose that grows steeper every month, wind in your legs, the speed and pull of gravity. The challenge is to stop before you reach the bottom; if you don't, your legs will hurricane you into the muscular lake where water moves like paper in the wind. (Abu can't swim.) Jump into the water, silent to your own splash. Break the wave's skin with ease. Knife downward, then float back to the surface, buoyant in weightless sleep. With sharp, clean strokes, swim the thick blind muddy lake. *Uncle John tosses you and Jesus into the live currents of the Kankakee River. The bank wafts sharp odors of gunpowder, worm, and fish. The two of you barely have time to draw breath before being sucked beneath the surface. Uncle John jumps in to pull you two back to the water's surface only after the water has filled the cups of your skulls. On the next fishing expedition, he tosses you two into the muddy water again. Lesson learned, you resurface at the same moment, trying to hurt each other with playful kicks. Flip over onto your backs. Eyes pinned to the sky, you swim the thick blind pond. With mud-black fingers, crawl out of the water. Sun sponges you dry. See, Uncle John says. See, now you know how to swim.*

Race done, fish.

You catch more fish than Abu, using your bait of locusts and wild honey, as Uncle John had instructed you on the banks of the Kankakee River. Uncle John prepared his reel, fishhook in his mouth, silver-shining like a new dime.


WITH FULL LUNGS, you blow on the covered pile of ashes. High clean flames lap up the spring chill and fill the air with fresh smoke.

They look like they ready, Abu says. Are they ready yet?

The meat lies on the grill.

I don't think so.

Maybe you should put some mo lighter fluid on the charcoal.

You aim the fluid and squeeze. The meat flies up from the grill and descends on you two, talons curled.

Damn!

Watch out.

Hey, Uncle John says, what yall tryin to do, burn up Gracie's yard?

Nawl.

He steps down from the back door, Dave behind him. He walks over and adjusts his eyeglasses. Examines the grill. Dab on some of that barbecue sauce.

You aim. Splatter red. The bird flutters sideways, shrivels and falls to the nest/grill.

Now take them off. They ready.

You take it off.

Man, Dave says, in the old days nobody used to buy ribs, cause the stockyard used to give away rib tips.

Yeah, and you used to be down there every day all day lookin fo a handout.

Fuck you, John. Dave sucks his Canary.

Uncle John looks directly at you. Don't they teach you nothing bout cookin in those Boy Scouts?

Nawl. We never cook on no grill.

Shit. You want Gracie to start complainin? Uncle John grits his teeth.

Abu's spit sizzles to the grass.

You spittin in my yard? Uncle John says.

Sorry.

Man, that's some nasty shit. Around where we eatin.

Sorry.

Uncle John, you say, you know I don't eat no pork.

You mean to tell me you ain't gon eat none of them ribs, the way you like barbecue. And I *know* you like ribs.

You say nothing.

That's what I thought.

This barbecue sauce smell like it got honey in it.

It does.

Uh, that's nasty. I don't eat honey. Bee's vomit.

Uncle John sticks his finger in the barbecue sauce. Pokes his sauce-covered finger between his closed lips, lollipop-like. Taste good to me, vomit and all. His eyes blink behind his glasses. So you an Eagle Scout now?

That's what they say.

How does it feel?

I don't feel it. Besides, I'm through with the Boy Scouts.

Me too, Abu says.

I thought you liked it. The camping part at least.

Man, forget that. Sleeping in that cold cabin. No toilet. If you got to take a shit, you gotta get out of yo warm sleeping bag and go out into the cold forest. Man, fuck that.

Yeah. Fuck that, Abu says.

Abu, you ain't gon get your eagle?

Why should I?

He ain't finished, you say. He courtin this honey. Cards, flowers, money—everything. Courtin. Tryin to earn him a Pussy Merit Badge. You salute Abu, two fingers formed in a razor-sharp angle at the forehead.

What? Uncle John says. He faces Abu. Courtin?

That's right.

Bout time, Dave says. Abu, you better get you some pussy before you turn eighteen or you'll go crazy. And that ain't no lie. Is it, John? Serious, Dave sucks his Canary, breathes it like oxygen.

Shut up, Dave, Uncle John says. Talks to Abu: Why you look all sad?

I ain't sad.

That bitch got you singin the blues?

Don't let the sun find you cryin, Dave says. Sings:

> *I wanna get close to you, baby*
> *Like an egg to a hen*
> *Like a Siamese twin*
> *Like fire to smoke*
> *Like pig to pork*
> *Like a bug to bed*
> *Like the hair on yo head*

She ain't got no hair, you say.

Uncle John and Dave stir the heavy air with their laughter. Wide-eyed, Abu looks for somewhere to hide.

What's her name? Uncle John asks him.

Elizabeth Chew, you answer.

Hey, I was askin him. Air closes over the words. Uncle John studies you for a moment—long enough to snap you shut—then turns back to Abu. So what's the deal?

Nothing, Abu says. Hatch jus talkin shit.

Yo mamma.

Ah fuck—

Hey, it's okay. Uncle John circles Abu's back with his arm. You watch Uncle John and Abu, still, together, frozen, in the same instant of time. Listen—Uncle John speaks softly, heart to whispering heart—forget all that courtin stuff. You don't sweep a bitch off her feet. You knock her off. He squeezes Abu closer, an inch deeper. His glasses reflect two clear walls that shut him and Abu off from the rest of the world. Remember, you treat a woman like a queen. But she got to realize, you a goddamn king.

SEE YOU, I wouldn't want to be you. Hatch opened the door to the absolute strength of streetlights.

Later. Abu stood, the scrim of the black doorway behind him. Garden leaves cut the wind to singing.

Hey, remember to practice that beat. Hatch hummed the tune to himself.

I will.

I'm serious.

Abu rubbed his chin.

Listen with your heart.

That's jus the problem. Abu's voice spun in the late spring night. I do listen with my *heart*.

Hatch thought and heard. Night birds pushed beyond the limits of their wings.

Sure you don't want to sleep here tonight?

Why should I? Hatch said. Then I gotta go all the way home in the morning and change clothes.

That's true. Well, you should take a cab home. It's rough out there.

Who got money for that? I ain't scared. I'll meet you back here tomorrow.

Okay.

Early. Seven o'clock.

Okay.

Seven o'clock. Cause the ticket window open at eight.

Bet.

Early. You better be ready. Don't you be sleepin or I'm gon slap yo ass awake.

Nigga, you the one who forgot to buy the tickets yesterday. Abu placed his hand on the doorknob, tugging it behind him.

I already explained that.

No problem. We good.

Ah, right. Later.

Oh, Abu said, I almost forgot. T-Bone said he want to see you.

The words held the door open. T-Bone?

Yeah.

Where'd you see him?

In Union Station, where he always is.

We gotta pass through there tomorrow. Man, that nigga can talk yo ear off.

He says it's serious.

Serious? What he want?

I don't know.

Nigga, he says it's serious and you almost forgot?

Sorry.

Damn . . . Well, what he say?

Something about Uncle John and Jesus.

Uncle John and Jesus?

Yeah. And Lucifer too.

Anything else you forget?

No.

You sure?

He ain't say nothing else. Cept he got to see you. It's serious.

# 27

CLOUDS CREATED PURE LIGHT. Lucifer stared out the small window and sifted through the white dark. Still heat—he could feel it through the glass—frozen smoke. A stalactite forced its hot point into his open mouth. He drank cold liquid that curdled in his hot stomach. Coughed. Covered the window with his white insides. He vowed, I'll never let a plane fly me again, fly me again. Live or die by these words.

The plane descended. White fanned out. Clouds thinned. Objects formed, stained with shadow colors. Ah yes, there was the sun, still. The plane sank through yellow-waved light. Features of landscape took position in Lucifer's mind. The city began to appear small, wavering, but distinct, a photograph quickening to sight, taking on text and texture in the fluid of development.

Wrong in transit, Lucifer entered the hollow ringing city. Changed. A trembling at the edge of cool awakening. The other world still warm in his mind. He felt like a man who sees a house he knew as a child: how much smaller it seems, the vast spaces of memory narrowed to the present reality.


SHEILA STOOD IN A SEGMENT OF LIGHT framed by the door. Home. He stepped into his own self-portrait. He had spent months digging a place for her inside himself.

He pulled her close. Her kiss measured to deliver the remembered warmth and wetness.

You're back, she said. She spoke into his shoulder.

Yes, he said. I'm back.

Lucifer rose at the first breath of sun and scrubbed his body until his skin sparkled. The old dark self floated in the white tub, jellyfish-fashion, dirty tentacles seeking what they'd lost. He pulled the rubber stopper. The old self lengthened and fought. Thinned. Lost its battle against centripetal motion (force) and circled down the drain. He ammonia-cleaned the tub twice so nothing was left. He had changed change. He was home now and could resume his life, leave the old Lucifer behind. But he would spend his remaining days *fearing* that he might change. Pain in his neck looking over his shoulder, watching for the old wet self that would slip him back into the world he'd left.

LUCIFER FINISHED LOADING THE LUGGAGE on the plane, returned the trolley, and loaded up for another run. Ben, the new supervisor, was leaning into a stack of luggage, a salt-covered radish in hand. He held up his other, radish-free hand. Lucifer stopped the trolley.

Hey, Ben said. He was twice Lucifer's age but half his height, his small head heavy under a high patch of steel wool.

Yes, sir, Lucifer said.

Try to load those bags a little faster. Ben bit a plug out of the radish.

The directive held in Lucifer's easy attention. Yes, sir. He put his shoulder to the wheel. No more hesitation and procrastination. He would perform well—the need smashed him in the chest—show Ben that he could pull his weight. Besides, he would be off work soon, go home. Sheila would stroke his tired back to life.

Hey, did you hear me? Ben said. I already asked you once. You tryin to make me look bad?

No, sir.

Well step to it.

Lucifer stepped to it. His body spoke speed.

You must be a smart aleck or something. One of these young black fools who think the world owe them grits and gravy. The sun beat through the hangar window against Ben's painful white shirt. Get the black molasses out yo black ass.

Lucifer leveled his eyes.

One side of Ben's face moved. Look, he said, I'm fifty-four years old. And I tell my wife when she's fucking up. I'm sposed to be closer to her than to you?

YOU SLEEP GOOD AT NIGHT? Lucifer said.

I sleep like a baby, John said. That's how you win.

What happened over there?

You tell me, bro. John wheeled the world with his hand.

No, you tell me, Lucifer said. I was jus a leg, a grunt. Unlike Spin, Spokesman (with his quick brain), and John (with his flashing remarks and insults), he hadn't walked the universe and returned with a constellation of sparkling medals. They had volunteered and could have chosen easy jobs, but their young foolish blood guided them to the most remote channels of danger.

What's to tell?

That world had left a green patina on Lucifer's memories and thoughts. But John, anchored in still waters, refused to budge from the present and ponder what he had done or what had been done to him. He and John never exchanged stories. (He bided his time to wait for those moments when he could eavesdrop on John passing stories to some interested listener.) That green world opened hollow and silent between them, a fertile space for speculation and imagination.

John trumpeted his horn and parted rows of moving metal. Stupid fuck! Learn how to drive. You ever heard of the Man?

Yes, the Man. He wears a white suit.

Vest and all.

He drives a white—

—Cadillac. He drinks—

—milk. He—

Words bounced back and forth between them: the evolving and endless story of the Man and his quest for a golden cotton field. Each morning, they would invent some new detail, add some variation, and laugh.


SCREAMS WARNING. Images flit batlike across the moving window. Running evidence of all he had witnessed. A long time between joints in the track. He would hear and feel the click, then a year would go by.

A change in the speed interrupted the current of his sleep. The window dazzled in the morning. The sun, a big bald head. Lucifer touched half-awake fingers to his forehead. Ah, his red—his fingers felt color—widow's peak had grown back during the night. He would have to shave it. Had he brought his shaving kit? His teeth felt pillow-heavy, coated with sleep. Had he brought his toothbrush? His bones cried from the stiff cold. He shook un-til his vision ran. He rubbed his legs to start the blood circulating again. He sorely needed refreshing. He rose—he was so stiff that he could barely lift himself out of the seat—and walked to the dining car, balancing himself with his hands against the shaking train. Ah, much more pleasant here. A room steamy with heated voices. He ordered a stiff drink. Downed it. Almost immediately, the whiskey burned in his belly, spread throughout his body, and he imagined himself a lamp, skin aglow. Bone-white flecks floated on the drink's surface. He relaxed in his seat, his eyes alive with seeing. Glassed in by reflections of the countryside. Sun walked in a field. Swam in the slow bend of a river. Cows stood in a motionless line. Ah, rest your weary eyes. (A carrier pigeon would lead him to John's hidden nest.) Slow, smooth, roll. Oiled rails ticking underneath. Speed would hold until the end.

AN OLD MAN sat in the seat opposite his, profile stamped by white light. His back facing the forward motion of the train. He directed his age-weakened eyes at Lucifer. Hi. He extended his hand, perfectly pointed and ridged, a flint arrowhead. I'm Reverend Van.

Lucifer took the hand, hard and cool as money. The reverend shook firm and sharp, machinelike. Lucifer Jones.

Glad to meet you.

You too. The reverend switched his long thin legs to the left, like a gate allowing a ship (Lucifer) to enter dock. Lucifer sat down in his seat—*How did he know that I was sitting here? How did he know that I wanted to sit down?*—and tried to be comfortable. Every nerve in his body alive. Strangers steel us.

Hope you don't mind me sitting here? The reverend returned his legs to their original position. The gate closed; only the reverend could open it.

Not at all. Lucifer's skin was hot. Fire stirred about him.

My car was too cold. So I decided to change.

Lucifer watched the moving words lift from the reverend's long phallic neck. *He's a preacher. I'm riding with a preacher.* Not what he had imagined: a long, quiet ride, the steady soothing rumble of the train.

Looks like we gon share this ride. The preacher's right eye was completely red, a broken blood vessel.

Yes.

I'm always happy to make a new acquaintance. The preacher's Dobb—ah yes, tight-fitting to hide his preacher head—sat on the empty seat next to him. Preacher-typical. His egg-shaped head contained the secret yolk of life.

Me too. Lucifer tasted his teeth. Whiskey had failed to burn away the sleep. He would have to brush them.

Where you headed?

New York.

Me too.

*I knew it. Jus my luck.*

I'm attending my brother's funeral.

Sorry to hear that. *Bet you gon preach his funeral. Probably be around to preach mine. Preachers never die.* The preacher smelled like the past in his dark—black? brown?—three-piece suit. *I bet he's had that suit twenty-five years.* Lucifer heard the tight heart beating inside his vest.

He lived on Amsterdam Avenue. You know where that is?

Uptown. Probably in Harlem.

Yes. Harlem. His wife gave me the address. The preacher fisted his left lapel and threw open his blazer, revealing the shiny vest. His free hand searched in the small vest pocket. Discovered a strip of paper luminous with grease stains. He handed—lines ran like dark roads on the old man's palm—Lucifer the paper. There. The preacher's finger indicated numbers scrawled across a bus transfer. Lucifer pretended to read them.

I see. Lucifer nodded.

She told me to take a cab from the train station. Said it should cost no more than eight dollars.

Probably so.

Sounds like you know New York City.

Not really.

You ever been to New York City?

Once or twice. New York and Home: two cities sailed together; he dreamed about one while he lived in the other.

Furrows in the earth last for three months. Furrows in the water come back together.

Lucifer sought slow understanding. The preacher's serious mood would not taint him. He would not allow it. Damn if he would.

I probably won't even recognize him.

Who?

My brother.

Oh.

He never sent pictures. He wrote or called me once a year. That was about it. We had no reason to see each other. This will be the first time he ever heard me preach. And I'm sure he'll be listening. Sure. He moved to New Orleans in 1928. Then Memphis for a few years, then Chicago, then Detroit, then Los Angeles, finally New York City, Harlem. He hated the world.

Lucifer thought about something courteous to say and thinking found nothing.

What about you?

Me?

Why are you going to New York City?

To see my brother.

He lives there?

No. Well, not exactly. It's a long story.

Well, we've got fifteen hours, I believe.

Lucifer said nothing. Nothing to be told.

I understand, the preacher said. The necessities of blood.

Yes, Lucifer said, not knowing what else to say.

What's your brother's name?

John.

John. The preacher broke the word between his fingers. John. Be kind to your brother, for he is just a ship in the ocean of time searching for a harbor.

Lucifer studied the preacher's wrinkled skin, legends or biblical passages written beneath it. *So the preacher thinks he's a prophet.*

I'm sorry. I'm not trying to pry.

No need to apologize.

I like to talk. The first sign of old age is all the talking cause you can't do much else.

Lucifer attempted a laugh.

Where you from?

Lucifer told him.

Oh yes. I often preach there. You know Mount Zion Church?

I used to know one called that, years ago, but it's probably not the same church.

It probably is. The preacher was looking directly at Lucifer's forehead. A red stalactite reflected in his white eye. Ah, the red widow's peak. He had forgotten to shave it.

Excuse me, Lucifer said. He tried to rise from his seat.

You see—the preacher's wing tips flopped like catfish—I got a few years—

I'll be right back.

—but I try to travel and spread the truth.

That's good, Lucifer said. Excuse me. I need to use the bathroom.

Maybe before God calls me home—the red eye was looking into a new country—I'll carry the gospel to another land.

The solid front of words knocked Lucifer back into his seat. *The preacher must be deaf. All that screaming in church.* That would be nice.

I'm from Memphis. Live there, that is. Born in—

Memphis? My wife's from there.

Maybe she knows my church. Here's my card.

Lucifer took it. Thanks. Pretended to read it. Buried it in his shirt pocket.

Being that your wife's from there, you've visited?

No. I've never been down South. Well, except when I—

You should visit.

I plan to. The world sped past. Lucifer wanted to sit here quietly and alone and watch it. Perhaps study his map of New York City. (So long since he'd been there.)

Memphis used to be a nice place. Now everybody got bars on their doors. The world's changed so.

Yes.

We hurt ourselves. Cain killing Abel. If we had any sense we wouldn't be stealin from other po folks. Socrates said, Teach your mouth to say no. Black people are petty thieves. That's the message of Jesus and the ten lepers.

Lucifer didn't know the parable.

But we still got some good folks in Memphis. You should visit.

I plan to.

Come by my church anytime.

Thanks.

You and your wife. You can stay with me.

Thanks.

My wife ain't living. God called her home.

Sorry to hear that.

She had bad kidneys. She had to drink one beer a day and keep her insides clean. By the time she lay back on her deathbed, she developed a round belly. Everybody thought she was pregnant, about to give birth to our sixth child. But you see, God been good to me.

*Oh no. Here it comes. Forcing me to go to church, right here on this train. Then he'll shout Lord! and pass around his collection plate. Why does everyone want to talk religion to me?* Lucifer was tired of the small predictable truths, gilded platitudes, humming homilies.

I got married in 1933. My wife was nineteen. We were married for forty-five years. God been good.

Lucifer smiled.

I was born in 1910. That makes me how old?

Lucifer told him.

And I still got my health. And I have plenty to live on. I collect rent on three houses I own. I get eighty-five dollars a week from my congregation. And I get eight hundred eighty-nine dollars a month in pension.

What sort of work did you do? *Why did I ask that?*

Railroad.

Oh yeah? One of my wife's uncles—he thought about And's relationship to Sheila: his wife's great-aunt's husband—worked for the railroad.

Which railroad?

I'm not sure. But he always talked about it.

I started out working in the roundhouse. That's where all the trains come in. I polished parts and kept the engines shining. Then they promoted me to switchman. My job was to open and close the track. I made forty cents an hour in 1941. In September I got a raise to fifty cents. In December I got promoted to seventy cents. Not bad money in those days.

Not at all.

Would you take my bag down? The preacher pointed to the luggage rack above their heads.

Sure.

The preacher adjusted his legs to allow Lucifer to stand. Lucifer slid the suitcase—old and heavy; *It'll last forever*—from the overhead rack, balancing his body against the moving train—the train was spinning through Pennsylvania; Lucifer could see the drift of it all, the black face of a ridge, then stretched land below tree-covered mountains—and gently placed it on the preacher's lap.

Thanks.

No problem. Lucifer retook his seat.

The preacher snapped the latches and disappeared inside the open suitcase. Placed two wedges of tinfoil on the suitcase—a makeshift table—and began to unwrap them. Have some. A pork chop sandwich blazed from the preacher's outstretched palm.

No, thank you.

Are you sure?

I already ate.

The best time of my life was when I was struggling. The preacher took an anxious bite from his pork chop sandwich. God has been good to me.

*Not God again.* Lucifer wanted to tell the preacher to shut up about God. He mouthed a silent prayer for God to shut the preacher's mouth.

He gave me five children. The preacher chewed white words. And almost a sixth. The preacher started on a second wedge of sandwich. My wife could make one chicken go far. And as we sat at the table, each child would tell a story. The preacher disappeared behind his open suitcase. Reappeared with a triangle of tinfoil. His careful fingers opened it. Revealed a piece of sweet potato pie with raisins. Have some.

No, thanks.

I taught my kids the importance of instruction. The preacher ate the pie with three bites. I always told them, Do your best. The preacher brought a handkerchief white to his face. Cleaned his mouth and hands. Picked orange string from his teeth. Sucked his fed teeth. You have kids?

The preacher's question ran through Lucifer's life like an accusing voice. Yes, Lucifer said. Two. A son and a daughter.

We were poor but my wife always kept the children clean. There's no excuse for not keeping yourself clean.

The preacher's voice strapped Lucifer in tightening circles of anger. Would you like something to drink? I could go to the dining car and—

No, thanks. I got something right here. For the third time, the preacher leaned into his open suitcase. Leaned back into his seat with a mason jar full of tea dark as the old leather suitcase. Buoyant cubes chimed against the glass. The preacher unscrewed the lid. And when we could, my wife made each child their favorite dish. The preacher tilted his head back. Drank slow and deep, his long throat working the liquid. He screwed the lid back on the jar. Things were bad. The preacher folded the tinfoil into neat squares. We had five kids to clothe and feed. Returned the squares and the mason jar to his suitcase. We had two girls in college. And the bill collectors threatened to throw me in jail. The water was up to here—the preacher held the edge of his hand before his nose—but God didn't let me drown.

OUTSIDE THE WINDOW, the slums of West Philly, rows of two-flat brick houses—two symmetrical windows on each floor, a small porch, wooden rails—twins of the flat brick houses in South Lincoln. Light made the houses transparent. Lucifer could see women with perfect breasts, men with penises naturally contoured, whiskey brawlings, bare vineyards, branching trees of crystal, tall limbs bending overhead, triangular groves, white grass, fat speckled fish, and violets he could not reach. The train shook the window up and down; images swam, paperweight objects gravity-free. And just as suddenly, green forestry, the Philly river, through the window opposite the aisle downtown Philly, its colonial spires, its arcades like a giant's stiff legs, arching cupolas and rooftops, and highways of blackened stone. The sun faded in a tunnel. The train shoved out the other side and pulled into a city of iron lace. A bridge curved black in blue air, both ends invisible. (Bridge cables?) Thirtieth Street station. The train pulled to a stop. Whistling trains punctuated the distance (silence). Some passengers exited. Others hurried on.

This must be a switching point, the reverend said.

I see.

We should be moving shortly.

Good.

The train started to move, in reverse direction.

Hey, Lucifer said. We're going in the wrong direction.

Relax, the reverend said. It always does that.

# 28

I'M GHOST.

I know. Ain't seen or heard.

I been busy.

Ain't we all?

So you found me.

Didn't think you'd come. Didn't homeboy—T-Bone aimed his bald head at Abu—smother word?

Yeah, Hatch said. Damn. It's seven-thirty now. How soon'd you want to get here?

T-Bone looked straight into Hatch's eyes, an iron path. His bald head gleamed like a chess pawn. He bit down on his toothpick. Held his barking bulldog tattoos in check with the leashes of his shirtsleeves.

Fast as I could get here.

T-Bone continued to iron-watch Hatch. He bit ridges into his toothpick. Tasted it. Savored it. Cool, he said. Held out his hand, a long black line between his thumb and forefinger. Hatch gripped the black scar with everything he had.

Good to see you, T-Bone said. T-Bone squeezed fire into Hatch's hand.

Same, Hatch said, pain beneath the word.

Abu. T-Bone extinguished the fire. Gripped Abu's palm. Squeezed Abu's fat thin for a moment.

What's up, T-Bone?

Kickin it.

How's life treatin you?

The same. See a lot. Hear a lot.

Damn, Hatch said. Is that a motor?

T-Bone studied Hatch's face, eyes unmoving. Stretched straight before him in a gleaming wheelchair. Silver spokes, silver hubs, and the wheels themselves, coated with black rubber. The motor tucked under the seat, small and black, neat as a gift, strong as a lunchbox.

That *is* a motor, Hatch said. Automatic. A first for T-Bone. Years of manual motion had molded muscle, and you would see him, see his bulldog arms dogsledding him all over the city.

So what. I don't really need it. I *want* it. Earned it.

Uh oh, you slippin.

Yeah, Abu said. You slippin.

Nawl. Earned it. Deserve it. A nigga gotta move up, that's all. I'm still me. You never grow out of being yourself. T-Bone thumped his leather chest.

The boom rocked Hatch, powerful waves. He steadied himself. So you found me. So I'm here. So what's up?

Same ole same.

Got to be more than that, Hatch said.

Yeah, Abu said. Tell us. I'm all ears.

T-Bone ran his eyes slowly over Hatch's face. That bitch still troublin you?

Hatch nodded.

What's her name again?

Elsa.

Spanish, right?

Puerto Rican.

Let me educate you. Cause you know I used to be out there. Race don't matter. If a bitch won't give—

That's why you brought me here? That's why you want me? You kickin word? You jus want to bust the hype? I thought it was something serious? Abu said you said that it was serious.

Yeah, Abu said. That's what you said.

T-Bone shot a glance at Abu, then returned his demanding eyes to Hatch's face.

Hatch caught his drift. Abu, Hatch said, I check you later.

What?

Why don't you go get the tickets. I'll meet you there in a few. Better yet, I'll pick them up. Meet you back at the house later.

I thought we was going together?

I changed my mind.

Why?

I jus did, that's all.

Abu looked at Hatch for a long balancing minute. Emotion bled from his face. Understanding set him in motion. Okay. Aw ight. Check you later.

Maintain, T-Bone called after him.

Abu said nothing. Went swinging along and alone.

He's gone, Hatch said. Abu's gone. So tell me.

I think you hurt his feelings.

You can't hurt Abu, Hatch said. He too fat.

That's yo homeboy. Learn how to be subtle.

He'll get over it. So tell me.

T-Bone's bulldog biceps bounced and leaped at invisible possums.

Come on, T-Bone. Tell me.

T-Bone smiled, showing toothpick between teeth.

He said it was serious. Something about Uncle John and Jesus.

How yo family doing? T-Bone spoke with night hush in his voice.

Damn, T-Bone. Hatch kept his voice calm. Held his anger and anticipation in check. No easy task. Skin hot, he wanted to scream. Damn. Why you holdin back?

Chill.

I am chill.

Ain't you never heard, patience makes virtue.

Patience is a virtue.

I said it right the first time. T-Bone's bright bald head threw Hatch's glances back at him.

Okay, Hatch said. You're right. I am chill. I really am. Chill.

Good. T-Bone spit out his toothpick; it arched and dropped, missilelike. John stole a bird.

Uncle John did what?

You heard me.

Come on, T-Bone. Come on.

T-Bone worked a new toothpick into his mouth. John stole a bird.

Damn, T-Bone. Damn. Why you playin?

You know I don't play.

Then somebody—

And Lucifer helped. Aiding and abetting.

Lucifer?

Yes, Lucifer. Aiding and abetting.

Lucifer? Hatch chuckled. No. That can't be right. Who—

I saw it, T-Bone said. Saw it with my own eyes.

Hatch's head traveled in a rotating pattern. Damn. Damn. You don't dispute fact, Hatch thought. Fact working through T-Bone. Eyes surprised into witness. Damn, Hatch said, his voice wavering. Damn. Whose bird did he steal?

Freeze.

Hatch felt something wet in his chest. Freeze?

T-Bone nodded.

From Stonewall?

You know another?

Uncle John don't even know Freeze.

T-Bone's toothpick curved limp and white, wet and heavy from spit and words. T-Bone tugged at it.

How?

Does it matter?

Hatch said nothing. His voice was buried deep inside. If he attempted speech, surely no sound would emerge.

Long as *you* know. Long as you know Freeze know. And long as you know that Freeze let *Jesus* know.

Jesus?

Jesus. T-Bone smiled again, less teeth this time. He read words in Hatch's face. Jesus? Why Jesus? Ask yourself.

Hatch looked outside of himself, like a passenger in a car. Yes, he thought. Yes. Jesus. No one else. It made perfect sense.

I just thought you should know.

There, Hatch thought. There. He had it all, the hard lump of truth. He could feel T-Bone's eyes on him like hands, shaking him, demanding response.


THE TRAIN SPENT THE GREATEST PART OF THE JOURNEY standing still. Stillness etherized the passengers. Jackals all of them. They floated now, on floods of bright talk. These jackals barely held together by cotton and steel, liquid and air. Their dens in weedy waste. Take a gun to all of them. Hatch waved off their shameful smell.

The black tunnel roared overhead. The train rocked over the clunking rail joints. Sped on, swaying to the curves. Hatch's mind eased away from his spine. Floating, flying. A clear feeling. It made things plainer.

T-Bone had solved one riddle even as he presented another. Ah, that explained it. Yes, that explained it. John. Uncle John. So that was why he'd made himself scarce recently. A disappearance both gradual and sudden. Each day, an oxidizing of a single cell, a single organ, a single limb, until — no more John. Uncle John. But Lucifer? Why would Lucifer aid and abet? Lucifer and John, brothers in the skin, but no closeness.

Light pitched upward, ran away from Hatch, quicker the farther it went. Each shaking train window mirrored blackness. Drawn by the seat's gravity, he was a body at rest. His mind signaled his body, Move, Act, but he could not. He ran his mind over T-Bone's smooth black tale, shining with lacquered luminosity. Bird. Betrayal. Lucifer. John. Jesus.

THE FAMILY HADN'T SEEN OR HEARD FROM HIM since last year, Christmas. Nor did they want to. Forgiveness had wings, but Jesus had ridden it to death. His fury, like a powerful storm, had carried him to heights that had permanently separated him from the family. Now—still unknown to them—he had orbited back into their life like a red meteor.

Even before he could walk or talk, he had exercised his red will. He refused to allow anyone to feed him. He would turn his face away from the feeding hand and food like poison. Cry in anger. *You had to wait for him to fall asleep, then sneak the food into his little mouth.* And once, his innocent teeth had tasted Lula Mae's big bare toe. She kicked (from reflex and fear)—*I thought a rat was biting me*—teeth and taste down his throat.

These events had come to Hatch's ears through the living mouths of his family. But he had no reason to question their validity.

His eyes fell on Jesus's long-fingered hands that balanced an old battered brown suitcase—Gracie's? Uncle John's?—across his high knees. Red, why didn't you check your suitcase?

I ain't want to, Jesus said. He turned to Hatch from the seat opposite, his face blurred and distant with sleep. They had been on the train for many hard hours. Jesus had refused to check the suitcase with his other baggage, refused to put it on the luggage rack above and kept it on his lap the whole time like a baby.

But ain't you uncomfortable?

Jesus laughed, a deep laugh that echoed inside Hatch.

Hatch let it drop. Silence seemed to pin them in moving place.

*Hatch, Junebug called, come here.*

*What? Hatch said. He approached. What you want? What you doing on my grandmamma's grass?*

*You don't like it?*

*Get off my grandmamma's grass.*

*You make me get off.*

*You better get off.*

*Shut up, punk. Junebug smacked Hatch's black face red.*

*Jesus cracked Junebug over the head with his milk-weighted baby bottle.*

*I'm gon tell yo granny, Junebug said. You crazy.*

*So what, Jesus said. Tell her. She ain't my mamma.*

The train checked speed, then jolted back. He knew what to expect, the pattern immediate, intuition, instinct. Lula Mae would greet them at the station—her white skin like light in the Memphis night—safe in something better and greater than herself. Two days later, her deepest heart would convert her warm smile into a permanent, burning frown. They were her prisoners for the summer, in her small, knowable world. Near summer's close her heart would cool. Her cold tears would greet their departure home. Yall call me, Lula Mae would say. Write me.

The same thing next summer. Predictable. Why do we visit her every summer?

Red—

Don't call me Red, Jesus said.

Hatch's eyes collided with his reflection in the train window. Jesus's face was so similar to his own. He sat up very straight and tried to smile.

*Nasty granny nasty granny, Junebug said. Whitelady, Whitelady. Briar-patch legs.*

*Better not say that again, Jesus said.*

*Whitelady. Briar-patch legs.*

*Jesus's fist exploded red.*

He had the feeling that Jesus was dissolving, disappearing. Again he tried to smile. The feeling deepened, widened.


Hatch listened to the secret whisper of Jesus's sleeping blood. Even in the dark he could see the ever-present suitcase. One end of a thin length of cord knotted around the handle, the other looped around Jesus's outstretched wrist that hung limply over the side of the bed. All day, he had refused to let the suitcase out of his sight, even carrying it to supper.

Lula Mae entered the room. With much racket—Jesus required the impenetrable sleep of the dead—she unlatched it (strangely, it was not locked), opened the lid, and revealed the shining secret, a pack of *Kool* mentholated cigarettes. Lula Mae woke Jesus with a resounding slap. She held up the pack. Boy, she said. You too young to smoke.

Jesus looked at her, her palm print clear and red in his cheek of fossilized stone. Bitch, he said, just like that, you ain't my mamma.

The early years, Red was closer to Hatch than his own skin. Gracie and Sheila dressed them the same for Sam's funeral (viewing?).

*Sam stands with one pants leg rolled up, offering his prized wooden stump for all the world to see. The stump moves with effortless, hidden will when he walks, like a hinged puppet limb. Stationary beneath him now as he mixes shaving cream in his old army helmet.*

*Yall niggas get bigger every time I see you. Soon I'm gon need me a chain saw to barber yall big heads.*

*My mammy say don't use no straight razor, Hatch says.*

*Is yo mammy here? . . . I'll cut you first since you got the brave mouth. Now hold still.*

*Sam works his sparkling straight razor between his fingers like a potato peeler. Shaves Hatch clean. Cleans Red the same. Two slick-bean twins.*

*Why you use that sword on my head? Red says. You ain't sposed to be usin no spear on nobody's head.*

Hatch signed both of their names—*Hatch Jones, Jesus Jones* in the same hand—in the Visitors' Book that slanted on a lectern under a remembered light. *Dearly departed.* In the scripted program, Hatch saw his great-aunts Beulah, Big Judy, Koot, and his grandmother Lula Mae listed as Sam's survivors. Had Sam beached these women from the drowning waters? Had this dead man carried them—floating them on the log of his wooden leg—but allowed life's tides to drag him into the dark drifting deep? Long ago, the dead man had planted himself in Hatch's and Red's hearts and grew; now, both of their heads yearned for the shining contents of the casket. Two faces and two eyes, they both peered into the coffin—

*Touch him.*

*Nawl. You touch him.*

*Chicken.*

*Scaredy cat.*

—hoping to view the undertaker's stitches that had reattached Sam's severed head.

*She ain't cut off his head, Dave said. Just buried that ax deep in it.*

*Like a log.*

*They found a bottle of Iron Ass next to his head. That's how they knew it was his woman that'd done it.*

Sam, if I'da just been there to lift up yo dyin head, Beulah said. You died too soon.

Damn, Hatch said. How old was he?

You died too young.

He was an ole-ass nigga.

Red, you be ole someday too.

Never.

Why was only one half of the casket—Sam's stiff powdered bust—open to sight? To hide Sam's wooden leg? *Perhaps a bird had laid tiny eggs in his tree leg.* He thought about Sam's wooden leg, waxed and shiny like Sam's dead skin—a birthday candle carrying the long, thick wick of Sam's years. Who would inherit it?

*Sam's wood leg stomp so hard on the floor that his empty Old Rocking Chair bottles and his girlfriend's Iron Ass bottles twink like chimes. Sam sit you in one chair, Red in another. Hand on hip, Porsha say, Uncle Sam, my mamma say, don't you be usin no straight razor on they head. Sam pull the straight razor from the sheath of his blazer pocket. Uncle Sam, my mamma say—*

*Girl, you gon cut they hair? Sam run the razor once twice across his strop. Flip it over. Run it once twice across his strop. Then peel you and Red clean as apples.*

*Sometimes he would threaten to cut you and Red with the dead Jap sword he kept under the bed.*

The next day, to lift their spirits, Uncle John took Hatch and Red to Fun Town—it was a satisfaction to take them about with him; *This is my son. And that's my nephew. My brother's boy*—the amusement park on Ninety-fifth and Stony Island. Three circus rings in a constant blur of motion with clowns, acrobats, and animals.

Nothing like Riverview used to be, Uncle John said. Boring. This might as well be the zoo.

Quick go-carts snapped popcorn sounds. A sweat-slick slide rolled your round butt like a ball bearing down five flights of friction—yes, you felt like a Coke bottle sliding down the chute of the red vending machine in Uncle John's garage—and a Ferris wheel afforded a giant's-eye view of Central and all the city's five boxes.

The one at Coney Island is better, Uncle John said.

It would be the only view and visit, for the city vaporized Fun Town soon after. From then on, Uncle John—this horse of an uncle and father carrying the two of you piggyback—took you and Red to the traveling amusement parks—trucks arrive with the first blink of sunlight; skinny white trash unload them; the park is open for business before the last fingers of sun scratch the horizon—that occupied the vacant lots on Church Street, Stony Island, or Jeffery Boulevard.

YOU AND RED straddled broomsticks and rode (yes, straw-maned horses) the plains—Giddy-up! Giddy-up!—of the small apartment on Kenwood in Woodlawn. The two of you rode hard and fast on your bikes, knees bumping against chests, through the decaying streets of Woodlawn, Englewood, South Shore on a single, shared breath of oxygen. Your need to know stretched an invisible telephone wire through time and distance, connecting sleeping mouth to sleeping ear; you and Red passed dreams back and forth like a joint. Wind expanded the sails of your windbreaker jackets and sent you coasting along through the hood, light, weightless, never losing breath, a race of radiance, running, watching the world blur past, forgetting that you are running, one corner followed by another corner, one street by another street, wrapped in the silence of flight, wind lathering your faces with cool air, blowing. Fevered days followed again and again. At Rainbow Beach or Oak Street Beach you sought sun-filled life, rash physical joy. The air filled with conversation. Waves galloped in like horses, and the two of you lay for hours flat against hot sand—fine, like brown sugar, shaking it out of your toes; damp sand that absorbed red root life, bloodlines—and watched the sun through the huge waves.

Flooded by images of the Gemini moon landing, you and Red—at *your* suggestion—raced into Sheila's garden, found two forked branches, and cut a circle in the grass so perfect you could have laid a foundation. Used the red of Sheila's roses to magnify the circle. Stood inside the circle and waved at the men on the moon. The men waved back. Porsha—*she wielded the body of a woman even then*—chastised you and Red with keen slaps.

Balanced, the two of you frog-kicked at either end of a seesaw, gravity-free, astronauts frog-leaping over the moon.

Come on, Red, you said. Let's get on the carousel.

Okay, Red said.

Bounced bowlegged to the carousel. You and Red grabbed the sides and ran with everything you had, shoving it, shoving, sending it around and around—Don't yall go too fast on that thing, Porsha said—the images blurring in a stream of speed and motion, and hopped on, round and round with dizzy speed, four hands gripped tight to the iron bars, four arms stretched full, elbows locked, roiling, shaking back and forth, the spin of a potter's wheel, you and Red leaning away from the center, heads all the way back, necks craned, straining the muscles, the world flicking swiftly in and out of vision, the steady backward rush of air, then Red sailing forth, cut from the line of motion, an astronaut sucked into outer space. You saw him for a moment, a moment lost in a blur of images. The carousel spun you back to the same spot. You let go too. Sailing. Landing. Your body cut a groove through the dirt. The two of you crying, more from fear than pain—later, Porsha treated a few nicks and scratches—and then an image waded into your wet sight. A double image. Your eyes tried to fix its outlines. What yall tryin to do? Porsha said. She smacked you. Smacked Red. Get me in trouble? Smacked you again. Smacked Red.

By day, you and Red would missile-pitch hot dogs—smothered with heat-seeking mustard—into stadium crowds. *Now, that Satchel, Beulah said, he could make a ball walk, make it slow down to a crawl, and his curves were so smooth his fingers leaked oil.* By night, catch sparkling lightning bugs. *Fire-*

*flies* you called them, for the fires glowed in the night with secret treasure. You would cut out the fuzzy sticky yellow lights from the thorax and store them shining in dull-glassed mason jars.

Once lived a nigga named Zoom, Red said. The fastest nigga on earth. So quick that he could beat his reflection in a mirror. Could catch his own farts in a bottle befo the poot escaped his butt and the air got funky. That's the end of my tale. Ain't no mo. Bang yo mamma til my dick get sore.

Who taught you that lie? you asked. Uncle John?

My secret to tell. Noah pissed and the water fell. The world ain't flat. The world ain't round. It's just one strip up and down.

THE CHURCH ROCKED. Soul-saving song. You and Red dropped into a split, then rocked back into position and grabbed imaginary microphones.

> *Michael row the boat ashore. Hallelujah!*
> *Michael don't wet yo draws no more. Hallelujah!*
> *Sister help to trim the sail. Hallelujah!*
> *Sister don't forget to cut yo toenails. Hallelujah!*

> *Jordan River is deep and wide. Hallelujah!*
> *Pussy and dick on the other side. Hallelujah!*

Red spit into the collection plate and passed the plate to you.

The spit watched you like a silver eye.

Spit! Red whispered.

No, you said.

Chicken, Red said.

No I ain't. Jus don't want to that's all. You tucked the collection plate under the wooden pew like a commode.

The choir sang dimensions. Cotton Rivers climbed the piano and Cleveland Sparrow mounted the organ. On wings of words, dead souls floated up above the podium, ascended, like sky divers. Tongue-tied angels flapped humming wings in the rafters. Two forks of sermon catapulted you from the hard wooden pew into the heavens. You saw God at work.

WHO WANTS TO GO inside the spaceship? Red said. He slapped the old refrigerator, earthbound and rusting in a glass-choked alley. A shock of red hair escaped beneath the visor of a red baseball cap jammed onto the back of his head. The visor pointed right at the sun.

Not me.

Not me.

Not me.

What's wrong? Scared?

Damn straight.

Let a man do a man's job.

It took three of them pulling on the handle to get the door open and expose the brown insides.

Uh. You gon go in there? Stinks. Somebody took a dump.

Shut up, stupid. That ain't no dukey. Mildew. Don't you know nothing?

Don't care what you say. I stays away from dukey. Hey, Abu, yo mamma been in there?

Nawl, yo greasy grandmamma.

Ain't nobody said nuthin bout yo mamma. I don't play that shit.

Shut up. I'm gon inside. Hatch—

Yeah.

You shut the door behind me.

Okay.

Red climbed inside, forcing his long body into a ball, the red cap still on his head.

Okay, shut the door.

You couldn't, so Abu and the other boys all leaned their weight into it. Door shut, they waited.

Red, you aw ight?

Yeah. Now open the door.

They tried.

Open the door.

They tried.

I said open the door.

They tried.

Quit fuckin around. Open the door.

They tried and tried. Much breathing and sweating.

Look, I ain't playin. Open the door.

We can't.

Open the door.

They tried.

Open the door.

They tried.

Open the door.

They tried. Then it came, the entire door breaking away like ice.

Red sat there, curled, not even trying to get out, the red cap wet with sweat. It would take you years to dilute the memory (never forget) of the tight twisted face under the baseball cap. The die was cast: this face Red would carry for the rest of his life.

JESUS'S CONICAL HEAD OF RED HAIR rose above the steering wheel of his car, sun on the evening horizon. Uncle John's surprise. Jesus hadn't asked for it since he would ask nothing of anybody, and Uncle John hadn't promised it, all he said, *Hatch, I'll get you one too;* he never did—a Frankenstein monster (a butchered white Volkswagen Rabbit) that Spokesman had pieced together with junk from Uncle John's Funky Four Corners Auto Shop. The muffler tied up under the chassis like a broke-dick dog.

You got to park it on level ground, Uncle John said. He filled the tank the same way he'd filled Gracie with his raging wine. The emergency brake don't work. Park it on level ground or it might roll away.

*The two of you, you and Jesus, Hatch and Red, loved to take it white-smoking through the hollow roar of the interstate—heard above the cracking of desiccated leather—bumps on the highway shaking laughter out of him, out of you. Drive all the way to Decatur—black cows dotting the landscape, farm quiet wrapped around you—zooming past farm boys in muscle cars and state police armed with chain saws and ten-gallon Stetsons. And on into the white trash section of Kankakee. (But never to Beulah's house itself. She pissed a fit whenever she saw Jesus.) Trailer homes propped up on concrete blocks. Rusted cars on deflated tires that had long forgotten motion. Look at them white motherfuckers! Can't drive for shit! Slow down and flash nigga grins at old ladies.*

HUSH, Sheila said. John, don't start that stuff bout how you don't celebrate Christmas.

Why not? Uncle John said.

Hush.

Why not? And, Hatch, I'm surprised at you. Sposed to be a man of the Book. Any fool who read the Bible know that Christ ain't born today. Ain't that right, Gracie?

Gracie showed no reaction, as if she hadn't heard the question.

Pagan holiday, Uncle John said.

It's only pagan if you pagan, you said.

What? Uncle John said.

Only if you believe in pagan things. Know that you are pagan.

What? Uncle John said. Hatch, thought you was smarter than that. He meant it; you gathered that from the look in his eyes. I expect more.

I know, you said.

Well, if you know, why you celebrate Christmas? Uncle John's fire hadn't cooled.

Tradition.

Tradition? You mean—

Nawl, that ain't what I mean. You trembled at the sound of your own loud voice. *Damn. I just shouted at Uncle John.*

Why you yellin at folks? Porsha said.

Who asked you? you said.

Boy, Porsha said, respect your elders.

Who asked you?

Both of yall be quiet, Sheila said. This is sposed to be a family get-together.

The family talked family things. (Holidays always helped the family's memory enlarge.) Time hung like leaden weights. Would Jesus appear? *The family thinking it, not saying it, cause nothing is hardest which treads on somebody else's toes.* No one had seen him in almost a month, since Thanksgiving, the scorched form of his body imprinted on Gracie's couch, her kitchen chair. His presence lay on Gracie's house—yes Gracie's house, the house that Uncle John had bought her, the home that he lost—thick and black. But his termite absence had eaten into the carved wooden armrests of her couch and chairs.

*Black Christmas. Snowless. Nipping frost. You and Red to build snowmen (always two snowmen cause one never seemed enough) with pointed icicle dicks. Christmas Eve, Santa's secret sled parked outside Gracie's sleeping house. You and Red wait for the clock to strike midnight, kneel beneath the tall sparkling tree that smelled of pine and artificial frost and unwrap present after present.*

Jesus would come. You knew it. Definite proof lived in the muscles, the secret blood.

Porsha poured everyone a fresh glass of eggnog laced with Crown Royal. Jesus stepped through Gracie's door. *He used his own key, yes he used his own key.* The family went mute at the renewed sight of him. For a moment, he said nothing, stood and held the family in his frowning eye, face fist-tight. His earring glittered like a single tear. You saw your own reflection swimming in the diamond surface. Sparkling tenfold on his shaved head. Yes, Jesus had shaved his head. Looked like a daddy longlegs with his clean curved skull and long skinny arms and legs. *Member how you and Red used to squeeze em? See how much pressure it took to ooze out the insides.* You studied the anxious line around Jesus's mouth. The eyes full of their usual clarity. (Yes, something had always been old about him.) A dull gleam of recognition filled Jesus's eyes.

What's up? he said.

Long time, no see, you said, keeping your voice steady and calm.

I know.

You and Jesus touched hands, softly, without the usual force.

Son. Uncle John met Jesus with an expansive hug, and the rest of the family offered tentative hugs and kisses.

Rest your coat, Gracie said.

Jesus did.

The perfect host, Gracie ushered everyone into the dining room, where a chandelier dripped crystal stalactites of light onto a bench-length table. Porsha cooked us a fine Christmas dinner, Gracie said.

*Thank God, cause you put salt in everything.*

Turkey and dressing, ham and chitlins (you avoided both, jackal meat), candied yams, greens, and (more) eggnog.

Hatch, Sheila said, you say blessing.

You looked at her. Thank you, O Lord, for these mighty beets that makes you taps you feets.

Sheila squinted her eyes to dangerous dimes. Is not life more than meat, and the body more than raiment?

God, Lucifer said, thank you fo this food we bout to receive.

God is good, God is great, Porsha said. Thank him for this food we are about to receive.

Show the other side of the shield, Uncle John said.

Christ wept, Gracie said. *Blessing the only time she was short-winded about the Bible. God had stamped the Bible on her bosom. And when the wind of conversation rose, the pages turned at blinding speed, and Scriptures blew from her lips.*

Jesus dug in, food dangling from the webs of his fingers. Everybody followed, chowed down, chewing, forks and plates clattering—the music of eating. Porsha struggled to keep each diner's plate full.

Food greased a smile on Uncle John's mouth. He jabbed his elbow in Lucifer's ribs. Lucifer, member how she—he nodded in Sheila's direction—slaved in labor with Porsha?

Yeah.

Go tell it on the mountain, Gracie said.

Slaved. Uncle John watched Porsha now.

Yeah.

No baby should make her mamma work like that. Uncle John shifted his quick eyes. You didn even want to see the baby. Sheila, what you tell him? The doctor?

Jesus ate, face bent over plate, as if deaf to the conversation.

I'll see her tomorrow, Sheila said. Shoot, after all that sweatin and pushin, I was tired.

Sheila, you was a mess. Eyes all red. *A river of blood vessels.* Blood everywhere. Shit everywhere.

Hatch almost let the huge wad of corn bread and collard greens he was chewing fall out of his mouth in amazement.

Please. Porsha eased her fork to the table. Not while I'm eatin.

Well, I'm sorry. When the doctor say push, you push. Can't help what comes out.

You was a mess.

Nawl. I was tired. Tired.

But I held it. It felt like a chicken.

Thanks, Dad.

No offense. A chicken. You know, plucked. When you hold it under the faucet.

*The slick red fetus.*

Tired.

And fell right to sleep.

John, how you know? You wasn't even there. Out in that car—

The red Cadillac.

—listening to the game.

What you mean I wasn't there? The first relaxing burp quit Uncle John's mouth. Sure, I heard the game but I saw the delivery too.

No you didn't.

Never forget it. Cause that was the night Dip scored two hundred points.

See, Lucifer said. See, you even got that wrong. It wasn't two—

People be talkin bout how bad Flight Lesson is. Dip smoke him any—

That doctor got it all wrong.

How you gon stop somebody made like Dip?

Yeah. He was tough.

Porsha, you was born eleven-fifteen, not no twelve-fifteen.

Dip. A basketball machine. Man, some mad doctor in a laboratory put him together.

Yeah. With some pliers.

I should know. I was there.

And Ernie's torch.

Yeah. Ernie's torch.

I was lookin at the clock.

And some of his oil.

And tall.

I counted every minute.

Yeah. Member that time Dip got hurt and they had to rush him to the hospital on a hook and ladder?

I counted every minute.

Yeah. Now, how you gon stop that?

But Dip used to hog the ball. Selfish. Today it's about team play. Flight Lesson could average fifty a game easy if he hogged the ball.

Mamma, why would the doctor change the time?

Give me another one of those sweet potatoes.

Porsha forked one onto his plate.

Every holiday, the family rolled onto one topic or another. You knew every stop, every junction, and the final destination.

Yall ready for dessert? Porsha asked.

Bring it on, niece, Uncle John said.

Jehovah, Gracie said. Jehovah.

Porsha brought it on. Served everyone a thick wedge of chocolate cake. Yours tasted paste-thick. *Gracie made this.* You looked at Jesus. Tight lines around Jesus's mouth told you that Jesus was thinking the same. *Gracie made this.* Jesus finished his cake. And yours.

Porsha, Sheila mouthed words between bites, when you was a baby, John couldn't put you down.

Jesus's eyes grew wide at the strain of listening.

Mamma, how many times you gon tell that story?

A little ladybug on his arm.

You remember that wagon? Uncle John said. I used to pull her around in that little red wagon? Lucifer, you remember that little red wagon?

Um huh, Lucifer said, mouth full. Sure. The red wagon.

Where'd you get that wagon?

The junkman, Porsha said. Mamma, wasn't it the junkman?

No. Lucifer?

Um huh. His words skimmed above the surface of the conversation.

Gracie helped Porsha stack the thick foul dishes and bear them to the sink.

Come on into the living room, Gracie said.

Radiant with food and spiked eggnog, the family rolled—shiny balls, Christmas ornaments—into the living room.

I'll be there in a minute, Porsha said. She fanned around in the kitchen.

Girl, leave those dishes. Come out my kitchen.

I'll be there in a minute.

Lucifer and Sheila sat and shared the love seat. Uncle John sat by him-self—with his silver-clicking lighter he fired up a square, *Kool, New Life,* his favorites, ancient as memory—cocooned in the smoke of his cigarette. A mark of space—solitude? contentment?—in his face. Gracie sat down in the rocking chair—her righteous clothing, garments unspotted by the flesh, and grief from her wig down to her shoes; and the red coals of her rouge, yes, cause her small body hid a huge heart, parent of the two small hearts red-glowing her coal-black cheeks—beside him. You and Jesus eased back on the couch. *Dream it to yourself. Smell it. Hear it.* You studied the red stop-light of Jesus's face. Studied the lamp-glared moons of Uncle John's specta-cles. Studied Lucifer's yellow glow. Something would happen. You could feel it.

Uncle John unscrewed the bottle cap and Lucifer's tight mouth.

Pour me another.

Uncle John tipped the bottle.

Don't forget the boys.

Jesus twitched at the words.

Men, you said. We men.

Uncle John filled each of your glasses. Then drink like men.

Don't give them too much, Sheila said. One drink.

Ah, Sheila, Uncle John said, when you gon let this boy outa your apron strings?

Liquor dripped from your full glass.

He ain't in my apron strings.

Let the boy have some fun.

The family told family tales. The tight red lines in Jesus's face relaxed af-ter a steady soaking of drink. Lucifer's face snapped a loose rubber-band smile. The Crown Royal—the family heirloom—made shining diamonds of his teeth. You knew what would happen: words would cascade from Lu-cifer's throat, and his hands wouldn't quit Jesus's back and shoulders. *Boy. Nephew. My nephew.*

The empty Crown Royal bottle glinted beyond Uncle John's reach. I'll get a fresh one, Uncle John said. He rose from his seat.

Be careful, Gracie said.

What'll you care? Uncle John said. His voice bubbled with alcohol.

Don't start, Sheila said.

Wait, you said.

Uncle John faced you, shoulders slouched forward, heavy with alcohol.

You felt the eyes of everyone on you, stage lights. Wait, you wanted to say. Don't go. Well, you said. Hurry back.

Uncle John quit the room for a new fifth, taking the empty bottle with him.

Porsha screamed from the kitchen, I need some help in here. Gracie and Sheila—twins in the flesh, the same reality-worn hands and dull false teeth (thank God they hadn't fallen out during dinner) but colored different and haired different—rose and went to assist Porsha in the kitchen.

Lucifer put Jesus's back into the circle of his arm. Tugged him close. Nephew. The alcohol had kicked in. You been taking care of yourself?

I do alright, Jesus said.

Nephew. Red, I mean. Red, how come you ain't been around?

You know, Jesus said.

Hey, Lucifer, you remember that time—Hatch began to talk, steering carefully away from dangerous waters.

Red, you look good. Lucifer grinned the words.

—me, you, and Jesus—

I mean, boy, you look good. Rocking to the rhythm of the words.

Jesus leveled eyes of drilling steel. Boy?

Lucifer tugged. Red, I remember when you was—

Jesus jerked free. Boy? What you mean boy? Always got something bad to say about me.

Lucifer didn't appear to be listening. Slapped him again.

You see a boy you slap a boy. Sarcastic motherfucker.

Lucifer freezes. Struck. You act. Rush forward and manage to drive both arms up into the crook of Lucifer's elbow, breaking the punch that crunches Jesus's chin, changing the trajectory so that it does not land cleanly. The blow has enough force to knock Jesus to the other end of the room, flat on his butt. Jesus's eyes fly wide, blinding metal—shock? disbelief? Motherfucker. Up now, crouched over and running, bald bullet head aimed dead at Lucifer's midsection. Lucifer catches him around the neck, just like that, a frontal choke hold. Applies pressure.

What's going on in here? A woman's voice, or several. The women are in the room now, Sheila, Gracie, and Porsha. Jesus, Sheila says. I shoulda known. Always spoiling the holiday. Don't I deserve some peace.

Let him go. Let him leave, Porsha shouts.

Lucky yo father ain't here, Gracie says. Lucky John ain't here.

Let him go, Sheila says. Let him leave.

He ain't got to leave, Lucifer says. He grunts, applies pressure.

What are you doing?

I'm gon give the boy what he shoulda had a long time ago. Constricts his thick boa arms.

Let him go so he can leave.

No.

Lucifer—

Butt out.

Eyes glazed with determination—yes, these eyes are hard and bright, flash like Jesus's diamond earring—Jesus swings wildly, an occasional blow connecting with Lucifer's thick legs and arms. Punk, lemme go, the words squeezed out.

Stop, you say. Wasted words. You try to wedge your hands beneath Lucifer's locked arms.

Gon away, Lucifer says.

Let him go. Using the sides of your fists, you pound Lucifer's shoulder and arms. Let him go!

Lucifer jerks his head to the side and butts you powerfully into the wall. The wall crowds space into your mind. You walk around, meet yourself there. You feel a sudden safeness descend upon you. No doubts, no reservations. You lift the receiver from its cradle, smooth and light to the touch, without texture or weight. Poke digits.

911.

All is quiet, only you and the other voice.

911.

Hello. Yes. Please send a car to . . . Flame fills your body. Your tongue so dry and weak it can hardly find any words.

Yes. 911.

You answer simple and clean: Violence. Return the receiver to the cradle as if you had never touched it. Open the door loudly to the full and wait. You don't wait long.

You called—

Yes.

What's the problem?

Over there. You point.

They push winter into the house—nightsticks drawn, two black men, faces underneath the shadows of their caps, smelling of tough black leather. You don't shut the door behind them. No reason to.

Hey, let him go. Cop hand slides to holstered pistol.

Can't you hear? The second cop approaches Lucifer, slowly.

Not him, you say. The other one. He started it.

Okay, let him go. Lucifer squeezes Jesus's head and neck still harder. I said let him go. A final squeeze—for good measure—and he does. Jesus drops into a crawl.

Praise the Lord, Gracie says.

Please take him. Please take him outa here.

One cop holsters his nightstick and bends low to examine Jesus. Jesus slaps his hands way. Rights himself, yellow face now purple, even the freckles. Bitch—swings for Lucifer. The other cop nightsticks him to the abdomen.

Don't hurt him, Gracie says.

Jesus drops to one knee, like a sprinter, holding his stomach.

Just take him outa here.

Never again, Sheila says. Never again.

Well, you shouldn have let him come in the first place, Porsha says.

Don't blame me. I ain't let him in.

A cop knee-pins Jesus to the floor. A strong cop arm jerks his arm to the small of his back. Snaps cuffs on both wrists, then hauls him to his feet. Jesus comes up choking, a cop on either side of him.

You want to make a report?

Transformer, Jesus says when he can speak. His face has resumed its normal color, a red road map of veins. He lifts his chin slightly, looks Hatch full in the face, his own face tightening. Transformer.

Shut up, the cop says, heavy, male.

Snitch. Jesus lurches forward. The cops pull him back.

Just relax. The cops apply muscle.

Jesus frowns, gash-deep.

My hands were tied, you say. You made me, you say, the words with life of their own.

Uncle John enters the room, paper bag in arm. Like beheaded chickens, two glass necks poke out from the open end of the brown paper bag. Uncle John and Jesus lock their eyes on one another. Uncle John's mouth expands, marshaling words behind the tongue.

But know this, Gracie says. Head bent back, neck craned and looking up into Jesus's face. That if the good man of the house had known in what watch the thief would come, he would not have suffered his house to be broken up.

Uncle John shifts the bag from one arm to the other—the two bottles inside the bag knock together—the only sound in the room. Uncle John's chest moves deep and slow, feeling and measuring every breath.

Who then is a faithful and wise servant, whom his lord hath made ruler over the household, to give them meat in—

Shut up! Uncle John says. His chalk-white teeth scrape the blackboard of Gracie's flesh. She shudders.

Take him, Uncle John says. Take him, he pushes the words out, somewhere and let him cool off, he says.

Jesus flashes his eyes at Uncle John.

This your house?

Uncle John says nothing.

You want to file a complaint?

Uncle John says nothing.

Look, we'll take him but we ain't got time for this. There real crime out there.

Take him, Uncle John says. He aims his mouth like a flashlight in Jesus's face. It won't kill him.

You heard the man. The cops tug Jesus into motion. You can feel your heart all through you. Eyes slide away from Jesus's hating face. The cops waver swiftly to Gracie's open front door. The cops slip and shamble with Jesus on the polished black oak front-porch stairs. Carry Jesus between and away from them like a scalding bucket.

Don't forget his coat, Gracie says.

Give it to me.

Gracie passes the coat to Uncle John. Uncle John follows Jesus and the cops to the squad car. Winter hovers like a bird. I'll come with you to the station, Uncle John says.

Come in the morning. The cop snatches the jacket from Uncle John. Sleep on it. And sleep it off.

The cops bend Jesus under the squad car hood. Push him into the back seat, throw his red coat over his head like a hood. Take their places in the front seat, doors slamming behind them, you and Uncle John watching from the sidewalk, the white headlights flicking bright—balloons in the night; light floating up inside to the inside place from where you watch — the engine growling and the car leaping forward onto the ribbon of road.

THAT WAS THE LAST Hatch had seen of him. On first finding out about the cancer eating away Lula Mae's body, Hatch was determined to journey to Jesus and let him know; he never raised one uncertain foot in search. But these many months Jesus had felt near. His presence clung like a damp shirt. Now Hatch understood why. His exile foretold. Jesus approached the full height of his weightless life, for Freeze had given him a high mission and he would fulfill it, his red will be done. Blood followed blood. Blood defined. Blood defended.

T-Bone had smothered word for a reason. Hatch's one spark of consolation. Through T-Bone, Hatch was wiser in the knowledge, perhaps safer too. *The future will tell.* But how to use this knowledge? Jesus was not within reach. Even if he was— Shifted, uprooted, Jesus would not drop back into what he had been for Hatch at the beginning. And Uncle John was gone from him forever. Lucifer too. And surely Freeze would not be swayed by reason, forget or forgive.

Hatch dipped, dived, turned—all without leaving his seat. One thing for sure, he had to heart it alone. The wheels were in his head now, carrying him, pushing him. The train curved around the tunnel, grinding iron wheels working filelike over his teeth. He sat there, hungry, digesting his own invisibility. The train straightened into moving silence. Red Hook. The words bobbed into Hatch's consciousness, shiny red apples. Hatch bit. Red Hook. He tasted. Red Hook. The words forced their way to his lips. He looked about the car to see if anyone had heard him. Assured, he savored the words on his silent tongue. He would walk beyond the knowable horizon. He would move, swift and definite. Red Hook. His bright mind cut through metallic glare. He would go to Red Hook. The thought came smooth, without effort, rippling like a boat over water. The train tilted up, unhitched from the world. The whole car filled up with joy so that it was hard to breathe. Yes, he would go to Red Hook.

# 29

BEAUTY DEMANDS MOTOR SKILLS. Like driving a car.

She feels, words tossed into her silent insides. Her head warms to morning. A listening glow. Infinite sunlight. Infinite window. How clearly the instructor stands out against everything going on in front of her, his lips moving quietly, birdlike.

White lines. Yellow lines. Steady hand at the circular wheel. Sight and touch equal, each with a job to perform. The instructor pours a cup of coffee—she can hear it, smell it, feel it—that gleams like liquid steel. Her nipples rise to quick attention. Heads bent over sketchpads, the students behave in exemplary fashion. Their hands move with ease, comfort in knowing exactly what to do.

The reassuring sounds of another vehicle or two. Caught in the stillness of speed. The eye of each man is on himself. But, please, be careful. Cautious. The instructor waves his hands like a magician. Don't blink.

The students shake with laughter, their pencils moving spastically. She would laugh too, if her flesh would permit.

Light, the most suitable of bodies, has the greatest extension.

The words she sees and seeing hears sink into a darkness past her telling. The instructor bends at the waist; with his thumb removes a dust speck from brown leather shoe, glowing tie extending down and away from his neck, a dog's wet tongue. She waits. Light ticks off the sun. *Spring forward. Fall back.* She sits in her own weather, private.

Optics is inseparable from the study of lines, angles, and figures that are realized in the propagation of light.

This still room (and her body still). Bright lake light tiding the window. Moved by the instructor's voice, words foreign in meaning. Depths she can't sound. Moved. She spreads thought on the morning. Water-deeps reflect opening roses, expanding (disintegrating) leaves, floating colors, petals larger than her hands.

Your eye seeds itself. His fingers circle a sun-charged cup and saucer. A chip on the rim, neat clean and precise from a distance, as if painted on. He sips (one sips tea not coffee) it black. *No sugar, I bet. Put money on it.* Of smaller details, he says, coffee steam on his words, no saying. He chimes cup to saucer. Moves to the window—white cup and white saucer balanced in the palm of one hand like a delicate flower—blackfired against the light. *Give me what you have.*

The window offers a visual path to Red Hook miles through air blindingly bright, clear as if she knew it firsthand. Her feelings expand. Her desire for Deathrow released and flowing.

No false colors.

Deathrow in a place memory picked out. His skin mirror to her own.

No fraudulent lines. He lifts cup from saucer and tilts it to his lips. His eyes close with the drinking. He returns cup to saucer. Opens his eyes. Sets cup and saucer on the plane of windowsill. Breathes.

Deathrow.

He stands before the city—small eyes (bits of green glass), face strong, brows and hair the same heavy black; his body, fat and lined—it behind him, as if he had painted it. The city built into the sky. He built it. *The calm of form,* he gestures, *the storm of imaginings.*

The serial glint of distances. Everything's far, except here. Even the instructor. A shape she can follow back to a source in the self. The students study her from the intimacy of distance, their voices faint and far. They—the same face repeated over and over, eyes gleaming—had entered quickly and silently, this long brown room full of sunlight and shadows, shifting trees outside. Her brown form took the podium, while silent praises trailed her from their desks.

*To paint is to draw boundaries. Each dot a simple bearing that tells us where and how we ought to stand.* He turns to face the window, his broad canvas of back facing the class. He takes it all in. Fresh. He lifts and sips. *Ah, yes. Fresh.*

Still-seated, seated-still, she listens and observes, only her eyes moving, and their eyes and hands: so many styles of breathing, varied shells dotting a beach. She hears against wind from a distance Deathrow speaks from, the earth (sand) between them. Her tenderest knowing. Deathrow far away, in that region inside herself, untouched and unchanged. Him belonging by how she feels about him. Yearning inward to be part, to be embodied.

*To draw is to shut your eyes and sing.* The instructor turns away from the window—light curling around him in the turning, curling, cocoonlike— back to the class. *Taste is the mother of beauty.* He takes up his cup and saucer, now yellow in the light. *Open your mouth. Pigment.* The instructor smiles, teeth large and round as eggs. *Not pig meat.*

Student heads bob laughter.

Time in the moment of waiting. This day barely different from the last. No Deathrow. No sight. No sound. No touch. Her heart shivers to stay her body. *How much longer will I wait?* She still—*this is my job*—letting wonder hold. (Could she afford less wonder?) Her mind, holding. Her body, waking and waiting, a gentle wearing down. The world gone over with the edge of sunrise, she had lifted her head from her exhausted pillow, bathed, dressed, baptized her earlobes with perfume, considered lipstick—tubular colors glittered in their steel bulletlike shells—taken the train, numb to the day, walked across the spring grass, the grass hissing at her heels, ducked under black boughs, angled through sections of the sculptured garden where hoses sprayed furious foam, where—above—pigeons turned again and again, air on air. So morning found her, serene and neat, fully upright in an armless chair (plain, hard, wood), her proud flesh exposed for training eyes.

What did I say or do? Maybe he met with an accident, black and blue. Deathrow. He never broods for days. So unlike him. Feel and feel in return. Only pain (or death) would keep him away from me, keep him from calling. She shivered at the thought, the inward turn of mind. Think the best. He is angry, even if lasting anger is uncharacteristic. Only one knows how two feel. She can ask, ask herself, how to the other she may appear, to his eyes and heart. Yes, the possibility of blind feeling when like-minded lovers harden, change.

Number is the key to harmony. Two perpendicular lines, one from nipple to nipple, the other the length of the torso. Simple ratios between the height of the columns and the spaces between the axes.

She could always go to Red Hook.

The surest way to a center is through a maze. The instructor drains the saucer to hollow whiteness. Burps. Catch light as a design on us.

Now the instructor's voice wakens her, awakens in her the need to know. Heavy in her chair, weighted with alternatives. Yes, she could go to Red Hook and end the uncertainty.

Once, she had driven there through freezing rain.

It was nine at night and had been storming all day. Heavy rain jumped like divers from the clouds and collided against the car's roof. (She would have to search it for dents. *Yes, the Datsun 280ZX was brand-new then.*) Her windows steamed, wind rushing the rain in. Bubbled in cowled sound, she drove slowly and carefully, illuminated by the dashboard's green light. Traffic was heavier than usual in the city streets and even slower on the highway. Stalled cars floated, water-soaked driftwood. Stalled buses like watering elephants. She put her foot on the gas—the rain accelerated—wheeled to the outside lane and speeded past the limit. It didn't take her long to reach South Lincoln. (Yes, she had seen it.) South Lincoln tilted into Tar Lake as

if a careless broom had shoved it there. The Red Hook Housing Projects—
*the jets*, so they called it, toilet flush and airplane roar—ringed it, a soaring
metal commode flooded with an invisible tide of heaving black brown yellow flesh.

She turned off at the exit. Entered a valley. The car whined down a black
strip of street. Touched waters curved away from the windshield, carrying wake behind. Sealed inside the car, she observed square metal giants
that looked down on small slumped-over houses set down boulderlike and
squeezed together in silent rows.

At the red-staring stoplight, she observed knucklelike roots that had
pushed up through the concrete pavement but no tree. Flocks of vivid children threw bread at one another, their laughs and taunts fluttering up. The
light blinked green.

She drove past the Wells Street Port with its railroad tracks extending onto
docks where Tar Lake raged black waters. She was close now. Deathrow
lived by himself—he had little to do with his family; long ago, he'd decided
that they were guppies, eating their young—in a row house that was part of
Red Hook but a good mile or more away from it.

Her wipers quit. The windshield cried with blind rain. She worked the
switch. The wipers refused to function. She would have to exit the car, enter
the rain, and manually set the wipers back in motion. Sighting out the passenger window, she swung car to curb and kept the engine running. Under
a blind streetlamp, corner boys tried to float an old gym shoe on a puddle.
And hooded boys (men?) moved lethargic, dreamlike, in the half-light of
rain and street.

She stood away from the memory. Kept it at a distance. Ah, Deathrow.
Deathrow.

The instructor cut his eyes toward her. His nostrils flared a little. Had she
said it out loud? Or moved with the thinking of it? Deathrow.

# 30

EVEN THE SKY WAS DIRTY HERE, canvas-colored, a rough sun pasted to it. Used papers fluttered about, giant moths. The morning full of sirens, moving in waves, crashing and rising again. Stonewall and Red Hook ran the distance of the horizon. Gatewayed in his eyes. Sparkled like two big buckets cast down in the middle of South Lincoln. He walked with measured steps. Every few seconds, his head wheeled back over his shoulder. He raised his arms like wings. Sticky sweat beneath his shirt. Many a time he had placed himself into the hollow form of a chalk-white sidewalk tracing, space that defined South Lincoln nightly on the TV news. He was alone here.

South Lincoln was like another country, cut off and remote from the one on the rim. He knew. Before the Great Fire of 1871, locals called this strip of land, which ran west from Stonewall all the way east to Red Hook, Mud Europe. Poor white trash lived in low wooden houses on pole foundations that kindled into fire nightly. After the Great Fire, the city replaced them with brick town houses. Then the city tapped rail upon rail to form highrises, a steel gift for veterans returning from the war. In a space of years, the once low shoebox houses had stretched to boot-tall projects.

A car rolled past and roared to a stop at the corner, turned, leaving behind the power of its sound. Red Hook rose up before him. A still red flower, sixteen buildings arranged petal-fashion. Wine-flushed niggas dogged a corner, leashed to a lamppost. Nerves went electric in his body.

What up, player?

What up, he said.

You straight?

I'm straight.

I got the best.

I'm straight.

Rock to you can't stop. Make you wanna drop.

I'm straight.

Aw ight, player.

At the next corner, another group of niggas stood. Silent. Sunlight slipped inside the caves of their bowed hoods. Gleamed off bald heads. He concentrated on keeping his pace.

The project walls had the thickest bricks he'd seen. Bricks made of iron, not straw. He could feel wet heat inside them. They could withstand a bomb blast. A bomb could do no more than age the sidewalks, add some cracks.

Voices speeded in. Voices of red song, red song. Sound on skin. Sounds of skin. Noise closer upon him than his own clothes. A chicken scratch of words clawed at his eyes and ears. A charcoal dog barked from the wall. Building One. The white-painted 1 ran a rough pattern over rough brick, crayon smeared on wax paper.

He stood before a door, two slabs of steel, at the top of each a box of thick glass window covered with iron wire. The lock buzzed, sending fire through his body, and the slabs opened, light to the touch, inward like a church. He stepped into a vestibule of red tile walls and cereal-colored tile floors. Ripe heat. A man sat short like a ventriloquist's dummy in the lap of a big wheelchair. Missing the lower halves of his legs. A second man sat next to him, his legs hidden under a metal block of desk. Wrinkles in his neck and face thicker than his mustache. A metal clipboard in reaching distance of his worm-wrinkled fingers. The fingers inched, crawled toward the clipboard. *This old motherfucker workin security?*

That's neither here nor there.

God was watching out for you. You were blessed.

Blessed hell. I wish he had killed me. In forty-five years, I ain't slept more than two or three hours a night.

Hello. The words barely quit Hatch's mouth.

What you want?

I'm—

You in the wrong place. This the senior citizens building.

I'm lookin for Mr. Pool Webb.

I said you in the wrong place.

If you'll permit me.

You got a hearing problem?

No, sir. I'm looking for Webb. Mr. Pool Webb.

What?

Mr. Pool Webb.

Silence sounds in the slowness of the pause. Pool Webb?

Yeah.

Why?

He's a friend of my father.

Who's your father?

Lucifer Jones.

Who?

Lucifer Jones.

The man watched Hatch longer than Hatch cared to return the stare.

Go into the Community Center.

Where?

The Community Center. Round there. The man pointed.

Thanks. Do I need to sign in? Hatch gestured toward the clipboard.

Did I ask you to sign in?


THE COMMUNITY CENTER was a small round checker of a building centered in the massive grid of Red Hook. Hatch cracked the silence of the faraway metal door with the barefaced window. A desk beckoned to his immediate left. *Desk or table? Who can tell?* The room fluttered white. He heard it and saw it, a window raised on rusted strings. Four white wings veiled Hatch's peeping eyes—had to peep (no fresh open sight), his pupils carrying the outside light inside. White doves.

Yall want this bread, yall better come get it. Damn if I'm gon chase you. The man held up two stubs of white bread. A gorilla head man with bear feet. *What kind of animal?* His body enveloped a leather chair in a shapeless mass of flabby flesh, a collapsed parachute. A black-tipped (rubber) brown (wood) cane slanted across his body, the curved head looping the circle of his lap. Hurry up, too. I gotta get back to the desk. The doves settled light onto the limbs of his thumbs. The man's bowed head raised quickly, as if he'd been kicked in the chin. Yes, his eyes had caught the shadow of Hatch's approaching shoes.

What you want? The voice thundered. The birds fluttered into white flight. You must be in the wrong place. This the Community Center. His eyes watched Hatch. Strained vision. Red overworked vessels. And yellow, possible jaundice. But more than red and yellow. Two globes of color. Dyed eggs.

You Pool Webb?

Yeah. Who you?

Aw, my name Hatch.

Who?

Hatch. Hatch Jones.

Don't believe I know you.

I come here about Lucifer.

Lucifer?

Lucifer Jones. You know, Blue Demons.

The man watched.

The basketball team.

What?

Blue Demons basketball team.

Oh, the team.

Lucifer coach—

Oh, Lucifer. Pool Webb smiled in recognition. Lucifer Jones. He extended his hand. Hatch accepted it, amazed at the tension of energy coursing beneath the skin, a secret torrent that bore no relation to the flabby torso, the rubber-band legs in crisp, pressed trousers. *Does he press them? With those hands?* Ain't heard from him in a while. How is he?

He fine.

He some kin to you?

Well, he my Uncle John's brother.

What?

John Jones. He my uncle.

Webb watched, questioning eyes.

Lucifer my father.

Oh, I see. So you want to join the basketball team?

No. I don't care much for sports.

Just visitin?

I guess. I heard a lot about you.

From Lucifer?

Hatch nodded his head.

He sho is a quiet one. Get more words out of one of these birds. And they ain't even parrots.

Hatch's face closed. He warmed to the joke, outer sun radiating upward from his inner belly. He released a delayed, high-pitched laugh.

I didn't even know he had a son.

Hatch said nothing.

How is he anyway?

Fine, I guess. *You already asked me that.*

That's good. He know we got a game Saturday.

I don't know if he know.

Bread-free, bird-free, Pool Webb rested his hands on the half-loop of his cane handle. Look, I gotta get back to the desk. Webb bowed forward—resting his full weight on the cane—kneeled, a sprinter preparing to drop low on his hips and haunches. The cane's black rubber foot pressed into the carpet. The wood shaft vibrated. Hatch thought he heard it hum. He extended an arm to assist Webb, but the arm wouldn't reach. Webb rose to full height. *He same size as me; maybe a little taller; can't tell with those legs.* Sit down right here.

Hatch dropped into Webb's still-warm leather seat.

I be off in fifteen minutes. Want some bread?

What?

Some bread. To feed them birds.

No, that's okay.

Pool Webb guided his cane, his knees projecting away from one another as if they were scared to touch. Yes, the O of his knees and bandied legs made him stoop and roll when he walked. His thick head bowed, watching his long arms and big fists. Hatch thought he heard a knuckle or two scrape the concrete. Hatch thought what he hated to think. *Pool Webb look like a gorilla.*

A NOISY VACUUM OF ELEVATOR sucked them in. Inner steel, cold, silver, and surgical. The doors banged shut. The elevator lurched into motion. *The spirit of gravity, Spokesman said, dancing, floating, freedom above things.* The vacuum sucked at Hatch's insides. Sucked out the butterflies. The elevator worked in pain. Breaking pain that gave a final push to open the doors.

Hatch followed slow Webb patiently down the hall. *Should I help him?* Webb pulled noisy keys from his pocket on a loop of steel chain and unlocked all three locks. The chain pulled the keys back into the darkness of his pocket. He pushed the door open and Hatch followed him in. Don't let the door slam, Webb said.

Hatch caught the heavy steel door. Closed it quietly. Locked all three locks.

The apartment was more window than wall. Four wide boxes—*yes, not picture windows cause they were more square than rectangle*—that filled the green-gray space with dust-flecked light and polished the furniture with sky-sharpened shine. A single space of room opening into other rooms. Webb's bed—puffed pillows and ruffled sheets, waiting—held parallel to a concrete veranda. And beyond the veranda, Tar Lake in the distance.

Nice veranda.

You mean the terrace. We all got that overhang. The senior citizens. In a slow, stooping motion, Mr. Pool Webb rolled across the room in round gorilla movements. Make yourself comfortable. You at home.

Thanks.

Pool sat down on the bed. Pulled off his slacks. Heavyweight boxer shorts over bantamweight skinny legs. The carpet was a black sticky swamp. Hatch guarded his steps. Pulled back the aluminum kitchen chair—parallel to the wall, parallel to the veranda—and sat down. A garden colored the veranda—*terrace, it's a terrace*—rows and rows of plants in rusted coffee cans. Tomatoes, collard greens, and peppers.

Wait a minute. Sit in one of those wood chairs there. They hold your weight.

Hatch did as instructed. A portable radio, a deck of playing cards, bottles of hot sauce and ketchup, a container of laxative, and a pencil or two were neatly arranged on the wide windowsill. Hatch saw other buildings, dead-white, stained by bird shit. So they gave you a hard time?

Hell yes. That was my last job. Worked there seventeen years.

I see.

Superintendent at Red Hook. Sixteen buildings. Ninety-six hundred families. Nine thousand and six hundred. Hundred thirty-four men worked under me. Custodians. But I couldn't take all that pressure. Told the doctor, I can't work no mo. He gon tell me I can. Fuck that. See my legs?

Hatch couldn't miss them.

I got rubber veins here and here. Webb pointed out long lengths of scars, yellow lines running up (and down) the brown skin of each leg. From when I had a stroke. And that doctor talkin bout I could still work. Fuck that. I told him, See if I work.


So how you like South Lincoln?

I can live with it.

Is it as bad as they say it is? I mean, South Lincoln?

Just like anyplace else. You got yo bad spots.

And Red Hook?

We got more security here, in the senior citizens building. Now Buildin Six, down on Federal. Webb shook his head. I wouldn live there for free. And Buildin Nine on Wells. Couldn't pay me to live there. They snuff you in a minute.

Damn.

But a lot of these young guys in South Lincoln just plain stupid. Small-time. If you can make corn whiskey, fix up a still in the backyard. That way you can bribe the sheriff. But if you cook it on the stove . . .

Hatch nodded. Make sense to me. It really did.

Yes, I seen a lot of shit in my day.

Centered on the dresser, a photograph of Pool Webb's son? grandson?—a fat-faced boy about Hatch's age—and daughter? granddaughter?—probably younger—equally healthy in the face. *This a eatin family.* And his grand-child—so Hatch assumed—with a black-skinned, white-bearded, and red-costumed Santa Claus.

Those yo grandkids?

No, that's my son and daughter.

Hatch saw a young, uniformed Webb—his sly eyes and mean pouted mouth—posed with a comely woman with a haughty face.

That your wife? She look West Indian.

Wife? Nawl. That's my mamma.

Hatch chanced a second look at the photograph. Yes, the heavy face, one sign of the aged, the same heavy face that Pool also bore.

She from Tennessee just like me.

I see.

Me and my mother used to have a helluva time. I called her Sister. Sister and I go get drunk. We come home. She clean the kitchen before going to bed.

Yeah, she died here in the city. Nineteen fifty-seven. I was ready though. I knew it was comin. If a bird flies into someone's house, someone will fly out.

A KNOCK ON THE DOOR roused Hatch's heart.

Who is it? Webb screamed.

Lee.

Shit. Hatch, let her in.

The floor was swiftly waiting to Hatch's feet. He freed the locks and drew the door open. Lee's breasts greeted him.

Hi, young man.

Hatch's tangled tongue came unloose. Hi.

Lee followed her breasts through the door. Hey, Pool.

Hey, Lee.

Hatch closed the door behind her. She was a good deal older than Hatch but a good deal younger than Pool. He was bad at tellin age.

I jus fed her. She sleep. Thought I'd come down here and see what you up to.

Jus waitin for you.

I know, honey.

Oh, Lee—Pool pointed at Hatch—this Hatch, my cousin.

Hatch almost spun his head at the word. *My cousin.* Why had Pool lied?

Hi, honey.

Hi.

Lee's breasts reached for him.

BUT MY GRANDMOTHER RAISED ME. My grandmother and my uncle. We did all the work on the land. The three of us. My grandfather worked at a sawmill. The steam fried his eyes. He went blind. He passed when I was five.

My grandmother made root tea from the woods.

*Drowned roots from a drained swamp.*

Sassafras tea, Lee said.

Castor oil, Hatch said.

Nowadays, they got castor oil you can't even taste.

WHEN I WAS SIXTEEN, I left town to work on the railroad. Webb spoke in a fat preacher's voice. But I didn't come to the city until after the war.

I came to the city for pussy I had met when I was stationed at Fort Square.

I came to the city in 1947. That's when the city was the city. You could have roof parties. Sit in Circle Park all night.

See, I got married in 1938. My wife messed round with every Tom and his dick.

Your wife musta had some good stuff, Lee said.

Nawl. She was just hot in the ass. One of those Creoles. Everybody but me knew she was hot in the ass. They say Pussy and she say Present. My wife's best friend told me how to catch her. I came home from work and caught her in the bed with a man. I put my gun on them. The man jumped up out of that bed and jumped out the window, dick whipping like a blind man's cane. I put the gun on him.

Pool, my wife said, why you gon shoot that man?

I put the gun on her.

Pool, please don't shoot me.

I put the gun in my pocket and left town that night, and that's how I got here. Nineteen forty-six.

Yo wife's best friend told, Lee said.

Yeah.

You know women are evil, Lee said.

The gospel truth.

Yo wife's best friend told all right. That's because she was gettin some of that big dick too, Lee said. Men with big dicks go from woman to woman. Mothers, daughters, sisters. My best friend I covered up for many times. But I ain't want none of her men. I wouldn't spit on a big dick man if he was on fire. It's not the size of the man's business that matters, but the service it renders.

I got service.

Pool, you bad. Ain't he bad, honey?

Hatch smiled, unsure about what to say.

I went back home and asked my wife for a divorce. She talking bout she ain't gon give me one. I put my gun on her.

Soon as I get back to the city, that woman throws me out. I done bought all of her furniture and I hear she got a new man enjoying it. I took out my knife and cut her across her stomach. Her girdle saved her.

See, I don't take no mess. Once I was at the movie theater with my wife—

*Whites sat on the first floor and blacks in the balcony, Beulah told.*

—and there was this son of a bitch cursing behind us. So I asked him, Mister, can you please watch yo mouth. I'm here with my wife. He leaned forward right next to my ear—

*You musta smelled his breath. Popcorn.*

—and started cursing all in my face. Called me everything but the Son of God. Then he put his knife to my throat. Nigga, I'll cut yo throat. He took the knife away and went back to cursing.

I told my wife, Let's go.

I want to see the other two movies, she said.

*Three movies for a dime, Beulah told.*

So I waited til that last movie was almost over and took my wife outside and found me a brick. See, my arm was in a sling.

*Why? What happened?*

I hid that brick behind the sling and waited for that son of a bitch.

Pool, please, my wife said.

Just stand out of the way.

That son of a bitch came out and saw me. Nigga, you want some mo? He reached for his knife. I threw the brick and hit that son of a bitch in the head. That son of a bitch fall right out, blood gushing from his head.

These two ladies come from the shithouse. Mister, you done killed that man.

Pool, Lee said, you bad. Ain't he bad, honey?

Hatch smiled.

See, I never took no mess from white folks either. Once I was in this bar and this half-drunk white man called me a nigga then kicked me. I grabbed him by his hair like this. Pool demonstrated. And beat his ass til I got tired.

*Naw, naw. Them white folks woulda got you.*

Think them white folks messed with me? See, they thought I was crazy. Boots, they say. They called me Boots. Boots, you crazy.

I worked with him. It rained the next day. He come up to me. Boots, we can't haul wood today. Let's go hunting. I went too.

What? Hatch said.

No you didn't, Lee said.

Yes I did. I had my rifle and he had his.

Why'd you do that? Hatch said. Why'd you go hunting with him?


WELL, I BETTER GET BACK TO WORK, Lee said. Time fo me to feed her her lunch.

You leavin already?

A woman got to work, Lee said. Ain't that right, honey? She winked at Hatch.

That's right, Hatch said.

Pool grabbed Lee's pointed tiddies. Lee, I may be old, but I can still shift the gears.

Lee retracted her titties. Pool, you bad.

Here, look at this. Pool worked his hand under the sheet.

Is it ready?

It's ready.

Well, Pool, you send that young man over to tell me when it's ready.

Hatch lowered his eyes.


YES, THAT LEE. Webb's old body laughed, an avalanche of spasms that began at his head and ended with his feet.

A snake bout the only thing I'm fraid of. Once I went hunting with this white man and he picked up this snake.

Pool, he says, I'm gon put this snake on you.

You better not, I says.

He threw it on me.

I shot him in the arm.


I HAD THIS COUSIN who killed him eight crackas. He was out on this little is-land in the middle of the lake, hiding in this woodpile. Every time a cracka raise his head, he blow it off. They sprayed the island with a plane.


ONCE, MY WIFE CALL THE COPS ON ME. Four cops. They say, Your wife say you pulled a gun on her. I tell em, Take your hats off in my house. They say,

Where's the gun? Don't put your hand on it. I tell them, Sit down. Don't
stand over me.

I BOUGHT MY HOUSE in Crownpin. White folks look at me but I just look at
them back. The first night, the man next door come ring my bell. He says,
I'm not like them. I'm not prejudiced. I slammed the door in his face. We
were best friends after that.

THE EL STOOD ON WOOD ARMS above downtown Central, the Loop. Fire engines roared down State Street, curved wings of red water onto already wet
sidewalks. Wooden horses—knee-deep in water—dammed-off streets that
imitated rivers. Cops helped lay black roads of fire hose. Firemen waded in
high black fishing boots. Aimed eel-thick hoses. Other firemen floated, red
rubber duckies.

*Divers had been inspecting all twelve rivers. The first reports suggest that
wood pylons broke through the freight tunnels. The freight tunnels run twenty
feet beneath the rivers.*

*The freight tunnels were used to cart messages and materials from building
to building. Then streetcars were housed there.*

*The mayor has formed a team of engineers. They want to plug the tunnels
with sandbags, then stick a rubber bladder in each. Work may begin as early
as midnight tonight.*

*All subways are closed. Expect partial service on the Els by morning.*

*The mayor has declared a state of emergency. CE has shut off all power in
the area. Firemen are relying on small generators. Water threatens the structural integrity of many of the buildings in the Loop. The Underground is completely underwater. Small colored fish swim there.*

Well, Pool said. Ain't that a mess? I guess you better be getting back.

I can wait a while.

Wait? Look at that mess. Webb nodded at the blinking blue screen. If you
don't leave now, no telling when you might get back. What you gonna do,
fly over all that water?

Hatch said nothing. He thought about it. I still got to get through Central, he said. They shut the subway down. I'll have to take the bus. Think I
can make it with all those streets closed off? He wished that he could answer
the question for Webb. *No. You won't make it.* No was the answer he needed.
A question had brought him here. Webb was close to answering it. He was
sure.

Maybe, if you leave now.

It'll be dark soon. It'll be dark soon but I can still try.

You can try it if you want.

Maybe, if I leave now.

Maybe.

Before it gets dark.

Before it gets dark.

Yeah. It'll be dark soon.

Well, you know, you welcome to stay here.

Hatch felt the words nest in his skin. You sure?

You welcome.

Thanks. His insides settled. He felt new space inside, space for the time he needed. I'll go back in the morning. They should have things together by then.

Call your mother and let her know you alright.

I will.

Call her now. Don't let yo mamma worry.

Hatch lifted the receiver to his ear. It felt cold, an ice compress. The line rang and rang, swelled into his brain. He counted the number of rings, hung up the phone, and settled back into the inner harbor of the couch.

No answer?

Hatch shook his head. Guess nobody there. She probably didn't make it home from work, with the flood and all. Got to come all the way from the suburbs.

You know her work number. You know it. Call her at work.

Hatch dialed another number. Let it ring a few times. Counted the rings. Hung up the phone. Nobody there, he said.

You sure?

Hatch nodded.

What about yo daddy? I know yo daddy worry, way he talk about you.

The words startled Hatch. *Lucifer talk about me?* Webb was wrong, his memory mixed up, one of those things old people do. *I didn't even know he had a son.* Lucifer never spoke his name to others. Webb probably meant Uncle John. Uncle John talk bout me all the time.

Call yo daddy at work.

At work?

Yeah.

Hatch thought fast. Maybe they had to go down South to see my grandmother. *Yeah, that's it.* They had to go down South to West Memphis to see my grandmother Lula Mae. She sick.

Oh yeah?

Yeah. Cancer.

Sorry to hear that.

Thanks. That's where they went. They go down there every two weeks or so. Hatch watched his own truth in Webb's eyes and face.

Well, try again later. Jus to be sure.

I will.

# 31

GIVE ME A COPPER, the bum said, and I'll tell you a golden story. Camouflaged in the city's dirt, the bum sat with the building at his back, his legs straight before him. (Lucifer had almost stumbled over them.) A cardboard sign hung biblike from his neck: I'M A VET.

Sorry, Lucifer said.

You look like a military man. Are you a military man?

Lucifer continued walking, silent in the slanting sun.

You *are* a military man. I can always tell a military man.

Sorry. Lucifer moved on. A plague of hot asphalt and city sizzle. New York, New York. The Big Apple. Back again. *You brought me back. Called.* There's an ocean of time between Lucifer's present and previous visits. The first many years ago. He left John and Gracie at the hospital after the doctor birthed them something that looked like a head of red cabbage. He pulled his savings from the bank (vet pay) and bought a plane ticket. He grinned broadly at the rush of takeoff. Speed hummed through his body. He settled into it. The stewardess—they were still called that then—smiled in the steam of the coffee she'd prepared. Neither female warmth nor coffee warmth relaxed him. He hated planes. Anxious boredom. He never knew if the plane was moving until it came to a stop. The plane hummed through a sea of clouds. New York was there somewhere beneath that sea. What would he see on descent? The Empire State Building? The Twin Towers? The Statue of Liberty? The Chrysler Building? The question vanished. He saw a swash of green and thought it green ocean, but as the plane descended, he recognized green-painted roofs. He saw what looked like houses, scattered over blocks of neighborhoods, but as the plane dropped closer, he saw these houses were really tombstones.

High windows steamed bright light. Thick crowds of people edged through blocks of concrete on concrete. Traffic flowed in slow coils. A big machine. Yes, New York was a big machine.

No one understood machines better than Spokesman. This was *his* city. He was the person to see. With Spokesman the facts were always the same.

Facts. Spokesman was always willing to sit you down in a corner of his thoughts.

Give me that shit say dynamite on the label, John said. I feel like something powerful tonight.

Dallas passed John the 40 Acres, John's and Dallas's favorite cheap wine. John tilted the bottle to his lips, one hand on the bottle, one on the wheel. It was in a car that John felt most at home.

Spokesman put his hand out the window, feeling the wind.

Pebbles shot up under the car and clinked. The road before them was one long curving surprise as John's red Cadillac zoomed through the hot white light of afternoon into tepid evening shade. Drinking and talking and philosophizing. Voices bubbling with alcohol. Spokesman said something and Lucifer said something and Spokesman nodded and smiled his approval and Lucifer felt like a bird flying above the car.

There was something fascinating about listening to Spokesman. You hold your breath to listen. He had the answers. All of them. But how to find him? Lucifer fingered the old envelope bearing Spokesman's address. Spokesman had supplied no phone number. Lucifer didn't know Spokesman's job title or place of work. What would he do, call or visit every Symmes Electronics store in New York? The only solution was to go directly to Spokesman's home. Camp out there if necessary.

What would he say to Spokesman? Words rushed through his head. So many ways to begin. Twice a month, Spokesman mailed Lucifer a letter thickly definite. Words bound to tell. Now, Spokesman's words come to mind like photographs. *Ancient words were written on durable clay tablets, and the Bible, parchment, a much more perishable material. Once the almanac is completed, I must publish it on some material that bridges the gap between ancient durability and modern flexibility.* Spokesman wrote, by airmail—always airmail—from *here* to *there, The gravity of physics rejects the presence of two identical forces staring each other in the eye.* The letter would always end: *If you ever get to heaven, I'll be there.* He would sign his simplest name, Spoke.

What had inspired the almanac? A reputable agency had investigated Spokesman's genealogy. Spokesman had discovered no less than fifty historical inconsistencies. No natural soil could have grown the proposed family tree.

WHAT DO YOU WANT? the doorman said. An old black guy who looked like a military sentinel in his uniform. You don't belong here.

Lucifer showed him the envelope.

Oh, Spokesman. Penthouse. Lucifer followed the doorman to the elevator. The doorman pressed the button P and waited for the metal doors to
shut. Tell him Bill says hello.

I will.

Lucifer used this final rising moment to organize his thoughts. Why was
he so nervous? Spokesman was an old buddy from the hood. Almost family.

*The way Spokesman skyed the ball, the way he palmed it high and made it
stick to air, made it stick like the sun. The way he drove to the hoop, bogarting,
all elbows, sharp elbows slicing at your guts and nuts. Short nigga spit science
on the ball, marked it his. Jumped on Jimmy the Cricket legs and slid the ball
in the hoop easy with grease off his palm.*

*Dallas let his tongue hang loose, as he always did whenever he got frus-
trated. Spokesman came in hard, black and smoking. Palmed the ball and
rolled it up Dallas's chin and tongue, leaving skid marks. Rolled that ball
smooth over the taller man's head.*

*Damn, John said. Damn. You gon let him do that shit to you?*

*Stay out of it, Lucifer said.*

*Damn. You gon let him play you like a chump?*

*John, Lucifer said, why you always tryin to start some shit?*

Elevator doors parted. Spokesman stood waiting. For the first time in
memory, he wore a suit, tailor-made from the looks of it. The same old bifo-
cals though, big as binoculars.

Lucifer and Spokesman stared at each other for a long minute. Lucifer
looked away first and Spokesman smiled to himself.

Lucifer, Spokesman said.

Spoke.

They hugged like old war buddies. Come in, Spokesman said. Long
time, no see.

Yes.

Spokesman took him through one room then another, all bare. The final
room seemed crowded after the previous emptiness. A large living room
with two plain wooden chairs (high backs but no arms) and a tall telescope
that looked into a drawn curtain. Lucifer remembered: the windows and
curtains were kept closed as light and circulating air would fade the furniture. But there was no furniture. Old habits.

Have a seat. Spokesman motioned to one of the chairs.

Thanks. Lucifer sat down in the chair.

Spokesman squatted down on the other chair in the long light. They
faced one another, a good thirty feet separating them, a second, curtainless
window directly behind Spokesman. In the open, bare room, Lucifer felt
that he could sit for days and absorb the atmosphere. The clear sky and me-

andering clouds above the green box of Central Park increased the mystery of being there. He had never felt this way in his life.

I don't believe it, Spokesman said. Lucifer Jones. Sitting right here before my eyes. Is that really you?

It's me.

I don't believe it.

Believe it.

I don't believe it.

Lucifer smiled. He felt a rush of warmth pass through him.

How did you travel?

By train.

Train?

Lucifer nodded.

I hope you brought along some good reading. One should always have something sensational to read on the train.

Lucifer said nothing. Made sense to him. Pure Spoke.

Man, I been trying to reach you. You never responded to my letters.

Been meaning to.

I'm glad you finally came down to see me. A pleasant surprise.

Glad to be here.

Where's your luggage? Behind bulletproof glass, Spokesman's weak eyes searched Lucifer's surroundings.

Lucifer cleared his throat. Back at the hotel.

Hotel?

Yes.

Spokesman said nothing for a minute. Oh, I see. You here on vacation?

Not exactly.

Spokesman seemed puzzled. He twisted his lenses as if to focus them. What brings you?

John.

John? Spokesman said. Speaking the name, the person, as if he'd never heard it. Spokesman's memory was infallible. He could look at *any* technological device once, take it apart, and put it back together again to the last screw, washer, or microchip without help of blueprints, notecards, or memos.

Where is he?

Spokesman's naked lenses floated before his invisible eyes. Why do you ask me?

You and John were always close.

Spokesman nodded in agreement. All that man dares do, I would do.

Lucifer smiled at the thought. Word had it John, Spin, and Spokesman had commandeered a hootch at base perimeter, fortified it with sandbags and an electric fence. Word had it they never wore boots or any rubber-soled footwear. *Rubber is dimagnetic.* Two of many rumors. You guys were famous, Lucifer said.

Yeah, Spokesman said. Things were wild over there. We were wild. John, Spin, and me—we painted like the eclipse of the sun, half black and half red.

Lucifer was aware of something inside him trusting Spokesman, trusting wholly and heavily. So John—

I can't help you.

The words fell to the floor at Lucifer's feet. But I thought—

I can't help you.

You know, he came for the march in Washington.

Is he in trouble?

Well, he—

Original relations, Spokesman said. He shook his head.

Yes, relations. He is my brother. That's why I'm here.

You look worried.

No. I wouldn't say that. Concerned. His wife is worried.

Still married?

Yes, Lucifer said.

To the same woman?

Yes.

Spokesman looked Lucifer up and down, making no effort to hide his disgust. Lucifer didn't hold it against him. He felt the same way about Gracie.

John said he was coming to see you. Did you go to the march?

Chickens can't fly, Spokesman said.

Lucifer held his breath, hoping that Spokesman would go on and say something else. Spoke, I thought—

Have you seen Dallas?

Why was Spokesman steering away from John? Lucifer answered him. I can't remember the last time.

You remember that time Spider got him a job at the Zanzibar Motel? The memory played itself on the two screens of Spokesman's glasses.

Yeah. And the manager found Dallas asleep in one of the beds, dead drunk.

Lucifer and Spokesman rode a wave of shared laughter.

Now John and Dallas, Spokesman said, they were tight.

So you haven't—

Wish I could help. To know more, we must assume more. Spokesman's eyes hovered over him. Lucifer could feel their energy. The eyes gave the talk weight. But they also made Lucifer uncomfortable. Had they always made him feel like this? Prediction is our best means of distinguishing science from superstition.

Please, Spoke. The words rushed to Lucifer's lips. I'm trying to clear up this confusion about John. When was the last time —

He asked me for a loan.

When was that?

A few months back.

Did you give it to him?

Do I look like Boo Boo the Fool? John rather cut out his heart than give you a dime.

This was true.

Spokesman began singing.

> *Captain, did you hear*
> *All yo men gonna leave next payday,*
> *Baby, next payday*

You remember that one?

Lucifer nodded. One of John's favorites.

Yes. I told him to fly down so we could do some hunting. Many good spots upstate.

Lucifer's mind churned as Spokesman spoke. Spokesman liked *spot* hunting. John would shine his flashlight in the deer's face and Spokesman would blast it.

I formed a new company. We stage live re-creations of the war for film, stage, and television. A lotta work these days, believe it or not. I offered John a job. He didn't refuse or accept.

Lucifer wondered why Spokesman hadn't offered him a job, too. Why he wasn't offering him a job now. So you haven't heard from him?

I wish I could help. Spokesman smiled, walrus teeth. Good fortune had not convinced him to correct his teeth.

Am I right?

I can't help you.

What are you saying?

I'm saying that I don't know why you came here to see me.

Because you and John were always tight. Close. Because —

Of course we were tight. Some things can't be destroyed. If a hologram is cut or blemished, it retains the image of the whole in each portion of the film. Spokesman nodded with the possibility.

Interesting, Lucifer said. But —

More than interesting. It's *real*. The war should have taught you that. Spokesman's angry eyes testified to the validity of every word.

Lucifer didn't let the anger bother him. It wasn't clear to him where this might lead, but he intended to keep on with it. Teach me what?

That life is based on awesome immutable laws. Ignorance of those laws does not excuse anyone from the consequences of the nonapplication of those laws or, worst, the breaking of those laws. Spokesman's head and teeth pumped a stream of words, a barking, spitting dog.

Lucifer sat and listened. He made an effort to vocalize his thoughts.

What? Spokesman said.

Lucifer rose from his seat and moved to the window behind Spokesman. He looked out on the green park and felt scared of the sky's beauty. Where's Spin?

Spin?

I need to speak to Spin.

He can't tell you anything.

Do you know where I can find him?

It's not what you know, it's what you can acknowledge.

Lucifer turned from the green and the sky and faced Spokesman. He leaned into the words. I need to know.

He lives in Queens, Little Asia.

Little Asia?

Yes.

But I thought he lived in Harlem?

No. His company—

The Royal African Company.

Yes. His company is there.

I see.

He lives next to the cathedral with the cemetery out front. I know that cemetery because I designed some of the tombstones. Plastic. They last forever. Spokesman smiled with fanged pride.

You have the address?

You have a pen?

Yes.

Spokesman gave Lucifer the address. Lucifer wrote it down.

You'll need the password, Spokesman said.

Password?

Yes. Spin only associates with those in the know. Fame will do that to you. Make you a prisoner.

What's the password?

Spokesman gave Lucifer the password. Lucifer wrote it down. Thanks.

Thank *you*.

Why was Spokesman thanking him?

Don't worry, Spokesman said.

I'll try not to.

No, I mean it. Don't *try*. Do it. No need to worry.

Why? Lucifer felt on the edge of something.

History is all matter, and matter cannot be destroyed. The moon pulls on the tides. The earth on a passing comet. But the object itself is not changed. Simply its path, the track or trace. And that track is external, nonessential to the object itself.

Spoke, Lucifer said, you're not human.

# 32

BUT YOU GOT TO GET AWAY from a woman who love you too strong. I used to have this woman who would drive my car after I fell asleep. Then in the morning, hide my shoes so I can't go back to my wife.

Damn, Hatch said. Damn.

Women is something.

You ain't married no more?

Yeah. Well, separated. Guess that's what you'd call it.

She left you?

I left her. Lazy. My wife got a good job workin for the city. A social worker. She be ready to retire next year. But she lazy. That's why I left her. I work all day and have to come home and cook for her and clean the house. All I wanted was a little help. She be out shopping.

Man.

And the kids tryin to talk back to me. My daughter so lazy she throw out the silverware with the garbage. And my son got a smart mouth. No respect. I told my wife, I'm gon leave you with these bad-ass kids. See how you like that. She go, Pool, you know you won't. I did too.

It bees that way sometimes, Hatch said.

Yeah, bout twice a week my wife come over here and I make her dinner.

What?

Yeah. See, my daughter don't cook and—

Your wife lives across the street?

Yeah, right there. Pool pointed. Peaches live right there.

Peaches?

That's her name.

Why ain't yall get divorced?

Divorce too much trouble.

Hatch thought about it.

My son talking bout he gon jump on me. I put my gun on him. Told him to get out of my house. My wife told *me* to get out.

Damn.

Now, my wife come over here anytime she want. But I got to call before I go over there.

She ever catch you?

Hell nawl. My old lady Martha live right down the hall. She got a big apartment. If my dick get hard, I go down there and do my business. I got enough respect for my wife.

Hatch thought about it. If it came down to it, he said, I bet you'd go back to your wife.

Pool grinned. Once, a husband jumped in the sea to drown himself. The wife pissed in the sea. Every little bit helps.


MY OTHER OLD LADY live out there in Crownpin, a few blocks from my oldest daughter, the one from my second wife. I was coming from down home and met her on the bus. She say, I'll be your wife for a day. I go to her house and we get naked and get in the bed. She keep her hand over her pussy. She got one of them little skinny dogs runnin around.

A Chihuahua?

Yeah. So, I pat the dog. I tell her. I'm gon get next to you the way I got next to this dog.

I used to take my kids to her house. They ain't speak nay word to my wife.

Yes, I've had my fun, even if I never get well no mo.

I used to have this one lady come over and I take her down in the basement and fuck her while my wife was upstairs washing dishes. You know, we didn't take all our clothes off. She wear a dress and I unzip my pants and bend her over the couch.

Battery acid flooded up from Hatch's groin. Trickles of heat in his legs.

You know, my wife could of caught us. All she had to do was leave the water runnin and sneak downstairs. Pool shook his head. Man, if I died today I wouldn't need nay more pussy.

Back home, I used to fuck these two sisters, Clara and Annabelle. They ask me, Which one of us got the best pussy?

I used to have this one girl and we'd go out in the field and screw in a cotton sack. Her father knew too. He knew I ain't walked no five miles for a kiss.

I used to work at this bakery. There was this white girl from Buffalo. A bookkeeper. It was her uncle's factory.

*Bakery.*

She used to come up to me. Pool, you know what I want.

White men thought I was screwin her. I look at em and say, You crazy?

WEBB'S PORTABLE RADIO scratched from the windowsill.

> *Holding on, holding on*
> *To God's unchanging hand*

Hatch hummed the melody. He didn't know the tune. He didn't go for the churchy stuff. But this song wasn't bad. Something about it. The choir inside the radio. Singing out. You like the blues? Hatch said. *All down-home folks like the blues.*

Never liked it. Nothing wrong with it. But I never liked it. Used to sing gospel, though.

I'll record you some tapes.

Thanks. You look bout as hungry as I feel. I'll cook us something.

Yall got any good Chinese food around here? Hatch asked. I could buy us some Chinese food. You like Chinese food?

I don't eat in restaurants. I used to work in one. We used to spit in the soup. Piss in the stew. And those white folks be, My, they got some good-cookin niggers here.

Hatch laughed.

I make you some fish, but you got to help me clean them.

Okay, if you show me how.

You ain't never cleaned fish?

Hatch shook his head.

Boy, where yo folks from?

Hous-

Don't nobody in yo family fish?

My Uncle John. He like to go down to the Kankakee River.

What he catch down there?

I don't know.

Trout. Probably some nice trout.

And he fish in this little pond out behind his house, well Gracie's house—she my aunt—Gracie's house on Liberty Island. He catch these lit-tle catfish.

Bullheads.

He put one on a log. Drive a nail through its head, then pull the skin off.

Ain't much to eat, is it?

Nawl. Uncle John a fishing fool. Just like his mamma, Inez. She my grandmother. She gave me my first rod and reel. *To replace the bamboo pole that Uncle John had bought you, like the identical one he bought Jesus.* Well, she and George. He my grandfather. Well, my stepgrandfather. Sheila—she my mother—she say Inez used to fish all the time. Georgiana—she was my—

Don't tell me who nobody else is. I'm old and slow. Can't keep up.

Well, Georgiana used to be a fishing fool too. So I heard. She and Pappa Simmons used to vacation in the Ca'linas, and they rent a boat and do some deep-sea fishing. Hatch had never seen the sea, but he could imagine it. Unrelieved blueness and a white, formless harvest of waves. They say she could catch crabs, shrimps, squid, scallops, clams, and oysters. Oysters and vodka was her favorite dish. She used to have it on her birthday, on Thanksgiving, Christmas, Labor Day, and Lincoln's Birthday.

Well, Inez—she my grandmother—they say Pappa Simmons—he my great-grandfather—he died before I was born—they say he like to fish. Maybe—

Webb put on his shorts and went into the kitchen without the aid of his cane.

You ain't got to do that, Hatch said. We both men here.

That ain't got nothing to do with it. I never enter the kitchen in draws.

Hatch followed Webb into the kitchen. Webb stooped and pulled a large bowl of fish from the refrigerator. He seated himself on a high stool positioned between the steel sink and the stove. His long arms reached into the steel cabinets above the sink for all the items he needed.

Be sure to cut from here. Webb held the fish with fingers gnarled beyond years. Dug the knife in. The asshole. That's why I don't let nobody clean my fish. Lotta people don't clean out the asshole.

A long-dead memory stirred to life. Knuckleheads in the Boy Scouts would catch lake fish and try to fry it. You found your teeth chewing on sand, grit, and—*now he knew*—shit.

Hatch saw the fish swim red in the silver-colored sink. I didn't know fish could bleed.

Bleed just like a stuck pig. Webb hardly had to lean forward. His long gorilla arms and hands did all the work.

Hatch watched and remembered. Studied the rhythmic sense. You don't have to skin it?

These is porgies. You don't need to skin em.

Porgies?

Yeah. You ain't never had no porgies?

Hatch shook his head.

Ocean fish. From the east coast.

Ain't never heard of em.

Sweet too. Now put flour in the bag, and some cornmeal, a little, but mostly flour. Shake em up good in the bag. Befo you put em in, make sure yo grease hot. The grease sizzled up. And be sure to use a spatula to turn em. Not no fork. Use a spatula to keep em whole.

I like smelts, Hatch said.

Smelts? Those nasty little fish?

Yeah.

Nasty.

Taste good, though.

You know, Jews eat filthy fish.

I know. Hatch grinned.

I mean, they got a fish they call filthy fish.

Oh, Hatch said. You mean *gefilte* fish.

That's what I said.

POOL, YOU CAN BURN.

Got to learn how when you got to eat what you cooks. Was gon open me a restaurant too.

Why didn't you? Hatch leaned forward on the night-stained couch, fish taste in his mouth.

Well, when I was in the army, I sent back all my money to my wife. My first one. We was gon open up a restaurant cause she could cook good too. She spent my money. She and one of her niggas. Or maybe all of em.

Damn . . . You sho can burn.

Can't be that good. You act like you ain't never ate no down-home fish.

You sho can burn.

When I was in the army, them crackas cheated my grandmother and my uncle out of the farm. See, they come along tellin black folks bout oil rights. My grandmother owned the farm. Bought it for a dollar an acre. We grew everything but flour, sugar, and salt. So we always had plenty to eat.

Peach, pear, and plum orchards.

*The locust grove bloomed in June.*

Many a day, I got up and hunted my breakfast. Possum is good and quail and pheasant—if you cook them right. Get that wild taste out of them. Lard quail with salt pork to get that wild taste out. And you got to boil pheasant in cream.

I used to cook for a man and his family but I couldn't eat with them. Seem like any son of a bitch could eat at our house but I couldn't eat anywhere but home. When I was older, my grandmother explained it to me. If you cook for one child, you can invite a family over. But if a family have six or seven children, you be eating their food.

Hatch stretched his legs. The plastic-covered couch moved beneath him. He said no more than he needed. Webb smoked cigarette after cigarette. *His lungs are black. A coal-town alley.* His words were Hatch's words too.

See, back home, we'd slaughter a hog and cook it in the earth. Dig a pit. Fire some hot coals. Man, that be the sweetest-tastin hog. Real barbecue. You ever had real barbecue?

No.

Hatch, you need to go down South.

I been—

We used to have everything on our land. My grandmother sold rabbits to white folks. Frogs too.

*Yuk! Taste like chicken.*

I go out to the pond and catch them for her. Hunt the rabbits. You ever been huntin?

Hatch shook his head.

See, rabbits hear you comin and jump up, run away, run in a circle back to the spot where they jumped. All you got to do is be quiet and wait for em. You ain't never been huntin?

No. But my Uncle John and Spokesman—

Hatch, I done hunted me some of everything. I'd shoot me a deer and drag it behind my truck to skin it. Ever have any venison? In Tennessee, I'd hunt me a bear. Little black bear. Skin it. Cut it up. Put it in my suitcase and fly it home on the plane.

But you need a good huntin dog. I used to have this dog that bark and twitch in his sleep. He dream about huntin. You know he gon catch something. But he liked to bite everybody. I put a bell around his neck to warn people he comin.


OKRA?

You don't like okra?

Hatch shook his head. *Okra trees harbor red ants.*

Boy, what yo mamma feed you? Down South, you better eat you some okra. Sorghum too. Bet you don't know nothing bout sorghum, do you?

No.

Up here, food just ain't the same. Can't find no good grapes. Now, back home, you chopped through the cudgery to find the scuppervine and muscadine.

What?

Grapes. Scuppervine these white grapes. And muscadine. You ain't never been down South?

Yeah, I—

I built me a grape arbor in Crownpin. Scuppervine. White grapes.


YES, I USED TO WORK HARD. If a donkey's ass was a Kodak, my picture would be all over the world. But I knew how to work and how to make money. I used to steal cotton seeds. They paid fifty dollars a ton. I had a thousand dollars in my pocket when I went in the army. I had the first sergeant in my belt.

I first worked loading ships. Then I drove a truck on convoy. We drove bumper to bumper at seventy or eighty miles an hour on these mountains. Didn't need the clutch either. We had our own signals. That was the only way you could stop in time.

We only lost one guy. He drove right off the mountain. All you could see was fire and smoke. We retrieved his body. The fire had melted his dog tags.

We drove ammunition to the front line and carried back a cargo of bodies. Many were headless. Couldn't identify them. So we used to get a tractor and dig these big graves.

We had to clean up at Hiroshima too.

*Pull the other one. Radiation. Cleaning up radiation ain't like wiping off yo shoe.* What yall do for protection?

We wore goggles.

Goggles? Hatch rolled his eyes. *Goggles.*

Spent some time in Europe too. The French women thought we had tails that came out at night.


PASSING THROUGH TEXAS those crackas threw rocks at you. Spit on you. You wanted to shoot them.

What about the officers? Hatch said.

In the States they treated you like shit, but overseas you were their brother. Many of them officers didn't come back.


YOU EVER KILL ANYBODY?

Like I say, we drove convoy. Now, at times— You ever seen a bayonet?

Yeah. At the Armory museum.

I mean really *seen* one?

Hatch said nothing.

They were sharp as razors. I could throw a bayonet so it twirled only once.

WEBB'S SNORES fell and rose.

From his distance, from this plastic-covered couch that would serve as his bed, Hatch could see four-leaf clovers sticking from between the pages of Pool's Bible. *Southern folks do that. Four-leaf clovers. Lula Mae.* Hatch opened the Bible. Someone had written on the white of the inner jacket, *"Miss Addie Lee Webb was borned June 15, 1900. Departed her life June 21, 1956, at 4:10 a.m. Age 56 yrs."*

A thin strip of paper poked out from the gold-trimmed edges. Hatch removed it. An old newspaper sketch. Hatch's age-fearing fingers gently held it up to sight. Beneath a tree in full bloom, a topless Eve—ugliest Eve he ever saw, with her hard man's face and buck wild hair—holds a branch to hide her vaginal bush. *Eve holding her twat.* A lion rests at her feet. Mouth-startled, Adam is drawing back, a firmly rooted shrub relieving him of the need to palm his privates from the viewer's eyes. In the distance, a deer drinks from a pond.

Hatch flipped the sketch over, like a hamburger on the grill:

# JARRED AND MOWED DOWN

### Burglar Got One On The House And Lead In The Leg

A well-aimed bullet from a police-man's pistol dropped a fleeing Negro burglar yesterday morning after an accurately tossed mayonnaise jar bounced harmlessly off the Negro's head.

Herbert Mayo, 22, of 705-707 Lyman, was shot in the left leg by

# 33

STORE SIGNS AND STREET SIGNS he couldn't read. Store windows that offered prolonged looks at suspended, gravity-free roasted ducks, chickens, and pigs. Fish resting on eternal beds of ice. Tray after metal tray of fried rice and noodles lined up like boxcars. And short people with fortune-cookie eyes. He had seen all this before. Lived it all before. A Yellow cab had brought him to this yellow place. Brought him here for answers. He moved on urgent feet, moved at the speed of a reborn man.

He found the cathedral and cemetery where Spokesman had said they would be. The gravestones looked like so many white boat sails anchored in a busy harbor. They faced the street where pedestrians and drivers could read them. So little regard for the dead and the bereaved. You had to walk through the cemetery to enter the cathedral.

*The largest Gothic structure in the world, the cornerstone was laid on December 27, 1892. The nave was dedicated on November 30, 1941, one week before Pearl Harbor. The war halted construction. The cathedral remains a great work-in-progress. Completion date is unknown.* Stained-glass windows as tall as two men cast pyramids of faint light. Columns marched in stone rhythm. Flying buttresses shot up into concrete heaven. Taut arches and groins stretched up into darkness. *The new churches slowed the movement through the nave by dividing and subdividing it into carefully articulated compartments.* Gray paradise at the top. A seemingly endless runway of velvet carpet led to the altar. Wood pews lined the stone floor. Ran into darkness like unscheduled trains bound for unknown destinations. So this was a cathedral. A world of distance. Space. And more space. Armageddon could happen here. Plenty of room for all God's angels and all the devil's saints to battle.

Lucifer found the house where Spokesman had said it would be. More like a hangar than a house. The structure took up one square block. *Perhaps Spin need all that room to hold all his wealth.* Dinkins Airport was only a few miles away, and Lucifer was certain that this hangar had been airlifted from there and set down intact here. He imagined what he would see inside.

Each object would show that Spin's fingers knew the touch of luxury. Objects from every corner of the globe, proof that Spin had nosed abroad. Lucifer also imagined how their conversation would end.

*See, Lucifer, everything is fine. That's just John. His way of doing things. Ease your mind.*

*I can now.*

*Good. Look, I've got to fly to the city tomorrow for the concert.*

*So soon?*

*Need to prepare. Why don't you spend the night here and fly back with me in the morning.*

*Thanks for the offer.*

*Here are some tickets for your family.*

*Thanks.*

*Tell Hatch to drop backstage after the show.*

Spin's words played inside Lucifer. He could wait no longer. He pressed the buzzer. An airplane roared by overhead. Lucifer searched the sky. Clear. Lucifer pressed the buzzer a second time. Another airplane roared by.

A wired voice cut through the sonic noise, Say your say.

It's Lucifer Jones. Lucifer spoke directly into a little black speaker. I'm here to see Spin.

Say your say.

It's Lucifer Jones. He spoke louder this time, shouting, lips close to the speaker. I'm Lucifer— He caught himself. He gave the password.

The voice laughed.

Lucifer gave the password again.

# 34

POOL, YOU TALK IN YOUR SLEEP.

Hatch was remembering the night before. Pool had talked the whole night—*Martha, park over there. I told you to park over there. Now park over here and see what happens*—while his chest rode the crest of a snore. Hatch tossed and turned. *Maybe the flood entered my dreams.* Spotted sleep. The unrest was still in him.

Yeah, I know. Pool spoke from the small cave of kitchen, the room awash with cigarette smoke where Hatch sat. *Hope Pool don't fire up another one.* And still dark from the previous night. But you couldn't make heads or tails of it, now could you?

Yes, I could. You was talkin bout how much you wanted your wife and how much you loved Lee.

Pool laughed. Now I know you lyin.

Hatch shared the laugh.

Seated on the high stool, Pool worked his invisible hands in the metal sink. I got to do some serious cookin today.

Pool, you like to cook.

The hell if I do. I learned from my grandmother. She put me in the kitchen and made me cook. Didn't have to show me nothing. When you have to eat your own cooking, you learn how to do it right.

I still think you like to cook.

Well, I got to cook these rabbits for my wife. Seasoned them last night.

Rabbit?

Yeah. You ain't never had no rabbit before?

Hatch shook his head.

Taste like chicken.

Yeah?

The dark in the room gave way to the first full light of morning.

Once you get the wild taste out. I told my wife, she buy em, I'll cook em. You wait here til tonight. You can taste them.

I'd like to, I really would, wish I could stay, but I got some things to do today.

And yo mamma probably worried. Did you call her?

Hatch lied.

Well, come on in here and make you some breakfast before you leave.


POOL, FRY ME SOME FISH, Lee said.

What you gon do fo me?

Pool, you bad. You a bad man.

See this gap between my teeth. Pool pointed to it with his finger. That's my nipple holder. I put your nipple between there, then flip my tongue like this—

Lee turned her head. You bad. You a bad man. Ain't that right, honey?

Hatch hesitated. Pool, are you bad?

Hell yes.

Fry me some fish.

Lee, stop beggin. Can't you see I'm resting here?

I'll fry you some fish, Hatch said.

You don't have to do that, honey.

No, it's okay. I'll fry you some. Hatch rose from his seat. You gon have fish for breakfast?

What, Pool said, you ain't never had no fish and grits for breakfast?

No.

Pool shook his head. Where you been all yo life?

Leave him alone, Lee said. Go on, honey. Go on. Hold the grits.

The kitchen drew Hatch in. He followed Pool's instructions from yesterday. Get the grease really hot. Put the flour in a paper bag with a little bit of cornmeal. Shake the fish around good.

Don't burn it up in there.

I won't. He fried the fish good on one side, then flipped it over with a spatula.

Don't flip it with no fork.

I won't. He fried the fish good on the other side, then lifted it from the popping skillet and laid it on a napkin-covered plate to drain the grease.

Don't forget to turn off that skillet.

I won't. He flipped the fish onto a fresh plate. He walked into the other room with the plate balanced traylike on his hand. He set it before Lee and laid out her knife, fork, and napkin.

Thank you, honey.

You welcome. Like something to drink?

No, thanks. This is fine.

Hey, Pool shouted, turn off that light in the kitchen.

Hatch complied. Returned.

Lee had already cut into the fish.

How it taste?

Good.

It better taste good. I taught him.

Now, Pool, how come you can't be nice to me. Like this young man? Fried me up some fish. You did something nice for me. Someday I'll do something nice for you.


THESE KIDS IS SHO LAZY, Lee said. I work eleven hours a day, five days a week.

Then why you over here runnin yo mouth?

Pool, you know you bad. You can sho talk some trash.

Ain't that the milk callin the sugar white.

Don't pay no tention to him, honey. He a bad man. Ain't that right?

Hatch couldn't decide whether to smile or nod. Pool, are you bad?

Hell yes.

Here, honey. I bought a book for you. Lee served the book on the table to Hatch. *The Trick Life.* Some people say this is trash, but you like to read. Don't you? I can look at you and tell. Read this book. Then tell me what you think.

Hatch opened the book, fingered the pages, seeing the words but not reading them.

That book is not trash. He just tellin it like it really is. The Muslims sell it. I bought three or four of his books from them. And you know they don't sell no trash.

Hatch nodded.

He just tellin it like it is. He used to be a pimp. You know that?

So I heard.

He talk about what the hookers have to do. Where the hookers hide their money. You know. How the cops treat them. And this man that dress up like a woman. And these women with the big bosom. You read it and tell me if it's trash. When you get finish, return it to me. I put my address and phone number inside.

YOU SAY YOU MET MY UNCLE JOHN? Hatch could talk now, now that Lee had left, now that they were alone. He would leave here, had to leave, leave and soon. He was shot through with things unsaid.

Once or twice. Lucifer brought him by.

What did you think of him?

Nice. We all vets.

Hatch thought about it. Tried to follow the wandering voice inside. You ain't seen him since?

No. I'd like to. You bring him by sometime.

I will. He studied Webb. Someday he would dress like that. He would wear old man's clothes. Wear these clothes daily without pride or shame, a uniform in a civilian world. He could feel it now. Inside him. The old man growing, inning the out, preparing for his day in the sun. Pool, he said, you been bad, you done wrong. What you gon say on Judgment Day?

Lord, let me in there. I ain't gon screw nwine one of them angels.

# 35

LUCIFER RENAMED NEW YORK the City of Trains. All rails glowed with
the memory of those speeding colorful objects his eyes had witnessed years
before. A babel of color inside and out. Scrawled tongues twisting into a
mute vision of motion and voice. So his nostalgia had formed. But the
trains had changed. New cars, clear cars. He found graffiti on concrete
highway embankments, eye-catching billboards, the sides of parked and
moving trucks, buildings—each brick a painted face—dolled-up girls sitting
on stoops, traffic signs, everywhere but the remembered place. Tiled mo-
saics offered something of the old color. He celebrated, in the city of memory.

In the same way bridge joined water to land, rails joined earth to sky.
(People here even called the El the subway.) You went deep inside to rise
high to the outside world, ass to mouth. Bridge and train stitched borough to
borough. New York was an island, all of it. In a city like this, each day might
be an adventure. Travel within to other places. Take a little bit at a time.
Archipelago to archipelago, pearl to pearl. He thought, I could live here. I
want to live here. I will live here. Someday. He had thought this years before
and was thinking it again now, a concentration of energy that vanished the
instant after the hope, the intention took shape. Ah, New York. The City of
Trains.

To be one of the first to enter the car and win a prized seat, you had to
box out the other passengers, the same way you boxed out another basketball
player to snatch a rebound. Back home, the seats faced to the forward or
backward motion of the train. Here, long bench rows of seats faced one another, the left side of the car watching the right—never look any of the passengers opposite directly in the face—and the right side watching the left.
An open middle between, standing room for millions.

He had spent the night in the City That Never Sleeps—the sky the deepest blue above the buildings and the buildings themselves, dimly lighted
from within, like jack-o'-lanterns—not sleeping, tossing and turning on a

hard mattress in a noisy Times Square hotel, the same hotel from his first visit many years ago. Only the rates had changed. A walk-up building—like so many others in the city—with wide stairwells, space in the landing, a fire escape zigzagging up the facade, and a printed warning to keep the escape window locked. *The hotel bears no responsibility for lost or stolen items.* A sailor and a hooker fucked in the sweaty shadows outside his room. *Pardon me, folks. Don't let me interrupt you.* Inside the room, he found a bed made for a man a foot shorter than himself under a hanging bulb with a saucer-shaped lamp. He turned off the bulb and fell on the bed, a rock hitting the softness of water.

The sink gargled its steel throat. Bed legs from the room above him bucked from one end of the ceiling to the other, and the ceiling showered peeling paint down on him. He curled into sleep. Dreamed close to the surface.

His bed drifted. He woke and turned on the lights. Rats—five or six of them—scattered for the dark. He pulled a candy bar from his shirt pocket and tossed the two halves into two corners.

The new day dawned fair and fresh. Found him here. Coney Island. To discover ocean in New York, lower Manhattan was the obvious, convenient choice. But the long train ride to Coney Island offered the illusion of journey. He journeyed here to ocean because over *there* he had never been aware that ocean was ocean, hadn't been convinced, even after he was told. Sea was just another word. Water was water. And the water *felt* like the waters back home, Tar Lake, hot summer waters, even if it had a salt smell and taste. He wanted to feel the ocean, *this* ocean.

A breeze strolled down to the boardwalk where the sand began. He dared not go barefoot on the beach. (He'd heard that dope fiends left their needles in the sand.) He walked, the impact of his steps darkening the sand, leaving puddles. The white sand broke loose in footprint after footprint. Clouds sailed in a westward armada. Gulls scratched through a rusty sky, circling ocean for minute after minute on a single wingbeat. Flocks of them wandered the beach on stick legs. The sea swelled, curled, broke in a long line, washing foam up on the beach, and slipped back down the beach to come back and re-form, break again in a long line, and slice back again, sound retreating with the wave to travel some invisible place and spill a great surge of noise. Lines of woven hemp trailed out into the ocean. Skeletal driftwood. And seaweed like discarded wigs. The green sea broke into silver on the beach. Lucifer stooped over sand—fish scales glistened like coins—grabbed a fistful, then stood, the sand dribbling out of his hand. He stooped again to gather pieces of seashell almost purple from the brackish water. Then he stood and looked at the sea, the waves now white and slow as sheep. All he saw was surf out there, more and more of nothing. He wiggled his toes, a wet feeling causing him to look down at his shoes. He had ruined them, a good pair. Sand spilled from the laces. The sides breathed like gills.

# 36

HATCH SMELLED THE CITY'S CHOKED SEWERS. He curled through the tangled streets of South Lincoln. John had brought him here. And Jesus. He had been drawn into the elongated circle of their will. He grafted unknowns to unknowns. If he had winged eyes, they could fly and find John. If he could make boats of his words, they would sail and find Jesus. How could he halt what had already been set in motion? Maybe blood ain't—

An angle of brick stabbed him. The concrete snatched him down. His eyes spilled spinning suns. He rubbed his head. His fingers felt no blood. The wheeling slowed to a stop. He and another boy both sat on their butts with their arms extended behind them. The boy pulled himself up on an invisible string. He was slow to follow.

Sorry, he said.

Bitch, why don't you watch where you going?

He felt sun on his shoulders. Listen, ain't no need fo all that.

You don't like it? The boy poked his hard face into Hatch's. *He's the same height as me. Why, he's the spittin image of*— He wore a hat, bomb-pointed crown aimed at the sky above, straps dangling like girl's pigtails. Bitch, I'm talkin to you. The boy had eyes like sucked-out shells. Dry ice or frozen spit. A nasty gray light glowing in them.

I was jus turnin the corner.

Bitch, I ain't ask you what you was jus doin. The words bat-flew out of the boy's black grave mouth. Hatch breathed in gravedigger breath. He saw. Face behind the words. Face behind the breath. Little fly hairs of mustache. A black hole of mouth. *Oh, he's smilin. That's what he's doing. Grinning. Sneering.* Crooked tombstones of teeth. I wanna know what you gon do now.

Hatch said nothing.

Bitch. I didn't think so. The boy's eyes traveled the entire orbit of Hatch's body. I oughta smoke you. The boy slid his hand in the breast pocket— Napoleon-like—of his athletic jacket. Least make you suck my dick. His eyes ran a second orbit. Bitch, get outa my face.

The words pushed Hatch away. Made his legs move as fast as they could.

But not fast enough. At the next corner, the boy leaned his face out of a red ambulance. Buck! Buck!

Hatch ducked to the safety of the sidewalk. Tried to camouflage himself in concrete. Laughter rose from beneath burning tires. Bitch. The ambulance speeded away.

# 37

THE SHADOW-SWAMPED TREES shimmered like black ghosts. Thinned against the stars. Moon burned over the rim of the horizon. Blackened headstones blazed in the night, cracked old people's faces, leaning, here and there a name or date barely legible. What did it matter? The years telescoping, he might have lived out the rest of his life in this single discovery.

He continued under the hot stars. Chill struck through his clothes. His veins drew it in, then spilled it from the faucet of his head, down the pipe of his neck, and throughout the basin of his body. He moved with no exercise of will, only the habit to endure. He looked down at his feet. They were far off, almost out of sight, under black water. He felt himself slipping away in the dead moment before dawn. I am no longer the same person I was, he thought. He was going home. A forbidden city.

# 38

THE STREETLAMPS STRUNG THROUGH THE NIGHT LIKE BEADS. Hatch and Abu stood in the yard, their still eyes following the back of the receding ambulance.

Keylo, Hatch said.

What?

That was Keylo.

Who?

He followed me here.

What?

Hatch looked at the star-filled night and breathed deeply. Nobody, Hatch said. He had already said too much.

You said Keylo, didn't you? Keylo from Red Hook?

Forget it.

How you know it was him?

Hatch said nothing.

What he doing round here?

Jus forget it. I was mistaken, that's all.

Where you been?

Who said I been anywhere?

Yo mamma called looking for you.

Hatch searched for an answer. I was over at Elsa's house.

Why you ain't call?

I was busy. I was getting my groove on.

Oh. Abu redirected his embarrassed eyes. You get the tickets?

What?

The tickets. You know, for Spin's—

Oh. *Forgot all about that.* They was closed.

Closed?

Yeah. You know, the flood and all. We'll get them tomorrow. Hatch turned toward the house.

Abu followed behind him, trying to keep pace. What did T-Bone want?

Oh, you know.

What did he want?

It ain't important.

If it ain't important how come—

Hatch gave Abu a look for an answer. Stared him down. *Looks have language.* Abu turtle-shrunk into himself. Hatch reached the housefront. He did not stumble. The low-rising steps were easy flying.

Once inside the house, Hatch phoned Sheila to ease her fears. (He knew precisely what to say. Much practice.) Then he clicked off the lights. Abu made no complaint.

They had the house to themselves until the morning. (Abu's parents worked nights.) In complete silence, he and Abu sat as one until dawn, their still eyes forming shapes to guard off the dark space of absence.

## 39

A BODY GETS AROUND. Traveling. To see the cities of men. Travel a little further and see as much as you can see.

Well, I hope you have a nice trip.

I plan to.

Porsha sat at the window—the sky has nearly forgotten the sun; how many days now? no sight no sound no touch—and watched the evening invade the avenue.

Why you so quiet?

Porsha said nothing. The receiver hummed at her ear like an empty well.

Hmm, I see. Um huh. I see.

The words echoed what she felt.

I'm sorry, Nia said. Sorry, I really am.

Porsha listened and waited.

I'm sorry but, you know, people shouldn't cross roads in heavy traffic.

Porsha searched each word for the meaning she wanted to hear. Perhaps Nia was right. Perhaps it was all her fault. Then again, she had only followed the natural flow of her heart.

Next time you'll know.

I thought we were talking about you.

Ain't no need to talk about me. Evil as always.

What happened?

Same ole.

I'm coming over.

No need to.

Nia had missed the point. *She* needed to. I want to come over.

Stay away from me cause I'm in my sin.

You ain't gon tell me what happened?

Who said anything happened.

Porsha could hear destruction in the words. But Nia was like that, secretive—something you either were or weren't—holding and nurturing it all inside until she was ready to let another taste her bitter milk. Okay, Porsha said, be like that then.

I will. And you do like I always do. Find a hole and crawl into it.

Porsha felt the words roaring like ocean in the phone, roaring, as if they had enough wet force to will her into action. Well, I'll talk to you when you get back.

Sure you don't want to come with?

Porsha smiled into the phone. She pictured Nia sitting at her office desk, looking like a package somebody else had wrapped. No.

It'll do wonders.

I'm sure it will.

Okay. I tried. Later, girlfriend.

Later.


THE WINDOW FRAMED A REMOTE WORLD. The day had drawn sure. The night was well along. But night is no hiding place. The earth and its corrupt works shall be discovered. What the cockroach has left, the locust has eaten. Cause the Good Book says that through the windows the locust shall go like a thief. She felt a hot melting urge. She greased her hands in petroleum jelly and eased them into the Lazarus 1 Ascension Aid, patent pending. She failed to levitate. Once again. She'd been unsuccessful for months. Nia had succeeded on her first try, her fat body bobbing balloon-fashion above the bare floorboards.

She returned to her seat before the window. She felt like a passenger in a waiting train. The hum of the air conditioner amplified her feelings. She clicked it off. Quiet. At that moment, she felt pain all over, pain that had been crouching and waiting in the silence and the dark. At first she thought her friend was paying the monthly visit, then the pain declared that it was different. She accepted this difference when the pain declared that it wasn't pain at all but acute lethargy. She drew the blind cords. Raised the window. Warm night air expelled the musty air of the room. Moonlight gave depth to the objects around her.

> *Got two minds to leave here*
> *Three tellin me to stay*

She lay down on the bed and stared at the ceiling. Half-formed images blinked in and out of the ceiling plaster. Head and face a patiently crafted globe directly in the ceiling's middle, glowing there in the lightbulb's place.

The face grew smaller and smaller until the features were indistinct. She had to think hard to imagine the eyes, the set of the mouth.

In all the folds of her body she felt tired dampness, summer weariness. But this was spring. Day had simmered down to brown evening and evening to blue night. She could string hours together in thin melodic lines but the rhythm had broken. Everything seemed impossible, far away, another world. To escape sleep, she took inventory of her physical being. Silence in her muscles. Her hands rubbed her legs in slow circles. She shut her eyes. Many a day he had met her at the train station. Piggybacked her home. *Damn, you heavy.* He would watch her walk about the room, loose her hair, take off her garments. Kneeling while she stood, he would kiss all her body. Now, he wasn't here. A mile away or a million, all the same. Her hands worked. He don't know what he's missing. Her open sea scent. A whole life would not be long enough to survey, discover, and explore her soft, curving geography. His loss.

With hidden force, she lifted her body from the bed. She took a long time getting dressed, hindered and slowed by pain. Clothed in cutting elegance, she stepped out into the night. Flowers shone stronger than the moon but she carried the night's chill—the first cool night in weeks—and trembled like a bird near a pond. She walked rapidly along the empty street beneath failing streetlamps where bugs crashed and whirled in halos of mist. Streetlamps that spread pools of soft fire at her feet. Her footsteps fell lonely and hollow. The night seemed a walking shadow. Her necklace shone like an illuminated noose. She admired herself in the mirroring dark.

How's Nia?

Porsha thought about it. Fine, I guess. Same ole. You know Nia.

She still datin all those men?

Yes.

Mamma shook her head. She keep that up, she'll be a used bill. Out of circulation.

Mamma and Porsha laughed above the river-running faucet. Truth in wet laughter. Where is everybody? Porsha said.

They ain't here. Mamma washed dishes, scrubbing hard, like they were made of iron. She rinsed them spotless under the running water. Lined up the cleaned dishes like soldiers in the drainer. Quieted the water. Porsha had seen it all before. Mamma, a woman of settled habits.

How come nobody's here this late at night?

Mamma dried her hands on her apron. Hatch over at Abu's house. She removed the apron and draped it over a cabinet arm. A plume of steam whistled from the teapot's spout. Mamma killed the flame, lifted the pot with a holder, and poured two cups. She lifted the cups and placed them on a plastic serving tray.

Need some help?

Sit back down. Mamma carried the tray and the cups over to the table on creaking knees and set them down dead center. Then she placed one cup before Porsha and one before herself. She pulled her chair out from the table and eased into it. Nobody's here, she said. Praise the Lord. She smiled into the steam of the tea she had made. I got some peace finally. Nobody to clean up after. She broke open two packages of artificial sweetener and poured and stirred them into her tea.

You deserve it. Tea steamed up into Porsha's face. She scooped two spoonfuls of sugar into her cup. She sipped tea hot and sweet on her tongue. Where's Dad?

Mamma raised—yes, raised, as if the hand were a machine; the fingers long and thin, the veins taut spokes beneath the skin   her steaming cup to her lips. Out of town. He went looking for John.

John?

Yeah. A few days ago.

What's going on?

Mamma tasted her tea. Ask *him* that.

Dad ain't called?

You think I been sitting around here waiting for him to call?

Porsha thought about it. You never knew what to expect when those two got together. Like two lil kids. Maybe all brothers are like that. She looked at the globes of Mamma's breasts. Dad remembered and told, Mamma would hold the infant Porsha to her breasts and recite all the places the baby would travel. Where did they go?

Well, John run off to that march in Washington, then Gracie come callin here at two or three the next morning sayin that she ain't heard from him.

Is that all? . . . What she expect?

I don't know what she expect. She thinks John disappeared.

Disappeared?

Her exact words.

Porsha shook her head. He disappeared all right. Wit some woman. *Beneath her sheets. Between her legs.*

Mamma sipped her tea.

Think after all these years she'd know.

Well, she don't know. That's why Lucifer up and run off to New York or Washington or wherever the hell he went.

Mamma, calm down. Porsha rubbed Mamma's rough hand—veins like ropes. You know John. And you know how *they* is together.

Mamma said nothing.

You'd be surprised if they acted any different.

Well, Mamma said. Well. She sipped her tea.

Porsha played the silence. I saw Inez the other day.

When?

Monday.

How is she?

Worst.

Well, Mamma said. Well.

She said that John had been out there.

You can't believe a word Inez say.

I know.

Mamma sipped her tea.

Though the night was cool, the kitchen was so hot it was hard to breathe. Porsha had something to ask. Her body trembled. Mamma. She blew on her tea.

Yes?

Did Clarence call?

Who?

Clarence. Deathrow.

No. Why you askin me?

Jus wonderin, that's all.

What, you ain't heard from him?

Did I say that?

You don't have to say it.

The phone rang. Mamma took her time about answering it.

Porsha leaned back in the chair and stared into the empty kitchen. In the quiet, she could hear ghosts flit across the ceiling, bump into walls, tiptoe from room to room. She touched each pearl of her necklace carefully like sore teeth. She thought about it all as if the thought would be answered in the asking. Whether by will or circumstance, a man leaves much when he leaves his own bed. She found much satisfaction in the idea. She heard Mamma approaching down the hall. She finished her tea, hoping that heat and taste would remove any trace of the thought from her face.

She's dead, Mamma said. She leaned her shoulder into the white refrigerator.

Who? Who's dead?

Lula Mae.

Porsha said nothing.

Now I have nobody.

# Part Three

# SOUTH

# 40

THAT'S NOT WHAT I SAID, Gracie said.

Well, what did you say?

Sheila, you think you know everything.

You jus don't want to admit when you wrong.

And you always right.

I didn't say that.

I know what you said.

I—

The flight attendant brought them both cups of water.

Sheila drank—the water was cool going down; it brought her back to her-self—and thanked. Gracie drank but said nothing. Her heavy Bible rested like a paperweight on her narrow lap to keep her from blowing out of her seat. She sat on the aisle. Sheila had allowed her that. Her comfort and more comfort in the knowing. But Gracie was ungrateful, face frowned up as if the water was poison.

Can I get yall anything else?

No, Sheila said. Thank you.

Just call.

The plane hummed through the deep sky. The sisters sat in remembering silence.

*He's a good boy, Lula Mae said.*

*I know, Gracie said.*

*He's a good boy, Sheila said.*

*She jus said that. You my mamma too?*

*Well—*

*She's right. He would make you a good—*

*Sides. He ain't no boy. He a man.*

*Marry him.*

*Nawl.*

*Why not?*

*I don't want to, that's all.*

*Quit thinking bout yoself.*
*Who said I'm thinkin bout me.*
*Think about—*
*I don't care.*
*But—*
*Why don't yall jus leave me alone.*

Sheila looked at the sea of shifting clouds outside the small window. Traveling clouds. Great flocks of memories. Flurry of claws. She fastened her seat belt. They would be landing soon.

THE MEMPHIS HEAT almost pushed her back onto the plane. She'd left home only an hour ago. The sky was sharp and clear and hot in the morning silence, telling you that, yes, you were someplace else. How many times in the last months had she made this trip? Now, she saw the pattern complete, first stitch to last. Lula Mae on loan, body and soul, both to be returned to her creator.

How you, Miss Pulliam? the white nurse said.

I been better.

Yo cancer actin up?

Lula Mae looked at Sheila, her secret revealed. She had hidden the cancer for five years. I didn't want yall to worry, she said.

In the following months, she waited patiently for death. This cancer gon kill us all, she said. Now she had passed, moved on to the world to come.

The bridge was steel and stillness and silence. A pyramid of rails and cables. Memphis this side, West Memphis the other. The river below was bright and clean, rocks on the bottom distant but clear, large and white as plates. Just a ways down the river, the dog track sat like a giant oil silo in the sun. Memphis's best greyhounds chased circular rabbit motion. Real rabbits once. But that too had changed.

The yard across the road was peaceful now, no longer crowded with scurrying chickens. A colorful rooster or two. You would go there and buy fresh brown and green eggs. Now it stood empty and yellow. And on this side of the road where Lula Mae lived an empty field had replaced John Brown's house. Both the man and his house gone—Brown first then the house—many years now. The promised construction had never begun. John Brown dead a good ten years or more already. Sheila couldn't say for sure. John Brown would stand in the yard and point up into the tree. See the monkey. See the monkey.

Shell-shocked, Lula Mae said. But he treated her good. Took her anywhere she needed to go in his old pickup truck (gray? blue?), shaking and shuddering and steaming like a train. He believed it to be the only vehicle of its kind in Memphis or West Memphis.

Sheila let Gracie go first on the splintery wood placement—like an old railroad plank, which perhaps it was—that offered a skinny path across the grass-covered drainage ditch. Gracie opened the chain-link fence and charged through the yard as if it all had ordinary meaning to her. Sheila watched from the sidewalk and fought to still her insides. A half-circle of spokes poked through the grass, straighter than peacock feathers. Wrought-iron lawn furniture, painted silver in the sun (*Lula Mae hid the red rust with seasonal coatings of silver paint*), was positioned in front of the green-and-white two-story house—well, the second story with the miter-shaped roof was an attic—for the right combination of sun and shade. A motherly awning reached over and sheltered a snug little concrete porch. No sides or banisters. Barely room for a chair. A porch for looking, not sitting.

Take care of everything.
I will.
Make sure Hatch has everything he needs.
I will.
You know how he forgets.
You don't have to remind me.
And try to get here Friday night at the latest. The funeral gon be Saturday morning.
We'll come well before that.
Don't be in such a rush. Give your father chance to return.
We will.
Maybe that damn fool John'll be with him.
More than likely.
You take care and I'll see yall when you get here.
Okay.
Bye.
Bye. Oh, Mom.
What?
Should we tell Jesus?
You decide.

This way, Reverend Blunt said. The young and handsome reverend took Sheila by the elbow. He led her down the hall. Sheila looked back to see Gracie still standing at the front door, her Bible tight at her side.

Aren't you going to come? Sheila said.

The reverend never stopped walking.

No, Gracie said. I'll see her later.

Well, stay away from that sun, the reverend said, looking back, still walking.

Gracie looked at him as if he'd spoken to her in a foreign language.

I'll have my boy bring you some tea.

Keep it, Gracie said.

The words caused the reverend to blink. Please, ma'm, keep over there in the shade or you'll catch heatstroke. Outside, the day's heat was still rising. Gracie didn't budge.

The reverend took Sheila where he needed to take her, then stopped and stood sentinel-still. I'll wait here, ma'm.

Sheila entered the room. She saw the body, open in a casket already chosen. Lula Mae's face was gray as the quilt that covered her. The dew of death on her breath. Sheila searched for the old image in the sunken face. Searched but did not find. The body had been emptied of both life and memory. She stayed as long as she needed to stay, then she went out.

We gon make everything perfect, the reverend said. He retook Sheila's elbow. Miss Pulliam already made all the arrangements. If there's anything you want to change or add . . . We'll bring her over to the church Friday evening for the viewing. Come on in here and we can go over everything. I'll just need you to give me cash or a certified check. My credit-card machine ain't seem to be workin today. His hand was a crane lifting her up at the elbow. Boy, bring her some cold tea.

Yes, suh.

And check on that lady out front there.


HOW SHE LOOK? Gracie said. She was a long time rising.

Fine. They did a fine job.

How she look?


LULA MAE WOULDN'T LIKE THAT CASKET, Gracie said. She returned the brochure to Sheila.

Well, we can go back and you can help me find one that you like.

It ain't about what I like.

It's the one she chose.

They sat for a long time. Sheila felt the silence all around her. When she spoke her voice was lost. Well, I guess we better be gettin on to the church.

Gracie leaned forward. She put both hands to her face. She sat like that, both shoulders moving.

THE SLOW GRAY PREACHER took Sheila's elbow to help her negotiate the collapsed steps leading up to the church. Gracie followed behind, carrying her heavy Bible like a suitcase at her side. The preacher took them into the small chapel and showed them all there was to see. The wake and funeral would be held here, the church that Lula Mae had attended just blocks down the road from her house.

Why we got to have it here? Gracie said. It's old. Dirty. Unclean. Stinks.

Lula Mae wanted it here.

I don't see why.

SHE WOULDN'T WANT TO BE BURIED IN THAT DRESS, Gracie said.

This is the dress she told me, Sheila said.

Well, she didn't tell me that.

She didn't have to tell you.

You know everything.

It's what she wanted.

You always right.

Gracie, what's wrong with you?

You always gotta have everything yo way.

I TALKED TO BEULAH. She'll be here tomorrow.

They driving? Gracie said.

Yes. Rochelle's husband rented a van.

That's a long drive from St. Paul to here.

I know. But that's the only way they can afford to come.

Beulah can't stand no long drive.

I offered to send for her but—

That's a long drive. Too long. Beulah is ninety—

Yes, well, Jacky and Lil Judy coming too.

Gracie half turned to her with some new complaint.

———

WASN'T NO LAUNDROMATS in the old days. Jus soap, water, and yo two hands. Wash the clothes in a big steel tub, scrub them hard across the scrubbing board, and lay em across the line to dry in the sun. Took a lot out of a person. That was the way Lula Mae had washed. That was the way Sheila was washing now. After she finished the laundry, she started on the floors, walls, and windows. She took little time to rest. Then she ironed the outfit she would wear Saturday, cut, color, and fabric chosen many months before. (She would wear it with Lucifer's gift, the yellow bird made of unidentified Brazilian stone.) That done, she went on to her next task. She knew what she needed to do beyond knowing, and knowing, knew that she had turned knowledge into obligation, duty, and the fulfillment of that obligation and duty.

Her hands are anything but idle. She must put the house in order. The house will be rocking with people come Saturday. And she has to sort through Lula Mae's belongings. What will she keep for herself? Those things dearest to her heart. Can she lug it all back to the city? What she doesn't keep Gracie and Lula Mae's friends can have. Whatever they don't want, she will try to sell. She will—

What are you doing? Gracie said.

Sheila turned and faced her. Trying to sort through all these things.

Why you ain't tell me?

Sheila looked into Gracie's eyes and saw the calculation in them.

I already told you.

Gracie said nothing.

Why don't you come help me? When Porsha gets here, she and Hatch can go through the attic.

Gracie said nothing.

They can do the little house, too.

Gracie turned and left the room.


SHE SAT ON LULA MAE'S BED and listened to the night frogs and crickets. She had accomplished all she could and deserved rest. She saw very clearly how her life had led to this moment. A moment that demanded perfection. It would take everything she had to grant a wish, but she would pay it. That much she owed Lula Mae. She had refused money from the Sterns, from Porsha, from George. She had bought her plane ticket and Gracie's. She had paid for the wake, the funeral, the burial arrangements. She could breathe easy and Lula Mae could rest without worry, knowing that her death had been placed in Sheila's loyal, dutiful, and determined hands. Sheila was the host that Death had promised her.

Tell Gracie to stay home, Lula Mae said. Don't come here no mo. All she do is set up in that rocking chair and accuse and pity.

When Cookie died, Sheila had had to make all the arrangements, pay all the expenses. Gracie moved slowly and stiffly, her heart beating at a heavy cost, carrying in her blood the lead fact of the death of her firstborn. After the funeral, Sheila helped Gracie put Cookie's wheelchair into the closet of the Kenwood apartment they shared. From there they pushed it to the patio of the May Street apartment and finally into the basement of the house on Liberty Island, where it waited in the corner, uncovered and empty. The house on Liberty Island with a real hearth where a fire could burn. Where Cookie's photograph held command on the mantel above: a will-less face and loose eyes that looked in two directions at once; a white-and-pink bow; a pink dress with white collar and black belt; black patent-leather shoes; a white cloud surrounding her body, Cookie standing out like a gem against cotton.

She had defended Gracie from Ivory Beach, the wicked Houston step-mother who staked claims during Lula Mac's New Mexico absence, the swamp woman who found daily satisfaction in tormenting Gracie. And, many years later, she exacted payment in Gracie's name and memory. She saw a woman standing old and thin and alone on Sixty-third and Church Street. The sight slowed then stopped her feet. No, it couldn't be. Surely her eyes deceived. Illusion. Mirage. She stood thinking that her cold desire for revenge and justice had caused the woman to crystallize. The woman's eyes jumped with recognition. She started to turn her face away. Thought twice about it. Why, why, Sheila.

Sheila listened to the remembered voice and said nothing.

Is that really you?

After all these years, Sheila said. Sheila had heard no word about the woman since leaving Houston. Now to find her here, in the city, on this very street corner.

Yes. How you makin along?

After all these years.

Ivory Beach lifted her nose with her old pride. Yes. After all these years. You was a mean one.

Sheila punched Ivory Beach in the face, feeling the ancient brittle bones go soft under her knuckles.

Gracie had forgotten all of this. Remembered only what she wanted to re-member, needed to remember, cause if she remembered it all the past might force her to forfeit her anger.

Sheila found Lula Mae's Bible where she thought it would be.

# The

# HOLY BIBLE

CONTAINING THE

## OLD AND NEW TESTAMENTS
(Authorized or King James Version)

## SELF-PRONOUNCING
*Words Spoken by Christ Printed in Red*

To WHICH IS ADDED

AN ALPHABETICAL AND CYCLOPEDIC INDEX
A UNIQUE SET OF CHARTS FROM ADAM TO CHRIST
LEADING DOCTRINES, HARMONY
OF THE GOSPELS, PARABLES AND MIRACLES
BIBLE DICTIONARY
ALL ALPHABETICALLY ARRANGED FOR
PRACTICAL AND EVERYDAY USE
ETC., ETC.

★ STARS IN TEXT REFER TO PROPHECIES OF CHRIST

A BIBLE OF OUTSTANDING
HELP—INSPIRATION—STRENGTH

PUBLISHED BY

## THE JOHN A. HERTEL CO.
CHICAGO

EXCLUSIVE PUBLISHERS OF BLUE RIBBON BIBLES

Lula Mae had inserted strips of white paper throughout the Bible, perhaps to catalogue important sections, clue her to crucial passages. Sheila found a yellowed newspaper clipping sandwiched between two pages.

**ARTY**

J. Paul Getty III, 19, grandson of the oil billionaire, smiles at a guest during an exhibit of his paintings in Manila. Above him hangs a self-portrait, one of 29 being shown by Getty, whose long red hair covers the scar marking the loss of an ear to Italian kidnapers two years ago. Most of the paintings were of Italian scenes done in sunny blues, with prices ranging from $3,000 to $5,000.

Sheila returned the clipping to its exact place. She ran her palm over the book's rough cover. She left it here for me to find, she said to herself, thinking, and thinking almost saying aloud. She put the Bible in her suitcase and locked the latches.

## 41

SHE MUST BUY NEW CLOTHES for the funeral. A plague of moths had eaten her old ones. (Could this be? Is it not true that moths eat wool and wool only? Perhaps certain varieties of moths feed on a range of fabrics.) An army of babies rode off in her shoes, tanks.

She fluttered, angels in her body. She blessed the railroad plank above the grass-covered drainage ditch. Blessed the ditch itself. Blessed the chain-link fence that surrounded Lula Mae's property, contained it. Blessed the lawn. The lawn furniture. Trees—apple, pear, and plum. Blessed the concrete walkway leading up to the house. Blessed the two concrete front-porch steps. Blessed the front porch. Blessed the lil house out back behind the house. Blessed the two railroad planks positioned side by side to offer a walkway to the three concrete back-porch steps. Blessed the back-porch steps. The back porch itself, an uncovered block of concrete. Blessed the kitchen. The bathroom. The living room. The bedroom where Sheila slept. The second bedroom where Mr. Pulliam used to sleep, the bedroom that Lula Mae rented out after he fled to heaven. She blessed the hall. The attic could wait.

Blessing done, she entered the second bedroom where Mr. Pulliam used to sleep, the bedroom that Lula Mae rented out again and again after he fled to heaven. She undressed and slid under the covers, full and satisfied. Sharp-edged silence. Sheila slept quiet across the hall behind a closed door. Memory wheezed in the darkness. She put her Bible underneath her pillow and heard Lula Mae talking.

# 42

DAMN, MAN. Can't you see that Indian behind you?

Gunfire crackled through Lula Mae's house.

Man, is you blind?

Turn that TV down.

What? Woman, you ain't left to get my medicine?

A folk can't even think round here. All that clamor.

Think what? Think bout gettin my medicine. Mr. Pulliam breathed.

Fool, get out of my face, Lula Mae said.

Woman, you make me, Mr. Pulliam said. The words bubbled, like he had something in his throat, phlegm, dammed spit.

You touch me, I steal yo life.

Mr. Pulliam grunted at Lula Mae. Turned back to the loud TV. Lula Mae left the room.

Mr. Pulliam sat bent forward on the divan, face almost touching, kissing the TV screen. He breathed beneath the TV's traveling volume. The sound of his breathing always reached the front door ten steps before he did. His belly bulging his ribbed, sleeveless undershirt like a white laundry sack. He plowed clean paths through his lathered face with a straight razor. *Fool, how many times I tell you to close the door when you in the bathroom. Ain't nobody interested in your business.* Lula Mae was careful to tell Porsha not to touch his food. (He had his shelf in the refrigerator, and she hers. So too the freezer.) Not to enter his bedroom.

Lula Mae returned with her largest skillet, black iron, creased with shining grease.

Woman, what you think you gon do wit that skillet?

Lula Mae rung the skillet against his head.

Damn, woman. You tryin to kill me. I'm callin the police.

Call them.

He did.

The white officer arrived with the speed of arterial blood.

Can somebody turn off that there TV?

Porsha turned it off.

You see what the woman done to me? Mr. Pulliam gestured to the white kitchen towel pressed to his head. I jus asked her to get my medicine. I'm sick.

Sick in the head.

Damn this woman. She sposed to be my wife. Look at what she done to me.

I can't miss it.

Take her to jail. I worked a good job. I'm sick.

He struck me.

Law, I swear I never touched that woman. I swear on a mountain of Bibles.

Don't let your nasty mouth mention the Good Book.

I'm sick.

He struck me.

Well, seem like what we got here don't add up. Somebody talkin out the side they face.

Law, it ain't me.

It is you.

You both want to go to jail?

I'm sick.

Not sick enough.

Well one of you is talkin sideways. Girl—

The white officer looked at Porsha.

—what happened here?

That's right. My granddaughter here can testify.

That's fine wit me. She saw what happen. Tell Law here what happen.

Porsha said nothing. She had something to say but the words wouldn't come.

Girl look scared to me.

She from the city. Up North.

Maybe that explain it. City life. Come on here. The white officer took Mr. Pulliam by the shoulder and moved him toward the front door. We better see bout yo head. Now, ma'm. You be nice. I don't wanna come back here. I do, both yall comin down wit me to the jail. We got plenty room.

Law, she attacked me.

The white cop looked at Porsha. Something mighty wrong wit that girl.

She's a mamma's girl. Lula Mae smiled. When she was a toddler, I used to call her Duck. Followed her mamma everywhere.

Well, pigeons never fly far from home, the white officer said. All wrapped up in them apron strings.

Young folks. Lula Mae smiled. What can you do? Who can you blame?

Blame? the white officer said. I know this, what you put down is what pops up.

Lula Mae gave the officer a hard look. Her brown eyes toughened like shit.

WHERE DID LULA MAE GET THE TREES? Porsha said. Did she plant them herself or were they already here?

I don't know, Mamma said.

EACH MORNING, Lula Mae angled into her white dress, pulled old lady stockings over her cotton-scarred legs, slipped on her white rubber-soled shoes—nurse's shoes she called them, tennis shoes she called them—fitted the helmet of her wig, clamped in her horse bit of teeth, stepped into her face—it shone like a powdered mask—checked her clam-shaped purse—*Where my pocketbook?*—then hustled off to clean some white folks' house.

You be good while I'm gone. Don't act up.

GRACIE STARTED IT.
No I didn't.
Yes you did.
You started the whole thing.
You started it.
No I didn't. You did. Mamma was crying now.
You a lie. You started it. Gracie was crying now too.
You the one that's a lie. You know you started it.
I ain't start shit.
Yes you did.
Why you wanna lie?
You know you started it.

SHE WOULD KEEP THIS FOR HERSELF. All those years she had never mustered the nerve to ask Lula Mae to give it to her. The photograph shows three card players in a bare-walled shack. Two brothers and a stranger. All three wear tattered clothing. The older brother, mustache and all, passes the younger brother a card under the table, passes the card with his toes.

COME ON HERE. We going to the dolla sto.

The dollar store on Main Street next to Kress's (the five-and-dime), next to the bicycle shop where Porsha purchased her first real bicycle (without training wheels), across the street from the Rexall, where you could buy anything you wanted. Lula Mae walked to the dollar store every day and spent money simply because the spending was cheap. Items two for a dollar, four for a dollar, ten for a dollar. Stocking up.

Come on here. We going to town.

Meaning Memphis. Down Main Street to the bridge and across the bridge, the river beneath reaching up to touch you like a live cold hand, into Memphis, John Brown bent forward over the steering wheel, his two withered hands moving near his throat like they were adjusting his tie. John Brown always looked at Lula Mae as if she was something rare.

YOU THINK THIS WILL BE ENOUGH? Sheila said.

Porsha looked at the seven bottles of Mogen David wine in Sheila's suitcase.

You got those from the Shipcos? she asked. *Steal* wasn't the right word. If it was she couldn't say it. Both she and Sheila knew that the Shipcos would hardly miss them. Even if they did, they had money to spare and could buy more.

Sheila nodded.

I guess they'll do. You know black folks like sweet wine.

YOU BUY THE DRANKS?

Yes.

You thought I didn't see you. Comin from Chinamen's. Actin a fool.

What I do?

Actin a fool round those mannish boys.

When?

I can't send you to the sto without you actin a fool?

I ain't—

You better be careful. Can't jus run fast and foolish when those boys bother yo principle.

I ain't do nothing.
What I tell you bout talkin back?
I ain't talkin back.
You mamma ain't teach you no better.
She teach me.
You need to be churched, Lula Mae said.
That's where we going? I don't want—
Hush yo mouth.
—to church.
We going.
You gon dress me?
Why, child, why?
My mamma said don't put none of them cheap earrings on me.
Lula Mae drew back her hand. Go on. Lip smart. Go on.

PORSHA STOOD IN THE KITCHEN and looked out the door to the backyard.
Not ready to enter the yard yet. Let her toes feel the sun-heated grass.

> *Little Sally Walker*
> *Sitting in her saucer*
> *Weeping and crying for someone to love her*
> *Rise, Sally, rise*
> *Wipe ya weepin eyes*
> *Put ya hands on ya hips*
> *And let ya backbone slip*
> *Shake it to the east*
> *Ah, shake it to the west*
> *Shake it to the one you love the best*

Skip a song down the two long railroad planks that flattened the grass in a
path to the lil house.

Here, kitty kitty. Here, kitty kitty. Lula Mae calling out the back door.
Calling her cats. Cans of dog food (Chuck Wagon) waiting in the grass. She
never let them in the house.

MAMMA? Porsha said. I wanna ask you something. How long was *she* gone?
*Trolleys that carried you down the serrated palisade of Main Street, carried*
*you past the poplar-filled and maple-filled square, by dingy brick three-storied*

*houses or smoke-grimed frame houses with tiers of wooden galleries in grassless plots, junkyards, greasy spoons with rows of noisy backless twirling barstools, a lone tree out front, lop-branched magnolia or stunted elm.*

A long time.

But how long?

I don't know, but it was long.

Beulah says two years.

Way longer than that.

And Gracie says ten.

Not that long. We went to Houston to live with Daddy Larry and his wicked heifer.

The wicked stepmother?

Mamma nodded. Yes, the wicked stepmother. Ivory Beach. She never messed wit me or R.L., but she jus couldn stand Gracie.

Why not?

Said she was two-headed. And the way she used to knock Gracie wit her fist, she like to give her a second head. So one day, I grabbed her fist. Squeezed it to crumble it to dust. And I told her, If you hit Gracie again, I'll beat you till you can't see. And that was the end of it.

Porsha said nothing. She let the new words soak in with the tea.

I saw that woman years later. She used to live on Kenwood.

She did?

Yes, she did. She said, Sheila, you wuz an evil child. I said, No. You the evil one. I hit that heifer. Like to kill her.

Porsha rowed her spoon in her cup and changed the direction of the conversation. Well, what did she do in New Mexico?

She ain't do nothing. Casey Love, the man she went wit—

You mean run off wit.

—worked road gangs. Construction. In Tucumcari.

Where?

Tucumcari.

Porsha made a mental note to look it up.

See, R.L. was her son by that man, Casey Love. Real name was Robert Lee Harris, but everybody called him Casey Love. So I remember. She wuz married to Daddy Larry, but she left him for this man.

Porsha felt the warmth of her teacup. How old was you?

Well, R.L. was eleven or twelve, I believe. So I was ten.

Then Gracie was seven or eight?

Yes . . .

*Why* she come back?

He went on to California and she came back to Memphis. We moved back into the house on Claybrook Street that she rented from her friend. She started working at the car factory.

Car factory?

Yes.

They had a car factory in Memphis?

And a lot else.

Thought she was workin fo those white people.

That was later.

You came wit Beulah? Porsha was heavy, full of questions.

Yes.

When Gracie come?

Bout a year later. She stayed wit Lula Mae in the house on Claybrook.

What they do?

You ask Gracie.

She say that Lula Mae put you in Catholic school but wouldn't let her go.

That's a lie. I paid fo my own schooling. Helped Beulah at those white folks' house.

Why she say it then? Why she lie?

You ask her.

Porsha thought about it all. How old was she when she had him?

Eighteen, I believe.

That means she was only sixteen or seventeen when—

Yes.

So R.L. was twelve when she left. That means she was about twenty-eight or twenty-nine?

Yes, that sounds about right. A year or two before the war . . .

Porsha thought about it all. *Lula Mae was sixteen. Sixteen. A mother at sixteen.* It was all starting to make sense. You said she left round the time the war started?

Yes.

But how could that be? Sam and Dave fought in the war.

They were older than R.L.

How much older?

Not that much older. A few years. They were still boys really. Couldn't have been older than sixteen when they went.

That young?

Yes.

Well, how did they get in?

They wanted to go. Trouble never had to find them if they could find it first. Beulah did her best to keep R.L. on the straight and narrow. The people she worked for were good people. The Harrisons. Those white boys treated R.L. like a brother. Took him everywhere wit them. Then when he got grown, he went out to California. That man, Casey Love, had a ranch out there. R.L. sent me letters.

Where the letters?

Don't know what happened to them. Beulah got them. Maybe Lula Mae.

How they get them?

You ask them.

Well, what did he say in those letters?

I don't remember much. It was so long ago.

What happened to his father, this Casey Love?

I don't know, but R.L. did take his daddy's name, Love. And you know Beulah got those letters from China, his Indian wife, and R.L. Junior his son. Yeah, they out there somewhere in California. Call the phone company or get a phone directory and see if—

Mamma, you know I ain't never tried that and you know why. You know how many Loves there might be in California? And where in California?

I don't know . . .

How R.L. end up in Brazil?

I don't know. R.L. was always ready to throw a saddle on a tornado.

There ain't no tornadoes in Brazil, Porsha said, her mouth serious and factual.

Mamma said nothing, seemingly stunned . . .

How old was he when he died?

Twenty-five. Twenty-six. I believe.

Sam and Dave never went looking for R.L. out in California?

They say they did.

They weren't with him when it happened?

No. They were already in the city by that time.

Why they chase Dave out of Houston?

I can't remember. It was so long ago. But Dave, Sam, R.L., and Nap was always gettin into something. They were young men looking for trouble. They chased Sam out bout a year after they chased Dave. Then Nap end up dead in that jail in Jackson.

Houston?

No, Jackson.

How'd he—

Never would take his medicine. Bout the same time, R.L. passed. That red Edsel. Dave, Sam, Nap, and R.L.—all them fools drive faster than next week.

Porsha played the silence. But why?

Why what?

Why did she take up with this Casey Love? Why did she leave Daddy Larry?

Ask her.


DID YOU BRING AN EXTRA SUITCASE LIKE I ASKED YOU?

Porsha nodded.

Well get it.

Porsha got it.

Put these things in it.

Why?

Hurry up.

Porsha did as instructed.

Quick.

Her hands moved quickly. A photograph flashed up into her eyes and made her quick fingers pause. A baby-faced man grinned up into the camera from a poker table. Three other men—smoking, drinking, winking—shared his company. He sat upright, no curve in his spine, upright under a stiff-brimmed hat, tweed blazer draped over the back of his folding chair. Is that R.L.?

Mamma looked at the photograph. Nodded.

Is this the only—

Put it in the suitcase. Mamma took it and put it in the suitcase. Look at it later. Put these things in there. Hurry up. Come on. Quick. Before Gracie take everything.

# 43

HATCH LED SHEILA to the casket, his hand in the small of her back. A pyramid of flowers. The casket was black with silver fittings, the trestles hidden by flowers in a mass of shapes: wreaths, crosses, bows. He leaned forward and looked into eternity. About what he had expected. She had shrunk since the last time he'd seen her a year ago. Her head almost too small for her black wig. He noticed a red dime-sized hole on her neck, a red scarf trying to conceal it. A faucet hole where they had drained her decaying insides? Damn that mortician!

He held Sheila up, kept her from falling. Helped her back to the pew. Had she seen the red hole in Lula Mae's neck? (Her old eyes weren't as sharp as his.) He was unsure if he should ask her. She cried next to him and he watched, knowing nothing better to do, jumpy inside himself but calmly waiting for her to settle.

Clothed in righteousness, Gracie walked quickly to the coffin, looked, and didn't linger. Sheila—resolved now, firm in herself again though still shaky, motion in every cell of her body—and Porsha carried Beulah up to the coffin, the way Lucifer and John would carry her from her bed to the front porch and the swing she enjoyed, though her legs were too weak to move it. Her frail body trembled as if she was soaked in cold water. Her smooth yellow face and long black Indian hair had escaped the snares of old age. Mamma, I been obedient, she said. I followed your words, Keep over your brothers and sisters. I'm the oldest and put the youngest in the grave. Carrie Sweet. Sheila and Porsha held Beulah up, kept her from collapsing into the casket.

Beulah!

Lil Judy, Jacky, and Rochelle—Hatch's first cousins, age exact versions of himself, Jesus, and Porsha but raised differently, living now in a place they had never been, possibly living a life they had never known and would never know; when had he last seen them? Surely at their father's funeral, old drunk Dave—followed Beulah up to the coffin, a mocking light in their eyes, indifferent to the proceedings. They had never been close to Lula Mae. Only Hatch and no one else from his family had attended Dave's funeral, and only he and Uncle John had gone to their grandmother's funeral, Big Judy, Dave's mother, the woman Dave's crumb snatchers called Mamma—they called Beulah that too—since she had raised them.

The church was crowded with people. Standing at the back and along the walls. Who would have thought that Lula Mae had so many friends and acquaintances? Who would have thought?

She walked in the road with her black umbrella open to the pounding sun. She spoke to everyone she saw.

How you duche?

Fine.

Alright.

And the next person she saw a few feet ahead.

How you duche?

Fine.

Alright.

And the next person.

How you duche?

Fine.

Alright.

Children greeted her. How you, Miss Pulliam?

Alright. Yall be careful playing in that road.

She knew everyone. All of West Memphis. Now all of West Memphis came to say goodbye, stopped by the first pew to offer their condolences to the family. Hatch didn't recognize most of the well-wishers. Perhaps he knew them beyond recognition. Memory knowledge.

The hot church made hotter with hot people, two small windows to let in the hot air and let out the sweat. The church was a small one-story structure with chipped and dusty stained-glass windows. A little piece of church pastored by a little piece of preacher. No white-robed nurse standing with one white-gloved hand behind her back to hold Sheila in her seat and fan her when she got the Holy Ghost. *Yes, Lord. Oh come oh come oh come oh come oh glory.* No ark that rocked to Beulah's shouts. *You may bury me in the east. You may bury me in the west. But I'll hear that trumpet sound in the morning. Lula Mae, dear sister, hear that trumpet blast.*

Porsha sat next to him bent forward on the pew, face in her hands, water escaping between her fingers. Lula Mae would greet Porsha with a hunk of grease in the palm of one hand and a straightening comb in the other, the necessary tools to keep her hair from going *back home.*

Hatch, put some of this Duke on yo head. Make you look like those nice boys I work for.

I hate white folks.

Hush yo mouth. You don't hate nobody.

How you know?

What I tell you bout talkin back! You have to love somebody before you can hate them.

Porsha had wanted to track down Jesus and notify him of Lula Mae's death. Reasoning swiftly, Hatch had persuaded her not to. *Remember how he acted Christmas? What if . . .* The family was none the wiser about the situation with Jesus, John, and Lucifer. He would keep it that way.

The choir sang:

> *Swing low*
> *Sweet Lord*
> *And carry all home*
> *When I shall stand*
> *Before the great white throne*
>
> *When he shall wrap me*
> *In the flapping wings of his robe*
>
> *If I make it home*
> *My saviour let me hold his hand*
> *You'll know, he satisfied me*

Their bodies swayed, following the motion of the spirit.

I AM THE WAY, the preacher said. No one comes to the Father except through me.

Yes, Lawd.

My sheep, hear my voice. Know and follow me that I give eternal life. No one shall snatch you out of my hand.

Wooh. Beulah let her soul escape through her mouth. If I could have been there, sister. Wooh. I would have seen you through. Mamma and Daddy told me to watch over you. Wooh, Beulah howled. Wooh.

Hatch looked at Porsha. They both wanted to laugh, Beulah's grief humorous to hear.

*Aw, Sam! Wish I had been there. To hold up yo head. To put a pillow under you. Mamma told me to take care of you. You were her only boy. The youngest. She told me to take care of you. And I did my best. But this wicked woman . . . Sam!*

O Grave, where is thy sting? Beulah, humming the words, preacherlike, singing them. O Death, where is thy victory?

The young organist—judging by the looks of him, about Hatch's age—dripped water from the wells of his eyes. He wiped his eyes quickly to keep from missing a chord.

Wooh. Ah, Lula Mae!

Sheila attempted to quiet Beulah. He understood. She had faith. Belief. But he would not give in. Both grief and belief deceived.

Let us rise now. Heavy though we are. Rise as on that great getting-up morning.

The words dimly echoed what Hatch was attempting to slip away from.

For as the sufferings of Christ abound in us, so our consolation also aboundeth by Christ.

Yes!

Stand now, and go, stand, having your loins girth about with truth, and having on the breastplate of salvation. Stand now, and go.

MISS JONES, Reverend Blunt said, we got a problem here. He took both of Sheila's hands with his long-fingered preacher hands. He wore a sky-blue suit made in heaven. I couldn't find nobody to fix the air conditioning.

Sheila said nothing.

Hatch gave the reverend his meanest look but the reverend wouldn't look in his direction. The reverend had promised that the faulty air-conditioning units in the two limousines would be fixed by the time the funeral ended. A promise he either couldn't or wouldn't keep. Now they would drive two hours to the Houston graveyard in the full heat. Lula Mae's instructions for her burial written in her own hand: BURY ME WITH MAMMA DADDY AND THE REST.

Now, I'm gon return some of yo money. The reverend rubbed Sheila's hand as he spoke. We can discuss that later. Why don't yall hurry on. It's a long drive.

They loaded up the limousines. Rolled down the windows. Prayed for a cool breeze. Started the engines.

Reverend Blunt leaned into the open driver's window and passed his mother what looked like a brick of hundred-dollar bills. In case of emergency, he said. The mother smiled. I'll see you when I get back, he said.

SUN WHIPPED THE LIMOUSINE FROM SIDE TO SIDE. Slapped him across the face. He struggled out of his blazer. Loosened his tie. The wet heat touched him everywhere at once, a hot bath. Sheila looked quietly ahead, determined. Intact and withdrawn and conscious all at the same time. Lula Mae's long spell in bed had prepared her for this moment. Death was a challenge, for that was what it was, a war. Beulah appeared to be asleep. Porsha was looking out the open window, wind moving her hair. Gracie and the rest of the family followed in the other limousine. Sweat moved in the wind and he thought of Elsa's fragrant rain of black hair. It came to him just like that. The first thought of her in days. Since . . . He leaned forward in the limousine to get a better view of the tall trees that lined the road and held the sky in place. (He would sit like this for two hours and let the heat prey on him.) Looking and seeing, everything neither familiar nor strange. Abu had never been down South, and Hatch had spent many hours talking up images of his southern experience. He wanted to tell himself these now, bring it all back, but that past was hidden behind a screen of trees. Mules and shadows of mules black-moving against the green. Black-moving into the red 'Sippi delta. Black images glided through the blue sky. He sat and watched from the black limousine. Black absorbs without reflection, roots itself in unreflecting calm.

Seemed like they always arrived in West Memphis to a sickle moon and the flutter of insects, Lula Mae with a big smile and an expansive hug. The yard drank black water at night and spat up dew in dawn silence. Birds bounced from tree limb to tree limb. You and Jesus searched the grass for dragon's teeth. Kept them on you as a secret. Rain always fell clear, solid, and slow. After the rain, the sun sailed out into a clear sky. Broad dented leaves—and winged seeds, birch? maple? elm?—sparkled light. Black cherries hung straight and heavy among foliage. You and Jesus pulled snails from their shells, then held up the freed shells to your ears to hear ocean roar. Frogs bellowed, their voices grave, deep, measured. Masters of the earth, they wandered out into the road—yes, the road, a rich mixture of red dirt and red gravel—to stop cars. You and Jesus tossed flattened frogs like Frisbees into the cornfield across the road. Stop that chunkin! Lula Mae screamed from the yard. A shower of leaves and Lula Mae with a mop handle knocking apples, pears, or plums from the trees in her yard. You had to guard your head from falling fruit. You had the same fear of falling when you passed beneath the horseshoe nailed above every door in Lula Mae's house. Her fruit made the best preserves for your morning toast, eggs, and bacon. Miss Bee's cornfield grew transparent in the setting sun's light. Lula Mae pulled the creaking attic stairs down from the ceiling—thick robot legs—unfolded them, and lit a kerosene lamp to a fragrant glow. You and Jesus followed her up the wobbly stairs. Her shadow quivered on the attic ceiling and walls.


MR. BYRON MET THE PROCESSION in Fulton, a good sixty miles from West Memphis, another state, 'Sippi, near Houston, the family's beginning place. A little red-colored white man in overalls and a Cat trucker's cap, the visor pointed right at the sun. He leaned into the window of each limousine and gave instructions to the driver. Follow close behind me, he said. You get lost, just honk.

Who's that ole white man? Hatch said.

Mr. Byron, Sheila said.

Who?

Mr. Byron.

Who's that?

Mr. Harrison. His son. Nephew. Grandson.

Who? I don't know no Harrison.

The people she —

What people?

Questions furled and unfurled into fire. Mr. Byron drove his black car fast as if the cemetery was in danger of disappearing. Fast in transport, fast in arrival.

Do you know how to find this cemetery? Hatch said.

Yes, Sheila said.

Is that white man the only one who know?

Sheila said nothing.

Mr. Byron guided the family through the cemetery. Nowhere else had Hatch seen earth so red. Gravestones shimmered in the high noon light. They followed Mr. Byron past a clutter of crippled tombstones,

SACRED TO THE MEMORY OF FLORA
A COLORED WOMAN, WHO DIED JAN. 5, 1826, AGED 104 YEARS
STRONG FAITH, STRONGER, TRUSTING IN HER SAVIOUR

then mounds with handmade crosses, then mounds with no crosses at all. Hatch knew. The Griffith family was buried here. All whose hearts had quit the job. Buried beneath red soil. Beulah had worked for the Byron (Harrison?) family. Koot and Big Judy too, for all Hatch knew. There Candice Griffith. Mr. Byron's voice banged like a gavel. He pointed to an unmarked grave. Hatch smelled brilliantine on the white man's hair. There Dave Griffith. There Carrie Sweet Griffith. There Judy Randle. There Buck Randle.

*Big Judy's husband.* There Arteria Stone. There Nate Stone. There Dave Griffith the Second. The weight of names. All buried in the same red constipated earth. All gone headlong in red clay holes. Only R.L. was missing, interred somewhere in California, foreign soil.

> *Whosoever will, whosoever will*
> *Hear the loving Father*
> *Call the wanderer home*
> *Whosoever will may come.*

We got to bring Sam home, Beulah said. Sheila and Rochelle kept her standing, holding up her arms like broken wings. Bring him here. Gather up the family. Yall ain't got to wait long. She was speaking to the graves now. I'll be with you soon. Follow you now if I could.

Hatch and three strangers dressed in black held two wide straps of canvas that cradled the casket over the grave's yawning red toothless mouth. On the headman's signal, Hatch released length after muscle-straining length of the strap, like undocking a boat to open water. He lost his footing and almost slipped into the grave.

A WHITE HOUSE comes to you from long-forgotten times. Floats, flutters, flies, a moth-eaten memory.

You reached it by a red string of road that snaked up through the hills—at the foot of the hills, neat white double-level houses, each perfect as a double scoop of ice cream—and from there up to the crown, flat houses like rotting boats, scaling walls, sagging blinds, torn window screens, pieces of curtain, sunlight blasting the exposed ribs and wafting mildew smells as Big Judy gunned her car along the narrow, curving road, yes, right up to the crest of the hill, where her house stuck out under the sunlight. Koot's house was just down the road, pushed back beneath the shadow of poplar and maple trees, like the oval portraits of every family member (except R.L.'s) pushed back into the space above Koot's fireplace—as if someone had mashed it there under their palm. A big range house—yes, how big it seemed to you then; years later, you returned to it (Dave's funeral) to discover that it had shrunken in size, like cotton under excessive heat—sweating in the Fulton summer.

A swirl of summer chickens. An invisible rooster strutting in the sun. *Used to have a rooster, Big Judy said. Henry, we called him. Never crow when he sposed to. Never at dawn. But five or six times during the day. But he ruled.*

*If you see my little red rooster, please drive him home. Been no peace in the barnyard since he been gone.* The vapors from three or four hogs fenced stomping and grunting in the pen. Big Judy dumped pails and pails of rotten fruit and kernel-depleted corncobs. Hogs roll, a boiling sea of stinking pink.

The ravine behind and just down the hill from the house everyone called the snake pit, a serpent-stricken hissing valley, smoke wreaths during the day and mist at night. Over the years, Big Judy had lost several hogs and chickens to the pit. But the old people would come and sit, bending the legs of the metal folding chairs under their weight of creaking years, in the shade of her concrete driveway, unbothered by the chicken and hog noises and smells or the threat of scorpions and snakes, and suck the sap of memory.

*Koot had a long life, Big Judy said. And Mr. Footy treated her good. Now, that Buck. He called me every kinda name, and ain't none of them in the Bible. Jus the meanest cuss. Couldn get him to walk ten feet down the road and ask Koot fo a cup of sugar.*

A flower blazed between an angle of roots. You took a close curious look. The yellow jacket stung you, your jaw puffed up and threatened to explode by the time you made it back to the house and Big Judy powdered it with tobacco—some of Mr. Buck's chewing snuff—to smoke out the swelling. Bandaged your face good with a shroud of handkerchiefs.

Your jaw swelled so your ears hurt. Pain new and undreamt of. Thankful that you had not been attacked by a snake or one of those blue-green lizards that Big Judy called scorpions. Better off than Koot, killed in a car accident—no, a *crash*, that claimed, *yes, claimed, staked with jagged glass and twisted spikes of metal*, the life of a pregnant white woman and the white baby black in her belly, and a second woman who was driving Koot to the hearing-aid store, thrown through a car's windshield—*If it means anything, if it can help, she was killed instantly; she didn't suffer*—her reluctant feet still planted to the passenger side of the floor where they had refused to follow her body roadside. *Feel yourself driving through a wet curtain (beads, yes, beads) of glass, like jetting from beneath a pool to break water's surface; feel yourself flying through air, a bird sailing wind in slow motion, then feel your face covered with crumbs of glass, and a numbing sensation in your feet.*

THE FAMILY SAT DOWN TOGETHER, their knees close under a table covered with a fresh white cloth. The room heavy with greasy odors. The delicate aroma of yellow watermelon that grew wild in unattended winds. Cool iced tea that people drank year-round. The graveyard preacher joined the family at the reception table. Word had salted down to him. Or he had invited himself. His plain black three-piece shined the satin gloss of a raven's wing. Small, but a big horse head and face of a man. Processed hair flowing mane-like. He found it easy to blend his religion and his appetite. (He wiped his mouth with a paper napkin after every bite.) Gracie matched him word for word. Angels angled out in their speech.

Sister, the preacher said, you know your Bible. His chin hung close to Gracie.

I try. She stirred with the start of a laugh.

Yes indeed.

The preacher's mouth smelled like money. Hatch had already endured two preachers that day. Now a third. Preachers troubled him. And the presence of this one strengthened his inclination to spit in every preacher's eye.

The preacher led the family in prayer, rising on food steam to heights invisible to the eye. With his paper napkin, he wiped the prayer from his lips.

Keep the faith. By and by God reveals his divine plan to man. And with that, he heaved himself up from the table and quit the house.

I HAD TO PUT THE GUN ON MR. BUCK, Dave said. I asked him, What you call my mamma? I told that motherfucker. Say it again. Big Judy screamin, Dave, it ain't worth it. Shit, it's worth it if I say it is.

The earth cooled. A heat-hushed night. The heavens low-hanging. Moonlight soft-showered the window. You rested under the white bed-spread, translucent from use, safe now, the wire screen having been checked and double-checked so that no bat would fly through the open window on a dark breeze.

*Jesus, you sure it closed?*

*Yeah.*

*Check it again.*

*I already did.*

*Them bats bite you in the neck. Flying rats.*

Pale moths and bright mosquitoes yellow-revolved around Big Judy's single porch light. John, Lucifer, and Dave, ghost-gray men in the night carrying their gin and beer, sat rough on Big Judy's metal folding chairs and lit up the dark with their cricket talk.

Uncle John blew magic lamp smoke from his mouth and nose. Why didn't you tell me that Fulton is a dry county?

I did tell you.

You ain't tell me shit.

Nigga, you got cotton in yo ears, that's all.

And what you got in yours?

Lucifer, you better tell this nigga.

He can't tell me shit.

Nigga, I'm older than you. Talk to me wit some respect.

You ain't sayin nothing.

Say what I got to say.

Say it then.

I'm gettin ready to.

You gon make us wait.

Did I ever tell you bout that time—

The men spoke brick upon brick, sharing mellow-golden stories—some about Sam, about And (who Hatch knew only as Beulah's former husband who visited her every free chance), about Spin, Spokesman, Dallas, Spider, Ernie; some about men Hatch didn't know (he hung on to their names); some about Bataan and Okinawa, where And, Sam, and Dave had fought and claimed blood, and others about that yellow-green place where Lucifer and John had done the same—building backwards, word after hard word.


WHY, SHEILA, THIS MUST BE YOUR DAUGHTER.

You know that ain't my daughter. That's Gracie.

Gracie? The drunk's red eyes widened in mock surprise. The drunk and Gracie sat squeezed tight together on the yard swing. The Gracie I used to know?

Cut that out, Mr. Man, Gracie said. You knew it was me.

I thought it looked like you but I knew you couldn be lookin that good after all these years.

Stop that, Mr. Man, Gracie said. You still a fool.

You still know how to love a fool?

Stop that, Mr. Man.

When had Hatch last seen Gracie show such girlish energy and exuberance? (Never in John's presence. Never.) Ready to lift her skirt and flirt.

When you going back home?

Why?

I'm gon drive up there to West Memphis to see you befo you head back.

You don't wanna do that.

You still know how to dance?

I don't dance.

You still know how to move yo body the way you used to?

Gracie grinned at the grass beneath her feet.

Why don't you move back down here? Why don't you come home? Why you want to live in a big city? City life, piss in a can. Bury it.


I LIKE EM SLIM. Streamlined. Built for speed.
St. Louis woman the best type. Way down from the Gulf of Mexico.
Can't hold a match to a Texas woman.
Who you know from Texas?
You'd be surprised.
You brought yo kids. Why didn't you bring Jesse?
I like my coffee in the morning. Crazy bout my tea at night.
What fo? So she can slow me down.
That's yo woman.
Like hell.
Sam should be here.
You know what he told Koot after Mr. Footy died?
What?
He said, Koot, you got to have somebody on the vine. Had to say it five or six times cause you know Koot deaf. Koot say, Sam, that ain't no vine. That a jimsonweed.
Well, I've given up chasin women.
I leave you there.
But I'll still go to a bar—
Dave, damn if we don't know that already. You a drinkin fool.
—have me a taste and talk to the womens. They'll give you some too, if you know how to talk to em right.


HE DIED TEN YEARS AFTER SHE CAME BACK.
No, it was fifteen.
You can't never get nothin straight.
Look who's talkin.
We can look at the death certificate.
Why don't you go get it.
I would if you hadn'tah lost it.
I ain't lost nothing.
That ain't what I recollect.
I don't give a damn—
Yall stop that arguin, Beulah said in her usual shrill voice. All yall do is argue.
You always agree with her, Gracie said. You always have.

I ain't tryin to take nobody's side.

You jus like Lula Mae. Take Sheila's side in everything.

Shut your damn mouth! Sheila said. All that happened a long time ago. What can I do about it?

THE ROAD HISSED under the black tires. They rode in the black limousine, silent as the dark they traveled through. The sun had fallen but the heat had not let up. The dark had absorbed it like black cotton.

THEY STOOD IN THE ROAD under the failed sky. Sheila passed Reverend Blunt a tip, slipping him the money quickly.

Why, thank you. Reverend Blunt had changed into a fresh suit. He smiled into Porsha's eyes. I'll drop by tomorrow and see how yall doing.

Porsha returned the smile.

Good night. Reverend Blunt charged up the road.

Why you do that? Hatch said.

Sheila said nothing.

Why you give that bastard a tip?

HATCH STEPPED INTO A HOUSE FULL OF MOVING VOICES.

You must be her granson. Is that her granson? Is he her granson? Why I ain't seen him since he was nay high. Where that other one, that red-lookin one? Her granson sure a handsome one. We gon miss yo granmother. Look, there Gracie's boy. A fine woman. I'm gon sho miss her. Ain't he the devilish one? You remember me? Why, I ain't seen you since I know when. Any kin to Lula Mae kin to me. You come down here to visit me anytime you want. Come on by my house and sit a while befo you go back. I bet you like pecan pie? You a fine young man. You a handsome young man. Look like yo daddy. You come down here to visit anytime you want. I live jus up the road there. You member where I live? Drop by and sit a while.

He couldn't wait for the house to clear of people. Juiced out by the sun, he needed sleep.

He found quiet escape in the kitchen. He would have shut the door but there was no door to shut. He thought about all he had seen and said and heard and done all that he had not seen said or heard or done and all that he would see say hear and do.

*Well, he said, if you ain't never been nowhere other than Kankakee, here, and West Memphis—*

*I been more places than that, Porsha said.*

—*Tucumcari might as well be Arizona and Arizona Brazil and Brazil might as well be France and France California and California Texas and De-catur New Mexico and*—

*What map you lookin at?*

He saw Mr. Byron standing and pointing and spitting his name. The past that wasn't past sparkled like a reminder above the kitchen shelf. Lula Mae's old serving set. He remembered it from his many trips here. She had purchased it in either Texas or New Mexico. The cocktail bowl showed a rodeo scene. The lid made like a cowboy hat, a Stetson. The ice tray was a chuck wagon held in place by black wire wheels. A coffeepot sat on a black wire stand with four matching coffee mugs. Each piece glassed in a western yellow-brown. The serving set had been waiting for him all these years. Waiting for his return.

Why are you sittin in here by yourself? Sheila spoke from the open doorway.

I want that.

What?

That dinette set. Hatch pointed up to it.

Well, get up and get it. You better put it up before Gracie see it.

# 44

TREES STOOD LIKE AN ARMY in the clear morning air, their leaves glowing rivulets of lava.

His sweat-dampened saddle fit easily into the horse's back. A horse can tell if a man is strong-willed. Give him a chance and he'll stand on your foot and let you know who's in charge.

He climbed on the horse in proper fashion and tightened his legs around the iron belly. He kicked the horse into motion. Man and horse galloped off in a mute cloud of dust. Ponds like glistening uniform buttons. Word of his talents had spread far. More than once he had talked gently, sweetly, and rubbed a calf's legs all night long.

The speed of the gallop watered his eyes. He looked into the shimmering distance and told his horse things about the world he knew to be true. The horse blew and rolled its eyes at all it saw.

# 45

PORSHA ROSE BEFORE THE OTHERS and moved quickly through Lula Mae's house, her quiet hammer taking down the horseshoes nailed above Lula Mae's doors. Each and every one of them. These she would have for herself. Luck. Magic doesn't fade. Maybe the magic could work for her, work in her life.

YOU CAN'T MISS WHAT YOU AIN'T NEVER HAD, Gracie said.

It's passed, Mamma said. What can I do about it? I've had forty years of dealing with that misery. Go on with your life.

You go on with yours.

THE LIL HOUSE was much smaller than Porsha remembered. Half the length of a city subway car. And even smaller inside, boxes and more boxes where seats might be, the space between the boxes only wide enough for one person to stand comfortably. She, Mamma, and Hatch rummaged through Lula Mae's belongings while Gracie stood in the grass watching through the open doorway.

*Gracie, why don't you stay in the house and keep an eye on Beulah.*

*Why don't you.*

The lil house had four small windows, all rusted shut. (Lula Mae had never opened them.) The open door offered the only light and air. Hatch had pleaded, begged to light one of Lula Mae's kerosene lamps and all had agreed, but the lamps were empty, long minus kerosene. No one could find a flashlight. So they worked in the metal dark and the heat, hauling out goods to the sun-heated lawn, cataloguing them by location on the grass.

Mamma discovered her wedding dress, Hatch's blue baby bonnet, Jesus's first rattle, Porsha's paddle-and-ball, Cookie's bib (Gracie wanted it), unidentified wigs, and Lula Mae's first partial, false teeth.

Look at this, Hatch said. He held up a green duffel bag by its canvas straps like a dead rat by its tail.

I believe that's Mr. Pulliam's old army bag, Mamma said.

I'm gon keep it.

Let me see it, Gracie said.

Hatch played deaf.

Porsha tunneled through hatboxes and shoeboxes. Lula Mae had thrown nothing away. She opened the last shoebox and found a mummified pair of shoes, peeling white leather that had long gone gray. She lifted the shoes from the box by the laces and found a thick, business-sized envelope. No stamp in the upper right corner, only a pale blue postmark, like watercolor. The envelope was burned black with the shoes' shape, the burn obscuring most of the words. She found a second envelope, twin to the first. Eyes working, she deciphered one letter, two letters, then two words or the semblance of two words. Brazil, Nebraska.


THAT WAS MR. PULLIAM'S DAUGHTER, Mamma said. She want the house.

Too bad. Lula Mae had willed her house, lil house, and everything in them to Sheila.

I told her she can have it.

Porsha cocked her ear. What?

Mr. Pulliam's name on the mortgage.

Mr. Pulliam been dead fifteen years. Lula Mae the one who paid off the mortgage.

Mamma said nothing.

Ain't you gon contest it?

It ain't worth the time and trouble.

I'll hire us a lawyer.

I don't want to go to court. For this old house.

But, Mamma—

Hush. It ain't worth the time or the trouble.


FOR THE FIRST TIME IN MEMORY, she saw the lil house stationed on grass not concrete, the trailer hitched behind a brand-new truck on the red gravel road before Lula Mae's house. Gracie had sold the lil house for a hundred dollars to Lula Mae's daily hospital transport.

I gave him a good deal, Gracie said. Since he was good to Lula Mae.

The truck and the lil house pulled away, leaving a thin gown of dust.

Gracie sold Lula Mae's stereo (for a dollar) to Lula Mae's best friend, an old lady with hands like a man, wearing a hearing aid like a spy. She sold Lula Mae's kerosene lamps, flower-rimmed plates, crystal pitcher and glasses, bread box, spice holder, red metal kitchen chairs and matching table. She sold the meat freezer for twenty-five dollars, frozen meat included. She sold the dishwasher, washing machine, and dryer (seventy-five dollars for the set).

Two middle-aged white women—daughters of Lula Mae's employers, kin of Mr. Byron, the white man who knew the Griffith family graves the way he knew his teeth—rushed through the house grabbing up everything in sight, like a tornado. Glass figurines, decorative baskets, vases, ashtrays, place mats, plates, and anything else Gracie had not sold.

Together they lifted a stunned and immobile Porsha off her feet. Hatch stayed their hands. They put Porsha down. Said, We jus wan something to member Lula Mae by.

MAMMA AND GRACIE fought for possession of the quilt, tugging at it, an angry game. A store-bought pattern—a tattered circus clown, once bright patchwork colors against a dull yellow background—now frayed at the edges that Lula Mae had sewn together in a matter of hours and stuffed with store-bought stuffing, an everyday quilt to keep you warm at night, protection against the air conditioner's winter cold. (Gracie had sold the air conditioner for twenty-five dollars.)

YOU SAY IT'S FUN?

Porsha thought about a favorable way to describe her line of work. Nothing came to mind. What about you?

Reverend Blunt smiled. There's no better job.

It must run in your family.

Why do you say that?

Ain't that how most people start?

He laughed. I guess so. I guess that is how they start. You must go to work and prepare the way of the Lord, he said in a deliberate humming preacher's voice.

She found it hard to laugh, laughter pinned down by everything heavy inside her.

It's a hard time for you. I know it is. Miss Pulliam was a special woman, very special.

His eyes were clear and kind, free open space.

Thanks.

I can—

She stopped him. I would like to. I really would. But to tell you the truth, she pushed the words up from inside her, I'm seeing somebody.

Reverend Blunt said nothing for a moment, his eyes showing no change. Well, he said, I hope he seeing you too. It never works when one person is invisible.

He said it the same way he said everything else, without malice or sarcasm. She listened and accepted it and thought about it and thought about other things she was thinking through and sat saying nothing not knowing what to say. Sat smelling the new car leather, supportive, firm against her body, Reverend Blunt smiling into her face—*got to admit, he is the perfect gentleman, ain't looked at my body once, short skirt and all*—the air conditioner blowing cool in the silence. How long had they been sitting here and talking? One hour? Two?

Sun shattered in flakes against the windshield. The reverend's mouth moved but she missed the words.

He was handsome, yes oh so handsome—but she found it hard to hear what he was saying. The sediment of the past floated to the top of her still memory. Memories thicker than a snowstorm, free-floating in the reverend's car, a single, contained space, a Christmas paperweight. His mouth moved again.

What was that?

I said why don't we drive to Memphis? Take your mind off things.

No. I really would like to. I really would. *You are so sweet.* But I better stay close to the house. In case they need me. You understand.

Of course. As it should be.

Reverend Blunt opened his door and exited the car, rocking it with his strength. He came around the front of the car slowly, giving her ample opportunity to observe him, take him all in and appreciate. He opened her door, took her hand, and helped her out of the car.

Well, he said, it has been a pleasure.

The same.

He held her hand, his eyes watching and holding. She read his heart in his handclasp. Well, I better be going.

Yes, he said. That is the proper thing to do. He kissed her hand. Under different circumstances we might have—

Yes.

He pulled her closer. She leaned and took his kiss as if it were her rightful due. Kissed him until the pleasure began to send her.

She turned to the house and made it to the front porch when he called her.

Oh, Porsha. Let me give you this. He crossed the small bridge over the grass-covered drainage ditch and waited for her on the road side of the chain-link fence. She walked to the fence slowly but without hesitation.

I'll be in the city in a few weeks for a mortuary convention. This is where I'll be staying. He extended a business card.

She took it and read it carefully. She turned for the house. Walked on in the fresh sunlight.

SOMEBODY TOLD YOU WRONG, Beulah said. I ain't never been po. Daddy always said, When you needy, eat the skin of a cow.

Porsha wondered if he meant this literally.

Yeah, Sam was a devil alright. But Mamma and Daddy couldn lay a hand on him. Our animals fight them. Our pigs and cows wouldn let Mamma and Daddy lay a hand on nwine one of us kids. Beulah's lungs wheezed above her words.

How you feel today, Beulah?

I had everything. Cancer. Stroke. Heart attack. Hypertension. Asthma. Diabetes. Arthritis. I feel as good as I should feel. What else is left? I'm too old to get the clap.

Porsha did her best to laugh. She had it in her somewhere. She wanted to laugh with Beulah, for her. Lil Judy, Jacky, and Rochelle had stayed in Fulton where grave and gravity conspire. Had promised to come up in a day or two to bring Beulah back to St. Paul—and her nursing home bed—where all four lived. Beulah had bought them all plane tickets. In her Decatur house, she had raised the three girls as her own. Their mamma, Jesse, just thirteen when she had Rochelle, thirteen with the chaotic brain of a five-year-old, a parentless drinking fool, made worse when a stroke shriveled up the left side of her body, threw her red eyes out of balance (one up, the other down, like losing cherries in a slot machine), shortly after the birth of her last child, Lil Judy. And their father, Dave, Beulah's nephew, Big Judy's son, ran the street with his uncle, Beulah's younger and only brother Sam, two stray dogs. So she had raised them as her own.

*How come Beulah never had any kids?*

*I don't know. Maybe she already had enough to handle.*

You ain't married yet?

I'm looking. I'm trying.

Well, take yo time. Don't be in no hurry. Soon as they get some pubic hair, folks figure they old enough to marry.

# 46

No. Lula Mae ain't have no money, and I aint's have none either. So we was gon ask Mr. Harrison to ship him. Never did. He had done enough.

Hatch thought about it. And he would do that?

Yes.

Why?

Kind.

What?

Kind. He kind. That was the best white man that ever lived.

I wouldn't go that far.

I would.

Hatch examined his shoes. Patterns there. So how was he gon ship him? Plane?

Train.

Train? All the way from California?

Beulah said nothing.

Hatch seethed, sunk, settled, let his mind clear. And you worked for him in Memphis?

Yes. He was good to work for.

Cleaning up after them is good?

Better than a lot of jobs.

When you'd come to Memphis?

During the war. Bought a ticket long as my right arm and hopped that locomotive. That locomotive pack. No room for nobody. No seats.

*The smell of everybody's life mixed together.*

So we ride wit the soldiers, sittin on our luggage in the aisles.

And you came to Memphis?

Colored folks bouncing babies to sleep on they knee. Some even draggin long the family hog. Huff and puff up the rise. Two points make a line and we gone ride em all. Where the Southern crosses the Dog.

Her voice thin as the sheet that covers her. *And is talkin. Andrew, her husband, the railroad man. Railroad talk. The beat in between the beat of her voice. His cigar puffing up the rise. Lil nigga, that the rail and that the tie and that the sleeper and that the rail chair. Come heah, lil nigga, so I can show you this.*

Oh, my soul got happy when I come out of the wilderness.

You went to Memphis? He said it louder this time.

Yes. Sam and Dave got jobs in the meat factory. I found me some day work.

*Yeah. Cleanin these white folks' houses.* But *why* did you come? She was the right person to ask. Her memory clean and clear. *I want to tell you and keep you told.*

Same reason we all came. The big river flowed from there to here, and they built the railroad right next to it.

*The rails are two rivers. Two watery trails.*

First came to the city—*Lord, I'm traveling. Lord, I got on my traveling shoes*—in the middle of winter. That cold liked to kill me. Cold city winds. Snatch off yo durn draws.

There was these two right evil hoodlums laid for me every Friday payday. Two cutthroats wit stockings on they face, lookin like onions. They knock me down in the snow and kick me til I rolled. Grab my pocketbook. And laughin. They yell, Stop thief! Somebody call the police! But this one Friday, I was ready for em. Put a straight razor in my bosom. I cut them every which way but loose. Shoulda seen the blood running away from they evil bodies. Glad to be free.

I WOKE UP THIS MORNING with my mind still on the Lord. You read your Bible?

Sometimes. He lied. He didn't want to hear nothing bout no Bible.

Those words ain't written in ink and paper. You go to church?

Sometimes.

Don't you know? Church is life and fire insurance.

Beulah had walked hand in hand with death most of her life. *Beulah will outlive us all, Sheila said.*

Turn on the game. Yankees playin today. Beulah never missed the Yankees.

You ever see them play?

Course I seen them play.

I mean did you ever go *there* to see them play? New York? The Bronx?

No. I'm gon wait for you to buy me some tickets.

He found no humor in her statement. Lula Mae was gone, lost, forever silent, and Beulah was alive, pillows propped up behind her in Lula Mae's bed—the creaking pain of old age—the windows shut, the shades drawn. Here before him now. She would soon return to St. Paul, resume her life there. He had little time. But why not? You rambled?

*First Houston, then Memphis, then the city, then Decatur, then Fulton, then St. Paul. No grass grew under her feet.*

Yes, I rambled. The hand of the Lord was upon me. I've never been to the seminary, but I've been to Calvary. I've had no education, but moved the Red Sea.


DROUGHT SUMMER, the topsoil gray and loose, light. Cracks wide, thirsty mouths, the desperation of breathing. Bent cane stalks like old men. No greening rains. Once, the plowed fields were like quilts in shades of green and brown. Now, a haze of thirsty yellow. He had to see the house, Beulah some other place now. Beulah's house, down the hill past the weed-choked cemetery, the crooked stones, past the train depot, the train shrieking through the intersection of road and track, speed eased or stopped with a red flag. He found a pile of ash-blackened boards where her house once stood, the hollow brick frame trying to swallow up the sky.

Uncle John always drove them to Beulah's during winter. Speeding out the city to cut gray slush paths through white winter space and silence. White flakes drop to the earth, fleeing the sun (just as black ashes rise to the sun's warmth). Square upon square of cornfield, the state hospital surrounded by corn, the crazies made crazier by the constant green beyond the window bars. These plains an hour outside the city, plains fitted for sweeping and rolling winds, twisting arrows that stick everything in their path and carry them off to the farthest horizon. Now the town itself. Decatur. Kankakee County. Snow brilliant white like a second skin on trees, rooftops, awnings, window ledges. The cement path to her house, winter-covered, sunlight blinding on white snow-thickened grass. The mound behind the house, the mound that you could enter through two wooden doors, pull them up and back, raised insect wings, and walk down four or five crumbling stone steps, descend into the earth itself. Cept it wasn't earth, but a concrete cave filled with dark cluttered junk.

*You and Jesus square off against Jacky and Lil Judy. Scratch each other's eyes in a tumbling-down clinch.*

*Don't yall play so rough, Porsha says. They girls.*

*Ain't nobody playin.*

And the two-story house itself where Beulah had raised Rochelle, Jacky, and Lil Judy, Dave's three girls—*Dave, that nigga, God durn his soul; he spend his check before he make it home; and Jesse would jus grin, Mr. Dave,*

*you so crazy; what she know; she weren't but thirteen and green as a grasshop-*
*per; Dave feed them babies sugar water; Jesse ask the neighbors fo some bread*
*and crackas, then that firewater take a holt to her and she have that stroke,*
*and Sam and Dave, God durn they souls, Sam and Dave runnin the streets*
*actin the biggest fool; Dave spend his check befo he make it home; them ba-*
*bies white as ghosts from all that sugar, sugar sticking to they diapers; and Lil*
*Judy sucking on Sam's wood stump leg like it some kinda pacifier; sure I took*
*them, raised them; what else was I gon do?* — who were quicker than Beulah's
old apron strings.

*Don't get too close to them, Porsha said.*

*They got worms again?*

*Yeah.*

*How they get em?*

*From eatin all that candy.*

*Worms live in candy?*

*No, in sugar.*

Thanks and praises. Pregnant and grown, Rochelle, Jacky, and Lil Judy
packed up babies and belongings, journey west, to St. Paul — to get the max-
imum government check from public aid — and left Beulah in an empty
house. Beulah musta gotten lonely. That's why she sold the house and
moved with Koot in Fulton; but Koot died; she moved up the road with Big
Judy; Big Judy died; where could she turn? Lula Mae? She and Lula Mae
didn't get along. Never had. So she moved to St. Paul, where Rochelle,
Jacky, and Lil Judy passed her from house to house, passed her around like a
hot reefer joint.

The sweet smell of her asthma cigarettes floated through the room and
refused to leave. Brown and green medicine bottles, still on the surface of
the nightstand next to her bed. Bedridden — *When you old and sick and*
*gotta stay in bed, ain't much else you can do* — in the silk Chinese robe that
Andrew, her first husband — two husbands, was this a family tradition? — had
brought her from Seattle, splotched with black-lined ginkgos, gold dragons,
jade rivers, and scarlet flowers. The smooth tan skin, the neck a hill of wrinkles sliding down to her big-boned torso. The years had preserved her hair —
*good hair,* Sheila called it — flowing in a silver wave down her back. *Used to*
*be longer than that. All the way down to her knees.* She would brush it in
long, slow, attentive strokes as if to bring the words out.

Dave say you had *really* long hair back then.

Yes, down to my ankles.

*Bird wings.*

I had to cut it when I started to work in the factory. Your hair get caught
in one of those machines.

Couldn't you just wear a cap?

All that hair?

Late in life (at age forty? forty-one?), she had met And in Houston and married him soon after. They came to the city together. When the gettin was good, she found a job in the war (car?) factory, while the draft shipped And overseas. *He speak Japanese, Dave said. Shit, I know a word or two but that nigga sound like he born a Chink.* War done, he found work as a Pullman porter. The marriage lasted five years. But the divorce (separation?) didn't end them. And drifted into town like smoke. *Aw, girl, what you doing up in that bed? Every time I come to see you, you up in that bed. How I'm gon look at yo butt?*

*Gon way from me, mister.*

Clicked open a gold initialed (AA) cigarette lighter and lit a sweet-smellin cigar, squirting smoke out of his hair-filled nostrils. (Did the hair filter the smoke?) Silk monogrammed (AA) socks, gleaming alligator shoes, shiny three-piece (his forefinger hooked in the vest), polka-dot tie with diamond stickpin (AA), sparkling and blinking like Christmas lights, blocked Dobb, cocked over one eye—he reached up a hand in salute, taking the hat edge onto his long-tipped fingers, then bringing the hat into the circle of his lap—initialed (AA) silk handkerchief, big sparkling cuff links—Hatch teased him, *What's those, handcuffs?* screaming the words wet in his face, as he was hard of hearing; *He listening to the sound of the railroad,* Beulah said—and a big cloisonné horseshoe ring (he liked the races, horse and dog) that glittered and wavered. *Always clean as a broke-dick dog,* Beulah said, through the worn threads of her voice, *plenty of jack.* Come here, little nigger, And said, worrying the railroad watch attached to his vest from a heavy silver chain. Hatch came. And put the big watch in Hatch's hand. Hatch examined it like some fossil. Engraved on the back, a double track between two crossed semaphores, stop signal. *You know how niggas is. Niggas loaded everything into they steamer trunks. No engine, I don't care how powerful, could move that train. We had to open up some of them trunks. See what inside. One nigga got his bathtub in there. One got his stove. Another got his horse in there. Another his house.* Got good tips, And said, but some white folks cheaper than Jack Benny. Give you a quarter or a cigar and pect you to do a song and dance.

Divorced (separated?), Beulah moved to Decatur and found a job in the local dog-food factory. Purchased a two-story (wood and brick, green and white) house with a length of green lawn where Hatch and Jesus could wrestle, chase Jacky and Lil Judy, and enough yard for a grove of pear trees. Her second husband, Mr. George, a co-worker at the factory—*I knew him before we decided to jump the broom*—was as plain as And was colorful. *The light of the body is the eye.* Overalls and snuff. Smoking his pipe—snuff *and* a pipe?—under the spreading pear trees. (Hatch could not recall a single instance of Mr. George speaking, the tucked pipe clogging back the words.) Wearing a basin-shaped hat and a black mortician suit on his way to church each Sunday. When she had the strength, Uncle John and Lucifer would walk her—one of them could have carried her without missing a breath, but she insisted on *Walking on my own two feet. That's what God give them to me for. Last person who carried me was And. Over the threshold. Mr. George too old to carry anybody and I don't plan to marry no more*—to the front porch, slowly, every inch of skin shaking with the effort as if she would crumble. The two of them, Beulah and Mr. George, the unlit pipe tucked between his lips, sitting in the cushioned rocking chairs on the screened porch, not a single word from the man, nothing escaping past the plug of pipe. And when And came to town, the three of them sitting on the long, noisy rocker/glider, where summer voices floated around them and fireflies flickered and faded at night. That was how Mr. George died one evening as the sun turned copper, heart exploding inside his chest, Beulah hearing the creaking rocker stop, seeing the angles of the chair freeze in place and blood thread from his nose.

Sugar. Hypertension. Heart attacks. Two operations to cut out the cancer. But I'm still here. Death try to sneak up on me when I sleep. But I go when the good Lord call me.

A wedge of light fell outward from the door. Found glints in her hair.

You hear bout people falling off a mountain and survivin wit nothin but a scratch, then you hear bout people dyin from a bump on the head. You go when it time fo you to go.

Her voice was soft and secret, almost a whisper, as if she were talking to herself.

When St. Peter say Come home, better put on yo runnin shoes.

She had outlived her one brother and many sisters (she killed one herself, when she was a girl, dropped the baby and busted its skull), some—Sam, Koot, Big Judy—whom Hatch had seen, heard, and touched, found various ways to die—though she was the oldest child.

*Beulah, you the firstborn?*

*No, the second. The first baby, a lil baby girl, drowned on Mamma's milk.*

All that remained, silent photographs, shadowy names, and inscrutable memories. Her family originated somewhere near Houston ('Sippi, not Texas), and she knew little more than that, knew nothing of her grandparents, so the family lineage began and ended at her maiden name, Griffith. (Some even spelled the family name differently. Griffis.)

Now they talkin bout men on the moon. Life motionless but alive, Beulah spoke between wheezes, cast talk in his teeth, a film of mist softening every word, the voice weak.

*They open a new highway, let it roll wide the earth, shake trees from their roots. Birds leave the edges of the forest, abandon the highway, carry pieces of the moon between their claws. Their sharp wings cut through the clouds. They fly up to mountaintops and from the highest peaks take in the widest landscapes. Foresee the space age.*

If God wanted men on the moon he woulda put them there. I ain't gon believe no men on no moon til I go there myself.

Beulah, they had it on TV. In the newspaper.

I don't have no truck with such nonsense. Them white folks think they got the sun and the moon locked inside a briefcase. But there are some things the Lawd wants all folks to know, some things jus the chosen few to know, and some things no one should know.

She could tell stories, though Sheila didn't want to hear them—*Hush; Beulah, don't go digging up the past; I been through enough in my life; that was then, this is now*—though Gracie stiffened at the voice, closed her eyes against remembrance, though Beulah took so long between words you didn't know if she had finished talking or was only resting, and you listened attentively, clutched every kernel from her throat, for she was *willing* to pass on greasy-fingered tales. Tales like houses, yards, gardens, other worlds, spaces to inhabit, hand-me-downs, generational clothes.

Thirteen of us in that shotgun shack, fifteen cluding Mamma and Daddy.

Hatch listened.

Fifteen. She watched him from across the lamp. People today don't know nothing bout being crowded. Fifteen of us. Fifteen. Thirteen—

Thirteen.

—chillun. The five oldest chillun stay and help Mamma and Daddy work the farm. The five younguns go to the fields. Crawlin through them fields on yo hands and knees. Tie some cloth patches cross yo knees so they won't wear down.

Talk bout hard times. People today don't know nothing bout no hard times. There was this one bad season, real bad, bad harvest. Our dogs Blackjack and Redman howled all day and night, bellies hanging off them like empty sacks.

One afternoon, Daddy came home all slumped up, bone-tired. He hadn't been to the fields that day. And he come in and take something outa his shopping bag and set it down on the table. A ham. All wrapped up neat and nice in butcher paper and smelling like sawdust. A big heavy one too. Make the table wobble.

What that? Mamma said.

Daddy looked at her. Woman, what you think it is?

Where'd you get it?

Where you think?

Well, can't eat that thing by itself. She removed a quarter from her bosom. Go to the store and get me a pound of greens.

Why can't you send one of these chillun?

Cause they busy doin stuff for me.

What about Beulah there?

Daddy looked at me.

Beulah gon help me fix this ham.

Soon as Daddy left, Mamma tucked that ham under her arm. Beulah?

Yes'm.

Follow me.

We walk and walk. I could feel the heat all along the back of my neck, that heat trying to get into my head and legs and arms. I never knew a person could get so hot. Mamma, where we goin?

To get some seasonin.

We walk bout a mile from the house. Mamma stop and let the ham fall to the ground. I start to pick it up.

Leave it, she say.

Mamma find her a thick branch and start to diggin at the ground.

Mamma, what you doin?

Preparin that ham.

You gon cook it in the ground? I ask. (Sure was hot enough.)

She didn't say nothing.

She dig her a hole and kicked the ham into it.

I says to her, Mamma, why you do that?

She didn't say nothin.

Mamma, why you bury that good ham?

DADDY LOVED THEM DOGS. Redman and Blackjack. What we ate, they ate. Never had a cold meal. Followed him everywhere, he just talkin away and they beside him, noddin they heads and waggin they tails. They be the first at the do when a guest come. Gon way from this door, Red. This caller ain't fer you. And what you, Blackman, his shader? They could howl so, like to scare off any thang come creepin long in the night. Walk us to school, one long each side a us. And be waitin outside the schoolhouse to walk us back. And them dogs could sniff out the devil down in the deepest hell. When the huntin be good, Redman and Blackjack liked to rob the woods of all coon, possum, and rabbit.

Nasty, Hatch thought, almost saying it.

Daddy even have enough meat to sell.

There was this mean ole cuss, Mr. Boatwright. Talkin bout a nigra shouldn do this, and a nigra shouldn do that. Even the other white mens couldn't stand him.

Hatch watched her in disbelief.

One day, Daddy and I take Redman and Blackjack to town.

Mighty fine hounds you got there, uncle, Mr. Boatwright said.

Yes, suh.

Mighty fine.

That Mr. Boatwright was a right nasty white man. He carry this brown snot rag hangin long out his back pocket. He pull it out and start to blowin.

Reckon a nigga can do right well for himself with such hounds.

Daddy keep walkin.

I figure five dollas a right mighty, uncle.

Thank ya, suh, but they ain't for sell.

Awright, ten dollas, uncle.

No, suh.

Damn it, uncle. You got somephun gainst money?

No, suh. Daddy keep walkin.

Next morning, Mr. Boatwright come out to the farm. Daddy greet him. I'm holdin back Redman and Blackjack, barkin.

Well, uncle. Come to bring you that ten dollas.

Suh?

Fer them dogs. We had a deal.

No, suh.

Now, uncle, you callin me a liar?

No, suh.

Well, bring me them dogs.

White folks, why don't we let the sheriff handle this.

Mr. Boatwright look at Daddy. Now, ain't no need to get the sheriff involved. Sure he got plenty to keep him busy. Be seein you, uncle.

Bout a week later, ole Redman and ole Blackjack out in the front a the house chasin each other tail. Round and round. Round and round. Then they start spittin up meat filled wit maggots.

*Moving like tiny white fingers.*

Turnin round and round in a circle. Then no meat jus maggots start to comin out they mouth, churnin like milk. You shoulda seen it.

He wished that he had.

Next morning, Daddy buried them out behind the house. Daddy never did talk much, and he talk hardly at all after that.

Mamma rubbed his shoulders. And rubbed. And rubbed.

Daddy said, Don't you go and Bible me.

*Verily, verily, I say unto you, He that entereth not by the door into the sheepfold but climbeth up some other way—*

Beulah worried the silence. And Daddy didn't say nuthin else. But he was the first one to enter the church when Mr. Boatwright died, all respectful, hat in his hands, walked right up to that white man's coffin and just stood there so long that the usher had to make him move long.

# 47

BIG JUDY WAS A MESS.

You remember the time she cut that woman for tryin to cut in with Buck? Don't remind me.

*Beulah, Lula Mae, and Koot tried to steer Big Judy away. Judy, you know that woman crazy. You know she done killed five peoples. But with that quick straight razor from her bosom she cut that woman ten red roads on her hands and arms—a good Christian, she spared the woman's face—before the tramp could even get the handle of her gun out of her purse.*

Well, Beulah, I guess we better get you all ready to go back to St. Paul.

Beulah's colored medicine bottles waited on the nightstand like missiles on a launching pad. No, Beulah said. I ain't ready to go back. They keep passin me round like a plate of green peas. They only interested in my pension check. You know they all on that stuff.

I kinda suspected that, Sheila said.

I don't know how much mo I can take.

Beulah's look pushed in at her. She recalled how Beulah had pleaded with Sam's woman, Don't kill him. He's my only brother.

Can I come live with you?

Beulah, I'm tired. You know that. Tired. I'll come up to St. Paul and help you find the best nursing home they got there.

I wanna come live with you.

Beulah I work every day. Who gon take care of you when I'm gone? I bet they got some good nursing homes in St. Paul. I know they do. Find you the best.

YOU'LL FEEL BETTER, Montel said. My father is buried just down the road. I talk to him as I could never do in life.

Sheila studied Montel's long, melonlike head—some hair left, not much, enough for a small Afro—and the body gone soft in a few places. A miracle that Montel was alive at all, here in Miss Emma's living room. (The same af-

ter all the years. More the same each time she visited.) Doctors had pre-
dicted, promised that the sickle-cell anemia growing inside would kill her by
age forty. She battled continual sickness and always bounced back. She had
remained a familiar, normal presence for fifty years. They became best
friends from day one at the Catholic high school during the war. Pencils in
their hands and legs proper under their desks. Stealing looks at the white
boys under the nun's habited faces, hovering above them, monitoring, anxious to punish. Girl things. Frequent Beale Street clubs, flirt with the men,
get the cute ones to buy them drinks. A beer or two, nothing hard. Drink,
giggle and flirt, dance. No sex. Just fun. Gracie had tried to strain their soli-
darity. Kept popping up in their path, a needlelike weed. You'd be having a
good time on the riverboat then turn and see Gracie watching you, angry
but calm, uneventful, natural and forceful like the waterwheel. *Ain't nobody
following yall.* She had a *right* to be there.

They had it on the news that big flood yall had, Montel said. Yall didn't
have any problems getting out of the city?

No. They say they got it under control.

That's good.

Never know, though. We might have problems going back.

I hope not. Pray for the best.

That's all you can do.

Where's Lucifer? Why didn't you bring Lucifer? I ain't seen him in so
long. I missed him at the funeral.

Lucifer, sound and name, entered Sheila and flowed like an unknown
substance through her body. You didn't miss him. He wasn't at the funeral.
He couldn't make it. She thought about telling all, all to tell, all she knew.
He had to work. Couldn take off.

I see. Working hard.

Yes. He don't know how to stop. Ditchdigger mentality. His co-workers always call the house. Slow down. Tell him to slow down. He makin us look
bad.

Montel laughed. (The blood and warmth of her laughter.) Sargent the
same way.

Sheila stirred in her seat, surprised at the comparison, Lucifer and Sargent. Sargent worked a good job, a well-paid superintendent for the Board of
Education. She had always believed that if Lucifer found a good job he
might slow down.

Some men are just like that.

I guess so.

An easy silence in the room.

Please wait for Mamma to come back. She sure wants to see you. Before she left this morning she was telling me how much she wants to see you. You know how much she likes you. I don't have to tell you that.

Yes. Miss Emma was the bouquet of the house, the growing force that kept it alive. (Miss Emma nursed a piece of money that her husband, a tavern owner, had left her.) You sat in the room with Miss Emma and felt force radiating from her, heat. She talked sparingly about the past but feverishly of the present, never advising, always asking about *you*, discovering, disclosing. Her look silently said that she knew more about your life than you knew yourself. Silent circumstances. I want to see her too. But we haven't finished packing.

That's too bad.

I wish I could.

Yes, Montel said. She'll be sorry. Hurt. But she'll understand.

Sheila smiled a genuine smile. Miss Emma's house looks good. Always does.

Sargent stays on top of things.

I hate that Miss Emma ain't here. Tell her that I said her house looks good.

I will. You can always come visit. Nothing has changed. We want to see you. Don't be a stranger. You have a *reason* to visit.

Sheila rode the deep currents of Montel's voice.

And you be sure to send Porsha by here. Maybe she can motivate Gregory. He got the cutest daughter. Did I send you her picture?

No.

I'll give you one before you leave. Remind me. Don't let me forget. Her mother ain't bout much . . . You tell Porsha to come on by here and see him.

Yes. She needs somebody good in her life.

Good? Good and broke. I can promise you that. All his money go into paying his car note. You see that fancy thing sitting out front there? Montel pointed. But maybe they would be good together. It happens.

Wouldn that be something.

Yes . . .

Seeing Montel before her, sitting and feeling it all in Miss Emma's house, Sheila lived the old life again, felt the old feelings, drawn by the new promise, driven, determined, energetic, expectant. She found day work and worked it, while Lula Mae exhausted her New Mexico savings and worked three times as hard to put and keep Sheila in the Catholic high school, her day carrying her from Memphis to Tupelo to Fulton and back to Memphis. After graduation, Montel went off to teachers college and Sheila followed Beulah North to the city. Her first Christmas in the city, she boxed some snow, wrapped it with ribbon and bow—web of excitement—to send Montel. See, the world really does get cold. Snow really does exist. Yes, it tastes like milk. I really am in the city, up North.

I think about it all the time, Sheila said. *A ghost of a chance. Invisible possibility.* Moving back here.

Believe me, Montel said. Memphis is nothing to move back to. We got the same problems here where you live. And West Memphis is even worse. They call it Lil City. Young people are crazy. Crazy. Changing change.

Montel said what Sheila already knew. Her eyes were open to the world's frightening changes. Even the blind couldn't miss them. But saying made the knowledge immediate, acceptable. Helped ease her terminal homesickness. *I'm gon buy me a suitcase. Leave this town.* A voice she trusted telling her never to return.

Maybe if I had stayed, she said. She sees it all before her now. Shapes only a foot away.

# 48

THE POLAROID INSTANT CAMERA hugged his eye. He shot the bare kitchen—
no red metal table, no red metal chairs, no white stove, no white refrigerator—the bare bathroom, the bare living room, Lula Mae's bare bedroom,
Mr. Pulliam's bare bedroom. He shot the front yard, now minus lawn furniture. He shot the pear, plum, and peach trees. He shot the backyard, the
thin clothesline—wind filled trouser legs and blouse sleeves, blowed them
about, whipped them light and dark—the railroad plank that flattened the
backyard grass, and the bald grass-free space where the little house had been
docked. He shot the back end of the house. He reloaded the camera. He
shot a frontal view of the house. Shooting done, he arranged the fresh photographs like a chessboard. He had what he needed, unyellowing artifacts.
He packed camera and artifacts in Mr. Pulliam's canvas army duffel bag.
Green force.

SUITCASE IN HAND, he opened the chain-link fence—he did not close it behind him—and crossed the wooden railroad plank—swollen but firm, the
belly of a sumo wrestler; splinters like prodigious hair—that offered safe passage over the grass-covered drainage ditch. He loaded the suitcase into the
cab's open trunk. Then he stood in the red gravel road—sun flowed down
his arms, out his fingers, and arrowed through the tips to stab the earth—
and took a final memory-absorbing survey. Miss Bee's house across the road,
her backyard once yellow with corn and chickens. Miss Witherspoon's
house on the corner on this side of the road, her backyard—flowers still in
the summer wind; he could describe the colors and textures but knew none
of the names—no further than a stone's throw from Lula Mae's front yard,
next to where the pear trees grew. Lula Mae's house itself. 1707 Monroe.
West Memphis. Summer. The South.

Go ask John Brown to carry us to town in that buggy of his, Lula Mae
said. (She called any automobile a *buggy*.)

Yes, ma'm.

John Brown's old blue pickup truck waited in the red gravel road. *Animated by its own rhythm. Humming grunting popping farting mumbling across the Memphis Bridge. John Brown leaning forward, arms bent around the huge steering wheel, the arcs of his tall knees pointing like mountains. The steering wheel moving between his raised knees. Lula Mae immobile beside him. You and Jesus in the open back, your feet hanging over and out the lowered door. Back-wheel boats churned a still black river—time fell off the great waterwheel but the ferry never moved—and steel stools spun smoke and talk before a wood counter in a steaming greasy spoon that served the best hamburger, something called a Hawaiian burger, and real soda from the fountain.* And looking through the low-hanging bushes of the tree before the sidewalk, you could see John Brown's rotting shell of a house. The sagging roofline. The worn porch steps like bad teeth. (One plank had rotted free.) The crooked mouth of porch. Peeling green paint, a shade darker than the uncut grass swamping the yard, as if the house were part of the very land itself, growing up from the earth.

See the monkey? John Brown circled the length of his property, fingering every link of the chain fence, every blade of grass, every rough edge of tree. See the monkey? he said again, pointing up into the treetops. A few hairs on his skull, head and hair like a coconut shell. Gnarled arms like vines. The veins wormlike beneath his dirt-colored skin. You could hear ghosts inside him, warring for control.

See the monkey? Boy, do you see the monkey?

You saw birds wheeling above tall trees.

Boy, do you see the monkey?

You saw sun like fire in trees.

Boy, you see the monkey?

You saw treetops filtering shafts of light. No, sir.

No, sir? No, sir? Course you see that monkey. There. John Brown stuck out a board-long finger.

Where?

There. John Brown shook his pointing finger for emphasis. Right there. Shakin his bare ass. Poppin it like a .45. Rattlin his hairy balls. Right there. Snappin rim shots wit his tail. Course you see him—

You ran like speed itself to Lula Mae's house.


THE HOUSE CROWDED WITH GHOSTS. Some dead, some alive. The brightness of their sunken eyes. Forever hospitable, they offer familiar praise, extend the usual invitations. Words spin in his head, marbles in a bowl. His muscles unravel like spools of thread.

Time whirling inside, he moved fast. The voices behind him. He entered the bathroom. Shut and locked the door. Sat Mr. Pulliam's indestructible green army bag on the white sink. Words flew off to nothing. Came indistinguishable through the door. The bathroom offered white solitude. His pulse slowed. There was the small gas heater next to the tub. (Every room of his grandmother's house had one.) *No flame. Flameless heat. The tile lit brown inside. Humming a soft smell.* The tub where Lula Mae demonstrated the proper method of washing the body. *Get a big washcloth. (The kind that could fold over your hand, floppy, like damp pizza crust.) Get it real soapy. Like this. And always use white soap cause it make the most suds. Fold your ends when you wash your face. Like this. Be sure to wash down there, wash your elephant snout. And dry off good. Be sure to dry your back off. Like this.* This small tub had once been large enough to hold both him and Jesus. Imagine that. For whatever reason, this thought, this fact, unnerved him, set him back.

The mirror held him in its still gaze. He studied his cool pose and expressionless mouth, the face he had brought to West Memphis and worn daily like a favorite hat. His skin pressed Lula Mae's outline. Over the past few days, he thought and thinking remembered everything. Stored up memories and studied them now in the mirror. Dreamed his way through all shapes and solids, for they were a map to get back by. He dwindled to a wet point in himself.

He heard it moving, water that refused to be stopped. Water that dimmed his features.

You ready? Sheila said through the closed door. You got everything?

With air and motion his head began to clear. Sheila rubbed his knee and said soothing things. Night touched him through the open window. The bridge hung by threads in the darkness. The iron grid made the cab's tires sing. Trawlers sparkled and winked on the water's black surface. The invisible water spoke no secrets. Under blinking bridge lights, the Memphis River took back its older form, its original name. It went on the same way, never hurrying, never hesitating.

He became aware all at once, the thought became clear though it was both wordless and beyond words: His tears were selfish. He was crying not for Lula Mae but for himself. Not her death but what he had lost, what was forever beyond him now because she was gone. *Summer. Her house. Her yard. Her kerosene lamps. Her lil house. Her trees. Her red gravel road. Her railroad plank that covered the grass-choked drainage ditch. Her railroad plank that led you from the back porch to the lil house. This bridge. West Memphis. The South.* His tears were private, selfish, for him only. He would never cry again.

# Part Four

# CITY

# DREAM

# 49

WHY YOU ALWAYS BE WEARIN RED?

Family stuff.

Which family? No Face the Thief speaks as if through an oxygen mask.

You wouldn't understand.

No Face studies Jesus with his one blind patch and his one seeing eye, the eye rotating like the steering wheel beneath Jesus's hand. His breathing fills the quiet spaces between the music. Then the eye spots a freak in bikini top and biker shorts, the sun oiling her skin. No Face rolls down the window. Leans his head out. Yo, bitch. Somebody got a big booty around here. The freak flicks her tongue at him, fast and dirty. Good goobly goo, he says.

Damn you stupid.

Hey, I'm like a squirrel tryin to get a nut.

Stupid.

I'm jus tryin to represent.

A retard.

Red Hook produces few gentlemen.

On they roll at the same unchanging speed. Each window of the red Jaguar alive with a frame of moving morning space. Many people wildly busy, coming and going. Vehicles stream like confetti. Tracks gleam. All the windows are eyes, watching in wait.

A strong sun pushes through the windshield, bright, burns through Jesus's eyes. His hand reaches inside his red blazer pocket and caresses the .9, warm and black, a bird hidden in its nest. His joints ache with wandering. His desire prickling, irritating his eyes, nose, and throat like a seasonal allergy. Shoving him through streets. Days had passed, much like one another. Searching. The city's rivers tilting into map shapes, reversing, evaporating. Days feeling the whole city around him. Flight-sense filling his nerves. Him at the wheel and No Face beside him, his copilot. A second shadow. No Face had refused to quit his side and Jesus had allowed his refusal. Fulfilling a promise, a prediction. *You said you gon put some weight in my pockets. You remember? You said that. You did.* No Face maintained a steady diet of oysters and hot sauce. Cried in his sleep; Jesus would slap him awake.

I like this suit, No Face says. It feels alive on my skin.

First thing this morning, Jesus had taken him to Jew Town—time to re-name it; the Jews had made their money and moved on; slopes, Pakis, and A-rabs had moved in on hot curry wind; sat on high camel humps behind their cash registers; paid the winos a dollar to shovel up water buffalo shit steaming beneath the shade of (real? artificial?) palm trees—got his ear pierced with a diamond stud twin to Jesus's own, bought him two new eye patches—white patch one day black patch the next: domino dots—and had him fitted for a fine ocean blue suit. Jesus could no longer stand to look at or smell the dirty warm-up gear, half-moons of sweat under the armpits. But No Face is like a child, the tailored suit jacket already wrinkled years beyond pressing.

Freeze wanna see you.

Freeze's name fell on Jesus like a thunderclap.

Freeze?

Yeah.

When you speak to him?

I spoke to him.

Jesus now has to think the obvious: over the previous days Freeze had come to believe that Jesus was buying time or, worse, that he had failed in his mission. Empty, the mission had filled him like city wind. And he ex-panded from within, for Freeze had chosen him—truth to tell, it is not clear to him if either of them had made a choice; circumstances had chosen them, commanded them—faith in knowing he would never disappoint. And he felt the gathering, his moving toward, growing closer toward his terminal point, where choices of destination narrowed to one, and where all possible movements and gestures became a single definitive act. He smiles more now than he had in the year previous, though he knows that he has done nothing to earn joy. He will. Better days are coming. Never has he been so certain about anything. Certainty moves red through his body like lasers.

He spoke to me.

Okay, Jesus says. I heard you. Powerless. The world is made of stone: pa-per, water, wind, and flame can do nothing against it.

Let's go.

You better not be lying.

Man, you don't know me from Adam.

If you are . . . I got to find a garage where I can leave my car.

No you don't.

You is stupid. You expect me to drive there? In *this*.

He ain't at Stonewall.

Where he at then?

He somewhere else. I'll take you.

No Face navigates to the location quick and precise, the red lines in his eye like map routes.

You bring me way out here to the boonies?

This where he at.

Jesus watches him. He better be.

Man, you don't know me from Adam.

An old red ambulance—white crosses on the doors—stretches long before the building, the silent siren like a half-buried missile in the roof. Jesus reads cursory letters printed in a glass arc above the door: Hundred Gates.

Are you sure this is it?

Damn, No Face says. Damn. He giggles uncontrollably, slobber flying everywhere, a dab catching the center of Jesus's forehead. Jesus wipes it away. Makes a mental note to wash his contaminated hand at the first opportunity.

They rise in a whining elevator commanded by a uniformed attendant to a room free from the day's heat.

Keylo hits No Face upside the head with his open hand, a loud and terrible blow.

Damn, Keylo. No Face rubs his head. Why you always be fuckin around?

Cause I want to, bitch. The straps of Keylo's bomber helmet dangle about his face like girl pigtails. Who suit you steal?

Jesus hooked me up.

His face the color of a sweet potato, Keylo looks at Jesus.

We tight like that, No Face says.

Tight like yo mamma's pussy, Keylo says.

Not as tight as you mamma's.

Keylo jerks his shoulders in a threatening manner. No Face starts. Keylo laughs.

Nawl, No Face says. You ain't scare me. I wasn't scared.

Jesus. Freeze emerges out of the well-lit but somehow shadowless interior. Extends a welcoming hand. Jesus takes it forcefully and without hesitation. He and Freeze shake hands, businesslike, professional, nothing like niggas on the street.

Have a seat.

Thanks.

Jesus seats himself on a white leather sofa. Keylo shoves No Face onto the sofa next to Jesus. Sit next to yo daddy!

He yo daddy.

Least I know mine.

Me too.

The apartment shows both a female and a professional touch. Light colors, a deep white carpet, a bubbly fish aquarium, decorative paintings, vases, books, aesthetic furniture.

A woman comes out of the bathroom, holding a man's shirt across her breasts. Something catches between Jesus's nose and throat. She glances at him from the corner of her eye and quickens her steps. On the sly, he tries to see her ass beneath the shirttails as she disappears into another room.

How you makin out? Freeze to Jesus. Disappointment in his bearing, the line of mouth.

Fine.

Glad to hear it.

The woman returns fully dressed now. Thin braids sculptured in circles around her head. Gold door-knocker earrings. A sleeveless top. Excessive baby powder on her neck and bosom forms a white bib. Discreet shorts. She rushes forward, silver bracelets flashing, and hugs No Face like a close relative. Her bare shoulder blades rise like wings. She pulls back to take a full view of him. You look nice.

Yeah. No Face fingers his suit. Jesus hooked me up. He smiles at Jesus and she does too.

Hi, I'm Lady T, hand extended.

Jesus. Looking at the hand, barely touching it, avoiding her face.

Jesus—Freeze begins.

Oh, Jesus said, could I use your bathroom?

Without speaking, Freeze points with both hands like a runway signalman. Jesus rises from the couch and moves past Lady T. Their bodies casually touch.

Excuse me, he says.

She smiles a smile, polite or genuine he can't tell which.

He pushes on to the bathroom, shuts the door behind him. Puts his ear to the closed door. Voices in the other room, the closed door muffling their meaning or the voices themselves deliberately low, secretive. The faucet rumbles, spills water into the clam-shaped basin. Dissolves the voices. He scrubs his hands with perfumed soap under warm water before a row of mirror that multiplies his red image. Leaves dirty residue. He pulls the stopper. The water drains quietly, dirty rings rotating, concentric fashion, circling, wheeling, whirling, pulling, drawing, force forcing him to feel their power . . .

He circles into the center of a conversation. Lady T is nowhere in sight.

No Face, what happened? Why you fuck up?

See—

Did you get hungry? Try to eat those rats?

See—

You musta tried to eat those rats. That's why you fucked up the job.

The gat jammed.

What?

The gat jammed.

No it didn't. You forgot to take off the safety.

No I didn't.

Stupid bastard.

How you know?

Retard.

Keylo laughs and laughs. Jesus doesn't think he will ever stop laughing. Mechanical hyena.

Jesus makes himself comfortable on the couch. Here now, here, and prepared for the clear mission.

So what you got good to tell me? Freeze says, white, Lula Mae's color.

Another day or two, Jesus says. At most. He clears his throat.

So what's up then? Keylo says.

Broken words speed through Jesus's mind.

You ain't worried, are you? Homes, it's easy. Keylo demonstrates. Like using a cigarette lighter.

Keylo, Freeze says. Go easy.

I coulda done it myself, Keylo says. Days ago.

Go easy. Jesus has his own way of doing things. Am I right? Freeze turns to Jesus. Puts the question in his face.

Yeah.

See, Keylo, like I said. He got his own way of doing things.

Keylo watches Jesus, bomber helmet straps in motion.

I'm here to help, Freeze says.

Thanks.

Don't mention it . . . Anything I can do?

No.

You sure?

Yes.

Freeze studies Jesus in silence—Jesus does his best to look him in the eyes, not turn away, show the steel he has inside—bright light crawling like ants over his bald head. I got some information that I want to share with you.

Yeah, No Face says. Yeah. He laughs, slapping his body at the private joke.

Freeze shuts him up with one look. He returns to Jesus. Is that okay with you?

Yes.

Your family is back in town.

Jesus's life flares backward.

Yeah, Keylo now. Saw them at the airport.

Freeze nods. No doubt.

The knowledge moves through Jesus's body. There. Freeze had done it. Bound together the hour and the fleecy sky.

Your lucky day.

I jus wanted to tell you that.

Thanks.

Don't be offended.

I'm not.

Look, I'm not tryin to push you or anything. I just want to speed up things, that's all.

Thanks, Jesus says. Thanks. *So they decided to return. The bird thieves. Lucifer and John.*

Let's just try to get this matter taken care of quickly.

I will.

Because, you know—

I will.

I'm glad to hear that. I took the trouble of getting you a car.

Yeah, Keylo says. Any fool know you ain't sposed to use your own.

I tried to tell him that, No Face cuts in before Jesus can reply and defend himself. He don't know me from Adam.

Keylo will drop the car off.

Where?

No Face laughed. Jesus took the laughter for a knowing answer.

And the keys?

Don't worry . . . Well, I think that's about everything.

Do it, Keylo says. Gather up your own.

Don't worry, Freeze says. He will. He will.

He will, No Face says. He got me. He got me.

And yo mamma's nasty draws.

Yo mamma's.


YOU TRYIN TO MAKE ME LOOK BAD BACK THERE?

Nawl, No Face says. I wouldn do that.

So why you was talkin all that shit then?

What I say?

Jesus speaks in a mocking voice. I tried to tell him this. He got me. I ain't gon let him fuck up.

I ain't say that.

You did.

Man, you don't know me from Adam.

Jesus says nothing. Feels red Jaguar motion.

We gon do this thing, No Face says.

No. *I'm* gon do it.

I'm with you. You know that.

Jesus says nothing.

You ready to do this?

Jesus lets the words pass in and out. Tell me about Lady T.

Lady T? You tryin to step to Freeze's bitch? You want them big draws, huh? Man, don't you know—

Jus tell me bout her.

No Face says nothing for a while. Breathes. That bitch had a rep. Word. Befo she start kickin it wit Freeze, she ain't give no nigga no play. Straight up. She go to a club, see a nigga she like then take a jimmy hat out of her purse like this. No Face pulls a condom from his blazer pocket. She be like, You think you can handle it? Then she slam the jimmy down pow! No Face slams the condom down hard on the dashboard.

The steering wheel jumps directionless under Jesus's hand. Damn! Is you crazy?

Sorry.

I ought to beat you down for that.

Sorry, I was—

You one stupid motherfucker. Know that.

Sorry.

Jesus shakes his head. Lets motion take the anger from his body.

She got pregnant.

Freeze got her pregnant?

Nawl. One of them 'Rabs.

An A-rab?

Yeah. She be fuckin em.

Jesus considers the likelihood of this. Can't picture it. He rides the silence. Hears No Face's whistling lungs. What happened to the baby?

What you think?

I don't know. That's why I'm asking you.

No Face laughs. Man, you don't know me from Adam . . . Stay away from her. Word. She an intersexual.

How you know?

I know.

YOU WANT TO GET DIPPED?

All the time.

Jesus opens a full bottle of his best and pours No Face glass after glass. It doesn't take long.

I'm higher than a motherfucka, No Face says.

I can see that. His skin is actually glowing with moonshine.

Jesus puts him to bed the moment he dozes off. His snoring mouth roars ocean, screams wind. Jesus removes his suit and shoes, covers him, and tucks him in.

HIS CITY REFLEXES, cunning, direct (tell, instruct) him to park his red Jaguar on a shady side street five blocks from Hundred Gates. He heads for the building, afternoon sun staggering along behind him. A truck's motor snarls somewhere and he wobbles. Calms himself. Continues. He feels Hundred Gates before he sees it. The building rises to him—it looks much larger than before, larger than it should—across yards of trees. High above the sharp roof corners birds wheel in a sky yellow and even. The old red ambulance is no longer parked out front. A good sign.

He melts ghost-fashion into fine glass and brick, vanishing. He isn't two steps inside when he pulls a deck of bills from his wallet and offers them to the uniformed doorman with a knowing smile. He rides up in the elevator confident that he has taken all the proper precautions, covered his tracks. The quiet hall fills him with quiet inside. He loses it all the moment Lady T opens the door.

Oh, is Freeze . . . is Freeze here? It comes out less than calmly.

Nawl.

Ah, um, when will he be back?

Lady T studies him—her eyes forcing nervous motion on his body—for a long time, as long as she pleases, a stone configuration. I don't know. You can wait. She pulls the door wide enough for him to enter.

Thanks. He enters the apartment with a tight turn and stands with back against the wall, stiff rods holding him in place.

Have a seat.

Thanks.

He sits down on the couch and unbuttons his blazer so he can move. You got a nice place here.

Everybody say that.

He tries to force his tense face to smile.

Can I get you something?

No, thanks. I'm straight.

You sure?

Yeah.

You thirsty?

A little.

Lady T gives him a glass of water made from honey. Thanks. He holds the drained glass out to her.

You welcome. Jus sit it on the table. Here. She positions a coaster near him on the marble coffee table. He places the empty glass squarely down on the coaster. Legs crossed on the love seat, she watches him from the other side of the table. Her eyes pry him away from a lifetime of certainty.

That's a nice suit, she says.

Thanks.

Nice color. (His usual red.)

Thanks.

Different.

Thanks.

She watches him. You bald as a stone.

Thanks. Saying it but unsure in the saying.

Is that all you know how to say, *thanks*?

What you want me to say?

You don't know how to talk to a woman? Beneath the T-shirt, her breasts move deep and full.

What makes you think that?

Lady T says nothing, visibly annoyed. The white baby powder has disappeared (evaporated? blew away?) from her neck and shoulders since he last saw her an hour or so ago.

What time do you expect him? Jesus studies the slim curve of her waist.

I ain't.

Well, Jesus says. Well . . .

You ain't got to leave. Chill for a while.

Thanks.

She sighs. Ugh. *Thanks*.

Sorry . . . So, how did you meet him?

The same way most people meet.

What is it that you like about him?

I don't know. Why do *you* like me?

The words rub hot against Jesus's skin. You seem like a nice person.

I am.

I mean it.

I do too.

Jesus doesn't know what to say.

You know why?

Why?

Cause I'm from the old school.

What school is that?

I stay home and protects mine. Back in the day, you *had* to stay home and keep it together while the man be out there kickin up dust. Now we be out there too. That's why things be the way they be. Fucked up.

Jesus thinks about it. It's like this, he says, what you do one day parlays into the next.

Lady T watches him: understanding, agreeing, admiring, confused, annoyed—he can't tell.

You have your own way of saying things.

I do. Factual, not boastful, but pleased that she finds him pleasing.

I heard about you.

Me?

*You.* You famous.

Jesus grins. Pokes out his chest. I maintain.

Lady T smiles.

I heard about you too.

Oh yeah. What did you hear?

Without a thought, Jesus tells all No Face had told him.

You believe that?

That's what he said.

If she sees something else in his face she ignores it. No Face is stupid.

Yeah, I know.

Stupid.

You from here?

No. Red Hook.

Oh. Jesus doesn't know what else to say.

You ever been there? I'll take you, she says before he can answer.

Take him, as if to Paris, Rome, some faraway place.

She taps his arm, a single detonation of touch. Let's go.

He rises and follows. Where?

To Red Hook. I gotta show you something.

Now?

Yes.

Oh, okay, he says, catching the drift. *Show me something.* So they would do it there, get mad busy. His safe sense shouts inside, tries to lock his feet. *What about the car? She expect you to drive it to the jets? You can't drive no car like that to no jets.* But why not *show him* at a quick and safe hotel? He wants to ask her. Can't.

Don't worry about yo car. I know a good garage.


TWO DOGS MEET, and a third. Lips curled, white fangs watering. They bark off after gray squirrel motion. The air is coming awake. The afternoon is drawing on. Human shapes flash in the streets. Lady T's eyes move about without real interest on faces, faces nearly invisible in the hot haze. Twelve red buildings rise like missiles against the red summer horizon. Ash images of burned-out buildings and houses here and there. Red Hook. The world is made of stone: paper, water, wind, and flame can do nothing against it. Like Red Hook itself. Inevitable. Indestructible.

Jesus moves heavy with omen. Unsure if he is safer with Lady T, a Red Hook homegirl, or more vulnerable. He doesn't want to be here but can't pull back. She speaks to no one. Heads straight for Building Six. He thinks he hears someone calling him through the cutting bitterness of the wind. Lady T's sandaled feet kick garbage out of their path. Beer cans crushed into the shapes of women. Diapers like padded boxers' helmets. Condoms like old, worn socks. He follows her inside the building, around one corner then another, down one hall and up a flight of stairs, through one door and out another. They edge through a rusted opening. Footsteps ring down metal stairs. Echo after them. They descend into darkness. (Her white blouse like a torch before him.) Travel down a long hall. He has to walk in a crouch, keep his head low. Smells bore through him: old storms and garbage, mildew and rot, sewage and fuel. This is the basement, he thinks. They are beneath Red Hook, all that life above. Trust leaves him. They could bury him down here, the world none the wiser.

Do we have to do this? he says.

Come on. It's not far.

They clamber up and over a ledge. Jibe left, right. Ascend level by level, story by story. The climb nearly chokes the breath out of him.

Is this necessary? he says.

Lady T laughs across the darkness.

He follows at a run, accelerating down a sloping corridor. Unsure that he can find his way out if he were to turn back.

Light finally. Light but no bulbs Jesus can see. A maze of plumbing, windowless walls, bright trash remains. Puddles where rats swim like fish. The farther they walk, the deeper, the thinner the air becomes. Ten miles high and rising. The thin air carries with it something else, something that cuts through all of what is tight inside. On they walk, the light forever changing. Light and air thread through him. Weave wish and weariness. He is actually enjoying it now, this journey, pleasure in each step. Adventure. He could stay here forever, wandering, opening doors.

Now another turn, another hall. A double row of runway-like lights leading to a white square up ahead. Closer now, he sees that the square is actually a room, lighted space.

In here, Lady T says.

He complies before the words are fully out of her mouth. Bright light comes slamming in out of the darkness. Holds his eyes hostage. He shades them with both hands. Stands waiting, white waves. Rinse open. The room spangles aflame. He feels he is at the bottom of a new steel pot. Circular steel. Walls so smooth that they show twin reflections of him and Lady T.

This is it, she says, twin voices of her, echoes.

Damn, he says. Hearing himself say it again.

The floor shines slick, clean, and bare. The walls flare and change colors like great curtains. His eyes slowly follow the walls up, the ceiling high above and almost lost in shadow. Stars blink in and out.

Look, Lady T says. Her pointed finger directs him.

Damn, he says.

Directly in the center of one wall, a circular cluster of TV screens, like a large eye pieced together with dozens of smaller eyes. Intimate images of people sleeping, eating, kissing, killing, getting juiced, pissing, shitting, fucking.

Is it *real*? Jesus says.

I guess so.

Now each screen starts flickering images so quickly that vision blurs. It actually hurts to watch. Burns. Visual torture. Jesus turns his eyes away.

Damn!

It does that . . .

A maze of levers, buttons, gauges, meters, dials, switchboards, keyboards, runs the length of the room. Amazed, Jesus walks over for a closer look.

Don't touch anything, Lady T says.

I won't. He pulls back, hands out, under-arrest fashion.

What does it do?

I don't know. I ruined yo suit.

Jesus examines his suit. Oh, that's okay. He dusts off his sleeves and pant legs—yes, it is ruined—turns and notices that Lady T shows no sign of travel: no dirt, no sweat, no rubbing of tired muscles. Why you know bout this place?

I found it a long time ago. Playin down here. When I was little.

Why don't they keep it locked up or something?

Lady T says nothing.

Sunlight comes in through small holes above, an iron grating in the rectangular shape of a window. Jesus can see shadows pass by. In the corner of his vision, he catches a flutter of red. He turns. It is gone.

Lady T holds out a steaming pipe. Jesus can read patterns in the fire. He takes the hot pipe, pulls smoke into his lungs, holds it in, feels it travel through his body, then he blows it out, a dragon. This is the bomb, he says.

I told you.

The bomb. He passes her the steaming pipe. She takes it slowly, making sure that their fingers touch. Sucks light into it. They share it back and forth, weave a braid of black-red smoke between them. With each hit of the hot pipe, the world melts away.

So is all that stuff true?

What stuff?

That No Face said.

Well, what do you think? Ask yourself. You know me now.

Do I?

Don't you?

Their voices arc through silence and solitude.

You should.

Yeah. I should . . .

Smoke carries their voices up into darkness. Jesus's bright reflection in the walls blinds him with color. Brightness bounces up and down once or twice before it settles in. Jesus realizes that he has experienced this before. Deep steel space. The captured German submarine at the Museum of Science and Industry from his childhood. Black torpedoes cut through ocean like great fish. Depth charges explode in silent water and crush hollow metal.

What about you? Lady T says. Is all that stuff about you true?

Who told you?

Everybody.

What did they tell you? No, don't tell me. You can believe it if you want.

Light in Lady T's hair like black doves. You want me to?

Yeah.

They walk and talk, enjoying the cycling of light and heat. Bounce into their own echoes. Light comes in from above and below at the same time so that they have two shadows. It is not clear if the light beneath his feet is true light or only reflected light from above.

You ain't scared of me no mo?

No, Jesus says.

When you first came to the apartment. I mean the second time, when you came back.

You could tell?

Lady T tightens up her body in imitation of Jesus. They share a good, long laugh.

He cranes his neck and sees a rainbow high above on the edge of darkness.

BIRDLEG RIP WE REMEMBER

You're easy to talk to, Lady T says.

Oh yeah?

Yeah.

So you enjoy my company?

Yes.

Good. Good. He stares into the colorful blackness above, feels the emptiness surrounding him, touching him with gentle, careful strokes. He feels his body expand, swell, the same feeling he felt when his dizzy form bumped from wall to wall, reached for a doorknob that was not there, fell into hard space, and crawled out of his mother's front door never to return, belled hope inside, free to begin again, to create himself.

Tell me something, Lady T says, almost laughing the words.

Tell you what?

Tell me something good.

Rainbow blinks color into Jesus's eyes. Rainy, vision washes in and out. I'll tell you about Birdleg. Images tumble downward through his head.

Birdleg?

Jesus nods. His finger points a straight line to the rainbow tattooed in steel flesh.

Birdleg?

He's inside of me, Jesus says. Right here. He rolls up his red sleeve and holds out his forearm as if for an injection, allowing her to witness rail-like scars, running, waiting.

Ugh.

Yeah, I know. Nasty-lookin, ain't it?

She does not answer.

Birdleg. He shuts his eyes. (So he loves the world, in darkness.) Calls all within. *We remember.* Red images flicker on his blind lids.

FAST-CLICKING TRACKS. Air rushing in at steady rhythm. The glare of passing stations. Metal walls closing in, squeezed in somebody's fist. The train curves through subway, tossing light then shadow. Explodes through the black tunnel, a fist shoved into a dark glove. Now, high above the expressway, zooming cars small beneath you. Spit you into light.

Wells Street. Next to the river. (One of the city's twelve.) Burned-out buildings and collapsing porches, rubble of ship frames and rusted pieces of rigging. An old black streetcar like a lost lump of coal, the streetcar that Birdleg said once ran the old trolley lines, then was converted into a restaurant, then a barbershop, then a health-food store, then *this*—junk. Hang a right. Brown water pooled before a red fire hydrant. Brown mud flowing from white diapers dumped in green grass. Seven sets of yellow brick buildings (grouped three to a set) rise like missiles above the horizon—*nuclear bombs stored in the basements, Birdleg said. That's why the jets look like filing cabinets. Cause they got nuclear bombs filed away in em*—each set opening onto a concrete park, steel swings, monkey bars, and metal slides like great silver tongues, and a basketball rig or two like skeletal robots guarding over a court. Stonewall. The jets. Sun behind a blue curtain of sky, drawing this world in a net of light. Building A. Birdleg's building. *Birdleg formed an A by curling his index finger into the base of his thumb, an A missing one leg. We the Stonewall Aces, he said.* Leaning on the corner of Wells Street, ready to fall like a drunk into the river. Let your sight curve with the river. Let it find Red Hook two miles or so upstream (downstream?). Stonewall's red metal twin. Stonewall. Red Hook. The jets. End of the road, end of the road, end of the road for nigga trash.

A swan-white sun floated radiant feathers down to the basketball court. You drove the ball to the hoop, only to let some nigga half yo size steal it from you, yes, snatch the pill from your hand and rob the pharmacy. This short nigga, guarding you, like white on a maggot, eating up the ball, forcing you to take shots. Flapping the wings of his arms, beating up a white blur of motion. Game point came before you knew it.

The swan flapped its wings, rippling wind. The short nigga rode white wind. Dropped the ball like an egg in the basket.

Damn, see the thread on that ball?

Yeah. Nigga must think that's his mamma's sewin basket.

Good game, homey, the short nigga said.

Thanks, Hatch said.

Thanks, Abu said, his fat titties bouncing better than he could bounce the ball.

Right, Jesus said.

Yo.

Jesus saw a belly, pushing at and poking through spaces of the shimmering chain-link fence which divided the court and the sidewalk.

Yo. Come here.

Jesus headed straight for the belly.

Jesus stopped before the fence and looked into the boy's chalk eyes. He looked something like a Halloween pumpkin. Though he wasn't orange enough. Sure, yellow, like the candlelight that illuminated pumpkin skin. A banana-colored nigga. *Dark skin is not darkness. Nor is fair skin illumination.* No, skin the color of Gracie's weak Chinese tea. Speckled brown like a butterfly's wing. Shiny as wax fruit. Knife-slit eyes. Hard and white like the river stones down South. Softened by sweat. *Nigga must have a water fountain hidden beneath his bald head.*

Yo. Try putting a flick in yo wrist, the round-bellied boy said. You know, like a fag. The boy demonstrated, raised hand curled, a praying mantis. And shoot in an arc. Like this. You'll never miss a free throw. Guaranteed.

Chirped words blew straight at the nests of Jesus's ears. He wanted to speak, but his own words stuck on his tongue.

And why you run around like somebody short?

What?

Learn to use your height.

Jesus felt the stabbing sunlight. Held up the basketball and watched his reflection, rippling, in shiny leather. *One of those rare things that happen two or three times a summer. The ball gets stuck between the rim and the backboard and somebody has to unstick it. Get Jesus, cause he can jump up and punch and blacken both the moon's eyes before he comes back down.* Who you?

Birdleg.

Birdleg? I ain't never seen you round here befo.

I ain't from round here.

Where you from?

Stonewall.

Nigga, stop frontin.

Do it look like I'm frontin?

It didn't. Birdleg's eyes were chalk-white, and his words were whiter, scrawling themselves across Jesus's chest. *Learn to use your height.*

*Stonewall.* Jesus knew, Birdleg might know a thing or two about basketball since Stonewall was but blocks from the Stadium, where His Highness, Flight Lesson, *the* basketball king, flew and ruled. How you get here?

I walked.

Walked? Sounded crazy to Jesus, but anything was possible: Birdleg came from Stonewall.

Stupid—

The white ice of the word put a cold pick in Jesus's heart.

—walked. I gotta go.

Wait. I wanna go.

Birdleg began walking, wide-legged and slow, like a pregnant woman. Jesus watched him through the cone spaces of the fence.

Hey—he shouted at Hatch and Abu. Come on.

Where we going?

Stonewall.

Nigga, stop lyin.

Yeah, Abu echoed, nigga, stop lyin.

Come on.

Hatch and Abu dragged their tired kicks from the court and followed. *Birdleg's kicks never touched a court. His white eyes watched from the sidelines. Walking was as physical as he ever got.*

You walked.

If Birdleg stood still too long, his string-bean legs might root in the ground. He liked to walk. *Once Abu saw him sprout wings and fly home, and Hatch saw him gallop off into the horizon on a pit bull's back.* His toes cut through his kicks and tracked claw prints in grass, mud, dirt, snow.

We the Stonewall Aces, Birdleg said.

The what? Hatch said.

Yeah, Abu echoed, the what?

The Stonewall Aces.

I ain't no Ace, Hatch said. I'm a spade.

I'm an Ace, Jesus said.

Yeah, Abu said. A red one. An ace of hearts.

Yo mamma like it.

You walked. Birdleg pointed to white smoke lifting from a manhole. That's smoke from the underground city.

From where?

Ain't yall never heard of the underground city?

Sure.

You walked.

Birdleg, what's that? You pointed at a blue-black bird with red bandannas around the wings.

Stupid. That's a redwing.

You walked.

Birdleg proudly carried his round belly, a real potbelly, steel, iron, cause you could hear the metal ringing when he walked. He smelled like food, like sugar, though he ate scabs candy-quick, scabs saved in an old M&M's box—plain, not peanuts; *I never eat peanuts, specially peanut butter, cause just look at it. It ain't nothing but shit, just like I never eat scrambled eggs, cause just look at it. It ain't nothing but somebody's brains.* All that food and belly and smell balanced on two stick legs. Two string-bean legs filled with pus.

You walked. Followed Birdleg through Central. Birds perched on spiked steeples and steel window ledges. Streets awash with people, merging into eddies and disengaging other paths, and the boys like slits in the swaying mob.

You walked. A lot bright with red dirt. That's the old negro cemetery. Yall heard of negroes?

Sure, Hatch said. My great-granddaddy was a negro.

Mine too, Abu said.

You walked. Summer burned in your lungs. You saw a pond with lightly starred lilies. You crossed a narrow dry gully. Followed a trail of yellow leaves. Heaviness hung low in the trees. Birdleg overturned ancient stones, exposing green worms wiggling in the footprints of Indians and dinosaurs.

Dinosaurs were birds.

Birdleg, Hatch said, you crazy. Dinosaurs were lizards. Reptiles.

Yeah, Abu said. Giant lizards. Reptiles.

Stupid. Dinosaurs were birds.

How you know?

I *know.*

You walked in heat without a breath of air. You reeled under the dazzling weight of the sun. Distance melted.

It was moving day. The afternoon white and pure. Birds black and light as smoke in the sky.

Yall wanna see some black squirrels?

Nigga, there ain't no such thing.

Follow me.

You walked. Birdleg's legs made a sound like twigs breaking. *And when it got cold, his legs would curve into a broken circle.* You walked for three days. Damn, Birdleg. We gon walk to China?

Shut up, stupid. We almost there.

Damn. Jesus sparkled, body glazed in warm sweat.

A bridge lifted above a black river. Birdleg started across, the wood creaking, sagging under his footsteps. Jesus put his feet down slowly, unsure if the planks would hold him.

Damn, Birdleg. You tryin to kill us?

You scared?

Nawl. I ain't scared.

The sun hung low in the branches. Slow shadows on the leaves. Points of grass directed Birdleg to his left. There it was. A little path.

Look. Birdleg stopped, bent his knees a little—a bridge's creak; no, a rusty sound, like Lula Mae's lawn chairs—and pointed a chunky finger. A black squirrel.

*What's that black bird?*

*That's a buzzard.*

*A nasty ole buzzard?*

*Yeah.*

*Why it nasty?*

*Cause it full of spirit.*

A day bright and clear as the leaves on the green plants which grew low and close to the ground. Dandelions clustered like stars. And the white Afros of milkweeds. Children filled the afternoon streets with their shouts. From the height of the park benches, the Stonewall Aces watched butterflies in the bright colors of girls' clothing and their floating cheeks. Hair braided tight with colored rubber bands, rainbows.

Man, I'm tireda watchin these silly girls, Jesus said.

Help me down from here, Birdleg said.

The Stonewall Aces stepped down from the benches. Made a net of arms and carried Birdleg to the ground. The Stonewall Aces stretched out in the grass, arms behind heads, watching the treetops, feet to feet, like bookends. The leaves were green and quiet, shimmering in a touch of sun. Jesus stole glances at Birdleg. Birdleg was sitting in his usual position, upright, legs forming a V from the center of his body, his pudgy hands clasped over his preposterous paunch like a protective shell. His mouth was twisted open and his breath came hot and short. Jesus wondered if he were asleep. He slept sitting up. Had to. Cause the stomach could crush him. *You imagine him sleeping like normal people, his fat belly rising above the bed, a fish belly-up in the bowl.*

Man, I'm tireda watchin these trees.

Okay, Birdleg said.

The Stonewall Aces helped him to his feet, Jesus and Hatch hooking on either arm and Abu shoving from the back. Birdleg moved in the hard afternoon light. Air bright and blinding. The boys followed. They walked along the old tracks. Alert to an occasional train, glittering silver between slices of light. They kneeled low in the green bushes, listening to the asthmatic poppings of pistons when a string of loaded freight cars came pounding along. Kneeled, because, at a distance, freight trains and commuter trains looked the same. Those commuters are deadeyes, Birdleg said. If you got heart and you look hard and heavy, you can see their gun glint.

My Uncle John was a deadeye, Hatch said. Still is.

Yeah, Abu said. He my uncle too. Hatch's best friend, he was proud to claim blood not his own.

He won a lot of medals.

Yeah? Who he shoot?

Gooks.

The train extended its streaked motion. The tracks curved off into the horizon along a long, white, hot sand road that split the flat green. They followed Birdleg's scrawny-legged walk through the flying landscape. The beaks of the road ate up the rubber soles of their kicks and unknotted their shoestrings. A stinging thirst clawed their throat.

Damn, Birdleg. We walkin to the moon?

Yeah, Birdleg. Where we goin?

Birdleg stopped, knelt forward, bowed down in exhaustion, hands supported against the forked branch of his bended knees. Pain squeezed the skin tight against the bones of his face.

Birdleg, what's wrong?

Nothing. Just tired.

Tears ran from his eyes, white, spilling sticky to the concrete. After six or seven hard breaths, Birdleg raised himself and pushed forward.

They walked to the end of a bridge. Climbed down a path under a small trestle where a creek had backed up to form a small pond. Fifteen feet away, a small shanty—a sloping, tar-paper roof, partly hidden by the low-hanging branches of a tree whose name Jesus didn't know, *sycamore, Hatch said*— shone white as a bulb.

Who made this shack?

That's fo me to know and you to find out.

Tell us, Birdleg.

The Stonewall Aces entered the shack, lit by light through holes that peppered the roof. The shack straddled a grass-filled ditch. Each boy made a seat on spike-shaped leaves on the ditch banks. Something was scratched into the wood walls—a fantail connected to a sphere? a fish? Jesus couldn't say for certain. Tall white sentinels, milkweed watched him from the grass.

Hey, Birdleg, why they call it milkweed? Jesus saw milk in Birdleg's eyes.

Stupid, Birdleg said. Don't you know anything?

Jesus studied the milkweed.

Yall loves milk?

Yeah, Birdleg.

Jesus saw flocks of clouds through breaks in the roof.

I loves milk like I loves white folks like a dog loves hickory.

What?

Why you love white folks? Hatch said.

Birdleg looked at him.

Damn, nigga. You got some funny-lookin ears. Jesus cocked his fingers and popped Birdleg's rabbit-long ears.

Bitch!

A bitch is a dog.

And you a bitch. Listen. Birdleg raised his palms. Yall know how white people got white?

Jesus watched the shack walls, twigs and splinters. A chill wind swept wide through the ditch, penetrating his feet and hands. But the ground was hot under his butt and the grass warm to the touch. *And you and Hatch sat fishing before the Memphis River. Feel water thundering near your feet. Hear fish invisible in the water, their shadows rising and turning into thick waves. Hatch afraid to touch the electrified worms.*

How?

From drinkin too much milk.

Above the roof, the sun blinked bright, immersed Jesus in a cascade of light. Pearl after pearl. *Like the way you cast sinkers of light into the Memphis River.*

How you know? Hatch said.

Yeah, Abu said. You lyin.

Straight up, Birdleg said.


ONCE YOU WALKED to the keen edge of exhaustion. Walked until the sun took on strange shape and color. *And Sheila met Hatch at the door, squeezing an ironing cord in her angry fist.* The sky rained boulders of ice and Birdleg demonstrated how to use a garbage-can lid for a protective shield. Use it as an umbrella—hard iron rain struck lid and ground with a hollow sound. The ice thinned to rushing water. And when the rain stopped, you as a team collected drowned birds. *Like the snails you collected in West Memphis. You and Hatch pulled them skinny from their shells. Held the shells to your ears and heard ocean.* Frogs burped, drunk.

Birdleg, where rain come from?

Stars. Stars are holes in the sky that let the rain through.

That's not right, Hatch said. Rain falls from clouds.

Yeah, Abu said. Rain falls into the clouds way up from Mars cause the devil be beating his wife and God squeeze the rain from the clouds.

Clouds ain't no sponges, Hatch said.

Know where babies come from? Birdleg tested.

From they stomach.

Out they navel.

Out they testine.

No.

Where, Birdleg?

A bubble of water. Inside a bitch's stomach.


BIRDLEG WOULD CLEAN HIS HANDS in dog slobber. Walk right up to a dog and put his hands under the slobbering faucet of mouth.

*Damn, nigga. That's nasty.*

*Shut up. Know what's really nasty?*

*What?*

*Blackbirds. Buzzards. They drip vomit. That's why you always see them flying in a circle.*

*Why?*

*Stupid. Ain't you never looked in a sink and seen a drain? The water flying in circles?*

*What?*

Birdleg had a way with dogs. His footsteps summoned them like drums. One snap of his fingers could make a raving dog heel. Two snaps could sic the dog on an enemy. Bear witness:

Stonewall Aces rolled proud and true through the red valley, the jets above reflecting menacing shadows. A rival crew rolled forward, six or seven big boulders, and blocked the path. Red-tied bandannas, threatening, gallows rope.

Damn. What yall sposed to be?

Natty lump lump lump.

Bitch plus three.

The four tricks.

So, nigga. Speak up.

Yeah. Represent represent.

Represent.

Well . . . Who yall—

Yo mamma, Birdleg said.

Bitch, I'm gon kick yo ass.

Birdleg stooped, rested his palms on his bent knees. Jesus must have blinked, because when he opened his eyes a pit bull shot out from between Birdleg's skinny ankles. Destruction took over. A black blur of violence, snapping teeth and crunching bones. Like a matador's cape, red bandannas bringing out the anger bringing out the hate bringing out the violence in the pit bull. And red blood drew more attacking teeth.

*Stupid. Bulls are color-blind. All animals are.*

*Dogs too?*

*That's right. Yo mamma too.*

The red boulders dissolved into black dust that took to the air, filled the sky. Justice done, the pit bull ran for Birdleg's skinny ankles and disappeared, yo-yo yanked back up into Birdleg's stomach.

WHO YALL REPRESENT

Sciples.

A laugh let go Birdleg's mouth. Stupid. That's a set.

Vice Kings.

Stupid. That's a set too. Not the source.

Who you callin stupid?

Don't you know what a source is?

I'm BP Nation. Chapter One.

Me too. Chapter Thirteen.

AK. Aerosol Kings.

TNT. Too Terrible Testaments.

Killer C's.

Cobra B's.

Stupid. Stupid. Is you People or Folks?

Jesus searched the faces of the circle of boys, seeing his face in theirs. Blinked into Birdleg's bold black outline.

Stupid. People and Folks. That's the source. Sets come from them.

Yeah, Jesus said.

How you know?

A timeworn train clanked in the distance.

Yeah, Birdleg, how you know?

Birdleg looked at Jesus, unblinking. White eyes. Frozen milk. Yall ever heard of Fort?

Yeah, Jesus said. The words flew from his mouth instant like vomit.

Hightop?

Yeah, Jesus said.

Sure, Hatch said.

Sure, Abu said.

Fort from Stonewall —

What was his real name?

Stupid. Fort, he from Stonewall.

Yeah?

Well, he ain't from nowhere. He dead. But he lived in my buildin. Buildin A.

Nigga, you lyin.

Let him tell it, Jesus said.

And Hightop from Red Hook.

Something ran a course, through, under, around, behind, and between the words. Crickets hummed. Grass whispered.

They were cousins. And they were sanctified.

The words fell to the bottom of Jesus's heart and what was at the bottom came out, swirling, turbulent. *Sanctified?*

They went to church eight days of the week. Sometimes nine.

What you talkin bout, Birdleg?

Yeah, Abu echoed Hatch. What you talkin bout?

Why you talkin bout church?

Yeah. Church.

Hatch scrunched up his face. You tryin to Bible me? The words blew hot as steam. Steam lifted.

I like the Bible, Abu said. I'm a Christian.

Jesus wet his tongue. Gripped his elbows to keep them from flying away.

Stupid. I said they *were* sanctified. Didn't say they *stayed* sanctified. Birdleg revealed a fan-shaped row of teeth. Stupid.

Why you always callin somebody stupid?

Shut up. I'm tryin to learn yall something. Do you talk in school?

What?

I say, do you talk in school?

No.

Well shut up then. Light caught the white in Birdleg's eyes. Fort and Hightop, they was way back in the old days. Way back. When niggas used to be sleeping on lawns in the summer and cookin in the snow in the winter. See, Fort and Hightop, they used to dance every Sunday in church. Then they started dancing at sets. Everybody knew these niggas had the best steps, so everybody get them to dance gainst one another. Course Fort had the best steps. This one time, he pulled his do-rag off his head, jumped way up in the air, clicked his heels twenty-five times, and polished his shoes befo he landed back on the ground. And he land on one toe and he hold his ground for an hour. He looked like a statue, a stone.

Damn.

Hightop tried to be like Fort. He jumped up and fell down. Well, his toes stuck right into the floor. Yeah, he standing up there on his tippy toes stuck in the floor. Like one of them ballerinas. Five big niggas had to pull him out. People be like, what kind of step is that? Hightop flashed the V sign. He yelled, Vice Forks Love, but everybody thought he said *Folks*. But since Fort held his ground, he yelled Power to the P-Stone Nation.

How you know?

Stupid, I know.

Jesus was saturated with a soft feeling. He didn't believe.

What the P stand for? Birdleg tested them.

P for people.

P for power.

P for peace.

P for prayer.

P for pussy.

P for punk.

Words disappeared in the sheen of sunlight.

Okay, pussy, punk. Better not let no Disciples hear you say that. They ain't as nice as me.

Hatch and Abu sat picture-still. Silent.

Who you represent? Birdleg blinked.

What? Jesus said.

Who you represent?

Well . . .

What bout you, Hatch?

. . .

Abu?

Damn, yall don't represent?

Friends.

Forks.

Persons.

Stupid. It's People and Folks. I'm People.

Then I'm People too, Jesus said.

I'm Folks, Hatch said.

Yeah, I'm Folks. Me and Hatch. Folks.

YOU KNOW KEYLO? Jesus asked. He remembered the name from the TV news.

From Red Hook?

Yeah.

Keylo. Big hat, no cattle.

What?

Stupid. He ain't shit.

How you know?

Stupid, he didn't even whack the raper man who sexed with his sister.

Ain't what? The green earth stole Jesus's words.

Now Fort changed the nigga that stomped on his sister.

He had a sister?

Yeah. She married this nigga. He made her stay in the house all the time. Used to invite his friends over and beat her up in front of them.

Damn.

Then he threw the baby food out the window. Then threw the baby. Fort threw him.

Damn.

What happen to the sister?

She jumped off the buildin.

Damn.

My buildin.

Damn.

Buildin A.

Damn.

My buildin.

Why she do that?

Why you think?

Damn.

And Fort shot the raper man who sexed with Hightop's sister.

What? But they—

Was enemies. Yeah, they was. But she was his cousin too.

What? Jesus said. What?

Whose cousin? Hatch said. She was whose cousin?

Yo mamma's, Abu said.

Yo greasy grandma.

Chill. Birdleg's glue-white eyes sealed lips. Listen and learn.

But they was enemies, Jesus said.

Who was enemies?

Yo mamma.

Stupid. She was his cousin. Cause this one time, Hightop's father, who was *his* uncle, he slapped his daughter who was Hightop's sister, he slapped her fo stayin out all night, and Fort happened to be there and Fort, he slapped him to the ground. Fort be like, Don't disrespect yo daughter.

The sun stroked a place deep under Jesus's heart and put all of his feelings to sleep. What Hightop do?

Shot Fort in the chest. Right here. Birdleg patted his heart.

Man.

Dag, he ain't have to do that.

Fort ran to the park. He took a ball of milkweed and stopped the wound. The words poured into Jesus's ears.

Stopped?

Yeah, stopped?

Next day, Fort cut up Hightop. Hightop came stumbling back to Red Hook with his guts in his hands.

Jesus pictured tangled fishing wire. Barking dogs and anxious rats. Why he do it? he asked.

Stupid. Why you think?

They enemies.

Who enemies?

The raper man and Fort.

What happened?

Stupid, this raper man sexed with Keylo's sister and he let it happen and ain't do nothing.

Damn.

The coroner, he be like, Hightop died of natural causes cause he got changed by a natural man.

Aw, nigga, Hatch said. That's corny.

Yeah. Natural. That's corny.

Natural, Jesus thought. Like a 'Fro.

Stupid. Yall corny. Yall weak, like Keylo.

Ain't what I heard, Jesus said. He changed a Roman with a long extension.

Yeah, he changed one, but he ain't do it wit no long extension.

How he do it then?

He threw a bathtub on him. Pushed it from the roof of Buildin C.

Damn.

Now, Fort was my nigga. Birdleg's eyes were big and wild and eyes reached a place in Jesus where the tongue could not. Fort changed this one Roman with a long demonstration. Changed this other Roman with a Jap chop.

Uncle John know karate. Learned it in the army.

He my uncle too.

No he ain't.

He is too. He said so.

No he didn't.

Jesus ignored Abu and Hatch's exchange. Hung to Birdleg's last words. *How he do that?*

Fort chopped and chopped. Birdleg mimicked the motion with the edge of his hand. And he kept chopping and chopping and chopping. Man, he sliced that pig up like a loaf of bread.

Hatch and Abu squealed laughs. Jesus sat silent, waiting for the words to return, continue.

Yeah, cut that nigga like a deck of cards. Then he shuffled and shuffled and shuffled that nigga.

Man.

Jesus remembered. Fort and Flight Lesson were partners.

What?

Shut up, Jesus.

Stupid. He's right. Yeah. They grew up together in Stonewall.

*How come you don't know him? Cause Birdleg showed you the alley with the fence behind the Stadium where you could see Flight Lesson and the other game-tall niggas lean into their low fancy cars. Where you shouted for an autograph but they couldn't hear your little shouts, mosquito buzzes to their giant ears.*

Am I supposed to know him? See, Fort—

> *I love you, baby*
> *Stay with me, then you'll see*

Birdleg waited for the song to melt away. You know the rest.

Jesus remembered the TV news. How Fort studded the teeth of his women with diamonds. Built an opera house on Wells Street.

What happened to Fort?

He dead.

Birdleg, I know that, Jesus said. Why he dead?

Romans shot him up.

That's right, Jesus thought, mind working.

Fort knew the Romans was after him. Think he cared? He walked around with his chest stuck out.

Like a shield, Jesus thought. A shield ready to bounce some bullets.

He went into the crib and waited. Number 111. Waited. The Romans told him to come out. Think he cared? He just laid back in the bed with his hands behind his head.

*A confetti of bullets preceded the confetti of the parade on Wells Street. The sky filled with white birds, slow-falling wiggly sperm.*

Yeah, Jesus said. He remembered. Found so many holes in him the undertaker thought it was buckshot. Nawl, the undertaker thought somebody had stabbed the muddafudda wit an ice pick.

Man.

Damn.

They buried that nigga in a gold Cadillac, Jesus said.

Nawl, Birdleg said.

Did too. Jesus remembered the news.

Gold-trimmed. And it weren't no real Cadillac. It only shaped like a Caddy.

Damn.

Yeah. Damn.

What happened at the funeral? Jesus drew up images from the well of his memory, dripping, wet, and blurred.

Everybody in Stonewall went to the funeral. Caribe Funeral Home. Everybody and they mamma and they grandmamma. A whole bunch of niggas squeezed in. Birdleg spread his arms wide. Almost knocked over the coffin. All the bitches—

Don't call them bitches, Hatch said. My sister Porsha say women ain't—

—in black miniskirts and fishnet stockings, crying, wetting up Fort's pink silk shirt. Them bitches went home and filled up they bathtubs with they tears. They bone was gone.

Man.

Damn.

Jesus let Birdleg's voice seep into ears. The words sank into him, spreading out, massaging his chest. He saw tears reddening the bitches' soft-talking eyes.

They buried him out there at Woodlawn Cemetery.

I know where that is, Jesus said. Knowing but not knowing why he knew.

Pushed him in the dirt. Then them bitches watered his seed with they tears. But Fort—Birdleg raised his shoulders like two pyramids for emphasis—that nigga, he remember everything.


BIRDLEG ANGLED HIS CANE POLE over his shoulders, guided them through blood-drawing thorns to the Tongue River. (One of the city's twelve.) The four boys frog-filled the muddy riverbank. *It rained frogs in West Memphis. And snails. And sometimes snakes. Hatch screamed running crying and Lula Mae got the garden hoe and with a short quick downstroke chopped off the snake's head clean and neat.* Bees buzzed overhead. Hatch and Jesus sat proud on the bank with rod and reel Inez and George had given them. The running river washed ocean waves. When the waves were still, Jesus could plainly see round rocks on the bottom, covered with red seaweed and looking as though they were floating close to the surface.

My daddy John like to fish.

Yeah? Birdleg said. He had bought a loaf of bread for bait. *John used worms and honey. Put you and Hatch in his boat-big car and drove to the Kankakee River. A silk line—glistening like spider spit—like the silk from his suit. Filling up basket after basket, stealing all the fish from the river. Cept the one time Dave came and poured E&J in the water and catfish and perch jumped up on the bank, burping and singing.* What he catch?

White perch.

Them taste good?

Yeah. The waves swelled, throwing shadowed patterns and refracted froth over the submerged red rocks. My grandmamma Honest—

Inez, Hatch said. Her name Inez.

—go fishin all the time.

Yeah? Birdleg said.

And me and Hatch used to fish down South, Jesus said. He could feel the river thunder. Feel blind subterranean fish, pulse and beat through smoky glass-water. West Memphis, he said. Two birds left a limb in the same instant. Circled the still air.

At our other grandmother's house, Hatch said.

Lula Mae.

She my grandmother too, Abu said.

No she ain't.

She is too.

The sun glowed on the stones, lit everything with color, drank up the water from the earth, played with the shining air that played with the leaves.

*Birdleg, why they call it a bank?*

*Cause water is gold. A rich river flow into a lot of fields.*

Birdleg, let's go, Jesus said. Ain't nothing biting. His line was motionless in the water.

Stupid, we only been here a few minutes.

So. Nigga, we sposed to be flying that kite.

Yeah, Abu said. He sat rubbing his hands and legs together like a fly.

That's some pussy stuff, Birdleg said.

Nawl, I wanna fly that kite. Forget this fishin.

I got one, Hatch said. Invisible, a fish tugged his line below a small circle formed on the water, tugged, and the rod bowed like a wino's head. Wind folded the grass into itself.

Uncle John can show us how to fly it, Abu said. He watched Jesus.

He ain't yo uncle, Jesus said.

But I got one, Hatch said. Wind clawed the water.

Okay. We'll go see your uncle.

But I got one.

Nobody like this fishing, Jesus said.

Damn, Birdleg. Do we have to walk?

Stupid. We gon take the train.

But I got one.

Yank it, Jesus said. So the hook catch in his mouth.

But we never take the train. *Cept when we coming to Stonewall, or leaving.*

Who got some money?

Birdleg reached beneath his stomach. His hand emerged, shining coins.

Birdleg led you to the subway. The train penetrated you like wind. *One of those old trains. Green with a white roof. Not the new ones. Silver, blue, and red.* Tour guide, Birdleg pointed and gestured. Tanks used these tunnels in the last war.

For real?

Word.

You mean my Uncle John's war?

Stupid.

The train slit the rail's throat. The rails screamed. The train rocked, swaying commuters from side to side like church choir singers. Sewer-smelling wind ripped from the tunnel's mouth and blew Jesus's cap off.

My cap.

Leave it.

Birdleg, my cap.

Leave it. You gon crawl down there and get electrocuted?

Jesus looked at his cap red on the rails. That's not the third rail. I can climb down and—

Leave it, Birdleg said. That's where it's *meant* to be. Didn't it fly down there?

Emerged from the subway, clouds crawling over the sky. Hatch led them to the depot. The bus gathered its wings, and swooped them through streets—Places, more Places than streets in Eddyland—like a hawk. That cold wind off the river. That cold wind that liked to sneak into Gracie's house on Liberty Island across the lake. Like a stork that knew the exact location of its delivery, the bus set them right before the Funky Four Corners Garage. Grime caked the car windows in the lot.

It was a strange establishment. An old Edsel perched on the very roof of the garage. The roof slanted inward with the pitch of the rafters—*like Lula Mae's attic; Lula Mae carried a kerosene lamp in one hand while crawling like a fireman up the ladder to her attic*—and the Edsel slanted all the way forward, a brim on a nodding junky's head, threatening to fall. Smelled like rubber from loops of fan belts hanging from the ceiling. Crowded with cases of motor oil stacked in front of the counter, coated with a film of dull oil, the desk behind the counter covered with yellow and pink slips of paper, and a red Coca-Cola machine that dropped bottled pop.

> *Flyin home*
> *Fly like a motherfucker*
> *Flyin home*
> *Fly*
> *Flyin home*
> *Fly like a motherfucker*
> *I said, flyin—*

John looked up from his song, eyes slowly rising from the counter like a plane on takeoff. Slid over Jesus's face like a searchlight. Well, he said. Well.

Hey, Uncle John.

Hey, Uncle John.

Hey.

Hey. John grinned. Yall thirsty?

Hell nawl, Hatch said. Looked at Jesus. Private joke.

Jesus smiled. Remembered car-crazy Ernie. In John's Recovery Room, Ernie would slide a shot of gasoline to a parched customer. Ernie's Special.

Uncle John, this Birdleg.

Birdleg? I heard a lot about you, Birdleg.

Birdleg showed his white teeth.

John held an oily cloth at his hip like a dishrag. Watched the boys. The Funky Four Corners, he said.

Nawl, Jesus wanted to say. Not the Funky Four Corners, John, Ernie, Spider, and old drunk-ass, dog-faced Dallas. *That time John and Dave found Dallas asleep on the court, inside the rim, dunk-drunk.* Five men, a basketball team, the Funky Five Corners. So call this garage the Funky Five Corners Minus One, Lucifer. Cause Lucifer didn't want to have nothing to do with the garage. *But he was there for the hunting trip. Remember? Ernie, Spider, Dallas, Spokesman, Lucifer, and John. A trip to celebrate the opening of the business. Remember? Spokesman's idea. Brought back rabbit and deer from the weekend, but John sold them to the butcher cause neither Sheila nor Gracie knew how to cook them. Yes, John selling them to the butcher but saving two rabbit feet, one for you and one for Hatch. Yall stuffed them in yall pockets til John came through with his promise, gold neck chains where the feet could dangle, even run a little up and down your chest. A week later, the feet were too stanky to wear and Spokesman had to fumigate yall clothes. Don't you know you just can't give somebody dead feet like that? Spokesman said.*

Nawl, Birdleg said. SA. The Stonewall Aces. He finger-flashed an A.

Okay, John said, amused. The Stonewall Aces.

What up, Uncle John?

In the garage proper, a car nested on the upper branch of a silver-colored, cylindrical, pneumatic dolly—black underside exposed. *The dolly an axle. Spin that car round and round. A seal twirlin a beachball with its flippers.* It was back there where Ernie had poured gasoline in a carburetor to fire up and test-run an engine—*gin, that's what they say he called it, a gasoline gin*—and the engine had exploded in Ernie's face. Ernie screamed his country whistle. A birdcall. The same whistle he used when he stood before Gracie's door and yelled—*Why can't he use the doorbell like normal people? Gracie said*—John! Yes, Ernie whistled, then carried his black face to the roof of the garage, felt his way inside the Edsel, slammed the door and locked it and locked all the other doors. John, Dallas, and Spider (and Lucifer?) banged on the window, but Ernie hammered his black face against the window again and again. Then the fireman came and red-axed the window. Too late.

Where Spokesman?

He at lunch.

He workin on that car? Hatch nodded to a car's raised hood.

Yeah. Yall stay away from there. I don't want nobody's mother cryin all in my face if somebody gets hurt.

Ain't nobody gon get hurt, Hatch said. We got this kite. He held it, wedge end pointed at the ceiling.

A kite? What yall lil niggas need wit a kite?

Can you show us how to fly it?

They insist, Birdleg said. He took a scab from his M&M box and popped it into his mouth. Chewed.

Jesus glared into the raised hood. Saw the open distributor cap. Like an intricate flower, the coils with thousands of turns leading to a handful of rubber-covered paths.

Mr. Birdleg, you can't fly no kite?

Birdleg acted like he didn't hear.

John shook his head. A bird in the hand is worth more than a bush.

Damn, Uncle John. Don't start crackin on him.


DRY OAK LEAVES tangled in the grass. Jesus and Birdleg tugged at the flying string with everything they had.

Damn, Birdleg. You stuck it in the cloud.

No, Birdleg said. That's where it wants to be. Didn't it fly there?

It's stuck. Jesus tugged at the string.

Go easy, John said. He watched the kite, his eyes liquid and golden brown.

Jesus tried to steady the spool of string.

Let it go where it want, Birdleg said, his breath tangled in Jesus's face.

Damn, Birdleg.

Let it go where it want.


WORD?

Word.

Birdleg, huh?

Birdleg.

Hmm . . . So that's who you represent?

Yep. From now til. The rail-like scars on his forearm disappeared into the tunnel of his shirtsleeve.

Interesting.

Yep.

Well . . .

Yep.

Well . . .

Excuse me?

Is that all?

Yep. Told and ain't no mo to tell. Threw yo mamma down a wishing well.

She giggled. You're funny.

I ain't funny. Never been. Never will be.

You make me laugh.

Do I now?

Yep.

I'm glad.

Are you?

Yes.

She thought about it, watching him, inside him.

Jesus cleared his throat.

Interesting, she said.

Well, I try to keep it real.

I'm not talkin bout that. *You*. She raised up like a mannequin on a string.

Me? An ax glint of light split his head in half. He could feel the silence.

Tell me something.

Yes?

She moves to put as much of their bodies in contact as she can.

HE CAN VIEW THINGS from a height. His view stretches to country distances. So he lies watching the rectangle of the high window, waiting for the glass to gray. Staring makes his eyes run.

He stares inside too, big lungs breathing in remembered sight, Lady T, magnifying her. He remembers. And more he remembers. He will say that he has seen her spoken words. He will say that she allowed him all the colors of her body. This he will say. He will also say that he had quit Lady T's secret place to discover that little time had passed. A fall of hours.

His task looms before him. He will erase Lucifer from the earth and condemn him to the place of memory, then he will go back there, to the secret place—free, relieved of his chronic angers, cut off from the family, existing only for himself—retire, and give up the world.

Freeze had raised his final resolve into an airtight structure and driven Jesus inside. For years, Jesus had lain awake at night and breathed the colors of Lula Mae's hair on the pillow. And for the length of this day, he heard Lucifer's grave voice broadcasting from another world, dreamed Lucifer's red widow's peak, a blade so sharp it would surely wound, when he closed his eyes. Now Freeze had shown him how to circle back, circle inside his plagued sleep.

There floods on Jesus an extraordinary understanding. His blood flows through the bodies of forty-four generations. Whenever he looks at any family photograph, he sees replicas of himself, Hatch, Lucifer, and John. All from the same wet vine, the circular eye of God's (or the devil's) dick.

His new understanding does nothing to lessen his rage. He closes his eyes. Remembers the future that will forever erase his past. Knows that his red will put him on the map, red lines red places. Large, out there: a red astronaut cut free from his ship, enough oxygen only for himself, floating in blackness.

THE SKY SEEMS CLOSE TO THE BUSHES. A sharp sickle moon. Red at the edges. Lights spill outward into the streets. Ghosts scuttle along in bone light.

What you do while I was sleep?

A little of this, a little of that. He moves through the night streets, his mind a pile of furious red shards.

No Face leads him to the car with prophetic certainty. A brougham, long and shiny red, smoke-tinted windows. He kicks the engine into life. We gon do this tonight?

No doubt.

How?

Elementary.

Surveyed locations from recent days go ripping by in the night.

We gon do this like Brutus, No Face says, belly-laughing the words, hardly able to contain himself. In the dark, Jesus catches glimpses of his face, his insane committed eye. Soon he will have what he wants more than anything else.

It seems the most intimate moment he has ever known. He can see back through the years, far back to a time that might have been the beginning of what he was feeling now. Everything now seems disconnected from what he had done before and what he will do after.

My style is tricky, No Face says, like spelling Mississippi. Ceremonially, he guides the brougham—the air conditioner full blast on this hot night— Jesus beside him with his .9, locked deep in concentration. Surprised at his skill at the wheel.

Darkness at the edges of broken shapes. Jesus lets instinct guide him. Faith. I thought I saw him, he says. His first glimpse of the red ruling target. And this he says: Circle back.

They circle back.

His heart grows hot against him. He searches the streets for the hidden shape he knows is there. Envisions the events to follow.

A red shape flickers across his path. That's him.

Where?

Right there.

Where?

Right there. The words fly from his mouth, magnetic, migratory.

That don't look like—

How you know what he look like?

Man, you don't know—

Circle back.

They circle back. No Face slows the brougham so that Jesus can jump out with the car still in motion, the gun like a heavy bird in his hands.

Do it. Put some head out. Peel his cap back.

Jesus runs up to Lucifer like an urgent messenger, close enough to recognize the bones of his uncle's red skull. Aims. Signals him with a birdcall. He turns. Meets hot surprise.

Birds take to the sky with the noise. Bright ribbons floating on the air.

Immediately, Jesus feels a moment of release. Blood singing in his body, this day marking the beginning of his seeing the world.

# 50

SOUND OF LIMB AND MIND, I leave:
1. My heart to my mother (Hope you deserve it)
2. My feet to my brother (Errand runner, keep humping!)
3. My penis to my wife
4. My mouth to my son (Sing poems)
5. My eyes to my daughter (See wisely)
6. My arms (for strength) to my grandchildren still unborn
7. My head to my sister-in-law (sorely in need of brains)
8. My teeth to my nephew (Eat and put on some meat)
9. My nose to the taxman (no other use for it)
10. My ass to a casket

# 51

EVERY SOLDIER TUGGED HOME A THICK HEAVY ALBUM of snapshots. Horse-playing with his war buddies. Flexing muscle in the flexing jungle. Or posed proud and pensive with weaponry. Even photos of kills. John brought back few frames from the war, all black-and-whites touched up for color, like (in the old days, years ago, years gone) the photos of jazz singers fronting the nightclubs on Church Street. Lucifer's favorite, the one angled in the corner of the bedroom mirror and so angered his wife: John arcing for a dive into ocean, arms thrown back like wings, frozen in time.

Sheila refused to look at it now. Caged her eyes and yielded to excess. Free. Vindicated. Her heart shaped something it could not utter. Her blind fingers discovered the thick world of Lula Mac's Bible. Black surface (artificial leather) and white depth. She touched the book with a tender sense of all it symbolized. She opened the cover and her eyes.

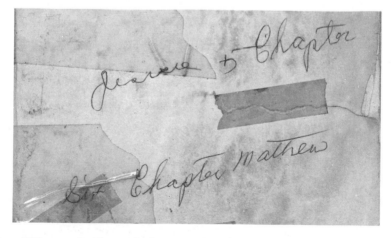

*Jesus Chapter 5?* No such thing. No Book of Jesus. Certainly in no Bible she had seen. She searched the Table of Contents to be certain. Found nothing. Hidden, protected, absorbed, she turned to the Sixth Chapter of Matthew and read to the end.

She flipped two or three slow pages. Then—

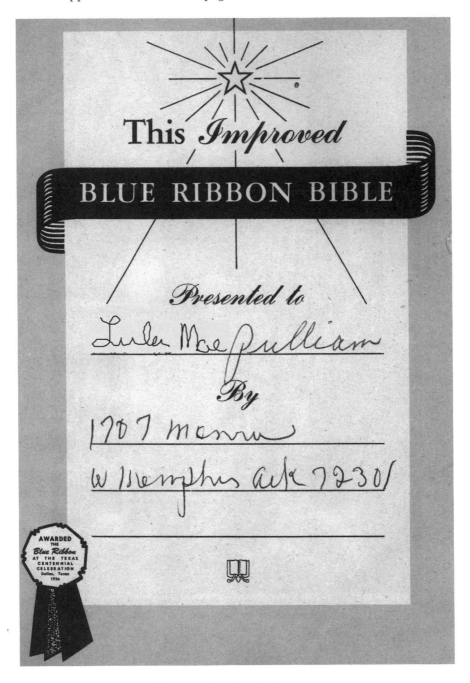

She spun the pages like a riverboat's wheel.

## FBI SPECIAL AGENT
### Men and Women
between 23 and 35 years of age years college degree and 3 yrs time work experience. Good health and U.S. Citizen. Salary over $27,000 with o/time to start. Available to relocate. Information and application. Call
**Agent Hayes 431-1333**

Spun. Wind and water. Spun. Motion. She floated freely. An undercurrent tugged at her. Some deep weight that anchored inside her so she could not advance. Why would Lula Mae save the FBI clipping? She searched for it, waded back, searched but found nothing. She searched again. Still nothing. She was heavy with her lack of discovery, heavy but held up, light, buoyant with possibility ahead. (She would have to find it at another time, some other day, hour. *It ain't going nowhere.*) She hurried to meet undiscovered pages.

The *Genealogy Record Family Register* was blank, untouched.

At the back of the Bible, at the very top of the page, written in blue ink in Lula Mae's hand:

She turned two pages.

Read from page bottom to page top. Reversed the book's direction. Read. Page bottom to page top. Read. None the wiser. Flipped on. Maps of the Holy Land, past and present. Faraway lands charted, penciled, reduced.

Journey on, eye and hand. Journey to the final page. Find there written in blue ink:

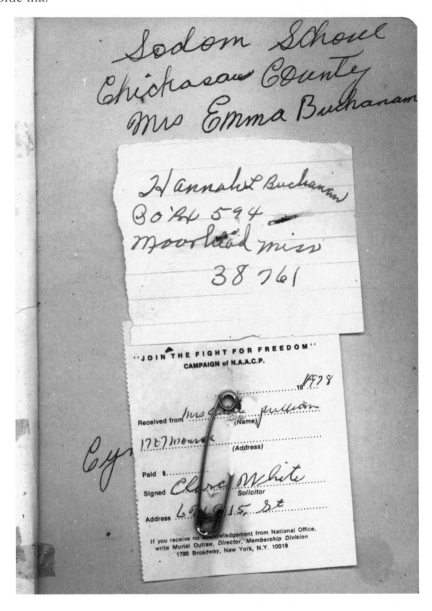

She lifted the NAACP receipt attached to the page by a baby's safety pin and revealed the name beneath: Cynthia. Cynthia? No name she recognized. No fact in her memory.

She worked her way backward through the Bible, hovering and hesitating, small strips and squares of paper positioned between pages, and small sheets of paper with handwritten verse headings, Lula Mae's private index. She closed the Bible. Enough for now. She had years to read it. Years.

LOOK, GEORGE, Inez said. It's Junior's wife. She spoke through tight teeth, teeth clamped down on invisible hairpins. Watched Sheila with a face framed in smooth yellow.

No it ain't, George said. That's Sheila. You remember Sheila. That's your other son's wife. Lucifer.

I know. My daughter-in-law.

Sheila could see through Inez's body, wax paper, see her cloudy insides. She was disappearing, disappearing into the same invisible space where John and Lucifer had gone.

My daughter-in-law. Gracie.

How are you, Inez?

Inez stared into Sheila's eyes. I think I'm dead.

Here, Inez, George said. Why don't you come on in here and lie down. He took her by one thin biceps, holding it like a broom handle, and guided her to the bedroom.

George, you want me to take her?

No, Sheila. You set down and relax.

Sheila pulled a chair out for herself and sat down at a small round glass table on the screened-in patio that overlooked the backyard and the garage with its own screened-in patio. She relaxed in the cool shade unbothered by summer insects. So long since she had been here. So long. Her eyes moved over the world map on the wood-paneled wall, red thumbtacks indicating all the places George and Inez had traveled.

How are you, Sheila? George stands in the raised doorway on a foot of concrete, waiting for her answer. He wears a pair of brown slacks that she recognizes from thirty years earlier. The years have taken away none of his sinewy muscle—he was always active, in motion—only weakened his eyes, dimmed them. He strains to watch her, as if she were far away, and his hair is grayed with a painter's touch.

Fine.

That's good. George steps down into the patio. Comes forward and seats himself on the opposite side of the table.

When did you all make it back?

Last night.

Everything go okay?

Yes. The way she wanted it.

That's good.

Yes.

So everything went okay?

Yes.

That's good. Everybody's okay?

You know. Sheila gestured.

Yes. Give it time. Give it time.

What were yall doing today?

Oh not much. I made us some breakfast.

I guess I should have called first.

No, Sheila. You know you don't have to call. We weren't doing nothing. I was jus about to turn on the news. George lifted himself from his seat, his strong arms trembling with age.

I can do it.

No, Sheila. That's alright. You set there and relax. He came forward and past her. Clicked on the television, an old black-and-white, the volume low. He had always preferred his hand-sized radio to the television. It lay quiet on the glass table. George passed her and retook his seat with the same trembling effort.

The television flickered light in the patio. Outside, the yard glowed with the brightness of the hot still hour.

George, the garden looks so nice.

Thanks. I try to keep it up.

What did you plant this year?

My usual stuff.

Well, it looks really nice.

You want me to get you some tomatoes to take home?

No, George. Don't bother.

Oh, it's no bother.

Maybe later then.

The television made small talk and small pictures about something or other.

You remember how Porsha liked to play in that bird pond when she was little?

Sheila chuckled. Yes.

Wasn't she the cutest thing?

Yes. Sheila saw Porsha bright and happy, her charitable hand holding out bread crumbs (Inez's leftover biscuits), waiting patiently, waiting, but birds flying in safe range on a steady sweep of wing, and Porsha crying out in anger and frustration, tears dripping into the marble pond.

*Don't cry, John said. Try a mouse. Birds like mice.*

And Hatch liked to sit out there on the patio by himself and read.

Yes. Sheila's fingers moved over her dress, followed the long black scar that ran up her belly. Rocking and reading, she said. Her vision was instantaneous. Hatch barely visible behind the garage's screen, rocking and reading in a rage of curiosity, his private hours at the helm of some great imaginary ship, glancing up now and again at the screened-in patio.

And that Jesus.

Yes, Jesus. She pictured Jesus's sharply cut features, then shoved the image out of her mind violently.

She had enjoyed coming out here as much as Hatch and Porsha. The moist air. Shadowed figures in the garden. The quiet and clean assurance of nature. The circular stones where—

You see that? George said. He directed her attention to the television news.

The anchor team reported the latest facts about the recent flood. A billion dollars in business losses. The threat of lawsuits. Another billion dollars in damage. The costs of repair and cleanup. Shifting blame.

Look at that mess, George said. Somebody screwed up.

Yes. They think they know everything. More than the man upstairs.

And no one wants to take the blame. No one wants to take the blame.

Organizers of the antiwar demonstration and Washington police claimed that the demonstration was the largest in history, at least 1,350,000 people. But the reporters estimated only 75,000. Camera angles made the demonstrators and counterdemonstrators look equal in size.

You heard from your brother?

Yes. He's fine. I haven't seen him in years. He wants me to visit him out there in California. But I can't leave Inez.

Why don't you hire a nurse.

You know how much they want? An arm and a leg.

*You have the money.*

And I'm not going to put her in a nursing home. At least right here with me I know she'll be alright.

I could come out and stay with her.

You don't have to do that.

I could.

Thanks, Sheila. You got your own concerns. Don't worry about us.

An unidentified man had been gunned down in a drive-by. Many clues but no suspects. Gang-related. Drug-related.

Look at them dummies, George said. Killing up themselves.

It's sad.

Dummies. Some of them young punks tried to steal our car.

Sheila's mouth opened in shock. When?

The other day.

From the garage?

Yes.

Did they—

That wasn't the first time either. So I sold it. I sold the car. Too much trouble to keep it. My eyes ain't what they used to be. And Inez can't drive anymore.

Well, I could come out and help you with Inez.

My niece stops by a few times a week.

Sheila said nothing.

This whole thing didn't surprise me.

What?

Inez. George spoke at the television. I married someone who couldn't help me. I was home from the war. Excited, I guess. And she didn't know why she was marrying. Excited about the uniform, I guess. I guess she fell in love with a uniform.

Sheila turned her eyes away from George's face. In all these years, she had never seen him lose his surface. She had come to expect of him words clean in remembrance.

I didn't even have a job. The army paid me a dollar and fifty a day since I was a noncommissioned officer. (Privates got a dollar.) I borrowed money from my best buddy to report to the base the next morning.

Sheila felt anger at the angry words. What gave George the right? What had pushed him so far? Why was he expressing such rage against Inez now, now that she was down, now that she wasn't *here*, wasn't able either to respond or to retreat, fight or defend herself?

And look at that Junior. *She* ain't his mamma. Ain't never been. He never called her Mamma. Old lady Simmons was his mamma.

Sheila weighed this against all else.

Her parents never taught her anything. Never made her go to school. She grew up like a weed.

Sheila stiffened with a sudden vibration of loyalty, duty, and courage. She opened her mouth to speak, but there was nothing inside her to measure and meet him.

Junior never was worth a damn. I knew that from the moment I saw him. I always thought that Lucifer had some get-up-and-go about himself. I guess he ain't worth a damn either.

———

THE TRAIN SHAKES HER to prove its force. Tracks whine down in stillness. The smells of the stockyards reach her now as they had long ago on her arrival in the city. Many years gone. Many. She remembers. Cows rode trains, passengers, rode them here to the country's bumping swinging heart, rest stop, where they were slaughtered and butchered, a single cow cleaved into a multitude of choice parts and cheap cuts, then shrouded in cellophane and reloaded on trains that drove them to distant reaches and anxious stomachs. The city didn't smell like promise.

52

OH, HI, MRS. STERN. How are you? Yes, I'm fine. I'm sorry, but I won't be able to come to work today. Oh yes, I'm fine. Jus a lil tired from the trip. No. That's okay. Please don't. I'll be in tomorrow. Give my regards to Mr. Stern. Thanks. Bye.

She returned the receiver to its cradle, then lay back on the tumbled pillows in the very center of the high white bed. The night had been hell and now the morning was no better. She would never get used to this. Never.

*OBSEQUIES*
*of*
*Mrs. Griffis Pulliam*
*1911–*

*11 A.M.*
*Rev.          officiating*
*Old St. Paul Baptist Church*
*504 S. 9th Street*
*West Memphis, Arkansas*

Gracie studied Lula Mae's photograph on the front of the funeral program. That looks like me, she thought. Death blackened her. That could be me. Black in death. She looks like me. She is me.

## *Obituary*

Mrs.     Griffis Pulliam was born Dec. 7, 1911 in Houston, Mississippi to the late Mr. Dave and Cardis Griffis.

She was united in holy matrimony to the late Mr. Lowry McShan and she moved to Memphis, Tennessee in the early 40's.

She was a very dedicated and devoted mother. She later maried the late Mr. Booth Pulliam and they resided in West Memphis, Arkansas until death. She was a member of Old St. Paul M.B. Church.          2 devoted daughters: Mrs.     and Ms.     of     , and the late Mr. R.L. Harris, sister; Mrs. Beaulh Dear, Mrs. Arteria Stone and Mrs. Judy Randle of Fulton, Mississippi. 9 grandchildren and a host of relatives and friends to survive in her passing.

*Poem*

*God saw the road was getting rough*
*The hill was hard to climb*
*He gently closed those loving eyes*
*And whispered peace be thine.*

*The weary hours, the days of pain*
*The sleepless nights of past*
*The ever patient, worn out frame*
*Has found sweet rest at last.*

## *Program*

Processional

Scripture and prayer

Song . . . . . . . . . . . . . . . . . . . . . . . . . . . . . . . . . . . . . . . . . . . . . . . .Choir

Expression . . . . . . . . . . . . . . . . . . . . . . . . . . . . . . . . . . . . . . (3 minutes)

Solo . . . . . . . . . . . . . . . . . . . . . . . . . . . . . . . . . . . Eurnice Robertson

Acknowledgements of cards . . . . . . . . . . . . . . . . . . . . . Mrs. Joan Winston

Obituary . . . . . . . . . . . . . . . . . . . . . . . . . . . . . . . . . . . . . . read silently

Eulogy

Recessional

*. . . There is no night in heaven in that blessed world above,*
*Work never brings weariness for work itself is love.*
*There is no death in heaven for they who gain that shore*
*Have won their immortality; and then can die no more.*
*There is no death in heaven, but when the Christian dies,*
*The angels wait his parted soul, And raise it to the skies.*

She reviewed the obituary facts. Name. Place. Date. Marriage. Survivors. Name and number. She added. She deleted. Corrected.

### Acknowledgements

The family gratefully acknowledges with sincere appreciation your comforting expressions of sympathy rendered through visits, cards, flowers and every act of kindness during this hour of bereavement. May God bless each of you. Family of Mrs. Pulliam.

### Interment

Houston, Mississippi

**National Funeral Home
120 South 8th Street
West Memphis, Arkansas
732-1300**

Sweet chariot had opened up its doors to her, wet in the Memphis heat. Shut its doors and leaped into the white world above. Sheila, Porsha, Hatch, and herself—all sat as strangers, swinging through the clouds. Her Bible (the funeral program buried inside, interred) weighing down her weightless knees to keep her firmly in her seat. Both the pages and her knees wet with Lula Mae's nonstop voice. *Swim out from my body. Search out your own water.* Sweet chariot swung her low to this city. The first to come. Called among the birds. Her fluttered pulse.

*What did you come out of the wilderness to see?*

She flew to her house on Liberty Island with its ancient implications of order, her rage at Sheila, so hot in West Memphis, already cold, drowned by the rushing in her skull. She emptied out Sheila and filled herself with John.

It belongs to both of us, she said. We both made it. Don't you want to touch it? Her palm moved in circles over her ripe belly.

John stood, the question holding him in place.

Touch it.

John blinked.

Touch it.

Okay, John said. He didn't move.

Put your hand here. She reached for his hand and he moved it beyond her reach.

Okay, he said. Okay. I'll touch it.

She eased her aching bones out of the bed, knelt in yellow sunlight, and mouthed silent prayers. Somewhere in the room, her Bible trilled tongues. She raised her head. Opened her eyes. Cookie's baby bonnet spread on the carpet like a discarded parachute.

She rose to her feet and went heavily down the stairs.

The morning air received her. Lake shape lying and lifting under a cupping sky. She moved in its direction. She felt her way easily. She had often walked here.

John met her on the path with only the crudest of necessities—a clean shirt, fresh socks, a change of underwear, razor and shaving cream, toothbrush, deodorant—in a flight bag. I'll be back in a day or two.

She refused to look him in the face. *Behold, I am of uncircumcised lips, and how then shall he hearken unto me?*

Don't act like that, he said. He stood there, eyes shining like brown diamonds. Don't act like that. I got to handle my business. It's only for a few days.

She heard silent prayer in the words. Yes, she said. I'll be here when you get back, she said, confident that he would return to her. He would often leave his body all over the place but he always returned to her, flight bag in hand. She wasn't much to look at and had little to say but he had an eye to see and an ear to hear.

Whenever he left her, she kept the pain of his absence locked up in her chest. But she could open it anytime she wanted, like a jewelry box, and watch the pearl-sparkling images inside. Her buried life.

Her thoughts were in advance of her body and she quickened her steps to overtake them. She found a quiet tree and stretched out beneath it, her back against the hard, rough trunk. Her bright red sandals and scarlet stockings made her thin legs look bigger. Two red rails that ran to Tar Lake. Trunks and trees made a black lacework around the island. Gray shadows and morning leaves. Silent light in shafts on bright grass. The morning sky bloomed above the blue horizon where black-bodied buildings formed a jagged wall. The city. Babies leaped high in the water, high above the city, like black dolphins. Birds studied their reflections in black water. For a long time she sat thinking.

It had been a week now since John had stepped out of her life forever (never to return), made her a ghost in a strange house where she would spend her remaining hours and days wandering. Perhaps she had driven him too deep inside herself to bring him back.

How slowly the water appeared to move. Lagging. Three steps behind the world. She recorded things never before perceived. The veining of each leaf and babies upon them like black locusts.

John gripped the steering wheel like an eagle gripped captured prey, Jesus and Hatch chirping in the back seat of his fast-flying red Eldorado. Flustered and afraid, she fluttered about with protecting wings.

John, please slow down. Can't you slow down?

Who driving?

I'm gon be baptized, Jesus said.

Why? Hatch said.

So I can save.

Save what?

Reverend Sparrow lifted Jesus high into his arms, kneeled down before the claw-foot bathtub, and leaned the boy across his arms, light, a shovel slanted above dirt. Except a man be born of water and of the spirit, he said, he cannot enter into the kingdom of God. He dipped Jesus into the water.

He heard his pleas even before his face broke the water's surface. John, help me! This preacher tryin to drown me.

John rushed forward and shoved Reverend Sparrow against the wall. The water sucked Jesus in. She heard the separate sounds of the water work on his body. John swooped him up kicking and blowing and blinded. She watched the clean waters, unmoving in the tub.


THE TREE LEAVES were too far apart to give any shade. The sun stood still and burned. Her black skin took on the orange glow of coal. Wet wind crawled off the ocean. Her body felt like dry ice, hot and cool.

A spirit must answer to his right name. Gracie tested the belief. She called John by his true name.

What? He put those brown eyes on her. What you call me? he said.

Nothing. She alone understood John's secret forms and transformations. And he made her part of that secret world.

I ain't think so. Deep eyes now upon the deep water.

She walked over to the railing and stood gazing down at the lake, gray, and slightly choppy in the wake of a distant tug. The lake was like a vast stage under the glare-filled sky above, and the boardwalk and beach, seating for the audience. She was unaware of the blazing sun, absorbed completely, caught up in the play of the washing waves.

Look, he said.

She looked. Saw what he saw, what he wanted her to see. Lined up like train cars, several objects rushed through the water below.

Rats, he said.

Vile, she said. Vile. She turned her eyes away.

He chuckled. For a long time he watched the water and said nothing. You know what?

What?

Dave, that sonofabitch remember everything. You know what he told me?

What?

Dave, well he told me that him and Sam drove out there to California to pay R.L. a visit.

Don't believe nothing Dave says.

So they visit him, thinking that ole pretty R.L. was fast enough to keep one foot ahead of the fast life. No, Dave said. That wasn't the case. Caught. His whole world tied up, tied up in Christmas tape.

Gracie listened with greedy ears.

All scarred up.

Scars?

Yep. His arms.

Gracie said nothing.

So Dave said. So there was ole pretty R.L. all pretty and fancied up and ditty-bopping down the street out there in pretty California and noddin so bad he couldn keep his hat on.

TAR LAKE MOVED with laser swiftness. Babies swam, raising their legs like powerful oars, the rush of their bodies parting the rushing water. Black riders came in off the lake beckoning for her red toes. New waves rose wildly, their height massed against the horizon, against the city. She could hear a battle far off, thunder and shouting. She could smell the ride of sin. Babies ran up trees, black squirrels. Shall two know the same in their knowing? All her life, she had believed that no two were closer than she and John. He had brought her into the world and she him. Entire with each other. Now she knew, their lives had never really touched. She was alive without equal.

She starts for the house in the serene extinction of light at sunset. The ground grows lighter and her feet move to meet it in the air. John passes up the white, wide walk, flight bag in hand. He looks at her with his marksman eyes. Touches her on the face and hands. She opens her mouth to speak, but he sends an answering smile before she can form the question.

The house receives them. Light, creaking, a house of twigs, a bird's nest. The floor rises under her feet. Rolls and pitches, rocks, a spray of witch's feathers. She sinks back, wet, weak and trembling, head expanding, the carpet moving under her feet. Pushes herself up to try again.

# 53

DEATHROW STANDS in the lobby of the Waldorf-Astoria holding his penis.
Why are you holding it? she asks.
I thought it was my shadow.


THE PARTIAL VIEW can reveal the strongest colors of the whole. North Park quilted in deep green through the window. Cloudy trees arching high in air. Huge bird nests built like penthouse apartments in tall treetops. She thinks she can see all the way to Red Hook. Buildings small, red, and hard in the distance. Fossils.

Red flickered in her eyes. Candle flame memories of Deathrow. She thought of herself, there (Memphis, West Memphis, Fulton, Houston, the South) and here, as holding on to him. She concocted scenarios where they would meet again. So certain that he would return to her on her return to the city.

Should she even be thinking about love now that Lula Mae was gone? And how should she feel about Lula Mae's death? How had it changed her? Did it diminish her life or increase it? She greased her hands with Vaseline and slid them prayer-fashion into the Lazarus 1 patent pending, thinking that she might have gained the power to levitate.

She had not.

She cleaned her hands, grease-free. Pressed a button on a mummy-shaped remote control and popped on her bubbled black TV, bright sight and sound. A drive-by shooting, the flood, the storm overseas. Hammered cadences ripped at her as masked and camouflaged entities transformed the desert into a huge movie set. Scaffolding, prefabricated structures, false fronts, precise machines. Rockets springing up over the horizon like toy snakes released from a can. Ah, here was a possibility. Perhaps Deathrow had been drafted—Do they still draft young men?—and stamped into a soldier.

With the television for company, she flipped through her stack of unopened mail. Bills, announcements, invitations, catalogues, and more of the same. A glossy postcard glowed like a priceless tempting jewel.

*Decided on Bahamas instead. The water is green. The sand is pink. I'm chillin. Enjoying conch fritters. Fried plantains. Strawberry daiquiris tall as mountains. Yum. Yum. And riding John Canoe at every opportunity. Need I say more?*

*Nia*

The postcard caused Porsha to remember the two letters she had found in Lula Mae's lil house. She opened her purse and searched through the contents. Receipt for the plane tickets. Boarding passes. Reverend Blunt's business card. (She put it aside for safekeeping. You never know. It might come in handy someday.) Funeral program. (Some extra copies for friends.) Rusty horseshoes. (She would need to mount them above the doorways for good luck.)

Finally the two envelopes. Why had she kept them for herself, not revealed them to anyone else, secretly lifted them from the shoebox and slipped them down her dress and between her breasts like a thief?

She quickly removed the letter from the first envelope. (The spine had been neatly cut with a knife or opener.) The envelope was stained and faded but the letter was not, the sheet of blue-lined notebook paper whiter than white after all the years.

*Dear Mamma:*

*Having many things to write unto you, the story of a man is lost and the story of his image loses a little interest every time it's retold. So I would not write with paper and ink: but I trust to come unto you, and speak face to face, that our joy may be full and the story complete.*

*I have many things to write, but I will not with ink and pen. I trust I shall shortly see thee, and we shall speak face to face.*

*Greet the kin by name.*

*Yours.*

The second envelope was much heavier than the first. She examined every detail before opening it. Size. Shape. Texture. Color. Two spots on the triangular flap. Like eyes. (Could it be watching me? He be watching me?) R.L.'s tears? His spit?

She removed the letter from the envelope. Fine stationery. Several folded pages—as many folds as a navigation chart—all unnumbered, no heading, no subscription.

*Brothers here, brothers there. Often did I think of the inhabitants of the deep much happier than myself.*

Words shimmered and wavered. Folded, collapsed into one another.

*To give an account of all I've saw, a thousand tongues would be insufficient; so please excuse my humble hand. Resolve as one may to keep to the main road, some bypaths have an enticement not readily to be understood.*

She stared as if staring would restore the words to sight.

*Though I am not present before you, my story wears an honest face. In the time of our fathers, writing was the voice of an absent person, and that absence bespoke another voice, the only voice.*

She told herself out loud, How am I sposed to read this?

*Read my little tale with reverence. Today, as I write it, all is quiet within me. You can see by my penmanship that I am not scribbling as I usually do. I'm not blessed like you. You could always write a pretty hand.*

For a moment, she imagined that the letter was written to her.

*All my life I've been absorbing bits of people around me. I have had business and conversation with wise folk, churchmen, laymen, fools and the like.*

Her fingers dream moist on the paper.

*It should be easy to follow the thread of my story.*

The moist pages move with wave rhythm in her fingers.

*The seams show.*

Words lift on light wings and settle like colorful butterflies on common objects in the room.

*Nobody can write their own life to the full end of it unless they can write it after they are dead. Some other must always judge us.*

The television wavers in the distance like far-off smoke.

*The pen employed in finishing my story and making it what you now see it to be has had no little difficulty putting it into language fit to be seen and read.*

She sees R.L.'s one surviving photograph, the crumpled black-and-white which gives up his form, his color, his hazel eyes.

*As you know I came out here for fresh fields to plough, new pastures. We martyr to motion. So here I am missing the changes of season.*

She sees his long legs sheathed in shining cowboy boots.

*What I have written is written. I drink this cup full to the end. And the water is sweet. I read. I think. I sleep. I read some more. God, enable me to proceed in this labor in the whole task so that when I render up at the last day an account of the talent you gave me I may receive pardon for the sake of Christ our Lord.*

She looks up from the letter and sees Deathrow in her window, his face a reflection of eternal dreaming life.


SHE LEFT HUNDRED GATES for the summer's first heat. Summer was already doing its work, for an old red ambulance, a long and low red hearse, was parked in front of the building, anxious for the sick or the dead. She drifted like a candle flame through the heated haze.

Taxi!

Where to, ma'm?

She entered the taxi to a humming air conditioner.

Where to?

She told him.

The cab pulled away under a sky that demanded to be noticed. Slow constellations wheeled overhead, fat swollen stars she had seen for twenty-eight years; none had any name or meant anything by shape or brightness or position. Thick trees bloomed on both sides of the expressway. (She's intensely alert to trees tonight.) The air rippled like camouflage. She said his name: Deathrow. He was somewhere definite, a dot on a map. She said his name: Deathrow. If voices had legs, they could crawl into all sorts of places, unexpected, unwanted perhaps, uninvited guests, willing and hungry. Deathrow.

She settled back in speed. Monday. The past week had rushed like a torrent. The flood had forced the new Cotton Rivers to reschedule the Great Awakening for today. (The media had it that he would declare Monday the new Sabbath.) And he had moved the location from downtown south to Woodlawn, to Mount Zion Baptist Church, which Reverend Tower had built and raised, a church high enough that every lowlife on Church Street could watch it from the deep gutter, Deacon Rivers his right-hand man, his first mate who took the helm when Reverend Tower died, directed a church where he was also to die and be remembered.

The thought sends her.

*One, two, three, four*
*Snap, snap, back, back*

*Put yo hands on yo hips*
*And let yo backbone slip*

*Shake it to the east*
*Shake it to the west*
*Shake it fo the one*
*You love the best*

How many years had it been since she'd lived in Woodlawn, lived where the Stone Park Rangers and the Crazy Insane Disciples waged war with death-hard fists, sharpened switchblades—steel drinks blood in the darkness—and single-shot zip guns? She remembers, they—Uncle John and Gracie, she and Mamma and Lucifer—shared a two-bedroom apartment (or a big one-bedroom that served as two) in a courtyard building on Sixty-third and Kenwood, a cramped, cavelike apartment with batlike moths, scurrying mice, slow arrogant roaches that ran antelope-quick at the sight of Mamma's curving broom, where the old, the original Cotton Rivers's tall pointy church rocked across the street, the church that King Kong climbed once in broad daylight, gnatlike fighter jets pestering him, while you watched from the living-room window. When you were alone, ghosts would flit across the ceiling, bump into walls, get tangled in the curtains, and tiptoe from room to room. One night a spaceship circled the building, spinning its rainbow of interplanetary lights against the drawn shades. Little men moved against the white shade screens. You threw the bedcovers over your head. Prayed for Uncle John's return.

Each afternoon, Uncle John would meet you in the schoolyard—Andrew Carnegie Elementary School—with the red wagon.

How was school today? Uncle John asked with his daring grin.

Fine. You always said fine.

What they learn you today?

How could you answer? Did you have a century to tell and he a century to listen? I don't know, you said. Your hands went quickly for Uncle John's pants pockets to discover the treasure of gold and silver coins hidden there.

What you want to buy?

Some potato chips and sunflower seeds and a 3 Musketeers bar and Now & Later and some wine candy.

The usual.

With his muscular stride, he pulled you and your sweets up and down Church Street, up and down Sixty-third Street, all over Woodlawn, all over the South Side, along the shores of Tar Lake, that great horseshoe curve west and east around most of the city, all over Central (Central was yours, belonged to the two of you, and would be yours forever), and backward and forward in time.

See that dead dog there?

Yuk.

I bet you it's a male. Dogs get run over crossin the street chasin after that stuff.

What stuff, Uncle John?

You know what stuff.

Perhaps to prove to you that he was as gallant with non-kin as with kin, he would offer other little girls a ride in the red wagon.

Two can't fit in this wagon, you said.

Share, girl. Learn to share.

To ease your jealousy, he would lift you above the wagon and bounce you in his arms.

Throw me in the air too, Uncle John, Nia said.

Don't throw her, Uncle John. She might float away like that big blimp.

A CONSTELLATION OF SIGHTS AND SOUNDS. A few hundred people were all trying to push through the wide church doors at once, their loud voices anxious and angry in the night. Long-headed TV cameras walked about freely like alien beings. Microphone booms floated above like black kites. Maybe she should turn around and go home. Besides, she wasn't feeling her best. Round and heavy with heat. She looked around and found that she had somehow waded into the crowd, surrounded, mosaic eyes. No turning back. Besides, what did she have to fear? The organ came from inside, a raised hand directing the visitors inside the church. Progress was slow. She floated through the doors, bodies and machines brushing against her, driving her, tossing her.

The church was large and high enough inside to hold every animal on

Noah's ark but all the pews were occupied and people stood in double rows against the walls. A kind reporter gave her his seat.

Thank you.

My pleasure.

If this was the old Cotton Rivers's church she didn't recognize it. Built by an architect with the will to adorn. Frescoes and murals of biblical scenes. Every board and beam gleamed. The oak pews greeted your backside with red cushioned leather. And the path of plush red carpet saw to it that you would never fall. Openmouthed speakers hung high off the walls like gargoyles. And blinking white runway lights directed your eyes and feet to the faraway chapel, a tree-trunk-thick podium on a stage of veined marble under three lean windows, moonlight swimming in colors through the stained glass.

The walls spoke: Please settle down and be seated.

Silence closed over the room.

I thank yall for coming. It has been a long time.

The podium was so far, far away that she could not identify the speaker. It has been a long time. On a wood beam above her the New Cotton Rivers spoke and moved on a stained-glass TV monitor. She studied his live double in the distance. The New Cotton Rivers was shorter than she had imagined he would be. And thinner. Barely enough skin on his face for a mustache. (How old is he now anyway? Fourteen at last count, last she remembered.) His white robe billowed like a sail.

Amen.

It's good to see so many of you here today though I know some of you are here for the wrong reason.

Tell them about it!

Though some of you did not journey here to worship in the Lord's house.

Tell the truth!

You are welcome. Keep coming back. God always got mo room for one more soul.

The congregation laughed long and deep, then laughter diminished, trickled down.

I welcome you.

She could not help thinking, Did the thin young body on the monitor truly house the booming voice? A voice heavy with age and insight. A miracle. The old Cotton Rivers was making himself known through his son's lungs and mouth.

Yall gon help me preach this morning?

Yes.

Said, yall gon help me preach this morning?

Yes!

Praise the Lord . . .

She praised him.

We are gathered here today in unique purpose. But let us remember, it is his loving kindness that has allowed us to be here.

That's right.

Some of yall don't realize that.

Yes!

I think I should say it again.

Say it!

I say, a lot of yall don't realize that. The preacher's voice searched out every corner of the church. Only his loving kindness, brothers and sisters. Some of us forget bout his loving kindness.

Tell it.

Don't lie.

He woke us up to glad daylight this morning, but some of us forget.

Teach.

He casts rays of pure joy over our problems and pains.

I know he do.

He bore us through the floods, kept us in a high dry place at his side, and still we don't thank him.

No we don't.

He fed our souls. He gave us children. He made us music. He gave us dignity. He bought our freedom.

Yes indeedy.

Why is it, brothers and sisters, that we don't thank him?

Why?

I say, why is it that we don't thank him?

The congregation waited in silence.

I'll tell you why.

Tell us.

I said, I'll tell you why.

Tell us!

Cause we are blind!

You said it.

I say we are blind.

Yes we are.

All things were made by him and without him was not any thing made that was made. But the world knows him not.

Tell it, brother.

It don't know him.

I said, he is in the world and the world was made by him but the world knows him not!

That's right, brother!

Did not Eve taste the sweet red skin of the apple?

Yes she did.

Did not Eve taste the sweet red skin of the burning apple?

Yes she did.

Why did she bite of the forbidden fruit?

Why?

What drew her lips to fire?

Tell us.

She thought she was safe in the garden. Did she not see the bloody foot-prints of the first remorseless soul thief?

No!

Yes, the Snake was in Eden before Adam.

You said it, brother!

Just like today. The Snake is here today.

I see him.

I said just like today!

Yes!

Hiding in the apple like an innocent worm. Isn't that always how he is? Satan waits in the shadows engineering his horrible plans.

Oh life is sweet!

Engineering his horrible plan to destroy the Lord Christ.

Sin!

So what did Eve do? Eve ate the worm-wet apple. And she knew she had done wrong. Yes, I say she knew she had sinned, for the devil's spit embit-tered the sweet waters of life.

Yes it did.

And Death stretched its dark wings over the land. God put Adam out of the garden. I said, Gawd—the boy preacher was humming the words, singing them—evicted Adam from the garden. Gawd looked at him and said, My son, I said, my son-on-on, you shall bear children the rest of your days.

Yes he did.

Bear children the rest of yo natural bawn days.

Yes he did!

And you know what? Brothers and sisters, we are all Adam in that garden.

We know it.

We are all sinners.

Um huh.

I am telling you that we all are sinners, so don't you ever think you can walk away from sin.

No.

I said, don't you ever think you can hop free of sin!

No, Lord.

The New Cotton Rivers began to hop around the stage, robe sleeves curved like a double-headed ax. He hopped back to the microphone. After all, how far can an apple fall?

A thunder of clapping hands.

I say, how far can an apple fall?

Preach!

The Lord says, The soul is a charioteer.

That's right, brother!

Preach.

The soul is a charioteer. See these two muscled arms—the New Cotton Rivers raised his thick curved robe sleeves like threatening scimitars—driving two horses, driving two horses. And you know what, brothers and sisters?

What?

One is ignoble—

Say it.

—and the other noble. I said, one is ignoble and the other righteous!

You said it!

The righteous learn to stay the hands of Satan.

Yes they do.

The righteous know that good and evil square off every moment.

Yes they do.

The righteous will fight for the big prize.

Fight!

Cause the children of light are wiser than the children of the earth.

Yes they are.

And the Lord tells us, Everyman is my name.

Everyman.

Everyman-an-an is my name!

Everyman!

In every breast my father planted the seed of me. A small seed so that you may gender gain and grow to seek salvation.

Tell it!

Don't lie!

Gain and grow-ow-ow to seek out your Lawd, huh!

Yes!

So place your salvation at the feet of Gawd, huh! Place your salvation at the feet of Gawd. Place your salvation at the feet of the Lord, who can wipe your sins away, huh! Cause your soul-oh-oul dangles over the licking fires of hell, huh! I said your heels-eels-eels pull away from the scorching fingers of hell, huh!

Yes, brother! Yes!

Take him, you wretched for good.

Take him, you starved for food.

Take him, you thirsty for your cooling stream.

Take him for your joyful theme.

Lay your complaints at his bosom.

Put your burdens on his breathing chest.

If you will walk in Grace's heavenly road,

he'll make you free.

If you walk the righteous path you'll know

Gawd is the only stability.

That's right, brother! That's right!

Because his power brings you power, and your Lord is still the Lord, huh! Give your life to the Lord; give your faith to the Lord; raise your hands-ands-ands to the Lord.

The church exploded in deafening applause. Porsha put both hands firmly on the pew in front of her.

The New Cotton Rivers raised his robe sleeves and dropped silence. His eyes opened terror-wide in farseeing vision.

Moses lifted up a people and tore a nation bawling and bleeding out of Pharaoh's side.

Yes he did.

What could ole Pharaoh say?

What?

What could ole Pharaoh do?

Nothing!

Cause Moses had fire in his head and a cloud in his mouth, huh! I say, Moses led the pilotage of a whole people, of an entire race, through the quicksands and breakers of spiritual degradation, led them-em-em, huffing and puffing, up to the plane of righteousness, huh!, led them-em-em up that mountain salvation-high, huh!, high and calculated to heighten the pulse and quicken the brain, huh!, led them to cool soul-cleansing clouds, cool to the sweat of a hot brow, for the soul's-ole-ole's salvation is hard work which calls for the coolest head, huh! So do not fear Satan, the Prince of the Power of Air, I say do not fear Satan, for God is the true power, Gawd-awd-awd, the sun radiating out the palm of his hand, huh!, Gawd-awd-awd lifts all, huh!

And know ye that neither the terror that flies by day nor the terror that walks by night shall overtake us.

The congregation rose from their seats, their praising hands blurred with speed, quick dizzy machines. Arms raised and extended like an Olympic diver, head thrown back, face lifted to the heavens, the New Cotton Rivers saw, and seeing, made the world shine. The brightness caused Porsha to shut her eyes for a moment. She felt a power, growing from the nexus of her belly button and radiating bright streams through the entire length of her body.

Gawd put reason in the head like the stars and planets in heaven!

Yes he did!

He put the passion in the heart and the heart in the chest like angels in the air!

The congregation stamped their feet.

He put worldliness in the kidneys, worldliness in the intestines, and worldliness in the abdomen like he put man on the earth.

The organ hit a heavy beat.

But the Good Book call chillun a gift from the Lord, huh!

The church grew suddenly hot. Porsha crossed her legs and her skirt stretched, revealing smooth brown thighs. She drew her skirt down like a shade. Her breasts shifted about in her blouse. She could feel her insides kicking out, kicking with guiltless violence, furious at the cramped heat. Then the church started to rock, tossed, a hot biscuit in cool hands.

Years have rolled on, and tens of thousands have been borne on streams of blood and tears to the shores of eternity. Years have—

Porsha felt the rocking increase steadily around her, gearing up, preparation.

For out of the abundance of the heart the mouth speaks.

A wave rose from her stomach to her lips. Rafters arrowed into the black sky. Water came.

## 54

STRONG-BLOODED, he quickens to the challenge. Rears back against the sharp veil. Constricts. Thickens. Cuts deeper. His throat swells. Once twice three times thicker than each cord of the veil. Forces his soft dry tongue— the tongue of a parched traveler—through hard dry teeth. Lashes along his body, lines, red paths that cut in all directions. And up above, way up, beyond and through the starlight-fine—

Sharp horns curve through the drawn curtain. He wakes with a sour taste in his mouth, like metal. Hot steel pokes from his pajama fly. He raises himself to the bed edge and sits in thin sharp light, he and the bed one. The pillowcases and sheets clean and new and scented with the fragrance of fresh powder. (Sometime last night before he'd retired, Sheila had entered his room and changed the linen.) The sheet smell, the early morning quiet, and the green trees waiting outside the window bring back West Memphis. Movement plays at the edge of his vision. He looks up to discover a mobile spinning in silent space. Half-moons tracking new half-moons, turning new sickles of light. A long apple peel that spirals the round rhythm of Elsa's walk. Turns Elsa's hot image over and over in his stewed skull.

A mobile? Where had it come from? Sheila had placed it there. That was the only possible answer.

He washed and dressed quickly. Left his room and filled the hall with his voice. Sheila! Sheila! No answer. He banged on her closed bedroom door, banged against blind wood behind which Sheila and Lucifer shared their bed. Sheila! Sheila!

He hurried downstairs to the kitchen, almost expecting to find Lucifer standing above the round table. Expecting to see him drink his coffee in six scorching swallows, jam four slices of toast down his throat then rush out the house.

Sheila! He waited. Let the words carry. Sheila! Sheila!

White paper beckoned to him from the refrigerator door:

*I went to Inez. Be back later.*
*Make you some breakfast.*

*Mom*

Damn!

He returned to his room, stuffed a carefully chosen assortment of compact discs, cassettes, and books into Mr. Pulliam's green army bag, and quit the house.

Knife-edged. Everything sharp, brilliant in the light. Cooler than yesterday. But less breeze. The air soft under hurrying clouds. (Hard to believe this the city of icy lake wind.) Birds drew heavy lines on the sky and the sky swayed with their loud noisy weight. A bird broke the line and dropped, stunned to the porch. Deceived, it had flown into the porch window that held the sky's reflection. Damn. He wanted to kick the red bloody thing but his shoes refused. His feet required motion.

A radio whined on the horizon.

> *Have you heard*
> *The rumors the wind's blowin round*
> *Tewenty thousand miles up in the shy*
> *Something's going down*
>
> *Get out of your grave*
> *Dance in the street*
> *Get up and go, learn more than you know*
> *Practice what you preach—*

Somebody's bustin Jimi, he said. Somebody's bustin Jimi.

He danced, marched to the beat, both asleep and awake. (John said that grunts learned to snooze between footfalls.)

He had sat up most of the night and watched dawn define the city with disconcerting swiftness. Sat, wavering between one plan and the next, his thoughts like loose shots. In the morning, he would ride out to Eddyland to see if John's cab was parked in his driveway. Check the garage. Break into it if he had to. An image floated up and remained like stagnant water in his memory: Jesus's teeth marks in the leather dashboard of John's gold Park Avenue. The shape of anger and absence. He would ride to Union Station and talk to T-Bone. Better yet, he would return to Red Hook and—

He tries to recall the plan now, a course of action as sure and certain as a man-made river. That river had dried up and evaporated in his sleep. He can see and feel it around him, ticker tape on cool city wind. In the city today, everything is new: hotels, clubs, restaurants, stores, and the buildings that house them, streets and the markers that name them. New. He can find few spots he knew only a few days ago. He remembers the city small and unreal inside the small square window, like a miniature model of itself. He remembers slow descending circles.

The roar of the engine brought a hot flush of relief. He was leaving Memphis, the South, for good. The plane taxied. Pure speed. The rush of takeoff. Try as he might, he could not help grinning broadly, broad as the plane's wingspan. Pure speed and the plane lifting into the air. He kept his open eyes trained out the small square window. Amazing how the large world shrinks in seconds. The plane found its altitude, leveled off, settled, cruised. Its shadow rippled over the white clouds like a black twin. A plane in flight offers the illusion of stationary life. You don't see motion. Your body feels it. And when you do see the motion, you act under the illusion that the plane flies slowly. White and distant, the sky moves and remains. This surprising lesson flew home with him.

Memphis last night and the city this morning. He had few facts but many feelings. There remained no trace of the former wish to see and save. The old desire like an early dream from distant centuries. No will to pursue and no fear of being pursued. Faith and intuition were both useless. What was left? A sense of flying longing. John had sailed off the edge of the world. Lucifer and Jesus had followed him. Not the smallest part of their existence reached him this morning.

ABU PEERED THROUGH THE ANGLE OF OPEN DOOR with yellow eyes, eyes topaz from the smoke of Boy Scout campfires.
    Damn, nigga. Why yo eyes so yellow?
    What? Abu rubbed them, his round belly bouncing once, twice.
    You still sleep or somethin?
    Nawl. I was—
    Smokin some weed?
    Ain't had none in a while. So you back in town?
    Nawl. I'm still gone.
    Funny. Real funny.
    We got in last night.
    Good. Abu looked like he wanted to say more. He didn't.
    So, what's up?
    Oh, same ole. Hey, you know the concert still on?
    What?
    Spin.

Word?

Abu nodded.

Man, I had forgot all about that.

They canceled it last night because of the flood. Now it's tonight.

Word?

Word. They even added an act. Klanfeds. That country rap crew.

So you got the tickets?

Right here. Abu patted his shirt pocket.

My nigga.

On point.

How much I owe you?

Abu told him. He gladly paid it.

He followed Abu down the hall. His mind moved. He wanted to ask, You heard anything?—meaning You heard anything about John, Lucifer, Jesus? Wanted to ask but how could he? For all he knew, Abu was none the wiser. He had to keep it that way.

Damn, where you get that bag? Abu's yellow eyes looked with high interest at Mr. Pulliam's green army bag.

From my grandmother's house. Ain't it the hype?

The bomb.

Hatch held the heavy green canvas bag to his chest and patted it like a burping baby. I brought some joints I want you to hear.

Cool . . .

They continued down the hall.

Your folks here?

No.

They at work?

No. Darnell here.

Darnell?

Abu nodded.

In all the years Hatch had known him, Abu hadn't spoke more than ten words about his father. Darnell traveled the country selling sports gear from his car trunk at rock-bottom prices; he came to the city once every two years or so, bringing Abu a pile of jerseys, T-shirts, caps, warm-up suits, gym shoes, you name it, bringing the old, scarred broken words of his life.

The long hall opened into the living room, where Darnell lounged on the couch with his woman (a girl really, Hatch's age or a little older), a baby snug in her lap. Darnell was just as Hatch remembered him. Youthful face. Thick arms and a tree-trunk neck protruding from a Cubs T-shirt. A tight Bulls baseball cap trying to contain his thickly wrinkled, near-bald head.

Hatch, what's up? Darnell rose from the couch.

Hey, what's up.

Don't I get a hug?

Sure. Hatch leaned in for the hug. Darnell squeezed him powerful and tight.

Darnell pulled back and opened the circle of his arms. Son, how bout another hug?

Abu gave him one, like a sigh, no force behind it. Darnell slapped him heartily on the back with his big-ass hands.

Hatch, it's so good to see you. You look good too.

Thanks.

Giving the women hell, I bet.

Hatch smiled. So when you make it in?

We arrived in town last night. Stayed at the Zanzibar.

Oh yeah? How you like it?

It did the trick, cause we went there for only one thang.

Darnell, stop, the woman said.

Damn. How was it?

Well, round one went quick. That first nut always quick. Niggas lyin talkin bout they went two hours. Yeah right, two minutes.

How many rounds yall go?

Well, round two, she had me on the ropes—

Darnell, you so nasty.

—but I came back, wit one of these and one of these. Motioning and twisting his hips. Now, round three—

The woman held up the baby to shield her embarrassed face.

—she got the better of me. I tried to run, but she wouldn't let me out of bed. She said, Come back here.

You got any children? Hatch asked, changing the subject, immediately realizing that he'd asked a stupid question.

I got more than Moses.

Hatch forced a laugh.

Let's see, I got six by my first wife, five by my second, three by my—

Damn, Hatch said. Darnell glowed like a mythical being in his eyes.

—third. And Junior. Darnell nodded at Abu.

*Abu*, Abu said with clear malice.

Abu there.

Thanks, Abu said, his fat lips forming a sarcastic pout.

Least those the ones I take care of. See, my first wife had two from another—

Okay.

Well, and this other one I don't even count.

Why not?

Cause he got a stupid mother. I go over there to visit him and she talkin bout, I ain't gon let you see him cause all you gon do is have him sittin up round yo other woman. I say, So goddamn what? Then she call me at work, Darnell, I jus got outa jail.

Jail?

Yeah, jail. Police arrest me cause Jim ain't been in school. He didn't have no shoes to wear to school. I tell her, What good that nigga you messin wit? She talkin bout, Bring me some money or you never see Jim. So I told her, Fuck you, fuck Jim, fuck yo mamma, fuck yo daddy and yo whole fucking family.

Hatch, Darnell, and the girl all started cracking up with laughter. Abu remained quiet.

Whose baby is that? Hatch said, settled now, directing the question to both Darnell and his woman.

The woman grinned.

His father dead, Darnell said. He's a bastard.

The woman cocked her eyes. Don't call my baby no bastard. You no good rotten —

Girl, keep yo panties on. Don't you know the meaning of the word?

She sat there, eyes smoking.

See, I'm honest wit her. Darnell nodded at his woman. She know I ain't gon leave my wife for her.

The woman smiled.

My oldest daughter called me the other day. Seventeen. She been going wit this boy for a while. So I tell her, You jus finished school. You doing well. I be glad to have him as a son-in-law. She say, Daddy, I don't know about him.

Why not?

He ask me for some.

What?

He ask me for some.

So I say, Damn, baby. Give him some. Yall been going together now for —

She live here? Hatch said.

No. In Yazoo.

Yazoo, 'Sippi?

Yeah.

My folks out of Houston.

I know where that is.

I jus came back from there.

Well, I hope you had a good time.

*Microphone check one two*
*represent*
*Microphone check*
*represent represent*

*Microphone check one two*
*represent*
*Microphone check*
*represent represent*

*Three four*
*Open up the door*
*Kid Attack is back and black so open up for more*

*I say I'm all that*
*Smooth and phat,*
*Lyrically developed, I'm like John Henry droppin the funky tracks*
*You can't sweat me*
*but you might catch me*
*See me perspirin*
*No I ain't cryin*
*See me flyin high like my man Flight Lesson*
*Don't mean to brag but you should see me confessin to all*
*these bytches I be stressin*

*Ah um*
*Listen to this lesson:*
*honeys be scheezin, honeys be weavin, honeys be schemin*
*The honeys who be abstract be givin up the ave*

That's pretty good, Abu said.

It's a little something I been workin on.

What about your guitar? You got some new phat licks? I bet you ready to tear—

Not really. Man, I ain't played in days. Hatch wiggled his mute fingers. Don't feel like it either.

Abu thought about the words with a disbelieving look. You'll be back. You'll play again.

Hatch said nothing.

The whir of wing in sudden flight. Birds lifted to the sky to join an eternal black stain that circled the horizon.

I been thinking, Abu said. Thinking. We should change the name of the band.

Oh yeah?

Yeah. How bout—

That's good.

The yellow day opened before them. They walked, their unlaced athletic shoes flapping about their ankles. Defeated, Abu took a while before speaking again. So what's up with Elsa? You talked to her since you got back?

Here, Hatch said. He shoved Mr. Pulliam's green army bag into Abu's chest. Carry this for a while.

Damn!

Yeah, I know. It's heavy.

They descended into the breathing subway. Enclosed behind a lengthy picture window, a subway map glowed like a great magical web. Steel rivers, red, yellow, blue, black, green. Sticky magnetism, spinning above, below, and through the city. Fast train wind blew loose flyers down the platform like racing horses.

DO YOU WANT TO DIE OVERSEAS?
GIVE PEACE A CHANCE
END U.S. IMPERIALISM!
HELL NO! LET YOUR MAMMA GO!
MOTHERFUCK THE WAR!

Hatch hummed a melody and swayed, fire-blue depths.

You'll get it back, Abu said.

A mouse scuttled into a crack of the tiled wall.

Ever notice something? Hatch said.

What?

How a mouse look like a Tampax.

Nigga, sometimes you think of some weird shit.

Seriously, his tail look jus like the string. And his body—

Okay, I get the picture.

YEAH. THERE WAS THIS LADY WIT NO HANDS AND NO FEET DRIVIN A CAR.

Nigga, you lyin, Abu said.

Straight up. One foot on the gas pedal. One foot on the steering wheel.

You lyin.

On the TV. In West Memphis.

No way.

They can do shit like that down South. On this other show, this man wit no hands and no arms was playin the drums.

Impossible.

That's cause you ain't never been down South.

Sure. Anything you say.

A trickle of water rolled down the train window. A second trickle staggered down as the train sped through the black tunnel.

You'll be back, Abu said. Hatch turned to see the other studying him with true concern in his eyes. Abu leaned over his stomach, leaned in close. You'll be back, he said. He lifted an invisible glass into the air, toasting to many more talented days.

Hatch allowed his eyes to travel the car. Look at that old motherfucker, he said, nodding at a white jackal who sat across the aisle intent on his newspaper.

Abu said nothing, clearly shocked at the swift shift in subject.

Man, jus look at him!

Ah, he's old.

Yeah, but I bet he's done a lot of damage.

At the next station, more jackals boarded the train, a pack, foul with the bowels of hell. Hatch pinched his nose.

What's up with that? Abu said. Why you pinchin your nose?

I can't breathe with all these jackals, Hatch said, nasal. He continued to pinch his nose.

Many of the jackals exited the train at the next station.

Good, Hatch said. He released his nose. Now we can breathe.

You too much, Abu said. Too much.

A nigga bopped onto the train. He walked stiffly on bowed legs, a cardboard skeleton, hinged limbs moving limply from side to side. He sat down and immediately fell asleep. The train pulled into squealing shaking speed.

That's No Face the Thief! Hatch said.

Where?

Over there.

That ain't him.

That's him.

Hatch recognized the black eye patch. Pin-striped like his tailored pin-striped suit.

He sure is funny-lookin, Abu said.

Yeah, Hatch said. He studied the sleeping No Face, nervous inside with secret knowledge.

The train slowed to a stop. Union Station. The doors ripped open.

This our stop, Abu said. He bounded to his feet.

Hatch remained in his seat, studying the snoring No Face—the eye patch a target, a map destination—between open spaces of the detraining commuters.

Come on! Abu said.

Hatch was still watching No Face, thinking, weighing.

Come on!

Abu's command pulled Hatch to his feet. A sea of arms pushed them onto the subway platform, their legs hardly moving. Hatch rooted himself on the crowded platform while Abu continued. The train began to pull away. No Face the Thief opened his one sleeping eye and winked at him. He shuddered, shocked. Watched the speeding train disappear into the curving tunnel.


A CLUSTER OF BRIGHT SHOPS branched about them. The Underground. Their rubber heels made dull bouncing sounds on the escalator's steel stairs. Hatch looked with hatred at the happy shoppers. Look at them, he said.

There you go again, Abu said.

I bet you they all Jews.

Now you gon start that Jew stuff.

They like mushrooms. Wherever you piss, they sprout up.

Abu shook his head.

Many jackals paraded outside the shops of Circle Square, spears rising like spokes from their snapped briefcases. Calling him. Mocking him. Defying him. Challenging him. Bums begged on the concrete sidewalks in the open heat, like lizards baking on a rock.

Kind sir, could you—

Not today, Hatch said.

Light breaks, red and pure. Night comes quickly. The sun falls like a cannonball and a red moon takes its place.

I knew we came the long way, Abu said.

Suspended on iron stilts, the elevated train led its passengers through the promised land of perspective.

I told you, Abu said. See, I told you. We should have taken the El.

So what, Hatch said. Stop bitchin.

You jus hate to be wrong.

Sabine Hall stuck up above the horizon like a needle point, downtown behind it. Buildings stacked up and arrowing toward the sky like chevrons. And Red Hook in the far distance, both splendid and monstrous, red bones glowing beneath its transparent skin.

A haze moved slowly in toward the horizon. Glazed it over, white sight.

Let's go.

I told you.

Hatch and Abu moved on through the shape-shifting night. A block or two later angry words came pouncing up the street to greet them.

What's going on? Abu said.

I don't know.

They continued.

Holy shit!

Abu and Hatch stopped, stood, and surveyed the scene before them.

Blue wood horses shaped the street into a massive boxing ring with demonstrators boxed off inside it. Cops in beetlelike armor crawled about the perimeter.

Come on, Hatch said. In one swift clean movement, he ducked under a horse. He would not be denied. He had paid an honest price.

Wait, Abu said. Wait.

Come on. Don't be a punk.

Hatch and Abu waded into the wet mob. Hatch left off thinking and let his body do the work. He tried to push forward—Excuse me. Excuse me. Coming through. Excuse me—push through the mob, push on to Sabine Hall.

Wait, Abu said, following behind him. Wait. Where are you going?

Faces turned to watch them with angry curiosity. Bodies closed around them. They could go no further.

Damn! Hatch said. Fuck! He stood sorting the city and Sabine Hall from his eyes, from the air, the night.

Dressed in colored spangles, the demonstrators knock him about, unbalanced, unsteady, left right, bell, pendulum. Their commands and demands on walls, windows, hands, backs, faces, bobbing in the air, spit into ghostly acts on the night.

The cops open their mouths to say, Come on, come through me. Their teeth are gates.

Hatch feels air damp with anticipatory sweat.

God cannot lie, Abu says. He stands trembling like a terrified tourist in a big, notorious city. God has no reason to lie.

Moonlight falls with a tarnish. The moon (or the fallen sun) holds like a red bull's-eye. Patterned stars dangle weblike in shafts of moonlight. Clothe bodies in subtle threads.

The demonstrators open their lungs to dark fire. One short rebel runs forward, throws a burning something, then darts back. The cops do not move or react, their foundation built of fire-resistant materials. Hatch wonders at the beauty of their blue bodies in the black night. Blue bodies proudly bearing new uniforms with blue crossed suspenders.

The demonstrators move forward without fear. The days cannot touch them. Hatch hears anger and repeats its sound. He absorbs the beautiful scent of standing, belonging, purpose. A light goes on in him, somewhere, inside. His call of discovery.

The lead officer shouts health-giving words through a bullhorn, voice crackling with feedback. The demonstration leader answers in words seasoned with salt. Hatch follows it all, enjoying himself, chuckling, taken from high moment to high moment.

Cops red-stain faces with straight-beamed flashlights. Blinded, Hatch brings language rightly to his tongue. You fucking pig!

The blue wood horses gallop off into shadows. The blue cops scuttle forward. The square street breaks into shapeless chance. Hatch stands silent and even, breathing in and out, staring at waves of cops. Uncertain. Possibilities flying apart at the speed of thought.

Butcher-fashion, a cop chops downward at Hatch with his billy club. Hatch meets the hatchet with Mr. Pulliam's old army bag. The nightstick recalls its circle and sets out again. Hatch can see the cop clearly before him, gnats crashing into his glass face mask. His eyes turn into stars. Hatch keeps his shield high and searches about him, searches, needing, hoping, wishing for more invisible darkness.

Abu!

He waits for Abu's returning touch.

Abu!

The crowd is half running, half flying like chickens. Pecking at the cops. Scratching. A nightstick settles red like a bird on some guy's face.

Hatch stumbles through the dizzy dark. Lives tumble into him. The doors go shutting in the distance, knocking like bowling pins. All the windows are webbed over. The city opens around him. The earth hanging in nothing.

## 55

SHOULDA SEEN THAT dog come flyin outa that burnin buildin. One of those ugly pit bulls, runnin red and wild and fast wit a fiery leash round its neck. Barkin flames. White foam drippin from its fangs like beer on tap. But Bird-leg didn't run. Couldnah run even if he'd ah wanted to. Damn cripple. Nawl, he didn't run. Hell, he didn't even *walk*. He jus stood there framed by fire. Jus stood in his window looking out, calm, unmoving, unhollering . . .

You approached the closed casket, cautious, keeping your distance, your body refusing to get close. You stood, your mind moving, telling you what you had to do. Pay respect. Pay homage to a fallen flyer. You took one step, two steps, and another. Closer now. You felt faint heat, like the warm hood of a recently run car. A sugar smell lingered in smoke scent. You leaned forward and placed your palms on the closed casket. Fire moved through the touch lines. Traveled up your arms. You pushed the casket open. Rising steam drew you back. He, the remembered, the departed, sloshed around, a soup of ash, shit, and blood.

Night birds cut the air to rags. He walks, breathing in the broken spaces, the memory that was more than memory, the image that was no longer image, sealed up tight inside him like preserves in one of Lula Mae's mason jars.

Voices around him like crickets. Strollers here and there, soft, fuzzy, out-of-focus flowers in the galloping world. And cops with snail-like faces retracting inside helmets.

He makes no attempt to hide himself. Safe in something better, greater than himself.

His clothes sag with the weight of blood. I'm here, he says, wanting to hear the sound of his own voice.

He sees stars lensed in perfect stillness. He can see clearly the way his invisible wounds are shaped. Shaped in the light of the likeness. Birdleg.

Gooseneck streetlamps drop nooses of slow swinging light. Mosquitoes pop and ping against hot, illuminated glass. The sun is still hours away. He will be gone by then.

Memory ambushes him, a drama of familiar names, faces, and scenes, which he translates into fact and feeling. He sees his own birth, the first flash of being, emerging from red 'Sippi clay. He sees his lungs, great bellows, stoking his first fiery words. Sweat gathers next to his eyes. Quickening moisture. He counts every hair of his former sickness with mathematical precision. Carries it all back to the old place, a distant well. He will not remember. He will not dream.

Entire, the Red Hook buildings stand close together like friendly neighbors. He is surprised at the ease it takes him to return to Birdleg's secret nest. A maze before when Lady T brought him here. A map now. He finds clean clothes—red—on the bare steel floor, neatly ironed and folded, waiting for him. He removes his old clothes. No use to him now. Naked, burns them in the center of the steel floor. Blood angers the fire. Flame rises tall and ragged, bear and claws. His body swells into open space around him. Red giant.

He wraps himself in the new clothes. They become him. A good clean color. His reflection wiggles and waves through the walls, red fish. He chuckles at his ability to multiply. A single red wave reinforced by another red wave and that wave reinforced by still another and on and on. All possibilities and probabilities.

Miles of switches, wire, and cable promise a glad net for the master fisherman. Glittering dials and buttons watch him like big frog eyes. He watches back with a renewed force of vision. Metal rubs against his hands, persistent and teasing, hungry dogs. His hands respond with heavy grace.

His naked feet rumble. Fire. Flame. Force. Foundation splinters. Concrete powders. Motion overpowers his stomach. He steadies himself. The city's roar sinks away, subsumed by silent rising. Birds arrow by, shaking space easily from their wings. He waves his hands at stars that begin to show over the trees. He directs his eyes down at the lamplit city miles below his bare powerful feet. Tar Lake no larger than a tear. Twelve rivers all thread-thin. Rhythmic cornfields like yellow waves.

Red Hook pulls away from the earth.

12/12/90–3/6/98
New York, Chicago, New York